Dear Arabesque Reader,

Thank you for choosing to celebrate 10 years of award-winning romance with Arabesque. In recognition of our literary landmark, BET Books has launched a special collector's series honoring the authors who pioneered African-American romance. With a unique 3-full-books-in-1 format, each anthology features the most beloved works of the Arabesque imprint.

Sensuous, intriguing and intense, this special tenth anniversary series includes four must-read titles. This special series launched with *First Touch*, which combines Arabesque's first three novels written by Sandra Kitt, Francis Ray, and Eboni Snoe. The series continues with *Hideaway Saga* by Rochelle Alers, and the book you're holding, *Falcon Saga*, by our award-winning author Francis Ray. The series concludes with the thrilling *Madaris Saga* by Brenda Jackson. We invite you to read each of these exceptional works by our renowned authors.

In addition to recognizing the esteemed authors, we would also like to honor the short succession of editors—Monica Harris, Karen Thomas, Chandra Taylor and, currently, Evette Porter—who have guided the artistic direction of Arabesque during our successful history.

Please enjoy these works and give us your feedback by commenting on our Web site at www.bet.com/books.

Sincerely,

Linda Gill
VP & Publisher
BET Books

Other books by Francis Ray

Break Every Rule

Forever Yours

Heart of the Falcon

Incognito

Only Hers

Silken Betrayal

Undeniable

Until There Was You

Published by BET/Arabesque Books

FRANCIS RAY

FALCON SAGA

BET Publications, LLC
http://www.bet.com
http://www.arabesquebooks.com

ARABESQUE BOOKS are published by

BET Publications, LLC
c/o BET BOOKS
One BET Plaza
1900 W Place NE
Washington, DC 20018-1211

All Kensington Titles, Imprints, and Distributed Lines are available at special quantity discounts for bulk purchases for sales promotions, premiums, fund-raising, and educational or institutional use. Special book excerpts or customized printings can also be created to fit specific needs. For details, write or phone the office of the Kensington special sales manager: Kensington Publishing Corp., 850 Third Avenue, New York, NY 10022, attn: Special Sales Department, Phone: 1-800-221-2647.

ISBN 1-58314-490-0

First Printing: August 2004
10 9 8 7 6 5 4 3 2 1

Printed in the United States of America

CONTENTS

ONLY HERS

To booksellers extraordinaire, Emma Rodgers
and Ashira Tosihwe, co-owners of
Black Images Book Bazaar in
Dallas, Texas. Ladies, you're the best.
Thanks for everything.

CHAPTER 1

"This may be your last chance."

Shannon Johnson heard the ragged voice and barely recognized it as her own. She was closer to the edge than she wanted to admit. But at least she had a chance to keep from completely going over. She owed that to a man who understood her better than her family or James Harper, the man who wanted to marry her.

"Thanks, Wade," she whispered, her throat tight with unshed tears. She had cried enough.

Hands gripped at her sides, she looked out over the flower-strewn meadow, heard the rushing water of a stream edged by towering cypress two hundred feet away, then brought her gaze back to the weathered log cabin to her left.

Arthur Ferguson, Wade's lawyer, had told her the cabin was habitable. The old shack looked as if any strong wind would blow it down. She had heard Texas people were rugged, but she thought this was going a bit far.

Her prominent family in St. Louis would be horrified to think she contemplated, even for a moment, the idea of actually living in such a desolate place. But then, she had horrified her parents a lot.

Only one person in her family had always understood her and now he was gone.

Unclenching her hands with effort, Shannon turned to get a flashlight from the glove compartment of her car. She wanted to inspect the cabin. Gripping the flashlight, she refused to think it was too late to salvage her life and her career.

But she hadn't wanted to come. That, too, had been forced on her. Two Code Blues and the subsequent loss of both patients in the ICCU unit where she was head nurse had sent her to the nursing lounge in tears. A job she once defied her parents to train for, she now dreaded.

"Go home, Shannon."

Shannon flinched, her eyes snapping shut as she remembered the gentle but firm words of the nursing supervisor who had found her in the lounge fighting tears and an aching emptiness. The underlying reason for the directive—her increasing inability to function effectively since the death of her maternal grandfather from cancer three months previously—had sent her to Texas.

Shannon had seen death many times in her six years of nursing, but it had never taken someone so close to her. Although the specialists had given her grandfather only six months to live after his diagnosis, she had known doctors to be wrong and had desperately clung to that belief. She wasn't prepared for the loss or the overwhelming sense that she, as a medical professional, had failed him.

Care of critical patients only intensified her emotional upheaval. Yet, somehow she knew moving to a less stressful unit wouldn't help. Her grandfather's death had taken its toll. She had lost her professional objectivity. She took things too personally and was preoccupied with her own loss. She wasn't helping those entrusted to her by staying. They deserved and needed the full focus of their caregiver and she could no longer give it to them.

Losing Samuel J. Rhodes had left her floundering and unsure of herself. The worst part was not knowing if she was grieving for him or for herself. She had lost her champion, her confidant, her ally.

Shannon looked at the rough exterior of the cabin and shook her head. "You and I both have seen better days," she muttered.

Without further hesitation she walked to the cabin, opened the stubborn squeaking door, then let the flashlight pierce the dim interior. It was spartan and filthy. A broken, built-in mattressless bed sat on the far side of the room.

Ten feet away an ancient-looking potbellied black stove squatted near a wood-filled apple crate. The only other piece of furniture was an overturned, three-legged wooden chair. Spider webs gleamed in the light; a wasp flew past her. It would require a lot of hard cleaning to make the place livable.

Weariness settled in. Another hope turned to bitter regret. No matter how foolish Wade had sounded, she had prayed that the healing power of his meadow would help her, as he had predicted. She badly needed to feel life instead of the anger and misery she couldn't shake.

She had planned on staying in the cabin and getting her life together again. Now she realized that was no longer possible.

The adrenaline pushing her to make the twelve-hour drive from St. Louis had evaporated. Returning to the car, she opened the trunk and pulled out the quilt given to her by Granddaddy Rhodes. It was the first thing she had grabbed when she decided to come to Jackson Falls. The lovingly hand-stitched squares of cloth was her security blanket. It was always to her grandfather that Shannon had turned when she needed reassurance and guidance.

As the shy, youngest child with two brothers who were as assertive and as brilliant as their parents, she had turned to her grandfather a lot. He had never let her down. Now he was gone and she was lost.

Spreading the quilt beneath the shade of a sprawling oak tree, she laid down for the first time in over thirty-six hours. A trail of blue clouds sailed past under the guidance of the gentle April wind. Hands pillowed beneath her head, she closed her eyes. Immediately, sleep claimed her.

Matt Taggart couldn't believe a stranger was asleep in his meadow.

Years of checking the Circle T's range had revealed some odd things, but nothing like the scene before him. The ranch was clearly posted, and people in the area knew he didn't make exceptions.

Puzzled by the woman's daring, he let his horse's reins trail loosely between his fingers and leaned over the saddle horn to study his uninvited guest.

Daniel's film crew from Denver wasn't due for another two weeks, so it wasn't likely she was with them. Besides, the Cadillac convertible parked by the cabin had Missouri license plates.

A frown marched across Matt's dark-brown face as his gaze swept from the sports car to the woman with skin the color of toffee. Her long legs were shapely and elegant in khaki shorts. Her hips nicely rounded. From the way her breasts pushed against her thin yellow T-shirt, he suspected they would more than amply fill a man's palm.

His hand tightened on the reins. Brazos brought his sleek head up and stepped sideways. A light touch of a booted heel settled the quarter horse. The corners of Matt's mouth tilted in wry amusement at his quick response to the woman. Must be past time for him to head to Kerrville for some R&R.

Dismounting, he dropped the reins to the ground. Quiet, measured strides quickly carried him to the sleeping woman. Up close, he saw the dark smudges beneath her eyes that the crescent shadow of her lush lashes couldn't hide. He knew those signs. She must have been burning the candle at both ends. Before he quit the rodeo circuit a few years back, he had burned the ends and tried the middle once or twice.

She appeared defenseless, almost fragile, lying there with her bare lips slightly parted, her thick mane of reddish-brown hair swirling in the afternoon breeze.

Studying her from another angle, he tried to see if he recognized her. Her face was exquisite with its high cheekbones hinting at a Native American ancestor somewhere in the family background. Her bow-shaped mouth begged to be kissed. She had a nice nose and her chin had just enough thrust to make it interesting.

He was certain he had never seen this woman before. She wasn't the type a man easily forgot . . . if at all.

Maybe she was the new waitress Moses had mentioned hiring for the Longhorn Restaurant and Bar. In the small ranch town of ten thousand, Moses Dalton owned one of the few businesses that kept growing and hiring.

If she was staying in town that meant she was off limits to him. He had made it a strict policy to steer clear of the local women. He wasn't the staying kind and he didn't want any problems when he moved on. As long as he kept it on the road, he didn't have to worry about causing bad feelings between him and his neighbors and friends or, worse yet, someone trying to push him to the altar.

Since this woman apparently felt enough at ease to fall asleep on his property, it seemed one of his hired hands didn't share Matt's philosophy on local women. Only three of the full-time men were single, but in today's society marriage didn't necessarily mean fidelity. It hadn't meant fidelity to Matt's ex-wife. Piercing anger no longer came with that knowledge, just an emptiness he didn't try to fill.

His questioning gaze again settled on the classic lines of the sleeping woman's face. He wondered which one of his men *thought* he had gotten lucky. Experience had taught him beautiful women weren't known for their staying power. For himself, he was too busy trying to make the ranch support itself to cater to a woman's whims no matter how tempting the outer wrapping.

"Hey, lady. Your date's not coming," Matt said. She didn't move, didn't blink. The toe of his scuffed boot nudged the sole of her expensive-looking sandal. No reaction. "Lady, wake up!"

Shannon sat bolt upright at the masculine command. Heavy-lidded eyes widened as they traveled up the long, muscular jeans-clad legs of a powerfully built man. Large hands were braced on a narrow waist. A partially unbuttoned chambray shirt allowed a tempting peek at an impossibly broad chest.

She blinked. No man's chest could be that wide. No man could have a voice that rumbled like distant thunder nor possess velvety black eyes that made her skin tingle. Deciding she was imagining things, Shannon closed her eyes to lie back down on her quilt-covered bed of bluebonnets and buttercups.

"Oh no you don't, lady."

Strong, callused hands circled her upper arms and set her on her feet. The black eyes were even more devastating closer, just like the man. "You're real."

The tall, handsome man laughed, a husky sound that vibrated down her spine. "Too bad you won't be able to find out how real."

"What?"

His sensual mouth quirked beneath his jet-black mustache. "A private joke."

"Oh?" Shannon said, somehow perfectly content to let him maintain his gentle hold on her arms. He had the most beautiful eyes. All dark and piercing.

"If you keep staring at me like that, I might forget you're off limits," he said, his thumb stroking her skin as his voice stroked her body.

"Off limits?" she repeated, clearly puzzled.

His face hardened. "Forgot the man you came to see already?"

Her confusion increasing with each second, she frowned. "I don't—"

"Save it, lady, I'm not interested. I know it's a long ways from town but Jay and Elliott are busy branding. Cleve has more sense and my other hands are married. So you wasted a trip and I don't like trespassers on my land."

Understanding slowly sank into Shannon's tired brain. "You must be Wade Taggart's nephew, Matt. I'm Shannon Johnson." Both her smile and her hand were ignored.

"Another one."

"Another what?" she asked.

"Another one of Wade's charity cases," Matt answered caustically.

Her chin went up. "I am not."

Heavy brows arched. "Lady, you mean to tell me you didn't come here expecting something from Wade?"

She flushed guiltily. "Yes, but if I could just expl—"

"Save it, lady," he interrupted sharply. "Wade died four months ago, and *I* have no intention of being duped the way he was by every pretty face with a sad story."

Hardcase. The nickname flashed into her mind. During Wade's hospitalization at Memorial Hospital in St. Louis he once told her that was the name some people called his nephew and partner. They didn't think he had any softness in him.

But Shannon had felt the gentleness of his touch, heard the warmth of his laughter. And certainly the nurses at Memorial wouldn't have been in such a continued frenzy to go out with the Walking Hunk, as they secretly called Matt, if he didn't possess some good qualities. His devastatingly handsome face and strong, lithe, perfect body would only take him so far.

"Mr. Tag—"

"You have two minutes to get off my land," Matt interrupted.

"If you would—"

"You're wasting time."

"You're the one wasting time," Shannon said in a rush. Perhaps she had overestimated the intelligence of the women at Memorial. "This is my land."

Surprise flashed across his dark features, then his face hardened into ruthlessness. "Whatever scam you're trying to run won't work on me."

"Mr. Taggart, if you'll just—"

"Lady, you either put your cute little behind back in your car under your own power or I'll do it for you."

Realizing Matt wasn't going to listen to anything she said, Shannon marched back to her car. So much for hoping they could be friends. She reached through the open window for her purse and withdrew a crumpled white envelope. "I think you better read this."

"Lady—"

"Call me lady in that tone once again and I'll do something we'll both be sorry for." He didn't look the least bit intimidated. Shannon sighed. There probably weren't many things that bothered a man with shoulders as wide as a door. "Please just read the letter."

Taking the envelope, Matt scanned the bold, black letterhead of Ferguson & Ferguson. His body tautened. Blunt-tipped fingers removed the paper inside. Midway down the page a heated expletive singed the air. Razor-sharp eyes stabbed into her.

"You won't get away with this. I'll fight you through every court in the country."

"I hope not, Mr. Taggart. Wade wouldn't have wanted that."

"How in the hell do you know what Wade would have wanted?" he challenged.

Shannon debated only a few moments before she decided to face the issue head on. "I was his nurse when he was hospitalized in St. Louis almost four years ago. We became friends and kept in touch after he was discharged."

Matt's perusal moved with deliberate slowness from her windblown hair down to her toenails polished Racy Red, then lifted to linger for a heart-stopping moment on her breasts before continuing to her eyes. "I don't remember him mentioning you while he was there."

Shannon refused to let his bold stare intimidate her no matter how her heart rate sped up. "I worked the eleven-to-seven shift."

A sardonic smile twisted the sensual fullness of Matt's mouth. "I bet that's not all you did, honey."

"Lady" sounded like an endearment compared to the way Matt sneered "honey."

"Now you've insulted me *and* your uncle. Wade was a fine man and you have no reason to talk that way about either of us."

"Being 'fine' doesn't mean he couldn't be fooled by a woman."

"No doubt not a failing you share," Shannon countered.

He ignored her taunt. "Why did you wait so long? That letter was dated a week after Wade's death."

Shannon looked away from his disturbing gaze and tried to speak around the sudden lump forming in her throat. "P-personal business kept me away."

"I'll bet."

She faced him. "Why are you being so rude?"

Hands on his hips, he glared down at her. "You have the gall to ask me that when you sashay in here and try to take the best grazing section of the ranch? The only one with year-round water? The original homestead site?"

"I had no idea what the land looked like until today. Of course, Mr. Ferguson sent me information on the property, but I don't know anything about ranching. I simply followed his directions and turned off on the first road to the left after entering the gate." She tried to offer a reassuring smile. "Don't worry, I won't be in your way for long. Just act like I'm not here."

"Not likely, lady." He leaned down to within an inch of her face, blocking out everything except his dark look of fury. "This land has been in the Taggart family for four generations. I'll fight you through court and hell for what's mine."

She took a hasty step backward. "I already *have* this land, and if the lawyer's office hadn't been closed because it's Sunday the final papers would have already been signed."

Some of the tension left Matt's face and his shoulders. "Then this farce hasn't been finalized. If it had, though, you'd be landlocked."

Shannon jerked her letter from his hand. She could almost see the wheels turning in Matt's devilish mind. "Only until I tore down the fence bordering the Farm-to-Market Road."

Matt looked thunderstruck. "You do and you'll chase every horse and cow that gets out!"

A tear rolled down Shannon's smooth brown cheek. Everything was going wrong. She hated arguing, she hated crying just as much. Tears implied a lack of control that, until the loss of her grandfather, she had prided herself on maintaining no matter what.

The faster she wiped at the tears, the faster they flowed. Her stomach growled. Watery eyes flew up to meet Matt's, and she turned away in embarrassment. How could her own body betray her like this? Easy. Working sixteen-hour days for weeks, sleeping badly, and eating worse would do it.

"Lady, are you all right?"

"I'm just dandy," Shannon sniffed. "Don't I look dandy?"

No, you don't Matt wanted to say, but he didn't think that would help matters. Tears were the oldest trick in the book used by women, yet somehow his usual immunity wasn't working.

Maybe because she looked so lost. Maybe because ever since his older brother Kane had married Victoria Chandler, Matt had to grudgingly admit that perhaps, just perhaps, there were a few good women left on earth.

Probably it was more the memory of Shannon Johnson asleep in the meadow looking beautiful and innocent. He stiffened. That kind of thinking wasn't going to get his land back. The Circle T was going to remain intact and his alone.

"Look, we need to talk. Where are you staying?"

Shannon couldn't suppress a shudder as she nodded toward the cabin. "I had planned on stay—"

"What!" Matt cried, cutting her off. "No one has slept in there for years. You're liable to wake up kissing a rattler."

Shannon's head snapped up and she stared at the cabin. "I . . . I was in there and I didn't see anything."

"You probably wouldn't until tonight." She swayed on her feet. His hand shot out to steady her.

"Mr. Ferguson said it was habitable," she said softly.

Matt snorted. "After Octavia and a couple of the hands tackled it all day."

"I see. Well that will change now that I'm here." Withdrawing her arm, she stepped away and instantly regretted the loss of the warmth and strength of his large callused hand.

For a split second Matt admired her show of courage and wanted to wipe the frightened look from her sad brown eyes almost as much as he wanted to keep feeling her silken skin. Skin that probably tasted as rich and sweet as its toffee color. He scowled. He must have been out in the sun too long. This woman wanted his *heritage!*

A beeping sound shattered the air. Matt snatched the pager from his belt and read the phone number. "It's almost six. Meet me at the ranch house in an hour so we can talk."

Her stomach growled again. Embarrassment overrode caution. Perhaps he wouldn't seem so overbearing after a meal. "I'll be there."

"Just follow the main road you turned in on and it will take you to the ranch house." The brim of his black Stetson dipped, then he turned away. With every step Matt berated his chivalrous uncle for putting him in a position of going up against a woman who looked as if she was on her last leg. Grabbing the dangling reins of his sorrel stallion, he mounted. Shannon was still staring at the cabin, the letter clutched in her hand.

Matt's eyes turned flint hard. She might be on her last leg, but like a lot of women, Miss Shannon Johnson still had dollar signs before her eyes and in her heart.

Matt's booted heel rapped loudly on the wide wooden front porch of the two-story ranch house. Opening the heavily carved door, he went directly to his office and dialed Arthur Ferguson's home phone number. The soft voice of Arthur's wife greeted him on a recording. Gritting his teeth in frustration, he left an urgent message for the lawyer to call him, then dialed the number on the pager. He and rancher Adam Gordon had talked back and forth so much in the past months that Matt knew the number by heart. The older rancher answered the phone on the second ring.

"Hello, Adam." Matt tried to keep the eagerness out of his voice. "I hope your call means I can buy Sir Galahad." Matt winced every time he said the name, but considering the bull's registered bloodline, it was his due.

"I didn't call to talk business, son."

Matt winced again. Adam had started calling him "son" ever since his daughter Vivian had made her romantic interest in Matt clear. She was a nice kid, but she was just that, a kid. "Oh."

"The wife has decided to give a little party to celebrate Vivian's graduation from junior college. We want you to come."

Matt's grip on the phone tightened. He needed that bull to improve his stock's bloodline but he wasn't going to dance a tune to Vivian's fiddle to get it. "It's hard to believe she's graduating already. Seems I still remember her in plaits."

"Vivian is a woman full grown and knows what she wants."

"I'm sure she does," Matt said, then added to himself, *but it's not going to be me.* "Adam, I hate to push you, but I need a decision on that bull. Getting closer to the time I have to start breeding."

"If Vivian lets us, we'll see if we have time to talk this coming Saturday night. She's so excited and looking forward to seeing you. I don't mind telling you that my little girl has taken quite an interest in you."

Matt's patience reached its limit. "Adam, we've been friends for years, so I'll be up front with you. You know I don't date the local women and, more important, you know why. With my reputation, would you and Peggy really be comfortable with me seeing your daughter?"

Silence stretched across the line for several seconds, then, "A man can change."

"Only if he wants to. If the sale of the bull hinges on my taking Vivian out, I'm withdrawing my offer."

"Now hold on, Matt." Outrage roughened Adam's voice. "You can't think I'd stoop to something that low."

"Ordinarily no, but I think you'd do anything to please Vivian and keep your wife happy," Matt said bluntly. "While I admire you for loving your family, I'm disappointed in you as a friend. You have until tomorrow to give me a decision on the bull or I'll look someplace else."

"Matt—"

"And I won't be able to make it Saturday." Matt dropped the receiver back into its base, then plopped in the chair behind his desk. He desperately needed that bull, but he wasn't going to be used or use a young woman's infatuation and her father's blind love to get the animal.

Adam was a good man, but his only daughter had always been able to wrap him around her little finger. He would bust a gut trying to get Vivian whatever she wanted. All she had to do was point. Apparently, she had pointed at Matt.

He really didn't think the girl wanted *him*. Since his uncle's death, Matt's appeal to the women in the area had increased a hundredfold. He had received more invitations in the past four months than he had in the past four years. Most of the women probably meant well, but he knew being sole owner of the Circle T, the largest ranch in the county, didn't hurt.

But you aren't the sole owner of the Circle T, Matt thought with a grimace. And the blame lay solely at the feet of his soft-hearted uncle.

Wade Taggart had been a robust man with an easygoing manner and a ready smile. A throwback to the bygone days when men protected women, pampered them. He was a sucker for their sob stories. Not even when Matt's wife had turned his life into a nightmare had Wade said one word against her.

Women, in Wade's opinion, were the weaker sex, and if they sometimes acted unladylike, it was their way of surviving. His belief had financed more than one woman out of trouble. No matter how much Matt tried to tell Wade the women were using him, he just smiled and did as he pleased.

Yet, never would Matt have thought Wade capable of giving away a section of their ranch. Wade's ties to the land were as strong and as deep as Matt's. It didn't make sense.

Matt's father, Bill, and his brother Wade were Matt's paternal grandparents' only children. The ranch passed jointly to both brothers. Since Wade was the oldest, when Matt's parents married and moved to Tyler, Texas, Wade stayed on the Circle T and kept the place going.

Ten years ago when Matt's world turned into a living hell, it was to the ranch that he had come to heal. At the time he wasn't fit to be around man nor beast. However, working the land had restored his sanity and given him back a reason for getting up in the morning. The week after the birth of Kane's twins, their father had signed over his share of the Circle T to Matt with Kane's blessing.

Wade had been there. "When my time comes, the Circle T will all be yours."

That was two years ago. What catastrophe in Shannon Johnson's life could have been enough to change Wade's mind? Try as Matt might want to dispute it, somehow he knew her claim was real.

Wade had gone to her rescue.

Matt pushed to his feet. Her story didn't matter. She wasn't getting his land. No woman was ever taking anything else from him again. He had made himself that promise the day his divorce was final, and in the years since, he had yet to break his oath.

But in order to fight Shannon, he had to learn more about her. Inviting her to dinner was the first step. He didn't like subterfuge, but if he had to put on the charm to find out what she was up to, his conscience could take it.

Reaching into one of the desk drawers, Matt pulled out a paperback novel, then strode into the kitchen. He needed the house to himself. Pushing open the swinging door separating the den from the kitchen, he saw Octavia Ralston stirring something with a wooden spoon in an old-fashioned crock bowl. He knew whatever she was making would be mouth-watering.

After burying two husbands, raising six children, and helping to care for twenty grandchildren, Octavia had always said mothering, cooking, and cleaning came naturally. Her gray hair was scraped back from her plump ebony-hued face that was free of makeup, leaving it as open as the owner. At least Matt had thought so until a few days ago.

"Octavia, I need you to leave the house for a couple of hours tonight."

"Why?" The housekeeper and cook for the Taggart household for the past forty years didn't pause as she dumped the soft bread dough onto a floured board.

"I've invited a woman over."

Octavia's speed in turning belied her sixty-odd years and her considerable bulk. "There'll be none of that going on in this house."

Matt returned her stare. "This is business. I've never asked a woman to the ranch. You're the one always inviting them over."

"It's about time you remarried." The housekeeper grabbed the rolling pin.

"At least just stay in your room."

"My TV is on the blink in my room and tonight's the conclusion of that miniseries."

Matt set his teeth. Octavia seldom watched her color TV. She had carried on for weeks to him about the waste after her children had bought it for her for Valentine's Day. She was just being stubborn.

"Strange. All this time I thought you were in your room reading books like these." He pulled the paperback from behind his back.

Wide-eyed, she advanced on him. "Give me that."

"Now, Octavia, don't be so savage," he said, eyeing the rolling pin in her hand. "Or did you get that from . . ." He paused and opened the book. " 'Serena, her black eyes glazed with passion, leaned into Jared's hard—'."

"That's my property," Octavia interrupted sharply. "Where did you get it?"

"In the easy chair." Black eyes twinkled mischievously. "Imagine my surprise when I reached down between the arm of the chair and the cushion for the TV remote I dropped and found a love novel with your name inside."

"Romance novel," she corrected.

Matt grinned. "Pardon me. Romance novel."

She held out her hand. "My book."

"You can have it and I promise to keep quiet about your reading material *if* you'll take the book and stay in your room tonight."

"Never thought you'd hurt a woman of my years."

Matt grunted. "This is the boy you took a broomstick to when I was sixteen, saying you wanted to even the odds."

Octavia smiled, showing strong white teeth. "It did, too." She took the paperback and pocketed it in her apron. "You win this time, but there's still two or three women I haven't invited back after church for Sunday dinner."

"And while they're here, perhaps they'd like to see what you do when you close your door."

"You're a mean man, Matthew Evans Taggart."

"It's a mean world."

CHAPTER 2

Shannon stopped in the driveway of the rambling two-story white house and gripped the steering wheel. Dread made her tremble. She had to make Matt Taggart accept his uncle's will. As silly and as desperate as it sounded to her own practical mind, she believed Wade's meadow could help her. A legal battle would only delay matters. She only had three weeks of vacation. Every day counted.

She chastised herself for becoming defensive. She should have made Matt understand that she had no intention of keeping the property. Her life was in St. Louis, not on a ranch in Texas. But he had the annoying ability of making her lose her composure.

People usually thought of her as the quiet, sweet Johnson girl. No one she knew would believe she had held her own with a man as commanding as Matt.

"You coming in or what?"

Snatched out of her musing, Shannon glanced around. Matt's handsome brown face was inches from hers. For a split second their gaze met and held. Shannon's stomach muscles tightened. Quickly, she looked away from the magnetic pull of his riveting eyes and grabbed her purse. She must be more stressed out than she imagined. The last thing she needed was another complication in her unsettled life.

As soon as she stood, his gaze moved with maddening slowness from her shoulder-length hair to her sandaled feet, then swept upward. The tightness in her stomach moved to her breasts. She fought the urge to hunch her shoulders beneath the same yellow T-shirt she wore earlier. "I . . . I didn't think it wise to change."

"Probably not. You can freshen up inside."

She was encouraged by his offer of hospitality. Perhaps they could come to terms.

Grasping her elbow, he started for the house. "Come on. Dinner is ready."

Shannon faltered on the first step of the wooden porch. "You said one hour. How long before you finish?"

His implacable gaze cut to her upturned face. "Do you think I'd sit down and eat and leave you cooling your heels?"

"I—"

"Don't answer that," he told her and continued up the steps.

Once inside the house Shannon let out a small sound of appreciation. She liked space, hardwood floors, and the durable softness of leather furniture. The front room boasted all three. "It's lovely."

"You expected cow hides and horns?"

Refusing to be baited, Shannon pressed her lips together.

Matt grunted. "Bathroom's on the left of the stairs. I'll be in the kitchen through those swinging doors. It's pot roast." He walked away before she could answer.

Shannon watched his long, measured strides, noticing the grace and ease of his conditioned body, the subtle shift of well-worn supple denim against his muscular legs and tight buttocks. Only after he disappeared through the swinging doors did she realize what she had been doing. Annoyed with herself, she hurried to the bathroom, flicked on the light and splashed water over her flushed cheeks.

She wasn't the type to pant over a man. James politely referred to her as "restrained." She had always assumed it was because the male body held no mystery for her. Matt had just shot down her theory.

Trembling fingers massaged her temper. *Stress.* Yes, that was the cause of her uncharacteristic behavior, and Matt's distrustful attitude was only making it worse. Confident that she now knew why she was reacting so strangely, she lifted her head, then grimaced at the face staring back at her in the oval mirror.

Gone was the happy, carefree person whose eyes sparkled with laughter and optimism. In her place was a pale shadow with dark smudges beneath somber eyes and lines of strain around a mouth that seldom laughed. If she didn't get Matt to listen to reason, she wasn't sure the image of the vibrant woman she once was would ever return. Snapping out the light, she closed the door and followed Matt's direction to the kitchen.

"Where should I sit?"

Standing at the stove, Matt pointed with a meat fork to a ladder-back chair at the circular oak table. A plate of food was in front. "I can't eat all that," she told him, her gaze on the overflowing plate of roast, new potatoes, carrots, and three steaming biscuits.

Broad shoulders shrugged. "Eat what you can." Bringing his plate from the stove, he sat across from her. "You look like you could use it."

She tucked her head in embarrassment and said grace. She initially picked at the food as she usually did, then found herself actually eating. The roast was delicious. Shannon moaned and closed her eyes in appreciation as she chewed. Swallowing, she flicked her lashes upward. She started to ask if he had cooked the dinner, but froze.

Piercing black eyes watched her intently. "What—what's the matter?" she asked, hating the breathless sound of her voice, hating worse that she was unable to do anything about it.

"You were making moaning sounds."

She flushed. "I'm sorry. I guess I was enjoying the food and got carried away."

His searing gaze flickered to her lips. "So I gathered. Are you always so easily pleased?"

Shannon's grip on her fork tightened. "I enjoy good food, if that's what you mean."

"It's not and we both know it," he said, his voice a lazy wisp of sound that caressed and promised endless pleasure.

Shannon felt flushed. Unsteadily she rose. "Thank you for dinner and good night."

Matt came upright. Unrelenting fingers closed loosely around her wrist. "We haven't had our talk yet."

Shannon felt the heat of his hand, the hypnotic pull of his black eyes. She fought to keep from swaying closer. God, what was the matter with her? "I—I think it's best that I leave."

"Which one of us don't you trust?"

She shied away from the answer to his question. Her chin lifted. "My arm."

For a long moment Matt studied the defiance in her eyes that was in direct contrast to the trembling of her body, the pulse leaping wildly in her delicate wrist. All he had to do was exert the tiniest pressure and she would be in his arms. He was sure of it.

His gaze lifted from her quivering lips to her wide, uncertain eyes. Fear mixed with desire stared back at him. Inexplicably, he felt the twin needs to console and possess. Both were dangerous. A grasping female like Shannon Johnson was the last woman on earth he wanted to become involved with. Long fingers uncurled; he stepped back.

"Ready for dessert?"

Two pairs of startled eyes swung toward the jovial female voice. Octavia stood by the kitchen counter with a lattice-crusted apple pie in her hands. The housekeeper frowned on seeing the barely touched food on Shannon's plate. "Didn't you like my roast?"

Shannon couldn't help from glancing at Matt's emotionless features. "It was very good, but I have to go."

"Nonsense," the robust woman told her. "Matt, sit the young lady back down and I'll put the pie within easy reach. Homemade vanilla ice cream is in the freezer."

Not wanting Matt to touch her again, Shannon quickly sat down on her own, but not before she saw the knowing look in his eyes before he took his own seat.

"Since Matt has forgotten his manners, I'm Octavia Ralston, the housekeeper."

"Shannon Johnson." This time her hand and her smile were accepted and returned.

"You two eat up." Octavia gave Matt a brilliant grin. "Don't forget to put the food up when you do the dishes."

Matt spluttered.

Shannon glanced from Matt's shocked expression to the retreating back of the housekeeper. No sound came from her, but her round shoulders were shaking as if she were laughing.

Shannon's quizzical gaze went back to Matt. He looked ready to take someone's head off. She smiled.

Something had transpired between Octavia and Matt. Shannon hadn't understood exactly what, but apparently Matt had been bested. Whatever the reason, she applauded anyone who could take down her opinionated host. Picking up her fork, she speared a potato and chewed with enthusiasm.

"I see your appetite has returned," Matt said.

"Yes, it has." She cut a sliver of roast. "I like Mrs. Ralston."

"Wouldn't have anything to do with her putting me on dishwashing duty, would it?"

Shannon smiled around a yawn. "I'll help you do the dishes. I haven't enjoyed a meal so much in months."

"I'll do them myself," he grumbled.

"Fine."

Black eyes widened. "You aren't going to argue?"

Shannon took a sip of iced tea before answering. "No."

Matt couldn't believe the whimsical smile on her face. Despite his obvious annoyance, she was fighting to keep from laughing. In his memory no woman had dared laugh in his face. They were too busy trying to get his attention.

He watched as Shannon lost the battle. Brown eyes sparkled. Her obvious weariness seemed to fade as her animated face began to shine with beauty and soft laughter started low in her throat.

"Did you make Wade laugh?" he asked abruptly.

The melodious sound ended as abruptly as it had begun. A shadow crossed her face. "We made each other laugh."

"If he meant that much to you, why didn't you come to his funeral?"

"I wanted to, but I just couldn't leave." Her hand clutched her glass. Her voice lowered. "There was so little time."

"Time for what?"

Her head snapped up. If there had been the least bit of softening in Matt's demeanor, she might have told him about her grandfather. There wasn't.

"Life," she answered, then laid her fork aside and stood. "If you don't mind, I'd like for us to have that talk now. I'm suddenly rather tired."

Matt slowly came to his feet. She was hiding something and he was going to find out what it was. "We'll talk in the den."

Leading the way, Shannon took a seat in a comfortable-looking over-stuffed leather chair. Settling back into the welcoming softness, she yawned.

"When did you sleep last?" Matt took a seat across from her and tried not to notice the way her T-shirt clung to the lushness of her breasts.

"In the meadow."

"I mean before that." He shifted uncomfortably in his seat.

She started to shrug and yawned instead. "I got a few hours early Saturday morning after coming off a double shift."

"What!" He came upright in his chair. "You drove all the way here on a few hours of sleep? You could have killed yourself."

Shannon straightened. Her family and James had called her foolish for driving instead of flying; she didn't need Matt adding his two cents' worth. "I'm here to talk about Wade's will, not my work schedule."

Matt's brief nod conceded she was right. It was none of his business what she did . . . unless it involved the meadow. "Why did you wait so long to make your claim?"

"I told you that I was busy taking care of personal business."

"Such as?"

She clamped her hands together. If she tried to discuss the loss of her grandfather with someone as cynical as Matt, she'd fall apart. Talking about Wade was enough of an ordeal. Tears stung the back of her eyes. Yet, to let them fall would only subject her to more of Matt's sarcasm.

"Such as none of your business."

"When you claimed Taggart land you became my business. I can hire someone to find the answers to my questions."

"Then hire someone."

Matt's heavy brow arched. Shannon might be down, but she was still fighting. "Why did Wade leave you the land? At least you can tell me that."

Shannon leaned wearily back in her chair "Wade was a very perceptive and caring man. Even when he was sick, he thought of others. We used to talk about his meadow. He called it a place of sunshine. After he was discharged from the hospital he invited me on several occasions to visit, but there never seemed to be enough time." Regret rang in her soft voice. She swallowed.

"About a . . . a month before he died, he called and we talked. I . . . I was going through a difficult time and he said I needed his meadow."

"Why did Wade think you needed his meadow? Had some man dumped you?"

"No, but a woman obviously dumped you." Matt's jaw clenched. Shannon shrank from her own cruelty. It wasn't like her to taunt someone, no matter the provocation.

Trembling fingers rubbed her pounding forehead. "I'm sorry." Wearily she pushed to her feet. "Thanks for dinner. It's time I started back."

Matt stood. "Back where? You're so tired you can hardly stand."

"Thank you for your concern, but I can take care of myself. Frankly I haven't been sleeping well lately," she confessed. "I didn't have any trouble staying awake until I reached the meadow. Now that I'm here, I can't seem to keep my eyes open."

Matt snorted in derision. "I guess you're going to tell me Wade left you the meadow as a sleep aid."

"I wouldn't dare tell anyone as judgmental and pigheaded as you anything."

Eyes narrowed, Matt glared down at her. "I don't like being called names."

"Neither do I, but that hasn't seemed to stop you."

"I never called you anything."

Eyes flaring, Shannon advanced on him. "Not outright, but you have a biting way of saying an innocent-sounding word and making the person feel like an inchworm."

"Lady—"

"Don't you ever call me lady again!" she yelled, so furious with him that she jabbed her index finger against his unyielding chest.

Matt wondered where this fiery woman had come from. Then his thoughts centered on something else, on the softness of her lower body pressed enticingly against his. Desire struck him low and fast. "Damn."

Shannon realized two things at once: that her thighs were pressed intimately against Matt's and that her body was enjoying every titillating second. She stumbled backward. The meadow might be helping her rest, but it was also turning her into an oversexed, argumentative shrew.

James Harper, the brilliant lawyer who wanted to marry her, the man she had known and respected for two years, had never made her body

react this way. He had never made her want like this. He also had never
made her lose her temper.

Of all the etiquette her mother had instilled in Shannon, the one lesson she never forgot was that no matter the situation or the provocation,
she must always remain a lady.

Then, too, her grandfather had always maintained that being in control of your emotions had little to do with breeding and everything to do
with intelligence. No one in her family shouted . . . except in court.

Even when her parents were at their steam-rolling worst, everyone remained polite. Whatever the situation, the Johnsons were always well
bred.

"I . . . I don't usually act this way," Shannon excused.

"Must be the meadow."

Shannon didn't know if Matt was trying for humor or sarcasm. She decided she was too tired to care. "Good night and thank you again for dinner."

"I asked you before, where do you think you're going?"

"To find a comfortable bed."

"You're not leaving this house." Her mouth gaped. His thinned.
"Don't flatter yourself. Octavia sleeps here."

"Thank you, but—"

Matt talked over her protest. "Jackson Falls is twelve miles from here
on some of the most winding two-lane roads in the county. There is no
sense in putting yourself, much less someone else, in danger."

Her chin lifted. "Thank you for the offer, but I can manage. If I can't,
I'll pull over and sleep in the car." Without another word she headed for
the door, well aware that Matt followed behind her. She quelled the urge
to run down the steps.

"You aren't going to let her go, are you?" Octavia asked from directly
behind Matt. "Sleeping in her car is ridiculous and dangerous, especially
when we have three empty bedrooms upstairs. The poor thing is so tired
she can hardly think straight."

Matt wasn't surprised by Octavia's appearance. Keeping anything from
her was like trying to hold a greased pig, frustrating and almost impossible. "What do you want me to do? Drag her back by her hair?"

The housekeeper sniffed. "All I know is that any man worth his salt—"

Matt turned. Something about the look in his eyes stopped Octavia
from completing what she had been about to say. She started back toward the kitchen. "I guess I better get to those dishes."

Shannon's car engine and her headlights came to life the same instant.

"Stubborn woman," Matt muttered. He strode from the house and
didn't stop until he stood directly in the path of the car. Tires screeched.

Shannon jumped out of the car, her voice and her body trembling. "W-what do you think you're doing? I could have killed you."

Ignoring her, Matt reached into the car, cut the engine, then removed the keys from the ignition. Opening the trunk, he grabbed her two pieces of Louis Vuitton luggage and slammed the lid.

She was right behind him. "Put those back."

"I'll be happy to in the morning. Now let's go inside."

Shannon moved away from his outstretched hand. "Why?"

"You're in no shape to drive into town, and it's too dangerous for you to sleep in the car."

"Not good enough. You've made it painfully obvious that you don't trust me or want me as a partner."

"That's right, I don't." Surprise widened her eyes. "But regardless of how I feel about you personally, I'd be less than a man if I didn't offer you a place to spend the night."

She folded her arms. "I'm not giving up my claim to the land."

"I didn't think you were and, for the record, I still plan to fight you, but not tonight, not when you're about to collapse."

Shannon wanted to argue, but she knew he was right. Matt looked like the type of man who was seldom wrong. He'd make a loyal friend or a bitter enemy.

She studied him a long time, measuring the man against his words and knew he'd keep his word, he'd wait until she was stronger. Then watch out. Opening the front door of the car, she drew out the quilt.

They both were silent as they reentered the house and walked up the stairs. Opening the last door on the right side of the wide hallway, he flipped on the light, then set her cases down. "Bathroom through that door. Sleep as long as you like." He turned to leave.

"Mr. Taggart?"

Knob in hand, he glanced over his shoulder. "Yes?"

"Thank you, but I still think my staying here is a mistake."

"Won't be the first for either of us, now will it." The door closed.

Clutching the quilt closer to her chest, Shannon sagged on the bed. "No, it won't be my first, but something tells me it might be my worst."

The blinding rays of the sun on Shannon's face snatched her from sleep. Panic seized her. She had to be on the floor at 6:45 A.M. Throwing off the quilt, she jumped from bed. Halfway across the room the sight of a double dresser instead of an armoire stopped her in midstride.

Slowly, then with increasing speed she remembered where she was and why. If she didn't get herself together, there would be no job to be late for ever again.

The prospect of leaving nursing and becoming a wife to James would please him and her parents, but not her, and certainly not her grandfather if he were alive. He was the only one in the family who encouraged her to pursue a career in nursing instead of going to law school.

When she held firm in her decision to become a nurse after graduating from high school, her family had urged her to attend medical school instead. If she was set on the medical profession then aim for a specialist. She had expected as much from her authoritarian parents yet they only wanted what they thought was best for her.

Yet, even after obtaining her degree in nursing her parents still harbored the hope that she might eventually go to law school and join the family practice. She had the brains and the tenacity; they thought hardness could be developed. She knew differently. She just didn't have the toughness she saw in James, her parents, and her brothers. They delighted in stirring things up and going for the jugular vein; she liked to soothe and comfort.

Or at least she had until she met Matt Taggart. Well, perhaps today would be different.

Looking around the room, she saw her suitcase. After Matt had left last night she had showered, then fallen into bed. She was asleep by the time her head hit the pillow. Opening the case, she picked up a pair of white shorts only to put them back, instead choosing slacks and a turquoise blouse. There was no sense tempting trouble. After she was dressed, she'd find Matt, thank him, then drive into town and get a room.

Not finding anyone downstairs, she set her luggage by the front door and went into the kitchen. A woman sat at the table, her face hidden by an open paperback. Its cover in vivid hues of mauve and gold showed a man and a woman in passionate embrace.

"Good afternoon."

The book jerked. Octavia, her eyes wide, appeared around the side. Scrambling up from the chair, she quickly put a dish towel on top of the book. "Ah, good afternoon, Miss Johnson."

Letting the swinging door close behind her, Shannon smiled and walked farther into the room. "Please call me Shannon. I'm sorry. I didn't mean to startle you, but you were so engrossed in your book."

The housekeeper tucked her head in obvious embarrassment.

"From the cover it looked good. One of the things I missed most when working long hours was not being able to curl up with a good romance book."

Astonishment lifted Octavia's head and widened her brown eyes. "You read them, too?"

"Used to. Every chance I got."

A wide grin spread across the older woman's charcoal face. "I knew there was something about you that I liked the second I saw you." Still smiling, she opened the refrigerator door and took out a plate of fried chicken and potato salad. "It's almost one. You must be starved. Sit down and eat."

"I really must be going," Shannon said, but her eyes were on the golden-brown chicken.

"Can't," Octavia announced, and set a glass of iced tea beside the place setting for one. "Matt said for you to wait until he got back. Usually once he eats breakfast I don't see him until late in the evening, but today he's been back twice to see if you were awake."

"Why didn't he have you wake me up?" Shannon asked. "I don't remember the last time I slept this late. I wouldn't have minded."

Octavia chuckled, a deep sound that shook her heavy body. "That may be, but he almost took my head off when he came back the last time around twelve and found me vacuuming. Told me to stop making so much noise because you needed your sleep."

Uncomfortable and oddly pleased, Shannon addressed the one safe issue. "I'm sorry I interrupted your cleaning."

"Don't be. As you can see, I made good use of the time. Anyway, having you in the house is good for Matt. Makes him remember his manners. Does my heart good to see that woman didn't kill all of his protective instinct toward females." Octavia pointed toward the ladder-back chair. "Now sit down and eat, so we can discuss books."

Shannon sat and half listened to the housekeeper discuss her favorite romance novels, but what Shannon really wanted to discuss was who "that woman" was and what had she done to Matt.

CHAPTER 3

Two hours later Shannon sat on the bank of a stock pond beneath the shade of a willow tree with a book dangling from her fingertips. A yard from her canvas-covered feet lay the end of her cane fishing pole, the red-and-white plastic cork barely moving in the tranquil water. Unfortunately, she wasn't as peaceful.

She would have preferred going in search of Wade's lawyer rather than dealing with the unsettling task of meeting Matt again. She was, if only temporarily, going to take his land away from him. And he was going to fight her with everything within him.

Peace was what she had come for and that was exactly what she had yet to obtain. Instead of leaving as she'd wanted, she'd let Octavia bamboozle her into going fishing.

After lunch and still no Matt, the housekeeper had thwarted all plans of Shannon leaving. Before she knew how it happened, the jovial Octavia had thrown some chocolate-chip cookies, a thermos of lemonade, and a paperback into a canvas tote, then led her outside. Several fishing poles leaned neatly beneath the overhang of the white house.

"Pick one."

When Shannon simply stared at the housekeeper, the older woman snatched the one nearest her, then shoved the eight-foot-long pole and a plastic bag of bait into Shannon's hand and pointed toward a clump of trees twenty-five yards away.

"Fishing is the best remedy for what ails you," Octavia said before she disappeared into the house. The banging of the screen door jarred Shannon out of her passivity.

She had reached the steps before she realized the woman was only being kind. More than once during their conversation Shannon had drifted into her own thoughts. Perhaps fishing wasn't such a bad idea after all.

Finding a shady spot, Shannon had baited her hook and prepared to do something she had never done in summer camp: catch a fish. However, the fish weren't cooperating. She picked up her book, then decided she'd rather just enjoy the countryside.

The meadow might have been Wade's favorite place, but the entire ranch, with its budding green grass, wide-limbed trees and scattering of rainbow-hued flowers, was just as peaceful. As long as Matt wasn't nearby.

Shannon winced at her unfair thought. The man was only trying to protect his heritage. In a way, she respected him for his tenacity, but not his attitude. If he'd stop being so judgmental, perhaps she could reassure him.

The fishing line moved so only the top half of the white cork showed. The cork dipped once, twice. Instantly Shannon forgot about her reluctant partner. Excitement bubbled within her as she scrambled to pick up the fishing pole. The cork disappeared completely beneath the water's surface. Two-handed, she jerked with all her strength. Line, cork, and fish came out of the water.

The fish kept going.

She sighed deeply. Even fishing as a child she had always pulled too hard. Usually the hook detached itself from the fish's mouth before it left the water. At least this time it had held long enough for her to finally get a fish on the bank. Dropping the pole, she went in search of her catch.

Several feet away in the grassy area, a grayish-brown bird with a black-striped chest flew into the air only to land again, walk a few feet, then fall flat on the ground making pitiful sounds. Shannon rushed toward the bird to help, but it got up dragging both wings on the ground.

Moving cautiously, she approached slower. Yet, again the bird moved farther away, gasped, then rolled over as if in terrible agony. Shannon saw a red spot.

"Oh, goodness. You're bleeding." She took another step. "Easy now. I won't harm you."

Out of nowhere another bird flew over Shannon's head screaming protest. She glanced at the bird in the air, then back at the bird on the ground. "I won't hurt your mate, but he or she needs help."

"It's a she and she's no more hurt than I am."

Shannon swung around. Matt, wearing a blue plaid shirt and jeans, stood a few feet away. He looked tall, handsome, intimidating. Her throat dried. No man should affect a woman that way. "I saw blood."

"What you saw was her rump. She's trying to lure you away from her nest." He inclined his black Stetson toward the squawking bird flying above them. "The male is getting into the act, too. Killdeer can put on quite an act when it comes to protecting their nest or their young."

"I certainly feel like an idiot."

"You shouldn't. Not many people care enough to try and help an injured bird, especially after the male gets into the act." He gave her a long, level look. "Were you that concerned and attentive with Wade while he was your patient?"

"I tried to be," she said softly, hoping this could be the turning point in their relationship. "Patients in ICCU often need healing in spirit as much as in body. Wade was an exception. It didn't matter that he was seventy-five years old with internal injuries and two broken legs from his automobile accident, he never doubted he'd walk out of the hospital and come home to the ranch."

The corner of Matt's mouth lifted in a fleeting attempt at smiling. "The physical therapist said she never had seen anyone more determined to not only walk, but run. He never did manage to run, but he could do a mean skip and a hop with his cane."

"He told me he let his horse Paintbrush do the running for him."

"He did. Every morning the two of them would head out and usually end up at the meadow." Matt shook his head. "No matter how I objected about him going alone, he went anyway. Turned up his nose if I mentioned me or one of the hands driving him."

"Why did you want someone with him?"

"Glaucoma," Matt answered succinctly. "Doctors found out early last year, but it was too late to be treated. Got so bad Wade could barely see his hand in front of his face. I understood riding Paintbrush gave him back his independence, but it was too dangerous for Wade to wander over a thousand acres by himself."

"Knowing that, you let him go anyway?" Shannon asked in disbelief.

"I had to."

"But—"

"Taking away Paintbrush or not helping Wade find his way to the barn would have been the easy way out for me, but not for Wade. He would have felt helpless, less than a man." Matt tugged on his hat. "So I hired someone to watch him from a distance. I couldn't take his pride away from him. He had lost too much already."

A wave of sorrow and regret swept through Shannon. One of the most heart-wrenching decisions a family member had to make was knowing when to set your own wants aside and do what the patient needed. "You did what was right."

"Yeah."

The one clipped word from Matt told her he didn't think it had been enough. She knew exactly how he felt. All her specialized training hadn't helped her grandfather. Her hand fisted to keep from placing it on Matt's tense shoulders and comforting him. "In all the times we talked, he never mentioned his failing vision."

"Wade wasn't the type to lay his problems on someone else; he was more apt to take on another person's problems. He never complained about the hand life dealt him. Only said that a man ought to be willing to take the bad times with the good." Matt glanced away, his voice gruff. "He was a hell of a man."

"Yes, just like Granddaddy," she mumbled. Her throat tight, she turned away and almost stepped on her escaped, gasping perch. Carefully, she picked up the foot-long fish and carried it back to the bank. Slipping the fish into the water, she picked up the fishing pole and the rest of her things, then started back to the house.

"He was a keeper. Why did you throw him back?"

She kept walking. "Life is precious in any form."

"That didn't stop you from eating that beef last night."

So the truce was over. "I didn't have to see it before it died."

"So it's all right as long as you don't have to dirty your own hands," Matt said, catching up with her. "I'm surprised you didn't send someone else to claim my land."

The unfairness of his taunt swung her around. The rebuttal sprang to her lips, but somehow she managed to swallow the words. "People in St. Louis consider me a nice, decent person. Why can't you?"

"Try taking one hundred acres of prime grazing land or, in your case, riverfront property, from one of them and see how long that opinion lasts."

He was right. Again. Her shoulders slumped. "Can't you understand? I had to come."

A callused thumb kicked his Stetson back on his head. "How could I have forgotten? As I said, it's your own personal sleep aid."

Shannon resisted the urge to bop him on the head with the canvas bag in her hand. "You are making it very difficult for me to like you."

Matt leaned down until their noses were an inch apart. Shannon quelled the impulse to lean away. "You didn't seem to have any difficulty liking me last night in the kitchen."

Face flushed, Shannon stumbled backward. Her canvas shoes caught in the underbrush. With a startled cry, she felt herself falling. Matt's hand shot out and pulled her upright against his hard chest, his other hand tunneling through her heavy mass of hair, his fingers warm and unsettling against her scalp. Her heart pounding, she stared up into glittering black eyes.

"Did you?" he asked, his voice a husky whisper of veiled hunger.

No words came. She was too busy feeling the muscular body pressed against hers. Sensations swept through her. Her mind shut down except for the narrow perimeter of the sensual outline of Matt's lips.

Would his lips be as abrasive as his taunt or as gentle as his hands holding her? Would they take or give? Would his mustache be soft or prickly? Unconsciously digging her toes into the grass, she lifted herself upward toward temptation and the answer to her question. Her eyelids drifted shut.

Trembling lips barely touched something warm and soft and tantalizing before she was snatched away. Her eyes opened. Matt glared down at her.

Comprehension of what she had done hit her like a fist. Heat flooded her face. She had acted on impulse, a sexual one at that. If she could bottle the meadow, she could make a lot of people happy. Apparently Matt, who was holding her at arm's length, would not be one of them.

"I'm all right. You can let me go," she offered, pleased that her voice didn't sound as shaky as her legs felt.

He continued to stare down at her, his stillness as unnerving as his tight face, the strange light glittering in his dark eyes. He seemed to be wrestling with his own emotions. She couldn't blame him. He probably wasn't sure what she was all right from, nearly falling or throwing herself at him. Slowly, he unclamped his hands from her upper arms and bent over.

Her face heated again as he picked up her fishing pole and canvas bag, then started toward the house. She hadn't even realized she had dropped them. Trying to ignore her trembling legs, Shannon fell into step behind him.

None of her mother's etiquette lessons had covered the proper method for recovering graciously from throwing yourself at a man who obviously didn't want you. From the peculiar way Matt acted afterward, he had only intended to annoy her.

Instead of being adept enough to read him correctly or strong enough to resist him, she had acted like a love-starved bimbo. If he hadn't pushed her away . . . She bit her lower lip and refused to let her mind go any further. One thing was certain, initiating the kiss had only given more credence to Matt's mistaken belief about her. There was only one way to let him know he was wrong.

"You can have it back as soon as I'm finished," she offered.

Stopping abruptly, Matt swung around. "What did you say?"

Shannon pulled up short to keep from walking into him. "I—I never planned on keeping the land your uncle left me. I decided when Mr. Ferguson first told me about the meadow that it wouldn't be right for me to accept. Nothing has changed my mind. I only plan on being here three weeks."

His dark brow furrowed. "If that's so, why haven't you mentioned it before now?"

"Because you aren't the nicest person to get along with."

Unlike the last time she had given a similar assessment of his character, Matt appeared undisturbed. "What do you plan to do in that time?"

"Live on the land."

"So you're telling me you just want to live in a run-down cabin for three weeks and then you'll sign over the place to me?"

"Yes."

"I wasn't born yesterday. Once you get the land, there'll be nothing I can do to stop you from selling or leasing the property."

"You have my word."

"Your word, huh? What if I promised you that if you renounce your claim to the meadow in writing, I'll let you stay for as long as you want."

She answered immediately. "I wouldn't believe you."

Matt nodded as if that was the answer he expected. "Neither one of us trusts the other, so it looks like we're at an impasse." He grasped her by the elbow and headed for the house at a faster pace. "Come on, Ferguson is waiting to see us."

She practically ran to keep up with his long-legged stride. "Us? When did he call?"

"About twenty minutes ago."

Her eyebrows furrowed. "But how did he know I was here?"

"I told him," Matt said.

She glanced up at the hard line of Matt's jaw. Something wasn't right. "Exactly when did you tell him?"

"Yesterday" came the flat reply.

She mentally called herself a naive fool for thinking for one second the stern-faced man dragging her back along a narrow path was kind. Arrogant, yes. Devious, positively. But kind, never.

"So that's the real reason you didn't want Octavia to disturb me. You weren't as concerned with my rest as my not seeing Arthur Ferguson and signing the final papers before you saw him. For a little while this afternoon I thought I might have misjudged you."

Apparently unconcerned by her opinion of him, he kept walking until he reached the side of the house where the fishing poles were kept. Without a glance in her direction, he replaced the gear, then dropped the canvas bag on the back porch steps.

Incensed at being ignored and duped, she put her hands on her hips and stepped in front of him. "It appears I was wrong."

"I never implied any different," he finally replied. Walking around her, he went to the front of the house where a dusty black truck was parked and opened the passenger door. "Get in."

Shannon folded her arms across her chest. "I prefer to drive my own car."

The door slammed shut. "Suit yourself, but you better be in Ferguson's office in thirty minutes."

Outraged, she snatched her arms to her sides. "I can't possibly get cleaned up and drive to town in that short a time."

"Look, la—*Miss.* I have a ranch to run in case you haven't noticed. I don't have time to sleep half the day and fish the other half." Brushing by her, Matt went around the end of the truck and got in.

She was right on his heels. "Sometimes I can't believe Wade was related to you."

"Sometimes neither could he." He started the motor and drove off leaving her staring after him.

"Where is she?" Matt tossed over his shoulder as his booted foot struck the hardwood floor of Arthur Ferguson's office. "I know she's anxious to stake her claim."

Watching Matt over tented fingers pressed against his beaklike nose, Ferguson continued to rock back and forth in his chair behind his desk. "You said she had to get dressed."

From beneath thick black lashes Matt shot Arthur a quelling glance. "Might have known you'd make excuses for her."

The lawyer's pensive expression never altered. "I'm merely making an observation. Like most women she probably just wants to make a favorable impression."

"She'd look good in a feed sack and she knows it," Matt blurted in rising irritation. "She just wants to annoy me."

Ferguson stopped in midrock backward and sat up straighter in his chair. His vague gaze of a moment ago was replaced by one of keen speculation. "Ms. Johnson sounds more interesting by the moment."

"Why?"

"In the years that I've known you since you came to live with Wade, I've never heard you compliment a woman or known you to let one take more than a fleeting thought in your mind. This one has done both."

"This one is trying to steal my heritage," Matt told him.

"I wouldn't jump to such a conclusion until you have all the facts, Matt," Ferguson said, and went back to rocking, all the time watching Matt as if seeking the answer to some difficult puzzle. "This is not her fault."

"Whose is it then? I need every cent to keep the ranch running until the beef can be sold in two months. I'm not paying off some little gold digger. The only thing I don't understand is why my uncle didn't want the bequest known to me until she and I were together."

"I'm sure he had good reasons."

Matt snatched aside the gauzy curtain on the office window and looked outside. "Yeah, I'll bet. I don't like the idea of meeting his lady friend this way."

A frown wrinkled Ferguson's deep-brown forehead. "There's no reason for that kind of talk. Wade Taggart was an honorable man."

"He was a man," Matt said flatly, remembering his own body's reaction to Shannon. Explosive.

When he'd baited her near the stock tank he had expected her to go prim and proper and indignant on him. Instead, she had looked at his mouth with a curious longing in her bottomless brown eyes. He felt himself falling in their glittering depth with nothing to grasp except her. A mistake. Her smooth, satiny skin was even more of a lure. Desire coiled through him as he watched her lips soften, part. Watched her long lashes flicker, then close.

He could have stopped what happened next, but he found himself as curious about her taste as she apparently was about his. It was a mistake. She tasted like his dream. A dream he was unaware of until Shannon's lips had touched his and made him want like nothing he had ever experienced. But life had taught him wanting wasn't enough and dreams had a way of turning into a living nightmare.

It had taken considerable willpower to push her away. Seeing the unbanked passion in her face, he had been tempted to damn the consequences and kiss her as her mouth and body begged to be kissed. Deep and hungry and forever. Instead, he had walked away because one kiss would never be enough with Shannon.

But the familiar heat in his loins didn't go away. Taking a deep breath, he continued to stare out the window. If he had to fight his own hunger, how could he have expected Wade to have resisted a woman whose sensuality was as much a part of her as her pretense of innocence and kindness?

His gullible uncle hadn't stood a chance against a grasping, seductive woman like Shannon Johnson. But this time she wasn't up against a man who would gladly give his last cent to any woman in need.

During the time his uncle was in the hospital, Shannon must have discovered Wade's weakness for helping women and used it to her advantage. The only thing Matt couldn't figure out was why she had taken so long to try to collect.

Scanning the two-lane street for her car, he finally spotted her convertible. The dark-blue Allante pulled into the space across the street from the law office. He glanced at his watch. 4:10 P.M. Fifteen minutes late.

The car door swung open. A pair of long, shapely traffic-stopping legs swung into view. Three-inch pale-yellow heels met the street seconds before Shannon stood and turned to face him.

Air hissed through Matt's clenched teeth. Involuntarily his hand fisted in the curtain. He damned Shannon Johnson as his body absorbed the full impact of her beauty.

Dressed to the hilt in a designer, figure-flattering pale-yellow suit, she looked elegant and beautiful and sexy. Barely four inches of material separated the hem of her skirt from the hem of the midthigh sculpted jacket. Without a woman's usual self-conscious swipe at her hair or her clothes, she headed for the street crossing.

Head high, she didn't appear to notice the people around her slowing down for a good second look. The women might be scoping out the clothes or the hairstyle, but Matt knew very well why the men were practically drooling. The same reason he was having trouble taking his eyes off her. She was a walking fantasy.

Releasing the curtain, he turned away. "Maybe I should be thankful Wade only gave her the meadow," he muttered.

"What was that?" Ferguson inquired.

"Shannon Johnson just arrived."

A knock sounded on the door, then a middle-aged woman entered. "Ms. Johnson is here."

"Show her in, Helen," the lawyer told his secretary and stood, straightening the slightly wrinkled gray suit jacket.

Shannon entered the office with a smile on her face and a subtle scent of an exotic floral perfume. Diamonds winked in her ears. Matt watched Ferguson's lower jaw become unhinged and knew Shannon had just scored points.

"Ms. Johnson, I'm glad you finally decided to come," Ferguson said.

"Thank you, Mr. Ferguson. I just wish it didn't have to be under these circumstances," she said softly.

Matt snorted. Her gaze sought him out. If he didn't know better he would have thought the sadness in her eyes was genuine.

The lawyer cleared his throat in the ensuing silence. "I believe you two are already acquainted."

"Yes, we are." Shannon gave her attention back to the lawyer. "I hope I didn't keep you waiting too long."

"Not at all." Ferguson patted the soft hand in his he had yet to relinquish. "Please sit down. Would you like something to drink? Tea? Coffee?"

"No, thank you." Taking the indicated chair in front of the antique wooden desk, she folded her hands over her small handbag. "I'd like to get this over as soon as possible."

"I told you she was anxious, Arthur." Matt strode across the small office and placed both hands on the arms of her seat. "What's the matter? Your last man woke up and now you need help in keeping yourself in the style you're accustomed to? On your salary you couldn't afford those clothes, the diamonds, and certainly not the Cadillac."

Her harsh intake of breath cut through the air.

"Matt, Ms. Johnson has been through enough in the past months without your adding to it," Arthur defended.

Straightening, Matt swung to the lawyer. "How would you know what she's been through?"

"I—"

"We're here to hear what Wade wanted, nothing more," Shannon interrupted, cutting off Ferguson.

The lawyer looked for a moment as if he wanted to say something, but at the almost imperceptible shake of Shannon's head, he clamped his lips shut. Going behind his desk, he took a seat, opened his desk drawer, then took out a heavy brown folder.

Their silent communication only gave more credence to Matt's belief that Shannon used her beauty and her aura of sadness to make fools of men. He wasn't going to be one of them.

"You're something else," he said, his eyes hard. "I bet your family is real proud of the way you turned out."

Shannon flinched.

Score a point for me, Matt thought. Then she lifted her tear-brimmed eyes to his. Misery stared back at him and he felt as though he had kicked a defenseless animal.

Calling himself a fool for falling for her act, he walked back to the window and leaned against the wall. "You have the floor, Arthur. But whatever happens, no one is going to get a square inch of Taggart land without a fight."

Ferguson paused in removing the legal document from the folder. "You haven't heard the will yet. On what grounds?"

"I think that's obvious."

Shannon finally looked at Matt. "Wade loved you like a son. Too bad you couldn't respect him like a father."

Matt came away from the wall in one fluid motion and crossed the room. Instead of cringing as he expected, Shannon jutted out her chin. The show of courage on her beautiful face stopped him more effectively than Ferguson's frantic voice.

"Matt, sit down," the lawyer ordered. "I know you don't like what Wade did, but he had his reasons. If you can't understand them, at least respect him enough to have his last wishes heard. Give him the same love and respect he gave you."

"It's not Wade I don't respect," Matt said, his meaning bitingly clear.

"Then we'll proceed as soon as you take a seat."

CHAPTER 4

"I don't care if you trust me or not," Shannon said with heat. "I do care that you keep going on as if Wade couldn't come out of the rain. He was one of the most intelligent men I've known. He was also one of the kindest. If you want to dislike me that's your privilege, but don't use Wade as an excuse."

His gaze drilled into Shannon's irate face. She returned the glare full measure. He *did* want to dislike her and he wasn't sure if the reason had to do with her wanting his heritage or because, despite his best efforts, he wanted *her.*

For the first time since his ex-wife taught him the bitterness of deceit, Matt was having a tough time suppressing his desire for a woman. He sat down.

Arthur Ferguson let out a tension-filled breath and looked from Shannon's tense body to Matt's. Lowering his gaze, he began to read Wade Taggart's Last Will and Testament.

Finished, he laid the papers aside. There were no surprises. Everything had been left to Matt except the original Taggart homesite of one hundred acres.

"How did you get him to turn his back on his family?" Matt asked.

This time he was the one who was ignored. "Please show me where I sign."

"Get ready for the fight of your life." Matt stood.

"You wouldn't let me have a moment of peace, would you?"

"No," he promised harshly.

"Just as I thought." She turned to the watchful lawyer. "After I sign, perhaps you can tell me where the nearest realtor's office is located."

"You're not going to sell my heritage," Matt thundered.

Surprise widened the lawyer's eyes. "Ms. Johnson, Wade wanted you to live on the property, not sell the land he loved. Perhaps I should have given you both these letters sooner, but Wade had instructed me not to hand them to you until after the will was read." Removing two letters from the folder, Ferguson rounded the desk and handed them out. "Because of his failing eyesight I offered to write them for him, but he wanted to do it himself. Not because of pride, but because he said the letters were too personal."

Shannon and Matt glanced at each other, then opened and began reading their letters.

Dear Shannon,

Life must be riding you pretty hard about now. The meadow will heal you. You did all you could for your grandfather. He was a lucky man to have had you. You may not believe it, but I felt just as lucky to have had Matt. Would you believe he thought he could hire Johnny Sanders to spy on me while I rode Paintbrush and expected me not to know it? Shows how gullible young people think their elders are. Many a day Paintbrush and I gave Johnny a scare or two. I didn't mind the watchdog because I knew it would keep Matt from worrying and it proved he wasn't as hard as some people thought.

That boy has had to get over a lot of heartache. At first, I had my doubts. But after watching him worry and fuss over me and all his shenanigans with Octavia, I know that other woman didn't tear the heart out of him, she just badly bruised it.

So while you're here don't mind Matt if he gets testy at times. Beneath that gruffness he's a good man. The roughest part in going is knowing he's still hurting because of that woman. He needs healing, too, just like you. I pray you can help heal each other.

Wade

Dear Matt,

Don't you make Shannon cry! If you do I'll get a pass from heaven and come after you. She needs all the help she can get.

When I woke up after that car in St. Louis piled into mine, the first thing I saw was Shannon's beautiful face. I thought I was seeing an angel. During the weeks I was in that hospital bed fighting depression, pain, and my fear of never walking again, I came to rely on her. With a gentle touch, a reassuring word, she helped me remember I wasn't alone. You and the family were my strength by day, but Shannon was my own special angel at night.

She is one of a kind. Do anything to make life worse for her and when I return, we're going behind the barn again. I can still best you and don't you forget it. So cut her some slack.

I know you're probably angry and hurt because I left her the meadow, but I owe her among other things. One day I hope you'll understand and forgive me. I loved you like a son and I came to think I was a pretty close second to your daddy. I'm counting on you to do what's right, but if you don't, remember I'm watching.

Wade

How long must it have taken you to write the letter, Matt thought. He shook his dark head in admiration and love. Wade was a tenacious fighter in more ways than one. Matt's mouth tilted slightly at the corners at the warm memories his uncle's letter evoked. When he glanced at Shannon, his blossoming smile vanished.

She looked utterly devastated. Her expression reminded him too much of himself when, ten years ago, Kane had brought a reluctant and angry Matt to Wade's ranch.

Matt had initially stayed because of his mother's tears, but it was his uncle's prodding and the land that helped Matt forget his wife's infidelity and turn his life around.

The painstakingly written letter clutched in her hand, Shannon recalled the peaceful expression on Wade's face, the wistfulness in his voice when he talked of his meadow. He called it a place touched by the smile of God. No, Wade wouldn't have wanted her to sell the land. Nor would he have been pleased to know she had taunted Matt with the possibility.

Wade thought she and Matt might help each other. That was impossible. Healing took time and trust, and Matt wasn't going to give her either.

Unsteadily, she pushed to her feet. "I'd like to think things over before I sign. I'll let you know my decision before I return to St. Louis." She turned to Matt. "In . . . in my letter Wade speaks fondly of you. Remember him the same way. He wasn't trying to take from you as much as he was trying to help me."

His continued silence hurt as much as the censure in his unrelenting face. She needed someone to recall the good memories instead of the sad ones. After reading Wade's letter, a part of her wished it could be Matt.

Sadness weighing heavily on her shoulders, she extended her hand to the lawyer. "Good day, Mr. Ferguson, and thank you for all your help."

"If there is anything I can do, please don't hesitate to call," Mr. Ferguson said. "Wade was more than a client, he was a close friend."

Shaking the lawyer's hand, she left very much aware of Matt's continued silence and the growing sadness within her.

* * *

"Where is she?" Octavia asked as soon as Matt walked through the front door of the ranch house.

"She who?" Matt never slackened his stride.

"Don't get funny with me, Matt Taggart," Octavia told him. "Shannon Johnson, that's who."

Matt flipped through the mail in his hand. "How should I know?"

"You had an appointment with her at Ferguson's office. I know you didn't expect Wade to leave her the meadow," she said, "but I guess he had his reasons."

"So I gathered, but there has got to be more to it than his letter explained. It also doesn't explain why the woman he left it to is ready to take my head off one minute and then before I can blink, she's trying to comfort me," Matt railed.

His mood had grown darker since he saw Shannon fighting tears. She hadn't acted the way he expected. Why hadn't she signed the papers in the lawyer's office? Why wait?

Suspicion narrowed the housekeeper's eyes. "What did you do to her?"

"Nothing." Matt barely kept from growling the word. Tossing the letters and magazines on his desk in his study, he retraced his steps to the front door. He hadn't felt so on edge since Kane dumped him at the Circle T. Octavia's nagging wasn't helping.

"She doesn't know anyone else here, where would she go?"

Matt spun around. "How would I know? She's probably someplace trying to con some man and make a fast buck."

Octavia opened her mouth, saw Matt's scowl deepen and said, "My arthritis is acting up. I won't be able to fix supper tonight or breakfast tomorrow."

"Fine." Jerking open the heavy front door, he headed for the barn. Whenever the housekeeper wanted him to know she was really upset with him, her "arthritis" acted up and she went on a work strike. In reality, she was as limber and as spry as a woman half her age. Let her get an attitude. He could fix his own supper. Shannon Johnson was no concern of his.

"I came to say good-bye, Wade, and to thank you," Shannon whispered as she stood amidst an array of wildflowers in the meadow. "I wish things could have ended differently."

She swallowed. The lump in her throat refused to budge. She hadn't ached this much since the day she lost her grandfather. Then, as now, she felt adrift, lost. Her family and friends hadn't been able to help, nothing had, and now she wasn't sure what would.

Hands clenched, she took one last look at the rustic cabin and walked to her car. Matt didn't want her around, and pushing the issue would solve nothing. She didn't have the time or the heart for a nasty court battle. And it would get nasty.

Matt might not be aware of it, but once he began proceedings to contest Wade's will, their private disagreement would become public knowledge. Both the Taggart and Johnson families were too well known and too prominent for the story not to grab attention.

News that Wade had left his former nurse, a single younger woman, a valuable section of his ranch and that his nephew was hotly contesting the will would send the media into a frenzy. Unfortunately some people were as suspicious as Matt and they would think the worst about her friendship with Wade. Wade's reputation would suffer, and the man who Wade had asked her to help would have another reason to mistrust women.

A horse neighed. Automatically she turned in the direction the sound had come from. Her heart stopped, then redoubled its beat. Matt, his signature black Stetson pulled low, sat on a horse fifty yards away watching her.

She'd know those broad shoulders and muscular build anywhere. She didn't have to see his face to know it was unrelenting in its disapproval. Whoever the woman was in his past, she had done more than "bruise his heart," as Wade had put it. She had wounded his soul.

Fumbling fingers opened her car door. Within seconds she was heading back down the road. Cowardly as it was, she didn't want another confrontation with Matt. Thank goodness she had put her bags in her car before she drove to the lawyer's office. She had intended to say good-bye to Octavia and thank her in person for making her feel welcome. A letter would have to suffice.

Glancing in her rearview mirror, she saw that Matt remained unmoved on his stallion. At least she hadn't had to suffer the humiliation of falling apart in front of him. She just wished she knew where she went from here.

With one arm draped over the open door of the refrigerator, Matt studied the well-stocked interior. Bone-weary, he couldn't decide if a hot shower or hot food called to him more. Every muscle in his body ached, but he hadn't eaten anything since breakfast and it was past nine at night.

Questing fingers lifted the corner of a foil-sealed glass dish. Roast beef. Recovering Sunday's leftovers, he picked up a quart-size plastic-covered bowl.

"I need you to take me into town," Octavia said from behind him. "My grandson has my car."

Having heard the housekeeper's heavy treads on the linoleum floor, Matt didn't even glance around. Instead, he tilted the clear container in his hand, recognized sliced canned peaches.

"It's important," Octavia continued, her voice strained.

"Riding in my truck might aggravate your arthritis."

"Shannon is in room twelve of the Paradise" came the tight-lipped reply.

His hand paused inches from the meat drawer. Broad shoulders tensed. The Paradise, known around town as the "no-tell-motel," had rates that were hourly and cheap. It was just the kind of place his ex-wife had frequented with men who could buy her the things Matt couldn't. So he had been right about Shannon after all. Something in his gut twisted.

He opened the meat drawer, then shoved it shut with more force than necessary. If his life had depended on the answer, he couldn't have named one item inside.

"I just knew something was wrong. She wouldn't have left without saying good-bye," Octavia reasoned. "So I called every motel in the vicinity until I located her at one I wouldn't let my dog stay in. That decent, caring woman I talked to this morning wouldn't go near such a place unless she had no choice."

"Have you talked to her?"

"The phone wasn't working in her room, so they couldn't connect me. But I know I'm right."

"I see." Absently, he moved a jar of jelly to one side. "Shannon didn't look like the type of woman to let herself get into a financial pinch."

"Looks can be deceiving." Octavia came around to the front of the refrigerator door and spoke to Matt's unyielding profile. "That young woman is here because your uncle left her Taggart property. That makes her partially your responsibility. You know what kind of place the Paradise is. What if some no-good man sees her and doesn't understand the word no?"

Matt's long fingers gripped the corner of the refrigerator tighter, but otherwise he didn't move. Shannon might have suckered his uncle and Octavia, but she wasn't adding his name to her list.

"Besides," the housekeeper continued, "since she has a claim on the meadow, it seems to me it would be in your best interest to keep an eye on her rather than letting her do God knows what with the property."

Finally, she had said something that got Matt's attention. He gave up all pretense of searching for something to eat and faced the housekeeper. Lines furrowed her forehead and crinkled the corners of her eyes. Obviously she was worried, and now he was, too. Not about Shannon, but about her future plans for the land.

That afternoon when he had seen Shannon near the cabin, he had been too angry to approach her. The thought that she had legal claim to the meadow and that he might have to pay her to get it back burned his insides like acid. After all these years, this woman was going to make him break a promise he'd made to himself because of another woman's deceit.

"She isn't going anyplace until she signs over all rights to the meadow to me." Slamming the refrigerator door closed, he headed for the front door.

"Now you're talking," Octavia encouraged, a pleased smile on her ebony face.

A mile from the motel Matt saw Shannon's car on the shoulder of the road. Since the car appeared undamaged, he reasoned it must be a mechanical problem. Recalling the last time he had seen her, how her miniskirt displayed her long, elegant legs, how her thick hair swirled wildly around her beautiful face, a face that sadness only made more compelling, he didn't imagine it was long before some man had stopped.

And now she was registered at the Paradise.

His grip on the steering wheel tightened. Her name might be the only one registered, but that didn't mean she was alone. The rage that splintered through him caught him off guard.

Loyalty and fidelity were two things he didn't expect from beautiful women like Shannon. His wife's had lasted only as long as he finished in the top money roping calves in the rodeo. But the more they argued over her spending habits and her refusal to travel with him on the circuit, the worse his concentration became, the more he lost.

By the time their nine-month marriage was over, he had gone from being ranked tenth in the country with a good chance at winning the National Calf Roping title to being unranked. At twenty-four he was a has-been and he owed it all to his stupidity and a greedy, unscrupulous woman. He had confused lust with love and paid the price.

So why did the confirmation that Shannon was exactly the same way anger him? He didn't look for an answer, he simply pressed his booted foot on the accelerator. The speedometer needle rocked to the right.

The purple-and-green neon-lit palm tree over the name Paradise winked on and off in subtle invitation and underlying promise of discretion and pleasure. The overgrown shrubbery, dingy windows, and cars of assorted ages and models told their own story of those whose carnal desires outweighed any other consideration. At least, on this night.

Matt passed the front office without slowing. His headlights on bright, he turned in a wide, searching arc in the one-story motel court. Number twelve was at the farthest end. An old dented Buick was parked at an angle in front, as if the occupants had been anxious to get inside.

Coming to a gravel-spitting stop, Matt jumped out of the vehicle. A heavy fist pounded on the door. "Open up!" A choked cry came from behind the peeling pink wood.

"Shannon! Shannon!"

Frantically, he twisted the knob. He stepped back with every intention of breaking the door down when he heard what sounded like his name and furniture being moved. Seconds later the door swung open. He only had a moment to glimpse Shannon's tear-stained face before she launched herself against him, her arms going around his neck.

"I—I thought you were that man who was bothering me earlier. Oh, Matt. I was so scared," she cried, her cheek pressed against his chest.

Something in his gut clenched again. His arms clutched around her shivering body drawing her closer. What if it hadn't been him? Fury at the unknown man—and himself—whipped through him.

For the first time in his memory, he didn't think right or wrong, he didn't weigh the cost. He simply held her. "It's all right, Shannon. I'm here."

Her grip tightened as she tried to burrow closer. Her voice quivered. "I . . . I was so scared."

"It's over. I'm here now." One hand slid down the smooth curve of her back, the other one tunneled through her hair. He soothed her with his voice, the steady rhythm of his hand.

The angry voices of a man and woman erupted in the courtyard. "I need to close the door, Shannon."

She tensed. "D-don't leave me."

"I'm not." Curving one arm around her small waist, he anchored her against his chest, moved just enough to reach the door, then slammed it shut. The instant the door closed, she released a tension-filled sigh. Her warm breath raked delicately over the side of his neck, the bare skin beneath his partially opened shirt.

Reluctantly, he set her on her feet, but kept her within the confines of his arms. "You feel better?"

She nodded, still not releasing her hold or moving away from him. With the full length of her body flush against his, he felt the lush imprint of each soft curve, the generous fullness of her breasts, inhaled the alluring fragrance of her perfume. Desire tore through him, but he ruthlessly controlled it.

Wrong time, wrong place, wrong woman.

The problem was she felt so right in his arms.

"No one is going to hurt you," he assured her.

"I—I knew that once I saw you."

Her words shouldn't have caused the strange feeling in his chest, but they did, and at the moment, there was nothing he could do about it except remember vulnerable women said things they often didn't mean. "When you feel better we're leaving."

A shiver ripped through her. "This was the only place I could afford after I couldn't find the rest of my money or my credit card," Shannon explained.

Every nerve in Matt's body went on alert. His hand in the small of her back paused. "You lost your money?"

"At first I thought I did. But after going over it again and again, I think I must have left the rest of my money and the one credit card I always carry on trips at home on my dresser." Sadness darkened her amber-brown eyes as she looked up at him. "I was in such a hurry to leave."

"To see the meadow," he said, ice sliding into his voice.

She nodded and lowered her head to his chest. "Everyone I called back home tonight was out. I just sat by the pay phone at the store and kept calling my family and friends in St. Louis with my calling card even though I had left a message on all their answering machines. Then it got dark and the store closed. There wasn't another place in town open for anyone to wire money to."

She took a deep, shuddering breath before continuing. "I thought about staying in the car, but after it got dark some men in a beat-up old truck kept cruising by. I had already asked the lady working in the store about the cheapest place in town to stay and she told me the Paradise. I should have suspected something from the surly way she answered my question."

"Why didn't you call Arthur Ferguson?"

"I tried. His office was closed and I got another answering machine at his house. So I decided to come here. Knowing how my family and friends would worry, I called everyone back before I left the store and told them I had run into an old friend."

"That was very considerate of you," said Matt coldly, his eyes narrow slits.

The terseness in Matt's voice finally penetrated Shannon's fear. Leaning back, she looked up into his starkly handsome face. His body against hers was as devoid of comfort as the emotionless black eyes that stared accusingly back at her.

"W-what's wrong?"

Matt studied the beautiful tear-stained face. If he didn't know better, he might think the puzzlement she showed was genuine. She had almost fooled him. Greedy like his ex-wife and a lot of other women he had known.

If she thought he was going to put her up at one of the hotels on the interstate, she had picked the wrong man to con. It was a good thing it suited his plans for him to be able to watch her or he'd leave her here with the roaches.

"Get your things," he ordered.

The stiffness of Matt's voice caused Shannon to hesitate for a moment before she rushed to get her overnight case and her purse from atop a rickety table. She didn't know what had gotten into him, but if he was taking her out of the Paradise that was all that mattered. The place made her skin crawl. "I'm ready."

"I see you didn't bother to unpack."

"I don't think a rat would stay in this place," Shannon said with feeling.

Matt glanced around the dingy room, the cobwebs on the one light fixture in the ceiling, the faded and chipped Mediterranean decor, then at the sizable diamonds in her ears. "Not what you're used to, huh?"

"No woman should have to get used to this."

"You'd be surprised at the number of women who like sleeping in low places." Taking her case, he grasped her by the arm and led her outside to his truck.

Unworried about decorum, Shannon pulled up her short skirt and climbed ungracefully inside as soon as he opened her door. Seated, she glanced at Matt's stiff profile as he slid in behind the wheel and wished the caring man who held her earlier would return.

She had told him the truth when she'd said she knew she was safe as soon as she saw him. He might make her angrier than she ever thought possible, but she couldn't deny he was the one person she had prayed would come and find her. And when he had held her in the shelter of his strong arms and soothed her with his deep voice, she had felt as if nothing could harm her.

At least she now knew Wade was right, that somewhere beneath Matt's cold exterior he had a heart. She hadn't missed his remark about a woman sleeping in low places. Had the woman Wade mentioned in his letter cheated on Matt? Was that why he distrusted women?

Absently, she wondered what kind of woman had taken away his ability to trust and what kind of woman it would take to restore his faith in a woman and make him smile. The sudden urge to be that woman jerked her back to reality almost as strongly as seeing them pass the motel's office without slowing.

"Stop!"

Tires screeched on gravel. "You forget something?"

"To check out." She held up the key. "I have to turn this in."

"If you think you'll get a refund, forget it."

"I don't, but I don't want anything to remind me of the last two hours." She opened the door, looked at the naked light bulb at the front door of the office, then back at Matt. Her voice hesitant, she asked, "You'll wait here, won't you?"

"I'll wait."

Offering a smile of gratitude, Shannon got out of the truck and went into the dingy office. The sight of the thin, unshaven man behind the counter caused her to shudder. She had been mentally groped by men before, but never had she wanted to rush home and take a scalding bath.

"I'm checking out."

Hands under his armpits, his back propped against the doorframe of a connecting room of the office, he slowly turned toward her. As when she had registered, his gaze dropped to her breasts and stayed there. His tongue ran across his narrow lower lip.

Shannon barely kept her disgust from showing. She wouldn't give him the satisfaction. The key landed with a soft thunk on the counter. "I'd like a receipt."

His gaze lifted. "Didn't take you long to get a better offer."

"The receipt."

Dragging his hands from beneath his arms, he went behind the counter and moved a sheet of paper. "Can't seem to find the receipt book. Wanna come behind the counter and help me look?"

"Not if my life depended on it."

"I'll just see about that," he snarled and started around the counter.

Shannon spun for the door. She heard a curse, then the distinctive clang of a phone hitting the floor. She looked over her shoulder. Not seeing anyone, she cautiously peeped over the four-foot wooden countertop. The clerk was sprawled on the cluttered floor, the phone cord tangled around his bony legs.

"Saved by Ma Bell," she said, and began to laugh.

The door behind her opened and she turned. Matt filled the doorway, his face harsh and relentless. "Having fun?"

"Hardly. The clerk appears to be having some difficulty finding a receipt book," she told him.

There was another clank behind the counter, then a string of curse words. "When I catch that bi—" A head shot over the counter and looked straight into Matt's dark, forbidding face. The man stumbled backward, tripped over the phone for the second time and went down.

Shannon laughed again. Catching her sides, she glanced up at Matt. Laughter abruptly ceased. She well understood the clerk's fright. Matt looked as if he could strangle her. She couldn't imagine what she had done this time to annoy him.

"Do you need help in writing that receipt?" Matt asked, his voice tight and clipped.

"No . . . no, sir" came the hasty reply.

Her eyes widened. Her gaze went to Matt. The pimply-faced, surly young man probably hadn't said "sir" in his life. At least it was nice to know she wasn't the only person intimidated by Matt.

True to the clerk's words, his head came back up this time with a body and a receipt shaking in his grubby hand. "Nice having you, Ms. Johnson."

Matt snatched the receipt with one hand and Shannon with the other. He didn't stop until he practically tossed her into the passenger seat of his truck. This time when he took off she had no intention of saying anything. Just breathing appeared to upset her reluctant rescuer. With no money she was at his mercy. She shivered. Not a comforting thought.

CHAPTER 5

Less than five minutes later Shannon realized she wasn't going to be able to keep her promise of not speaking to Matt. A small groan slipped past her lips as he slowed his truck and pulled off the highway behind her Allante. She had hoped he had forgotten about her car. The way her life was going she should have known that wouldn't happen.

Cutting the engine, he twisted in the seat toward her. "Which light came on?"

"Light?" Long, sooty lashes veiled her eyes.

Beneath his mustache sensual lips thinned in annoyance. "The red warning light in the dash."

"Oh." She twisted uneasily in her seat. She had known exactly what he had meant. Stalling wasn't something she usually did, but she had never been up against anyone who inspired such conflicting emotions within her.

Matt could be as compelling as he was annoying. For the last five minutes he was definitely the latter. "It's late. I'll just have the car taken care of in the morning."

He grunted. "The same way you took care of your sleeping arrangements?"

Bristling, she faced him. "I did the best I could with the money I had."

"If you couldn't afford a decent hotel, how are you going to get the car repaired?" he asked tightly.

"I'll manage." She resumed staring straight ahead. "I really thank you, but can we please just go."

"Give me the key."

Her head snapped around. Matt's face was determined, inflexible. He wasn't leaving until he checked her car. He held his hand out palm up. He wasn't the type to wait long.

"What difference does it make?"

"Jackson Falls may be a small town, but we still have car thieves. Your Cadillac would be too good to resist if one of them came across it," Matt explained impatiently. "You need your car to get home."

She looked into his resolute face. It didn't take a genius to decipher his words. He planned on her leaving soon and he wanted to make sure she had a way of doing so. He might have rescued her, but he still didn't trust her.

For a short time at the motel she had dared to hope things might be different between them. Another regret to add to her growing list. Opening her purse, she located the keys and dropped them into Matt's palm.

"Stay in the truck."

Shannon knew it was useless to continue with the charade. So what if he yelled at her again. She could take more of his condemnation, couldn't she? "It's out of gas."

Matt's muscular body paused halfway out of the cab. He sat back in the seat and just looked at her for a long moment.

Shannon found herself fidgeting and instantly stilled the nervous motion. She was stronger than this. "I discovered I was almost broke when I went into the service station to buy gas. Finding someplace where money could be wired to me took precedence. Then by the time I realized I wasn't going to be able to contact anyone, finding a safe place to stay seemed more important than the possibility of walking."

Her nose wrinkled in disgust. "At least I thought it was safe."

A flicker of something crossed his face so swiftly she couldn't read it in the dim cab. "You make a habit of running around on fumes?"

"Oh, no. In fact it's just the opposite since I work at night," she explained. "It's just that everything has been so hectic here. I didn't think about gas until it was too late."

Straightening, Matt started the engine and pulled back on the highway. On the interstate, he pulled under one of the eight bays of a brightly lit gas station.

"Thank you. I'll pay you back," Shannon told him as he got out of the truck.

"You can count on it," he promised harshly.

The door closed. Despite temperature in the upper seventies, Shannon shivered. She was safe and that was all that mattered. Matt's poor opinion of her shouldn't be important, yet somehow it was.

* * *

Octavia met Matt and Shannon at the front door of the ranch house with a nod of approval for Matt and a hug for Shannon. "You look tired, child. Go on up to your room and I'll bring a tray."

"Won't climbing the stairs be difficult with your 'arthritis'?" Matt asked.

"Nope," Octavia answered with a sassy smile and headed for the kitchen. "It's in remission."

Matt's grip on Shannon's luggage tightened. He was afraid this might happen. Octavia had accepted Shannon as one of her charges, which meant no matter what Shannon did or said Octavia would staunchly stand by her. The woman didn't give her friendship lightly, but once given it was irrevocable.

The moment Matt heard the words "child" and "her room," he knew Shannon had gained an ally. Shannon had managed to work her magic on the housekeeper, just as she had on Wade, just as she had tried to do on Matt himself.

"She did it to you again, didn't she?"

Matt glanced at Shannon. She was smiling. Again he experienced the almost imperceptible softening. "Did what?" he finally asked.

Her smile wobbled. "Got to you somehow. You had the same expression on your face last night."

"And that was?"

"A mixture of admiration and pique."

Grunting, Matt started up the stairs. Her intelligent brown eyes saw too much. "Men don't have pique. If we're angry we show it."

"Tell me something I don't know," she mumbled.

Matt heard the softly spoken words and decided to ignore them. It was just as well that he was immune to her. He hadn't realized it before, but he admired a spirited woman. Too bad she wasn't honest as well.

Shannon stepped inside the room and experienced an unexpected sense of peace. The homey room filled with heavy maple furniture and scattered rugs on the hardwood floor was nothing like her own Italian decor, yet somehow it felt right. She felt right being here.

She turned with a smile. "I can't thank you enough."

"Thank Octavia." He closed the door and placed her luggage by the dresser. "She's the one who called all the hotels until she found you."

"But you came for me." The breathlessness of her voice surprised and annoyed her. Matt might be one of the handsomest men she had ever met, but he was also one of the most unpredictable.

"I had my reasons."

"Whatever they were, I'm grateful." He looked stern, untouchable. The peace she had found began to fade. She knew the unbending man in front of her was responsible for that. His opinion of her mattered. She wanted the caring man to return and hold her one last time.

On impulse, she pressed a light kiss against his cheek. The sudden stillness of his body told her she had made a mistake. Eyes wide with apprehension and embarrassment, she took a step backward.

Something about Matt's entire demeanor changed, grew more calculated. Unsure of how to deal with this new aspect of an already unpredictable man, she decided to put more space between them. "I . . . er . . . good night."

Matt matched her step for step, his avid gaze watching her every movement. "How grateful?"

His husky voice vibrated down her spine. It was at once a lure and a challenge. "I don't understand."

Matt took another step. The heat of their bodies mingled. Shannon's lungs seemed to be fighting to suck enough air into them. And with each attempt her breasts came uncomfortably close to brushing against Matt's shirtfront.

Her foot eased back and struck a low cedar chest at the foot of the bed. She was trapped.

"I think you do, Shannon."

The sound of her name affected her almost as much as the pad of his thumb grazing across her lower lip. She had heard him say her name at the motel, but at the time she had been too frightened for it to register. Now she was too aware of him not to notice. Heat pooled in the center of her body. Desire made her legs weak.

"I think you understand very well. You need a place to stay and a man in your bed." The long, lean fingers of his other hand trailed along the collar of her suit. "I can give you both."

The blatant insult cleared the sensual haze from one heartbeat to the next. For a moment she was too surprised and too hurt to speak, and when she did it was barely above a shocked whisper. "You think I'd sleep with you for a place to stay?"

"We won't be sleeping," Matt told her bluntly. "You should have waited a little longer to tell me about your missing money and credit card."

Understanding hit, and with it came the bitter knowledge of what kind of woman Matt thought she was, and despite that knowledge, even now she couldn't keep her body from shivering from his touch. "Take your hand off me."

"There's no reason to keep—"

He was talking to air because Shannon had ducked beneath his arms and headed for her luggage. She reached them within seconds.

"Where the hell do you think you're going?" He stepped in front of her.

"Since I won't pay your price, why should you care?"

Surprise at Shannon's seemingly displaced anger made Matt's brow arch. In spite of himself he watched in reluctant fascination as her flushed cheeks and jutted chin made her face even more striking. "It's a little late to be playing the shocked innocent."

"I guess the same could be said of you playing the gentleman." She gritted a false smile. "Looks like we both guessed wrong."

"What did you expect?" he practically snarled. "You were all over me."

"Tenderness," she told him, her voice strained. "A hint of kindness. Foolish of me, wasn't it." Her chin lifted. "Please move."

He didn't budge. "So now I'm supposed to believe you're going to walk twelve miles back to town and sleep in your car over a harmless pass."

Shannon remained silent and stared at the door over his wide shoulders.

Her silence infuriated him. She was the one who had started this. "I don't force women. There's a lock on your door. Use it if you want, but I won't beg you to stay."

Placing her overnight case under her arm, she secured her hold on the larger suitcase and stepped around a grim-faced Matt. Opening the door, she started through it only to come to an abrupt halt. Octavia, a tray of food in her hands, blocked the way.

"Thanks, child." The heavy woman frowned. "Why are you still holding your suitcase? Matt, where's all that training your mother and I tried to give you? Take her things," Octavia instructed as she placed the tray on the dresser.

Taking a step away from Matt's outstretched hands, Shannon said, "I can't stay."

"Why?" the housekeeper asked, clearly puzzled.

Shannon glared at Matt. His jaw tight, he looked away. At least he wasn't without some shame. Yet, there was no reason to embarrass Octavia. "I don't have any money."

"I knew there was a reason for you staying at that place," Octavia said with conviction. "Don't worry about a thing. You don't need money to stay here. Besides, since Matt's cattle have been grazing in *your* meadow, he's the one who should be paying you."

"Anytime Shannon wants to pay her share of the taxes on this place, I'll be happy to pay her a grazing fee." Matt stalked from the room and shut the door on the silent women.

After Matt's late supper and a bath, sleep still eluded him. The letter on the nightstand from Wade wouldn't let him. There was no way in hell his uncle or any of the Taggart men would have approved of the way he had treated Shannon.

No matter what she was, he shouldn't have stooped to her level. He didn't threaten women. He had no intention of making his suggestion a reality. He had just wanted her to know she couldn't keep pushing her lush little body against his and not expect any consequences. He was an all too human male.

She evoked needs in him that made a mockery of common sense. He didn't trust her, but for the first time since his divorce ten years ago, his mind and his body weren't in complete accord in dealing with a woman. Shannon tested his control and tried his patience with every glance, every touch, every enticing sway of her shapely hips.

No matter what he thought of Shannon, his uncle had thought well enough of her to leave her his favorite place, the place of the Taggart original homestead. Matt's anger had cooled down enough to realize there had been nothing romantic between the two, but that still left a lot of questions. There was more to it than just Wade owing her.

Apparently Arthur Ferguson was privy to Shannon's past and Matt was almost positive Octavia was, too. She wasn't surprised by Wade's will and what's more, she had never taken to a woman the way she had to Shannon. He was flying blind on this one and making mistakes.

He couldn't forget the hurt look on Shannon's face when he made his crude suggestion. It was too much of a contrast with the aroused look of moments before. Somehow he had badly misjudged things. Anger at life assaulted him again for pitting him against a woman beautiful enough to make his body clench each time he looked at her and mysterious enough to doubt himself.

But she wasn't taking his heritage. He'd help her get back on her feet and then she was leaving . . . after she signed over her claim to his land. Yet somehow he had to accomplish the first goal in such a way as to help him accomplish the second and most important objective.

The idea came out of nowhere. Shannon probably only thought of the monetary gain in owning part of a ranch, not the hard work it took to keep it in the black. Obviously she lived well above what her nursing salary provided.

It stood to reason someone else was paying the price for her expensive tastes. This time she was going to work for what she wanted. She was about to find out firsthand the back-breaking work it took to make the ranch run smoothly and return a profit.

Within a week, she'd be begging to go home. He had already broken his golden rule and bought her gas, he might as well give her enough money to get to St. Louis . . . after she signed over the meadow. Without another moment's hesitation, he went to Shannon's room and knocked.

Opening the door at her assent, he saw her sitting on the side of the bed, her back to him. "You needn't have bothered coming for the tray, Octavia. You've done too much already." Rising, she turned toward him. The weak smile on her face froze, her body went rigid.

Matt accepted the accusations in her wary eyes and the bitter taste of self-disgust in his mouth as partly his due. The other part was hers. "Next time don't send out signals unless you're willing to back them up."

Shannon flushed guiltily and glanced away. In the aftermath of their argument, she had time to think about what she had done and realize she shared a large part of the blame. Matt knew nothing about her except she was trying to take his heritage . . . not a very good character reference.

At least he had been honest enough to tell her beforehand what he thought of her instead of *afterward*. Her cheeks heated. She wasn't sure what the afterward would have been, but there definitely would have been one if he had returned her kiss. Twice, by the stock tank and in this very bedroom, he had showed more restraint than she had. He hadn't taken advantage of her.

Finally, she nodded. Matt wasn't as dangerous to her as she was to herself.

Callused fingers brushed across his hair. She should give up nursing and go into acting. Averted eyes, trembling lips, slumped shoulders . . . she really had mastered the art of appearing the uncertain, sexually awakening virgin. If Shannon was a virgin, he was from outer space.

"We need to talk about the meadow."

Her head came up. "Yes."

He wasn't surprised he had gotten her attention. "The meadow as I told you has the only year-round water on the thousand acres of the Circle T. Yes, the cattle graze there, but if it wasn't for the alfalfa hay that is bailed in another section of the ranch for winter feed, the ranch couldn't sustain the large number of cattle we run.

"Since nothing in the meadow is sold, the profits from the ranch have to supplement this house, the wages for the hands, and all the other things needed to make the ranch solvent, including the meadow."

"I see."

"I hope you do. The ranch and the meadow are interchangeable. One can't prosper without the other."

"You're asking me to sign over the meadow?" she asked, aware of the slight tremor in her voice.

"I'm asking you how badly do you want the land? Bad enough to sweat and get your hands dirty?" Seeing her stricken face, he rushed on. "After breakfast would you be willing to work for the land you want to claim?"

Shannon watched in stunned amazement as Matt slammed out of her room. Gradually what he had said began to sink into her tired brain. She had just been issued a challenge. Living in St. Louis all her life, she knew nothing about a ranch. She could only ride a horse because her mother insisted she have riding lessons as a child.

Work in Matt's mind was probably the grungiest, dirtiest job he could find. She'd be crazy to take him up on his challenge. She should call her parents in the morning and have them wire her her money and leave.

Then what?

Shannon sat back down on her bed. If she ran this time, how long before she ran away from another problem? She had run away from her grandfather's death, her profession, her family, and the man who wanted to marry her. Her head lifted, her shoulders straightened. She wasn't running a step farther. She was accepting Matt's challenge.

She'd be less than a Johnson if she didn't beat him at his own game. A slow calculating smile tilted the corners of her mouth in anticipation of the coming battle. Apparently she had more of her parents' tenacity than she thought. She was going to make Matt Taggart take back every insult he had ever flung at her.

The arrogant, distrustful scoundrel didn't believe she had left her money and credit card at home. At the time she hadn't wanted to believe it either as she had frantically searched through her wallet, her purse, and her suitcase.

Recalling her haste to leave her parents' home, she remembered cleaning out her wallet, laying the one all-purpose credit card she always took on trips and the green-and-white bank envelope with five hundred dollars on top of her dresser. And that's where she had left them.

So, she had run out of gas getting to the only place in town she could get a room for the twenty-five dollars and odd cents she had left. One look at the run-down motel, the slovenly clerk, and she knew what type of place the Paradise was.

Matt might have rescued her, but obviously he had not reversed his opinion of her.

There was something about his handsome, unsmiling face that called to her. She wanted to see him smile. To see him look at her with something other than mistrust in his piercing black eyes.

She couldn't possibly accept James Harper's marriage proposal. Not when Matt affected her so.

The two men were alike in so many ways, yet so totally different. James was charming, gracious, and witty; Matt snarled and sniped. Both were handsome, aggressive, and reveled in taking charge.

James usually planned the evening for them. It was "I have tickets for" or "we're invited to." To give James credit, he did ask for her preference early in their relationship, but since she didn't have any interest in most of the social whirl of see-and-be-seen, he usually ended up making the decision anyway.

As he explained once, it was important to his career as a lawyer that he be visible, and since he was going to have to make the decision anyway, why go through the motions of asking her. If his take-charge attitude irritated her sometimes, it wasn't enough for her to make an issue of it.

She didn't like arguments. In fact, she usually went out of her way to avoid them. It was the one flaw in her character Granddaddy Rhodes regretted not being able to change.

With the exception of Granddaddy Rhodes, the rest of her family adored James. Not one of them was going to like the decision she was about to make, but she had made unpopular decisions before. Granddaddy Rhodes was always there to back her up before. Sadness slumped her shoulders. He had always been there for her, with a smile of approval and love.

The two of them had always been closer than he was to her brothers. Her mother often said it was because both Shannon and her grandfather had stars in their eyes. Coming from a family of practical, hard-nosed lawyers, her success in nursing and Granddaddy Rhodes's in real-estate speculation was something talked about frequently, and always with wonder.

Now those same stars in her eyes had gotten her in trouble with her reluctant partner. In the future she'd have to remember to keep her lips clamped together and her hands in her pockets around Matt.

Walking over to the dresser, she picked up the roast beef sandwich Octavia had brought and took a small bite. Her appetite had returned. Of course Matt expected her to fail. He wasn't the type of man who liked to lose. She knew that from his reaction when Octavia bested him.

Well, he shouldn't issue challenges because he was in for the surprise of his life. Obviously he didn't know the long, grueling hours nurses worked bending, lifting, stooping. This time he was going to lose. She took another bite of the sandwich and smiled despite her full mouth.

CHAPTER 6

"Shannon dear, are you sure you're all right?" asked George Johnson.
"Perhaps you should come home," Henrietta Johnson added.

Seated in a chair in the den, Shannon almost regretted calling her parents tonight instead of waiting until morning to reassure them. They had put her on the speaker phone in their bedroom and she could just imagine them pacing the floor, each ready to fire questions at her as if she were on the witness stand.

"I'm fine and I'm not coming home," she finally said. "I'm old enough to take care of myself."

The minute the words were out of her mouth she knew she had made a mistake. Her parents were too sharp to miss an opportunity to come back at her.

She was right.

"Leaving your money and credit card is hardly responsible," they parroted.

Shannon slouched lower in her seat. She had debated whether or not to mention the money and credit card, then decided she had no choice if Melanie, her best friend, was going to pick them up in the morning from Shannon's parents and send them to her by overnight mail.

"Mother, Daddy. I'm with friends, I've just eaten and I'm about to go up to my room and go to sleep."

"What's the name and phone number of these friends?" her father asked.

"Where do we send the money? You know how I feel about that,"

Henrietta said almost frantically. "I shudder each time I think of what might have happened."

Shannon smiled. Despite everything, she never doubted her parents' love. They might disapprove of her actions at times, but their love was constant. Her father as usual wanted to know the who and the what, but her mother, her mother believed a woman should never be at the mercy of fate or a man. No matter how nice or upstanding her date, Shannon always had a quarter in her shoe and a twenty-dollar bill pinned to her bra when she went out in high school.

"I love you both."

"You know we love you, too, baby," answered her mother. "So does James."

Shannon straightened in her chair. "Mother, I don't want to go into that now."

"Of course," her father placated. "Just give me the name and phone number of these friends who helped you and we'll wire you some money. There's no need to bother Melanie."

"Nice try, Dad. You'd also call me every day." She continued to talk over their protests. "You mean well, but this is my life and at the moment I need to take a good long look at it. If I get into something I can't handle, I promise, you'll be the first to know."

"But, baby—"

"Shan—"

"Please give the money and credit card to Melanie when she comes by in the morning and don't badger her with too many questions. I love you." She hung up the phone, then leaned back in the chair and stretched out her legs. Her parents were probably dialing her brothers' phone numbers now. They'd hook up a three-way and discuss her life. As always, they thought they knew what was best for her.

Their answer to her emotional upheaval since her grandfather's death was for her to quit nursing, accept James's marriage proposal, become a social butterfly and have two beautiful, well-mannered children. The idea had even less appeal now than it did when he first proposed six weeks ago.

James was nice, but he didn't excite her like—

"What are you doing downstairs?"

Shannon jumped up from her chair. As if she had conjured him up, Matt stood in the den. Bare-chested, jeans unsnapped and perched on his hips, he looked tempting. Muscles rippled as he braced his hands on his waist. The man had one fine body.

"I asked you a question." His eyes were hooded, but there was a hint of something in them that made her heart race.

She tried to work up some moisture in her mouth so she could speak.

"Using the phone." She held up her calling card. "I hope you don't mind."

A dark brow arched. "Reassuring everyone again."

She smiled. "That's right. Sorry if I disturbed you."

"If you're finished, I'd like to get some sleep. *I* have to work."

Shannon continued smiling despite the barb. "Good night." She brushed past him and went up the stairs. If she could control her attraction to Matt, it was going to be a pleasure to teach him a lesson.

"Shannon. What are you doing here?"

Heavy-eyed with sleep, Shannon lifted her head and greeted the housekeeper around a yawn. "Good morning, Octavia."

"Child, why aren't you asleep in your bed instead of at the kitchen table? It's seven-twenty."

"I got up to fix Matt some coffee," Shannon explained, stretching her stiff arms over her head.

Octavia's gaze went to the automatic coffeepot. "Oh, Lord. I forgot to get things ready last night. That boy never could make good coffee."

Shannon smiled. "So I gathered from all the grumbling and banging I heard when I entered the kitchen. I'm surprised all the noise didn't wake you up."

"Once I'm out, I'm out. But my eyes open at seven each morning and there's no getting back to sleep. Matt comes in from working outside for breakfast a quarter to eight." Opening the refrigerator door, Octavia took out a box of sausage patties and a package of bacon.

"If I had known you were a deep sleeper I would have cooked breakfast." Shannon stood. "Is there anything I can do to help?"

"Hand me that big black skillet from the cabinet under the stove." Octavia placed the meats on the counter, opened another cabinet and took out a large crock bowl. "You never did tell me why you were asleep at the table."

Rinsing the skillet under tepid water from the faucet, Shannon smiled over her shoulder. "Showing Matt his partner is no slouch."

"Would you mind explaining that?" Octavia asked as she folded her arms across her wide girth.

Shannon smiled. Something she couldn't seem to stop doing. "Last night Matt asked me if I was willing to sweat and get dirty for my claim. He left before I could give him my answer. Getting up with him was my way of showing him that I can hang just as tough as he can."

Laughter burst from Shannon. "You should have seen his startled expression when I came into the kitchen. I've never seen a man so starved for coffee and too stubborn to ask for help."

"He's stubborn all right, but he's tricky, too," the housekeeper warned.

"I can handle Matt."

The housekeeper looked at her quizzically. "Seems you and *Matt* got along pretty well this morning."

Shannon ignored the comment and busied herself with opening the package of bacon. "How many slices should I put in the skillet?"

"Six for Matt and whatever you want for yourself. None for me, my cholesterol is up again. I sure do miss my bacon," Octavia lamented. "Some things are hard to give up, but you got to know what's best for you in the long run."

Shannon wondered if the housekeeper was talking about her cholesterol level or Shannon's situation with Matt. Not sure if she wanted to know, she didn't ask.

Matt had wolfed down four fluffy biscuits before he learned his unwanted junior partner had made them. The hungry side of him said it didn't matter, the suspicious side of him said this one knew all the tricks to get to a man. Dressed in an oversize bright-red-and-white striped shirt with the collar turned up and a pair of jeans, she shouldn't have looked elegant and chic in his kitchen, but she did. Well, he was adept at a few tricks himself.

Taking another sip of coffee from the stoneware cup, he pushed aside his plate and rocked back slightly in his chair. He was about to knock that confident smile right off Shannon's beautiful face. He didn't even mind Octavia's glare.

"Ready to work, Ms. Johnson?"

"Since we're in this together, why don't you call me Shannon and I'll call you Matt." Across the table, she folded both arms. "And to answer your question, I can't wait."

"Glad to hear it." Matt took a sip of coffee before continuing. "First, muck out the twenty-four stalls in the stable and lay in some fresh hay, then polish the tack in the work room. After that there's some brush down by the creek that needs clearing."

"And after that?"

Coffee was gliding over his tongue when Shannon asked the question. Matt, who knew the stables would probably keep an inexperienced person busy most of the day, choked on his coffee.

The flat of Octavia's hand slapped him hard between the shoulder blades. "What's the matter, Matt, something go down the wrong way?"

Matt scowled up into his housekeeper's cheerful face. Her grin widened.

"Are you all right?"

His head whipped around. Shannon was bending over him, her face filled with concern, her lips too close. Hastily, he pushed to his feet. "No need to make a fuss. Let's go outside and I'll introduce you to the hands."

"Shannon needs some work gloves and a hat before she goes to work." Octavia glanced at the younger woman's tennis-clad feet and shook her head. "Once you wear those shoes cleaning stables, you might as well throw them away."

Shannon bit her lower lip. "They're the sturdiest shoes I have. I don't have any money . . ." She didn't have to see Matt tense to know where his thoughts were leading. Melanie was going to wire Shannon her money and credit card in care of Arthur Ferguson. When she had called both of them this morning, each had been too glad to help. But in the meantime she only had thirty-six cents.

"I'm not asking you to buy me anything."

"Glad to hear it," Matt said.

"I know where you can find everything you need and not worry about paying a cent," Octavia said. "You just come with me and I'll fix you up."

Grabbing Shannon's hand, Octavia left the kitchen and started across the den. Shannon looked back to see Matt wearing a scowl as black at his Stetson. Shrugging her shoulders, she allowed the housekeeper to lead her up the stairs.

Less than ten minutes later, Shannon came back downstairs wearing a faded blue shirt and jeans, scuffed boots, and a beat-up straw hat. Standing in the den in front of Matt in his younger sister's discarded clothes while his critical eyes skimmed over her was not easy.

"You look like a scarecrow."

"Perhaps you'd like to assign me to the alfalfa field instead of the barn?" Shannon asked politely. She'd eat worms before she'd show how much his remark hurt.

One dark brow lifted, but all he said was "Come on, you've wasted enough of my time."

Shannon followed his long strides out the front door and wished sticking your tongue out behind someone's back wasn't considered childish. Besides, with her luck, he'd catch her or, worse, think she was coming on to him again.

She saw the car as soon as she stepped off the porch. Moments later a smiling Arthur Ferguson emerged from the vehicle just as they reached the bottom steps.

"Good morning, Matt, Shannon. Wade would be proud of you, Matt. Shannon called me this morning to let me know she was all right thanks to your timely intervention."

"Hello, Ferguson," Matt said thinly. "Shannon prides herself on reassuring people."

Shannon spoke to the lawyer, then clamped her teeth together to keep her tongue from getting her into trouble.

The lawyer nodded. "Wade always said she was one of a kind." Ferguson reached into his breast pocket and pulled out two letters.

"Since you two seem to have come to some sort of terms with the will, I have something for you from Wade."

Matt and Shannon looked questioningly at the lawyer before accepting the envelope, then lifting out the single sheet of paper.

Dear Shannon,
   Thank you.

                                                                    Wade

Dear Matt,
   Thank you.

                                                                    Wade

Matt's fingers curled around the letter as he lifted his head and asked, "You have any more of these?"

Ferguson's smile grew. "Might. You two have a good day." Getting back into his car, he drove off.

Shannon watched him leave, then shoved her letter into her hip pocket. She watched as Matt did the same. "I wonder if there was a letter for us if we didn't reach an agreement?"

"I can only hope," Matt said, and took off across the yard to the barn thirty yards away.

Unable to help herself, she made a face at his retreating back, than started after him. Trying her best to keep from looking as if she were running, which in fact she was, Shannon snatched her straw hat off her head so she wouldn't lose it. By the time they entered the dim interior of the barn, she was slightly winded.

"Jay, Elliott, Griff, Cleve. Get out here."

Four men emerged. One came from the hayloft, two from the interior of the barn, and one out of a stall. All came running. The three youngest men were first to reach Matt. Although they couldn't have been much younger than their boss, it wasn't difficult to see the adoration in their eyes. The last to arrive was a bearded elderly man who could have been Uncle Remus's twin.

"Men, I'd like you to meet the newest hand, Shannon Johnson." Four pairs of eyes bugged, then went from Matt to Shannon. "This is Jay Fisher, Griff Walker, Elliott Fox, and Cleve Redmon."

The elderly gentleman, Cleve Redmon, was the first to step forward. "Pleased to meet you, ma'am."

His gaze was as cautious as the hand he extended. Their hands barely touched before the light pressure of his hand was gone. Stepping back, he ducked his head.

If Cleve was reticent, the three other men were not. With their hats clutched to their chests with one hand, they pumped Shannon's arm with the other as if they were priming a pump. She hoped it meant they were going to accept her.

At least all of them were friendly except Cleve. For some reason her gaze strayed back to him. She was surprised to find him anxiously looking at her. "Is something the matter?"

"No, ma'am, I better get back to my chores."

"Shannon is going to muck out the barn for you," Matt told him.

Cleve straightened his slightly stooped shoulders. "You aren't pleased with my work no more?"

"You know if I hadn't been you would have heard it before now," Matt said.

"No offense, boss, but I'd rather do it by myself," the elderly cowhand argued.

"She cleans the stalls, Cleve." The flatness in Matt's voice brooked no argument. The other three hands found the pattern the toes of their boots were making in the dirt enticing.

The older man's shoulders slumped for a second, then surged upward. "Yes, sir." There was no surliness in the tone, just hurt.

Wounded pride. Pride Shannon understood. She took the few steps that would bring her face-to-face with Cleve. "Cleve, I know it's an imposition, but I hope you can please put up with me for a little while. Since I now own a piece of the Circle T, Matt insists I learn what it takes to run the place."

Three dirt-staring heads popped up, their jaws unhinged. The scowl on Matt's face would have made most men run. Shannon smiled. He wasn't as fierce as he appeared. She had seen his face earlier and knew he hadn't wanted to hurt Cleve, either.

She turned to the elderly man. Lightly, her hand touched his stiff arm. "So, if you could please tolerate me and show me the ropes, I'd appreciate it."

"Well . . ."

She smiled. "I'd be so grateful." In a side whisper that everyone could hear, she said, "I might need to brush up on my riding, too, before Matt sends me out to scout the range."

Cleve looked horrified. "Ain't no such thing as scout the range. Where did you come from?"

"St. Louis. Where the West begins."

"The West begins in Fort Worth, Texas. You've got a lot to learn, girlie," Cleve told her.

"That's what I've been trying to tell her," Matt said. "You can give instructions, but I want her to do everything by herself."

"All right, boss. But don't be surprised if she don't last the day." Cleve turned and walked deeper into the barn's interior. "Ranching is man's work."

This time it was Shannon's jaw that came unhinged. After trying to help Cleve, he had turned on her. A bark of laughter swung her around.

Mesmerized, she watched Matt throw back his head in laughter. He was framed in silhouette of the morning light. He looked like a dark angel, tempting and unbelievably handsome.

"I could have told you, Shannon. Some men are immune to your charm." Tipping his hat, he walked away.

Angel my foot! Devil was more like it. With determination in every step, she stomped off to find her reluctant teacher.

CHAPTER 7

Matt crossed the yard in ground-eating strides. His foul mood was his own fault. All morning he had tried to forget the picture of injured pride on Cleve's face, but it wouldn't go away. In Matt's attempt to get rid of Shannon he had inadvertently hurt a man he loved and respected.

Cleve Redmon had been a fixture on the Taggart ranch for as long as Matt could remember. Like Wade, Cleve had never married. Unlike his uncle, Cleve tended to enjoy being by himself. Matt couldn't remember the elderly cowhand ever taking a vacation or a few days off. Working on the ranch seemed to be all he wanted. Even on his day off, he was never idle.

Yet, while Cleve's heart might be willing, his body was tired. His arthritis wasn't helping. More days than Matt wanted to remember, he had seen Cleve wrap his horse's reins around his wrist when his fingers were too stiff and pained him too much to hold the narrow leather strips. His pride was as big as the Texas sky. Pensioning him off would have slowly killed him. Easing him into taking care of things around the house and barn had required delicate maneuvering.

Wade had helped by constantly reminding Cleve they had worked in their youth for twenty-five cents a day and a rock-hard biscuit for lunch. Through rainstorms, broiling sun, and bad health they had stayed in the saddle and got the job done no matter how hard or how long it took. Without a word being said, Matt always knew Cleve was thinking Wade had been working for his father, then himself while Cleve had simply been one of the hands.

It surprised no one that Cleve had kicked against slowing down, but gradually he had settled into his new responsibilities off a horse. But he didn't like help from anyone. And in Matt's haste to get rid of Shannon, he had forgotten all that. Grudgingly, he had to admit she had been sensitive enough to Cleve's feelings to try to ease his mind.

Or was it another game she was running?

His mood darkened. Yanking open the back door, he entered the kitchen. From somewhere in the house he heard the vacuum cleaner shut off. The screen door banged shut behind him. Opening the refrigerator, he took out a pitcher of tea, then reached for a glass.

"Is that you, Shannon?" yelled the housekeeper.

"Nope, it's me."

Moments later Octavia entered the kitchen, her face wrinkled in a frown. "I thought you'd be out plowing most of the day."

"So did I," Matt said, then took a huge gulp of the ice-cold drink. "The clutch went bad on the tractor. I brought it back in to work on it."

"I don't suppose you got time for a bite to eat?" the housekeeper questioned.

"No, but thanks." Setting the glass down, he headed for the door again.

"If you see Shannon, send her in for lunch."

One hand on the knob, he glanced at his watch. "It's after one."

"I know, but I haven't seen her since the two of you left this morning," she answered. "You did tell her to come back for lunch, didn't you?"

"Any fool would know to stop for lunch."

Octavia crossed her arms in a familiar gesture. "That's the same thing I've been trying to tell *you* for years. Yet, you don't listen."

He scowled. "I'm working for what's mine."

"So is Shannon." The housekeeper nodded toward the kitchen clock on the wall. "Looks like she's willing to work just as long and as hard as you are."

"That remains to be seen." Opening the door, Matt headed for the barn. This was one time he was going to delight in proving Octavia wrong.

If there was one thing he had noticed about Shannon, it was her neatness. In contrast to the sassy red toenails, her fingernails were short, rounded, and had a glossy shine. He'd bet his truck they were professionally cared for.

He hated to admit it, but she had the softest hair he'd ever touched. It smelled good, too. Whether ruffled by the wind or a man's hand, the lustrous, shoulder-length auburn hair somehow managed to look tempting. Automatically his mind conjured up the picture of the last time his hands had glided through her hair and pulled her body flush with his. Immediately, his body responded.

With ruthless determination, he brought his mind and desire under control. Shannon might be tempting as sin, but she was also manipulative, untrustworthy, and out for what she could get . . . the easiest way possible.

Nope, a woman like Shannon wouldn't like being sweaty and dirty. She'd probably spent most of the morning in the tackroom, not working, but washing her face and hands. Matt had no doubt she had already eaten with Cleve and the rest of the hands.

Cleve might not like women working on the ranch, but he wasn't mean-spirited. He'd offer her lunch. Shannon would accept; she wasn't the type of woman to pass up an opportunity to gain more allies or another conquest.

Matt entered the barn. A few feet inside he blinked, then blinked again.

A wheelbarrow was midway down the wide aisle. Dangling from one of the handles was the straw hat Shannon had been wearing that morning. His brows furrowed. She couldn't have gotten that far. Continuing, he didn't stop until he was at the open stall in front of the wheelbarrow.

Instead of using a pitchfork, Shannon was on her knees distributing hay and mumbling to herself. "I'm never going to think it's romantic to see a couple making love in the hay again. This stuff itches and it's dusty." She scooted over a bit. "You'd have to be in the depths of lust to forget where you were."

"Are you saying you've never forgotten where you were while making love?"

Her shoulders stiffened. Her eyes closed. Why couldn't it have been anyone but *him?* All too aware of how sweaty and dirty she was, she spoke without turning. "After I finish, I'll go to work on the tackroom."

One broad shoulder leaned against the stall door. "You didn't answer my question?"

His deep voice did strange things to her heart rate. "Don't you have work to do?"

He did, but at the moment he was oddly content to stay where he was. Shannon had a nice little backside. "You haven't chosen your lovers very well if not one of them could make you concentrate just on him."

The derision in his voice propelled her to her feet. "Oh, and I suppose your lovers wouldn't mind if they were on a roller coaster."

"High, hot, and wild. Why would they?"

Her body heated from one word to the next. She only had one defense. "And probably just as fast."

His darkly handsome face leaned within an inch of hers. "Keep pushing me and you're liable to find out the answer for yourself."

She staggered back. Her mouth felt bone dry. Her skin tight. "I . . . I. . . ." Her voice trailed off. She didn't know what she wanted to say. Worse, she didn't know if she wanted Matt to carry out his threat or leave her alone.

The sensual gaze left his eyes as quickly as it had come. "What did Cleve fix today for lunch?"

"B-beef stew."

Matt almost smiled. Better and better. If Cleve had fixed stew it meant he didn't plan to cook anything else for lunch until it was all gone. That could last a couple of days to a week.

"Octavia was concerned that you hadn't had lunch. I'll tell her you ate with the boys."

"But I didn't."

"You just said Cleve had beef stew."

"I did, but I didn't eat." Shannon stared down at her feet. "I wanted to get a bit more work done before I stopped for lunch."

Matt wanted to shake her. Why couldn't she act the way she was supposed to? She didn't appear a bit concerned that she had straw in her hair or that her jeans and shirt were dirt-smeared. He had too much to do to try to figure Shannon out. "Go in the house and eat."

Her head lifted. "I'd like to finish this first." She wiped a trickle of sweat from her brow. "I'm a little behind."

"That wasn't a request."

A glance at Matt's taut features told her arguing was useless and potentially dangerous. Not danger to her body, but danger to her emotions. Her feelings were too chaotic to risk another confrontation.

It was just her luck that Wade's nephew was the most sensually handsome man she had ever met. If that wasn't enough, something within her yearned to see him smile, to make him happy. She didn't know if it was her instincts as a nurse or as a woman.

He wouldn't appreciate either.

Stiff-backed, she walked past Matt. She had so wanted to impress him and she had failed. The thought had barely registered in her mind before her chin lifted. The day wasn't over. Her pace picked up as she hurried into the house.

"I saw you coming across the yard." Octavia set a plate on the table. "Chicken salad all right?"

Shannon grinned. "I'm hungry enough to eat a horse."

"Better not let Matt or the boys hear you say that." The older woman chuckled. "Go on and wash up."

Shannon glanced down at her soiled jeans and shirt. "I don't imagine I have time to change clothes."

"Just pretend you've been gardening."

Shaking her head at the housekeeper, Shannon quickly washed, returned to the table and said grace. The first bite of salad was delicious. "It's a wonder Matt doesn't weigh three hundred pounds."

"That boy barely eats sometimes," Octavia sniffed as she took a seat.

"Why? Is something wrong?" The words tumbled out of Shannon's mouth before she could stop them. "Forgive me, I have no right to pry into Matt's personal business."

"You didn't ask to be nosy. I know you care about him."

Sooty black lashes flew upward. Sherry-brown eyes widened.

Octavia patted Shannon's fluttering hand. "It's all right, child. Nurses are caring people."

She didn't answer. Instead, she concentrated on quickly eating lunch.

"Slow down or you're gonna choke," the housekeeper warned.

"I'm sorry, but I have to get back and finish." Draining her glass of iced tea, she stood and took her empty plate to the sink.

"I'll get that." Octavia took the plate out of Shannon's hand. "How far did you get?"

She made a face. "Only half through cleaning the stalls."

Black eyes rounded, Octavia grinned. "I knew you had it in you."

Shannon frowned. "Didn't you hear me? I still have to do the rest of the stalls, polish the tack, and clear the brush before I'm through for the day."

Leaving the dishes in the sink, Octavia faced the puzzled woman. "Did Matt give you a timetable or just tell you what he wanted you to do?"

"Just what he wanted me to do, but I assumed—" She stopped short as she said the taboo word in nursing. No one *assumed*. You went on facts. Period. If you didn't understand, you asked. A patient's life necessitated you make the correct decision based on fact not assumption.

"Depending on the experience of the person, cleaning those stalls can take anywhere from six to seven hours. Matt knows that." She chuckled. "That's why he choked on his coffee when you asked him what else he wanted you to do after you finished."

"He didn't expect me to finish, did he?"

"I told you he could be tricky."

"The rat! I told him I had skipped lunch to try and finish," Shannon railed. "He could have said something."

"I don't think Matt exactly knows what to say to you."

Shannon's gaze narrowed in on the housekeeper. "What are you talking about?"

For a moment Shannon thought Octavia was going to sidestep the question as she had done before. "Matt's opinion of women, especially beautiful women, isn't the best. Can't say I blame him after what he went through with that woman. Never thought I'd see the day he'd meet one halfway, the way he has Victoria."

"Victoria?" The pang Shannon felt wasn't jealousy, she argued with herself. It wasn't.

"Victoria Taggart. Married to Matt's older brother." Octavia smiled. "Those two are so much in love they glow. Even a cynic like Matt had to admit Victoria's crazy about Kane. His size doesn't intimidate her a bit."

"Because I worked the eleven-to-seven shift I never met any of the family members. But I heard a lot. Matt might have set the women's hearts aflutter, but they were in awe of Kaṇe and so were the doctors," Shannon recalled.

"That's Kane," Octavia said proudly.

"Even after Wade was discharged he talked mostly about the ranch and Matt. His uncle was worried about him."

"He wanted for Matt what Kane has with Victoria," Octavia said softly.

"That might take a miracle."

"Or the right woman."

Shannon bit her lower lip. "I guess I better get back to work. Thanks for lunch." Shannon escaped to the barn.

Her cheeks still burning, she finished scattering the rest of the hay in the stall. Plopping the hat on her head, she picked up the pitchfork and shovel leaning against the wall, placed them in the wheelbarrow, then went into the next stall.

She might feel a healthy dose of attraction toward Matt, but that was all. He was different, a challenge. What woman wouldn't be attracted to him? Just because she wanted to see him smile didn't mean she felt anything on a deeper level.

"Staring into space won't get the job done."

Letting the wheelbarrow drop, she turned to Cleve. "How was the beef stew?"

Bushy eyebrows lifted. "Filling."

"They're lucky to get it with all the work you do." Picking up the shovel, she began cleaning the stall.

"Forgot your gloves."

Propping the shovel against her leg, she put on the gloves and went back to work.

"You got good wrist action and swing."

Shannon smiled. "Didn't think I'd last the day, huh?"

"Day ain't over yet," he tossed back. "By the way, it's easier scattering the hay if you use the pitchfork."

Laughing, Shannon glanced over her shoulder and watched him walk away. This morning Cleve had pointed out the wheelbarrow, pitchfork, and shovel, then showed her where to dump the refuse. His battered straw hat jerked toward the loft where the baled hay was stored.

"How do I get it down?"

With a deadpan expression on his grizzled face he had said, "With your hands."

When the time came for her actually to get a bale of hay down from the loft, she saw Cleve standing nearby currying one of the horses she had brought back into the barn. He'd probably deny it to the last, but she had a feeling he had watched her take every cautious step upward.

Trying to move the hay was awkward; lifting it would have been impossible. So, she took a chapter from her nursing training. She rolled it off the loft.

The hay hit the barn floor with a solid thud. Cleve looked from the broken hay bale to her standing with her hands on her hips.

"I used my hands just like you told me," Shannon yelled.

"See that you don't waste any of that hay," Cleve admonished and left.

Shaking her head at the memory, Shannon went back to work. She liked the crusty old man. He didn't give her an inch, but she had the notion it wasn't because she was a woman. Clearly anyone who knew nothing about ranching was next to worthless. Before her three weeks of vacation was over, she was going to learn plenty.

"All finished. Ready to come see?"

Matt looked up from the belly of the tractor. Shannon was grinning from ear to ear. Her hair was pulled up on the top of her head by a rubber band, and she had managed to collect more straw and dirt all over her. Somehow she still managed to look beautiful.

He returned his attention to repairing the clutch. The sun had gone down an hour ago. He had spent too many hours repairing the thing. He wasn't in the mood to see Shannon gloating.

"Nope."

"Don't you want to see if the barn is up to your high standards?" she questioned, the cheery note in her voice scraping on his nerve endings like fingernails on a chalk board.

Callused hands closed more securely around the wrench. "Doesn't take a genius to muck out stalls."

"How about what you're doing?"

His head snapped up. Black eyes glittered. "Meaning?"

She had the grace to flush. "It's just that I've been seeing you working on this thing when I take the wheelbarrow out. How is it coming?"

"It's not." Giving her his back, he returned to tightening the bolt.

"Is there anything I could do to help? Like hold something?"

Matt gave the wrench one last yank, then turned his full attention on Shannon. "As a matter of fact there is."

"Yes?" she answered eagerly.

"Let me work in peace."

Shannon's expression faltered. "Oh."

Matt pushed away the twinge of guilt he felt at her shattered look. Shannon played the game better than most, but it was still that, a game where the woman walked away with everything, leaving a man nothing, not even the remnants of his pride.

He'd thought his ex-wife was the most beautiful, the most perfect woman he had ever met. He'd bragged to anyone who stood still long enough to listen how wonderful she was. He'd worked two jobs during the week and on weekends had followed the rodeo circuit to give her all the things she asked for.

She kept their apartment clean, meals on the table, and the sheets hot. She was a very inventive and tireless sexual partner. His grip on the wrench tightened. There was only one problem: she didn't mind whose bed she happened to find herself in . . . as long as the man in it had money. Once his popularity and his ranking started to decline, so had his wife's interest. The money problems that had ensued hadn't helped.

They had their disagreements when money had gotten tight, but he never suspected her infidelity. He had just worked harder to get his concentration level back up where he could finish ahead and stop his downward spiral in ranking as a calf roper.

He had been a fool going on blind faith and a stupid emotion called love. Never again. He chose honest lust and women who made no demands. Those who tried were left talking to thin air. He would never allow another woman to make a fool out of him. Never.

If he was a little hard on Shannon, she'd just have to learn that he couldn't be swayed and look for an easier mark.

"He's *so* rude!" Shannon said, the moment she entered the kitchen and saw Octavia. "All I did was ask him about that monstrosity he's been working on."

"That monstrosity is a top-of-the-line tractor that cost in the neighborhood of eighty thousand dollars. Without it working, Matt can't finish plowing the early crop of corn and he can't fertilize the alfalfa in the hay meadow for the cows' winter feed," Octavia explained patiently. "Matt's trying to fix it himself because if he can't . . . well, what kind of bill do you get when you take your fancy car in?"

"I thought he was . . ." She bit her lower lip. Once again she had assumed.

"Rich," Octavia accurately finished for her. "Depends on what you call rich. But even a rich person won't be that way for long if they don't watch how they spend their money. Especially on a ranch."

Shannon accepted the housekeeper's gentle reprimand. No one in the Johnson family had to work; they did so because they enjoyed the challenge. In the early thirties, forties, and fifties when many people were selling their land, her great-grandfather was buying it. The family still owned real estate in downtown St. Louis and on the riverfront.

From an early age she had been taught never to judge someone by the zeroes in their bank account but by their character. Her parents were always cognizant of how blessed they were and aware of the needs of those who were less fortunate.

"I owe you a hug after I'm cleaned up." Opening the door, Shannon went back outside.

At first she didn't see him, then she heard a clink from beneath the front of the tractor. Looking underneath, she saw him screwing on a bolt. Not wanting to interrupt him again, she dropped to her knees, took a deep breath and spoke to the top of his dark head, "I'm sorry for that crack earlier. Octavia just explained how important the tractor is to the ranch."

Not by one movement did he indicate that he had heard her. Or worse that he cared if he had.

Determined to apologize, she plunged on. "I worked very hard in the barn. It was childish of me to expect praise, but I did, and when you didn't give it, like a spoiled child, I struck back." Her shoulders squared. "Please accept my apology."

Matt moved, but it was to screw on another bolt. Her shoulders slumped in defeat. Her hand braced against the warm belly of the tractor to push to her feet.

"Come down here."

Without a moment's hesitation Shannon stuck her head underneath the tractor. It was as much of a concession as she was going to get from Matt. "Yes?"

He blew out an exasperated breath. "Down here, Shannon. With me. Go on the other side and scoot under beside me."

When she had ensconced herself under the tractor beside Matt on the well-worn blanket she asked, "What should I do?"

Unceremoniously, he dumped a handful of nuts and washers on her stomach. "Put those on all the bolts on both sides and I'll tighten them."

It sounded easy and it would have been if she hadn't kept brushing against Matt. Working in the small space together, it was impossible not to.

His hip bumped hers, her shoulders touched his, their thighs brushed together as one or the other turned. His touch inflamed her senses. With each contact, Shannon fought the temptation to conjure up what it would be like to leisurely explore the hard, muscled warmth of the man next to her, what it would feel like for him to explore her in return.

Hot. She was hot everywhere and it had nothing to do with her sticky clothes or the temperature outside and everything to do with the man next to her.

"You're hot?"

"W-what?" Her gaze jerked to his.

"Is the heat getting to you? You haven't moved in the last minute," he explained. "Your cheeks look flushed."

If she could have sunk through the ground, she would have gladly

done so. "I'm finished. I was waiting for you to tell me what to do next."
Great. Now she could add lying to the list of uncharacteristic things she
had started doing since she came to the Circle T.

"Right behind you," Matt said. He tightened the last nut. "Now to adjust it."

Matt stood before she did, then helped her up. His hand only touched
her arm for a second, then it was gone. The warm imprint, however,
lasted. "Start it up and hold down on the clutch." He dove back under
the hood.

Shannon didn't move. She didn't know what the clutch was.

Matt's dark head popped up. "What's the matter?"

"My car is an automatic."

His eyes rolled heavenward. "Climb on and I'll show you. Pay attention
because you may have to drive it before you leave."

"I . . . I don't think I could. I have problems with judging distances,"
she confessed, climbing onto the tractor

"Since you'll be in a field, that won't be a problem." He started the engine and pointed to the clutch. "Keep your foot on that and let me know
how the tension feels."

She didn't know about the tension in the clutch, but hers was wound
pretty tight. But slowly she relaxed as they worked.

"That should do it. Cut the engine," Matt told her.

Shannon climbed down. "It's fixed?"

"It's fixed." He began picking up tools and putting them away.

"I guess I better get cleaned up. Any suggestions about these?" She
held up her grease-stained hands.

He started to lift his hand toward her face, then glanced at hands that
were greasier than hers. "You also have it on your nose."

She rubbed the sleeve of her shirt across her nose and tried to ignore
the stab of disappointment that he hadn't touched her. "There's probably not an inch of my body that doesn't crave a hot, soapy bath. So could
yours," she suggested with an impish smile.

"You're offering to wash my back?"

Frantically Shannon tried to vanquish the images of her doing that
and more to his body. "T-that's not in my job description."

Black eyes narrowed, and for a wild moment she thought he might tell
her it was. "Ready to quit and head back to St. Louis?"

"And leave you short-handed? No way."

"The green bar of soap in the utility bathroom will cut through the
grease. Under the sink in a pink jar is some cream for your hands."

Surprise and pleasure swept through her. "Thanks."

He shrugged. "No sense getting the grease all over the place for Octavia to clean up, and I don't want to hear you complaining because your
soft hands are becoming as tough as mine."

She smiled and his jaw clenched. Imagine. *Matt had noticed her hands.*

"The ranch comes first," he said tightly.

"I quite agree. Never crossed my mind otherwise. Now, if you'll excuse me, I think that water is calling my name." Turning, she started for the house.

Halfway there she yelled, "Anytime you need an extra pair of hands, holler. That's what partners are for."

This time when she imagined Matt's scowl, she smiled instead of worrying. Every muscle in her body might ache, but she had showed him she wasn't a cream puff. She was going to make a believer out of him. Her smile faded as she recalled his irritation after he mentioned her soft hands. The mysterious woman must have really done a number on him if he had to rationalize being thoughtful to a woman. Deep in thought, Shannon entered the house.

"If I have to reheat this food again it won't be worth eating," Octavia warned from the stove.

"Sorry, but I had to help Matt fix the clutch." She held out her grease-smeared shirt. "Matt told me about the special soap. There's no way I can sit, let alone eat, until I get cleaned up all over."

"Hurry up then."

Upstairs in her room, Shannon resisted the urge to linger in the scented water. Instead, she quickly finished her bath, then washed and blew dry her hair. After liberally using the pink hand cream, she dressed in shorts and a blouse, then gingerly picked up her dirty clothes and went downstairs. Returning from putting them in the washing machine, she saw the place setting for one.

Her happy spirits faltered. "Did Matt already eat?"

"No. He went to the field," Octavia replied as she lifted boiled cabbage onto a plate.

"It's after eight. It'll be dark in less than an hour." Shannon looked out the window, frowning.

"The tractor has lights and he lost a lot of time today."

"He can't make it up by killing himself."

"I've been trying to tell him that for years. He won't listen."

"Did he at least come in for a sandwich or something to drink?" Concern laced Shannon's words.

"He wouldn't have eaten at all if I hadn't taken some food to him." The stoneware plate hit the table with a soft thud.

"Why don't you go catch up on your reading?" Shannon suggested. "I'll clean up after I finish."

Octavia smiled in appreciation. "I think I'll take you up on your offer. Good night."

"Good night." Shannon took her seat, but she made no move to eat. Her mind was still on Matt.

Men and women pushed themselves past the limits for different reasons. Her parents and brothers for the sheer exuberance of winning, and the glory. The financial reward was icing on the cake.

None of them knew how to relax and enjoy themselves. Enjoyment for her family was zeroing in on a witness for the opposition and making them sweat. Relaxation was a breakneck-paced game of racquetball.

Her mother despised idleness as much as preachers despised sin. More than once, her grandfather had to rescue Shannon from some "project" her mother had assigned her. The two of them would escape and enjoy their time with each other. What they did didn't matter as long as they did it together. She'd miss him forever, but they had built some good memories. Her thoughts skidded to a halt.

How had she forgotten that?

Good memories lingered. She leaned back in the chair and remembered the happy times. The long talks, baking cookies, helping her study for a test, playing a game of chess. She smiled. He hated losing and hated it worse if she let him win. He was a special man.

It had been so very hard letting him go. Letting him know that it was okay to stop fighting, that it was okay to seek a place without pain. She had fought against it at first, begging him to fight although his body was racked with pain.

It wasn't until one night he had looked at her and said, "I'm ready to go, Shan girl," that she realized he was trying to hold on for her. And her alone. She was the one selfishly keeping him in pain. So she had taken his hand and told him it was all right. She'd swallowed tears, railed against life and told him how much she loved him, and then she'd let him go.

He had taken part of her with him. But he had also left a part of himself with her. Tears rolled down her cheek and she made no move to stop them.

The healing process had finally begun.

A long time later she looked out the window. Darkness had descended. Maybe that's what Matt needed, to create some good memories to overshadow the bad ones.

But first she had to find out what drove him past the limits of other men. She had to admit she hadn't had much down time herself lately. When your mind was busy you didn't have time to think about yourself. That was the reason she pulled double shifts, to keep her mind occupied. And it hadn't done a bit of good. Her mind would drift: tears would fall.

She glanced out the window again and wondered at the reason behind Matt's long grueling hours of work. She knew somehow that she was going to find the answer.

CHAPTER 8

It was after ten-thirty when Matt made his way toward the stairs. He was tired, but it was a good kind of tired. He had managed to plow a large section of the young corn, and the way he figured it, he was only a couple of days behind schedule. Everything would be going well if he didn't have to worry about Shannon.

He had to admit, she hadn't backed away from hard work or from getting herself dirty. After putting the tractor up he stopped by the barn to see the stalls. She had done a surprisingly good job.

Just as she had done a good job helping him with the tractor. He thought to push her a little further by getting her to help with the greasy, tedious clutch job and miscalculated badly. Instead of quitting, she stayed and put him through sheer torture squirming and rubbing against him.

Determined not to let her see how much she affected him, he had ordered her to stay and help him adjust the tension on the clutch. By the time she'd left, his body had ached for release.

He saw her as soon as he turned down the hallway. Dressed in a silky-looking pale-blue pants outfit, she leaned sideways against the wall facing him, her slim arms crossed beneath her generous breasts. If not for the pensive look on her face he would have thought she had seduction on her mind.

"Why do you do it?"

"What?" he asked, surprised at the slight edge to her voice.

She pushed away from the door and met him halfway. "Why do you work through meals and push yourself so hard? Is the ranch in some financial trouble?"

Now he understood the reason for her concern. "Worried about your profit margin?"

"Should I be?"

"This may come as a surprise, but I like what I do. I like pitting myself against all the capriciousness of Mother Nature and whatever else tries to take this place from me."

Her shoulders snapped back, her lips pressed together. Obviously she had caught his meaning. "If you keep on working these hours you won't be healthy enough to fight anything."

"Why should you care?"

"I asked myself the same thing."

"Care to share the answer you came up with?"

"Because Wade loved you."

The smug smile left his face.

"Good night and thanks for the hand cream."

She walked away leaving behind her a whiff of her exotic perfume and a burning ache in his body.

"I can make my own coffee," Matt announced without preamble as he entered the kitchen the next morning and saw Shannon standing by the counter.

"But can you make this?" she asked, and turned with a cherry-topped coffee cake in her hands.

So that was the mouth-watering smell he'd inhaled the moment his boot struck the bottom step of the stairs. She didn't give up easily, he'd admit that much. But to get his land away from him she'd have to do more than show him her skills in the kitchen.

Unbidden came the thought of other skills she knew all too well, skills more suited to scented sheets and long hot nights. Unbridled need rushed through him. With an iron will, he brought his desire under control.

"Coffee will be fine until breakfast."

She shrugged slim shoulders beneath another oversize shirt, this one yellow and white, and set the pastry next to the coffeepot.

"Suit yourself, I'm a sucker for sweets." Leaning back against the counter, she picked up a slice of coffee cake and took a bite. Bread flakes clung to her lips. A pink tongue flicked them away.

Matt watched in hungry fascination as her tongue disappeared inside her mouth and yanked hard on his slipping control. Lifting the cup, he took a drink. "Ohhh."

"What's the matter?"

"Nothing." He wasn't about to tell her he was paying more attention to her mouth than the hot coffee.

Her elbow propped on her bent arm, she took another bite. Crumbs fell. She lapped them up. "Are you sure you won't have a slice?"

He picked up a wedge to stall for time until his coffee cooled and to get his mind off her lush lips. The pastry had barely settled on his tongue before he realized Shannon could be a rich man's dream or a poor man's nightmare.

So far hard work hadn't scared her and she cooked as mouth-watering delicious as she looked. His ex-wife hadn't cooked half this well or worked as hard, and she had put his life into a tailspin. Shannon was in a class by herself.

It would take a rich man to keep her happy. A poor man would try and end up feeling less than a man because he couldn't.

"Do you like eggs rancheros?" She handed him a napkin.

He wiped his mouth and wished she'd stop looking at his lips. "Why?"

"Since I'm already up, I thought I'd give Octavia a break and cook breakfast."

Black eyes narrowed. He put the pastry down. "Why?"

She sighed. "Have you always been this suspicious?"

"Why?"

"Because I'm creating extra work for her by being here. It's the least I can do for her making me feel so welcome."

"You're still going to clean up the tackroom and polish the gear."

Her eyes rolled. "I can't believe you sometimes. Of course I'll do the tackroom. This isn't a trade-off, it's an act of kindness."

"Yeah." Sarcasm tinged the word. "What act of kindness did you perform for Wade to get him to give you the meadow? Or was it another kind of trade-off?"

Her eyes widened in shock, then darkened in pain. She started to flee the room.

Unyielding hands grasped her forearm. He was surprised to feel her body tremble, surprised even more to feel a twinge of guilt for hurting her.

"Turn me loose," she mumbled, her head downcast.

"Not until you understand I didn't mean it that way." He waited until his words sank in and she lifted her head.

"I've had some time to consider the situation and I admit I said some things without thinking them through. But the fact remains that you touched Wade enough for him to leave you the meadow," Matt stated, bewilderment in his voice. "He had a soft spot for women in trouble, but his connection to the land was unshakable. I want to know what trouble you were in and why he thought the meadow would help?"

"I'm glad you changed your mind about Wade," she said softly. "That bothered me more than your anger and mistrust."

"What did you expect me to do?" he asked coldly. "Lay out the red carpet and throw a feast in your honor?"

She sighed, her head lowered again as her body seemed to shift closer to his. "I expected peace."

"Why, Shannon? Why did you need the peace?"

Her bangs brushed against his blue shirtfront. "Things happened I had no control over and I had trouble accepting them. And before you ask, I don't want to talk about it."

Secrets and pain he understood. There were things in his past only Kane knew about. Some things, like his talking through his ex-wife's deceit, he had never been able to discuss with anyone. His pride had been hurt too badly. Yet, there had been times he would have gladly given a piece of his soul to make the ache in his gut go away.

Shannon's head turned, her cheek pressed more solidly against his chest. The warmth and softness cut through the barrier of his clothes and his cynicism with lethal effectiveness. His thumb absently stroked her arm beneath the cotton fabric.

With a trembling sigh, she leaned her upper body closer to his. Blunt-tipped fingers flexed with every intention of bringing her even closer. Before his actions became a reality he realized the risk. Abruptly, he pushed her away.

Feeling sorry for Shannon was as dangerous as being seduced by her body subtly shifting closer to his with every heavy thud of his heart.

"As long as you want to take what's mine, you won't get the peace you're looking for here."

Heavy lids blinked. Sooty lashes lifted over slightly dazed amber eyes. Her gaze shifted. "There are different kinds of peace, Matt, I'm just beginning to figure that out." She turned away. "I need to fix breakfast and your coffee is getting cold."

Matt crossed the room, dumped the coffee without tasting it, then poured himself another cup. "You're hiding something and I'm going to find out what it is before you leave."

"Why?"

He didn't like his word turned on him. "I don't like surprises."

The doorbell rang. She started from the room.

"Leave it. We're not finished talking."

"It's not even seven. It must be important if someone is calling this early."

"It'll wait. This won't."

The chime came again. "There is never any excuse for rudeness."

This time he didn't try to stop her. Crossing his legs at the ankle, Matt leaned against the counter and sipped his coffee. *Run all you want, Shannon,* he thought with conviction. *But sooner or later, I'm going to run you to the ground and find out all your secrets.*

Taking a deep breath, Shannon raked an unsteady hand through her hair as she crossed the den. She had done it again, gone from boiling mad to hot and bothered in 0.9 seconds.

Try as she might to deny it, she could resist Matt no more than the increasing desire to get past his distrust and have him see her and not the woman he thought she was. And that was just the beginning of her problems. Being around him was only going to make it more difficult for her to ignore her feelings.

Arthur Ferguson had delivered the money and credit card Melanie mailed to her so she could leave if she wanted to. She didn't want to. She wasn't running a step farther from whatever life tossed her way. And that included Matt Taggart.

What a time for her slumbering hormones to go on overdrive. She knew that's what it was. No woman in her right mind would fall in love with a suspicious, overbearing cowboy. A dependable, soft-spoken man like James Harper was more like it. With James fixed firmly in her mind as worthy of another look, she opened the front door.

The tall, rawboned man on the porch blinked in surprise on seeing her, then quickly jerked off his cream-colored Stetson to reveal a thinning patch of salt-and-pepper hair.

"Er, morning, miss. I'm Matt's neighbor. Is he home?"

Shannon smiled to put the older man at ease. "He's in the kitchen. Please come in." Closing the door behind the visitor, she led him back to the kitchen. "Matt, there's a gentleman here to see you."

The rancher stepped from behind Shannon. "Good morning, Matt."

The last person Matt expected was Adam Gordon. It was Wednesday. The Monday deadline had passed for them to agree on the sale of Sir Galahad. "Morning."

Shannon glanced between the two, her curiosity increasing. The elderly man's nervousness had increased, not decreased. Matt looked hard and uncompromising.

The rancher's gaze flicked back to Shannon, then swung to Matt. His grip on the brim of his hat tightened.

"Could I get you a cup of coffee or some coffee cake?" Shannon asked. She, of all people, knew how unnerving Matt could be.

"No, ma'am." He looked at Matt, then back at Shannon.

She offered a slight smile of encouragement.

Adam gulped.

Matt scowled. The speculative gleam in Adam's face when he entered the kitchen had gradually become one of male appreciation. He wasn't as interested in the relationship between Shannon and Matt as he was at looking at a beautiful woman.

"Something you wanted, Adam?"

The rancher jerked his attention back to Matt. "It . . . it's about the talk we had the other day."

"The deadline passed. I said all I had to say."

Gordon shifted from one polished ostrich-skin boot to the other. "Can we go someplace and talk in private?"

"Of course, I'll le—"

"You'll cook breakfast," Matt told her. "I don't intend to waste any more time today than I have to."

Head high, Shannon yanked open a cabinet door, then slammed it shut. Matt ignored her and the noise. "If you've changed your mind, it doesn't take privacy to tell me you're going to sell me the bull."

"Sir Galahad is worth a lot of money."

"Fifteen thousand dollars is a lot of money."

"Fifteen thousand dollars for a cow!" Shannon screeched, staring at both men as if they had lost their senses. Matt returned the look with one of censure, the older man with wry amusement. "Sorry," she mumbled and turned away.

"Pardon me for saying so, ma'am, but you must not know much about prize bulls."

"She doesn't know much about ranching period. But she will before she leaves," Matt promised.

"I'm not the only one who'll learn a lesson before I go," Shannon shot back, one hand on her slim hip, the other clutching a skillet handle.

Gordon's eyes skirted another glance between the two. Curiosity triumphed over good manners. "You're just visiting then, miss?"

Shannon gave up all pretense of cooking and extended her hand. "Yes. I'm Shannon Johnson."

"Adam Gordon." He pumped her hand up and down. "Welcome to Jackson Falls."

"If you two are finished . . ."

Gordon hastily withdrew his hand. Shannon faced Matt with a syrupy smile. "Drink your coffee. It might improve your disposition."

"Shannon," Matt gritted out.

"I know. Breakfast."

His jaw tight, Matt faced the rancher who looked stunned. Matt knew the women Adam usually saw around him went out of their way to please Matt. Shannon took pleasure in opposing him at every turn. "I'm waiting," he growled.

The man jumped, then blurted, "I brought someone for you to see."

Matt couldn't believe such audacity or callousness. His body became as rigid and cold as his voice, "Then you've wasted a trip and my time."

"I deserve that." The rancher looked at Shannon. "Miss Johnson, if Matt can spare you a moment from cooking breakfast, I'd like to show you the finest bull in the Southwest."

"Sir Galahad is here?" Matt thundered.

Gordon finally stopped gripping his Stetson. "I thought he could say it better than I could." He took a deep breath that strained the pearl snaps on his red-checkered shirt.

"At first I was angry with you and then I thought long and hard about things. It didn't take long to figure out you were right." Adam Gordon held out his hand. "You can't buy love or friendship. No one should try."

"I know." Matt clasped Adam's hand, but his steady black gaze was on Shannon. "But you'd be surprised at the people who haven't figured that out yet."

Matt's words stayed with Shannon all day as she worked in the tackroom. The reason for his distrust was clear. Money. She hung up a bridle she had just finished polishing and reached for another one.

Sitting down, she picked up the soft cloth and began rubbing cream into the leather. Telling him she had a trust fund that would see her very comfortably through two lifetimes wouldn't help. Maybe a certified letter from her father's law firm might, but she shied away from that idea.

Sighing, she leaned back in the wooden chair. As crazy as it seemed, she didn't want him to trust her because he knew she didn't need the meadow or his money. She wanted his trust because he was powerless to withhold it. It hardly seemed fair that she reacted so strongly to him and he barely noticed her unless it was to interrogate her or give her a command.

Her lips pursed. After breakfast he had ordered her to follow him to the small room in the back of the barn and told her that he wanted everything polished by the end of the day. It was almost two o'clock and she had barely made a dent in the numerous bridles, harnesses, and whatever else hung from the curved hooks scattered around the room.

Her stomach growled. There was no sense in skipping lunch. The gear would still be here. Maybe Matt wouldn't come back until late and she'd be finished by then. Even as her thoughts formed, she hoped he'd return for dinner. She had gone into the house for a glass of water earlier and knew he hadn't returned for lunch.

Whatever else she could say about Matt, there was no doubt he worked hard.

Laying the bridle aside, she rolled her head to loosen stiff muscles, then stretched her hands over her head. She ached in places she had forgotten she had. Lunch, and then back to the grindstone.

Crossing the yard, she saw a late model Camaro coupe pull up in the circular drive in front of the ranch house. A young woman got out of the car and started for the front door. With each hip-swinging step the wind lifted the flared hem of her floral sundress to reveal a pair of long legs.

Shannon sighed. She had always envied women who could wear those flirty little numbers or body-hugging spandex. She had always been too conscious of the wind catching her at the wrong moment and too conscious of her upper proportions. She had only recently worked up to short skirts.

Sir Gallahad bellowed from the corral. The young woman's sandaled foot paused over the first wooden step on the porch. Shoulder-length, blunt-cut black hair swung around in an arc. Her gaze stopped on Shannon and for several seconds stayed there. Sir Gallahad bellowed again. The woman started toward Shannon.

"I'm Vivian Gordon," she said, her voice a slow, seductive drawl that was a captivating mix of the deep South and the West.

Shannon smiled at the pretty, cinnamon-hued woman and introduced herself. "I met your father this morning. I guess you came by to say good-bye to Sir Gallahad."

"I came to see Matt."

Shannon reassessed the unsmiling young woman. Obviously her father had mentioned Shannon and she was here to see what she thought might be the competition. "He's been out plowing since this morning. I don't expect him back until tonight."

Glistening red lips tightened. "*You* don't expect him back? What are you to him?"

If nothing else the woman was direct and Shannon had no intention of being caught between Matt and another woman. "Just what I look like. A hired hand."

The woman's calculating eyes traveled over Shannon who was in her work outfit of faded jeans, a sleeveless knit T, and an oversize shirt. "Is that Matt's shirt?"

Shannon laughed in the suspicious woman's face. She couldn't help it. Anyone who was that rude didn't deserve anything else.

Vivian bristled. "Daddy was wrong, there's nothing special about you. Matt wouldn't look at you twice when he can have me. I'm rich, prettier, and younger than you."

And spoiled rotten. Definitely not the type of woman Matt would choose. He wasn't a man to pamper a woman.

Shannon felt sorry for Vivian. The girl looked to be about twenty. Matt was probably the first thing in her life she wanted and she hadn't gotten. She wasn't dealing very well with the real world.

A girl's first love was often painful. Just because the person was older or entirely out of your reach or not an acceptable object of affection didn't stop you from wanting and hoping. Shannon's fixation had been on the captain of the high school football team who wanted her to be another notch on his jock strap. Her brothers had quickly wised her up.

"Mr. Gordon didn't mention he had children."

Her chin lifted. "I'm an only child and he gives me anything I want."

The conversation between the elderly rancher and Matt now made sense. Mr. Gordon might have come to his senses about Matt not being right for Vivian, but his daughter still needed convincing. And her father clearly wasn't up to telling her what you want isn't always best for you.

"I'm not a threat to any relationship you might have with Matt. He hardly knows I'm around." Vivian looked doubtful. "If there was anything going on here, do you think I'd be cleaning out stalls and polishing harnesses?"

The younger woman looked horrified. "Daddy said you were helping Octavia."

"Matt doesn't like for his workers to be idle," Shannon said sadly. If she was going to play the part of advice-giver she might as well do it right. Her brothers hadn't spared one rotten detail about the high school football captain.

"That's awful," Vivian said, looking at Shannon in a different way. "I don't have to do a thing around my house if I don't want to. Daddy would never ask me to do anything menial. I always thought Matt was just as considerate of women."

Shannon chortled. "Obviously you haven't disagreed with him on anything."

"We really haven't talked much." As if realizing what she had said, Vivian rushed on to add, "He's busy a lot on the ranch."

"If he's too busy to spend time with you, then he isn't worthy of you," Shannon said. "I bet there are plenty of young men around here who would jump at the chance to talk with you."

"Yes, but none of them are like Matt. They all seem so immature and insignificant compared to him. Matt has it all . . . money, success, a gorgeous body, and looks to make any woman's knees weak. He is one fine brother," the younger women said, her voice a breathy rush of adulation and yearning.

"I can't deny that, but I think I'd rather have a man who cared about me above everything else." Shannon's eyes twinkled. "Then again, I'm greedy at times. I bet you can find a man with it all."

Vivian laughed. Shannon joined in. The roar of the tractor drowned out the sound. Vivian's large brown eyes widened as she looked from a grim-faced Matt on the farm machinery to Shannon.

"Please don't tell him why I'm here." No longer did she sound like a self-assured woman trying to warn off another female from her man.

"He has a big enough ego as it is."

Matt stopped the tractor beside the women. As soon as he cut the engine, Shannon said, "I see the clutch I helped you fix is working fine on the tractor."

Vivian's eyes rounded in renewed horror. "He made you work on the tractor, too?"

With a long-suffering sigh, Shannon nodded.

The young woman glared up at Matt. "You shouldn't work her so hard. Daddy would never do that to a woman."

"What have you been telling her?" Matt growled and came off the tractor in a controlled rush.

Vivian stepped back from the harsh intensity of his glare. Shannon lifted her chin. "Only my work schedule."

"Apparently it's too light if you have time to lollygag," Matt told her.

"You're not the man I thought you were, Matt Taggart," Vivian said. She turned to Shannon. "My father's ranch is down the road about six miles on the left-hand side. Gordon's Angus Ranch. You'll always be welcome there."

"Thank you, Vivian," Shannon said. "And good luck."

Without a glance in Matt's direction, the young woman went to her car and drove off.

"What the hell was that all about?" Matt demanded. "That girl's been following me around with those big eyes of hers for the past three months. Now she acts like I'm the devil incarnate."

"Angry that you lost an admirer?" Shannon asked.

"Heck, no," he said, his face spreading into a wide grin. "I was just wondering if you could do it again."

His smile stole the air from her lungs. Her heart lurched in her chest. God. If he had smiled at Vivian that way, no wonder the young woman was so captivated.

"How did you do it?"

Shannon moistened her dry lips. There was no help for her throat. "I—I told her how hard you worked me."

He frowned and she smothered a small groan at the loss. "That's all?"

Shannon came out of her haze. "You aren't that irresistible."

The look he sent her obviously said he didn't care what she thought. "We're going to a party Saturday night."

"Why?"

"To meet your neighbors, of course."

"Try again?"

"Now who is being suspicious?"

Silence was her only answer.

"Adam and his wife are throwing a party in honor of Vivian's upcoming graduation from junior college," he explained. "Since you two hit it off I'm sure you'll want to go."

"And if I just happen to spread the word of what an arrogant, obnoxious tyrant you are, that wouldn't hurt," Shannon said tightly.

His lips thinned. "Hard taskmaster would be enough."

"Ohhhh! I can't believe you," Shannon railed. "That foolish young woman had some stupid notion of how fine and gallant you were. As much as I pity anyone else witless enough to believe such an idiotic idea, I am not, I repeat *not* going to tell them what a jerk you are. You'll just have to be man enough and tell them yourself."

She turned to walk away, then abruptly swung back. "Or just open your mouth and they'll find out for themselves."

Black eyes blazed. His body became as taut as a plucked bow string.

Too late she realized she had let her temper run faster than her brain. One look at his hard face and she knew running would do little good.

Before she could draw another breath, unrelenting fingers closed around her forearms. "Let's just see how irresistible I am."

His dark head descended.

CHAPTER 9

"I bite."

Barely leashed passion flared in his riveting black eyes. "So do I."

Shannon refused to give in to the sudden heat centered in her lower body. "I mean it, Matt. You don't want me, you only want to punish me."

"Maybe I just want to see what else that quick little tongue of yours can do."

The heat became a flame. "You deserved everything I said about you. I can't believe you'd be so unfeeling. I thought you were a better man than to lead a young woman on."

"You don't know what you're talking about."

"Yes, I do," she said. He had lifted his head, and she gave only minor thought that he continued to hold her upper arms. "I've known men like you who are thoughtless of women. Just because you're fairly good-looking doesn't mean you can treat women any way you want. You have no difficulty telling *me* what you think. I can't imagine you not setting Vivian or any other woman straight," she told him with certainty. "Failing that, all you need do is look at one of them the way you're glaring at me and they'd run for the hills."

"I have my reasons."

"Yes. I bet your giant ego is one." She shook her head sadly. "One day you're going to find out what it is to love someone and not be loved in return."

"I already have," he said, his face bleak, his voice raw.

"What?"

Releasing her arms, he started for the tractor. Shannon only hesitated a moment before she went after him. The pain in his face before he turned away had been devastating. And she had caused it in her anger, an anger she had used to keep her mind from the growing desire she felt for him. In trying to protect herself, she had hurt him.

Her fingertips touched his sleeve. He swung around, his expression remote. "You have work to do."

"The trouble with trying to judge people is that often it makes you take a good look at yourself. I don't like what I see," she told him. "I'm developing a bad habit of striking out at you when I'm angry. My problem, but you're the one who suffers. I'll try not to let it happen in the future."

"That's all?"

"Unless you want it in writing," she told him with frank calmness.

His Stetson-covered head tilted to one side. "What, no words of pity or polite inquiries?"

"You're too strong to need pity and too arrogant to accept any," Shannon told him quietly. "As for the inquiries, I won't deny I'd like to know the whole story, but you don't trust me enough to tell me. So why waste both of our time by asking?"

"You always have the answers, don't you?"

The way he said it wasn't a compliment. She smiled sadly and shoved her hands into the pockets of her jeans. "Once I thought I did, but life showed me how little I knew."

"Yeah, life is as fickle as any woman ever dared to be." He climbed on the tractor.

"Aren't you coming in for lunch?" she asked over the roar of the engine.

"No."

Shannon watched Matt drive the tractor over to the fuel tank and begin pumping gas. She started for the house. When she entered the kitchen, Octavia was nowhere in sight. Knowing she wouldn't mind, Shannon found the canvas bag and thermos the housekeeper had given her when she had gone fishing, fixed a ham sandwich, wrapped the last piece of coffee cake, and filled the thermos with iced tea. She took it all outside to Matt.

"Do you want to eat while I pump or do you want to take it with you?" she asked. If *she* was tired, he had to be near exhaustion. An empty stomach wouldn't help.

"Octavia send you?" he queried.

"Does it matter?" She dismissed the slight feeling of hurt.

"Leave it," he told her.

Hanging the canvas bag on the headlight, she started back. That woman had really done a number on Matt, cutting him more deeply than any surgeon's scalpel.

"Shannon."

Surprised to hear Matt call her name, she spun around. He stood with one hand on the wheel of the tractor, the other holding the canvas bag.

"Thanks."

"You're welcome," she called, knowing she was grinning foolishly and not caring one bit that he was scowling again. For a moment Matt had remembered what it was like to repay kindness with politeness not suspicion, and best of all he had shared it with her.

Shannon Johnson had to go and soon, Matt thought as he parked the tractor under the galvanized shed and cut the headlights. Darkness settled around him. It was almost nine, he had been up since six. His body should be ready to shut down. It wasn't. It hummed with a strange mixture of something. Whatever, Shannon Johnson was the reason.

It made no sense. Hell, who said life or women made sense?

One thing he knew, it was becoming more and more difficult to remain emotionally detached where she was concerned. This afternoon, she had been right. He had wanted to punish her, but he also wanted to taste her lips and go from there.

Climbing down from the tractor, he started for the barn. His mind knew she was out to take what she could, but his body wasn't listening.

Maybe it was time he went into Kerrville, have himself some fun. Just as quickly as the idea formed he discarded it. He wouldn't use anyone like that. And despite Shannon's accusations, he didn't lead women on. God knew he had ample opportunity.

Telling the women in the small town of Jackson Falls he wasn't interested was a lot trickier than telling the other women he met across the country. For starters, he respected the townswomen's families and didn't want to create hard feelings. The prodding of well-meaning family members like Adam Gordon was just what Matt wanted to avoid. Then, too, the women in town were too marriage-minded, and he was too easy to find.

He could just imagine the gossip if he flatly rejected one of them. Besides, he'd never forget the laughter and the scorn in his ex-wife's face when she told him she had never loved him, had only used him to get what she wanted. When he couldn't fill her needs, she used other men.

He could never do that to another person. He didn't understand why Shannon had sounded genuinely disappointed in him or why it continued to bother him. Like she said, she had no right to judge anyone. Strangely, at the time she had told him that, she really looked as if she wanted to comfort him, when moments earlier she had been chastising him.

He shook his head. Shannon was a chameleon. Somehow she had learned to adapt and change as the situation demanded, going from innocent to defiant to seductive before his eyes. And by doing so she interested him as no other woman ever had.

An interesting woman was a dangerous woman. A man tended to go on feelings, on what he saw instead of what he knew.

Wishing he'd never seen Shannon, he entered the barn and saw the one person he wanted to avoid.

"What are you doing?" he asked.

Startled, Shannon swung toward him and away from the stall she had been about to enter. "I think there's something wrong with your horse."

"What do you mean?" he asked, brushing past her and going to the horse who stood on three legs.

Shannon followed him inside. "This morning when Jay brought him out of the pasture, he was all over the stall. I could hear him stomping around while I was in the tackroom. As I passed just now, I realized I hadn't heard him in a long time," she explained.

Matt's hand slowly swept downward from Brazos's back to his rump to his leg, then finally to his hoof. His fetlock was hot to the touch and slightly swollen. Matt straightened "How long has he been this way?"

"I don't know." She looked at the horse's leg, then up into Matt's harsh expression. "He was standing in the same position he is in now when I went inside to get a drink of water at seven. I didn't think anything about it until I was passing just now."

"Very observant."

Shannon shrugged. "Will he be all right?"

"I think so. It's just tender. Nothing seemed broken or pulled. Cleve does wonders with his remedies," Matt said, sliding his hand over the horse's rump. "If he isn't better by morning, I'll call the vet."

"I'll go get Cleve."

"I'll stay here," he said, staring back down at the horse's leg.

"I thought you might," Shannon said with a smile and headed for the bunkhouse.

Shannon alerted Cleve to the problem.

The frown on Cleve's face quickly turned to one of concern. "I'll get my hat." With that, he was out the door of the bunkhouse and down the steps.

Inside the barn, he went straight to the sorrel stallion and inspected him just as Matt had. "He was kickin' up his usual fuss about being in the stall when I went to the bunkhouse a little after six."

"Shannon noticed he was quiet when she went inside around seven." Matt squatted by the older man. "What time did Jay bring him in?"

"Midday," Cleve answered. His gnarled fingers lightly ran over the stallion's leg, then he gently raised the hoof and just as gently, flexed and extended it. "Looks like he might have kicked the stall too hard and bruised himself. Don't look like it's botherin' him enough to worry about a fracture. I'll go fix up somethin'. He should be fine since we caught it early."

"Thanks to Shannon." Matt nodded in her direction. "She noticed the quiet."

"It was nothing," she said from the stall door. "Anyone would have done the same."

Cleve's free hand clenched, his battered gray hat tipped forward. Slowly he stood. "Meanin', I should have?"

Her eyes widened at the implication. "No. Of course not. I was here, you weren't."

"I guess we're lucky you were here then," he told her, then glanced down at Matt. "I'll fix the poultice."

Shannon stared after the elderly cowboy. "I didn't mean to offend him. I wouldn't intentionally do that to anyone."

"So you keep saying."

She faced Matt. "I know it might be hard to believe, but you're the only one who can make me forget reason."

Since she made him behave the same way, it wasn't difficult at all for him to believe her. "Yeah."

"We just rub each other the wrong way," she stated, folding her arms and catching her lower lip between her teeth.

"Rubbing each other the right way would create just as many sparks. Maybe more," he told her, his voice unnaturally gritty.

Her hand flew to the base of her throat where her pulse leaped wildly. "You . . . you shouldn't say things like that."

She was right, but hearing the breathless catch in her voice made the sudden tightness in his jeans worse, not better. Pivoting away from temptation, he stood facing the horse. "I wonder what's keeping Cleve."

"If you want, I'll go check."

"No, he likes fixing his remedies alone." Matt's hand ran over the horse's flank. "He takes his responsibilities seriously. This ranch is his life, the family he never had."

"Matt, I didn't mean to infer otherwise," she said earnestly, watching Matt's large hands glide reassuringly over the animal.

He glanced over his shoulder. Her face was filled with entreaty and a strange kind of hope. Shannon might be a lot of things, but so far he had yet to see her be deliberately cruel. She was just as quick to soothe as she was to annoy him with her sharp tongue.

"I believe you," he finally answered.

Her face lit up. "Thank you."

"Cleve will probably come to the same conclusion once Brazos is all right." The horse neighed and Matt stroked him. "Although he knows it's not his fault the animal is hurt, Cleve feels guilty he wasn't the one to notice the problem."

"Just like family members feel guilty when a loved one becomes ill and they hadn't noticed sooner," Shannon said, remembering her own feeling of guilt about her grandfather.

Matt looked at her intently. "Sounds like you've been there."

Her breath came out shakily. "Yes, I have."

Matt watched her brown eyes darken, watched her struggle for composure and win. She had loved someone, and if he didn't miss his guess, she had lost him. Questions pounded in his brain, but he wasn't sure if he wanted to know the answers for himself or for the ranch's benefit . . . or why he felt the urge to pull her into his arms and console her.

"You better go on in. Cleve and I can finish things here."

"A men-only thing, huh?" she questioned with a laugh.

He struggled to keep from being affected by the twinkle in her eyes and the laughter. "I won't have you sleeping on the job tomorrow because you stayed up needlessly tonight."

"I've pulled double shifts before. I can take it," she told him. "I'll go see if Cleve needs any help."

"Shannon, go to the house." She kept walking. Matt shook his head. "And she called *me* stubborn," he muttered.

She opened the door to the tackroom and saw Cleve sniffing the contents of a quart-size brown bottle clutched in his right hand. She tensed. "What are you doing?"

He whirled around. Shannon was confused. Instead of the glazed look she had often seen in the eyes of people who had inhaled substances, Cleve's were sharp and accusing. "You ruined everything."

He was still upset with her. "You've got to believe me when I say I didn't mean anything earlier."

"I mean this," he said angrily, the wide arc of his arm encompassing the top two shelves where various bottles and metal containers sat.

Shannon looked at the shelves she had worked on most of the early morning rearranging and cleaning. From over-the-counter liniment to grooming needs, all the various bottles, jars, and cans were now neatly in groups instead of the chaotic mess she found this morning. She could find anything she wanted without . . . Her mind came to a halt.

This was Cleve's domain, not hers.

"I'm sorry. Before I moved anything I should have asked first. I needed some extra saddle soap. While I searched for another can, I started cleaning and rearranging." She studied his unhappy face. "If you'll tell me where, I'll put everything back tomorrow. Right now Matt is waiting."

"Tell him I'm comin'," he said sharply, and set the bottle on the table with several other similar-looking ones and turned away.

She started to go, then frowned when she read the label on the bottle. Iodine. "I'll straighten things out tomorrow. Matt is waiting."

"I know what I'm doin'," he told her flatly. "You just tell the boss I'm comin'."

"I'm glad to know it," said Matt.

On hearing Matt's voice, the cowhand tensed and slowly turned. Lines bracketed his mouth and raced across his dark forehead. He glanced at Matt, then away.

"It's my fault," Shannon blurted. "I rearranged the shelves and now he can't find anything."

"You what?" Matt shouted. His gaze swept the neat shelves, then Cleve's tense body before coming to rest on an anxious Shannon. "I told you to polish the harnesses and other gear, that's all."

She explained what had led up to her cleaning session.

Matt's stony expression didn't soften. "Go to the house, Shannon, and this time I mean it."

She started across the room. "Cleve—"

Matt blocked her path. "I'm not going to tell you again."

Shoulders back, chin lifted, she accepted his angry glare unflinchingly. "I messed up. The least you can do is let me apologize."

"You've already done that." Matt took her by the elbow and led her to the door. "I don't have time to waste arguing with you."

"But I could help. I know where I put things."

"We'll find them."

Digging her heels in did little good. His callused hands were gentle and powerful and determined. "The old bottles like the ones on the table are in the back of the second shelf."

Matt stopped. "You didn't throw them away?"

"What kind of an idiot would do that without asking?" She wrinkled her nose at his raised eyebrow and answered her own question. "The same kind that would rearrange someone's work space without asking."

She twisted to look at Cleve. His shoulders sagged. She had done that. "I really am sorry. The only reason Octavia hasn't thrown me out of her kitchen is that she feels the same way about keeping things in order. I forgot men aren't the same way."

Once again she was on her way to the door. "Good night, Shannon."

Looking up into Matt's unrelenting face, she bowed to the inevitable. "If you're not too tired, please let me know how they both are when you come up to bed."

His hand clenched on her arm.

She swallowed. The tip of her tongue ran across her lower lip. Matt's narrowed eyes followed. "I . . . I mean when you come upstairs."

"Good night." Spinning on his heels, he went inside the tackroom and closed the door, shutting her out.

"Need any help?" Matt asked on reentering the tackroom.

Cleve lifted his head. His eyes were old, tired. "You think she suspected anything?"

Matt gritted his teeth to hold back a curse word. He had learned a colorful array of words on the rodeo circuit and as a rancher. But respect for his elders was bone deep. "No."

Nodding his head, the elderly man began pulling bottles from the second shelf. "I know what you told me, but I can't help how I feel."

"I shouldn't have sent her in here," Matt replied, turning on the faucet and filling a bucket with water. "I never thought she'd do more than what I asked her to do."

"She looks like fluff, but she's as scrappy as I've ever seen."

Matt shut the gushing water off with a snap of his wrist. "Sounds like you like her."

Taking three quart-size brown bottles from the shelf, Cleve hugged them to his chest. "Just speakin' the truth."

The bucket of water plumped on the table. "She won't be here much longer. In the meantime, I'll set her to riding fence or something."

A battered straw hat came upward sharply. "Meanin' I can't handle one female."

Matt had seen that stubborn look before. "Meaning I had already planned on seeing how well she liked being in the saddle for eight hours." As soon as the words were out of his mouth, his body reacted with predictable swiftness.

Cleve's laughter sounded more like a rusty cough. "Might have known you wouldn't let that those big brown eyes get to you."

"You noticed her eyes?"

Cleve shot Matt a long, level look. "Might be old, but I ain't six feet under." Opening the bottle in his hand, he sniffed the contents, nodded his satisfaction, then poured about a cup into the water. A medicinal smell wafted upward. "She's got grit to go along with all them other things a man my age can only admire."

"You about ready?" Matt asked, his words sharper than intended.

The cowhand didn't appear to notice. "Yep, a man regrets a lot of things when he gets old," Cleve reminisced.

A younger man also had regrets.

Matt wanted Shannon with an increasing fervor that kept him awake at night, then invaded his dreams when he finally fell asleep. The taste, the feel, the scent of her was never far from his mind. Somehow he knew with a gut certainty that if he took her to bed, his need for her would only increase.

Once before he had been suckered in by wanting a woman so badly he wouldn't listen to his family, only the wild clamoring of his body. He had paid the price. This time he was staying in control. "Come on, Brazos is waiting."

Cleve quickly poured from the other two bottles he had taken from the second shelf. "Grab some clean towels from the drawer over there. This might be a long night."

"In more ways than one," Matt mumbled and followed the older man out the door.

Shannon was waiting for him at the top of the stairs. She had on another of those silky pants outfits, this one the color of peaches. Her knees were propped up, her folded arms across them. A faint exotic scent drifted to him as his booted foot touched the bottom step. "It's after midnight."

"I couldn't sleep."

"The meadow losing its magic already?"

She rocked. "Cleve's remedy must have worked faster than you thought."

Matt peered at her closer. If he didn't know better he'd think there were dried tears on her cheeks. "Morning is going to be here before you know it."

She nodded and slowly stood. For some reason, she hadn't wanted to be alone. She had never minded solitude before. Her grandfather wasn't the reason. She just felt incredibly sad.

Before she knew it, she was on the steps waiting for Matt. But his aloofness made her feel worse, not better. Without another word she started down the hall.

Knowing he shouldn't, but somehow unable to help himself, he followed. "What's the matter? Are you sick?"

Head down, hands jammed in the pants pockets, she continued down the hallway. "I'm not sick."

"Then what's wrong with you?"

"Good night, Matt." She reached for the doorknob.

His hand shot out and closed around her delicate wrist. "All right? I'll bite." Her head lowered even more at his choice of words. "You were waiting for me so the least you can do is tell me what's wrong."

She shook her head. It was too late.

Two fingers lifted her chin. Her skin was velvet smooth, but what caught his attention were the tears shimmering in her sad brown eyes. They affected him more than he wanted to admit.

"Shannon, what is it?" he asked, unaware of the husky note of entreaty in his voice.

She swallowed around the lump in her throat and the desire to ask him to hold her. "I just wanted to say good night."

Sadness stared back up at him. He should leave her and go to his room. Yet something tore through him. "Ah, hell. Come here." Strong arms closed around her. Instantly her hands came up to push him away. Using his greater strength, he pulled her closer. Again and again in one continuous motion his hand brushed from the base of her spine to her shoulder.

She shuddered, then relaxed against him. "I'm sorry," she gulped.

She fit perfectly beneath his chin. It seemed natural for his cheek to rest against the top of her head. "You smell like some exotic flower."

"You don't."

Matt tensed, then laughed, a deep rumbling sound. Once again she had caught him off guard. "I don't suppose I do."

Shannon leaned back and looked up at him. A smile started at the corner of her mouth and blossomed into a laugh. "That wasn't very nice of me."

"You certainly don't pull any punches."

"Neither do you."

"You offering to wash my back again?"

"No, and you know it."

They stood smiling at each other. Then the smiles were gone, replaced by an intensity neither wanted and neither could deny.

Air became harder for Shannon to draw into her lungs. Every place their bodies touched, her skin tingled. She suddenly knew why she had waited for Matt. The realization made her take a hasty step backward.

She didn't need this. Dear Lord. She didn't need this. "Thanks for helping me to laugh. I—I think I can sleep now."

"Don't bet on it."

Shannon escaped into her room, away from the blazing fire of Matt's eyes. She glanced at her bed, then away. Matt was right.

Sleep would not come easy.

CHAPTER 10

She couldn't go down to breakfast, face Matt across the table and act as if he hadn't touched her last night as no man ever had.

He scared her. He excited her.

Sitting on the bed, Shannon tucked her lower lip between her teeth. Matt disturbed her in ways she didn't want and didn't understand. She finally had to admit those feelings he drew from her had nothing to do with her instincts as a nurse, and everything as a woman.

Sixteen days remained of her vacation. Sixteen long days of pretending that Matt didn't set her body afire with a look, make her want with a simple touch.

And he didn't trust her as far as she could throw his horse.

Her stomach rumbled. A not-so-subtle reminder that she hadn't eaten since her late lunch yesterday. After leaving Cleve and Matt last night, she hadn't been hungry.

She glanced at her watch. Seven fifty-five. She stood. Matt should be finishing breakfast. She'd go down and get her assignment. Whatever detail around the ranch he put her on today she'd find time to grab a bite once he left. She knew she was being a coward, but at the moment being a coward was safer than being vulnerable.

Grabbing her straw hat, she went downstairs and into the kitchen. Matt's unreadable gaze touched her the instant she opened the swinging doors.

She smiled and spoke despite the familiar lurch in her stomach, the catch in her breath. "Good morning, Octavia, Matt."

"Good morning, child. I was just going up to wake you for breakfast," said the housekeeper, smiling.

"She doesn't have time." Matt sat his coffee cup down and stood. "Let's go."

She accepted the brisk command with relief. If she was having difficulties resisting a suspicious Matt, a tender, caring Matt would melt her like snow on a hot stove.

"She hasn't eaten," Octavia protested.

"Shannon knows what time work starts." Setting his Stetson on his head, Matt headed for the door.

With a reassuring smile at the housekeeper, Shannon followed. Let him stay annoyed with her. That way, she'd keep out of trouble.

Halfway to the barn they were met by the three range hands, Jay, Elliott, and Griff. Five horses trailed behind them. Matt grabbed the reins of a huge black satin-skinned animal and swung up in the saddle in one graceful motion. Gazing down at her, he looked at once intimidating and compelling.

"You'll be riding the fence line today with Griff," he informed Shannon.

"Boss, you gave *me* that assignment," said Jay, the youngest and best-looking of the two single ranch hands. His appreciative gaze on Shannon, he smiled. "I never thought I'd ever see the day I'd be looking forward to riding the fence line."

"You'll enjoy moving the cattle to the north pasture just as much." Matt's tone was curt, final. "Trade horses with Griff."

His confusion obvious, the young cowboy's brows bunched together in his rich mahogany face as he glanced over his shoulder at his boss. The implacable face wasn't reassuring. Jay hastened to do as he was told. Griff and Elliott wisely said nothing.

"The roan's yours, Shannon," Matt indicated with a curt jerk of his Stetson. "Mount up. We're wasting time."

Her eyes rounded. "I haven't ridden for years."

"Riding is something you never forget." When his spirited horse side-stepped, Matt controlled the blaze-faced animal with effortless ease. "Give her the reins, Griff."

"Morning, miss." Griff, tall, homely, and happily married, tipped his hat and extended the reins.

Gripping the leather strips, she stared at Matt. He stared back, his face resolute, inflexible. Another challenge. Being on the Circle T made her remember something she had forgotten in the past months. Once you commit to something never give up until either the job is done or the last breath is gone from your body.

Looping the reins over the horse's docile head, she put her left foot into the stirrup, grabbed the horn cap and swung into the saddle. She was certain she heard a sigh of relief from Griff.

Matt's expression didn't change as his encompassing gaze swept from her booted foot resting comfortably in the stirrup to her face. "What if I didn't know how to ride?"

"The fence in the south pasture needs checking. You're assigned to do it. One way or another, you would have gotten the job done." The heel of his dusty brown boot touched the horse's flank. Instantly, the black animal sprang forward. The ranch hands took off after them.

After one longing look toward the back door of the kitchen, Shannon urged her horse to follow. This wasn't exactly the way she had planned her morning. Matt had outwitted her.

She just wished she knew if it was because of the incident with Cleve or he had decided to turn up the pressure and make her quit. Either way she hoped her gluteus maximus didn't give out before Matt gave in.

In ICCU when she had been too busy to take a break let alone eat lunch, she had worked through hunger and thirst. There was no reason for her not to do so today. It was after ten and Griff said they'd head back for lunch around twelve. She could make it until then. As when she was on the hospital floor, she just needed to focus on getting the job done.

After giving herself the pep talk, Shannon gazed dispassionately at the meandering line of fence stretched out before her. She sighed. Getting excited about barbless wire was simply beyond her capability.

Now she understood Jay's earlier comment. This had to be the most boring and monotonous job on the ranch. If it wasn't for the beautiful countryside and the lanky cowboy beside her, she would have had a hard time continuing.

Griff Walker was forty-something, balding, and as thin as the proverbial rail. He was also soft-spoken, kind, and loved his family. She knew all about his three sons ranging in age from four to nine, his wife who worked at the hardware store, his hope of buying a place of their own one day. He was a talker and good company.

"You wanna get down and rest a minute under one of those oak trees, ma'am?" Griff asked, looking sideways at the stooped shoulders of the slender woman riding beside him.

Shannon wiped her shirtsleeve across her perspiration-damp forehead before answering. "If I get off this horse, I may not get back on."

"You're doing fine, ma'am. The boss will be real proud of you."

"Somehow that doesn't inspire me at the moment." She shifted from one hip to the other. Thank goodness she was in pretty good shape.

"The boss might work you hard sometimes, but *he* works just as hard," the tall cowboy said with conviction. "Ain't nothing he asked you to do, he won't do himself."

She wasn't surprised Matt had the loyalty of his men. He certainly had jumped to defend Cleve and reassure the elderly hand. It was *women* Matt didn't trust. "I'm sure he treats his *men* fairly."

Leather creaked as Griff shifted in his saddle. "That he does. Never looks down on us or treats us different because he's the boss. If we're running a little short until payday and need money and have a good reason, he'll advance us the cash without interest. Ain't many a worker who can say the same thing."

From personal knowledge, she knew he was right. Although the hospital frowned upon loan transactions between employees during working hours, it was common practice. Sometimes the borrower just signed over their paycheck to the lender.

Wade also had been right. Matt wasn't as hard as he pretended. "He doesn't sound like Hardcase to me."

"The boss don't deserve that name," Griff said with heat. "Without him my youngest wouldn't be alive."

Slender hands clenched on the reins. "What happened?"

The cowhand looked embarrassed he had blurted out the information. "He don't want me telling folks, but I don't like hearing things 'bout a man who helped Clint when no one else could or would."

"I understand, it's just that I'm having difficulty understanding Matt," Shannon told him.

"No wonder since you two are partners and all. Must be hard for him to get used to." Griff shook his head. "I've lived in Jackson Falls all my life. Never thought anyone but a Taggart would own Taggart land."

"I'm only a temporary owner," Shannon confessed, holding her hat against the sudden gust of wind that tried to blow it off. "I'm leaving in a couple of weeks, but before I go, I'm signing the land back over to Matt."

"I'll be." Griff grinned and guided his horse around a clump of stunt cedar. "The boss will be happy to hear that."

"If you don't mind, I'd rather you not mention it to him or anyone else." Matt wouldn't believe Griff any more than he believed her.

The cowhand nodded. "You're good people, ma'am."

"Thank you."

"The boss is the same way." Griff looked away for a long moment. "Clint was stung by a bee. I didn't think much 'bout it. I been stung lots of times and so had my other two boys. Told him he'd be all right." The cowboy swallowed. "I left him in the truck while I went in the hardware store to pick up my Millie from work. By the time we came out, Clint was having trouble breathing. The boss had walked outside with me.

"He took one look at Clint, grabbed him from me and ran back in the store giving instructions for the other clerk to call 911 and Dr. Carter. Then my boy stopped breathing. My wife started screaming. I was shaking so bad I didn't know what to do. Everyone stood back, not knowing what to do. The boss bent over Clint and breathed for him."

The cowhand looked at her with eyes that unashamedly shone with tears. "He saved my Clint's life. Every day I thank him and thank God for giving me another chance."

"Not many people know what to do with a second chance."

"I know. Come on, we better get to checking this fence." He urged his horse from a walk to a canter. "The boss don't give second chances."

She grunted. "Tell me something I don't know."

He had been right to send Shannon off without breakfast. She hadn't overslept as Octavia suspected, she had stayed in her room to avoid him. When he didn't see her in the kitchen when he first went down, he had gone upstairs to check on her. Outside her door, he had heard her pacing the floor, yet when he knocked, there had been no answer.

Maybe she regretted last night's encounter in the hall as much as he did. He had spent a miserable night, and when he did fall asleep, it had been to dream of Shannon as a living flame in his bed.

His gritted his teeth at the memory. No breakfast was her choice. Yet he couldn't get out of his mind the sound of her stomach rumbling as they crossed the yard. It was too much of a reminder of when they first met and how exhausted she was and how stubborn.

His horse jumped a small ditch, and the canvas bag on his saddle horn bumped against his knee. He wasn't taking her food because he cared. Shannon had to learn that she didn't have the stamina it took to help run a ranch, but at the same time he didn't want her fainting from lack of nourishment and falling off her horse. He had enough on his mind without dealing with an injured woman.

Matt came over the slight rise and saw Griff and Shannon standing by the fence. Shannon was gesturing toward the fence with something in her hand. Griff was shaking his head. Matt urged his horse toward them.

They turned to him when Matt was several yards away. Stopping in front of them, he saw a break in the barbless wire fence. Shannon had a wire stretcher in her hands. A hammer lay on the ground.

"Is there a problem?"

Shannon shot a look at Griff. Her chin lifted. "No."

Matt leaned over and crossed one arm over the horn, then propped the other arm on top. Griff looked uncomfortable. He wasn't going to get his range-riding partner in trouble. Score another conquest for Shannon. Matt had known the impressionable and unmarried Jay would be easy prey for a captivating woman like Shannon, but Matt figured a happily married man like Griff would be a little stronger.

Hell. He had a hard time not being suckered in by her beauty and her spirit, and he knew she was after his land. He couldn't expect a goodhearted man like Griff to resist falling under her spell. But as boss, Matt expected the hands' first loyalty to be to him.

"Griff, if there's a problem I want to know about it. Now."

The cowhand ignored the plea in Shannon's eyes. Matt wasn't known for his patience. "Miss Shannon wants to help."

Matt straightened. "Then let her help. That's what she's here for."

"She don't have any gloves."

Matt looked at Shannon's delicate hands. In spite of himself he recalled their softness. Without gloves, the firm grip needed to use the wire stretcher would blister her hands in no time.

"Why didn't you say something before we left the ranch?"

The impertinent chin went higher. "How would I know I needed gloves? You said check the fence, you didn't say anything about repairing it. Besides, if you'll remember, you were in a hurry."

Matt barely bit back an expletive. "Let her nail in the staples."

Griff appeared even more uncomfortable. "We, er . . . already tried that."

When Matt's probing gaze went to Shannon, she stuck her hand behind her back. He swung out of the saddle. In the two strides it took to reach her, he removed his gloves.

Superior strength easily pulled her hand from behind her back. The knuckle of her thumb was bruised, slightly swollen. Tenderly, his thumb stroked hers.

Air hissed through her teeth. Huge brown eyes stared up at him.

"I didn't mean to hurt you." He was surprised his voice came out so husky, surprised more that he didn't want to release her hand.

"You . . . you didn't." Her lips were slightly parted as if she was having difficulty drawing in air. The pulse in her throat leaped wildly.

He recognized desire not pain, but if he didn't stop this craziness, one could quickly lead to the other. Releasing her hand, he stepped back. "Go back to the ranch house and put some ice on your thumb."

"I haven't fin—"

"Yes you have," he interrupted her. "Afterward, help Octavia. Today is her half day."

"Gladly. When I finish here."

"I don't give an order twice."

"Neither do you send a hired hand home and give them light duty simply because their thumb got in the way of a hammer." She went to the fence and, using the wire stretcher, tightened the wire. "Ready, Griff."

The cowhand didn't move.

She sighed. "Matt, I'm not being argumentative or stubborn. I've done worse and survived. When I bang my knee against a bedrail at work I can't take time to pamper myself any more than you or one of your men can." He didn't move. "I don't like walking away from something until it's done. You assigned me a job, now let me do it."

He studied the determined features of his unwanted junior partner for a long time. Short of throwing her on her horse, he didn't have a choice. Touching her was the last thing he wanted to do at the moment. Even with her battered straw hat punched down on her head, reddish-brown hair whipping around her face damp with perspiration, she was too tempting for his peace of mind.

He handed her his gloves.

Surprise widened her eyes, then she smiled. "Thanks, boss." Sticking the wire stretcher under her arm, she put on the too-large gloves, then resumed holding the wire.

Matt watched her eager expression and tried not to read too much into her calling him boss. She sure as hell wasn't going to take his orders without letting him know her opinion. He decided to stop trying to figure out this woman for now, and bent to pick up the hammer. Without asking, Griff handed him the staples.

With one glance to make sure Shannon held the wire securely, he drove in staple after staple, then moved to the next wire and the next. Each time Shannon had to adjust the oversize gloves, and each time Matt waited. At last the break in the fence was repaired.

"We did it." She grinned, testing the wire. "My best friend Melanie will never believe this."

"Perhaps you should send her a picture," Matt suggested dryly.

Shannon tilted her head to one side. "Maybe I will. Do you have a camera I could borrow?"

His mustache flattened. "Go home, Shannon."

Her heart lurched. As much as she didn't understand her feelings about Matt, the thought of leaving him sent her into a panic. "You can't make me go back to St. Louis. I've done everything you asked me."

"I meant the ranch house," Matt explained curtly.

"Oh, my mistake," Shannon mumbled in embarrassment. Pulling off his gloves, she handed them back. "I'm going. Sorry, Griff, to leave you without help."

"That's all right, Miss Shannon, I done this before by myself," the cow-hand placated.

"But I bet the time goes faster when you're not by yourself," she told him with a mischievous grin.

"That it does, ma'am," he agreed.

"Griff, you still have work to do," Matt said.

Gathering the tools from Matt and Shannon, the hand put them in his saddlebag and mounted. "Nice ridin' with you."

"You're a gallant man, Griff." Shannon wiped her shirtsleeve across her brow as she watched him ride away.

"Is there a man you can't wrap around your finger?"

Since there was no accusation in his voice or in the midnight-black eyes watching her so intently, she answered him. "Men *and* women seem to find it easy to talk with me. My nursing instructor called it my special gift."

"You thirsty?"

The question was so far afield, Shannon blinked. "What did you say?"

"Are you thirsty?"

"What do you think?"

"What I think doesn't bear saying." Matt walked over to his horse, took off the canvas bag and handed it to her.

Shannon's avid gaze went from the bag to Matt. A tongue moistened her dry lips. "I'll wait. That has to last you until tonight."

Guilt struck him like a physical blow. Yet, he could no more admit the bag was for her than he could admit wanting her was slowly driving him crazy. Reaching inside, he handed her the thermos. "It's enough."

She didn't need any further urging. Unscrewing the lid, she poured the cap half full and drank. Finished, she recapped the thermos and handed it back to him with thanks.

Blunt-tipped fingers closed around the container. "Can you find your way back?"

A disarming smile lit her face. "I thought I'd give my horse his head and he'd lead me home like in the movies."

"More likely to the spot with the sweetest clover," Matt told her. "Follow the fence until it juts sharply to the left, then head due west for about two miles. The ranch is over the next rise."

"Okay."

"Remember, due west."

She nodded. Still unmoving. Two hours ago she hadn't wanted to face him and now she didn't want to leave him. The hot sun didn't seem to matter. "How is Brazos today?"

"Fine."

"Cleve."

"Fine."

"Is he still upset with me?"

"He thinks you have grit."

"He does?"

"He does."

"What do you think?" The question was out before she had time to stop herself.

"I think you should get on your horse and leave while we're both thinking at all."

Shannon recognized the dark, smoldering passion in Matt's eyes and quickly went to her horse, mounted and rode away. She rode fast because she so wanted to stay.

God help her. How was she going to last until her vacation was over?

CHAPTER 11

"I'll do that."

Shannon glanced around to see Cleve behind her. She stepped away from the horse she had been trying to unsaddle. "Thanks."

Gnarled hands finished uncinching the horse, then removed the saddle and blanket. "Saw you ride out this morning."

"He put me to riding the fence line." It was easier to think of Matt impersonally.

Cleve straightened the blanket on the rail to dry. "And?"

"I seem to have a knack for doing the wrong thing." She held up her thumb. "I'm on light duty."

"Better go inside and put some ice on it."

"You sound like him," she said, pleased that Cleve didn't appear upset with her any longer.

"Well, if us men don't take care of those with less sense, who will?" Untying the horse's reins, he walked off.

"You sure you two aren't related?" she called after the bow-legged cowhand. She didn't expect an answer and she didn't get one. Shaking her head, she headed for the kitchen. Octavia glanced up from the kitchen table. The frown on her face curved into a smile.

"Oh, Shannon, I'm glad you're back."

"It's nice knowing I'm wanted somewhere."

The frown returned. "Matt giving you a hard time? I thought he was coming around. I know he fixed you some food."

"That was for him."

"No, it wasn't. He might fill a canteen with water, but that's about it no matter how long he plans to stay out." Octavia's smile returned. "He certainly would never put a napkin and a wash cloth inside."

"He only offered me a drink. He didn't say anything about food," she said.

"He didn't have to since he was sending you back to the house. That way he didn't have to admit he was wrong this morning or that he was worried about you. Told you he was sneaky."

Shannon suppressed a warm rush of happiness. "He's only worried that I won't sign over the meadow and leave."

"Wouldn't be so sure about that." The housekeeper's level gaze studied Shannon for a long moment. "Matt pays about as much attention to women around here as a horse does to a fly. Less. For him they simply don't exist. I'm sure it's a different story with women away from here, but for whatever his reason, the women in the area are off limits. Since you're living here, logic says he should ignore you, too. But he doesn't. You have his attention and I don't think the land has anything to do with it."

Shannon didn't like the way the conversation was going. "Was there a particular reason you're glad I'm back?"

"I can take a hint," the housekeeper said. "The ladies auxiliary is having a call meeting and I need to go. I had already switched my half day off from yesterday to today because of my hair appointment. I just called the beautician and, thank goodness, she can work me in tomorrow. Lord only knows how long I'll be there. Matt won't care if I take off, but I had planned on going grocery shopping."

"Say no more. I'll do the grocery shopping."

"Oh, Shannon, that would help me out so much. I truly hate going to the grocery store, so we're almost out of everything," she confessed and handed Shannon a three-column list on a sheet of paper.

"You weren't kidding."

"If it's too much—"

Shannon shook her head. "I was just wondering how I'm going to get all this in my car."

Octavia brightened. "Cleve always drives me in his truck, so he can help with the groceries."

"Oh, wonderful," she said drolly.

"Like Matt, he just takes a bit of getting used to."

"Define a bit."

The corner of Octavia's mouth twitched. Shannon's lips curved upward. Simultaneously both women broke into laughter.

"Cleve, this would go a lot faster if you'd just read over the list and help me find the right aisles." Shannon remembered why she stayed with her old grocery store back home after a new superstore opened. Even with the signs overhead, she still had to find the exact spot the item was located in.

"I just push the cart," he said, moving his chewing tobacco from one side of his jaw to the other.

She sighed. "You cook for the other hands. You must know something."

"I just tell Mrs. Ralston what I need and she adds it to her list. She understands how a man feels about grocery shopping."

"I wonder how that same macho man would feel if there was no food on the table when he came home."

"Mighty upset," came the reply.

"Then I suggest you find your memory or your boss is going to know why there's no food prepared when he comes home for dinner tonight." She tore off the third column, handed it to a startled Cleve. "I'll do the rest of the list."

Halfway down the next aisle, Shannon stopped. She shouldn't have done that. She had promised Octavia she'd do the grocery shopping, it wasn't Cleve's responsibility. Perhaps if he didn't act as if she didn't have sense enough to come out of the rain, he wouldn't upset her so.

He thinks you have grit. Matt's words came back to her.

Wheeling the basket sharply, she went in search of Cleve. She turned the aisle to see him unmoved from the spot she had left him, the list clutched in his fist, his eyes shut tight. Misery radiated from him like a physical thing.

His eyes opened. He turned away, but not before she saw the pain and confusion in them. Suddenly, she remembered Cleve sniffing the bottles, not reading the labels.

He can't read.

Her chest tightened. He couldn't read and she had embarrassed and hurt him. She started toward him, praying somehow she'd find the right words not to injure his pride further.

"I was thinking, Matt isn't going to be too pleased with me if I don't get this done and I sure don't want to let Octavia down, so how about we do this systematically and compromise?"

Gently, she pulled the rumpled list from his hand and put it with the other one. If he knew what she wanted, she didn't doubt he could take her to every item. People who couldn't read were visual learners.

"Let's see, baking products are next. You can get the flour, cornmeal, sugar, and I'll get the rest."

Dark-brown eyes shifted away from her. "Pardon me, but I don't feel like grocery shopping no more."

The elderly cowboy slowly walked away from her as if every step was an effort. She had never felt so helpless in her life. He had seen through her subterfuge as easily as seeing through spring water. Without giving the groceries another thought she walked after him.

As soon as she opened the door of his truck, the engine roared to life. Her door closed and the vehicle took off. She stole one furtive peek at Cleve's rigid profile and slumped against the leather seat. He wasn't up to listening to her. Besides, she had had her chance and blown it. There was only one person who could help him now.

Matt.

This time when he yelled at her, she knew she would deserve every second of his condemnation.

"Octavia, I need Matt to come back to the ranch at once," Shannon said as soon as the housekeeper came to the phone. She didn't know what she would have done if Octavia hadn't left a number where she could be reached.

"Child, what's the matter? You all right?"

Shannon spoke around the lump in her throat. "I can't explain things now, but it's very important that I talk to Matt immediately." She took a deep breath. "Do you have an emergency code or something? I tried to catch that stupid horse, but he wouldn't come."

"Shan—"

"Please, Octavia. I don't have time for questions." Twisting the phone cord around her finger, she stared at the entrance of the barn. Cleve had gone inside about fifteen minutes ago and she hadn't seen him since.

"Just tell me you're all right."

"I'm fine. I'm not the one . . . I'm fine."

The housekeeper gave her Matt's number, then instructed, "Put in 911 and your name. He'll know it's you calling and come running."

Shannon sniffed. "Thank you for not demanding an explanation."

A none too delicate snort came through the receiver. "I'm not sure you would have given me one. I guess I'll have to wait until you're ready to explain things."

"That's not my decision to make," she said softly. Pressing the disconnect button, she put in Matt's beeper number, the emergency information, then went outside on the porch to wait.

Matt came thundering over the rise looking down on the ranch in less than five minutes. Low in the saddle, he leaned over the horse's long neck as if they were connected in some way. Shannon's breath caught in her throat when she saw he was headed straight for the white wooden fence of the outer corral instead of taking the time to go to the gate.

Horse and rider cleared the fence with room to spare and Shannon let out a grateful breath that he was an excellent rider. Her gaze glued to him, she watched him take the next fence with the same reckless ease. He was aiming straight for her.

Her eyes widened in apprehension as he swung from the still-moving horse with an agility and skill that left her breathless again. In seconds he was on the porch. His gloved hands closed around her forearms, his black eyes drilled into her.

"What's the matter? Are you hurt?"

Despite his voice, the gentleness of the hands holding her finally got through to her. "He's hurting."

"Who?" he barked, clearly at his limits.

"Cleve. He and I went to the grocery store together." She took in a huge gulp of air. "I thought he was acting macho and I gave him part of the grocery list."

Matt's fingers tightened on her arms.

"He's hurting, Matt. He's a proud man. I didn't know what else to do but call you."

"Where is he?"

"The barn."

Matt turned and started back down the stairs. Grabbing the reins of his horse, he tried to slow his drumming heartbeat and get the bitter taste of fear out of his mouth.

He had never been so frightened in his life. Seeing the concern in Shannon's teary eyes had been like someone twisting his insides. The fear hadn't been for herself, but for a man she had only known a few days.

Nearing the barn, he wondered if he'd ever know the real Shannon, or if he dared. He saw Cleve sitting a few feet inside on a small stool, three strands of hemp in his dark, callused hands.

Making handmade rope was time-consuming. To Matt's knowledge, Cleve had never made over a few dollars' profit from a single one of the highly prized ropes he "sold" to friends. The elderly cowhand considered it a dying art, and since he had no children, he was leaving a part of himself behind. He blessed the good days when his arthritis allowed him the strength and dexterity to work without pain. He'd always said it proved he wasn't useless.

Cleve certainly had a need to feel useful today.

Matt leaned against the stall door beside Cleve and glanced out the door. Shannon still stood on the porch, her slim arms wrapped around her, her gaze fixed on the barn door.

He looked at the top of Cleve's battered, sweat-rimmed hat. Matt would rather be locked in a chute with an angry bull than see the old man hurt.

"You all right?"

"She call you?" Hemp twisted around hemp.

"Yeah."

"Haven't seen you ride that crazy in a long time."

Matt propped his elbows on top of the stall door. "She put in the emergency code."

The battered hat lifted, then swung in the direction of Shannon. "You should have seen her tryin' to catch Flapjack again. Had a carrot in her hand."

"She watched a lot of westerns."

Cleve's head lowered. A long time passed before he said, "I never wanted anyone else to know."

"She won't tell anyone."

"She knows." The words came out tightly, embarrassment mixed with resentment.

"She knows and she's so worried about you that she has tears in her eyes."

The arch of the old cowhand's neck brought Matt into his line of vision. "You must be wrong. Why would she cry for an old nobody like me?"

It was all Matt could do not to yell he wasn't a nobody, that the person, not the education, not the money, made the man. But he had yelled before and Cleve hadn't listened. "A nobody wouldn't drop out of school and stay at home to help with his four younger brothers and sisters after his father was killed when a mule kicked him. A nobody wouldn't work from sunup to sundown for the price of a soft drink in today's money. You gave up your education for your sisters and brothers. Without you, they wouldn't have made it."

"They're gone now, but all of 'em got an education," he said proudly.

"They had you to thank," Matt said, his hand clamping on the older man's shoulder. "A nobody couldn't have done that."

Cleve's hand gripped the rope. "A grown man should know how to read."

"I told you I'd teach you anytime you're ready."

The elderly man's sigh was long. "What if I don't have it in me to learn?" His shoulder moved helplessly beneath Matt's strong hand. "That's a failure I don't want to face in this lifetime. I don't even know if I can face her again."

"She regrets what happened," Matt said.

"She's sassy, but she's got a good heart."

Matt's gaze followed the direction of Cleve's. Shannon hadn't moved from the porch. She might be concerned, but he wasn't ready to concede her goodness. A good woman would be more disruptive to his peace of mind than a selfish one. "She's stubborn and opinionated."

A dry bark of laughter erupted from the old man. "Just like you."

"Now who's calling the kettle black?" Matt asked.

"She don't know spit about ranchin'," Cleve snorted.

"I don't know what Wade was thinking to leave her the meadow."

Cleve came to his feet, his eyes wide. "She wasn't kiddin'? She really owns a part of the Circle T?"

Matt lips tightened. "Yeah."

"Why?"

Matt gave the only truth he knew. "She was Wade's nurse."

"I'll be," the older man said. He looked back at Shannon with new interest. "So she's the 'angel' in the hospital Wade talked about. He thought highly of her. Can't say he said the same thing for her beau."

Matt had been about to ask why everyone seemed to know something about Wade and Shannon when he didn't, until Cleve said "beau." Every nerve in his body snapped to attention. He came away from the stall and faced the cowhand. "Beau?"

"Yep. Wade spoke of some citified fellow up in St. Louis. Should have made the connection sooner." Rope in one hand, Cleve took his hat off and scratched his balding pate with the other. "Wade thought she might marry the fellow. Guess he was wrong. Didn't see no ring."

Something inside Matt tightened. His ex-wife had kept hers in the coin holder of her billfold. After he filed for divorce she had pawned her rings and sent him a useless part of the ticket to show him just how little she thought of him. Enclosed with the torn receipt was a note telling him how angry he had made her by not fulfilling her dreams of fame and riches as the wife of a top rodeo star.

The laughing, caring woman he had met in line at the grocery store and married a month later didn't exist. He had been suckered all the way by her beautiful face and lying lips. He wasn't going to be that gullible or that stupid again no matter how tempted.

"I better get back."

"You shouldn't have come," Cleve told him. "I ain't made out of fluff."

"Never thought you were." Untying the horse, Matt went to the waiting Shannon.

"Is he all right?"

He wanted to ask Shannon questions of his own, such as who was this man Wade had mentioned. Matt shut the words away because he shouldn't care about the woman whose gaze kept darting from him to the barn. Or care that the perspiration dampening her face indicated she was uncomfortable in the heat. Most of all, he shouldn't have the strangest urge to run his tongue across the moisture beaded on her brow, the curve of her upper lip.

His jaw hardened. Hell, he'd like to taste her all over and then start again.

"Matt?" Concern etched her face, echoed in that one word.

Somehow he drew his rampaging mind from his fantasy of her body to the need in her face. She cared and she was worried.

Unbidden came the memory of being in the emergency room with a broken collarbone. With his shoulder feeling like someone had taken a branding iron to it, he kept asking why his wife wasn't there. She'd been in the stands when the bronc threw him four seconds into his ride; she should have been there.

Kane had told him she probably didn't like to see Matt in pain. He had wholeheartedly believed his big brother, because he hadn't wanted to face the alternative. Two months later, he had no choice.

A tornado wouldn't have kept Shannon away. She was capable of caring, possibly even loving. Somehow he knew, if she had been in the stands, nothing would have kept her away.

"Matt, please say something."

He shook off the memories with practiced ease. "He'll be all right."

"I knew you could help him." She reached out her hand to touch him, then as if realizing what she had been about to do, jerked it back. "He respects you so much."

"Hard to believe, huh?"

Her smile was tremulous. "No. You can be nice when you put your mind to it."

The smile, the rosy lips, were too much. She smelled good and looked better. He turned and swung up on his horse.

"Wait!" she cried, and stepped off the porch. "At least come in and eat something."

"I haven't time." He gathered the reins tighter in his hands.

She grabbed the canvas bag and stepped back. "Then I'll fix you something fresh. I won't be but a minute." She whirled and ran up the steps.

He should go. He didn't.

Shannon's big brown eyes staring at him one moment as though she'd like to lay his head on her soft breast and comfort him and the next as though she'd like to eat him with a spoon was too much of a temptation to see again.

He waited and, of course, it took longer than a minute. A smile on her face, she came rushing out of the house and handed him the bag.

"You eat every bit of it."

"You're beginning to sound like Octavia." He hooked the bag over the saddle horn. She was in her comfort mode. His gaze flickered to her breasts.

Her smile widened. "Maybe you'll listen to one of us."

"I'm hardheaded, remember."

"You're a lot of things, I'm just beginning to learn," she said softly and went into the house.

Matt had one leg over the saddle before he realized his intention of going after Shannon and asking what she meant. Calling himself crazy, he regained his saddle and took off. He didn't care what she thought of him. Even as the words formed in his thoughts, he knew he lied.

Good or bad, he wanted Shannon Johnson with a soul-burning urgency. It was stupid, it was dangerous. His mind knew, his body just wasn't listening.

Her grocery basket was exactly where she had left it earlier. Thank goodness there had been nothing perishable inside. Hands clamped on the handle, she headed to aisle 4. Baking products. Rounding the corner, she came to a halt.

Cleve. A smile started at the curve of her lips and spread.

He put a ten-pound bag of flour inside his cart next to the cornmeal and the sugar. "What else is on that list?" he asked.

Grinning, Shannon started toward him. "Cleve."

He backed up a step when she lifted her arms. "Ain't no call for all that."

Her arms lowered. "I'm glad you came."

He shrugged. "Ain't much gonna fit in that little toy car of yours, so I followed in my truck. I got a taste for a German sweet chocolate cake."

"I'll fix you one tonight."

"Hmph. Hope you cook better than you can catch a horse."

She laughed. "Cleve, you're priceless. You and Matt must have given Wade a run for his money."

His smile was warm with memories. "Wade was one of a kind. Left me that truck of his." He fixed her with a stare. "Left you the meadow, I hear."

She hadn't told Griff the exact location of the property or why she owned Taggart land. "Matt told you."

"He did."

"You needn't worry. I'll be gone soon and, when I go, the ranch will be his alone." She said the words calmly, as if something inside her wasn't protesting at the thought of leaving the ranch, leaving Matt.

Cleve picked up a box of pancake mix. "This on the list?"

Glad to have the matter dropped, she scanned the list. "Yes," she answered, then named several other items.

Without pausing, Cleve plucked them from the shelves. For the first time, she really looked at the various items and realized how difficult it must be for someone to memorize labels, especially when some products by the same manufacturer were packaged in so similar a manner.

She was just beginning to fully understand something Matt already knew. A man's character was measured by many things. Strength and courage and intelligence were shown in many different ways.

Matt cared about the person inside, not what he was, not who he was. A hardcase wouldn't care or know the difference. Wade had been right. But was it possible to find the gentleness inside Matt and bring it to the surface?

"You gonna daydream or what?"

Cleve's terse voice snapped her back to the present. "Sorry."

"You thinking about that feller of yours?"

Shannon blinked. "What!"

"Wade said you had a feller you might marry."

Shannon's mind flashed not to James but to Matt. Strong, compelling, and so handsome he made her knees weak. She looked away from Cleve's sharp gaze. "We're just dating."

He nodded tersely. "Glad to hear it. Wade wanted better for you."

So did her grandfather, but she felt it disloyal not to speak up in James's defense. "James is a very successful lawyer and well respected by everyone."

Cleve's gaze sharpened. "Is that the only way you take the measure of a man?"

"No," she answered without thought.

He nodded. "You'll do. You're not like the other one."

"What other one?" she questioned, afraid she already knew.

"If you don't know, ain't my place to say." Wheeling his basket around her, he started down the aisle.

Abandoning her cart, she caught him in two steps. "You can't make a statement like that and leave me hanging."

Cleve's lips clamped tighter than a two-year-old's mouth with a spoonful of spinach in front of him.

"Everyone alludes to a woman in Matt's past. What did she do to him?" she asked, unaware that her voice trembled.

"You got your feller back East," Cleve finally said. "Why so interested in the boss's life?"

"I-I'm just concerned."

Bushy eyebrows rose. "You're sure that's all?"

"Yes." Matt wasn't for her.

"Probably just as well. A city lady like you wouldn't be much good to a hard-working rancher like the boss," Cleve said. "He needs a sturdier woman."

"Is that how you measure a woman, by her sturdiness?" she asked sarcastically.

His crackling laughter boomed. "You give as good as you get, girlie. Does that mean you're interested in the job?"

She jerked back. Her mouth worked several seconds before any words came out, and when they did they were filled with indignation. "Matt means nothing to me."

"You don't have to hurt my ears. A simple no would have gotten the job done."

"You shouldn't ask such personal questions."

"I figure if you don't ask, you won't learn." Cleve started down the aisle again. "Anyway, it would take a mighty special woman to get the boss to the altar, mighty special indeed."

CHAPTER 12

"Melanie, I think I'm in trouble," Shannon said softly into the receiver.

Her best friend laughed. "That's usually my line."

Shannon leaned against the wooden chair in the kitchen and almost smiled. She could picture this woman who had been her best friend since college with one foot draped over the side of her hammock in her living room, her tortoiseshell glasses perched on her nose, a mischievous smile on her coffee-colored face.

But that smile could turn intimidating in seconds if she was thwarted. The staff and patients in the rehabilitation center where she headed the physical therapy department quickly learned to respect both.

"I'm serious. There's a man—"

A loud screech came through the line. "Way to go, girl. I always knew James was too stiff for you. Now, tell me every delicious and dirty detail, and don't leave anything juicy out."

Shannon cast a glance at the oven where Cleve's German sweet chocolate cake was baking, as if to make sure the loud noise hadn't made the cake fall. He was the cause of all these doubts resurfacing. Matt wasn't for her. She couldn't heal his heart. But Lord, how did she stop herself from wanting to do that very thing?

"Shannon?" Melanie prompted.

"Well, there's nothing much to tell ex—"

"What! After I've waited all these years for some guy to knock your socks off, you're telling me you're still at the looking stages?"

"If you'd stop cutting me off, I'd tell you."

"So talk."

Impatient. Melanie had always been impatient. She rushed headlong into everything. She wasn't afraid to take chances. Shannon marveled at her best friend as much as she envied her free-wheeling spirit. Nothing intimidated Melanie, especially not a man.

Yet, she never thought less of Shannon because she weighed everything carefully before making a decision. Melanie had always said it was because of Shannon's single-minded determination once she made up her mind. Melanie's friendship and loyalty were unwavering. "Thanks for sending me the money."

"You're welcome. Now, tell me everything before I start thinking your parents might be right about you being in trouble. Has this brother got it going on or what?"

Shannon had no difficulty answering that question. "He's the most compelling and the most irritating man I've ever met."

"Oh, girl. I wish I could see the man who finally melted your butter."

"You've seen him."

"When?"

Shannon sighed. "Four years ago. He's Matt Taggart, the Walking Hunk, the nephew of Wade Taggart."

"You come home right now or, better yet, I'll fly down and we can drive back together," Melanie told her, all playfulness gone. "That man disrupted the entire department every time he came to therapy with his uncle. Work virtually came to a standstill. There were so many tongues hanging on the floor you had to be careful where you stepped."

"I heard it was the same way on the unit," Shannon admitted.

"Exactly. No woman was immune to him, and although he took several of the staff women out, once his uncle was discharged they never heard from Matt Taggart again. You worked the night shift so you didn't get to see all the pitiful weeping and moaning when he moved on to the next woman or if he chose one woman over another." Melanie snorted delicately.

"I thought," she continued, "they were all being foolish until his uncle introduced us. If his good looks didn't get you, that molasses voice or those devilish eyes would. Let's not even get into his body. Oh, Lord! That's one man who looks as good going as he does coming."

"I know."

"You're too vulnerable to tangle with a heartbreaker like that. Lord only knows if any woman could," Melanie said flatly. "He's the kind of man who'll give you heaven for a few days, then drop you straight into hell for a lifetime. Come home."

"I can't. I can't explain it, I just can't leave." Shannon might be unsure of her feelings, unsure of her control, but one thing she was sure of was that if she ran this time it would be the worst mistake of her life.

"No, you didn't, Shannon Elaine Johnson," Melanie riled. "Tell me you didn't go and fall in love with this guy."

She had never lied to Melanie and she wasn't about to start. "I don't know."

"Then don't. Get your soft-hearted behind out while you still can," her friend advised. "Marry Mr. Conservative and be happy."

"Melanie, you know how I feel about marriage. It's forever. I couldn't do that to James."

"So you're gonna stay and let Taggart leave his boot marks on your back as well as on your heart," her friend said tightly.

"Matt hardly pays me any attention unless I do something wrong," she confessed.

"What's wrong with that man? Men fall all over themselves trying to get your attention. We had to have an unlisted phone number in college because of all the guys trying to hit on you."

"The way I remember it, half of those calls were for you."

"From men trying to get to you through me. And they're still doing it," Melanie said. "It's a good thing my ego can take it or I might end up in therapy."

"Men don't ignore you, but Matt does ignore me."

"He must have fallen off his horse one time too many. You're the best thing that could happen to a hard man like Taggart."

Shannon smiled at her friend's quick defense. "He doesn't think so."

"His loss. Come home."

"I can't. I just needed to talk to someone." It went unsaid that it had always been her grandfather whose counsel she sought.

Silence. "How's it going?"

"Better," she answered, and for the first time since she lost her grandfather, she actually meant the words. "I'm going to be all right. I know that now. I'll miss him forever, but I can make it."

"I never doubted."

The oven timer dinged. "I better get off the phone. Thanks for listening."

"Anytime. Just guard that heart of yours."

"Good-bye, Melanie." Slowly she hung up the phone and realized her best friend's warning had come too late.

"Is Brazos's fetlock worse?" Matt asked as soon as he entered the barn that evening and saw Cleve standing by the horse's stall.

"Nope," the cowhand answered. "Just walkin' off two big slices of German sweet chocolate cake."

Matt dismounted with a smile. Cleve's sweet tooth was well known. "How did you talk Octavia into baking on her off day?"

"I don't recall sayin' Mrs. Ralston baked the cake."

Strong fingers paused in the middle of tying the reins. "Who else could . . . Shannon?"

The dusty brim of a battered hat dipped. "Yes, siree. She may not know squat about ranchin', but she shore can bake. Best tastin' cake that ever passed these lips. The man who puts a ring on her finger is gonna be mighty lucky."

"Or mighty miserable," Matt said, throwing back the stirrup to unbuckle the cinch.

"I bet that successful lawyer feller in St. Louis doesn't think so."

Matt stilled, then turned, his eyes intent. "How do you know so much about him?" he asked, unaware of the sharpness of his voice.

"I asked while we were grocery shoppin'," Cleve answered with satisfaction.

"You two all right now?"

"I reckon. Figured anyone who'd shed a tear for me deserved a second chance. Besides, that fancy car of hers couldn't have brought back all the groceries Mrs. Ralston usually buys." A crafty smile brightened his lined face. "Got me a cake out of it, too."

Matt grunted and turned back to his horse. Looks like he was the only man in Jackson Falls who wasn't tripping over himself trying to sing Shannon's praises. "She seems to have a knack for making some men happy."

"That feller in St. Louis must have a lot of competition," Cleve said thoughtfully. "When it came time to check out, we had more sackers than a dog has fleas."

"That must have made *her* happy." The saddle landed with a solid thunk on the wooden rail.

Cleve shook his head. "Miss Shannon didn't seem to notice. She was laughing at some silly front-page story in one of them tabloids. She sure has a pretty laugh."

Matt had had enough. He faced the elderly cowhand. "You sound as if she's your best friend."

"I'm just tellin' it like it tis. She's a mighty interesting lady even if she had the misfortune not to be born a Texan."

"Somehow I think she would take exception to hearing that."

"Reckon you're right." Cleve grasped the horse's reins. "I'll take care of Sundance for you. You better get inside and see if any of that cake is left. Jay and the boys were just ridin' in when she came out to tell me to come and get mine."

"I'll pass."

Cleve lifted a heavy eyebrow. "Since when didn't you like anything chocolate?"

"I don't want any cake. I'm not going to eat some just to please Shannon. I'm sure the rest of you have praised her cooking skills enough. She doesn't need mine."

"Well, I'm sure Miss Shannon won't force any down your throat." With that remark, the cowhand turned and led the horse away.

Matt started for the house at a ground-eating pace. He had over-reacted. Cleve knew it and he knew it. He just hoped the elderly cowhand didn't know the reason.

Shannon.

He wasn't able to get her out of his mind. No matter how hard he tried, he couldn't dismiss her as easily as he had other women. It was more than the softness of her skin, the tenderness of her touch, more than her beautiful face, her shapely body.

He kept remembering her stubbornness in repairing the fence, her tears for a man she barely knew, her admonishment for him to eat his lunch. She was like no other woman he had ever met. She fascinated and confused the hell out of him. He may not have succumbed to Shannon, but he was sure teetering on the brink.

Somehow he had to keep from going over. His life wasn't what he wanted, that was for sure, but he wasn't about to go through the hell his ex-wife put him through trying to get it. Having his niece and nephew, Chandler and Kane Jr., was almost as good as having his own children. Against a gut full of pain, almost wasn't so bad.

Snatching open the door, he entered the kitchen and came to a dead halt. Shannon stood by the stove, a shy smile on her toffee-colored face, a plate of steaming, delicious-smelling food in her hand. Without asking, he knew it was for him. She was not going to get to him as she had all the other men.

"Where's Octavia?"

The smile on her beautiful face slipped a notch. "Eating dinner at Mama Sophia's with her church auxiliary group."

Matt's gaze swept the stove noting the skillet and the two pots. "You cooked."

"Octavia wanted to stay. She didn't have time this morning to cook something for you." Shannon tucked her lower lip between startling white teeth. "She said you liked stuffed pork chops."

"Sometimes." They were one of his favorites. "You can go. I can handle things from here."

She turned back to the stove. "That's all right. I have to get mine."

He glanced at the clock. Seven-thirty. "You haven't eaten?"

"No. I got kind of busy. While you wash up, I'll set the table," she told him, her voice oddly breathless.

Placing his hat on the back of his chair, he went to the kitchen sink. Water gushed out of the faucet, and he stuck his hands underneath.

"You know Octavia doesn't like for you to do that."

Matt glanced over his shoulder to see Shannon setting two plates on the table. "So we won't tell her."

She smiled and brought him a towel. "Do you always get your way?"

His gaze roamed over her face. "Am I going to get my way with you?"

Her eyes rounded. Her sharp intake of breath cut across the small space separating them. She took an unsteady step back.

He had meant the ranch. At least that's what he *thought* he had meant. But watching the tip of her tongue glide across the sensual fullness of her glistening red lower lip, the rise and fall of her full breasts beneath her sleeveless beige blouse, he wasn't sure.

It was suddenly very important that he made sure. "Are you going to sign over the meadow?"

Disappointment. Surely that wasn't disappointment in her brown eyes. "I—I told you I would when I leave."

He studied her closely as she went to the refrigerator, returned to the table with a pitcher of tea and filled their glasses with a hand that trembled. Tonight, instead of her usual long pants, she wore wheat-colored shorts that clearly showed her long, shapely legs. Legs that could easily wrap around a man's waist.

"I just thought you might have a special reason to sign now so you can leave here sooner."

"No. No reason," she answered, her gaze as direct as his.

Her answer shouldn't have mattered. It did.

He shouldn't have asked the question. He had.

There shouldn't be a need to sit down before she noticed his jeans had gotten considerably tighter. There definitely was.

"We better eat before it gets cold," he said, his voice rough with suppressed need.

Shannon took her seat and said grace for them. Without glancing across the table at Matt, she picked up her fork. So much for waiting to share dinner with him. He didn't notice her any more than he usually did. Nor did he notice the wildflowers she had picked for the table. He would be glad to see her leave.

Perhaps that would be for the best.

"Aren't you hungry or are you one of those people who eats while they cook?"

Her hand paused on cutting another floret from the broccoli stalk. Gathering her fraying courage, she finally glanced up. "I guess I'm just tired."

"From doing what?" he asked, cutting into the second pork chop on his plate.

She blinked. "I beg your pardon?"

"All you did was go grocery shopping and cook." He forked the pork chop into his mouth and reached for a biscuit. There had been seven on the plate. Only four remained.

Shannon snatched the plate away from his questing fingers. "Let me have another one before you put more on."

"I have no intention of putting any more on." She stood and reached for his plate. "In fact, the kitchen is closed."

"That's not funny."

"It wasn't meant to be," Shannon said, incensed he thought so little of all her time and effort. Learning how to cook had been as much of a requirement as etiquette in her house. A meal to her practical-minded mother was more than nourishment, it was a necessary business asset.

At a well-appointed table set with sparkling crystal, polished silver and fresh flowers, careers were advanced, deals made, lifelong friendships cemented, tempers and hurt feelings soothed. Apparently, her mother had yet to meet a man like Matt Taggart.

"If you hurry you can get to the grocery store before it closes, then come back and peel onions, chop celery, bake cornbread for your stuffing, make biscuits, wash broccoli. Shall I continue?"

Matt noticed the glint in her eyes and knew he had better be careful how he answered her question if he wanted his dinner back. With one wrong word, she'd have his hide and his supper. Cleve was right, the woman could burn.

Cleve.

"This is how Cleve got into trouble at the grocery store, isn't it?"

The glint in her eyes brightened.

Matt looked from Shannon's rigid stance to his plate. He probably could put together a meal, but he wanted his pork chops. "Octavia expected you to feed me."

"She suggested leftovers."

Matt wondered if he could get to her plate before she could, then dismissed the idea. No self-respecting man would fight over food . . . unless he hadn't eaten more than a couple of mouthfuls in the last twenty-four hours.

He scowled. Shannon's fault again. He hadn't been able to eat breakfast because he had been worried about her. Now, she wanted to deprive him of his dinner.

Just like I deprived her of breakfast.

"Is this your way of getting back at me for this morning?"

"No. This is for your chauvinistic attitude toward women doing housework," Shannon told him. "Your mother would probably brain you with a frying pan if she were here."

Matt flushed. There was no *probably* to it. From his earliest memories, everyone in the Taggart family had shared the household duties. He still remembered hiding the mop when one of the guys had dropped by unexpectedly.

"Then you'd have to administer first aid," Matt said, the corner of his mouth curved upward.

"Oh, you're incorrigible." Plopping the platter and the plate back on the table, she turned to leave.

Matt stood. Gentle fingers closed around her arms and brought her to him before she took one step. "Wait."

"You can make me so angry sometimes."

"You seem to have the same effect on me."

"I—I don't want to fight with you."

"Something tells me the alternative would only create more problems." His thumb stroked the smoothness of her forearm and he felt her shiver.

Breathless. She felt breathless and lightheaded. She also felt the blunt hardness of his body against her and, God help her, she wanted to press closer. Heat zipped through her like lightning, oversensitizing her skin.

Matt wasn't ignoring her now and neither was his body. *If* she wanted him, all she had to do was step closer, lift her lips to his and . . . step off a precipice.

He offered no guarantees, no happily-ever-after. He offered nothing but an overpowering passion that would probably sear her very soul. Although she had no sexual experience to speak of, she didn't doubt he would be a magnificent lover, but, God help her, she wanted more, much more.

Fighting herself, fighting need, she glanced away from compelling black eyes that made her ache. "I forgot the salad."

Callused hands released her before she completed the sentence. "Sit down. I'll get it."

Shannon sat. He had a better chance of finding the salad in the well-stocked refrigerator than she did of walking on her shaking legs.

"Which dressing?"

"Th-the vinaigrette. It's the clear bottle with the green top next to the salad." Her voice sounded almost normal.

Matt placed both items on the table, then refilled his plate before taking his seat. "Can I get you anything?"

She was as surprised by the question as she was by the total indifference in his eyes, eyes that had earlier seared her soul. Then, she experienced the loss. Her fault. She hadn't been willing to take a chance.

"No, I'm fine." Since he continued to watch her, she picked up her fork and began to eat. The food had grown cold. It didn't matter. She wasn't tasting it anyway.

The phone rang. She pushed her chair back to answer it. Matt was already up.

"Hello."

He straightened. Black eyes drilled into her. "Who's calling?" he asked, his voice harsh.

Dread tripped down her spine as he continued to stare at her.

He held out the phone. "It's for you."

She didn't like the way Matt was looking at her. "Who is it?"

"Lover boy."

Her brows bunched, then she drew back. "The man from the motel?"

"I forgot, you probably have trouble keeping all of them straight," he said sarcastically. "I'll give you a hint. He says you're engaged."

"James."

"Bingo."

CHAPTER 13

"What?" Shannon cried in disbelief as she ran to the phone and snatched the receiver from Matt.

Heavy black brows arched. "I don't think I've ever seen you move so fast."

She sent Matt a quelling glare, then spoke into the phone, "James?"

"Oh, Shannon, it's so good hearing your voice" came James Harper's cultured voice. Then it took on a cutting edge he usually reserved for the courtroom. "Who answered the phone? I had to tell the man who I was before he'd put you on."

"Never mind that. Why did you tell him we're engaged?" she asked, turning her back on Matt. He could have the decency to leave.

"Now, sweetheart," James said and laughed cajolingly. "Although it's not official, everyone knows it's only a matter of time."

He was patting her on the head again and making her decisions. Only this time she didn't like it. She had told James and her family she wanted this time alone with no interference from either of them. Both had a tendency to try and pressure her into doing what they thought best for her. Because she didn't like arguments, more times than she liked to remember, she had given in to them. No more. "Then everyone knows more than I do."

Worry finally sounded in his voice. "I'm sorry if my call upset you, but you know how much I love you. You've changed since your grandfather died, become preoccupied. You've spent more time at work than with me and now you're gone again," he said, accusation creeping into his tone.

"If there is a problem, I'm the one you should be with. I want to marry you."

"James, please, I've told you before, I can't think about marriage now."

"Darling, I'm sorry. I didn't mean to distress you any further. I know how devastated you've been and I didn't want you to do anything rash."

"Taking a vacation is hardly rash," she said. "I told you when I left that I needed some time by myself."

"I know, but it isn't like you to be so secretive," James explained. "I want you to come home."

Shannon stiffened at his commanding tone. "I'm staying until the end of my vacation."

"Then I'm coming to you," he stated flatly.

"Melanie told you where I was?" Shannon asked, astonishment in her voice.

"Not yet," James said. "But she's just as worried about you as I am. As is your entire family."

"Put her on the phone."

"We haven't finished talking."

"Please, James. Now is not the time to try and win an argument."

A defeated sigh echoed through the line. "All right, but I want to speak with you before you hang up."

"Shan—" Melanie began.

"I trusted you," Shannon said, cutting off her best friend.

"He was worried," Melanie defended. "I had him turn his back while I dialed. He doesn't know any more than he did five minutes ago."

"We both know that's not true." He knew there was a man with her.

"I told him a married couple ran the lodge where you were staying and the place had only one phone," Melanie placated. "I just thought you needed to hear from him."

And remember he was safer than Matt Taggart.

"Melanie, I know you meant well, but you've only made matters worse for everyone."

"Sorry."

"I am, too."

"You mad?"

"Because you worried about me? No. Annoyed that you, like everyone else thinks I can't handle my own life? A little. But you're my best friend and I love you."

"I won't interfere again."

"Thank you. Now please put James back on." Shannon cast a glance at Matt who had finally moved a few feet away. Arms folded, legs crossed at the ankle, he leaned against the counter watching her like a hawk watching a mousehole.

"Shannon darling, if I have upset you, please forgive me," James coaxed. "We'll talk when you're up to it."

So nice, so forgiving . . . so very wrong for her.

Shannon closed her eyes at the thought of what she had to do. She should have been stronger and never let things get this far. For months she had known what she felt for James wasn't enough. Instead of putting an end to it, she had succumbed to the coercion from both him and her family. She'd had the foolish idea her affection for him would increase with time.

It had taken midnight-black eyes and a voice like subdued thunder to let her know she had deluded both of them.

"It's all right, James," she told him softly. Her forehead rested against the wall by the phone. She couldn't end things between them over the phone. But was it kinder to let him hope or set him free?

Melanie, why couldn't you have had more faith in me?

"Shannon, are you still there?"

"Yes, James, I was just thinking."

"Take your time. I'll be here when you get home," he told her as if sensing her doubts.

But you'll never be the man for me, she wanted to say and knew she couldn't. How do you explain to a man that when he held you, you felt no more than a faint warmth, not the white-hot heat of a raging inferno? How do you explain to him that it had taken another man to make you realize the difference.

"Yes, James, we'll talk when I get back."

"I'll be waiting for your call." Relief sounded clearly through the line.

"Just promise me there'll be no more talk about an engagement. Please."

"Whatever you want, Shannon," he assured her.

She heard the swinging door close and glanced around. Matt was gone. "Take care of yourself, James. Please put Melanie back on."

Her friend came back on the line. "Next time I'm minding my own business."

"Take care of James. Good-bye." Gently, Shannon replaced the receiver. As if on cue, Matt reentered the kitchen. If he said one nasty remark, she wasn't going to be responsible.

"Sit down and eat. Afterward I'll take you to your meadow. You look like you could use your sleep aid." When she didn't move, he crossed the room, took her by the elbow and gently urged her to sit. "I'll even do the dishes."

They drove to the meadow in silence.

Every once in a while Matt glanced at his passenger. If she was any stiffer, the next rut they'd hit, she'd break. She had looked so lost in the kitchen that for some inexplicable reason, he had wanted to take her in his arms and offer solace.

He had no idea where that crazy idea had come from, so he decided to do the only other thing he could think of . . . which was almost as crazy as the first. Despite what she and his uncle thought, the meadow didn't have any special powers.

He couldn't see her face clearly in the dark cab, but he didn't think she was crying. The woman shed more water than a leaky faucet! But after she hung up the phone she looked more melancholy than teary. He pulled out a clean handkerchief and handed it to her just in case he was wrong.

"Thank you."

Polite. Just the way her conversation had been with Harper. Matt had heard enough of the one-ended conversation to figure out she wasn't going to marry the guy. Matt didn't know why the thought pleased him so much or why it had angered him just as much when he thought she was.

He pulled to a stop in front of the cabin, pressed a button to roll down the automatic windows, then turned off the lights and cut the engine.

The scent of wildflowers drifted inside the truck. Through the cypress trees moonlight glinted on the surface of the stream two hundred feet away.

Now that he was here, he felt like an idiot. Women sure had a way of messing with a man's mind, especially this particular woman sitting next to him. He couldn't even enjoy his stuffed pork chops for trying to make sure she ate her dinner.

He stilled. Was that a sniff or her shifting on the leather seat? Out of nowhere came the urge again to pull her close.

"How do you do it?"

He frowned and tried to see her face more clearly. "Do what?"

"End a relationship and remain friends?" she asked so quietly he had to lean closer to hear her.

"I'm not sure that you can," Matt answered honestly. "That's why I never mix the two. But the longer you stay in one the more difficult it is to break off."

"I see," she said, not knowing if the sadness in her voice was because of her conversation with James or knowing Matt's involvements with women were brief and sexually motivated. She was very afraid it was the latter. She wasn't as worried about breaking off with James as she was at the frightening possibility of never having a relationship with Matt or, worse, having one and watching him walk away.

"You cool enough with the air-conditioning off?"

"Yes." She clamped her hands in her lap, because she wanted so very much to wrap them around Matt and ask him to hold her. Friendship was better than nothing. Her head lowered.

The impulse was stronger this time to offer her the comfort and strength of his arms. He needed some air.

"You want to get out?"

"I haven't gotten used to the total darkness in the country," she admitted softly. "It makes me feel small and rather insignificant. Except for the few stars there's no other light in the sky except the moon."

Propping his arm on the back of the seat to keep himself out of trouble, Matt stretched out his legs. "I like the isolation, the quiet."

"That's because you have never probably known a moment of fear in your life," Shannon said.

"Anyone who says he's never been afraid of something is a liar."

"You don't impress me as a man afraid of anything."

"A man without fear is a fool waiting to get his comeuppance," Matt said with feeling. "There's not a man or woman who has ridden the rodeo circuit or ranched who hasn't been a tiny bit afraid of the animal they drew, afraid they won't make the slack, or worried about the weather, or fluctuating beef prices. I went from one profession to another, where each new day brought new problems."

"And you wouldn't change it for anything."

The certainty in her voice somehow pleased him. "No. There's not another place I'd rather be."

Shannon leaned her head against the seat. "It must be nice knowing where you belong, where you're going."

Something about the wistfulness in her voice pricked at him. His fingers touched something soft and silky. Her hair. Instead of moving away as he planned, he wrapped a curl around his finger. "You don't?"

"I thought I did, but now I'm not so sure." She glanced out the window. "I'm ready to go back if you are."

She'd shut him out. She'd done it politely, but she had done it just the same. Just as she had the jerk who wanted to marry her. Somehow that angered him. He didn't want her to treat him like every other man in her life.

He knew one way to get her attention. Warm fingers settled more firmly in her hair, then turned her head toward his descending one. He felt the warmth of her breath, inhaled the exotic scent that seemed so much a part of her, savored the gentle touch of her lips against his.

He stopped thinking.

His arms gathered her closer, his mouth slanted across hers. Her lips opened without hesitation. He needed no further invitation. His tongue swept inside the dark interior. Forbidden and delicious and hot.

At the first taste of him Shannon forgot everything but the need to get closer. He kissed her relentlessly, taking from her, giving to her until her mind was filled only with incredible sensations that began and ended with Matt. She felt as if she were being enveloped in a thick, sensual haze of passion.

Under his nimble fingers, her blouse eagerly parted. The touch of his hand on her stomach wrenched a low moan of pleasure from her. Her breasts tingled and tightened in anticipation as his searching hand slowly moved upward. Then, he was there, cupping her.

She arched against his hand, her entire body quivered in mindless pleasure. He caught her lower lip between his and suckled. She felt restless, needy, hungry. She needed to touch him the way he was touching her.

Hands that trembled somehow unbuttoned his shirt, then touched almost reverently the hard, hot muscled flesh beneath. His mouth found her again. She whimpered and strained against him.

She was burning him alive and he was enjoying every consuming flame.

His thumb raked across the tight bud of her nipple, and he caught her low groan of pleasure. He never knew a woman to be so responsive or her skin to be so soft. He didn't seem to be able to get enough of touching her, of tasting her.

He wanted to taste her everywhere and then start again. The agony was exquisite torture. He had never wanted anything as badly as he wanted to bury himself in Shannon's sleek body.

The last thought rocketed through his brain. With wild desperation he tore his lips from hers and fought for control. Somehow he had forgotten she wasn't for him.

Her breathing as labored as his, her eyes dazed, she stared up at him. Her hands remained on his skin, her soft curves pressed to him. With more power than grace he set her across the seat from him. And prayed she stayed there.

She did, but it wasn't far enough. His senses were too attuned to her. He still smelled her, still remembered the satiny texture of her skin, still tasted the honeyed sweetness of her lips, still wanted her so much he ached.

Every button she slowly did in the lengthening silence he wanted to undo. All he had to do was . . .

He gripped the steering wheel instead of reaching for Shannon. His head spun, his body was in torment.

Shannon kissed like she did everything else, with power and passion. She put her entire body into it. More than his next ragged breath, he wanted to pull her down on the seat and make love to her until nothing else mattered.

He started the engine, backed up and took off to the ranch. He left the windows down. Maybe the wind whipping across his face would cool him off. As delectable as Shannon's body was, she wasn't worth his ranch.

The truck tires screeched as he came to a halt in front of the ranch house. He stared straight ahead. The passenger door opened, material glided over the leather seat. When he didn't hear the door close, he glanced around. And wished he hadn't.

The porch light behind Shannon threw her into sharp relief. He saw her tousled hair, her kiss-swollen lips, the mismatched button on her blouse. She looked rumpled and needy.

"Somehow I don't think going to the meadow will help either of us sleep tonight." The door closed.

Matt stomped the accelerator and took off for the garage. That was the last time he'd try to be nice. From now on, Shannon was on her own. He didn't care if she flooded the entire state with tears.

Matt was avoiding her.

Sighing, Shannon lifted the curtain in the kitchen and looked out. Lightning streaked across the night sky followed by an ominous rumble of thunder. The weatherman had predicted a rainstorm. And Matt was out there somewhere. She shivered and let the curtain fall.

Today he had assigned her to Octavia and Cleve. This morning over the strained atmosphere of the breakfast table she had tried to talk to him about her duties, but he had brushed her aside saying he had more important things to do than listen to her complain.

The unfairness of his remark hurt. He was the one who said she needed to learn about the ranch. Somehow she didn't think he meant tending the vegetable garden or taking over Octavia's job as cook. She wanted to be out working on the ranch. She had enjoyed being outdoors, enjoyed knowing she was helping Matt in some small way.

But the kiss last night had changed things.

Now there was an awareness between them. Almost like an electric charge. All it would take was a tiny spark to set it off.

Matt was going to make sure that didn't happen.

In principle she agreed with his decision. When he touched her, her brain turned to mush. She wished this awareness didn't keep them from being friends.

She wanted to get to know him better. There was a tenderness beneath Matt's tough exterior just as Wade had said, just as she was slowly discovering.

For all his gruffness and arrogance, he had cared that James's call had upset her. In Matt's own way he had been trying to help her.

Then they had kissed and everything had changed.

A loud clap of thunder shook the house. Startled, Shannon lifted the curtain again, praying Matt wasn't still out there moving the herd as Cleve had told her earlier, praying he was safe in the barn.

In her mind came the memory of a horse spooked by lightning, an unseated rider injured and alone as the rain unmercifully plummeted his body. It had been in a movie, but it was still a real possibility.

Shivering, she strained her eyes to see past the slight drizzle of rain that had begun to fall. He was probably all right. She had seen for herself how well Matt rode. Octavia wasn't worried. The housekeeper had retired to her bed an hour ago. Shannon had gone to her room, but she hadn't been able to stay put. So she had come to the kitchen, the first room Matt always entered when he came home.

A flash of lightning illuminated the yard. Shannon gasped. A cloaked figure in a duster-style rain slicker and Stetson strode toward the house. Head bent against the rain, he came toward her.

Matt.

She wanted to run to the door and berate him for scaring her, hold him to make sure he was safe. She could do neither. It was after nine. He'd know she had waited for him. She started from the room.

The back door opened. Light flooded the kitchen. It was too late. Slowly she faced Matt. Hat in hand, his black rain slicker glistening with water, he looked dangerous. A dark angel.

"What are you doing here in the dark?"

"I'm thirsty." It wasn't exactly a lie, her mouth was dry. Deciding to brave it out, she crossed to the refrigerator. She had taken two steps before she remembered she was wearing pajamas. Her steps faltered. The oversize boxy top and above-the-knee leggings in a rose print covered everything, yet knowing she didn't have on any underwear caused her to wish she had been a coward and gone to her room.

Out of the corner of her eye, she glanced at Matt. He hadn't moved. His stillness unnerved her. He was watching her, his black eyes stripping away her clothes, touching her, wanting her, making her body tingle and burn and want his.

"Y-you're making a puddle."

His head jerked up, then down. Water ran from his duster and pooled on the floor around him. His gaze arched upward. His mouth tightened beneath his mustache. Shrugging off his slicker, he headed for the utility room.

Trembling so badly she could hardly walk, Shannon somehow managed to get a towel and clean up the floor. The door to the utility room reopened. Her skin felt hot, prickly, too tight for her body.

"Get your water and leave. I'll take care of the floor."

Gripping the towel, she stood. This was one time she was glad to take orders from Matt. She needed to leave while she was still thinking clearly. Placing the towel on the far end of the counter, she washed her hands, then got a glass of water.

The glass clinked against her teeth. Hoping Matt hadn't heard the sound, she clutched the shaking glass tighter and lowered it from her lips. Preparing to make her escape, she took a steadying breath and faced Matt. "I . . . er, think I'll take this upstairs."

"Night." The word was low, husky, as if forced through clenched teeth.

"Good night," she said, and began inching her way across the room, her eyes unable to keep from roaming over his powerful body one last time to reassure herself he was all right.

He needed a haircut. There were dark smudges beneath his eyes. His shoulders, encased in a faded green shirt, were as wide as she remembered. The wide silver belt buckle emphasized his trim waist. His hands—

"You're hurt," she cried. Crossing the room, she reached for his bandaged hand.

Matt moved it out of reach. "It's nothing."

Shannon glanced from the blood-specked white handkerchief tied around the palm of his left hand to Matt's tight features. *This* she felt fully confident to handle. "Then you won't mind me taking a look."

Setting the glass down, she retrieved the first-aid kit from beneath the sink. After putting away the groceries and cooking, she knew where everything was located in the kitchen. Without giving him a chance to protest further, she caught him by the arm of the injured hand and led him to the sink.

"I can do this myself."

"I didn't say you couldn't." Her back to him, she pulled his arm under hers and began untying the bandage. She breathed a sign of relief as the bandage easily slid off. "How did it happen?"

"Barbed wire" came the succinct reply.

She glanced at him over her shoulder. "Why weren't you wearing your gloves?"

Black eyes drilled into hers. "Are you gonna fix my hand or ask foolish questions?"

She glared right back. "Is your tetanus shot—"

"Yes," he snapped.

"At least you remembered something important." With that parting shot, she opened the first-aid kit with one hand, held Matt's hand with the other, then turned the water faucet on low. "This cleaning solution might sting a little."

Matt remained silent.

Slanting his hand downward beneath the stream of water, she cleaned the two-inch wound at the base of his palm, then gently probed the area. It wasn't very deep; the sides easily met. But it must have hurt, must still be hurting. The thought of him in pain caused her stomach to knot.

She shut off the water. The pads of her fingertips brushed across his upper palm, the callused ridges of his hand, trying to soothe away the pain. Once, twice.

Matt shifted from one foot to the other. The front of his thighs brushed against her hips. Awareness shot through her like lightning. The hand that had been so steady moments earlier trembled.

His uninjured hand came to rest on the sink by her waist, effectively trapping her. Her throat dried. Trying to regain her professionalism, she took a deep breath. And felt his muscled hardness from her shoulder blades to the bend of her knees.

Air wobbled out of her lungs.

Fingers that refused to remain steady and cooperate finally dried his injured hand, applied too much antibiotic ointment, and put on the adhesive bandage about as well as a four-year-old could.

"Th-that should do it." Not wanting to step back against him, she glanced over her shoulder with what she hoped was a professional smile.

Hypnotic black eyes smoldered. "Not quite." His head slowly lowered, giving her enough time to stop him if she wanted.

His lips brushed against hers. Once. Twice.

With a sound between a moan and a groan, she turned fully toward him. Parting her lips, she welcomed him inside. Her arms circled his neck, her hands clasped his head bringing him closer.

His large hands found their way beneath her top, stroking her warm skin. His thumb grazed across her pebble-hard nipple and she shivered with pleasure.

He smelled of wind and rain and his unique male scent. She was surrounded by him, by sensations she had only imagined until last night. His hand cupped her hips, pressing her closer to his hardness, then lifted . . . and hurt his injured hand.

"Ouch!"

Shannon's eyelids blinked upward. Her body stiffened an instant before she pushed away. She hadn't meant for this to happen.

Matt reached for her.

"N-no. Please." She staggered backward, her palm thrust out in supplication.

"You want this as much as I do."

"I don—" She couldn't finish the lie. She wanted him more than she ever thought it possible to want a man. With the realization came fear. If there was one thing she had learned about Matt, it was his distrust of her and his cavalier ways. She wasn't going to be any man's castoff.

"I'm sorry." She turned and ran from the kitchen.

Matt started after her, then stopped at the swinging doors. His growing need was a danger to his self-control. Needs made a man weak. Another lesson his ex-wife had taught him.

But with Shannon he had difficulty remembering. Shannon tempted him as much as her mixed signals puzzled him. One second she was getting away from him as fast as she could, the next she was insisting on taking care of his hand.

He hadn't meant to brush against her; somehow he just had. He had tried not to be affected by the exotic scent of the woman so tenderly taking care of him, to disregard her soft curves brushing against him, to dismiss the warm brown eyes filled with concern.

He hadn't lasted two minutes.

"I thought I heard you," the housekeeper greeted as she entered the kitchen.

"Hello, Octavia," Matt said, glad she hadn't entered a minute earlier. He walked over to the first-aid kit.

"Hurt yourself?"

"Barbed wire."

Picking up his hand, she inspected the bandage. "You never could get one on straight. You want me to put another one on?"

His hand fisted. "No."

"Sit down and I'll get your plate."

After putting away the first-aid kit and the towel Shannon had used to wipe up the water, Matt took a seat. A steaming bowl of beef vegetable stew was waiting.

Instead of leaving, Octavia took the chair across from him. "Why don't you take Shannon to the dance at the community center tomorrow night so she can meet her neighbors?"

"They aren't her neighbors. Besides, she'd probably be bored stiff." He reached for a piece of cornbread.

"As long as she owns the meadow, they're her neighbors," the housekeeper pointed out. "And I don't think she'd be any more bored than she was today stuck here with me and Cleve."

"Octavia, not tonight."

"Shannon is a beautiful, caring woman. What's the harm in taking her out?"

The harm was, if he came within two feet of her, his brain went South. The harm was, he had been thinking about her instead of paying attention when he had injured his hand.

"You know I don't date women this close to home."

"Make an exception. Any other man would jump at the chance."

"Octavia."

She studied his set features for a long time, then heaved her bulk from the chair. "I'm going. I can see you're tired. Just think about it. Good night."

Matt returned to his meal. If he didn't know better, he'd think Octavia was matchmaking. She should realize by now, he never planned to remarry. There could never be anything between him and his unwanted partner except mind-blowing lust.

A lust that he had to deny or risk losing more than the meadow.

CHAPTER 14

The last thing Matt expected to see as he came over the ridge was Shannon's car parked in front of the rustic cabin in the meadow. He frowned as he pulled his horse to a halt.

He hadn't seen Shannon at breakfast, but since it was Saturday he thought she was either sleeping late or avoiding him. He had secretly hoped it was the latter.

The morning after their first kiss she was in the kitchen acting as if nothing had happened. When she hadn't shown up this morning, he had been strangely pleased. He thought he had finally gotten to her. Now he wasn't sure.

But what was so important to Shannon that would bring her out so early? The only reason he was out was to see how the livestock and the crops had fared following the storm. It hadn't rained hard at the house, but years of experience as a rancher told him that didn't mean it hadn't caused some damage elsewhere on his ranch.

Suddenly the answer to Shannon's presence hit him. Despite everything, she still planned to take the meadow. White-hot anger swept through him. He urged the horse down the incline.

The cabin door stood open. He didn't knock, just walked inside. Immediately he smelled the strong scent of cleaning agents and saw that the cabin had reaped the benefits of them. Shannon stood by the open window.

Wide-eyed, she stared at him, paper towels in one hand, a bottle of spray window cleaner in the other. "W-what are you doing here?"

"I might ask you the same thing."

She faced the only window in the cabin and began rubbing the dingy pane. "I think I should stay here."

"So your claim on the meadow will be stronger?" he clipped out.

Her hand paused, then resumed rubbing the glass. "So last night won't happen again."

Her answer drowned his anger and left him speechless. It had been his experience that women didn't like to admit their vulnerability to a man, yet Shannon had just admitted hers. She was up to something again. "It was just a kiss."

"I—I know, but it has happened twice. There mustn't be a third time."

A scowl swept across his face. She knew damn well it was more than just a kiss. It had left them hot, breathless, hungry. He knew he couldn't trust her. "Don't worry, it won't."

She sprayed the pane again and rubbed. Sweat trickled down his back. Dressed in a sleeveless knit shirt and shorts, Shannon probably was only a little cooler.

"There's no electricity for even a fan." he pointed out.

"I'm sure it will be cooler at night."

"I thought you didn't like the darkness."

"I'll manage."

She was being calm and polite again and Matt wanted to shake her. Then, he noticed something else: she had not stopped spraying and scrubbing that same plate of glass.

He rocked back on his heels and crossed his arms. "Are you running from me or yourself?"

Her shoulders tensed, then she faced him with the spray bottle clutched to her chest. "All right, Matt. We'll have it your way."

She had the lost look again. He pressed his arms tighter to his chest. He was not falling for that again. "I'm waiting."

"You asked questions about my past that I wasn't up to talking about before. Now I'm going to tell you because I hope you'll understand and know why I can't have any more complications in my life."

Her eyes closed briefly, then opened. When she spoke her words thickened. "The—the reason Wade left me the meadow was as I told you. He believed it would heal me."

Brown eyes glittered with unshed tears. "I desperately needed to be healed."

Matt's arms came to his side. His chest hurt. He barely pushed the words past his lips. "You're sick."

"In a way. My grandfather, the man who believed in me when I didn't believe in myself, the man who was never too busy to listen to my dreams, the man who was always there for me, was dying." A tear slipped down her cheek. "There was nothing I could do to help him. After all the times he had helped me, I couldn't help him."

Matt crossed the room and closed his arms around her. He was sure he was hearing the entire truth this time. Somehow he wished he wasn't. "Don't."

"All I could do was hold his hand and tell him it was all right to let go." Tears soaked into his shirt. "He was worried about me more than he was about dying. I couldn't leave him to come to Wade's funeral. I was afraid he wouldn't last until I got back. I wanted every precious second."

His hand swept up and down Shannon's rigid back. "Don't, Shannon. Everything is going to be fine."

She pushed frantically out of his arms. "No, it isn't. That's the problem. I was a damn good ICCU nurse, but the thought of going back to the unit or anywhere with direct patient care is too much of a reminder of losing my grandfather. I know in my head that I did all I could, but in my heart . . . my heart just aches." She drew a deep, steadying breath. "Yet, if I don't return to nursing, I'll let my grandfather down, let myself down, let Wade down."

"Only if you give up."

"What is that supposed to mean?"

"If you don't like how your life is going, change it," Matt told her. "No one is going to do it for you. Feeling sorry for yourself is a waste of time. Believe me, I know."

"Who was she, Matt?"

His face became shuttered. In trying to help Shannon he had revealed too much. "I'm sorry about your grandfather. You obviously loved him very much, so maybe you'll understand where I'm coming from." His gaze piercing, he kicked his Stetson back with his thumb. "I love the land, the ranch, the same way. It's a part of me. It's in my blood. Just like you fought to save your grandfather, I'll fight to save what's mine."

"There's no need for us to be enemies. I told you I plan to sign over the meadow when I leave. You'll just have to trust me."

"Women can't be trusted."

"Wade didn't believe that."

"Yeah, and look where that got me." Spinning on his heels, he left the cabin and mounted his horse.

Shannon walked to the door and watched him ride off. In a way, Matt was right about one thing. Feeling sorry for herself wasn't going to change her life. She had to do that for herself. That meant taking charge. Deciding to end her relationship with James had been a start. She just didn't know what to do next.

One thing she knew, she wasn't ready to admit defeat and leave. She had accepted Matt's challenge and she was staying to see it through no matter how much of a dangerous temptation he was.

Sighing, she returned to the window. Matt wasn't for her. He excited her, left her breathless with wanting, but she would only be another notch on his bedpost. He might want her body, but he wanted the meadow more. She was certain if she signed it over to him, he'd put her off the ranch before the day was out.

Spraying the window cleaner on another pane, she scrubbed the glass. Her life was in St. Louis. She just wished her heart agreed with her.

Several hours later, Matt sat at the Horseshoe Bar nourishing his anger with a beer. How could Wade have saddled him with a stubborn, irritating woman like Shannon Johnson?

"Hello, handsome. You finally ready to see what you've been missing out on?" a sultry voice cooed.

Matt slowly turned to see Irene Nobles, a Saturday-night regular, in gold spandex and lace. Bosomy and nicely curved, Irene had been known to jump-start more than one man's heart, but not his, and not for want of trying on Irene's part.

"Sorry."

Irene pouted passion-red lips, then ran two-inch gold-lacquered and glittering nails up his muscled thigh. "Give me three minutes."

His hand caught hers before it reached its objective. "I'm not in the mood."

She leaned over, her breast rubbing against his arm, her heavy perfume cloying. "Two minutes."

"I don't think so." He moved her hand away.

"Your loss," she said, and glided across the room to another male customer. This time the man was all smiles. Irene settled in the man's lap instead of the chair.

Matt knew she had probably forgotten about him before she took two steps across the room. She didn't care who paid for the things she wanted, just as long as she got them. Just like his ex-wife.

Although he wanted to think the same of Shannon, it wouldn't fit any longer. Which made matters worse for him. It wasn't money she was looking for, but peace of mind. While she sought hers, she tampered with his.

Finishing off his beer, he left the honky-tonk and headed outside. It was completely dark and the parking lot was beginning to fill up. Getting into his truck, he pulled out of the graveled parking lot onto the main highway and headed back to the ranch.

Shannon and Octavia should be gone by now. He could go home to some quiet.

His housekeeper had been like a broken record once he came back to the house. "Take Shannon to the dance." "Take Shannon to the dance." To escape he had to leave his own house. He'd put in a perfunctory appearance at Vivian Gordon's party, then headed for the door. She might have given up on him, but the other single women had not.

He glanced at the clock in the dashboard. Nine fourteen. The monthly community social should be in as much of a high gear as it was going to get.

Matt knew that the pot-luck gathering with a fifteen-year-old record player wasn't what Shannon was used to. Perhaps her going to the social would be to his advantage. She'd see another reason why living in a ranching community wasn't for her.

Parking the truck in the garage, he entered the house. As usual, Octavia had left the lights on downstairs. She said seeing the lights gave her the sense of being welcomed home. He hoped that wasn't for at least another hour and a half. The ranch accounts needed to be updated, and he had a feeling Octavia wasn't through with him. Once she learned Shannon planned to live in the cabin at night, he was going to be in for the chastising of his life.

Opening the door to his study, he was halfway across the room when he realized he wasn't alone. He spun around.

A shy smile on her face, Shannon uncurled her sock-covered feet from beneath her. "I didn't mean to startle you."

"What are you doing here?"

The smile slipped as she held out a thick black leather-bound book. "Reading."

"Why aren't you at the dance?"

Slim shoulders shrugged beneath an off-the-shoulder oversize top. The knit material dropped another inch, baring smooth brown skin. "I didn't feel up to meeting a lot of new people. Octavia said she understood."

Matt gritted his teeth. Irene had practically crawled into his lap and it hadn't bothered him at all. Now he sees a couple of inches of Shannon's bare shoulder and his jeans get tight. He was going to get Octavia for this. "I'll bet."

"I hope you don't mind me borrowing some of your books," Shannon said hesitantly. "You have quite a collection."

"Most of the books belonged to Wade." Continuing across the room, he took a seat behind his desk, opened a drawer and took out a large red-and-gold book. Pen in hand, he began writing. No woman was going to make him lose control.

If Melanie could see Matt now she'd know she didn't have anything to worry about, Shannon thought. She barely kept from sighing aloud.

Deciding if he could act as if she didn't exist, she could do the same thing, she sat back down with her book. However, she couldn't concentrate with him in the room. Standing, she began to roam around the oak-paneled room filled with plaques, trophies, and pictures.

"All these trophies and things belong to you?"

"Yeah."

"Wade said you were a champion calf roper a few years back."

"I was."

"I've never been to a rodeo."

That remark earned her a long, level look.

"It's a shame I won't get to see one while I'm in Texas."

"I can tell you where several are being held."

Shannon gritted a smile. "I'm sure you could."

Matt grunted and went back to his books.

Her fingers trailed over a pair of binoculars, a collection of silver belt buckles, a lariat. She moved to a picture on the wall. Matt sat on a magnificent black stallion holding two toddlers, a boy and a girl. All three were grinning from ear to ear. "What beautiful children."

He glanced up, saw the photograph and smiled. "Kane Jr. and Chandler. My nephew and niece."

Her heart knocked against her chest at the beautiful smile on Matt's face. "You sound as proud as their parents must be."

"I don't think that's possible," he said, a wistful note in his voice.

She moved to the next picture on the wall. Matt stood beside a man as tall and broad-shouldered as he. Both stared directly into the camera as if they barely tolerated the imposition. Both were strikingly handsome. "Who is he?"

"Daniel Falcon."

"Is he a rodeo performer?"

"Hardly. He owns several firms across the country. You probably heard of Falcon Industries. His logo is a falcon, legs outstretched, talons poised to capture its prey."

"Not a very nice picture."

"That's exactly what Daniel intended. If he comes after you, he's coming for blood."

"I'm glad I won't be meeting him."

"Then you better leave before next Monday."

"What?" She whirled to face Matt and noted the strangely pleased expression on his face. Probably the happy thought of her leaving.

Matt reared back in his chair. "Daniel and a film crew he's hired are coming to the ranch to get footage of the African-American cowboy of today. Too much of our heritage has been lost and Daniel intends to set some records straight."

"For instance?"

"Black men and women contributed to the settling of the West as much as anybody. Nearly one-third of all the cowboys in the West were black. The word cowboys comes from ranchers telling the black man to 'go into the brush and get the cow, boy.' Many black cowboys were hired to do the hardest work, busting broncs. The typical trail crew of eight usually included a couple of black cowboys. Many came West after emancipation, hoping they would be judged by their skills and not by their skin color."

"It must have been extremely difficult for them."

"It was, and most people don't even know the true history of the black men and women in the West. Their trials and tribulations might be in the history books, but not their triumphs."

Shannon glanced back at the picture. "It seems I was wrong about Mr. Falcon. I'm looking forward to meeting him after all."

"When you do, don't forget his logo."

"Is that a warning?"

Matt went back to his book. "Take it any way you want."

"I will." Going to the built-in bookcase, she replaced the book in her hand. "Good night."

"Shannon."

"Yes?" She glanced over her shoulder.

"When do you think the cabin will be ready?"

She looked stricken. "Soon." The door closed softly behind her.

Matt's hands clenched atop his desk. His desire for Shannon was testing his control with every breath he took. Finding her on the couch reminded him too much of the first time he saw her in the meadow, looking both beautiful and innocent.

All the ranch hands certainly liked her. The men watched their language around her and were as polite as choir boys. The bunkhouse no longer looked like a tornado just blew through, and all of the hands had taken to cleaning up and wearing cologne.

She certainly had made an impression on everyone, including him. He didn't understand why. He steered clear of women he couldn't walk away from. Becoming involved with one under his roof was crazy. He had his share of lady friends and past lovers, but to date no woman had ever managed to be both. He and Shannon weren't friends, but neither could they be lovers.

Picking up his pen, he went back to the account books. Maybe if he kept telling himself that enough, he might actually begin to believe it.

"You look stunning in that navy suit. And how about that white blouse. I love the draped collar!" Octavia said.

Shannon's brown eyes sparkled. "Thank you, and you look good, too. I love that hat."

The housekeeper beamed with pleasure as she turned her head from side to side for Shannon to get a better look at the pale-pink wide-brimmed straw hat with two large, deep pink roses in full bloom on the crown. "Besides my romance books, hats are my weakness."

"I hope it's all right that I'm not wearing a hat to church."

"Sure it is. Lots of the young folk these days go bareheaded," Octavia said as she picked up her gloves, purse, and Bible. "Matt, better hurry or we'll be late."

The smile slid from Shannon's face. "He's going with us?"

"Of course. My grandson has my car again."

Breakfast had been difficult enough, she didn't want to have to sit by a silent Matt for the next couple of hours. "Octavia, why don't we go in my car?"

"Waste of gas to take both cars. Here's Matt now. We better hurry or we'll be late for prayer service." Without waiting for an answer, Octavia went out the back door of the kitchen.

Sensing Matt's eyes on her, Shannon followed. Outside, Olivia waited by the truck with the passenger door open. "I'll sit by the door," Shannon said.

"I have to ride by the window or I'll get sick," the housekeeper told her.

Shannon's steps faltered. This definitely wasn't a good idea.

"Will you two stop dragging your feet?" Octavia ordered.

All of a sudden Shannon realized Matt was as reluctant as she. He didn't want to be near her, either. She had more pride than to let him know how much that hurt. Head high, she continued to the truck. Her courage faltered as she put one foot on the running board and realized how high her skirt would rise and how difficult it would be for her to get inside gracefully.

She turned back to suggest they take her car and looked straight into Matt's piercing black eyes. The fluttering feeling returned to her stomach. Dressed in an almond-colored suit that fit his powerful body flawlessly, he was magnificent. And totally out of reach. She didn't want them to be enemies anymore.

"Matt?"

His sensual mouth compressed into a thin line beneath his mustache. Strong hands circled her waist and lifted her into the truck. As soon as her bottom touched the seat, he stepped back.

"Move over, child."

Afraid to look at Matt again, Shannon did as requested. Octavia settled in beside her. Matt closed the door and went around and got inside.

Matt's muscled warmth touched her from shoulder to knee. She swallowed and tried to pull her skirt down from midthigh. It wouldn't budge. Placing her small box purse in her lap over her sheer navy hose didn't help hide her exposed flesh.

Matt leaned forward to start the engine and brushed the outside of her breast. Shannon froze from trying to inch down her skirt. Her heart rate doubled. Swallowing again, she stared straight ahead.

Something soft touched her hands. A large lilac handkerchief bordered with lace covered her lap.

"I have four teenage granddaughters," Octavia said and grinned.

Shannon smiled and some of the tension drained away. Now, if Octavia had a two-inch steel divider that Shannon could place between herself and Matt, she might stay sane.

Pastor Billows never had a chance. He paced in front of the pulpit, shouted in his fine bass voice, called sinners to repent, Christians to rejoice. He had never been in finer form. He rose to the occasion, but it wasn't enough.

He was no competition against Shannon.

Matt had never been so annoyed in his life. You'd think the citizens of Jackson Falls had never seen a woman. So much rubbernecking was going on, it was a wonder some of the participants didn't get whiplash.

More children had to be taken outside by a parent than in the past year. The second a baby whimpered, out it went. Each time with a different person.

Not even Leola Price and her glare could quiet the murmurs. Leola liked the audience to pay attention. They usually did. None wanted to make the unofficial matriarch of Jackson Falls upset with them. Today she might as well have been calling hogs. In an effort to gain control, she decided to direct her attention to the person who was causing the problem. Shannon.

Shannon smiled encouragingly at the singer and nodded as if every word went straight to her soul. Soon Leola stopped glaring and sang her heart out. Leola finished on a note that shook the wooden beams.

Nobody seemed to notice but Shannon, the pastor and Octavia, who certainly hadn't helped by forcing Matt and Shannon to sit together. He hoped he didn't sink to such low levels when he got older. He and Shannon could sit hip to hip, flesh to flesh until hell froze over and . . .

"Let us pray."

Matt bowed his head, his eyes going instinctively to the lilac handkerchief. Since hell hadn't frozen over as far as he knew, he asked for God's forgiveness and turned his head slightly and saw three other men looking exactly where he wasn't supposed to be looking.

He plopped his hat in her lap. Shannon glanced at him from beneath her lashes. He flexed his leg.

Leaning over, she whispered to Matt, "Would you like to go outside and stretch your legs?"

There was nothing he'd like better, but he was sure if they left, the entire congregation would follow them outside. "We'll stay."

She looked so disappointed, he smiled. She blinked, then smiled back.

"Brother Taggart, please introduce your guest."

They jumped and their heads jerked up and around. Every adult and some of the children watched them with undisguised interest. Matt wanted to howl. He didn't need to see Octavia's pleased expression to know he and Shannon had been caught grinning at each other like two idiots.

And how in the hel— *heaven* was he supposed to introduce her? People knew Wade helped people, but they also knew how he loved the ranch. Talk was going to run through the community like a brush fire. He didn't want that for either of them.

While he was trying to think of something, Shannon stood. "If you don't mind, Pastor Billows, since I was more a friend of Wade's than Matt's I'd like to introduce myself."

CHAPTER 15

*Y*ou *could hear a pin drop.*
  Shannon had often heard that expression and, until this moment, had laughed at the fallacy. She wasn't laughing now. She didn't have to see Matt's face to know he probably wanted to pull her down in her seat. She wasn't so sure about this herself.

Octavia gave her an encouraging smile. Shannon's hand clenched the stiff brim of Matt's hat. He'd never stop shouting if she ruined his Sunday Stetson.

Her fingers relaxed and she met the expectant gaze of the pastor. "My name is Shannon Johnson and I was fortunate enough to be assigned as Wade Taggart's nurse while he recovered in St. Louis. He was a fine, caring man. I wanted to come and see the place Wade loved."

She glanced around the congregation. "I've met so many wonderful people since I've been here and now being in church today, I see why Wade loved Jackson Falls. Thank you."

The church exploded in applause as she sat down. The person on her right stuck out her hand, and so did the next person.

"Please stand for the benediction."

Shannon came to her feet still clutching Matt's hat, her purse strap slung over her shoulder. As soon as Pastor Billows said, "Amen" she was surrounded by parishioners.

"Welcome to Jackson Falls."

"Wade and I go way back."

"Nice having you at church."

"Hope you enjoy your stay."

Out of the corner of her eye, she noticed Matt had drawn his own crowd. Three attractive women and two matronly ladies hemmed him in. She couldn't make out what the females were saying, but she had no difficulty hearing Matt repeatedly tell them how tied up he was with the ranch.

"Shannon can tell you how busy I am; she's even riding fence."

Everyone stopped talking. Once again she became the center of attention. She had told Matt she wasn't going to help him discourage women, but she could see his problem since Octavia said he didn't date the local women. Those five weren't taking no for an answer. If he wanted to be painted in a bad light, who was she to say no.

"One morning he was so anxious to get started, I didn't have time to eat breakfast or get my work gloves." Every eye whipped to Matt. Shannon smiled into his scowling face. "But he did put me on light duty after my thumb was a bigger target than the staple."

"He hit you with a hammer?" the woman next to her asked in horror.

"No, I did that myself." Maybe she was laying it on a bit thick. "Matt took one look at my bruised thumb and sent me back to the ranch. He cares for his people very well. Wade was justifiably proud of him."

All around people murmured their agreement. The women resumed gazing adoringly at Matt. He pulled his hat from her hand. His face was smiling, but his eyes promised retribution.

"If you'll excuse us, we have to be going." Catching Shannon's arm, Matt started out of the church. Sneaky. Nobody seemed to notice that flaw in her character except him.

"Matt, Pastor Billows and Sister Price want to meet Shannon," Octavia called.

Matt clenched his jaw and halted. People clustered around and waited. He cast a sideways glance at Shannon and saw her smiling. Sneaky as they come.

Octavia quickly made the introductions, beaming at Shannon as if she were her own child. "Shannon's the head nurse now in the ICCU unit where Wade was a patient. You can tell just by looking at her what a warm, gentle lady our Shannon is."

There were several loud amens. All from men.

"You only see the goodness in people because you're so nice," Shannon said. "Pastor Billows, I really enjoyed your sermon, and Mrs. Price, you touched my heart."

Pastor Billows stuck his chest way out. His round, dark face glowed with pleasure. "I'm but the instrument of God."

"I give all praise and glory to Him," added Leola Price, glancing around the audience as if to let them know she was taking account as to who agreed and giving them a second chance.

Women took the hint and sent out another chorus of amens and praises for Leola's voice.

Matt had had enough. "Octavia, we need to be going." Thanks to Shannon he still hadn't updated the ranch accounts.

"Any chance of you staying with us permanently, Miss Johnson?" Pastor Billows asked.

Matt wasn't the only one who stared at the pastor. Tall, midforties, widowed, and handsome, he had the respect of the entire congregation. Matt always admired him for his ability to keep so many women in the church happy and willing to work.

Shannon moistened her lips before answering firmly. "No."

"That's a pity. We need someone of your obvious experience in our community. Our only doctor retired last month and referred all the patients to a colleague forty-five miles away. It's tough on our senior citizens getting there."

"I'm sorry, but I'm only here for a short time," Shannon told him.

"How long?" Leola asked. "Maybe you could help out while you're here."

"I don't have the authority to practice nursing in Texas," Shannon explained with more calm than she felt.

"Is taking a blood pressure practicing nursing?" asked a frail woman holding the hand of a equally frail man. "My name is Rose Badget and this is my husband, Henry."

Shannon said how pleased she was to meet them.

"I bought that pressure thing, but I can't hear the sound. Now I have to drive my Henry every week to the doctor because he has glaucoma and they have to watch the medicine he takes for his pressure. The traffic and the drive are a bit much for me, Henry, and our car."

Shannon saw the desperation in the woman's face, felt her need. Dressed in a print cotton dress and small straw hat, she appeared to be in her early seventies. Henry wore a crisp khaki shirt and pants. Her grandfather had been seventy-two when he died.

"Couldn't someone in the church or in your family take his blood pressure for you?" Shannon asked hopefully.

"The doctor has to regulate the medicine sometimes and he says he won't take the responsibility unless it's taken by someone he trusts or a professional person," the woman said. "Our daughter lives in Atlanta."

"I'm sorry." Shannon crossed to the older woman. "Then that means I would be acting as a RN because I would report directly to your husband's doctor. For that I'd need reciprocity."

"Reci—what's that?"

"Validation of my nursing license to work as a RN in Texas, since I took my nursing exams in Missouri. I'm not even sure how long that takes." She rushed on at the woman's crestfallen expression. "I'd be happy to come over and I'll try to help you learn to take your husband's blood pressure."

The woman looked away, then back at Shannon. "I spent two hours trying already with those double things where the nurse and I both could hear the sounds." She blinked. "We'll make it. Have a nice stay, Miss Johnson."

Helpless to stop them, Shannon watched them leave. Callused fingers curled around her arm. She didn't have to glance up to know it was Matt.

"We're leaving."

This time no one tried to stop them. Once in the truck, Octavia spread her handkerchief in Shannon's lap.

"I'm sorry."

Octavia patted Shannon's knee. "Ain't your fault, child. Nobody's blaming you. We know you'd help if you could."

But she could help . . . if she wasn't afraid of falling apart again.

"You think I'm a coward, don't you?"

"What I think doesn't matter," Matt said and braced his shoulder against the trunk of an oak tree. "Dinner is ready."

"I'm not hungry." Arms clasped around updrawn legs, Shannon laid her cheek against her knee.

She was hurting and he didn't know how to help her. Shannon might be a lot of things he hadn't figured out, but mean wasn't one of them. As soon as they had reached the ranch house, she had gone upstairs.

She had passed him going back downstairs as he was going up. Wearing the same yellow T-shirt and shorts as when they met and carrying her quilt, it wasn't difficult for him to figure out where she was headed.

After changing, he told Octavia to eat without them. Now that he was here, he didn't know what to say. After his divorce, his family telling him to get himself together hadn't helped him a bit. He had to work through his anger.

The land had been his salvation. He wasn't sure if it was Shannon's. He looked around the flower-strewn meadow, saw a jackrabbit scurry for safety, heard a blue jay in the trees.

It was a peaceful place, but sooner or later you had to leave. And when you did, your peace had to come from within. He knew that better than anyone.

"Did you really enjoy Leola's singing?" Matt asked.

"Yes."

He picked up a rock and threw it in the direction of the stream. "Those high notes of hers always remind me of a whooping crane."

She lifted her head. The wind playfully tossed her thick auburn hair. "That's not a very nice thing for you to say."

"I'm not a nice guy."

"Yes, you are. You just don't like anyone to know."

"How did you come up with an idea like that?"

"Wade. You helped. I didn't mean for that lady to think you hit me with a hammer."

"Forget it." She was trying to comfort him again when she was the one in need of consolation. Lowering her chin to her knee, she stared out across the meadow. "You better go back and eat. You know how Octavia hates to rewarm food and there's no one there to eat."

"She knows we might be late." Matt sent another rock toward the stream.

Her lush, plum-colored lips curved into an alluring smile. "I said you were a nice guy."

Another rock went sailing. "Your grandmother give you that quilt?"

"My grandmother died before I was born. My grandfather gave it to me when I spent the night with him for the first time." She looked wistful. "I was four years old. I had the chicken pox and couldn't go on the family vacation to Disneyland."

"He kept you by himself?"

"Yes."

"Brave man."

Shannon looked at him as if unsure if he was serious or joking. "Granddaddy Rhodes was the best. He wouldn't like knowing his only granddaughter turned her back on people in need."

"He'd probably understand better than you think." Matt squatted down beside her. "People who love you are less judgmental than you are of yourself."

Shannon wrinkled her small nose. "You haven't met my parents or brothers. They all think they know what's best for me better than I do."

Matt tossed the one remaining rock in his hand. He wanted to ask if her ex-boyfriend was one of the things her family thought best for her, then discarded the idea. He didn't want to become entangled in Shannon's life any more than necessary. Trying to help her through this bad time was the same as he'd do for any of his other ranch hands who faced a problem.

He pushed to his feet. "Are you going to show them they're wrong or sit here and feel sorry for yourself?"

Amber eyes glinted. "I take back what I said about you being nice."

"You only have to decide one thing: can you live with yourself knowing you could have helped and didn't? I don't think you can. You had no control over what happened to your grandfather. You do over this. I'll see you back at the ranch."

He had gone only a short distance before he heard her say, "I don't think I could, either."

He turned to see her folding up her quilt. He waited until she caught up with him.

"Granddaddy Rhodes would have liked you." On tiptoe, she kissed his cheek. "Thanks." Getting into her car, she drove off.

It took Matt a full thirty seconds to realize he was smiling. The smile vanished in the next heartbeat.

She wasn't adding him to her list of admirers. He had only done what was best for the ranch. She would be unable to do her job effectively if she was upset all the time.

Walking to his truck he ignored the voice that whispered, she might have left sooner if she was unhappy.

"Come in," Matt called from behind his desk.

The door slowly opened and Shannon hesitantly stuck her head inside the room. "I know you're busy, but could I talk to you for a minute?"

"What is it?"

"Stop frowning, I'm not going to ask for a raise."

"Very funny."

Shannon had thought this was going to be so simple, but the stern-faced man staring at her wasn't the same compassionate man who had helped her in the meadow this afternoon. Matt looked at her now as if he didn't care if she dropped off the face of the earth.

"Shannon, if you have something to say, please get on with it. I'm busy."

"I wanted to thank you again for this afternoon. Octavia and I just got back from visiting with Henry and Rose Badget. They're a wonderful couple."

He tossed his pen down. "I've known them most of my life. You interrupted me to tell me that?"

No, I interrupted you because I just wanted to see you smile at me again. Maybe say I knew you could do it, Shannon.

"Octavia took me to meet two other elderly people. I'd forgotten how frightened of the unknown and doctors the elderly can be," she confessed. "We're going to see a Mrs. Snyder tomorrow. She's recovering from a stroke, but she's depressed and her daughter can't get her out of bed."

Heavy brows arched. "You seem to be jumping with both feet into something you were scared witless of a few hours ago."

"I still am, but whenever it gets too much, I think of Granddaddy and thank God someone was there to help him." *Just as I thank God you were there to talk me through a difficult time just as Granddaddy did.*

She stuck her hands into the back pockets of her shorts. "Like you said, I couldn't live with myself if I didn't help."

"What about reciprocity?"

"I talked with the director of nursing where I work in St. Louis and she doesn't see a problem. Once I made a promise I wasn't thinking of leaving, she was a lot of help," she told him, becoming more animated. "She even thinks I'll be able to take Mr. Badget's blood pressure as a lay person, but because of my background, the doctor will probably accept the reading."

He rocked back in his chair. "You seem to have it all worked out except when you're going to have time for all this."

Her smile faltered as she drug her hands out of her pockets. "I'm sure I'll manage."

"That's your little spiel for everything, 'I'll manage.' Now I see why you came in here." He pushed to his feet and rounded the desk. "If you think I'm going to cut back on your duties so you can run around the country-side playing Shannon Nightingale, think again. Tomorrow you ride fence with Griff and you better remember to wear your gloves."

Her chin came up. "I've never shirked my duties. You're the one who assigned me to work around the house."

"Consider yourself unassigned."

"I don't know why I'd thought you'd understand." She left the room, slamming the door.

"What's the matter, child?" Octavia asked as she stormed into the kitchen.

"He can make me so mad."

The older woman chuckled and went back to readying the automatic coffee maker for Matt to use in the morning. "I get the feeling you do the same thing to him. Better to strike sparks than complacency, I always say. At least you know the person knows you're around."

Shannon grunted and picked up the plate of chicken and dressing with a huge wedge of lemon cake on the side. "I guess I'll go take this to Cleve."

"You're gonna spoil that old rascal."

"What about you?" Shannon asked with a smile. "I saw you add more food to this plate when you thought I wasn't looking."

"I'd just throw it out," the housekeeper defended. "Now take that on over and be back before it gets full dark."

"Yes, ma'am." Still smiling, Shannon left the kitchen. Everyone was so nice to her. Why did Matt have to be such an obstinate . . .

Her shoulders sagged. It wasn't Matt's fault that she wanted more from him than he was willing to give—or could give for that matter. She wanted his trust, his laughter, his love.

She stumbled as the full impact of her words struck her. To want Matt's love she'd have to care deeply for him. She'd have to be . . . in love with him.

She wasn't. She wasn't. Each way she tried to escape the truth, no matter how she ran, it was always there waiting for her.

She loved Matt. Wildly. Passionately. Endlessly. And he would never love her in return. Despair as deep as a bottomless pit swept over her. She had found the love her heart always knew was out there and it would only bring her heartache.

Matt didn't trust her and showed no signs of changing his opinion. But then came those rare moments like this afternoon. She could see the tenderness in him, feel him reaching out to her, but then it would disappear behind a shuttered mask of indifference. It was almost as if he were *afraid* to reach out to her.

Which was crazy. Although he had told her otherwise, she didn't think anything on earth could scare Matt. Least of all Shannon Johnson.

Loosening her grip on the plate, she continued to Cleve's house. There was nothing she could do about loving Matt, except hope he never learned her secret. That would be the ultimate humiliation.

Why did she have to fall in love with someone who couldn't love her back?

"Daydreaming again?"

Shannon jerked out of her musing to see Cleve sitting on his porch. She grasped at the chance to get her mind off Matt. "Hi, Cleve. I guess I was."

His booted feet on the step below, he reached for his plate. "If you're bringin' that to me, I better take it 'fore somethin' happens to it."

Giving him the plate, she sat down beside him and handed him a fork. "In case you didn't want to wait."

After removing the plastic wrap, Cleve reached for the utensil. "For that I might put you to muckin' out the stalls again."

"Matt has me riding the fence line with Griff." Bringing up her knees, she circled them with her arms, then held up her face to the gentle evening breeze.

The hand that had been bringing a cake-laden fork to his mouth paused. "You're a good worker."

His boss didn't think so. "For a woman from the city, you mean."

"For anybody." He laid down the fork.

"You don't like my cake?"

"Just thinkin'." Carefully, he replaced the wrapper.

"About me teaching you to read?" She had taken a chance and brought up the subject the day they were weeding the vegetable garden.

She had glanced up to see him with a package of seeds in his hand, his thumb grazing over and over the letters for cabbage. "I could teach you."

His head had lifted, hope glittered in his eyes, then died. Replacing the package on the stick at the head of the row, he began hoeing again.

His not saying a flat out no encouraged her. "If you ever change your mind, the offer remains. It'll just be between the two of us."

Returning to the present, she gently touched his arm. "Cleve?"

Gnarled fingers smoothed the plastic wrap over and over. "I've been thinkin' about it a little, I guess."

She strove to keep her enthusiasm down. "First we start with what you know and go from there."

"I know a few letters, but not any words."

"It's a beginning. Once you learn the alphabet sounds you're going to learn to sound the words out. All we'll need to start is pencil and paper."

"I already have that stuff and some books, too. I told the saleslady I was buyin' 'em for my grandchildren," he admitted softly.

Her heart went out to him. "You can learn, Cleve, I know you can."

"We won't have time if you're out on the range all day."

"We'll manage," she said, then grimaced as she thought of Matt's reaction to her words and the reason why. She looked at Cleve's wishful expression and brushed aside any doubts. She couldn't turn her back on him. If he had enough courage to ask for help, she could get up an hour earlier each morning.

"I promised Octavia to look in on a couple of people in the afternoons, but I could come around seven each morning."

"The boss would suspect somethin'." Cleve shook his head. "I couldn't stand him knowin' I tried this and failed. I don't know why, but he's always thought highly of me, I kinda like him to keep thinkin' that way. That's why I never let him teach me."

"He offered to teach you?"

Cleve looked offended by her startled reaction. "Course he did. Offered again just the other day. Don't many come finer than the boss."

Matt cared for his people on the ranch, she just wished he cared for her as well. "Then we'll just put things in reverse."

Bushy salt-and-pepper eyebrows lifted. "What are you talkin' 'bout?"

"Instead of me teaching you how to read, you'll be teaching me how to make rope," she told him with growing enthusiasm.

Cleve looked at her as if she had said he'd teach her to belly dance. "I don't know why I thought you were smart." He pushed to his feet and stomped into the bunkhouse.

Shannon was right behind him. He reminded her of Matt so much, sometimes she wanted to shake him. "What's so unbelievable about that? You told me it's a dying art. Doesn't it stand to reason you'd want to pass it on to someone?"

"An Easterner?"

Momentarily, she lifted her eyes heavenward. "If I didn't care about you so much, I'd walk out that door after an unfair crack like that. You just said I was a good worker."

"Don't get your feathers all ruffled," Cleve said, putting the plate on the table. "The boss is too smart to believe you'd want to learn how to make rope."

"Matt doesn't pay attention to me except to give orders or ask if I'm ready to leave the Circle T," she said, unaware of how wistful her voice sounded.

"There you go talkin' foolishness again."

Shannon braced her hands on her hips. "As long as I'm there by eight to take orders in the morning he'll never miss me."

Dark-brown eyes sparkled as leathery fingers rubbed a stubbled jaw. "A peach cobbler says he will."

"What do I get?"

"The satisfaction of bestin' me."

She extended her hand. "Done."

"Done."

"Where're you going?"

The whiplash in Matt's voice stopped Shannon in midstep going down the stairs. "It's not eight yet."

Booted feet pounded on the hall runner. Firm fingers curled around her forearm and turned her to him. "I didn't ask you for the time, I asked you where you were going."

Her explanation fled as she gazed at the heavy matting of chest hair visible through his unbuttoned red shirt. He must have been dressing when he heard her leaving. The curly black hair looked soft and crinkly at the same time. Her hand lifted toward beckoning temptation.

"Shannon."

Her gaze flew up to his face, dark and uncompromising. Guilty, she stuck her hand behind her back. "Out."

A muscle leaped in his jaw. "My patience is wearing thin."

"You have my time from eight in the morning until my job is done. The rest of the time belongs to me or did you forget?"

Charcoal-black eyes searched her face, noted the way her glance kept sliding away. His sensual mouth hardened. "Who is he?"

"You always think the worst of me. I'll tell you one thing, if there was a man, he'd treat me much better than you treat me," she snapped without thinking.

He struck without warning. Both hands lifted her to him so they were eye-to-eye. "Is that a challenge, Shannon?"

The lazy sensuality in his voice curled around her body and held her tighter than his hands. She wanted and couldn't have. "Matt."

He shuddered, then briefly closed his eyes. When they opened, his eyes were as devoid of emotions as his voice. "Did I hurt you?"

"No. You could never do that," she told him softly.

He set her on her feet. "You think the best of people too easily."

"Only when it's deserved."

"Be careful you don't trust the wrong person. See you at eight." He left her on the stairwell and started for his room.

Shannon bit her lower lip. He wouldn't bother her again if he saw her leaving, but she couldn't stand the thought of him thinking she was sneaking out to meet someone. "Cleve's teaching me how to make rope."

He faced her with an expression on his dark face much like's Cleve when she had suggested the ruse. "Rope?"

"Now you see why I didn't want to tell you? I knew what your reaction would be." It wasn't difficult to look irritated. Cleve would never let her forget this.

"You're getting up before seven to learn how to make rope?"

"It's a dying art form," she unnecessarily reminded him. "I thought I'd make one for a friend back home."

"So you've added something else to do." His scowl returned. "When did you plan to rest?"

"I'll man—"

"Manage," he finished sharply for her. "You get hurt while you're working because you're tired and you'll answer to me, is that clear?"

"I don't pl—"

"Is that clear?"

"Yes."

Spinning on his heels, he went back to his room. The door closed with a crisp thump.

Sighing, Shannon continued down the stairs and out the back door. That's what she got for trying to reassure him, someone else to treat her as if she didn't have two brain cells. Next time he could think what he wanted.

Going up the last step to Cleve's house, she crossed the porch. The door opened before she lifted her hand to knock.

Cleve opened the door, took one look at her mutinous expression and laughed. "I like lots of peaches."

CHAPTER 16

He had acted like a jealous maniac. He had never touched a woman in anger in his life. Not even when he caught his ex-wife in the bar with her body and her lips plastered against her boss's.

The bastard hadn't been so lucky.

"Gritting your teeth is bad for them."

Matt snapped his head up. Shannon sat across the breakfast table from him, her comforting smile firmly in place. He didn't want to be comforted. "They're my teeth."

"The dentist's drill will remind you of that quite nicely."

"Now, children," Octavia chuckled from her chair between them.

Being chastised in his own home was the last straw. His chair scraped against the floor as he rose. "Let's go."

Shannon picked up her hat, gloves, and the canvas tote bag and was at the door before he was. "If we're going, let's go." Then, she was gone.

Octavia's chuckles grew louder. "I prayed for this day."

"For Wade to saddle me with a stubborn woman who doesn't have the sense God gave a chicken?" Matt railed, trying to calm down before he followed Shannon.

"For you to meet a woman you couldn't ignore. A woman who could stand toe-to-toe with you and make you like it."

Matt scowled. "Lay off the house-cleaning today. You've been inhaling too many fumes." Laughter followed him out the door.

All the hands including Shannon were mounted and waiting for him.

He didn't waste time giving orders. They rode off as soon as he finished. Over the noise of the hoofbeats, he heard Shannon's laughter.

He caught himself turning his head trying to catch the captivating sound. His hands tightened on the reins. She had to go before he completely lost it.

"Somethin' wrong with Brazos again?"

Startled, Matt glanced around to see Cleve making his way toward him from the barn. "No. Just thinking."

Cleve cocked a brow. "Miss Shannon does the same thing sometimes."

Matt held on to his temper with both hands. "Shannon and I have nothing in common."

"Try tellin' that to my ears." He tugged one earlobe, then the other. "It's a wonder I ain't deaf."

"Don't you have work to do?"

"We both do," Cleve said, and started back to the barn. "Ain't no shame in likin' a pretty woman," he called over his shoulder.

"Cleve."

"Have a nice day, boss."

Booted heels touched the horse's flank and he took off. Was everyone around him crazy? He did not like Shannon. He might feel a little sorry for her at times, but he certainly didn't like her.

He could, however, understand why her parents thought she needed guidance. She took too much on herself. She had let this comforting business get out of hand. If helping the senior citizens wasn't enough, she had added Cleve to the list.

He had thought she had lied to him at first about learning to make rope, but the more he thought about it, the more he reasoned she might be telling the truth. It was just like her to help Cleve preserve the craft he loved so much.

Matt would have to remind Cleve to teach her with cured leather instead of sisal or hemp. The amount of strength and tension it took to keep the twisted strands together might be too much for Shannon's delicate skin if they used anything else. Matt didn't want to see it marred—

Shannon's skin was of no concern to him!

He gritted his teeth, remembered what Shannon said about the dentist's drill and pulled his horse to a halt. No woman had ever gotten to him the way she did. He didn't know whether he wanted to berate her for being so stubborn or pull her down and bury himself deep inside her.

A trickle of sweat glided down the side of his face. He was worse than a kid. He glanced around, saw the cabin and bit back a groan. He was nowhere near where he had planned to be today.

Beseeching eyes lifted heavenward. "Wade, I never would have thought you'd do this to me." Whirling Brazos, he headed for the south pasture two miles away.

* * *

Sometimes she didn't understand Matt. And now was one of those times. Honking her horn, Shannon turned into the road leading to the ranch house. The sound was answered by the truck behind her. In her rearview mirror, she watched the vehicle back up, then go back the way it had come.

Her escort had gotten her safely back on Taggart land. Matt's orders. No one had wanted to admit it at first, until she insisted she didn't need anyone following her home. No one had listened. Matt had said she needed an escort and that was what she was going to get.

The respect his neighbors had for him gave her a warm glow. There was talk of his financial help in putting a roof on the church, sponsoring a summer camp for teens. He wasn't a hardcase. She wanted to see him happy and loved. With all her heart she wished she could be the one to help him discover both. Parking the car, she went inside and knocked on Octavia's door and told her she was home.

"Good night, child."

Shannon smiled. No one had waited up for her since high school. Shoving open the swinging doors, she wasn't surprised to see light spilling from beneath the door of Matt's study. He worked too hard.

She started in that direction, then changed her mind and continued toward the stairs. He didn't like to be interrupted. She'd tell him an escort wasn't necessary in the morning. Absently rubbing her neck, she started up the stairs.

"Kind of late, isn't it?"

The rich timbre of Matt's voice sent a shiver down her spine and compelled her to face him. Her breath caught. Silhouetted in the doorway of his study, his powerful body was a study in masculine beauty. "Time got away from me."

"Was there a problem?"

"No. Things couldn't have gone better. The people I saw gave me as much as I gave them. I'd forgotten how older people have a certain way of looking at things, of expressing themselves that is practical and thought-provoking at the same time."

He stepped closer, his eyes searching hers. "Why do you keep rubbing your neck?"

She snatched her hand away. "Stiff muscles. I wish Melanie were here to give me a massage."

"Isn't she the one you wanted to send a picture to?"

Shannon lifted a delicate brow. She had no doubt Matt remembered Melanie from the night James called as well. "Yes. She's my best friend and the head of the PT department at Memorial." Shannon smiled in remembered pleasure. "She can give you a massage that will make you curl up and purr."

A strange expression crossed his face. He took another step. "I don't know about making you purr, but I can give it a try."

Shannon felt hot all over, her knees weak. "I—I wouldn't want you to go to any trouble. A good soak will do just as well."

"A massage would feel better," he said, his voice as dark and compelling as his eyes.

"W-we couldn't do it properly." She forced the words past her dry throat. His heavy brow quirked as his searing gaze ran the length of her. She gripped the banister for needed equilibrium. "Th-there's no hard surface to lay on."

"You can sit in a chair and I can do it from behind."

Images immediately formed in her mind. Matt, bare-chested with a carelessly wrapped white towel around his lean waist, standing behind her as she sat on a backless chair. The heat and hardness of muscular thighs pressing firmly against her back while callused hands caressed her bare shoulders, then slid with aching slowness to gently close over her breasts.

She plopped on the step, her breathing erratic. Her entire body tingled in hopeless disappointment and growing need.

Instantly, he was there kneeling in front of her. "I told you you couldn't do all this."

"I . . . I . . ." She fumbled for words. She couldn't very well tell him it wasn't her work schedule but the passionate promise in his midnight eyes and velvet voice that caused her weakness. Her mind frantically sought a way out of her predicament.

"I don't want an escort."

"He stays," he told her, thrown not at all off balance by the change in topic.

His warm, minty breath bathed her face. It took all her willpower to stand instead of leaning closer to taste his mouth. "I can take care of myself."

Matt straightened. "If anything happens to you, Octavia would blame herself."

Why had she thought for a moment that he might care a little bit about her? "I've driven at night by myself before."

"The escort stays."

He was too close, her feelings too new. Turning away from the blazing intensity of his eyes, she fled up the stairs and to her room. Loving Matt was the easiest and the most difficult thing she had ever done.

Matt set a time record in removing his boots. Next came his shirt, followed closely by his pants and briefs. Stepping into the shower, he turned the water on full blast.

Shannon was killing him.

What the hell possessed him to offer her a massage? Stupid question. The opportunity to touch her soft skin without feeling guilty had been too much of a temptation. But something within him had also wanted to ease the lines of tension around her mouth.

He shouldn't care about easing her discomforts or seeing her smile. But he did. If he wasn't worried about her he was lusting after her or irritated with her. Somehow she had slipped past his ability to remain indifferent.

Throwing his head back, he let the blast of cold water hit him square in the face. This crazy wanting, this mindless need for her had to stop. She was not going to get to him. He was not going to break his staunchest vow of keeping his involvements casual. He was not going to make love to her.

His head lifted. Water pelted the thick, corded muscles of his arms, shoulders, chest. And it wasn't doing a bit of good. He wanted Shannon, wished she were with him now, sleek, wet, willing.

He tried to think of something else . . . the haying, taking the cattle to auction, Sir Galahad's breeding schedule. Matt groaned. This wasn't working. The only thing that would work was the woman down the hall.

Only her.

Matt was avoiding her again. Shannon had hardly seen him in the past three days. With the torrid dreams she was having about him, perhaps that was for the best. Her face heated just thinking about the lusty things he did to her in those dreams. Sweet little Shannon Johnson was turning into a wanton!

Shaking her head, she turned off the FM Road onto the Badgets' driveway. Her car had barely straightened when Mrs. Badget stepped out of the house, then came down the flower-lined walk. Shannon frowned. The elderly woman had made a habit of meeting her at the front door with a smile. Today, she was doing neither.

Unease swept through Shannon. She forced herself not to slow the car to a crawl and put off whatever waited for her. As she pulled to a stop and saw the lines of strain bracketing Mrs. Badget's mouth, Shannon's dread intensified.

Inside the tiny frame house, Shannon took one look at Mr. Badget's flushed face, the subtle flaring of his nostrils as he tried to draw more air into his lungs, and knew she had been right.

She could not handle this.

"I'm so glad you're here, Shannon," Mrs. Badget said, the relief on her face easily discernible. "Henry hasn't been well since lunch."

"D-don't go worrying the girl," Henry admonished, and tried to rise from where he reclined on the couch.

Without thought, Shannon went to him. The uncertainty in his pain-filled gaze reached out to her. She was all he had. Once she had been the best. Gentle but firm hands kept him from rising. "Why don't you let me judge that? I want you to lie quietly while I take your blood pressure and vital signs."

"I'm fine," he said.

Shannon gave him a reassuring smile as she quickly wrapped the blood pressure cuff around his arm. "Then you shouldn't mind me taking a reading."

Henry nodded and relaxed.

Shannon quickly took the vital signs. They weren't good. "Let's prop you up a little so you can breathe better," she told him and did just that, all the time asking questions that required only a monosyllabic answer. Finished, she turned to Mrs. Badget. "I forgot to ask Octavia to take my things out of the dryer," she said to the elderly woman. "Can I use the phone?"

Mrs. Badget glanced sharply at the phone on the end table by the couch and began to tremble.

Shannon took the frightened woman to the kitchen. There was no time to pull punches. "I think your husband is having a heart attack. He needs immediate medical attention and he needs you to be strong." Reaching for the phone, she called the emergency medical service and Mr. Badget's doctor, all the time keeping an eye on the man through the open door.

As soon as she hung up the phone, Rose Badget clutched Shannon's arm. "I'm scared."

"I know and it's understandable, but you can't let your husband know." Shannon closed her hand over the woman's frail hand and squeezed. She of all people knew what Mrs. Badget was going through, but this time Shannon was determined to win. "Help is on the way, and for what it's worth, I'm here."

"Thank God. I don't know what I would have done without you," Mrs. Badget said.

After another brief squeeze of Rose's hand, Shannon led her to the living room and urged her to take the seat by the couch. Shannon drew up the piano stool.

"Mr. Badget, I think you need to be seen by Dr. Gaines. The fastest way is by ambulance."

Fear and denial stared back at her. "I-I'm fine. Just indigestion."

"Then I'll feel foolish and you can have a good laugh on me."

"I . . . need to feed . . . the chickens," he told her, and once again tried to rise.

Again firm hands restrained him. "Please, I know this isn't easy, but I want you to lie back and try to relax. Don't talk."

"You listen to her, Henry. Be glad she's here."

His gaze found his wife's. She caught his left hand. Her eyes were suspiciously bright, but no tears fell. "Just be glad she's here."

Henry gave a half-nod, then his eyelids drifted shut. Mrs. Badget's worried gaze flew to Shannon, but Shannon assured her he was fine.

Mrs. Badget watched her husband for a few minutes, then looked at Shannon. "Nursing is clearly more than a job to you."

"Yes," Shannon answered.

"Wish I had some of your training. I thought it was indigestion from the red beans he talked me into cooking for lunch. He didn't start having trouble breathing until a few minutes before you arrived."

"Without training you couldn't be expected to know. Don't blame yourself for what you have no control over." As soon as the words were out of her mouth, Shannon felt them deep in her soul. That was exactly what she had done. Blamed herself for something beyond her control. Matt had been right on target. She could only help to the degree of her ability.

"I'm thankful you decided to come see Jackson Falls," Mrs. Badget said. "I'm glad you're here with us."

"I am, too," Shannon said, and meant it.

Matt walked into the ICCU waiting area, not knowing what to expect when he saw Shannon. Her call to Octavia from the Badgets' house had been brief. As soon as he received the emergency page he had known Shannon was involved. All the way to the hospital he had worried and wondered and prayed as much for Henry as for Shannon.

Her saw her immediately. Standing beside Mrs. Badget and Dr. Gaines, Shannon looked self-assured and competent. She hadn't buckled under pressure. Somehow she had found the strength and courage to face her fears. He didn't know why the knowledge both pleased and bothered him.

He watched Octavia rush over and hug Shannon, and wished he could do the same. She looked up and their eyes met. Shannon might have gained her peace, but she had taken his.

Matt was waiting in the kitchen early the next morning when Shannon walked in. Leaning negligently against the countertop, arms folded across his wide chest, he looked unbearably handsome. And utterly unobtainable.

Last night at the hospital, he had left her alone once she assured him she was fine. Dr. Gaines, Mrs. Badget, and others praising her only made Matt's aloofness more difficult to understand.

Although Henry Badget was resting comfortably and the preliminary tests results were good, her mood had grown somber. Before she knew it, she had been on the pay phone in the waiting area to her parents. Faced with the uncertainty of life, she wanted to see them. She hung up with a promise to be home for the weekend.

Gathering her courage, she walked over to the coffeepot. "Good morning."

"I told you you didn't have to work today," Matt said, never taking his eyes from her.

"I couldn't sleep." He seemed more remote than ever.

"Probably a combination of last night and the prospect of going home." He picked up his cup of coffee. "Have you made your reservation yet?"

Hurt splintered through her, and her hands were unsteady as she poured her coffee. "I thought I'd make them this afternoon."

"I've got a better idea," Matt said. "If you leave now, you should be able to visit Mr. Badget and still get an earlier flight out to St. Louis."

Knowing her emotions were easily read, she kept her eyes averted. "I don't know if there's a flight then."

"There is. I called. Your parents will be happy to see you."

"Yes, they will." The pain deepened.

"If you get home and decide to stay, just contact Arthur," Matt told her. "I'm sure we can work out something about the meadow and see that your car gets to you."

Her head came up. "I'm coming back. I have a week left of my vacation." Her voice trembled with the effort to remain calm.

Hard black eyes impaled her. "Why? Jackson Falls isn't what you're used to, and obviously you don't have any more doubts about what you want out of life."

"How do you know that? Before now you haven't said ten words to me in the past twenty-four hours. No, make that the last three days." The incriminating words were out before she could stop them.

He gripped the mug. "Last night you seemed totally in control. Mrs. Badget and everyone there looked to you for support and you gave it without a moment's hesitation."

Some of the anger left her. She didn't think he had noticed. "In caring for Mr. Badget last night and trying to help him and his wife deal with his illness, I finally accepted something you told me in the meadow was true. I had no control over what happened to my grandfather. My training has limits. Last night I realized how important just being there is."

She drew a hand through her hair. "I'll always feel empathy for the people I care for and their families, but it won't tear me up inside. It won't interfere with my effectiveness as a nurse."

"Then you've found what you came for, Shannon. Peace. There's no need to come back."

He didn't want her. She gripped her cup to fight against the crippling misery. "I haven't finished learning how to make rope."

A muscle clenched in his jaw. "I'm sure Cleve will understand if you didn't return."

"I'm coming back."

His face chilled her as much as his voice, "There's nothing for you here." Moments later he was out the door and striding toward the barn.

Her entire body shaking, Shannon watched Matt leave. He couldn't have made it any plainer. He didn't want her, didn't need her in his life. There was nothing for her to return for. Nothing except the anguish of seeing him every day and knowing he'd never love her as she loved him.

She hurt and it was her own fault. Melanie had tried to warn Shannon, but she refused to listen.

Turning away, she went to her room to pack. She had some pride left. He didn't have to toss her off the ranch. Snatching up her overnight case, it opened. A can of hairspray rolled across the room and came to rest below the window. Stomping over, Shannon picked up the aerosol can. Blinking back tears, she looked out the curtained window toward the barn.

A lone figure stood just inside the door. Although the person was in the shadows, the fluttery sensation in the pit of her stomach told her who it was.

Matt. His utter stillness was unnerving. What was he watching? He seemed to be looking toward . . . Her breath caught, hope blossomed. Tossing the spray can on the bed, she rushed downstairs to Matt's study, grabbed his binoculars and went around the side of the house.

Trembling hands lifted the glasses. She located Matt, then followed his line of vision. Her room. The tremors of her hands increased as she panned back to him.

He was gone. Slowly, she lowered the binoculars. His face had been in the shadows, but the tautness of his body had been obvious. It was almost as if he were preparing himself to receive an unexpected blow.

And he had been looking at her room.

Going back into the house, she returned the binoculars, went to her room and stared out the window again. What if the idea forming in her head was wrong?

Leaning her head against the pane, Shannon closed her eyes. She had barely gotten her life back together. Why deliberately open herself up to more heartache? Turning away, she began to pack.

Inside the barn, Matt's gloved hands clenched into fists. He had been careless. Light glinting off the binoculars had warned him a second too late. She knew he had been watching her window but not the reason why.

If they were both lucky she never would.

"Don't come back, Shannon. Just don't come back."

CHAPTER 17

She wasn't coming back.

Matt glanced at the clock on the kitchen wall. It was five past eight. If she was going to return, she would be here by now. She wouldn't be late for work or to help Cleve.

From somewhere in the house he heard the distant hum of the vacuum cleaner. Octavia was getting an early start on her Monday morning house-cleaning. Everything was back to normal. It was almost as if Shannon had never been at the ranch.

Over the weekend, neither Octavia nor Cleve mentioned Shannon's name. Matt had thought she would have called one of them to let them know she had reached home safely. If she had, they didn't tell him. But why should they? He had assured them there was nothing between him and Shannon.

But the first night she was gone, it had taken a considerable amount of willpower to keep himself from going into her room to see if she had taken all her things. He had wanted her gone. He just hadn't known how . . .

His mind searched for a word other than the one hammering against his skull. Empty.

He did not feel empty! It was the quietness that made him so contemplative this morning. With Shannon around he never had a moment's peace. He settled more firmly in the ladder-back chair with the comforting assurance that he had figured out what was bothering him.

Suddenly the sound of an engine had him jumping up from the table. Instead of her car a blue-and-white motor home the size of a Greyhound bus pulled up. The tightness in his chest was not from disappointment; he probably needed to cut back on the caffeine.

Opening the kitchen door, Matt went to meet Daniel Falcon and his film crew. As expected, Daniel's custom-made red lizard boots were the first to hit the ground. Also as expected, he wore a smile on his honey-bronzed face.

Daniel smiled more than anyone Matt knew and meant it less. But when he stopped smiling it was time for the other person to start praying.

"You're right on time," Matt said, extending his hand. Daniel caught it in a firm grip and both men grinned.

"If not for the horse trails you call roads, I would have been here sooner," Daniel said, kicking back his pearl-gray Stetson.

"What's life without a little challenge?" Matt bantered, and for some odd reason thought of Shannon.

"Why the frown then?" Daniel asked, his black eyes probing.

Matt waved his question aside. Next to his brother Kane, Daniel was one of the most perceptive men Matt ever met. "You want some breakfast or coffee before you and your crew get started?"

One dimple winked in Daniel's cheek. "Now you're talking." He glanced around at the two men approaching. "Matt Taggart, meet Carter Simmons and Price Lofton, my cameraman and historian."

"Where's the woman? I thought you hired a woman to keep a daily record," Matt said after shaking the men's hands.

Daniel's smile slipped to half-wattage. "She found she didn't like riding around the countryside as much as she thought."

"Meaning she discovered you're slippery even in a motor home," Matt said, laughing.

Carter and Price joined in.

"I don't notice *you* getting any closer to the altar," Daniel said teasingly.

Matt's smile died. "Nor will I ever."

Daniel arched a brow. "Never is a long time, friend."

"For some things, it's not long enough."

"Men, wait over there and I'll be with you in a minute," Daniel told the two men, then to Matt, "I thought you were through with the past."

Matt's face went blank. "I thought I taught you in Albuquerque to stay out of my business."

Crossing his arms over a chest as wide and muscular as Matt's, Daniel's smile was part taunt, part teasing. "A pity Kane had to intervene."

"Saved you from getting another broken nose," Matt said without heat.

"My nose has never been broken." He fingered the slight rise on the bridge of his elegant nose. "Nor have I met the man who can accomplish that feat."

Matt's smile grew slow and menacing. "We'll have to see about that once the filming's over."

Daniel's smile finally disappeared. "It's probably none of my business, but who the hell left you spoiling for a fight?"

His friend's statement was so on target, it caught Matt off guard and without a comeback. He and Daniel had half-heartedly thrown a few punches when they first met, but it was more roughhousing than anything else. Kane had ended it before it began. Matt couldn't even remember why or how it started.

"Your men are waiting," Matt finally said.

"I'd let them wait if I thought it would do any good."

"Come on, I'll introduce you to my housekeeper." Matt started for the house.

Daniel fell into step beside him. "That's why I like you, Matt. You're nearly as stubborn as I am."

They had gone only a few feet before the sound of a car caused both men to turn. A Cadillac convertible came to a screeching halt behind the small truck attached to the motor home.

Shannon jumped out on the driver's side, started for the front door, saw Matt and ran to him. She stopped a short distance away.

"Sorry, I'm late. I know I told you I'd be on time, but Mr. Hodges saw me when I passed and he waved me down. He had hurt his finger fixing his car and he wanted to know if I thought it was broken." She took a breath. "It wasn't, but I splinted it for him. I'm already dressed so as soon as you tell me what to do, I'll be on my horse and gone."

Joy.

Matt felt it in every fiber of his being. She had come back. Dressed in gently worn jeans, a chambray shirt with the collar turned up, new boots, and a hat with a daisy on the brim, Shannon looked more ready to go gardening than mend fences.

Her face danced with so many emotions he couldn't catch them all. Excitement, embarrassment, yearning. A gentle breeze brought to him the subtle scent of her perfume and he couldn't help inhaling deeper. The same breeze teased a lock of her silky hair.

Absently, she brushed it away from her cheek, her gaze still fixed on his. A wariness had entered her brown eyes, but her eyes still clung to him. Shannon had grit, just like Cleve said.

She was also wreaking havoc with his life.

"Aren't you going to introduce us, Matt?"

Matt glanced around at Daniel, but his friend was looking at Shannon with a smile that made most females over six lose reason and follow him around like lost puppy dogs.

Matt jerked his gaze to Shannon. To his pleased amazement, she wasn't looking at Daniel any differently than she had Matt's hands when she first met them.

"Shannon Johnson, Daniel Falcon."

"My pleasure, Shannon," Daniel said, grasping Shannon's hand in his. "I hope it's all right to call you Shannon."

"Hello. Only if I can call you Daniel."

"That will do for starters," Daniel said easily, still holding Shannon's hand.

She blinked, then laughed and pulled her hand free. "You're certainly not shy."

"But I'm very gentle," Daniel's deep voice dipped. "I'll let you pet me if you want."

"If you two are finished acting like teenagers, we have work to do," Matt barked.

One corner of Daniel's sensual mouth lifted. "Aren't we grouchy this morning. I wonder why?"

Matt damned the dentist's drill and gritted his teeth. He hadn't kept his hands off Shannon for Falcon to get her.

Grabbing her arm, he started for the kitchen. "Come on. Octavia will probably be thrilled to see you're back."

"I'm glad somebody will," she muttered.

"Shannon, you missed our lesson this morning."

She glanced over her shoulder and saw Cleve, hands on hips, scowling. Grinning, she ran and hugged him.

He patted her shoulder awkwardly. "That's enough of that."

"You didn't forget me," she said.

"You've only been gone a weekend," Cleve said, eyeing her critically.

"I missed you, too." She turned to the other three ranch hands behind him and gave them all a hug. "I missed all of you."

The back screen door opened, then banged shut. Octavia joined the happy group as fast as her legs would cover the distance. Her arms went around Shannon's waist. She let out a holler and kept grinning.

Daniel leaned over and whispered to Matt, "Where's your hug?"

If looks could kill, Daniel would have keeled over on the spot. His pitiful attempt to smother his amusement set Matt's teeth on edge. By the time Shannon left he wouldn't have to worry about a dentist's drill because he wouldn't have a tooth in his head.

"You eat anything, child?" Octavia asked.

"No. They didn't serve anything on my flight and I didn't have time to stop," she said.

"Then come on inside," Octavia urged.

Warily, Shannon glanced at Matt. "It's after eight."

The hands, Cleve, and Octavia all turned in unison and glared at Matt. Yep. Toothless as a baby. "Since we're off schedule anyway, you might as well," Matt said and winced at the callousness of his words.

Daniel joined the others in glaring at his friend. "She'd eat if we had to wait all day."

"Shannon works for me, not you," Matt said.

"If you refuse to let her eat, perhaps she'd like a change of employment," Daniel said, his brown eyes narrowed.

"Thank you for your concern, Daniel, but not eating was my fault," Shannon explained. "I overslept, but Matt took it upon himself to bring something out to me."

"I don't need you to defend me," Matt snapped. How did she know he had brought her some food? One glance at a smirking Octavia and he had his answer.

"Matt, if you're gonna get anything done today, you need to let this child and your guests eat breakfast," Octavia said in a placating tone. "It wouldn't hurt to introduce everyone either."

Calling Daniel's crew over, Matt did just that. By the time hands had been shook all around, his temper had cooled considerably. "Cleve and Griff have the horses ready to leave in ten minutes. Does that meet with everyone's approval?"

Daniel was the only one brave enough to say yes.

Grabbing Shannon's arm, Matt went into the kitchen. Octavia, Daniel, and his two men followed. Daniel removed his hat.

Shannon gasped. A cascade of salt-and-pepper hair fell over his shoulders and down his back.

"Lord a mercy," Octavia breathed.

Daniel smiled his killer smile. His men exchanged long-suffering looks as if they'd been through this before.

Matt's jaw tightened. He had forgotten about Daniel's secret weapon.

Although he was only thirty-two it was lightly streaked with silver. His African-American mother had given him just enough curl in his hair to make it interesting. His Creek father had given him the pride to wear it stylishly cut in front and offer apologies to no one. In the summer months when he was traveling and doing African-American western heritage research, he usually let his incredible hair grow long.

"Your hair is beautiful," Shannon said. "You must create quite a stir."

Daniel took a seat beside Shannon. "Depends on who's in the room with me."

Octavia hooted and set a plate in front of Shannon. "A sweet-talking devil if I ever heard one. You watch this one, Shannon child. Slippery as they come."

"Don't worry. I'm on to Daniel."

"So, tell me Shannon. What leads a beautiful woman like you racing back to work on a ranch?" Daniel asked mildly.

"It's a long story." She glanced sideways at Matt.

Thanking Octavia for the cup of coffee, Daniel leaned his muscular frame closer. "I've got time. Carter. Price. Finish your coffee and check to make sure everything is ready."

The two men were gone in seconds. It was all Matt could do to stop himself from telling Daniel he had seven minutes. Then, he heard Shannon repeating the same story she had to the church congregation. She ended by saying she had a week of vacation left.

"Earlier you said something about being ready to ride out. What exactly do you do on the ranch?" Daniel asked.

Shannon sipped her coffee. "Anything Matt asks me. Mucking stalls, riding fence, clearing brush."

"What a waste," Daniel said meaningfully and shook his mane of salt-and-pepper.

Shannon flushed and lowered her head.

"Daniel, remember your nose. Shannon, I thought you were hungry." The other man smiled.

Shannon picked up her fork, then dug into her scrambled eggs. "Just like old times."

Matt was in a bad mood.

And it had worsened as the day progressed. Shannon looked at him through the fringes of her lashes as he stood off to the side of Wade's cabin with Daniel. Matt's jaw was so tight you could bounce a racquetball off it.

Sighing, she glanced around the flower-strewn meadow and tried to recapture the peace it once gave her. All she saw was Matt. Hard and unyielding. Her eyes briefly shut in misery.

Maybe she shouldn't have come back. Maybe she had misinterpreted what she saw with the binoculars. If having her here was making him unhappy, she had to leave.

But how could she walk away from her heart again?

After all the mental acrobatics she had gone through to come back, he seemed more remote than ever. Although her parents and Melanie thought Shannon was crazy when she told them about Matt, she hadn't wanted to give up on him. Not even after she officially broke off with James were they willing to listen. Surprisingly he took the news better than her family or Melanie. He wanted a devoted, obedient wife. Shannon clearly was going to be neither.

Her mother and Melanie's conspiracy was the reason she was late this morning. First her tickets were misplaced, then Melanie called to say she had a flat on her car. Shannon had missed her flight.

She had made another reservation and taken a taxi to the airport. She had come back to try one last time to win Matt's love, only to discover despair greater than she had ever known.

She glanced down and saw an area where some of the flowers were bent and broken, and remembered sitting in the grass, Matt kneeling beside her, pushing her to face her fears and meet life head on. Out of nowhere she recalled her grandfather's telling her, if it wasn't worth fighting for, it wasn't worth having.

Her head came up and around until she saw Matt, one hand propped against an oak tree, his handsome brown face intent, the sleeves of his white shirt rolled back over his forearms, faded blue jeans taut over muscular thighs. The sight of him would always cause her heart to race faster, the air in her lungs to stall, but it was the man beneath who called to her, who she wanted to touch and love.

She had seen handsome men before. She had never met a man who called to her soul as Matt did. He needed love and laughter in his life and she had to be strong enough to risk giving it to him.

Taking a deep breath, she moved toward the men. Daniel's brow lifted questioningly, Matt's face remained implacable. "If you wanted history, Daniel, you couldn't ask for better than the original Taggart home."

"I couldn't agree more. I've decided to come out later this afternoon and film it against the setting sun," Daniel told her. "Then in the next frame get the ranch house. I can't think of anything stronger to show how one family kept and increased their heritage over four generations."

Matt sent Shannon an icy glare. "What belongs to a Taggart should stay that way."

"It will," she said with more calm than she felt.

"Black roots on the Texas plains go back even further. A Spanish census in 1792 stated that it had two hundred and sixty-three black males and one hundred and eighty-six black females in its populations of sixteen hundred, yet to read some of the history accounts you'd never know it," Daniel said, the intensity clear in his voice. "They won't be able to ignore the films."

"How long do you plan to be here?" Matt asked.

"Think you can put up with me for a couple more days?" Daniel answered with a smile in his voice.

"No problem." Matt tugged his Stetson. "Come on, we better get back to where they're filming the men ride herd."

"I still think Shannon should have been in that shot. Women were and are just as important to our history as men," Daniel told him. "Don't you think so, Shannon?"

"I agree with you about the history, but the Circle T belongs to Matt. It's his call." Shannon stuck her hands in her pockets. "I just work here."

"You've done very little of that today," Matt said tersely.

Her hands whipped out of her pockets. "You're the one who wouldn't let me help repair the barbed-wire fence. And you're the one who said I couldn't help with the herd."

"With good reason," he roared. "You're also the one who banged her thumb. A two-year-old is more coordinated than you are."

"You should know about two-year-olds. You've been acting like one all day," she snapped.

Daniel roared. "She's got you there, man."

"Nobody asked your opinion," Matt snarled.

Palms up, Daniel tried to smother his laughter. "Leave my nose the way it is. I'm the narrator for this project. But if you insist, I'm sure Shannon will nurse me back to health."

"I'm going back to the herd." Matt mounted his horse and rode off.

Shannon shivered. She had only made things worse. "I'm sorry. I didn't mean for you to get caught in the middle of our disagreement."

"Don't be. You're making progress with him."

She went still. "I—I don't know what you're talking about."

He studied her a long moment. "Are you going to deny you're in love with that stubborn cowboy who just left here?"

"Oh, no," she groaned in embarrassment. "If . . . if you guessed, then Matt surely knows."

"Your secret is safe with me." His led her to the trunk of a fallen tree and sat down beside her. "Besides, Matt's so busy trying to deny his own feelings he can't see anything else."

Her gaze clung to his. "You think so?"

"Trust me on this. I haven't seen Matt for about six months, but I've been with him enough to know how he is around women." Daniel shook his head. "I've never seen him possessive before."

Shannon sighed and dropped her head in defeat. "For a while I thought you might know what you were talking about."

Strong fingers lifted her chin. "Matt watches you like a hawk. You're not riding with the herd because he's afraid you might accidentally get hurt, the same for the barbed-wire. It's wicked stuff."

Her smile grew until it reached her eyes. "You think so?"

"Positive. I've made a study of my friends who fell in love so I won't fall into the same trap."

"Love isn't a trap," Shannon said with feeling. "Love doesn't bind, it heals."

"For some people, but not for me." Daniel pulled her to her feet. "We better get going. I like the way my face is arranged."

Brushing off her jeans, she started to where their horses were tied to a scrub oak. "Matt's not the jealous type."

"You'd be surprised at what some people will do when they're pushed far enough." Daniel's face harshened. His eyes were as sharp and as piercing as talons. "Never underestimate your opponent."

"B-but Matt's not my opponent. He's the man I love."

"Anytime someone withholds something from you that you want, they become your opponent."

Shannon was not sure if she liked the hard-sounding man in front of her.

A shift of his mouth, a flash of strong white teeth, and the jovial Daniel reemerged. "Ready to go?"

"Matt was right. You can be ruthless."

"If I wanted you as much as Matt does, I wouldn't deprive myself. I'd kidnap you like my father did my mother and damn the consequences."

She gasped.

"Just teasing."

Shannon got on her horse, then looked at Daniel. Something about the lingering glint in his eyes made her wonder if he had been telling the truth after all.

CHAPTER 18

Matt's booted feet pounded out a steady but uneven beat as he stalked the length of his study from the heirloom rug in front of the massive stone fireplace to the hardwood floor that stretched to the door. With every step his fury grew. A fury so hot the air seemed to crackle around him and block out everything but the cause, his deplorable lack of control whenever he was around Shannon.

He couldn't deny he had been ridiculously pleased to see her drive up this morning. But his pleasure had quickly turned to unbridled jealousy when Daniel began paying attention to her.

Matt clenched his fists remembering his behavior when the three of them were at Wade's cabin. His crazy feelings for Shannon were hindering his ability to think clearly. He had been ready to punch Daniel out. He still might do it.

Ever since they joined him at the herd, she had been casting those comforting glances of hers at Daniel. Somehow he had managed to get to her. If Falcon touched her, he'd have more than a broken nose to worry about!

Shoulders sagging, he stopped in front of the fireplace and clamped his hand over the mahogany mantel. Shannon was making him crazy. She had to leave and soon, but the thought of never seeing her again made him just as crazy.

Emotions as confused as he'd ever known, he did the one thing he thought might help. He dialed his brother's number.

Kane never lost control. Well, except for the time Victoria, his wife, almost got hurt at the rodeo arena. Kane had lost it then, but good.

The phone clicked as someone picked up the receiver. Instead of a greeting, Matt heard the beckoning sound of a woman's laughter, the husky command of Kane's voice telling her to hang up.

The polite thing would have been for *him* to hang up. Matt leaned back against the corner of his desk. Come to think of it, there was another time Kane hadn't shown very much restraint. That time also concerned Victoria.

Two months after Kane and Victoria were married, Matt had entered the back door of their house without knocking and caught the two locked in a heavy-duty embrace. Kane's bare broad shoulders blocked his wife's body except for her slender arms clinging to her husband's neck.

When Kane turned to face him, Matt had been sure if he had been any other man seeing Victoria in only Kane's shirt, he would have been seeing the emergency room next.

Victoria's laughter abruptly ended and pulled Matt back into the present.

He grimaced. After three years of marriage and two kids you'd think they'd be used to each other. A picture of Shannon popped into his mind. His body hardened. Maybe a lifetime wasn't enough.

"Kane. Victoria. Cut it out. This could be Mama or Victoria's grandmother," he said into the receiver.

"Matt?" Victoria said breathlessly, "Is that you?"

"Good-bye, Matt," Kane growled.

"Kane, stop that," Victoria ordered. "Matt, is everything all right? It's after ten."

Too late Matt remembered that because of the twins, Kane and Victoria asked family members and friends not to call after nine unless it was important. "Yeah, I just need to talk to Kane."

"This better be important, Matt," Kane grumbled as he came on the line.

Matt smiled. "Hello to you, too, big brother. Catch you at a bad time?"

"It's a good thing I can't get my hands on you now."

"I had that same thought."

"I talked with Mama, Daddy and Addie this morning. Everything all right at the ranch?"

"Yeah."

"You're sick?"

"Nope."

A loud sigh came through the phone. "Did you have a reason for calling?"

"At the time I called I did," Matt said, unable to keep his uncertainty out of his voice.

"You all right?" Kane asked sharply, his irritation gone.

How do you tell a man you've looked up to all your life that a woman has scared the hell out of you? "I guess. I don't know."

"I can have Howard ready the plane and be there in three hours."

"Aren't you in the middle of a major marketing campaign with your company?"

"You're my brother."

Matt's chest felt tight. Those three words had carried him through some hard times. He felt the same.

"Matt?"

"I'm here. How are the twins?"

"Ruling the house as usual. They'd love to see their favorite uncle."

"Their only uncle."

"They couldn't have better."

"Glad you think so." Lights passed his window. Shannon was home. "I gotta go."

"Matt?"

"Yeah."

"I'm here. Whenever you need me."

"I know. Good night. Sorry for the interruption." He dropped the receiver back into the cradle. Talking with his brother only confirmed what Matt already knew: women sure changed a man's life.

He glanced over his shoulder at the account book and grimaced. If he didn't get to it soon, he'd never get caught up.

There was a brief knock on his door before it opened. Daniel, his eyes glowing with excitement, entered with Shannon next to him. "You won't believe what just happened."

Shannon had yet to look at Matt. "Perhaps you'd like to tell me."

"I just got a call from Bracketville. If I can get there by Wednesday afternoon I can meet with two of the descendants of black Seminoles whose ancestors were scouts." Daniel was almost dancing.

"I guess they finally forgave you for being part Creek," Matt said absently, his gaze on Shannon.

Her head came up. "What has that to do with anything?"

Daniel grinned. "Seminoles and Creeks were bitter enemies. One of the reasons the Seminoles resented being on the reservation so strongly was probably their placement next to the Creeks. That and the government's refusal to recognize the black Seminoles as part of their tribe," Daniel explained. "Their resistance in the Florida swamps lasted eight years. The black Seminoles fought bravely and led beside their Indian brothers in the Seminole War."

"I read about the black or Negro Seminoles in a couple of Wade's books on blacks in the West," Shannon said. "Black men and women fled to Florida for freedom, then eventually came to Texas after the government tried to force them on reservations. They came by way of Mexico in the 1850s?"

Matt nodded. "They were intelligent and fearless. Because of their knowledge of the Indians, firearms, and horses, it was natural for some of them to become scouts for the Army. The Commanches were a fierce group in Texas, but the black Seminoles met them head on. Three of the scouts received the Medal of Honor, the highest for combat bravery."

"That's why it's such a shame that many of them have become main-streamed into society. Much of their culture and their unique language of African-rooted Gullah dialect mixed with Seminole, Spanish, English and French Creole is in danger of being lost forever. I'd like to capture it before that happens," Daniel said with fierce determination.

"You will. We'll be ready to ride out at eight sharp and work straight through to get you finished," Matt told him. "You can pull out Wednesday morning."

"I knew I could count on you. Thanks." Daniel left and closed the door behind him.

Shannon took a step toward the door. "I'll be going. Oh, Daniel was on his way to see you when I pulled up and insisted I come with him to see you. I guess he wanted me to hear his good news, too."

"You two seem to have developed quite a friendship," Matt's tone sounded accusatory instead of casual as he had intended.

"Daniel is a complex man," she answered.

Her answer told him nothing and keeping her there was too danger-ous. She looked too tempting and he was too hungry for her. "I'll see you in the morning," he said dismissively.

"Good night."

"Night," Matt muttered, and watched her close the door.

The way he saw it, he had two choices, make love to Shannon and hope once was enough or keep on fighting the urge and let the ranch go to pot because he couldn't think of anything else. Slowly the tension in his body eased. He owed it to four generations of Taggarts to see that it didn't happen.

There was something different about Matt. It wasn't that he wasn't ig-noring her or that he and Daniel were acting like Monday had never hap-pened, it was something more subtle. Once he caught her watching him at the breakfast table and the look he gave her all but melted her into a puddle.

Shannon was still trying to figure Matt out when she followed him to the barn for her orders. Remembering the day before, she was sure she'd be left behind to clean the stalls. Seeing Cleve sitting tall in the saddle surprised and pleased her. Matt hadn't forgotten about the proud, older man.

"Mount up, Shannon."

Her lower jaw became unhinged as she turned to Matt, but he was getting on his horse. She glanced at Daniel for a possible explanation and found herself staring into the lens of a camera. Praying her sudden nervousness didn't cause her to mess up, she swung up into the saddle.

Beside her, Cleve nodded his approval.

"I've got the best crew in Texas. Let's show people what ranch life is all about," Matt said, meeting the eyes of each hand, then Shannon's. In the next moment he was riding off. She felt so proud of him, tears pricked her eyes. He deserved to be loved.

Daniel or his cameraman kept one or both of the cameras going all day. Everyone on the ranch was captured on film. Whether the cameras were stationary or shoulder-held, they were constantly rolling. Even their short lunch break under an oak tree was recorded. After they had eaten, Matt had sent her back to the ranch. She hadn't minded. She had her own agenda for the rest of the day.

Once she learned Octavia didn't need her, Shannon drove into town for some shopping, then headed back to the cabin. Near sundown, she surveyed the room with a pleased smile.

The three-legged chair had been replaced with a new one, which had a peach throw pillow for a cushion. The table remained, but its scarred surface was covered by a peach-colored twin sheet overlaid with one panel of a lace curtain. All the material pooled on the freshly scrubbed floor. On the table next to a bouquet of wildflowers in a clear vase was, according to the hardware salesman, the strongest battery-powered light made.

Her gaze strayed to the bed that now had enough nails to attract a magnet from fifty yards away. But it was sturdy enough to withstand Shannon bouncing up and down on its new six-inch-thick layer of comfort. Draped over the newly screened window was the other panel of her lace curtain. More nails on either side of the window anchored the swagged material.

She had left the stove and apple crate filled with wood once she cautiously checked both to make sure no vermin had found a home there. In the corner sat her most inspirational idea. An ice cooler, filled and waiting.

Everything was ready to carry out her plan.

After one last look, she closed the door and got in her car. A distant rumble of thunder sounded overhead. She eyed the sky apprehensively. Rain wasn't going to make things easy for her.

When she got back to the ranch Matt and Daniel were sitting at the kitchen table. Afraid Matt might be able to read her as easily as Daniel, she concentrated on his friend. "How did everything go?"

"Fantastic. The shooting is a wrap," Daniel said. "We're all going out to celebrate. Including you."

"I can't. I have to see a couple of patients," Shannon told him, unable to keep the disappointment out of her voice.

Daniel stood and draped both arms over her shoulders. "I won't take no for an answer. Matt and Octavia have already cleared things for you." Dropping one arm, he turned her toward Matt. "Tell her she has to come or our celebration won't be complete."

The tentative smile on her lips died. Matt's face held a furious expression.

"You seem to have more influence over her than I do." Matt stood and left the room.

"If I thought you did that on purpose, I'd hate you," she told Daniel, her voice and body shaking.

Daniel's eyes narrowed. "Go get dressed. Wear something that will put a smile on Matt's face."

She didn't move. "Don't ruin this for me just because you don't believe in love."

He drew in a sharp breath. "You learn fast, Shannon. Never let anyone stand in your way. Matt is a lucky man to have a woman who will fight for him."

"One day you'll be just as lucky."

His smile was as cold as his eyes. "Luck won't have anything to do with it. Now, if you'll excuse me. I'll go change. And I promise to stay out of your and Matt's way."

Shannon's facial muscles ached from her forced smile.

A woman's high peal of laughter rang out in the quiet family restaurant. Shannon flinched as if the sound were a lash across her back. Heads turned toward Shannon, not the woman. Shannon felt the pitying gaze of every person at her table. They were all witnesses to her humiliation.

She felt conspicuous in her peach-colored slip dress, auburn curls cascading from the crown of her head. She had wanted to look beautiful, wanted Matt to notice her. Instead, people had only noticed how foolish she was. Hands clenched beneath the table, Shannon blinked her eyes to keep the stinging moisture at bay.

"If I thought it would do any good, I've give him the fight he's asking for," Daniel said tightly. "I'm sorry."

Shannon gave a slight nod to indicate she'd heard the comment. If she opened her mouth she couldn't vouch for her control. Dessert had been served; all she had to do was hold on a little longer.

"Thank you for the party, Mr. Falcon, but I think I'll call it a night."

Cleve tossed his napkin on his plate and stood. One by one he was joined by the other men. Their dessert was barely touched.

"Let's go, child," Octavia said.

Shannon didn't move until Daniel's hand grasped her by the elbow and pulled her upright. She swayed. His arm circled her waist. She jerked away.

"Would you rather crumple in front of him and that bitch who's crawling all over him?" Daniel hissed.

Shannon leaned against Daniel. Somehow she made her feet move past Matt and the woman he had gone to sit with a short time after their party was seated. He had remained there for the rest of the evening. That was the cause of her humiliation.

Outside, Daniel led her to her car. "Give me your keys."

"N-no, I—"

"I'll get them." Octavia took Shannon's purse, located the keys and handed them to Daniel. "I'll ride back with Cleve. Don't you worry about a thing."

Opening the passenger door, Daniel helped Shannon inside, then went around and got in. He started the engine and took off. "I'll say this once. I'd take you with me, but I don't think you'd enjoy living with three men. But I have several homes around the country and friends with more property in and out of the country. In the morning tell me where you want to go and one of my jets will get you there. No strings for as long as you like."

Shannon said nothing. It wouldn't matter where she was, the pain would follow her, ripping her apart, killing her. She had gambled and lost.

Once at the ranch house, she went upstairs to her room, grabbed a few things, then came back downstairs. Cleve, Daniel, and Octavia were still in the living room talking softly.

"I can't stay here."

Cleve stepped toward her. "I'll drive you wherever you want to go."

Shannon fought tears. "I . . . I'm going to the cabin."

All three protested.

"Please. I can't be here when he returns." She took a steadying breath and tightened her hold on her blanket roll. "I've worked on it all afternoon."

"Shannon, there's a storm coming," Octavia said.

"I'll be fine." She walked past them; no one tried to stop her. She wasn't surprised to see headlights in her rearview mirror as she drove to the cabin. Either Cleve or Daniel or perhaps both wanted to make sure she reached the place safely.

She had friends and family who loved her. She was grateful, but at the moment it couldn't stop the pain.

He had shown Shannon he didn't care about her, so why did he feel like someone had kicked him in the gut? Matt's hands clamped and unclamped on the steering wheel as he pulled over the cattle guard to his ranch and stopped.

Because you sent her straight into Daniel's arms.

Matt hadn't missed how closely Daniel held Shannon or how she leaned into him. They could be in Daniel's motor home now. Rage swept through Matt as he pressed on the gas and took the road to the left.

He couldn't see the two of them together. Daniel wasn't the type to trespass on another man's territory. Matt could have set Daniel straight, but pride and uncertainty had kept him quiet.

Now Shannon was in the arms of another man.

And Matt felt like someone was tearing out his insides. He hit a rut without slowing. When the truck stopped bouncing, he noticed a light where there shouldn't have been one. He frowned. Where could the light be coming— the cabin.

His frown deepened as he saw Shannon's car reflected in his headlights. She didn't like the darkness. She hadn't mentioned sleeping in the cabin since Sunday before last. Why would she suddenly decide to come up here at night?

Only one answer came to him. The same reason his wife had gone to motels. Rage swept through him. Matt stopped in front of the cabin and slammed out of the truck.

The pounding of the door mixed with the rumble of thunder. "Daniel, you have five seconds to get out here or I'm coming inside."

"Go away," came the shaky sound of Shannon's voice.

"I'm not leaving until I see Daniel."

"Daniel isn't here."

"Then you won't mind opening the door."

"Go back to that woman in the restaurant and leave me alone," Shannon told him, her voice oddly muffled.

"I'm not going to ask you again."

The door jerked open. Shannon, her quilt wrapped around her shoulders, stood in the doorway, tears glistening in her eyes. "All right, come in and look, then get out."

Matt's gaze never left Shannon's. "I thought you were through crying."

Shannon looked away. "Leave."

"Not until you tell me why you're crying." Automatically he dug his handkerchief out of his back pocket and handed it to her.

She flinched from the white cotton square as if it were a snake. "I want nothing else from you."

The words sliced him to his very soul. "Shannon, talk to me. Is . . . is it

Daniel? Are you crying because of him? I saw you two leaving the restaurant?"

Fire flashed into her eyes. "So naturally you assumed we'd run to the nearest bed."

"Shan—"

"Don't touch me," she shouted, jerking away from him. Tears streamed down her cheeks. "Not after you let that woman touch you. Did you enjoy humiliating me?"

"Shan—"

"Did you?" she interrupted sharply. "If you had really wanted her, you wouldn't have stayed in the restaurant. I finally figured that out. You stayed to punish me because you thought I liked Daniel." She shook her head. "Didn't you realize you could hurt me only if I cared about you?"

Stunned, Matt tried to understand what Shannon was saying.

"Somehow, someway, I'll get over it, though. That's a promise. I'm leaving in the morning and I never want to see you again." She shoved the door closed.

CHAPTER 19

The flat of Matt's hand kept the door from closing. "You've had your say, it's time for me to have mine."

"What could you possibly have to say that I'd want to hear?" she cried, her eyes blazing again.

"I don't want you to leave."

Shannon went still.

Matt closed the door. "I didn't mean to hurt you. I didn't even know I could. I was trying to protect myself, not hurt you."

"Protect yourself from what?"

"From you, what else," Matt shouted and yanked off his hat. "You started to disrupt my life the moment I found you asleep in the meadow looking so damned innocent and beautiful."

"You really think I'm beautiful?"

He meant to glare at her idiotic question, but she looked so unsure of herself it was all he could do not to drag her into his arms. "I can't think of anything more beautiful."

"Matt," she whispered.

Unable to resist he took her into his arms. His lips found hers, and her mouth opened, welcoming him. Her arms slid around his neck. The quilt fell to the floor.

Faintly, he heard the patter of rain against the asphalt roof, felt the rain-cooled air coming through the open window. His arms tightened as he drew her closer, his lips moving to the curve of her cheek, her slender neck. He couldn't seem to get enough of her, he wanted to fulfill his fantasy and taste her everywhere. Before the night was over, he promised himself he would.

Shannon couldn't get close enough. He had come to her. He really cared— she sniffed and almost choked at the cloying perfume. She stiffened. He had come straight from that woman!

"Let go of me!"

"What?" The haze cleared and he stared down into Shannon's angry face. "What's the matter?"

"You lied to me." She pushed out of his arms.

"I told you, I don't lie." Arms folded, she looked sultry and beyond beautiful in her long white nightgown. He wondered if she knew the diaphanous material revealed the curves and shadows of her body.

"What you care for is the meadow," she finally said.

"I wouldn't sleep with you to get the meadow."

She snatched her arms to her side. "Don't flatter yourself. I'm not as easy as the woman you obviously just left. Her perfume is all over you. Go back to her."

"I didn't go to bed with her."

Shannon's chin lifted. "Who you sleep with is no concern of mine."

"Who *you* sleep with is damn sure my concern. If the scent on the shirt is bothering you, I'll get rid of it."

Pulling the shirt out of his pants, he unsnapped the fasteners in front, stalked to the door and tossed the shirt into the rain. When he turned, Shannon was watching him with wide, uncertain eyes.

Her gaze roamed across his chest, then lower where hair thickened and disappeared into his jeans. Lower still to his obvious arousal. She snapped her head up. She swallowed. Any other man she would have shown the door. Matt was too sensually masculine, too handsome . . . and she loved him too much. She shook her head in silent defeat.

"You're right about one thing, if I really wanted Irene I would have left. I used her as an excuse to get away from the table. For the first time in my life I was jealous of another man. I wanted to punch Daniel out and take you to the nearest bed."

Her sharp intake of breath cut across the room.

"You scared me as much as you drew me to you. My ex-wife soured me on women. I was foolish enough to believe in everlasting love and fidelity. She taught me differently with any man who could buy her more than I could."

"Matt, don't."

The words had been held in too long to be contained. "I was so blinded by lust, I would have done anything to make her happy. Working two jobs and riding the rodeo circuit on the weekends was worth it as

long as she was happy." His face and tone harshened. "I bragged to anyone and everyone what a wonderful, loving wife I had. Then I caught her
with her boss at a bar next door to a motel I learned she frequented."

Shannon went to him, her arms going around his waist, hugging him
tightly. His hand brushed a lingering tear from her cheek. "She was a stupid, vain, petty woman. And she fooled me completely."

Hearing the contempt and bitterness in his voice she leaned back and
looked into his set features. His ex-wife had done more than make him
mistrust women, she had made him doubt himself. "Her mistake, not
yours. You don't expect lies and deceit when you give love. She tried to
ruin your life. Don't let her succeed. I'd never use you."

"Not intentionally."

She frowned at his phrasing. "I wouldn't hurt you at all."

"I don't want to talk about it." His head dipped, his lips finding the
sensitive hollow in the curve of her neck.

Shannon shivered. "Matt, we need to talk."

He nibbled the lobe of her ear. "Later."

"No, now." Using the last of her strength she pushed him away. Ebony
eyes blazed down at her. "I need for you to believe me."

"Shannon," he said tightly.

"I need to hear you say it."

"You won't hurt me," he said, his lips taking hers.

Shannon's thoughts stumbled and fell. Matt's arms went around her,
she felt the softness of the bed against her back, the hardness of Matt
above her, pressing her down.

Before she had time to be nervous, their clothes were gone and he was
kissing her as if he'd never get enough of her. His mouth left hers and
she whimpered at the loss. Then, his avid lips closed around her nipple
and sucked. Shannon arched off the bed, a low moan coming from the
back of her throat.

All her senses were alive to the touch, the lingering taste of him on
her lips. Sweat beaded on her brow. There was something she had to tell
him.

"Matt, I . . . I . . ."

"Shh. I want you to want me as much as I want you."

"If . . . if you did, you wouldn't torture me this way."

He laughed, a deep, husky sound that teased her heated flesh. He
feasted on her lips again. When she thought she could endure the aching
hunger no longer, his mouth came back to hers and at the same time his
hips thrust once, sharply.

The ache became pain. Her body tautened, her fingers flexed, then
closed. Nails bit into his muscled shoulders.

His body stiffened. He stared down at her with a mixture of wonder,
amazement, and joy. "Why?"

Shannon's hands trembled as she touched his lips, the curve of his jaw. "Because I was waiting for you." The same wonder, amazement and joy were echoed in her words.

He tenderly smoothed the hair from her sweat-dampened face with a hand that trembled. "I waited just as long."

Before she had time to decipher his words, he moved again, pulling away from her quivering warmth only to return, each slow thrust longer and deeper. Again and again he measured the velvet length of her, driving her to sweet madness, driving her closer to something she had never experienced before.

Her legs locked around his hips. Soon she felt her entire body tense, gathering like a giant storm cloud. When her release came it rocked her. A scream tore from her throat. Moments later Matt found his own release.

Shannon slowly surfaced from her haze. She opened her eyes to see Matt's intent gaze on her. She shyly lowered her gaze.

"You all right?"

She nodded.

"You mind looking at me?"

Her eyelashes lifted. He was frowning. Her heart twisted. "I disappointed you."

"If you had disappointed me any more, I'd have had a coronary," he replied, a slow smile spreading across his face.

She threw her arms around his neck. He let her pull him down on top of her, their laughter filling the small room. She shoved him away again, her eyes shining.

"What's the matter?"

"You never laughed with me before," she confessed. "I can't believe it. I wanted your smile and your laughter, now I have them."

His brow quirked as if to say that wasn't all she had. Shannon ducked her head. "W-would you like something to drink?"

"Not if it means I have to let go of you to get it."

"I'll get it," she offered.

His thumb brushed across her lower lip. "You'd still be out of my arms."

"I didn't think of that."

"Wonder what was on your mind?"

Her hips moved against his burgeoning arousal. "Same thing that's on yours."

He blinked, then laughed out loud. "You're right, but that's about as far as it's going to go. My mind. I don't have a way of protecting you again."

Puzzlement turned to a smile. Once again, she was pushing on his chest. Matt moved off her. She picked her purse off the floor, rummaged inside, then without looking at Matt, handed him something.

Matt glanced down at the two small foil-wrapped packets in the palm of her hand and picked them up. Shannon plopped down on the bed, dragging the comforter with her, her gaze fixed on the flower arrangement.

His gaze followed. Shannon had turned the dingy cabin into a cozy room. His hand fisted. "You planned to move out of the house."

"I planned to kidnap you," she said quietly.

"What?" Thumb and forefinger turned her face to his. "Repeat that."

"I figured if I could get you alone, you might forget you didn't quite trust me."

The foil crackled. "And these?"

"You never know what might happen."

"Shannon?"

"Yes?"

"How many times can this happen?"

Grinning, she reached under the bed for a paper sack, then emptied the contents on the bed. Five boxes of condoms tumbled out.

Matt laughed and drew her down on the bed. "That'll do . . . for a start."

"No."

"Come on, Shannon, it won't be so bad."

"How do you know? Have you ever done something like this before?"

"Of course not, but—"

"I can't."

Sighing deeply, Matt held Shannon in his lap, her head beneath his chin. She was the most stubborn woman he had ever met . . . and he cared for her more than he ever thought possible. "I'm not leaving you here alone."

"You could stay with me."

"If I stayed, we'd be in bed and I'd be loving you most of the night."

Warm brown eyes stared up into his face. "Would that be so bad?"

Somehow he resisted the urge to kiss her. "Honey, I've been at you for most of the night. You need a warm soak and a soft bed. If we stay here, we'll be back in bed with me inside you in no time."

She wound her arms around his neck and kissed it. "I'm not complaining."

"Shannon, stop that." His tone brooked no nonsense. "You have your gown back on and we're having this talk in this chair instead of bed, because my control is being held by a thin thread as it is. I'm taking you back to the ranch house."

"I couldn't face Octavia." Snatching her arms down, Shannon stood. "She'd know, and so would everyone else."

Standing, Matt pulled her into his arms. "No, they wouldn't."

"They'd have to be blind not to see when I look at you my legs get weak and I go limp all over."

"Fortunately you have the opposite effect on me."

"Matt, be serious."

He kissed the top of her head. She fit perfectly against him. He felt protective and possessive. His woman. Only his.

"Once we get to the ranch house you'll go straight to your room. In the morning I'll tell everyone I went to your room to apologize for last night and discovered you weren't feeling well. In light of how I acted, I insisted you stay in bed the rest of the day."

"I can rest here."

"And everyone will be worried. Octavia and Cleve are probably tossing in their beds worrying about you," he reasoned. "If they see your car in the morning that will put their mind at ease. Think of them."

She bit her lower lip. "They were worried and so was Daniel."

Matt hadn't wanted to include Daniel. Matt took her dress from a nail hook and handed it to her. "Hurry up. I'll tidy up the place."

She gathered the light rayon dress to her chest, but made no move to take off her nightgown and put it on. "I couldn't stand it if they looked at me any differently."

The uncertainty in her face tore at his heart. "That won't happen."

Still clutching the dress, Shannon walked to the bed and slipped off one shoulder of her nightgown.

Temptation was a woman called Shannon.

Clutching Matt's hand, Shannon followed him through the front door of the ranch house and up the stairs. With every step she expected Octavia to appear and ask where they had been. Or more to the point, what they had been doing.

To make matters worse, she had been so worried and distracted, she didn't realize she hadn't put back on her panties and strapless bra until they were outside the cabin and the rain-scented air touched her skin. She had been nervous all the way to the ranch house, and her nervousness increased with each beat of her heart until they were in front of her room and Matt opened her door.

"See. No problems." He handed over her quilt. "Rest and sleep late. That's an order."

Shannon watched Matt turn away without so much as a kiss on the cheek. She needed his kiss, his touch, to reassure her things would work out for them.

Halfway down the hall, he glanced over his shoulder. In several long strides he was back by her side. "Stop looking at me that way."

She dropped her gaze and heard him swear. She flinched at the harsh sound.

"If I kiss you, we're going to be in your room and in your bed and I won't care if the entire county comes banging on your door. Do you understand?"

She did. She felt the same way when he touched her, out of control and loving every second of it. "Yes."

"I can see I'll have to do this myself. Come on."

Shannon followed him into her bathroom. Hunkering down, he turned on the faucet over the tub, then dumped in a generous portion of bath salts. Foaming bubbles immediately formed, but Shannon was more interested in the play of muscles on Matt's shoulders and the loving way his jeans cupped his hips.

Matt dipped his hand in the water, then held the fading bubbles to his nose. "My tub is bigger. We'll have to use it sometime."

The picture of them naked in the tub weakened Shannon's legs and sent desire racing through her. Her hand gripped the corner of the built-in wash basin to keep upright.

Swiping his damp hand on his jeans, he came to his feet. "Do I need to make sure you get in?"

"No," she choked out. "Thank you."

"Good night." He brushed past her.

The bedroom door closed. Shannon released her grip on the quilt, slipped off her dress, and stepped into the scented water. She'd never understand Matt's mood changes. He went so quickly from caring and gentle to gruff and distant.

Some time later, Shannon climbed out of the tub and dried off. Putting her clothes away, she slipped into a white satin nightshirt. Although she was tired, she didn't want to go to bed. Walking over to the window, she stared out. Except for the single light in her room, darkness surrounded her.

She had never felt so alone and lonely in her life, not even when her grandfather died. Tears stung her eyes, but she told herself she wouldn't cry. Matt did care for her. Letting her rest made perfect sense; she just wished leaving her hadn't appeared so easy for him. Eyes closed, she fought the tears and loneliness.

The creak of her door opening snapped them open. *Please don't let it be Octavia.* She couldn't stand— "Matt."

His gaze captured hers and they simply stared at each other. Wearing only black pajama bottoms, his hair damp from the shower, he looked as uncertain as she felt. That small hint of vulnerability touched her as nothing else could.

The tears she had been trying to contain slipped from her eyes and rolled down her cheek. Closing the door, he was across the room in seconds, holding her securely against his bare chest.

"Shh. Don't cry." His broad hand swept up and down her back. "I don't have a handkerchief, so stop that."

Nodding, Shannon inhaled his clean scent and clung to him. No matter how he pretended otherwise, he was as unsure as she.

"Knowing how new you are to this, I thought you might feel abandoned." He pushed her gently away. "I'm going to stay with you, but that's all. Tomorrow you're going to stay in bed and rest."

She nodded again. He looked so stern and held her so gently.

He led her over to the bed and pulled the covers back. "Get in."

He didn't have to tell her twice. The light on the nightstand went off, throwing the room into complete darkness. The mattress dipped, his arm loosely circled her waist. Taking his hand in hers, Shannon scooted backward until the solid warmth of his body stopped her.

"Shannon, cut that out."

She settled against him with a contented sigh. "Good night, Matt."

Early the next morning, Matt carefully withdrew his arm and his body from Shannon's sleeping warmth and slipped from her bed. He hadn't slept a solid thirty minutes the entire night. Every time he moved, she moved with him, wiggling her hips against him until he was as hard as a rock. The only thing that kept him from burying himself deep inside her was the knowledge that she was asleep and didn't know how she affected him.

And she wasn't going to know.

Without looking back, Matt quietly let himself out and went to his room to dress. Shannon made him feel too much. He'd known from seeing her face when he left the bathroom, she felt deserted. He'd lain in bed staring at the ceiling for as long as he could.

Except for his ex-wife he'd never spent the entire night with a woman, preferring to wake up by himself. He'd gone to Shannon because of a desire to comfort her that was too strong to deny.

Shoving open the swinging door to the kitchen, he went straight to the automatic coffeepot. He grimaced. No coffee. Looking through the cabinets didn't yield any, either.

Matt had a hunch it was more than an oversight on Octavia's part. After last night, he'd be lucky if she fixed anything for the next month. That might work to Shannon's advantage. As long as Octavia was upset with him, she'd have less time to notice Shannon. He didn't want her upset. He scowled at the protective, instinctive thought and opened the back door, then abruptly pulled it closed.

Going to the window, he watched Shannon pause near the back of Daniel's motor home. Equal parts of jealousy and annoyance swept through him. She was supposed to be resting, not going anywhere near

Daniel. Matt didn't know he had held his breath until she passed the hood and kept going. Air gushed over his lips as he watched her.

The saucy spring in her walk was gone. Instead, her movements were more deliberate. He remembered the reason, the open generosity of her body. She had touched him as no other woman ever had and her stubbornness set his teeth on edge.

Seeing Shannon disappear behind the barn, Matt headed out the door. She was going to rest if he had to tie her in bed. His gaze on the spot where Shannon had disappeared, he didn't hear Daniel until the other man spoke.

"You look like you're in a big hurry."

Matt never slackened his pace. "I am."

"When you catch up with Shannon don't make her cry again," Daniel told him, a slight edge to his voice.

Hands fisted, Matt spun to face Daniel, who was leaning against the front of the motor home. "Stay out of something that's none of your concern," he ordered.

"I was worried about her last night, so I drove up to the cabin and saw your truck. You two didn't come back until hours later."

Matt went still. "Mention one word of this to Shannon and I'll tear you apart."

"Do you really think I'd do that?"

"No," Matt clipped out.

Daniel studied his manicured nail, then glanced up. "So when's the wedding?"

"I'm never getting married again."

"Does Shannon know that?" he asked mildly.

"Daniel, you don't want to push me this morning."

"I saw her face last night when you were with that other woman. Shannon doesn't understand how the game is played. She's too honest to use subterfuge, too good to hurt someone intentionally." Daniel laid his hand on Matt's tense shoulder. "This could blow up in your face."

"I know what I'm doing."

"I really hope you do. For some men there's only one woman." His expression hard, Daniel walked into the motor home.

Matt shrugged off Daniel's warning and started after Shannon. He had made no promises and Shannon hadn't asked for any. It was easy to confuse love with lust. He knew.

He took the steps two at a time at the bunkhouse, then knocked on the door. "Cleve, it's Matt. I'm looking for Shannon."

"Just a second," Shannon called, but it was more like sixty before she answered the door. "Good morning, Matt."

Her gaze was centered on his chest. Cleve remained at the table, a cup of coffee in his hands. Matt glanced down at the top of Shannon's head. "I thought we agreed you were going to rest."

"I'm resting sitting down."

She thought of others before she thought of the consequences to herself. But she had given him her word. "I won't argue semantics with you, Shannon. Can I trust you to keep your word or not?"

Her head lifted. "After I leave here I was going back to my room."

"Yes or no?"

Hurt flashed into her eyes before she glanced over her shoulder. "I'm not feeling as well as I thought, Cleve. Do you mind if we put the lesson off?"

"Don't worry about me, Miss Shannon. You go on back to the house."

Stepping around Matt, she went down the steps. His gaze followed. He noticed everything about her, particularly the slight droop of her shoulders. He had meant to push her into going to bed, not hurt her.

"Pretty hard on her, weren't you?"

Matt sighed. Another of Shannon's champions. He had had enough, but when he saw the censure in the eyes of the man he respected and loved, all Matt said was, "She takes too much on herself sometimes."

"That's the kind of woman she is."

"Today she rests."

"Glad to hear your concern. I took a drive out to the cabin last night to check on her."

Knowing what was coming, Matt groaned. At least Octavia wasn't with— "Were you alone?"

"Yep. Good thing I was, too." Cleve's eyes were as hard as jagged glass. "A man has certain responsibilities. Don't you go forgettin'."

Matt's ears and face grew warm. With unnecessary haste he went back down the steps. And Shannon had worried about them seeing *her* face.

CHAPTER 20

Shannon heard Matt's footsteps behind her and paused in front of the kitchen door. She hadn't meant to break her promise, she had only wanted to help Cleve. Somehow, Matt had to understand.

A hand reached around her and opened the door. "Go on inside."

She faced him. Dread pounded through her as she saw his harsh expression. "I know how important trust is to you. I don't want you angry with me."

"You were supposed to stay in bed."

"Matt, I admit I'm a little sore, but that's no reason to become an invalid," she told him. "Frankly, you look more in need of rest than I do."

His eyes narrowed. "Something kept me awake last night."

"What?"

"You using me as a back warmer."

Shannon flushed, her gaze lowering. "Oh. I didn't . . . er, realize. I'll be more careful tonight—" She laced her trembling hands together.

"If you rest today, you won't have to."

Her lashes lifted. What she saw caused her breath to catch. In Matt's hot gaze was a desire barely held in check, a hunger that matched her own. Her fingertips lifted to press against his lips.

"Not if you don't want to shock Octavia and everybody else within sight," he said roughly.

"Can I touch you tonight?"

"Anywhere and everywhere."

Shannon shivered and withdrew her hand. Silently she entered the kitchen and tried to calm the wild cadence of her heart, the need churning through her body. Not wanting to leave him, she started for the coffeepot. "No wonder you're so grouchy. I'll fix you some coffee."

"I couldn't find any. We must be out."

"That's impossible, I opened a fresh bag yesterday." Looking in the usual spot where the coffee was kept revealed nothing. Undeterred, Shannon opened the cabinet over the refrigerator. "Eureka."

Matt plucked the can off the shelf. "I can handle it from here."

He was certainly being protective and stubborn. She worked hard to keep from grinning. She took the coffee. "I'd like a cup myself. I'm also hungry."

"I cook worse than Cleve."

Shannon laughed at his disgruntled expression. "I heard. Now sit down and stay out of my way." After preparing the coffee, she took out two big skillets. "I'm sure Daniel and his men would like breakfast before they leave," she explained. Opening the refrigerator, she removed a package of butter, a can of biscuits, rolled sausage, and some bacon.

"I can cook for them," he said, a smile in his voice.

"If you don't mind, I'd rather not have to use my nursing skills this early in the morning," she said drolly. "I wouldn't want to tax myself unnecessarily."

Black eyes narrowed. "You'll pay for that."

She laughed. "Oh, Matt. Where's your sense of humor?"

"Gone South."

She laughed so hard her stomach hurt. Who would have thought Matt had a sense of humor? She leaned her head against his chest and felt his body shaking with his own laughter.

"Don't you dare forgive that scoundrel."

Shannon whirled to see Octavia, hands on ample hips, glaring over Shannon's shoulder at Matt. "G-good morning."

The housekeeper advanced on them with firm steps. "If I had my broomstick handy, I'd teach you a lesson about respecting women."

Shannon held her breath. Octavia knew.

"Shannon forgave me for my bad manners in the restaurant, why can't you?" Matt said.

"I'm immune to that smile of yours." She looked around the room. "That skillet will do just as good."

"Octavia, no," Shannon yelled and caught the other woman by the arm. "He apologized, really he did. He even gave me the day off because I'm not feeling well."

The housekeeper looked back at Matt. He hadn't moved. "See what you did."

"I know. That's why I'm not trying to stop you," Matt said calmly.

"Please," Shannon pleaded. "He apologized and just offered to cook breakfast."

"He did?" the older woman questioned, surprise in her voice.

"He did."

The expression on Octavia's face went from censure to approval. "It's about time you came to your senses."

Shannon didn't like the sound of that and from the way Matt's brows bunched, he didn't, either. She flicked on the gas burner under the skillet. "Octavia, do you think a pound of bacon is enough?"

"Better cook two." She beamed at Matt. "We don't want our men going hungry."

Rolling her eyes, Shannon began placing the strips of bacon in the hot skillet. Talk about jumping from the frying pan into the fire.

Matt unsaddled his horse and headed for the house. He tried to tell himself the account book was the reason he had stopped work so early in the day. He wasn't quite able to convince himself. Ever since Daniel left and Octavia mentioned Cleve was taking her into town to do some shopping after lunch, the thought of coming home and just holding Shannon had never been far from Matt's mind.

It was going to be dangerous as hell to hold her and not make love to her, but worth every nerve-wracking moment. He was crossing the den when he noticed the door to his study ajar.

Shannon. She was probably searching for something to read.

Opening the door, he saw her lying on her stomach on the couch, a pencil poised in her hand, staring at his account book. He had let his body rule his mind. Look where that had gotten him. Now she knew everything about the ranch's finances.

"Looking for anything in particular?" he asked.

She jumped and almost fell onto the floor. Eyeing him warily, she sat up. "I was hoping to have this finished before you came home."

"I don't like anyone working on the accounts except me." The door snapped shut.

Anguish flashed across her face. "I should have asked if you wanted my help." Picking up the hand-held calculator and the account book, she placed them back on his desk.

He stepped in front of her when she would have left the room without speaking again. "Where're you going?"

"My room," she said softly, her gaze meeting his squarely.

"Sulk all you want, but I haven't changed my mind about tonight."

"I don't remember asking you to. At least when you make love to me I don't have to see the mistrust in your face," she told him.

The anger left as swiftly as it had come. He didn't understand her. He had offended her, but she was staring at him as if he was all in the world that mattered to her. His hand curved around her neck, anchoring her, searching for deception in the depth of her eyes, hating the thought of finding it.

"A woman's body doesn't lie as easily as her tongue."

"Let me go."

When he did, Shannon picked up his hands and placed them over her breasts. Never taking her eyes from his she curved her arms around his neck and pressed her lower body against his. "I'm ready to take a lie detector test."

Before he had a chance to reason, to think, his hands closed around the soft mounds, his thumbs stroked over her nipples. Her breasts blossomed in his hands, the tight bud of each nipple straining toward his hand, seeking. Some force compelled him to look down to where he held her.

The erotic sight of his hands on her made him feel humble and tender. A desire so strong it shook him to the deepest level of his soul coursed through him. She wore another of those loose-fitting blouses. This one was made of some kind of turquoise clingy material that hung off the shoulder. All he had to do was . . .

His hand opened, then he hooked one finger over the top of the scooped neck and tugged. The blouse slid down revealing the lush swell of her naked breast.

"Y-you better ask your questions while I'm still able to think."

"I thought I was." One arm slid around her waist as his tongue stroked across her nipple. Then he sucked long and hard.

"M-Matt!" He caught her in his arms as her legs went out from under her. "M-maybe we should do this sitting down."

"You want to continue?" He couldn't keep the surprise out of his voice.

Her arms tightened around his neck. "Whatever it takes. Besides, you may look ready to shake my teeth out, but you only touch me with gentleness."

"Why would you say something like that?" he yelled, fighting the tender warmth of her words.

She kissed his cheek. "Because it's true. Even with the test, you didn't grab and take, you gave to both of us."

"You confuse the hell out of me," he admitted grudgingly.

"You're not so easy to understand yourself."

He eyed her. "I'm a reasonable man, and if you don't stop smiling I'll drop you."

"I'm going to give you a chance to prove it. But first I think you better put me down," she requested.

He put her down. She drew her blouse up on her shoulder and backed away a couple of steps. "That bad?" he asked.

"Not if you're going to be reasonable, and I hope you are because what I'm about to say also concerns me." She took a deep breath. "I couldn't help but notice that buying the bull almost depleted your operating expenses for next month. Since the meadow is a part of the ranch—"

"Name your price for the meadow and I'll get it," he cut her off, his voice cold and curt.

She continued as if he hadn't spoken. "I think it's only fair that I pay my share of the operating expenses. I didn't get a chance to figure out the percentage, but you and I could come up with a figure. Of course, I also insist on helping with the taxes."

Stunned. When he opened his mouth, nothing came out.

"I am a junior partner and you're the one who told me how integral one part of the ranch is to the other." She fidgeted when he continued to remain silent.

"You want to give me money?" he finally got out.

"It seems only fair."

"It also doesn't make sense. Unless you plan on keeping the meadow." She clasped her hands in front of her. "My vacation is over at the end of the week. When I leave, the meadow is yours."

"Where had you planned on getting the money? Daniel?" He didn't wait for an answer. His face became harsher with each word he uttered. "I don't need any help taking care of the ranch. That's not what I want or need from you."

She flinched, but her eyes flared. "No, you don't want any woman's help. You want an obedient bedmate. Shall I lie on the desk or on the couch?"

The torment of her words, the sparkle of tears in her eyes, lanced through him. He handed her his handkerchief and she snatched it out of his hands. Why did her tears always get to him? "I didn't mean that the way it sounded."

She sniffed. He touched her and she moved away.

"You want to give me a lie detector test?" he asked.

"I'd rather punch you in the nose."

"Then you'd go get me an ice pack and defeat the whole purpose." When she didn't bother to deny it, Matt shook his head. Shannon was generous, kind, and easily hurt. Too soft for a hard man.

"Maybe we shouldn't discuss the ranch or the meadow for the time being," she suggested, removing the last traces of tears with his handkerchief.

"Maybe not."

She bit her lip, her face solemn. "Would you like some lunch?"

She was also polite, kind, willing to forget, to forgive. She was too soft-hearted for her own good. It was about time someone tore those rose-colored glasses off her eyes.

The world was cruel and life sure as hell wasn't fair. And most men were heartless bastards when it came to getting a woman into bed. He stood at the head of the line.

"I've got a better idea." He picked her up, laid her on the couch and followed her down, planting soft, fleeting kisses on her lips, her cheek, the curve of her cheek. Nearing her mouth, but never fully joining their lips.

With a little whimper Shannon arched against him and tightened her arms around his neck, trying to bring his mouth to hers.

The honest need in that sound rocked his body and made a liar out of him. He wasn't teaching *her* a lesson, she had taught *him* one. Even heartless bastards had a conscience with the right woman.

Lifting his head, he stared into her eyes. "Do you know why they call me Hardcase?"

"What has th—"

"Do you?"

"Wade said it was because nothing affected you. That your emotions were encased in ice."

"You should have listened. I kissed you just now to teach you a lesson that men and life aren't going to play fair. Hell, I sure didn't. Last night I wanted you and I took you," he said tightly.

She punched him as hard as she could on the shoulder. To her increased anger, he didn't even grunt. "Of all the arrogant braggarts. You didn't take anything. I *gave*. I am sick and tired of people thinking I'm some kind of nitwit because I try to be nice. Get off me!"

"Shan— Ohhh." From his sprawled position, Matt watched Shannon head for the door.

He reached it before she did. For some reason, he couldn't stop grinning. "Now, honey, don't get so upset."

"I'm not your honey and that smile is wasted on me."

"I was only trying to protect you."

Her arms crossed over her chest. "By insulting me. Get real."

He looked uncertain. "It sounds kind of strange I guess, but I was angry that you forgave me so easily after I hurt you. I was trying to teach you to be less forgiving, but when you made that little sound in the back of your throat, I couldn't go through with it."

Smiling, Shannon launched herself into his arms. "Matt, that's the nicest compliment anyone ever gave me."

"Trusting isn't easy for me, Shannon."

"I know." Her tongue stroked across his lower lip. "So we'll work on something we both enjoy and go from there."

His mouth sought hers, his lips molding against hers with gentle pressure in a kiss as slow as it was deep. With a little sigh, she opened to him, luring him deeper to explore at his leisure the taste and texture of her mouth's sweetness.

He couldn't seem to get enough. Then it was her turn to savor him. The tentative glides and strokes of her tongue became more aggressive, more demanding.

His hands in her hair, he gave her all she asked for and more. When he finally lifted his head they were both breathing hard. He stared into her passion-filled eyes and pressed his forehead to hers.

"You go straight to my head, among other places."

Shannon stroked his back. "You seem to have the same effect on me."

Sighing, he reluctantly opened the study door, the other hand draped loosely around her waist. "Will you come to the cabin with me tonight?"

"Yes."

He kissed her. Shannon was nobody's pushover, and for the time being she was only his.

Shannon was nervous. With each rotation of the truck's tires taking them closer to the cabin, her agitation mounted. It was one thing to agree to a rendezvous but quite another to deliberately carry it out under the nose of people you respected. She had never snuck around like this in her life. Although she wanted to be with Matt, she wished it could be different.

His continued silence wasn't helping.

She cast a glance at the shadowed profile of the man sitting next to her. He'd only spoken two words to her since she arrived back at the ranch tonight: "You're late." He had proceeded to put her in the truck parked a little ways from the house and drive off.

The truck came to a halt. Matt cut the motor. "I'll see about some light."

Without waiting for an answer, he got out and went inside. After what seemed like forever, he came back and opened her door. The light coming through the window was barely discernible. She started to ask him about her lantern, then decided perhaps it was best they couldn't see each other clearly. Whatever closeness they had shared earlier was gone.

Head down, she let him lead her to the cabin door, praying, hoping, when he took her into his arms, the power and passion of his touch would make everything all right.

Two steps inside the cabin, she came to a dead halt. Her mouth formed a silent O of wonder. She couldn't believe it. Scattered around the cabin were more than a dozen large candles. Peach fragrance permeated the air. On the table was a bottle of wine in an ice bucket and two long-stemmed glasses.

"Say something," Matt demanded.

"I—it's beautiful."

"If you cry, I'm going to blow out all these candles and keep my surprise," he told her.

Shannon brushed the moisture from her eyes and gave him a watery smile. "Thank you."

Going to the ice chest in the corner, he lifted the lid, came back, and shoved a bouquet of spring flowers at her. "Here."

Shannon glanced at the bouquet, then at Matt's stern expression. Her brows furrowed. Matt didn't do anything he didn't want to. Yet, he acted as if he had been dragged kicking and screaming all the way. The reason hit her all at once.

He was as nervous as she was. Not about coming here, but about how she would react to his gifts of tenderness when he wanted her to think he was incapable of such acts.

More than anyone she knew he needed and deserved love, but he would deny it with his last breath. His willingness to be vulnerable to please her calmed her fears and strengthened her love.

"Matt. How did you know?"

"The more Octavia dropped hints about us during dinner, the more subdued you became. By the time you left tonight, your chin was dragging on the floor." His shoulders hunched. "You looked like you could use some cheering up."

She wanted to know how he'd thought of the scented candles, but most of all she wanted to be in his arms, his lips on hers. She lifted her face to his.

His mouth was hot and soft and utterly intoxicating. She could kiss him forever. The taste, the feel of him curled through her body as much as the slow building of heat.

He lifted his mouth enough to mutter, "What about the wine?"

"I'd rather taste you."

His eyes narrowed and darkened. "We'll take turns."

"Anywhere and everywhere," she breathed softly.

Matt's entire body went still, then he repeated her words: "Anywhere and everywhere."

His lips took hers and it was a long time before either thought of anything, but each other.

CHAPTER 21

I'm in trouble.

And Matt didn't have the foggiest notion of how to get out. He had come up against unpredictable calves, killer broncs, blind judges, bad weather, failed crops, deceitful people, but nothing had prepared him for Shannon.

In the four days since they had become lovers she had gotten under his skin but good. It wasn't just the sex, though Lord knew it was hot enough sometimes to blow his mind, it was Shannon herself. He had never met a woman more open, more generous, more compassionate, or more attuned to his needs. A lot of the time, he lay awake just holding her, listening to the even sound of her breathing, feeling oddly content.

But then there were times he was as greedy for her body as he was for her teasing smile, her disarming laughter. The shape of his jeans changed just looking at her. He worried about her when she was out of his sight. Like now.

He'd been pacing the porch for the last fifteen minutes waiting to catch a glimpse of Shannon's headlights. Last night she'd flatly refused the escort any longer. At the time she'd presented her argument, he was on his back in the hay. She was straddling him, her blouse hanging open with nothing underneath except temptation, her lips working their way down his chest. He'd agreed before she reached his navel.

He had taken her to the hayloft instead of the cabin because he re-membered her comment about not understanding how people could make love in the hay. He had planned to show her. Instead, they had ended up showing each other.

Her vacation would be over this weekend and she'd be gone. The thought of her leaving filled him with an anger which made no sense. He refused to dwell on it. The ranch was what mattered. In the distance he saw a flash of light. Excitement and anticipation drummed through him.

He took a step off the porch before he realized it. He paused, only then measuring the undeniable response of his body to a woman he didn't completely trust. How had he forgotten the lesson his ex-wife taught him?

Letting another person have control over your emotions was asking for a kick in the teeth. He had to remember that. Stepping back up on the porch, he turned to go into the house, then noticed the headlights were different.

The late-model sedan stopped directly in front of the house. The door on the driver's side opened and out stepped a broad-shouldered man a good three inches taller than Matt.

"Gazing at the stars or wishing on one?" drawled a deep, velvety voice.

"Kane." The brothers met halfway, hugged unashamedly, smiling at each other. "What are you doing here this time of night?"

"Visiting my brother," he answered.

Matt's eyebrow lifted. "If it's about the call, I have everything worked out."

"Glad to hear it." Kane reached into the front seat and drew out a small suitcase. "That'll give us more time to catch up."

Matt, who knew how stubborn his older brother could be, turned toward the house. "Come on inside."

"Looks like you've got more company."

Those headlights Matt recognized. Shannon. He cast a quick glance at his brother. This was going to be as tricky as hell. "She works here."

"What is she doing here so late?"

"She happens to live in the ranch house," Matt explained. Although Kane didn't say anything, Matt felt the weight of his stare.

Shannon stopped behind Kane's car and got out, her smile tentative, her lower lip tucked between her teeth. Kane, used to people being fascinated or intimidated by his size, backed up closer to Matt. Her gaze widened, slid to Matt, then away.

Matt realized their relationship, not Kane's size, was causing Shannon to chew on her lip. When they were alone, she held nothing back, but around other people he often caught the dread in her eyes that someone would find out they were lovers. No matter how much he told her they had nothing to be ashamed of, he wasn't able to convince her.

From the suitcase in Kane's hand, it was obvious he was staying. As much as Matt loved his brother, he wasn't going to let her get all tense. He might not completely trust her, but no one was going to cause her be uneasy, not even Kane.

Stepping forward, Matt gave her a smile hot enough to melt steel. The change in Shannon was instant. Her eyes softened, her lips parted.

"Keep that thought and you'll be all right," he whispered.

"If I don't melt first."

He grinned and brought her to where Kane was standing. "Shannon Johnson, Kane Taggart, my brother."

Shannon extended her hand first, her smile open and warm. "Hello, Kane. I've heard a lot of good things about you."

His large hand completely enclosed her smaller one. "Hello. Apparently you weren't talking to my brother."

Matt noticed the way Shannon's eyes widened, her head tilted to one side as Kane spoke. His voice and his size always demanded a second look. It annoyed him a little to know Shannon was affected, too.

"Octavia," she finally admitted.

"Come on, let's go inside." Matt's hand still in the small of Shannon's back, he led the way into the house.

Shannon stepped away from Matt as soon as Kane closed the front door. "Good night. I know you two must have a lot to talk about. I'll just let Octavia know I'm back."

"She adopted you, too," Kane said with a smile.

"Yes. Good night again."

As soon as she disappeared through the swinging doors, Kane started for the study. "I need to call Tory and see how she and the twins are doing."

"How long have they been out of your sight? Three hours?" Matt said drolly and followed his brother inside.

"Laugh all you want. Your turn is coming." Kane picked up the phone. "Real soon, it seems."

Matt tensed. "What do you mean?"

"Shannon is a beautiful woman."

"She's okay, I guess."

Kane replaced the phone without dialing, his laughter booming around the room. "Matt, your eyes were following her like a homing device. And she was trying so hard to keep from looking at you, I kind of felt sorry for her."

"You must be really tired to be seeing things." Matt flung himself into the chair behind the desk.

"Daniel said you were in trouble, but I never thought it had anything to do with a woman."

Matt came out of his chair and around the desk in a flash. "Daniel needs to keep his mouth shut and stay out of my business."

"Since he usually does, his call this morning concerned me a great deal." Kane folded his arms and leaned against the desk. "He was worried that you were going to mess up somehow. He wouldn't be specific. Now I understand what he meant."

"The only reason he's meddling is because he wants Shannon for himself," Matt blurted, then scowled at his admission.

"From the little I saw, it's *you* Shannon wants. And for her to be staying here with Octavia's obvious approval, she must be a nice young woman."

"That nice young woman wants to steal my land!"

Kane straightened. "What?"

"She was Wade's nurse when he was in the hospital in St. Louis. He left her the meadow. All she came here for was the land."

"Is she going to sell it back to you?"

"She claims Wade left it to her to help her get her life back together and once her vacation is over the end of this week, she's going to just sign it over to me." He stalked across the room. "I'm not that big of a fool."

"I don't know, Matt. Wade was a pretty good judge of character."

"Not when it came to women. Shannon can twist men around her little finger without trying. You see how quickly you jumped to her defense," Matt accused tightly.

Kane studied his younger brother intently. "Are you angry because you're scared you love her or angry because she has a claim to part of the ranch?"

"I'd rather be kicked in the head by a bronc than let another woman tear my heart out. Shannon can leave tonight for all I care. The only thing I care about is keeping the ranch intact," Matt hurled.

A small gasp had him turning toward the sound. Shannon stood in the doorway, a tray of sandwiches and iced drinks in her hands. Anguish bracketed her tightly compressed lips. She stared mutely at Matt. He sensed she wanted—needed—him to deny his words, but he couldn't.

"Matt," Kane said. "Don't let the past ruin this for you."

Matt walked to Shannon. He had tried to warn her. "I'm too hard to care for anyone. The ranch is the only thing I need."

With a whimper of pain, she thrust the tray at him and fled up the stairs.

Matt's hands clenched the wooden tray. His chest felt tight.

"You're a fool if you don't go after her."

"Just let it go." Matt placed the food on the coffee table. "The bedroom across from mine is empty. I'll be back in a little bit."

"Need some company?"

"No thanks." The tightness of his chest increasing with each breath, each step farther away from Shannon. Finally he reached the front door and opened it. Surprise widened his eyes.

Victoria Taggart gasped, then smiled on seeing her brother-in-law.

"Hello, Matt. I didn't know the twins and I were making that much noise coming up the steps."

A stunned Matt barely had time to glance down at the sleepy-looking toddlers leaning against their mother's legs, before he was brushed aside.

Kane scooped up a child in each arm. Their drooping lids drifted closed as they settled against the familiar muscular warmth of their father. "Tory. I thought we agreed you were going to stay home."

Victoria, stunning in a white linen suit accented by gold jewelry, smiled into the scowling face of her husband. "It's a woman's privilege to change her mind. Give me a kiss before I start thinking you aren't just as happy to see me as I am to see you." Catching him by the narrow space of shirtfront between the twins, she pulled his head down to hers.

When she released Kane, he reluctantly lifted his head. "That wasn't fair."

She smiled ruefully. "It wasn't meant to be. We've never spent the night apart and the more I thought about it, the more I knew I didn't ever want to."

"I wasn't looking forward to it, either," he confessed.

"Then it's a good idea I had the foresight to expect such an occurrence and get flight reservations and rent a car to get me and the children from the airport," she told him.

Kane chuckled and kissed her on the nose. "This is what I get from being married to a businesswoman. Sassy and smart. Don't ever change."

"Hello, Victoria. Excuse me and make yourself at home." Matt stepped around the happy couple. It wasn't envy he felt. He didn't need a woman's love.

"Is he all right?" Victoria whispered.

"No, and he's too stubborn to admit it."

Matt walked faster. It was best, safest, to be alone. All he needed was the ranch. Getting in his truck, he drove off. The strange tightness in his chest somehow had moved to his throat.

With trembling hands, Shannon threw her possessions into her suitcase. She had to get away before she completely broke down. If she let the tears start, she didn't know if she'd be able to control them. The only person who could help was the man who had caused them.

The searing knowledge eclipsed everything else. Her love hadn't been enough to heal his heart as he had helped to heal hers. If she thought there was a chance, she'd stay. If only they had more time, if only the meadow wasn't between them, if only his first wife hadn't scared him so badly. If only . . .

Snapping shut the overstuffed suitcase, she groaned under its weight as she picked it up. She'd have to come back for the rest of her things.

Closing her door softly, she made her way quietly past Matt's room and his study.

Outside, she breathed easier, but the tension returned when she saw Matt's truck missing and a car parked behind hers. Getting her car out would be a tight squeeze. She had no choice, though. The alternative of facing Matt was too painful. Putting her luggage inside the trunk, she went back upstairs for her overnight case and her quilt.

She was on her way back downstairs when the door across from Matt's room opened. Kane. She wanted even less to see the man who had witnessed her embarrassment.

He stepped into the hallway. Shannon was sure she didn't make a sound, but he suddenly looked over his shoulder and saw her. His gaze immediately went to the case in her hand. Softly he closed the door.

"I don't guess I can get you to reconsider."

Trembling fingers tightened on her luggage. "No."

"Where do you plan to spend the night?"

"One of the hotels on the interstate."

"What if there aren't any vacancies?"

Shannon stared straight ahead. "I'll manage . . . be fine."

"That may be, but I can't let you leave."

"What!"

"Running away is not going to solve things between you and Matt," he said bluntly.

"You heard him yourself, he doesn't want me," she whispered, the words making her ache.

"He wants you too much. That's the problem."

Shannon refused to let herself hope he was telling the truth. The bedroom door Kane just closed opened. He turned in that direction.

She started for the stairs. Out of the corner of her eyes she caught a glimpse of a woman, then she heard Kane call her name. Her speed increased. She had to get away.

"Shannon. Stop!"

She swung around, the case banging against her leg and throwing her off balance. She was too close to the landing. Her eyes widened as she dropped the things in her hand, her arms windmilling to keep her balance.

Kane's hand shot out to grab her a second too late. She felt herself falling backward. A scream tore through her throat.

Her body hit something hard but yielding. She heard a muffled sound and felt the shock of landing. Her body trembling, she shut her eyes.

"Say something," demanded Kane.

Shannon opened her eyes to see Kane and a beautiful woman kneeling by her side. Both of their faces were filled with concern. "I . . . I'm only winded."

"How about you, Matt?"

"I'll live."

Shannon tensed. The sound had come directly behind her. Rather beneath her. The warmth and hardness of a man's chest, Matt's chest, came through her clothes. She had fallen on top of him.

She scrambled to her knees beside him. Her hands ran over his chest, his arms. "Do you have any trouble breathing? Does anything hurt? Dizziness?"

"Yeah," Matt said.

"Where?"

"Here." He laid his hand over his heart.

Shannon hadn't dared let herself look at his face. Now she slowly allowed herself to do so. In his eyes she saw a tenderness he made no attempt to conceal.

"You . . . you must have bumped your head."

Matt sat up, his arm going around her waist. "For once I'm thinking straight. You can take those things back upstairs."

"So that's all you want." She pushed out of his arms and reached for her overnight case. Matt pulled her back in his arms, and before she could do more than gasp, he held her down with his body. "Let me go."

His grin infuriated her. "I'm not that big of a fool."

"Matt, are you all right?" Victoria asked.

"Never better. If I'm not, Shannon can take care of me. She's a nurse."

"Couldn't you tell from the way she was so, ah . . . thorough in checking him over," Kane said with a smile in his deep voice.

Shannon groaned. She wanted to disappear through the floor. It wasn't fair that they could laugh at this any more than it was right for her body to betray her. Her nipples had hardened and she had to grit her teeth to keep from arching her hips toward his.

"You want me to use my broomstick, child?" Octavia asked. "I heard all the commotion in here and grabbed it just in case."

"Told you twern't necessary," Cleve pointed out.

"Why are you here then?" the housekeeper questioned.

" 'Cause I saw all them cars, and then after the boss left I got to thinkin' somebody might be sick or something," the ranch hand answered.

Matt glanced around to see Octavia in her robe and Cleve by her side. He felt Shannon tense, then wiggle her body trying to hide under him. He wished she'd stop that. He wanted her bad enough as it was, and if he stood up everyone would know it.

"If you don't mind, Shannon and I would like some privacy," he finally said.

"Matt's right," Victoria agreed. "Octavia, Cleve, good night. We'll talk in the morning."

After exchanges of good nights, there was silence.

"Get off me!" she snarled.

Matt came to his feet and immediately swept Shannon into his arms and held her securely against his chest.

She glared at him. "I'm leaving no matter what you say."

"If I can find the right words, I don't think you'll want to."

Shannon was so surprised by what he said that she didn't resist when he carried her into the den and sat in his desk chair with her in his lap. Opening the drawer, he took out the account book, a second larger thin blue leather-bound book, and a brown folder.

"The ranch is the only thing I ever owned that gave back. Even when I'm working sixteen hour days, the ranch brings me a sort of peacefulness I've never known before. I never thought I'd need or want anything more until I saw you asleep in the meadow." His hand stroked her from hip to shoulder and she was powerless to withhold a shiver of response.

"I tried to control my feelings, but it was as useless as trying to hold the wind. I didn't want to believe your kindness didn't have a price. Even when we made love, I refused to believe you just wanted me. It was easier to look for deceit in you than face my own feelings. Diana, my ex-wife, had taught me too well. Before tonight I didn't even want to say her name and I became enraged if anyone else did."

So that's why everyone referred to her as "that woman." Shannon turned in his arms. "I understand, Matt. You don't have to explain. I know you gave me all you could. You can't love me the way I love you."

His hand paused, then began the slow steady glide again. "When you ran up those stairs, I felt like a vise had clamped around my chest. I didn't know what it was until I drove to the cabin, walked through the door and realized we'd never be there together again."

He set her away, his hands cupping her face, a tender smile on his. "Do you know what it was, Shannon?"

Too full to speak, she shook her head.

"It was my heart breaking free. Diana doesn't have any power over me any longer because you banished all the anguish with your unconditional love. Daniel was right when he said for some men there is only one woman. For me, you're that woman." His knuckles gently brushed across Shannon's damp cheek. "I finally figured out it wasn't you who I didn't trust, but myself. I love you, Shannon. Only you. With nothing held back, no reservations."

"Oh, Matt, I hoped, I prayed. I love you, I love you," she repeated, overjoyed to finally be able to say those precious words aloud to him. The flow only stopped when his mouth covered hers hungrily.

After a long time he finally lifted his head. With one hand, he pulled the books closer. "Nothing I own will ever be off limits to you again. My checking account should reassure you that I can take care of the ranch in a crunch, and if not, my investment portfolio can. It's just that I want the ranch to be self-sufficient."

She never took her eyes from his. "Then I guess I'll have to come clean, too."

A moment of wariness flickered in his dark gaze, then it was gone. "Shoot."

"My great-grandfather and Granddaddy Rhodes loved land also. In fact, they sort of collected it. Some of it turned out to be very valuable. When Granddaddy died, he left a large chunk of his estate to me."

"You're rich," he almost shouted.

"Like Octavia once told me, rich is relative."

"So you bought the Cadillac and diamond earrings for yourself."

"Graduation presents. The car came from my parents, the earrings from Granddaddy," she told him. "I'm really conservative with my money. You needn't worry that I'm going to waste yours, either. I'm not like my mother who spends hundreds of dollars on clothes and lingerie."

"Don't let Victoria hear you say that. At least not about the lingerie."

"Why?"

"She owns several lingerie boutiques, and from what Kane tells me, the prices are as high as a cat's back."

Shannon laughed at the dismay on Matt's face. "Don't worry, if I want something, I'll pay for it myself."

"You'll do no such thing," he told her sternly. "I can buy you whatever you need. In fact, I'm looking forward to it."

"Matt—"

"I mean it, Shannon, I can buy my wife her clothes and nightgowns. Not that you'll keep a nightgown on very long."

Her face glowed. "Your wife?"

"Yeah, and that's final. But I might as well tell you that I don't plan to sleep single until we're married. So we better have a short engagement."

"Anything else?" she asked, wanting to sound stern, but knowing she was too happy to hide her excitement. She had a very good idea how to get around any objections he might have.

"Yes, there is. This going around at night is going to stop. I know you love nursing, so you and the families will have to work something else out."

She kissed the frown from his face. "I think that can be arranged."

"We'll call my parents and yours in the morning." He looked thoughtful. "I better warn you. Before Kane and Victoria eloped, my mother and her grandmother were trying to plan their wedding for them."

"My mother will be just as bad." She smiled down at him. "I'd opt for eloping, but she'd never forgive me. She's waited too long for someone to put a Mrs. in front of my name."

He turned serious. "I'm glad you waited for me."

"So am I." Beguilingly, Shannon looked up at him through a sweep of lush lashes. "I know it's rude to leave house guests, but could we go to the cabin?"

Abruptly, Matt stood with her still in his arms and headed for the front door. "All you ever have to do is ask."

EPILOGUE

The bride was breathtakingly radiant in white silk satin and French alençon lace. And the groom was devastatingly handsome in a morning coat.

The mother of the bride and the mother of the groom cried through the entire candlelit ceremony. Everyone agreed it was the most romantic and beautiful wedding they had ever seen. No one remembered such a splendid array of flowers. The scented peach candles added a nice touch. And weren't the Taggart twins precious.

Kane Jr. refused to give the ring to his uncle and instead presented it to the best man, his father. That brought a chuckle from the father and a groan from the mother. Not to be outdone, his sister, Chandler, left the other bridesmaids and handed her father her empty flower basket.

The father had squatted down, thanked each child, then plucked the ring from the pillow and handed it to his brother. When Kane stood, both children were standing dutifully in front of their father, who somehow managed not to look awkward with a tiny flower basket in his powerful hand.

The two busloads of guests from Jackson Falls and the three from Tyler would certainly have a lot to talk about on their trip home from St. Louis. Imagine, three ministers had officiated. One from each of their respective towns and the bride's minister.

But the three ministers didn't stop the groom from giving his bride a kiss that was as boldly erotic as it was meltingly tender. No one expected them to stay long at the reception and they hadn't. Cleve Redmon, the groom's new foreman and groomsman, and Octavia Ralston, helped the newlyweds slip away. And didn't Cleve and Octavia look happy dancing and smiling up at each other. Could there be another wedding in the making? Time would tell.

While the wedding guests were downstairs in the Crystal Ballroom sipping on vintage French champagne, eating prime rib and lobster tail, and speculating on the absent newlyweds, the two in question were on the top floor of the five-star hotel in the honeymoon suite instead of the cabin the bride had requested. For once Matt had held firm.

Low, feminine laughter, followed by a deep masculine growl, came from the entwined couple in a tangle of sheets on the king-size bed. Bare skin touched bare skin. A kiss here, a nuzzle there. For once there was no rush to explore the other's body.

"I'm glad you talked me out of the cabin." Shannon nipped Matt's earlobe.

"No gladder than I that you decided to wear one of the nightgowns from Victoria's shop. Once my heart slowed down, I enjoyed it on you. Brief as it was."

"You were quite demanding," she laughed.

The smile slipped from Matt's face. "For a while, I didn't think I'd make it."

"I'm sorry, Matt. My family descended on the ranch the day after you called and mother insisted I come home."

Some of Matt's good humor returned. "Smart lady. She took one look at me looking at you and hustled you away. I thought I had her when I insisted I drive back with you. She nipped that in the bud by telling your brother to drive your car and you to take his plane ticket."

"She's a lawyer," Shannon said by way of explanation. "By the time you came to St. Louis we could have been together."

Matt shook his head. "No way was I going to take you to my hotel room. I knew you wouldn't feel comfortable facing your parents afterward. Besides, you deserved better than that."

Shannon kissed him. "I have the best. I have you. You'll have to thank Daniel for getting the ballroom for the reception, and the suite. I still don't know how he pulled it off on just two months' notice. Too bad he couldn't be here."

"My sister was disappointed, too. She thought she was finally going to meet him. When Daniel and I talked this morning he said the suite was a wedding gift and to stay as long as we wanted. That reminds me, I have something for you." Getting up from the bed, Matt went to the suitcase and brought back a thick white envelope. Ferguson & Ferguson letterhead stood out in bold lettering.

"Oh, Matt, I already took care of it." Not as comfortable with her nudity as her husband, Shannon slipped on her peach-colored lace gown before going to her suitcase. "With the wedding preparations I forgot to tell you."

Locating what she wanted, she came back to the bed and handed Matt the envelope. The letterhead on the outside of the envelope was also Ferguson & Ferguson.

"Now, the ranch belongs only to you," she said with a smile.

He nodded toward the envelope in her hand. "I think you better open that."

Frowning at the strange expression on his face, she opened the letter and gasped. Her startled gaze went to Matt. It couldn't be. It just couldn't be.

"It seems we've traded ownership. The ranch now belongs to you and I have the meadow."

Tears streamed down her cheek. "You can't do this."

"I already have."

"I won't have it. The ranch is yours. It belongs to you."

"It belongs to a Taggart and you're now a Taggart. You can pass the ranch down to our children just as well as I can." He kissed the tears from her cheeks. "It's still hard to believe Wade planned all this from reading one of Octavia's romance novels and that she and Ferguson were in on things from the start."

Shannon nodded and snuggled closer in his arms. "Octavia admitted she kept her romance books hidden because she was afraid you might find one, read the back, and figure things out. She certainly succeeded. I couldn't believe it when Mr. Ferguson gave us another letter from Wade after our engagement was announced. I hope he knows his plan worked and that we're so happy."

"I got a feeling he does, and your granddaddy, too."

"I never knew I could be this happy. I love you, Matt, but I'm signing the ranch back over as soon as we get home."

Grinning, he lay back on the bed and folded his hands behind his head. "I look forward to you trying to persuade me, Mrs. Taggart."

"So do I, Mr. Taggart." Coming to her knees, Shannon faced Matt. A sultry grin on her face, she began to slowly inch the lace nightgown over her thighs, past her waist, over her breasts. By the time the nightgown floated over her head to land on the plush carpeting, Matt knew he was in trouble. And he was going to enjoy every second of it.

The last coherent thought Matt had as Shannon staked her claim to his willing body was eternity wouldn't be long enough to love this unique woman of his. He wondered if she knew how special she made him feel, how loved. As soon as he got enough breath back into his lungs he was going to tell her and keep telling her every day of their lives.

She was his woman and he was only hers.

HEART OF THE FALCON

To Monica Harris, my extraordinary editor who has extraordinary patience. Thank you.

Special thanks to Nina Yancy and Alda Pool.
They know the reasons.

CHAPTER 1

Madelyn "Addie" Taggart awoke by slow degrees, turning from her left side to her back, then stretching languidly on the plush comfort of the king-sized bed. Slim arms circled her tousled head of shoulder-length black curls and rested on her pillow.

Slowly thick lashes lifted to reveal eyes the color of rich, dark chocolate. Leisurely she scanned her luxurious hotel suite. She was as impressed with her surroundings as she had been when she checked into the Hilton Palacio del Rio in downtown San Antonio yesterday afternoon.

Muted shades of beige and off-white suited the restful setting. Not one piece of carbon-copy furniture, assembly-line lamp, or misshapen, flimsy drapery marred the perfection of the room. The richness of cherry wood gleamed throughout. The lamps were heavy and brass. The draperies hung perfectly and closed snugly. And it was all hers for an entire weekend.

A smiled lit her caramel-colored face. Life was good.

At times during the past three years, she hadn't been so sure. Working as a production engineer for Sinclair Petroleum Company had been the ultimate test of her professionalism and her determination to succeed.

She had done it though. She hadn't let the gray-haired critics on the job intimidate her, or the good-old-boy system discourage her. She had taken whatever they had given her with a smile on her face and taunted them to bring on more. They hadn't known she had cried herself to sleep more than one night. Not even her close-knit family had known how difficult it was for her.

There were countless times she had wanted to call them or simply quit, but something within her, whether pride or stubbornness or anger, hadn't allowed her to do either. Her parents had always taught her life was what you made it. You took the good with the bad and succeeded in spite of everything and everyone.

Those words had sounded fine through high school and college with her family standing behind her. But on her own in a large corporation, they were scary as hell until she remembered the odds her older brothers, Kane and Matt, had had to overcome to succeed.

Being a woman wouldn't lessen her brothers' or her parents' expectations. God had given her intelligence, but she had to have the faith and the backbone to use it. However, it had taken a while for her to reach that realization.

She had thought she had been prepared for the cutthroat, dog-eat-dog world of business since she had done an internship at another large petroleum firm in Dallas. She had been wrong.

Then she hadn't been a threat to anyone. She had been the baby sister of Kane and Matt Taggart, both respected men of some influence and wealth. She hadn't traded on her brothers' names to get the job, but the first week Kane and Matt had just happened to drop by to take her out to lunch.

Separately Kane and Matt could be intimidating; together they were awesome. Both understood being a minority and female; some narrow-minded people put limits on her as soon as they saw her gender and her race.

She had known such people existed—she just hadn't known how overtly subtle and demeaning being treated like a nonentity could be. She soon found out, but she also discovered she had whatever it took to show the intolerant skeptics she wasn't going anyplace. The lesson hadn't been an easy one, but she had learned—and not once had she run crying to her family.

Her brothers' tendency to watch over her was one reason she had chosen to relocate to Houston when she graduated summa cum laude from Texas A&M University. Kane had expected her to come to work for him at his cosmetics firm, Cinnamon. But developing products to help some woman's lipstick stay on longer wasn't what she had gone to school five long years for. Actually the research was too tame.

She liked something a little more dicey. Like designing the pipelines to draw oil and gas out of new wells at different pressures and depths. Accountability was high. A mistake could cost millions and your job. With her company finding and developing new oil and gas fields, she was never idle.

Oil and gas, once the boon of the Texas economy, became the bane in the eighties. The nineties had heralded a comeback. The industry was coming on strong. Energy was back, and Madelyn was doing her part to see that it stayed that way.

Madelyn's smile widened as she glanced around the spacious hotel suite again. She had done well for herself in the three years she'd been at Sinclair. Too well to suit some.

Laughter bounced off the ivory-colored walls as she remembered the shocked expression of her immediate supervisor when she was named Employee of the Month. She had been almost as shocked.

Only people in management nominated employees, and she knew he'd eat dirt before he'd do that. Even saying her last name seemed to cause Carruthers difficulty. She always got the impression he wanted to substitute the *T* for an *M*.

So naturally when she accepted the plaque and the expense-paid weekend to San Antonio, she'd given him her brightest smile. His mouth had been drawn so tight, he'd looked as if he'd been eating alum.

After accepting the presentation, she had learned his immediate superior, Howard Sampson, submitted her name. Two months earlier she had been temporarily assigned to Sampson's team to help on a systems-analysis report.

Sampson was a hard taskmaster, but he didn't care about color or gender. He cared about results. He often commented he got his gray hairs the old-fashioned way—he earned them. She had enjoyed every minute working with him and had dreaded going back to work under Carruthers. Now she didn't have to.

Once she returned to Houston, she was being permanently transferred to Sampson's department. Best of all, she had done it all by herself, without the help of her brothers.

She thought of the bouquet of roses from her parents, the silk nightshirt from Kane and his wife, Victoria, and the ten-pound box of her favorite chocolates from Matt and his wife, Shannon, that had arrived the day after she phoned them with the news. Her family might not have helped, but they certainly were proud of her.

Life was good, and on this sunny Saturday morning in February, she was going to sample some of it. Throwing back the covers, she bounded out of bed and headed for the shower.

There was so much going on around her, Madelyn couldn't take it all in. Her morning had been a whirlwind of sights, sounds, and colors. She was turning her body into a pretzel, trying to make sure she didn't miss one nuance of San Antonio's colorful history with its diverse people.

San Antonio was doing its best to accommodate her. The city was in the midst of the stock show and rodeo. The area was crowded with jovial people in western and native garb outside the coliseum, intent on having a good time and eating as much high-cholesterol food as they could. With ethnic foods from Mexico, Germany, Czechoslovakia, and China, they weren't going to go away disappointed.

It had taken the rumbling of her stomach to remind Madelyn of the passing of time. The tempting aroma of sausages-on-the-stick grilling over a mesquite fire drew her gaze. With determination, she continued. She had gorged herself at the hotel's scrumptious breakfast buffet, and she had promised herself at the time that she'd eat a nice, sensible lunch. Sensible meant low-cal and low-fat.

Out of the corner of her eye, she saw a vendor spraying whipped cream over a funnel cake heavily layered with powdered sugar, then spooning on lush, ripe strawberries. Her tongue circled her lips.

She might be having a sensible lunch, but she knew exactly what she was having for dessert. Looking around to note the spot where the booth was located, she continued making her way through the crowd toward her hotel.

A short distance away on a tree-lined street, she noticed the sky had become cloudier. Hoping the rain showers forecasted for the afternoon would hold off until she reached her hotel, she grimaced and increased her pace. Each hurried step carried her farther from the crowd and the distinctive mariachi music of the strolling Mexican street band.

She cast another belligerent look at the rolling, dark gray clouds. Maybe she'd have to substitute strawberry-topped cheesecake for her funnel cake. She hoped not. Not that she wouldn't enjoy both, she just didn't like the idea of the rain keeping her inside. Spending an afternoon alone in her hotel room wasn't her idea of fun. And that wasn't the worst of it.

She could just imagine the thoughts of some of her friends and coworkers when they asked about her trip, and she had to tell them she spent most of it in her hotel room by herself.

A few might not be bold enough to say it, but Madelyn knew that every one of them would be thinking being cooped up in a hotel room on a rainy day wouldn't have been a hardship if she had brought a man with her.

But Madelyn didn't have a man.

She watched the laughing young couple in front of her—with four fingers of their hands tucked in the back pocket of the other's jeans, their hips brushing with each step—and admitted that finding someone special to love would be wonderful. The problem was her demanding job left little time for a social life. The situation was only going to get worse.

Sometimes she didn't leave work until well after seven in the evening. If she and her coworkers weren't too tired, those who didn't have family to go home to would meet someplace for dinner. Since there was no one special in her life, she always went with them. In college she had gotten into the habit of going out in groups and saw no reason to change. So far she hadn't seen one man she wanted all to herself.

Well, she had seen him. She just hadn't met him.

Until a couple of years ago when she had seen a photograph of Daniel Falcon with her brother, Matt, she hadn't known Daniel existed. Since then she hadn't been able to forget him.

Daniel's eyes had captured her first. Dark, passionate, piercing . . . challenging. Then she had let her own eyes roam over his strong features shaped by his African-American mother and Native American father, shaped by time, shaped by life. It had been an eyeful.

Daniel Falcon was jaw-dropping handsome. She had seen handsome men before, had grown up with two men she considered unbeatable . . . until she saw Daniel Falcon's photograph. She couldn't explain the wild cadence of her heart then any more than she could now just at the thought of him.

The problem was since the corporate headquarters of Falcon Industries was located it Denver, and he was from Boston, she wasn't likely to meet him. She had looked forward to finally meeting him at Matt and Shannon's wedding since Daniel had worked a miracle in securing the ballroom for the reception, but he had been a no-show at the last minute. The thought that she might never meet him always saddened her.

Daniel Falcon had touched her in ways no other man had, and he had yet to touch her or she him.

Lost in thought she didn't feel the first drops of rain. The sound of people shrieking was her first indication that something was wrong. In a second she realized the promise of rain had become a reality while she was daydreaming of Daniel Falcon.

Holding her tiny purse over her head, Madelyn sprinted for cover. Unfortunately other people had the same idea and had been faster to react. In less than a minute, her midcalf, gauzy white cotton sundress was soaked. With each running step, her white leather sandals slapped noisily against the concrete.

Realizing she'd have to find a place to wait out the rain or a taxi, she paused beneath the dubious covering of a palm tree to get her bearing. Directly across the street the deep burgundy awning of a stately hotel nestled between a travel agency and a French restaurant caught her attention.

Taking only a moment to check the traffic, Madelyn made a run for it against the traffic light. Surely in a tourist city, the hotel staff wouldn't begrudge offering her sanctuary.

The elderly doorman in a heavy black rain slicker and black cap circled at the crown in gold braid didn't bat an eyelash when he held open

the heavy glass and gold chrome door for her. Flashing him a smile of
thanks, she entered absently, noting the feeling of opulence and spa-
ciousness of the lobby. Getting dry was uppermost in her mind. Luckily
she spotted a bellman almost immediately.

"Where's the rest room?"

"To the left of the bank of elevators around from the restaurant," he
told her, his dark eyes running over her in one encompassing sweep.

Madelyn glanced down and flushed. The off-the-shoulder dress was
plastered to the front of her body. The lacy bra was no match against the
rain and the frigid temperature of the hotel. Dusky nipples thrust
brazenly against the fabric.

Flushing again, Madelyn headed in the direction the bellman had indicated. Head bent, shoulders hunched forward in an attempt to conceal her predicament, she hurried around the indicated corner and ran
into something solid and immovable.

She heard a soft grunt, felt herself falling backward, and instinctively
reached out in a frantic attempt to keep herself upright. A steel bar
clamped around her waist. The spark of awareness stunned her as much
as being anchored against something equally unyielding and hard.

Startled and confused she gasped, her eyes widening. Staring down at
her were a pair of mesmerizing black eyes she recognized instantly.

Madelyn blinked, then blinked again. Had she somehow conjured up
Daniel Falcon? The heat and solidness of muscled flesh beneath her
splayed fingers told her this was a flesh-and-blood man. Her hands, pushing against an impressively wide chest to break the enforced closeness,
stilled.

Her searching gaze quickly cataloged thick black hair lightly streaked
with silver secured at the base of his neck, heavy black brows, chiseled
cheekbones, strong nose, and the sensuous lips of the man holding her.
They comprised an incredibly handsome face. The photograph hadn't
captured the essence or the sensuous vitality of the man.

She wasn't sure anything could.

"Daniel." His name came out in a throaty whisper of awe.

From somewhere off to her right came an amused bark of laughter.
"Mi amigo, is there not one beautiful woman in Texas you do not know?"

Madelyn heard the deeply accented voice, but she was unable to look
away from Daniel's compelling features. After thinking and speculating
about him for so long, she was finally meeting the legendary Daniel
Falcon.

Midnight-black eyes were studying her just as intently. "Apparently I
missed one, Carlos."

Instead of the Bostonian accent she expected, his voice was dipped in
velvet and laced with infinite possibilities, all of them dangerous. Un-

characteristically she responded to the danger. "Only one. You must have gotten a late start this morning."

Deep dimples winked mischievously in his bronzed face. "Old age will do that to you," Daniel returned easily.

She burst out laughing. He was only thirty-three. Daniel's laughter joined in. She felt the deep, smooth sound all the way to her toes. Definitely dangerous.

"What's going on here?"

Jerking her head around sharply, Madelyn saw a beautiful young black woman, her pouting red lips pressed together in disapproval, her dark eyes snapping angrily. It didn't take Madelyn longer than her next breath to guess the reason.

Daniel Falcon.

According to her brothers, women stuck to Daniel like cockleburs— that is, when they could catch him. Why shouldn't they? Besides being gorgeous and having enough sex appeal and charisma for ten men, he was a very successful and influential businessman. Madelyn could just imagine the arduous task of keeping other woman at bay while attempting to keep Daniel's attention.

She almost felt sorry for the irate woman. "Please put me down," Madelyn instructed.

"If you insist," Daniel said, a note of regret in his voice. Gently he set Madelyn on her feet. Immediately she regretted the loss of his warmth and muscled hardness and wanted to return to his arms. The unexpected yearning astonished as much as shocked her. Hastily she stepped away.

The woman gasped.

Carlos whistled.

Madelyn cringed. In Daniel's embrace she had forgotten her revealing wet dress. Embarrassed, Madelyn crossed her arms across her chest and took a sidestep toward the refuge of the rest room.

She had chosen the dress and several like it because they were light and airy, the full skirt making it unnecessary to wear a half-slip. Now, ironically, the same reasons she liked the dresses were now putting her on display.

Heat flushed her face again. She took another step.

A man's tan jacket settled around her shoulders and stopped at her knees. She glanced around to see Daniel, his dimples winking at her again.

"I always wanted to rescue a damsel in distress," he explained, a grin tugging the corners of his sexy mouth.

If she hadn't already been halfway infatuated with the man, his gallant gesture would have certainly started her on the road. "Thank you." She drew the coat tighter around her shoulders, wondering if there was a female alive who could resist his smile or those dimples.

"She's dripping all over the floor and getting your coat wet," the woman accused. "It's a Versace."

"Then, Lydia, I'm sure you'll excuse us and understand why I'm taking her to her room." Daniel's large hand on Madelyn's shoulder, he urged her toward the elevator several feet away.

"But you were going out to lunch with us," Lydia protested loudly.

"I already told you I had other plans," Daniel replied, pushing the button for the elevator. "Give your father my best. We'll talk later, Carlos." The elevator pinged open, and Daniel hastened Madelyn on. The door closed on Lydia's angry face. A silent Carlos stood by her side.

"Which floor?"

"I'm not staying here," she confessed, pulling the jacket closer to her body. "I came in only to get out of the rain and dry off a little."

Incredible black eyes studied her for a moment, then he turned toward the panel. A lean brown finger punched seventeen.

"What are you doing?" Madelyn exclaimed, her anxious gaze going from Daniel to the panel clicking off the floors.

"You may be out of that rain, but you have yet to achieve your second goal." Folding his arms, he leaned against the highly polished paneled wall. "From your reaction downstairs and the way you're clutching my coat, you now have a bigger problem."

Madelyn glanced at a dangerously attractive Daniel Falcon, a certified stealer of women's hearts and common sense, then away. "I'm not going to your hotel room."

The elevator door slid open smoothly on seventeen. Madelyn remained unmoved.

Daniel pushed the button to keep the door open. "Whatever you've heard about me, did anyone ever say I took advantage of women?" he asked, his voice infinitely patient.

Her head came around to face him. "How do you know we haven't met?"

"Some women you don't forget."

A tiny shiver of pleasure worked its way down her spine. She shifted uneasily under his intent regard. "The woman downstairs seemed upset."

"Not my doing, I assure you. Now do we get off, or do we go back downstairs and I call you a cab?"

Nervously she chewed on her lower lip. "I don't suppose I could keep your coat, could I?"

"You can keep the coat until you're ready to give it up. I wouldn't want you to think you needed rescuing from me as well," he told her with the same patience he had displayed earlier.

It wasn't fear she was feeling, but something totally different and new.

Her problem. Her brothers trusted this man. He wasn't about to try and take advantage of her or any other woman. He didn't have to. Women fought for the chance to get his attention and be in his bed. The angry woman downstairs was a case in point.

Madelyn shivered again from the cold, from something she wasn't ready to examine too closely. One thing she couldn't ignore was the wet dress clinging to her body like a second skin.

Water ran in silent rivulets from her hair down the sides of her face. More water dripped from the hem of her dress to the carpeted floor. Irresistible she was not. She stepped off the elevator.

Lightly grasping her elbow through his coat, Daniel led her down the wide, carpeted hallway to his room. Opening the door with his plastic key, he stepped back.

Swallowing, Madelyn slowly entered. One step inside, she knew her room was nothing compared to Daniel's suite. Her feet sank into lush white carpet. Chinese art graced the walls, and art deco pieces sat on the intricately carved entry table.

Wide-eyed she stared up into Daniel's bronzed face. "I can't."

Black brows drew together. "I thought we had settled that you were safe."

She shook her head, then stopped and flushed again as water sprayed the front of his cream-colored shirt. "It's not that. I'll mess up the place."

Relief washed over his handsome face. "I'll leave a generous tip for the maid. Come on, let's get you into something dry."

Madelyn was so shocked by what he had said that she didn't resist the strong hand propelling her past the spacious living room with a dining table seating eight into a bedroom that screamed luxury and comfort.

"There's a bathrobe on the door. Do you want coffee, tea, or chocolate?"

Trembling fingers clutched his coat. "Chocolate."

Nodding he gently but firmly urged her inside the bathroom. "I think you'll find everything you need." Smiling, he closed the door.

For a long moment Madelyn simply stared at the door. Trusting Daniel was one thing—taking off her clothes in his bathroom was another. Swallowing nervously, she glanced around and gasped at her reflection in the immense mirror.

She had seen drowned rats who looked better. Rain had taken the curls from her hair, the light makeup from her face.

It didn't take much to remember the well turned out and beautiful Lydia from downstairs and her elegance in a bright yellow silk sheath. Of the two of them, Madelyn had to admit the other woman would be chosen hands down. Daniel was only being nice. The same way he had been nice to her sister-in-law when she had needed rescuing.

Shannon had told Madelyn on more than one occasion how protective and solicitous of her Daniel had been when they first met. At the time Shannon had been in love with Madelyn's stubborn, hardheaded brother, and he had been fighting it all the way.

Matt had tried to deny his feelings for Shannon, but that hadn't stopped him from being intensely jealous of Daniel. After Matt came to his senses, he realized all Daniel had offered Shannon was friendship when she had needed it the most.

Madelyn knew when she fell in love, she'd be more like Kane. From the first moment her oldest brother had held Victoria, he'd known she would be important in his life. Their first kiss sealed their fate. Falling in love for Madelyn would be just as simple and satisfying.

A knock sounded on the bathroom door. "Someone's here to pick up your things."

"Just a minute," she called. She was a grown woman, for goodness' sake. Going back downstairs and waiting for a taxi, dripping water all the way, was idiotic when she didn't have to. Daniel was an honorable man.

Taking off the coat, she reached for the elastic shoulders of the white dress. Quickly pulling her arms free, she pushed the clinging dress down over her legs and stepped out. Making sure she didn't look in the mirror again, she pulled on the robe and tied it securely around her waist.

Cracking the door slightly, she held out the dress wrapped in a towel. Seeing his large hands close around the bundle almost had her snatching it back. Instead she closed the door. Some of her friends would laugh themselves silly if they knew how nervous she was.

Daniel wasn't going to see any more of her now than he had before. In fact, he was going to see less. It was just the idea that he knew she was taking off her dress that had her so jittery.

Moments later another knock sounded on the door. "Was that all you wanted to send?"

A wave of heat swept from her breasts to her cheeks. "Yes," she said crisply.

His answering chuckle was part teasing, part sinful, and wholly intriguing. "Just checking. Hurry up or your chocolate will be cold."

The scoundrel! Madelyn thought, but she was smiling. She glanced into the mirror, and her heart sank. She looked like a lost waif, a very wet lost waif.

Why couldn't she have met Daniel when she was dry and had a smidgen of makeup on? She might not want her name added to his long list of past lady friends, but that didn't mean she didn't want him to find her attractive.

Fat chance she had of that happening now. Taking a towel from the roll on the marbled vanity, she mopped up the water from the floor.

CHAPTER 2

She looked adorable standing in the door of his bedroom in the over-sized white bathrobe. Adorable wasn't a word Daniel equated with women in his life, but it seemed to fit the hesitant woman staring at him with huge chocolate eyes.

"I was beginning to think I'd have to drink all this chocolate by my-self," Daniel said, hoping to ease some of her obvious tension.

"I thought about letting you," came the soft reply.

Daniel smiled. He had been doing that a lot since the woman now chewing on her bottom lip had literally fallen into his arms. "I'm glad you didn't. Have a seat and I'll pour."

Clutching the neck of the robe, she crossed the room. Toenails painted a deep burgundy emerged from beneath the dragging hem with each step. Gracefully she sank into one of the four easy chairs positioned around the coffee table.

"Why don't you put your feet up?" he asked her, pouring her choco-late and handing it to her.

"This is fine, thank you." The cup and saucer rattled slightly in her hands. "How long will it be before my dress is ready?"

"Soon." He took a seat next to her. Obviously she wasn't used to sitting around in a robe in front of a man. On one hand he was pleased; on the other he was hoping to change that. "I told them to put a rush on it."

A shy smile flickered across her beautiful face. "Thank you. You've been very kind."

"I try to take care of things that are important to me."

Her smile slipped a notch. "Octavia was certainly right about you being the silver-tongued devil."

He jerked upright in his chair. "Octavia. Octavia Ralston, Matt Taggart's housekeeper?"

"The one and only."

"You aren't one of her granddaughters or something, are you?" he asked. *Please, don't let her say yes,* he thought fervently.

"No. Why?"

Relieved, he settled back in his chair. "Just checking. Is that who you heard about me from?"

For a few moments she stared into her cup, then lifted her head turbaned in a white bath towel. "Actually I've heard about you from a number of people."

"Such as?" Daniel questioned, uneasiness creeping back over him.

"First from Shannon—then of course Matt had to put in his two cents' worth. Kane said very little, but Victoria added a few points." She sipped her chocolate. "Cleve was almost as closemouthed as Kane, but Octavia talked enough for all of them."

"Who are you?"

"Can't you guess?" she asked, setting her cup aside.

He studied her beautiful caramel-colored face again, the winged brows, the lush lashes, the supple lips, the sparkles in the deep eyes a man could get lost gazing into. More than that, he recalled what she had said. The Taggarts weren't given to gossip, neither were Cleve or Octavia.

That left one damning and unwanted answer. "You can't be Kane and Matt's little sister."

She grinned impishly at him. "And why not?"

"Because little sisters don't look like you!" he said almost accusingly. The moment the words were out of his mouth, he thought of Dominique. His wandering younger sister created a minor stir wherever she went. Presently she was in Paris doing a photo shoot—only this time she was behind the camera instead of in front of it.

Daniel's guest laughed, a full, throaty sound that delighted and annoyed him at the same time because he knew he wasn't going to hear it while she was lying next to him in bed. "Oh, Daniel, I believe you've given me a compliment. But little sisters do grow up."

His hot gaze raked her body again. He remembered the lushness of her breasts—the soft curves of her body that the wet, clinging dress made impossible to ignore and silently groaned. That was putting it mildly.

She held out her hand. "Madelyn June Taggart."

Daniel rose to take her small hand in his, noting the fine bone structure, the softness, the unexpected jolt of awareness. "I thought they said your name was Addie."

Madelyn made a face. "As a child I had difficulty pronouncing my name and left off the *M* and the last syllable. I refused to answer to anything but the mangled form of my name, Addie. Since graduation from college, I've refused to answer to anything except my given name."

A slight smile tilted the corner of his mouth. "Stubborn just like your brothers, huh?"

"I choose to see it as determined."

His expression became grim. "When I asked Matt about you, he said they were still trying to get your teeth straight."

Pulling her hand free, she showed him perfect white teeth.

Both hands on his hips, Daniel scowled. "He really had me going."

"You and every male over the age of eighteen. What is it they say about rogues and rakes making poor husbands? They make even worse older brothers." Wrinkling her nose, she pulled her feet under her.

Daniel saw a flash of smooth brown leg and seriously thought of giving Matt that broken nose they always joked about.

"He probably told you I was nearsighted, kept my head buried in a book, and was so shy I seldom went out in public." Madelyn folded her arms. "Kane's not as bad, but they're both overprotective."

Daniel finally reclaimed his seat. "That's like saying a hurricane is a strong wind."

"Matt doesn't usually lay it on so thick. Your reputation must be worse than they let on or even Octavia suspects."

The words were said teasingly, but from the way she looked at him, he suspected she was half convinced he couldn't make a step without tripping over a woman. He usually didn't care what people thought of him, but the woman across from him made him think differently.

"Since the only time I met Octavia was shortly before Matt and Shannon's engagement, I don't suppose what she had to say was too complimentary," he explained.

Those perfect white teeth flashed. "Actually Octavia likes you. Matt likes you, too, as long as you're not within a hundred miles of Shannon."

"I never trespass. Matt should have remembered I have certain rules I live by. Rules I never break," Daniel said. "You have chocolate on your upper lip."

Madelyn ran a finger across the area, then flicked her tongue over her upper lip. "Did I get it?"

"Yes," Daniel said, shifting restlessly in his chair. He had rules he lived by, and he had never been tempted to break them. Until now.

He was being tempted now to get up and taste the chocolate on her lips and go from there until he intimately knew the taste and shape of every inch of her body.

"You were dealing with the old Matt," Madelyn told him. "Marriage agrees with him. I've never seen him happier."

"I hope it lasts," Daniel replied, glad they were on a subject guaranteed to cool down his blood.

Madelyn frowned. "Why shouldn't it? They both love and respect each other very much."

"Sometimes love isn't enough," he said.

Her frown deepened. "You can't mean that?"

"I do."

She shook her head. "If Matt could change, there's hope for every man. He thought love and marriage wasn't for him until he met and fell in love with Shannon." She tilted her head and openly studied him. "The same thing will happen to you. You'll probably fight harder than he did, but you'll lose."

He crossed his arms across his broad chest. "You sound like you're looking forward to my downfall."

She flushed and clasped her hands in her lap. "I-I simply meant I believe in love and think people are happier in love. Matt is proof that love can change anyone."

"Has love changed you?" Daniel asked, unfolding his arms and leaning forward to hear her answer with more interest than he cared to admit.

Her head ducked. "I haven't found him yet."

"But you believe he's out there?"

Her head lifted. Brown eyes met his with boundless assurance. "With all my heart."

Somehow the idea of some faceless man waiting for Madelyn didn't set well with Daniel. That man would have the right to slide the thick robe off and lay claim to her silken body.

But he could never be that man.

"You're frowning. I'm sorry." She shifted uneasily in her chair. "After all you've done for me, I didn't mean to offend you."

"You didn't."

A knock sounded on the door. Grateful, he rose. It was past time to send Madelyn on her way before he did or said something they'd both regret. "It must be your dress."

Instead of a bellhop, an enraged Lydia stood in the hallway. Without a word she brushed by him as if she had every right to do so. Tight-lipped and apologetic, Carlos slowly followed.

At another time Daniel would have put a stop to Lydia's nonsense. Presently he needed a buffer.

"Do come in," he drawled and closed the door.

"Just as I thought," Lydia snapped. "Why isn't she in her room?"

Large brown eyes sought Daniel's. Madelyn's delicate hand went to the collar of her robe. Daniel might need a buffer between Madelyn, but he'd be damned if he'd stand by and see her embarrassed.

"I wasn't aware that either I or my guest had to give you an explanation for our actions." Stepping around the other woman, he went to stand by Madelyn.

"How heroic, Daniel. Apparently you didn't waste any time getting to know each other better," Lydia said snidely, glaring at Madelyn.

"Not as much as we would have liked before you arrived," Madelyn said, surprising herself by the loaded innuendo. Her hand left the collar of the robe to rest negligently in her lap.

Something about the haughty arrogance of the woman grated on Madelyn's nerves. She didn't dare let herself think it was because Lydia's presence made Madelyn feel even more drab and unattractive in front of Daniel.

Daniel's head jerked toward the breathy sound of Madelyn's voice. He blinked in amazement, then grinned. Perhaps she wasn't the innocent he thought. One thing he was sure of was that being around two strong-willed, no-crap-taking men had apparently rubbed off on their little sister.

Carlos stopped pretending to study the watercolor landscape and instead studied Madelyn.

Lydia's scarlet lips clamped tightly at seeing both men's attention shift to another woman. Perfectly manicured nails, the same bright red as her lips, flexed in agitation on the gold chain of her handbag.

"Daniel and I were just having some chocolate, would you like to join us?" Madelyn asked, uncurling from the chair and reaching for the pot.

"I don't want any chocolate," Lydia snapped.

Madelyn straightened. "So, Lydia, what exactly is it you want?"

The woman turned toward Daniel, her face unexpectedly softening. "So you've been talking about me."

"Sorry to disappoint you, Lydia, but your name never came up," Daniel answered truthfully.

A frown marred the woman's beautiful face. "But how did she know my name?"

"I have a knack for remembering names. Yours as well as Carlos's was mentioned downstairs," Madelyn told her.

"And what is yours?" Lydia flung.

Madelyn pushed to her feet. This waspish woman would never get a man like Daniel. She probably didn't even notice Carlos's longing looks at her. He was a good-looking guy with warm brown eyes.

"Madelyn Taggart." This time she didn't offer her hand. She knew it would be ignored.

Lydia's expression went from sneering to speculative. "You're related to Matt and Kane Taggart?"

Madelyn hadn't expected the woman to know her brothers. A moment of uneasiness swept through her. If either found out she was in Daniel's room in a bathrobe, she was in for a hard time—and Daniel was looking at a possible trip to the emergency room. "Do you know them?"

Lydia smiled with pure malice. "No, but I have heard of them. They're Daniel's friends, aren't they?"

Not knowing where the conversation was leading, Madelyn said, "Yes."

Lydia laughed. The harsh crackling sound coming from the mouth of such a beautiful woman was unnerving.

Still smiling, Lydia faced Daniel. "You didn't know who she was in the lobby, did you?" She continued as if she didn't expect an answer. "Of course not, or you wouldn't have rushed her up here." Laughter erupted again. "Now you will know how it feels."

Continuing to smile, she turned to Madelyn. "My family has controlling interest in this hotel. If there is anything you require, please don't hesitate to ask. I'll leave word at the desk."

Madelyn couldn't understand the sudden change in the woman. "Thank you, but that won't be necessary."

"I think it might be. He hasn't told you about his little code, has he?"

"Lydia, it's time we left. Your father and the others will be waiting for us at the restaurant," Carlos suggested, gently grasping her elbow.

Black eyes flashed angrily. Lydia brushed off his hold. "Since he hasn't told you, I will. Daniel has a thing about not becoming involved with relatives of his friends. So your little scheme downstairs won't work."

The unmitigated gall of the woman! If Madelyn knew how to work her neck, this was one time she'd do it and give two snaps to boot. "Unlike some women, I don't have to resort to subterfuge to catch a man."

Lydia gasped at the implication. "You'd have to do something. You look like a skinny, drowned chicken."

"Now wai—"

"Lydia."

The woman whirled toward Daniel, and Madelyn had to give her points for courage. If he had called her name in that same cold voice, she would have been running in the opposite direction.

"I don't care who owns this hotel," he continued just as coldly. "This is my room, and I want you out of here."

Outrage marred Lydia's perfect features. "You can't throw me out of my father's hotel."

"He'd do it for me, if he were here."

"I'm not go—" She gasped and jumped back as Daniel took a step toward her. Her eyes became malevolent. "How dare you treat me like this!"

"You brought it on yourself. Now leave," Daniel said flatly.

"I'll leave, and I'll make sure everyone at lunch knows what went on up here!"

In two steps he towered over her. "Say one word that might embarrass Madelyn or her family, and I'll make sure you regret it for the rest of your unhappy life."

Lydia staggered back, her hand going to the heavy gold necklace at her throat. "Carlos, do something. Carlos?"

"I am. I'm doing something I should have done long ago." He turned to Madelyn. "Goodbye. I wish we could have met under different circumstances," then to Daniel, "I'll see you later." Opening the door, he was gone.

"Carlos," Lydia screamed, but he kept going.

"If I were you, Lydia, I'd run after Carlos and try to get him to forgive you," Daniel said. "Although personally I think he's finally realized you're not worth the effort."

Lydia looked at Daniel with heartless eyes. "One day I'll make you pay for this."

"You're welcome to try, but make your first shot count because you won't get another one—and then it will be my turn," Daniel finished with deadly promise.

The woman shivered, her hand once again clutching her throat. Turning, she fled and almost ran into the bellhop who carried Madelyn's dress. The young man's questioning gaze went from the escaping Lydia back to them.

Daniel took the dress enclosed in clear plastic wrap in one hand, tipped the man with the other, and closed the door. "Your dress. Looks like they did a pretty good job."

"I thought Kane was joking, but he wasn't," Madelyn said, staring at Daniel.

"Joking about what?" Daniel asked, inwardly preparing himself for her censure. He could be a ruthless bastard. No one knew that more than he, but he usually managed to control it better.

"He said the emblem on your plane of a falcon with claws outstretched was a warning to anyone who crosses you. He said when you go after someone, you go for blood."

Daniel never wanted to see fear or revulsion in this woman's eyes when she looked at him. "You have nothing to fear from me, Madelyn."

"Afraid of you?" she scoffed and rolled her brown eyes. "Apparently you've never seen Kane or Matt on a roll. I have. They're no harder than they have to be. Neither are you. But like Kane, you don't like repeating yourself or having your authority questioned."

Daniel studied her with renewed interest. "You're full of surprises."

"Just being realistic," Madelyn said, taking the dress from his hands. "Matt and Kane might like you, but they wouldn't like hearing I was in your room in a bathrobe."

The corner of his mouth kicked up in a half smile. "The same thought crossed my mind."

"You're pretty good at rescuing women, Daniel." She smiled up at him with all the warmth he wanted and could never have.

Daniel's face settled into grim lines "I'm a rogue, and innocents like you shouldn't forget it."

Her smile faded as he knew it would. "I'll go change and get out of your way. I'm sure you must have a lot to do."

"I've already done it." At her puzzled look, he continued. "Seen my bootmaker. My mold was damaged, and I had to come down and have it redone."

Frowning, she shook her head in disbelief. "You came from Denver to be fitted for a pair of boots?"

"I'm particular about what I put on my feet. A bad pair of boots—"

"Can ruin your feet," she finished. "I know that, but it's still hard to imagine someone coming all this way for boots."

"If you want something badly enough, too far or too much doesn't enter into it."

The way he said the words had Madelyn clutching the dress closer to her. No woman would be safe if he decided to come after her. The idea was fascinating and frightening.

"I'll be out in a minute." Whirling, she hurried to the bathroom, her heart racing. She was imagining things. Daniel had no special interest in her. Hadn't Lydia made it perfectly clear he didn't become involved with relatives of friends?

But what if Lydia didn't know what she was talking about? What if Daniel handed her that line to get her out of his face?

Madelyn lifted her face to the mirror. There was only one reason she was asking herself all those questions. She wanted Daniel to look at her and see a desirable woman, not the little sister of his friends. She wanted a man who, rumor had it, had no heart. Heaven help her.

"I'm lost."

Several minutes later Madelyn emerged from Daniel's bathroom. She felt more in control of the situation now that she was in her own clothes, her hair was dry, and she had on her lipstick.

She made a face. Maybe she had been too hasty in her thoughts on the unimportance of lasting lip color.

"Something wrong?"

Her head jerked around to see Daniel rising from the chair . . . all six-feet-plus of him. She might have been too nervous to appreciate the sheer male beauty of the man when he was in his bathrobe, but she wasn't now.

He exuded a raw magnetism that was disquieting. Those midnight-black eyes were as sharp as talons. The intelligence in them shone just as brightly and kept her from bolting back into the bathroom.

"You've changed."

"There's another bathroom off the dining area," he explained.

Jeans suited the muscled hardness of his long legs. The white shirt complemented his dark, good looks. He looked sinful and forbidden, and much too tempting.

She moistened her lips. "Well, I guess I better be going."

"What are your plans?"

Madelyn glanced toward the windows before answering. The draperies were partially drawn. She couldn't tell if it was still raining, but the sky didn't look so gloomy and dark.

"They were for a sensible lunch and strawberry-topped cheesecake, but if the weather cooperates, I think it'll be Tex-Mex food with salsa that will take the skin off the roof of my mouth followed by a funnel cake loaded down with strawberries and whipped cream."

"Care for some company?"

There was no way for her to hide her shock. "You?"

"I know this little restaurant that sounds exactly like what you're looking for," he told her.

Briefly she thought of what Lydia had said, then pushed it to the back of her mind. She'd never know if she didn't try.

"After I go back to my hotel room to change, you're on."

CHAPTER 3

Cafe Mexicana was everything Daniel promised. The freshly prepared food was delicious. From where their table was located, Madelyn could see an elderly man in the back making tortillas.

She and Daniel had stuffed themselves on salsa and chips, refried beans, Spanish rice, enchiladas, and fajitas. By the time they left the restaurant, Madelyn was sure she had gained two pounds.

"Daniel, you're a mean man," she groaned.

"What did I do?"

"Condemned me to rethink my position against eating sprouts and granola bars for lunch."

"We'll walk it off."

"Walk? I'm not sure I can go another ten feet."

Laughing he slung his arm companionably around her shoulders. She tried to ignore the tingling sensation winging its way down her spine. "Then how about riding?"

At her puzzled stare, he pointed toward a river taxi gliding by. "How about it?"

She smiled despite her rapidly beating heart. "You're forgiven."

It was a short walk from the bank to their point of embarkment. The rain must have kept most people indoors because they were able to board the colorful red and orange boat within minutes of their arrival.

Gratefully Madelyn climbed aboard and sank down into one of the cushioned seats. Lush vegetation and palms lined the bank along with sidewalk cafes, shops, galleries, hotels, restaurants, and clubs.

"Feeling better?" Daniel asked, settling his black Stetson more securely on his head as the boat picked up speed down the canal of the San Antonio River.

"Yes, thank you. I shouldn't have eaten so much. First breakfast, then just now." She leaned back against the railing. "The only excuse is that I don't have time for good meals at home."

"Where's home?"

"Houston. I work for Sinclair Petroleum Company as a production engineer."

Daniel's broad shoulders tensed. He stared down at her. "You work for an oil company in Houston?"

"Yes. I have for three years." She frowned. "You have something against Houston or the oil industry?"

Facing straight ahead, he leaned back and propped his arms over the railing. "Neither. I was just surprised you weren't living in Dallas or Fort Worth. I seem to remember Kane mentioning he wanted you to work for him."

She relaxed again, enjoying the ride through the Rivercenter. "I know, but I wanted to be on my own. Houston is close enough for us to visit, but far enough away where they can't try and run my life."

"Or screen your dates?"

She gave him a sharp look of disappointment. "Actually I was thinking more of interfering with my job. As for the dates, if a man can be intimidated by my brothers, he's not the man for me."

Daniel's disturbing gaze found her again. "You're quite a woman."

Madelyn flushed with pleasure. "Glad you approve."

"Oh, I approve. Kane and Matt must be very proud of their little sister."

The softly spoken words touched and saddened her. He still thought of her as the little sister of his friends. If she wanted more, that was her problem.

Gathering her slipping composure, she lifted her face to the bright rays of the sun for a minute. "I'm glad you suggested this. I didn't get a chance when I came on a field trip in high school."

"Came to see the Alamo, I'll bet." Daniel shifted slightly and stretched his long legs out in front of him. His red lizard boots were polished to a rich sheen.

She nodded, trying to concentrate on the peaceful ride through the Rivercenter instead of the hard length of Daniel's muscular thigh pressed against hers. "The Alamo and the state capital in Austin are practically unwritten requirements to graduate from a high school in Texas."

"Why didn't you get a chance to go on the river taxi?"

Madelyn shifted uneasily before answering. "Things just didn't work out."

"Did it rain then?"

"No."

"Are you going to tell me why, or do I keep on guessing?" he asked mildly.

Unsteady fingers plucked at the hem of the shorts she had changed into at her hotel before finally meeting Daniel's enigmatic eyes. "One of our chaperons was a really nice man. He thought, along with the history, we should experience some of the unique flavor of San Antonio.

"He talked the teachers into letting some of us take a river taxi ride. It quickly became a couples thing, and since I didn't have anyone to go with, I stayed in the hotel room with some of the other girls and we ordered pizza instead," she explained, the occasion indelible because her date had dumped her for another girl.

Daniel pulled up his legs and gave her his full attention. "Are you telling me in high school you didn't have a boyfriend?"

"I had them. I just wasn't able to keep them," she said, glancing away. Her inability to keep a boyfriend wasn't something she wanted to discuss with a man like Daniel Falcon.

"Kane and Matt the problem?"

"Partly." She studied the shops lining the walkway. "There's a T-shirt shop. I promised to bring the twins one."

He frowned down at her. "The twins? Kane and Victoria's children?"

"Yes. You should have seen them at Matt and Shannon's wedding. They were adorable. We were all disappointed you couldn't come."

"Something came up," he said, his voice remote. He stood as the boat docked. "We can get off here."

Madelyn allowed him to assist her off the boat, but didn't speak until they were in front of the shop. She extended her hand, hoping her smile didn't appear as forced as it felt. "Thank you for lunch and the taxi ride."

He stared at her hand, then lifted a dark brow. "You wouldn't be trying to get rid of me, would you?"

"I'm sure you hadn't planned on doing touristy things with the little sister of your friends," she told him, her hand wavering.

"Nope." He gathered her smaller hand in his. "I had planned on a boring lunch with some business associates. This is much better."

Madelyn fought to sound normal when her insides were shivery. "Are you sure?"

"Didn't someone mention I never do anything I don't want to?" he questioned mildly.

A smile and a tiny ray of hope lit her face. "I believe it came up once or twice."

"Well, then."

"All right, but remember, you asked for it."

* * *

The afternoon turned into evening and evening turned into night. Madelyn couldn't remember ever having so much fun. Somehow the tenseness between them seemed to leave as they tried to pick out the right T-shirts for the twins. They finally settled on one with San Antonio emblazoned in bright colors on a white background.

Continuing down the sidewalk, they passed a shop and saw a piñata. Madelyn mentioned the twins' birthday was coming up and how much fun a piñata would be for each of them. Off they went to the Market Square. Daniel was as finicky as she was in finding one with the right colors and shape.

After wandering down the aisles, they finally found two donkeys that were exactly what they had been searching for. Against her protests, Daniel paid for the piñatas.

After depositing everything at her hotel, they were off again, ending up at the street fair surrounding the coliseum. Passing the funnel cake concession, Daniel had asked if she wanted one. She had punched him playfully on the shoulder.

Seemingly without a moment's hesitation, he draped his arm around her shoulders again and they continued down the aisle. Her heart beat faster, her skin tingled.

They were strolling past the game booths when Madelyn stopped and watched an excited teenage girl clutch an enormous lion the young boy with her had just won for her. Both of them had to carry the toy as they walked away.

Madelyn watched them fondly. "I've always wanted someone to win one of those animals for me—one so big it would be hard to drag home."

"Your boyfriends didn't seem to be around when it counted."

She grimaced. "One did win me a four-foot fuzzy green snake at the State Fair of Texas in Dallas when I was sixteen."

"I think I can do better than that."

"Daniel, I wasn't hinting."

"I know. That's why I'm going to win you one." Taking her arm, he steered them through the crowd toward the counter.

Before they were halfway there, the sharp-eyed booth huckster saw them approaching and began his pitch about how easy it was to win the young woman the stuffed animal of her choice from the top two rows. All the strong man had to do was completely shoot out the red bull's-eye on the target in twenty pellet shots.

Taking out his wallet, Daniel turned to Madelyn. "How many?"

"Two dollars for twenty shots," replied the worker, placing a pellet gun on the scarred wooden counter.

Daniel didn't take his eyes from Madelyn. "I was asking you how many stuffed animals you wanted."

She barely kept her mouth from sagging. Not for a moment did she think he was bragging. He was utterly confident in his ability to do anything he set his mind to. It was an awesome realization.

Although shredded target centers hung from one end of the booth to the other, she didn't doubt the difficulty of accomplishing such a task. Each time a pellet struck the target, the paper would fan backward, making it more difficult to hit the red center with the next shot.

Madelyn glanced at Daniel, noting his patience, his confidence. She was just as confident in him. She switched her attention to the display of elephants, lions, and bears. There wasn't a green snake in sight.

"The brown teddy bear."

"That's on the bottom row. You'll have to hit five in a row. No misses," the man said.

"Dan—"

"Line them up," Daniel said, cutting her off.

"Ten dollars."

Daniel handed the man a ten-dollar bill. Only then did the attendant move to set up the targets, then he placed four other pellet guns beside the first.

"Remember if you miss one, you'll have to start all over again," the attendant reminded him.

"He won't miss," Madelyn said, her arms folded across her chest. She glared at the man behind the counter.

Daniel winked at her, then picked up the gun. Her confidence in him shouldn't have made him feel a foot taller, but it did. If he didn't watch himself, Madelyn could become more of a problem.

He should have left her hours ago, but there was something about her smile that was irresistible and made him want to keep her smiling. He had come to San Antonio to donate funds and finalize plans for a work-study program to be overseen by Carlos for Hispanic, Native American, and African-American high school students—not fool around with a woman. Yet here he was, trying to win her a darn teddy bear whose fur would probably fall out in six weeks.

Hoisting the gun upward, Daniel sighted down the barrel and began pulling the trigger. Paper popped and danced as the small black pellets tore into the red circle. Picking up another gun, he began firing again. He continued until the last gun was empty.

Madelyn's slim fingers closed around his arm as the attendant slowly removed the clothespins holding the targets. By the time the grim-faced man laid the last tattered remains in front of Madelyn and Daniel, a crowd had formed to see the results.

Madelyn squealed like a schoolgirl. In each one the red circle was completely obliterated. "You did it! You did it! We won! We won!"

She threw her arms around Daniel's neck, intending to kiss him on the cheek. His head turned. Their lips met, clung.

Fire swept through her. Need warred with common sense. Move closer or pull back?

Every instinct in Daniel shouted for him to push her away. He couldn't. Her lips were too soft, too sweet and alluring. He knew he was headed for disaster, but he was powerless to keep from pulling her into his arms and deepening the kiss.

It was the best and worst decision of his life. Her body seemed to melt into his, offering herself to him without reservation, without coyness. Daniel accepted the gift with reverence, with barely leashed desire.

"Way to go, man."

"Wow!"

"See what winning can do for you men? There's nothing like a grateful, happy woman. Who's gonna be the next man to step up and play?"

The loud voices snapped Daniel back to awareness of where he was and what he was doing. Abruptly he lifted his head. Looking into Madelyn's dazed, desire-filled eyes, he wanted nothing more than to take her someplace and make love to her.

None too gently, Daniel pulled Madelyn's arms from around his neck and set her away from him. The look of rejection on her beautiful face tore at him and almost had him pulling her back into his arms. Almost.

He faced the grinning attendant. "I believe you owe the lady a teddy bear."

"Don't you want to win the mate and make her twice as happy?" the carnival worker questioned slyly. "It would be a shame to separate them since they're the only bears I have."

"Some of us don't need mates," Daniel snapped.

The man quickly rushed to pick up the bear and set it on the counter. "Whatever you say, mister."

Feeling irritable, Daniel handed the stuffed animal to Madelyn. "Here you go."

"Thank you." Her fingers sank into the soft brown fur. Glassy black eyes stared up at her. She glanced at the other teddy bear behind the counter and bit her lip. Although she knew the man was trying to con them, she still wasn't immune to his suggestion. She looked at Daniel.

"If you want the other one, I'll win it for you but not because of what he said," Daniel told her tightly. "It's silly to think of a stuffed animal needing a mate when most people can't find and don't want or need one."

Madelyn's fingers tightened. Her happiness of moments ago disappeared. He was upset with her. She shouldn't have kissed him. "No thank you," she replied politely.

His jaw clenched. "If there's nothing else you want to see, I think I should take you back to your hotel."

Madelyn swallowed the lump in her throat. "No, I'm ready to leave."

Taking the animal from her, Daniel started from the area. Fighting tears, Madelyn followed. By the time they reached the door of her hotel room, Madelyn's nerves were ragged. Daniel hadn't said one word since they left the festival.

She had barely opened the door before he stepped past her to place the animal in her room. "Good night. Have a safe trip home."

"Daniel," she said as he stepped back into the hallway. The expressionless face that turned toward her wasn't reassuring. It certainly didn't invite conversation.

"Yes?" The word was clipped.

She clutched her purse in her hand, gathering her courage. "Tell me one thing. Are you leaving me at the door because I'm Matt and Kane's sister or because I'm a lousy kisser?"

Heat flared in his slumberous eyes, then centered on her lips. Her body quickened.

Slowly his gaze lifted. "I'm not one for long-term relationships."

Madelyn took her courage in both hands. "I don't remember asking you for one."

He smiled sadly. "Everything about you asks for one. You're not the kind of woman to go from one affair to the next. I'm not the kind of man who offers a woman anything else."

"Would we be having this conversation if I weren't who I am?" She knew she was pushing it, but when you were hurting inside, you'd fight for survival at all cost . . . including laying your pride on the line.

"Good night, Madelyn."

Her throat stung. "Thank you for the stuffed animal. I had a won—" She swallowed. "Good night."

"Don't do this to either of us."

She gazed at him with mute eyes, then swallowed again.

"If I give you what you're asking for, neither one of us is going to be able to look the other in the eye in the morning."

He couldn't have said it any plainer. She could have him for the night, but only the night. She wasn't that courageous or that stupid. "I'll be sure and tell the family I met you."

Blunt-tipped fingers touched the brim of his black Stetson. Turning he walked down the hall toward the elevators.

With each step, she felt the tightness in her throat grow more unbearable. Swallowing did little good. Just before the hallway ended, he stopped and glanced over his shoulder.

"Close the door and go inside," he ordered.

She bit her lip.

"You aren't a little girl any longer. Don't ask for something you can't handle."

Nothing he could have said would have worked any better. Stepping back, she closed the door. Pressing her back against the smooth wood, she stared at her teddy bear.

It occurred to her as tears rolled down her cheek that for the second time in her life, she had been left alone in her hotel room in San Antonio because she didn't believe in casual sex. The other time it hadn't mattered—this time she was afraid it mattered too much.

Daniel's tense shoulders slumped. Who would have ever thought he'd have trouble keeping his hands off a wide-eyed woman like Madelyn Taggart.

She called to him in ways he had never experienced before. Her smile charmed. Her laugh invited him to join in. Her voice stroked him. Her touch fired his blood.

Madelyn Taggart wasn't for him. So why was walking away one of the most difficult things he had ever done in his life?

The answering machine was blinking in Madelyn's bedroom when she arrived home Sunday afternoon. She wasn't naive enough to think it was Daniel calling. He didn't have her phone number. That he hadn't asked for her unlisted number even before the kiss continued to bother her. She couldn't help feeling as if she had failed to interest him as a potential friend as well as a woman.

After hauling in her luggage, the gifts for the twins, and the teddy bear, she punched the recall button. As the messages played, there were no surprises.

Her parents wanted her to call when she arrived home. The same instructions from Kane and Matt . . . only their wives had made the phone calls. The fourth message was from Jeremiah Gant. His irritatingly cocky voice made the same request.

Madelyn screwed up her face. If he asked her out again, she was going to scream. He was a successful accountant who attended her church, but he was also full of himself. He couldn't seem to understand why she and every other woman wasn't beating his door down.

The next caller had her smiling again. Sid Wright, her neighbor from two doors down in her apartment complex, wanted to remind her that they had tickets to the Houston Grand Opera to see *Carmen* the next night. Going out with Sid wasn't dating. His girlfriend, Gloria, was an international flight attendant and was gone a great deal.

Picking up the phone, Madelyn began returning the calls. She put off the most difficult call . . . Kane . . . to last. Somehow he always knew when things were bothering her. Casually mentioning she had met Daniel Falcon to her parents had elicited only mild interest. Her oldest brother would be another story.

"What was he doing in San Antonio?" asked Kane.

"Getting a new mold made for his boots."

Kane chuckled. "He likes the finer things in life, but flying over nine hundred miles is reaching even for Daniel. There had to be another reason."

Madelyn glanced at the teddy bear. "If there was, he didn't confide in me."

"Don't feel bad. He confides in few people," Kane said. "I didn't know until I heard the news this morning that his company is moving from Denver to Houston."

"Houston?" she almost shouted.

"I take it he didn't tell you."

Madelyn's misery increased on recalling his unease when she told him she lived in Houston. He probably thought she would be one of those women chasing after him. Kissing him had only confirmed his speculations.

"N-No, he didn't."

"Sounds like the Daniel I know. Can't blame him though. Looks like the oil and gas industry is about to go boom again, and he's going to be a big part of it. Letting the competition know your plans would be business suicide."

"Yes."

"Looks like you'll be seeing him again then."

Madelyn chewed on her lip. "I doubt it. He's a busy man."

"You're both in Houston. Both in the petroleum business. You'll see him from time to time."

She managed a shaky laugh. "The underlings don't often mingle with the top brass."

Kane snorted. "Daniel's not the type to judge a person by their job description or their salary. You'll see him again."

Madelyn was unsure if she was feeling better or worse when she hung up the phone five minutes later.

Daniel was coming to Houston.

Heaven help her.

CHAPTER 4

Heaven might help her, but the news media wouldn't.

Daniel Falcon hit Houston with a media blitz that was unprecedented in recent history. Everyone wanted to interview him, see him, press flesh with him. The mayor and the city council members loved anyone who was legally bringing millions of taxable dollars into the city.

He was an instant hit.

Not since the Houston Rockets won the NBA title had the media covered an event so thoroughly. Only now one man held center court, and he did it brilliantly.

The camera loved him. He didn't have a bad angle to photograph or film. The press and citizens of Houston couldn't seem to get enough of his effortless charm or his exotic male beauty.

Friday afternoon at Special Occasions Beauty Shop proved no exception. The moment his smiling, handsome face appeared on the TV screen, everyone paused to watch, listen, and speculate.

"Now that's what I call one fine man."

"Look at those big hands. I bet that man could do a lot of damage."

"Hands nothing," shouted a dyed redhead getting a wave. "I wanna see the feet to see if he's gonna go the distance."

Special Occasion Beauty Shop erupted into bawdy laughter, foot stomping, and finger snaps. The wide open elongated room, done in purple and white, and filled with a profusion of cascading ivy and lush tropical plants, invited conversation and interaction between its clients—which they took full advantage of.

Refusing to join in, Madelyn hid her face behind a copy of *Our Texas* magazine. Scrunching down farther in her overstuffed purple floral chair, she wished she were still under the dryer.

Daniel Falcon had struck again—this time on a live broadcast with the local TV station. It was almost impossible to turn on the TV news or read the paper without seeing his face. Although she admired him and his accomplishments, she just wished seeing him didn't remind her of how little she had impressed him.

Not one time had he mentioned to her his plans to relocate Falcon Industries. Yet he was telling the interviewer the move had been planned for months. Add to that his plans to pitch his considerable wealth into finding the next mega oil fields, and she felt almost betrayed.

He could have said something, given her a hint. He hadn't. His silence couldn't have made it clearer that he didn't trust her or expect her to be a part of his life when he reached Houston.

Although she tried to concentrate on the editorial by Gemeral Berry in the magazine, it was impossible. The announcer's words drew her like the proverbial magnet. In almost reverent tones she described Daniel as brilliant, intelligent, and charismatic. Madelyn noted she left out ruthless in getting what he wanted. The reporter last night on the ten o'clock news hadn't, but the newscaster had been a male.

> Mr. Falcon has an uncanny knack for tapping into the next big-money venture before it hits big. His record as an industry forecaster and trendsetter is unprecedented in the business world. If anyone doubted that after a decade of lean years for the energy industry that energy would be back, then I suggest you look at Daniel Falcon.
>
> I know this reporter will be watching closely. This is Erica Stone reporting live from the temporary headquarters of Falcon Industries in downtown Houston. Back to you in the studio, Elvin.

"Somebody give Erica a bib, I think the woman is drooling."

"I bet she won't be back in the studio for a while."

"You think he likes 'em chesty?"

"He's a man, isn't he?"

"My man says more than a mouthful is a waste."

"That's because you're still wearing double-A's."

More laughter, including the teased woman wearing double-A's.

Surreptitiously Madelyn glanced down. She was all right in that area. But it wasn't likely that Daniel had any interest in finding out. He had been in Houston two weeks, and he had yet to contact her.

She snorted. As if he'd take the time. He was too busy giving interviews and grinning at chesty females like Erica Stone, who probably wore a push-up bra.

Instantly Madelyn was ashamed of herself. It wasn't like her to be waspish or vindictive. Daniel had her as confused and off kilter as she had ever been. She didn't know what to think of him, and apparently she wasn't alone.

It was a testament to his craftiness that he had virtually snuck into the oil and gas industry unnoticed. The same day he broke ground for his five-acre business development, he announced his purchase of Slate Oil Company, stunning people again. Slate Oil had been family owned for over seventy-five years and no one expected George Slate to sell a company his grandfather started despite its financial woes.

George Slate couldn't be reached for comment, and Daniel Falcon wore his perpetual smile just before saying, "No comment."

"Madelyn, I'm ready for you."

Madelyn almost leaped into the black leather chair. In thirty minutes she'd be out of here and on her way home. Tomorrow she planned a quiet day at home, and she wouldn't have to listen to one person comment about Daniel. Her relief was short-lived.

"You work for Sinclair Petroleum Company, don't you?" questioned the beautician blow-drying Madelyn's black hair.

Beneath her pink blouse, she rolled tense shoulders. "Yes."

"Any chance you might meet that good-looking hunk?" Stephanie asked, her speculative gaze meeting Madelyn's in the oval mirror in front of them.

"I doubt it. We move in different circles."

Sectioning Madelyn's hair Stephanie picked up the curling iron, expertly curled the black strands, then replaced the iron in its stand. "Too bad, I'd love to get my hands in his hair."

The beautician beside Stephanie snorted. "That's not all you want to get your hands into."

Stephanie, who was gregarious and easygoing, threw out one slim hip in exaggeration and struck a pose with the rattail black comb in her right hand. "I never said I'd stop there, now did I?"

The women hooted. Madelyn made herself smile. Stephanie had more men friends than she knew what to do with. There wasn't a doubt in Madelyn's mind that the other woman knew exactly what to do with Daniel if she got her hands on him.

Refusing to give in to self-pity or cattiness, Madelyn said in all truthfulness, "I'm not sure a man like Daniel Falcon would want to get in your long line."

Stephanie grinned and leaned down. "I'd let him go to the front."

"You and half the women in Houston," said the attractive woman who was sitting in the chair next to Madelyn, getting her hair braided. "A lot of them are rich, society women. Women who work for a paycheck don't have a chance."

"You think the brother is a snob?" asked the redhead from across the room.

"Whether he's a snob or not, how are you going to stand out among all the women trying to get a piece of him?" she asked. "When you've been used to the best, why settle for less?"

"Daniel's not like that," Madelyn said before she could stop herself.

Twenty-one pairs of eyes converged on her. Including women under the dryer.

Stephanie whirled Madelyn around in the chair so fast she had to clutch the armrests to keep from falling. "Daniel? I thought you didn't know the dude."

Madelyn fought the vision of leaving the beauty shop with her hair half done. "I said we move in different circles."

"So do you know the man or not?" asked the talkative redhead.

"We met briefly in San Antonio," Madelyn admitted reluctantly because she knew what was coming next.

"When you were on that weekend trip by yourself? You mean you let a fine-looking, rich man like that get away from you?" Stephanie questioned as if Madelyn had done the unforgivable.

Glancing around the shop, she wasn't sure she hadn't. Some of the faces wore surprise that they had met someone who had met Daniel, others were openly appraising. "We just didn't hit it off."

The look of sympathy that crossed her beautician's pretty face was unmistakable. "Probably a snob, like Eula thought. You're better off without him."

There was a distinct quietness in the shop before the conversation turned to the day's soaps. Madelyn stared straight ahead. Now the entire beauty shop knew Daniel Falcon had found her lacking. For a man she had never met until two weeks ago, he had certainly screwed up her life.

The phone was ringing when Madelyn opened her apartment door. Rushing to pick up the receiver, she answered breathlessly, "Hello."

"Hi, sis. Caught you coming in, huh?"

Madelyn smiled at the sound of Kane's voice and perched her hip on the arm of the sofa. "Just walked in from the beauty shop. How're Victoria and the twins?"

"Fine. I'm a lucky man." The pride and love in his deep voice was unmistakable.

"So are they. You're the best." She tossed her purse and keys on the cushion beside her.

Kane laughed, a rich, booming sound. "As long as you think that, I know some man hasn't stolen your heart."

She bit her lip. She wasn't so sure about that sometimes, but she wasn't about to discuss her feelings with Kane. He was too perceptive, and Daniel was too close a friend. "I'm too busy for that."

"At twenty-four you're also too young and naive. A lot of men out there can't be trusted. I almost asked Daniel to look out for you when he called."

"What!" she shouted jumping to her feet. "Tell me you're only teasing."

"Calm down," Kane said. "I know how you value your independence."

She bit her lip again. "Why did he call?"

"He wanted my input on some names he was given to head a work-study program for the minority youth in Houston."

Madelyn frowned and slowly sat back down. "I haven't heard anything about such a program."

"You won't," Kane told her. "He insists on total anonymity so he can pick the men and have full control. He wants the money going to the kids and not to bureaucratic red tape. He was in San Antonio finalizing a similar program. The Dallas/Fort Worth area is next, then Austin."

Madelyn fleetingly wondered if the boot mold was just a ruse, then another thought struck. "That will cost hundreds of thousands of dollars."

"I know. He had the same programs in Denver while he was there," Kane told her. "He feels as strongly as I do about helping to put something back into the community and state that has given him so much."

"He really isn't as ruthless as he pretends," Madelyn said, her voice soft.

Kane snorted. "Until you cross him, then watch out. But he protects his own. I respect him."

"He thinks highly of you and Matt, too."

"He's a good friend to both of us. Well, take care of yourself."

"I will and thanks for not telling Daniel to check on me," she said.

"You're welcome. Just don't make me regret it. Bye."

"I won't. Bye," Madelyn said and hung up the phone. So Daniel had a soft side. He called to her on so many levels. Now she had added another one. Growing up she'd always known she'd choose a man like her brothers: tough, aggressive, intelligent, but always aware of those weaker individuals who needed your help.

Picking up her things, she wondered why Daniel wanted her to think he was so ruthless—and more importantly, would she ever see him again to learn the answer.

Daniel Falcon tried to sit patiently while the long-winded gentleman at the podium extolled the return of the oil and gas industry. It was difficult. Especially when he wanted to get up again and see if he had actually seen Madelyn Taggart in the audience or just imagined her.

It wouldn't be the first time since he had arrived in Houston three weeks ago. He had almost spoken to one young woman. She had laughed just before he reached out to touch her. Instantly he'd realized his mistake. The laugh was pleasant enough—it just didn't make his heart beat faster or his blood run hotter.

Madelyn and her laugh had done both. Too well.

He should forget her, but somehow he couldn't. She had appeared so lost and alone standing in her hotel room doorway in San Antonio. He didn't regret walking away—he regretted that she didn't understand why he had to.

Judson Howell, the man at the podium, took a sip of water, shuffled his notes, and was off again. The man seated beside Daniel sighed.

Daniel studied the tip of his Bally loafers, then crossed one leg over the other. While doing so he barely refrained from glancing at the eighteen-karat gold and stainless steel Cartier watch on his wrist.

Now wasn't the time to appear impatient. Being asked, even at the last minute, to speak at the annual Cambridge Energy Research Associates meeting being held in Houston was a coup. Cambridge was a leading industrial consulting firm, and being on their agenda meant Daniel's foray into the energy business was being taken seriously.

It had better. He didn't do anything by halves.

Perhaps that's why he couldn't forget how badly things had ended between he and Madelyn. Kissing her hadn't been wise. The taste of her lips still haunted him. Sometimes he'd catch himself running his tongue over his lips to see if he could find a trace of her sweetness still there.

Knowing the idea was crazy hadn't helped him stop. With one erotically charged kiss, she had done more to upset his plans to remain emotionally uninvolved than any woman before her.

The polite smattering of applause alerted Daniel that the gray-haired gentleman had finally wound down. Straightening, Daniel added his own applause, then listened to the moderator introduce him as their "special, unannounced guest."

Daniel stood while the applause was still being given. Sharp black eyes searched the luncheon crowd of over five hundred with an intensity and concentration that his employees had learned to dread. Fortunately the people in the audience didn't know that. Unfortunately he didn't see the one person he had been looking for.

As soon as the applause began to dim down, he began speaking. His strong compelling voice reached to the back of the room as clearly and as easily as if he were speaking to each person directly. Placing one manicured hand on the podium, he spoke to the people as if he had always known them.

A quietness settled around the room as people stopped whispering at the tables, stopped trying to get one more bite of carrot cake, stopped clinking their spoons against the sides of their cups or glasses to stir sweetener into their coffee or tea. Daniel Falcon had them in the palm of his capable hand.

"Worldwide the demand, the need, for oil and gas is growing. We are in a position to meet that need. The profit potentials are staggering. You are to be commended for your faith, courage, and fortitude in standing firm in your belief when others loudly proclaimed the doom of the oil and gas industry. I salute you and welcome the opportunity to work alongside you in the coming years. Energy is back. Thank you."

The applause was thunderous. Before he could reach his seat, the ten men and women on the stage with him were there to shake his hand.

Daniel accepted their praise and congratulations with true appreciation. Working with friends was infinitely preferable to being in the midst of enemies. With a final handshake to the elderly speaker before him, Daniel headed for his seat. Something made him glance at the audience again.

This time he spotted her immediately. She sat near the back of the large ballroom. Dressed in a champagne-colored double-breasted suit with a portrait collar, she appeared to stiffen, then she glanced away.

His teeth clenched, Daniel continued to his seat. He had paused only a few seconds, but it was enough to tell him there was still something unfinished between them.

Thankfully the speaker after Daniel was short and to the point. With a fond farewell, the moderator adjourned the meeting and said he hoped to see everyone that night at the Petroleum Ball.

Daniel was out of his chair in an instant. His gaze locked on Madelyn until someone moved into his line of vision. Afterward he never stood a chance of catching her. People crowded around him, wanting to shake his hand, wanting to congratulate him.

With a patience he was far from feeling, he smiled and thanked them. Thirty minutes later when he finally left the raised platform, Madelyn's table was empty.

He should let it go at that and count it as a narrow escape. What was he going to say to her anyway? He honestly didn't know. All he knew that once he saw her, he had to see her again.

Madelyn was shaking as she stepped into the glittering ballroom that night. The immense room where they had eaten lunch had been transformed. Fifty-foot oil derricks were scattered throughout with the name of the most famous oil and gas strikes in Texas emblazoned on them.

On each side of the long tables laden with everything from succulent roast beef to poached salmon were nine-foot trees glittering with tiny white lights. Round, linen-draped tables, each with a stunning floral centerpiece in cylindrical crystal vases, were in a semicircle, leaving the middle open for dancing, milling around, and the all-important networking.

Walking farther inside, Madelyn searched the crowd for one person: Daniel Falcon.

Seeing Daniel on the podium at lunch had been a complete surprise. She, like everyone in the room, had been entranced by his voice. He was as dynamic as she remembered. When he had stopped on the stage and looked at her, every nerve cell in her body went on full alert.

She had remained at her table a full five minutes after everyone left, hoping he might come over and say hello. She left when it became obvious some of the people in the room were reluctant to let him go.

She had gone home and immediately started looking through her closet for a dress to wear to the Petroleum Ball. Before seeing Daniel, she hadn't planned on attending. Afterward she couldn't think of anything else.

All her mental anguish had been forgotten as she pulled a long, black crepe creation from her closet. Daring, sleek and sophisticated, the gown fit lovingly over her breasts, leaving one shoulder completely bare before skimming down to her narrow waist to flare from the knees down.

The other women would probably be wearing sequins and glitter. She'd rely on simplicity to capture Daniel's interest. She could no longer deny she wanted his attention and much more. The woman in the beauty shop was right . . . flash and dash wasn't going to do.

"You wanna dance?"

A man's voice jerked her around. In front of her was a man in his midtwenties, blatantly staring at her breasts. Besides bad manners, his cologne made her head ache. The jacket of his black tuxedo hung on thin shoulders. "No, thank you."

"Are you waiting for someone?" he persisted, giving her another once-over.

"Yes," she answered without a moment's hesitation.

"If he doesn't show up, I may still be available." Snickering at his own humor, he moved farther into the room and asked another woman to dance. He must have received a similar answer because he walked away.

"Madelyn, glad you decided to come after all."

Glancing around she saw her boss, Howard Sampson. Robust and balding, he smiled down at her. Working with him on a full-time basis was everything Madelyn had thought it would be. Each day he challenged her and accepted nothing less than her best.

She smiled warmly in return. "Hello, Mr. Sampson."

"This is my wife, Jane," he said proudly of the matronly woman by his side. "Jane, Madelyn Taggart, the newest member of my team. If she can stand the heat, she might make a darn good production engineer one day," he offered in a bit of oil humor.

His wife, in understated lavender chiffon, smiled indulgently. "Don't you let him intimidate you, dear. I've known him for sixty years and been married to him for forty-three of those. His bark is worse than his bite."

Madelyn liked the gray-haired woman instantly. "I'll try to remember that."

"Do you have a seat?" asked Jane.

"No, I just arrived."

"Then come and sit with us . . . if you don't think we'd bore you to death," Mrs. Sampson said with a teasing smile.

Madelyn didn't hesitate. "I'd love to."

Later that evening Madelyn couldn't quite believe she was sitting with some of the top executives at Sinclair. She had seen more than one person from the office send envious looks her way.

One of those was her ex-boss, Robert Carruthers. He was staring so hard he bumped into another gentleman. Madelyn loved it. Sending him a little wave over her shoulder, she straightened in her seat and looked directly into Daniel Falcon's fathomless black eyes.

Once again she had that breathless feeling. He made a woman consider sitting on her hands to keep from grabbing him.

Dressed in a tailored black tux that fit his tall, muscular body to perfection, he exuded sex appeal. Madelyn didn't have to look around the table at the women to know each one of them was affected. They all might be happily married, but they weren't dead.

"I hope I'm not interrupting. I just wanted to say hello to Ms. Taggart," he said, his voice a rich mixture of velvet and sin.

She felt a ripple of excitement. Maybe, just maybe.

Then she noticed the woman next to him: glittering from the crown of her head with an overdone tiara, a clunky gemstone necklace, and drop earrings to match. Madelyn couldn't see the woman's feet, but she was sure her evening shoes were just as sparkling.

Aware of the attention around the table on her, Madelyn forced herself to smile and make the introductions. She finished by saying, "I'm sorry, I don't know your companion."

Squeezing Daniel's arm, the dark-haired woman didn't wait for him to introduce her. "You must not attend the opera. I'm Natalie Kemp."

The words were deliberately condescending. "I love the opera," Madelyn explained. "One of my fondest memories is meeting Katherine Battle after she gave an outstanding performance at the Metropolitan Opera. The acoustics are marvelous. But I'm sure you know that since all the greats have performed there."

Uncertainty touched the other woman's face. "Not yet."

"Then what might I have seen you in?" Madelyn asked pleasantly, too aware of the conversational lull around the table. She'd be nice if it killed her.

Natalie glanced nervously around the table, then at Daniel before answering, "Mercedes in *Carmen.*"

"Ah, one of the gypsy women," Madelyn said, clearly astonishing the other woman with her knowledge of one of the minor roles in the opera. "Some of my friends are going tomorrow night. I'll have to tell them to look for you."

Natalie flushed.

"Come along, Madelyn, I think I've been sitting too long," Jane said and stood. "I'm not sure how long we'll be gone, so I'll say my goodbye to you now, Mr. Falcon, Ms. Kemp."

"Goodbye, Daniel, Ms. Kemp." With her hand on Jane's arm, they moved across the room.

"Don't worry, Madelyn, real men don't stay around vicious, catty women," Jane offered, accepting a flute of champagne from a white-jacketed attendant. "I'd say Ms. Kemp won't last the night."

Madelyn's hand trembled on the long stem. "I don't suppose it would do me any good to say I don't know what you're talking about."

"Please don't. I detest people who lie, and I already like you a lot."

A smile tugged the corner of Madelyn's mouth. "I like you, too."

"Good, then let's give them five more minutes and then we'll go back." Jane took a sip of wine.

"Thanks for the rescue," Madelyn replied softly.

"Women have to stick together." Jane lifted her glass in a salute. Madelyn joined her.

"Hey, this is pretty good," Jane said after downing half the contents. "I usually have only half a glass because it goes straight to my head, but since Sinclair is helping to underwrite this affair, we should do our best to have a good time."

"I agree." Madelyn drained her glass. Grinning, they placed their empty glasses on the tray of the circulating waiter and reached for full ones.

When they returned to their table several minutes later, Madelyn was feeling comfortably mellow. Her boss took one look at his wife's wide smile and decided it was time to go home.

Not wanting to stay, Madelyn followed them outside. "Good night, Mr. and Mrs. Sampson. Thanks for allowing me to sit at your table. I had a wonderful evening."

The older woman patted Madelyn's hand. "Call me Jane. We like each other, remember?"

"I remember." With a wave, Madelyn started toward the parking lot.

Mr. Sampson called after her, "You didn't valet park?"

"No, the line was too long." *And I was foolishly impatient to get inside and see if Daniel was there.*

"We'll take you to your car," Jane offered, her expression worried.

"It's all right. I'll be fine."

With a wave, she headed for the packed parking lot. When she had arrived it had been twilight, now darkness shrouded the area away from the bright gold and chrome hotel entrance. It was just her run of bad luck that the overhead light was out on the aisle where she had parked her car.

Chastising herself for her earlier impatience, she stopped near the outer perimeter of light shining from another part of the hotel to search in her bag for her car keys. A noise behind her spun her around.

Less than seven feet away was the ill-mannered man with the horrible cologne. "Thought you were waiting for someone."

"That wasn't your concern then or now."

He shrugged and the too-large jacket almost slipped off his shoulder. "Since we're both alone, what do you say we go someplace."

"I'm going home. Alone."

He stepped closer. "Don't play so hard to get. You and me could have a lot of fun together."

"You're pushing it." She was more angry than frightened. Men could be such egotistical jerks.

The man snorted. "Like I'm scared. What are you gonna do to me any—"

He never completed the sentence. He might have if he hadn't reached for her.

She reacted instinctively to the threat. Grabbing his hand, she used the momentum of his off-balance body to flip him over on his back. His wrist secure in her hands, she pressed her foot to his chest to keep him down.

"You were saying?" she asked mildly.

Angry curse words singed the air. However, another deeper, angrier voice had no trouble being heard.

"Shut up, you piece of trash. Count yourself lucky she got to you before I did," snarled a cold voice.

Madelyn jerked her head up and around. She'd know that voice anywhere. Daniel stood glaring down at the man who had suddenly quieted.

When Daniel looked at her, she saw black rage burning just short of control in his dark eyes. She swallowed.

"Are you all right?"

She swallowed again before she could answer. "Yes."

His gaze swept over her like silent, invisible fingers. "We'll talk about your part in this later." Taking the man's hand, he moved her aside, yanked him off the ground, then twisted his arm high up behind his back.

"Ohh! You're breaking my arm."

"Shut up and move."

The man moved.

Daniel called over his shoulder. "I'm not in a very good mood, so I suggest you follow us inside."

What did she care about his mood? He had messed up hers three weeks ago. And where was Miss Congeniality?

Picking up her purse and the scattered contents, Madelyn remembered Daniel's high-handedness in taking the man once he was down. Show-off.

Then she remembered something else: Daniel's close connection to her brothers. If they or her parents heard about this, she'd never hear the end of it.

"Daniel, wait a minute. We need to talk." Her skirt raised up over her knees, she sprinted to catch up. Her comfortable state of mellowness had lasted all of ten minutes.

CHAPTER 5

Madelyn couldn't believe what was happening. She had seen Kane on a tear, but he was mild compared to Daniel. She didn't blame the on-duty executive manager for looking uneasy. The chief of hotel security didn't escape his wrath, either.

Daniel's tone was scathing when he mentioned the light out in the parking lot and the stupidity of not putting on extra security people to patrol the parking lot on the night of a big event.

Both men had initially tried to defend themselves, but after Daniel got through with them, they simply listened. Madelyn didn't blame them. She wasn't about to forget his words about her part in this.

As for Jerome Turner, the man who had started all this, he remained slumped in his chair, his thin shoulders hunched forward in the ill-fitting tux. He worked in the janitorial department of one of the oil companies and had stolen the invitation out of the wastebasket. He probably hoped Daniel had forgotten him.

The thought was wasted. Every few seconds Daniel would turn those steely, black eyes of his on the man, and the tension in the room would almost sizzle.

Madelyn had thought of leaving the private office they were quickly and quietly escorted to, but as if he had a sixth sense where she was concerned, each time she began to ease up from her chair, Daniel's attention immediately shifted to her. Considering she had to ask a favor of him, she decided after being caught for the second time, she'd stay.

"If Ms. Taggart had been harmed in any way because of your carelessness, you would have answered to me," Daniel said, his voice crackling with dark promise.

He was a magnificent warrior, she admitted reluctantly. He intimidated and commanded respect. No one in their right mind would antagonize him. She'd read that traits such as fearlessness and daring were inheritable. He'd certainly gotten his share.

"I'm sorry, Mr. Falcon," David Flowers, the executive on duty repeated, his Adam's apple bobbing up and down in his thin neck. "Maintenance is taking care of the light, and extra security is on the lot. We've pulled off some of the valet attendants to escort unescorted ladies to their cars."

"The police are on their way," offered the middle-aged security guard, his hands noticeably by his sides instead of hooked in the waist of his pants as when he had arrived. He had ripped them out two seconds after Daniel tore into him.

"Police," Jerome shouted, straightening in his chair. "Now wait a minute. Ain't no call for that. I just wanted to pick her up for a little fun."

Daniel whirled and reached for him.

"Stop him," Jerome yelled, toppling his chair backward in an attempt to get away from Daniel. It was useless. Tossing the straight-back chair to one side, Daniel kept going.

"Daniel, if you touch that man you'll end up in jail, and I thought you wanted to talk to me," Madelyn said, trying to sound calm when her entire body was shaking.

He stopped, but didn't turn. "I know where to find you." The implication was that the cowering man might not be so easy.

Both hands defensively in front of him, the young man scooted until his back hit the wall. He swallowed repeatedly. "Look, man, I'm sorry. I didn't mean no harm. I was on my way to the bus stop, saw her and thought I'd try one more time."

"Bus stop," Madelyn cried in disbelief. "You were trying to hustle me, and you didn't even have a car?"

"What's this about one more time?" Daniel asked coldly.

"I-I asked her to dance. She turned me down." He shook his head. "I didn't mean no harm. I just reached for her, and she pulled that judo crap on me."

"I thought Mr. Falcon subdued you," said the executive.

The man on the floor shot Daniel a glance before answering. "I-I forgot."

Madelyn returned the speculative looks of the hotel executive and the security guard with what she hoped was an I'm-just-a-helpless-female look. It galled her to do so. But the thought of having her name on a police report wasn't thrilling.

"Daniel, can we go now?"

With one last lethal look at the cowering man, Daniel turned. "Let's go."

"Man, please—don't send me to jail. I ain't got no record, and I'm gonna lose my job as it is," Jerome pleaded.

Daniel jerked around, his eyes as ruthless and chilling as his voice. "You should have thought of that before you tried to attack her."

"Man, I told you, I just wanted to pick her up. My partner said he came to one of these things last year and scored. He didn't have no car, either."

"And you believed him?" Madelyn asked incredulously.

"Greg's a player. Says he always scores. Said they left in her ride. I figured I could do the same. Please," Jerome cried, "I apologize. I was being cocky, but I didn't mean to scare your woman, man. I swear. My mama would take a broomstick to me."

"Your mother?" asked Madelyn softly, her curiosity growing with every word the young man spoke.

As if realizing his hope lay with Madelyn, the young man gave his full attention to her. "I live with my mother. If I didn't have to give her a hundred dollars every two weeks for rent and take out health insurance, I'd have a car—and Keisha wouldn't have kicked me to the curb."

"You might have needed the health insurance if you had touched Ms. Taggart," Daniel reminded him.

The young man began shaking. Madelyn wanted to swat Daniel. Any man who paid his mother rent money wasn't all bad. "Have you ever missed paying rent?"

His gaze touched the floor. "Once—but she had my clothes packed two days later. I had to borrow the money from my partners."

"Was Greg one of the men you borrowed money from?" she asked.

"No. He said his ex-wife was hassling him about child support. He wanted money from me," Jerome admitted.

"Greg sounds like a person I'd stay away from," she said.

"That's what my mama says."

"Then perhaps I should call her and let her know you didn't listen," Madelyn threatened.

Wide-eyed, he came off the floor. "You can't. My mama would kill me if she knew about this."

Daniel had matched movements with the man, his huge bulk defensively in front of Madelyn. Scowling at his broad back, she stepped around him. The man's fear was obvious. Somehow Madelyn knew he didn't mean "kill" literally.

"I won't, if you do some things for me." The man was bobbing his head in agreement before she finished. "Apologize to your employer, scratch Greg off as a buddy, and give your mother a hug when you get home."

He hung his head. "If I hug her, she'll know I did something wrong."

"Then you'll just have to suffer the consequences. It's better than going to jail," she told him. "In case you think about forgetting . . ." She paused adding, "Remember this man standing by my side, because he certainly won't forget you."

"I won't forget," he promised, looking as unhappy as any teenager made to own up to his misdeeds.

Madelyn touched Daniel, felt the tenseness in his arms, and forged ahead anyway. "I believe him. There are enough young men with police records. Life for a young black man can be rough enough without that. You believe in giving young people a chance, or you wouldn't have started the work-study programs," she finished softly for his ears alone.

His surprised gaze jerked toward her.

"Please," she said. "I think he's telling the truth. I don't want to press charges."

A muscle leaped in Daniel's bronzed jaw, then he spoke to Mr. Flowers. "If it checks out he has no prior arrest records, we won't press charges."

"Thank you. Thank you," Jerome cried.

Daniel turned cold eyes on him again. "Don't make me regret my decision."

"You won't. And, miss, I'm sorry."

"I hope you are, but another thing you can do for me is start treating women with respect," she told him.

"Come on." Daniel urged her out of the office and down the lush carpeted hallway to the immense atrium lobby. Passing the two rushing Houston policemen, they kept walking.

"You don't want to talk with them?" Madelyn questioned.

"I've ranted enough for one night," Daniel answered.

From beneath her lashes, Madelyn glanced sideways at his stern profile. "You mean you don't always have men sweating bullets."

"I'm glad you can smile about it," he said, steering her around a group of chattering people.

She heard the tightness of his voice and knew she shouldn't have teased him. He had been concerned about her safety.

"I'm all right, Daniel. I was too angry to get scared. I overreacted." Her lips twitched. "Imagine him trying to pick up someone while riding a bus." Laughter bubbled from her throat.

Daniel stopped and stared down into Madelyn's animated face. She could laugh—and he was still shaking. His rage against the hotel staff had been misplaced. He was the one really to blame.

The instant he had seen the light go out of Madelyn's dark eyes when he introduced the opera singer, his guilt had begun. The woman had meant nothing to him. Another woman who wanted to add his name to her list of lovers. He had met her at the ball and had escorted her back to her table after she had tried to insult Madelyn.

She should have saved her breath for her arias. No one got the best of the laughing woman in front of him. Not some cocky jerk trying to pick her up, and not Daniel Falcon.

He had seen her leave with the Sampsons and followed. People stopping him to speak had caused him to lose sight of her. The valet had pointed Daniel in the right direction. Hearing the man boast, then seeing him reach for her, had enraged him. He didn't know who was surprised the most—him or the man on the ground with her foot in his chest.

He shook his head. "You're something."

"Glad you noticed."

"I noticed." He started walking again. "I'd appreciate it if you wouldn't tell anyone about my involvement with the work-study program."

"I won't. Kane explained everything to me." She glanced up at him through a dark sweep of lashes. "I think it's very generous of you."

He shrugged. "Don't go picturing me any different than I am."

"Why won't you let me think anything good about you?"

"Because there isn't," he said, leading her down three marbled steps. "We'll get my car first, then I'll follow you home."

"That isn't necessary. Besides what about Miss Congen— Kemp?" Madelyn quickly corrected.

"I met her only tonight," he said, ushering her through the outside glass door held open by a uniformed attendant. "I'm not going to renew the acquaintance."

"Mr. Falcon, Mr. Flowers called and your car is waiting." The smiling young man looked at her. "I'll be happy to escort you to your car."

"Thank—"

"That won't be necessary," Daniel said, cutting her off, then urging her to his Bentley coupe parked by the curb. He opened the door. "Get in. I'll take you to your car."

Madelyn lifted her chin. She was tired of him seeing her as his friends' helpless little sister who always needed rescuing. "I can see myself home."

"Do I call Kane or Matt first?"

Madelyn got in the car without another word. Closing the door, Daniel tipped the attendant standing a respectful distance away.

"You really aren't going to tell on me are you?" she asked, gnawing on her lower lip.

"That depends," he said, setting the car in motion.

"On what?"

He shot her a glance before turning in the direction of the parking lot, glad to see a security guard on foot patrol and the burned-out bulb replaced. "On whether you appease my appetite or not."

A soft gasp echoed in the car.

Daniel didn't know if the sound pleased or displeased him. "I didn't get a chance to eat at the banquet today or tonight. Any chance on fixing me a sandwich or something?"

Madelyn vacillated between anger and disappointment. She took both out on the French bread she was slicing on the cutting board. How could she keep letting herself in for disappointment?

Easy—she got within an inch of Daniel, and her brain shut down. Too bad his didn't do the same.

"You sure I can't help?" he offered.

She glanced up and wished she hadn't. He had made himself comfortable. His jacket was gone, his shirt unbuttoned at the collar, and the sleeves rolled back. But the worst thing he had done was to take the band from his hair.

Shannon, her sister-in-law, hadn't exaggerated when she described it as being sensual. The lustrous black hair lightly streaked with silver moved with a supple grace that was almost hypnotic.

She didn't know if the reason was because she wasn't used to seeing men with long hair, the hair itself, or because everything about Daniel seemed to make her heart beat faster.

"My beautician wanted me to tell you she wanted to get her hands on your hair," she said, thinking she'd better leave the other part out. "I told her I'd tell her if I saw you."

Pushing away from the door, he came to stand beside her. She barely kept from jumping when he touched her hair. "She did a good job with yours, but I think I'll pass."

Nodding, she went back to making the submarine sandwiches. Daniel's blunt-tipped fingers picked up an olive and popped it into his mouth.

"These will be ready in a minute." *Faster if you'd move.*

"No hurry. You're sure I can't help? Even I can slice and dice," he said.

She shook her head, piling on shredded lettuce, pickles, tomatoes, and onions. "Matt burns water. Kane is a fantastic cook."

"How about you?" he asked.

She smiled in spite of the tension. "Somewhere between Kane and Matt. I was in a lot of activities at school, and I just didn't seem to have the time. You're lucky I went to the store yesterday. Mama's care package isn't due until Friday."

Picking up the round platter of sandwiches, she placed them on the table. "Is cola all right, or do you want a beer? I mean is beer okay?"

"Alcohol has never been a problem for me, although I seldom drink." He smiled and Madelyn's heart did a little flip-flop. "Do your brothers know you drink beer?"

"It belongs to them," she told him with an answering smile.

"Then cola is fine. Matt probably keeps count."

She laughed and sat down in the chair he held for her. "You know him well, don't you?"

"He's a good friend," Daniel said, no longer smiling.

Madelyn placed her hands in her lap, her appetite gone. "So I can't be one, is that it?"

Black eyes bore into hers. "It wouldn't stop there, and we both know it."

"We could try," she offered.

His laughter was rough. "You couldn't be that naive."

"I'm not naive or afraid of what I want."

"You should be." Rising, he pushed his chair back under the table. "I'll get something on the way back home. You need to rest."

She was right behind him as he went to the door. "Stop telling me what I need. I can take care of myself."

He whirled, his eyes blazing. "Just because you put down that guy tonight doesn't mean it might not have been a different story if he had been armed or more determined."

"I've taken tae kwon do classes for four years. Any man who touches me better have his life insurance paid up."

"Is that so?"

"That's so!" She knew she had challenged the wrong man the instant the words left her mouth.

She expected him to come after her, no holds barred. She knew she wouldn't be any match for Daniel. Skill might count for a lot, but he outweighed her by a good ninety pounds. Besides, something about the way he carried himself let her know he could walk into the meanest bar in Texas and come out unscathed.

"You like challenges, do you? Let's see how you like this one." Abruptly he pulled her into his arms. His head dipped.

She closed her eyes, expecting an assault on her body. She should have known better.

The assault came, but it was against her senses. The tiny, nibbling bites on her lips—the slow, rough glide of his hot tongue against the seam of her lips—stripped her of her defenses and left her hungry.

He was feasting on her lips, and she was starving.

Her hands loosened their hold on his shirt and slid around his neck, pressing closer to his masculine strength and warmth. She wanted more. Her lips parted, trying to join their mouths.

His lips kept moving, always an instant in time ahead of hers. Frustrated, she reached up and grabbed handfuls of thick hair and kept him still. His mouth finally closed fiercely over hers. The fit was perfect, natural. Instead of assuaging the hunger as she thought, the mating of their tongues made the ache spiraling from the middle of her body intensify.

Whimpering, she pressed her body against his, trying to make the ache go away. His hands pulled her hips firmly against his blunt arousal. Air hissed over her teeth at the utterly arousing and erotic contact.

Her knees sagged. Her head fell backward.

Daniel took the opportunity to press kisses against the slim column of her graceful neck, the rapid pulse beating at the base of her throat. Her tempting, full breasts were only a short distance away. His lips skimmed downward on her bare skin.

Locking his arm around her tiny waist, he lifted. Startled, she cried out, then cried out for another reason as his teeth closed around her nipple and tugged.

Abruptly his head lifted. "Did I hurt you?" Daniel asked, his voice hoarse.

Her eyelids blinked open. Her eyes were black with passion. "I—I—"

"Did I hurt you?" he repeated, his face an anguished mask.

Trembling fingers touched the rigid line of his mouth. "N-No. I was just surprised. I never knew. I never knew," she said, replacing her fingertips with her lips.

"Mad—"

Whatever he had been about to say vanished when her tongue touched his. He drew her to him again. One more kiss, and then he was out the door. He simply meant to teach her that she couldn't keep on provoking him. One more sweet taste.

He felt Madelyn's small hands on his bare chest and started to pull away. When had he unbuttoned his shirt?

Warm lips closed gently on his hard brown nipple. He groaned instead. When his shirt had been unbuttoned no longer mattered. He was wildly glad that it was.

Her head lifted, and he found himself torn between regret and salvation, then her tongue licked the nub delicately, before she whirled her tongue around the turgid point.

He shuddered.

By the time she had moved to the next nipple, Daniel was holding on by a mere thread. His entire body was shaking with need. He had been a fool to start this. He had wanted her too badly for too long.

"M-Madelyn, we have to stop this."

She kept right on driving him out of his mind with her delicate little tongue, seemingly lost in the touch and taste of him. Thinking to stop her, he pulled her up to him and kissed her. She melted against him like honey on a hot day. Her unbridled response snapped the last thread of his control and sealed their fate.

She was a woman burning in his arms, and he needed her fire to survive.

Stopping was impossible. The need had built inside him, picking up force like an avalanche thundering down the mountainside, mercilessly taking everything in its wake, its power awesome and frightening.

He didn't know where the bedroom was, and it was pure chance the first door he entered held a bed. They tumbled on top of the covers. Daniel swiftly rolled, bringing her beneath him. Feeling her full length against him was pure ecstasy.

He wanted to taste her, taste all of her . . . later. Now he ached too much. He rolled again, this time standing as he unzipped her dress. Thankfully she seemed as impatient to undress him.

Sweeping the covers aside, he lay back down, taking her with him. He prepared himself, moved her thighs apart, and thrust into her.

The thin barrier easily gave way. Disbelief tautened his body.

No, she couldn't be! Wide-eyed he stared down into her strained features. Her lips were tightly pressed together, her eyes shut.

She had been a virgin.

Cursing, he started to withdraw. She arched against him, locking her legs around his hips.

Breath hissed through clenched teeth. His forehead rested on hers. "Please don't move, Madelyn."

She heard him. She just wasn't able to stop trying to find some ease from the feeling of being stretched and filled. It had been so nice before— Maybe if she lifted her hips.

Control slipped beneath the seductive call of her body. Daniel met her halfway. She tried to pull back but he followed, his body plunging deeper, then withdrawing.

Pleasure snuck up on her. Instead of shrinking from the intimacy, she was greedily demanding more.

Their mouths and bodies fused. Her arms wrapped around his neck, her legs locked around his hips, she met him stroke for incredible stroke. Madelyn felt her body spiraling out of control, the feeling frightening. Instinctively, she began to withdraw in mind and body.

"No, come with me."

The husky entreaty of his voice caused her fear to recede. Her fingernails bit into Daniel's perspiration-dampened back. Her head arched, her body tightened as she reached toward the spiraling sensation, knowing Daniel was with her.

As soon as the last aftershock left her body, Daniel rolled to one side and held her tightly in his arms. Madelyn snuggled closer. She had never felt so happy, so complete. She had known almost from the first moment he had held her that she would love him.

Feeling shy and bold at once, she ran her hand down his back. The stiffness of his muscles surprised her when she was feeling so mellow. "Daniel, what's the matter?"

Suddenly he released her and sat up on the side of the bed, his broad back to her. "I'm sorry."

The tiny ray of fear receded. He was only concerned about her. "You didn't hurt me," Madelyn said, sitting up in bed and clutching the sheet to her breasts. She reached out to touch him.

He jerked at the contact, stood, and began dressing. "Yes, I did. In ways you don't even understand yet."

"Daniel, what's the matter?" Fear crept over her, stronger this time. "Did I do something wrong?"

"No. Never think that." Finally he faced her, his face tortured. "This shouldn't have happened."

She flinched, but kept his gaze. "I-Is that all you have to say?"

"What else is there to say?" he questioned, roughly buttoning his shirt.

"How about 'Madelyn, I'd like to see you again.' Or 'Madelyn, this was just a one-night stand.' "

His grim expression told her he could say neither of those things. "I tried to warn you in San Antonio I'm not the staying kind."

"So you did." Hurt beyond measure, Madelyn glanced away. "I'm sure you can find the front door. You seem to have excellent radar in finding the bedroom."

"I didn't mean for this to happen."

"Goodbye, Daniel." The words were tight.

"Mad—"

"Just go."

For endless moments he stared at her, then her huddled form turned away from him. The sight tore at his heart. He was already reaching for her when he realized his mistake. If he touched her, they'd probably end up doing the same thing she was crying about now.

A virgin. He hadn't expected that. She had been too responsive and somehow knowing in his arms. There hadn't been any of the awkwardness he'd have expected from an inexperienced woman. She had come to him with fire and passion, making his feeble attempts to deny himself her sweetness impossible.

Even now he still wanted her. Yet more than the wanting of her body, he wanted to see her smile, hear her laugh.

"Mad—" He broke off abruptly. The instant he began speaking, she flinched and curled tighter into a fetal position.

Guilt weighing heavily on his shoulders, he turned to leave and saw the teddy bear he had won for her in San Antonio. The animal's flat black eyes seemed to stare at Daniel accusingly.

Closing his eyes, Daniel glanced upward. What had he done? How could an innocent like Madelyn deal with something like this? No answer came. Opening his eyes, he left.

Madelyn heard him leave and wondered how she could still breathe with her heart ripped out. The front door opened and—after what seemed a lifetime—closed.

With a whimper of pain, she tucked her chin into her chest.

CHAPTER 6

Head bowed, Daniel's hand clamped and unclamped around Madelyn's front doorknob. He couldn't leave her like this. Not in misery after she had trusted him.

But what could he say? Do? That he valued her gift, the generosity of her sweet body, but he had been the wrong man to give it to. A sound from the direction of the bedroom had him whirling sharply.

Crying. No, crying wasn't the heart-wrenching sounds he heard. She was sobbing. He'd hurt her. A hurt he didn't know how to mend or fix or even if it were possible to correct such a wrong.

It didn't take a genius to figure out that she probably thought she cared about him. In her inexperience she had confused lust with love. A woman didn't wait that long and then give herself to a man unless she thought there was some permanency to the relationship.

She had picked the wrong man. Marriage was out for him. Even when two people loved each other, it wasn't enough. Madelyn was looking at her brothers and her parents as examples. Unfortunately he had his parents as examples.

Love hadn't kept them together. They couldn't live together and couldn't live apart. They'd tried dozens of times to make it work, until a couple of years ago. The final break had been physically and mentally hard on both of them . . . and on him and his sister, Dominique, who hurt for them both.

No wonder neither his nor his sister's plans included marriage—although Dominique had had to learn her lesson the hard way.

The wrenching sounds from the bedroom gave no indication of lessening. Daniel's hand rubbed the back of his neck. Jewelry, flowers, or a designer original wouldn't fix this. She'd probably try to stuff it down his throat if he tried.

All he had was the truth and the hope that she'd understand. Slow steps took him to the bedroom. His knuckles rapped softly on the wall by the door.

"Madelyn?" The sobs stopped abruptly. "Can I come in?"

"Go away."

"Madelyn, please."

"You don't want me. What could be plainer?"

He stepped into the doorway. The sight of her sitting with her back pressed against the headboard, her knees drawn up, frantically wiping tears with the corner of her sheet, tore the words from his throat. "I wanted you. I still want you."

Her head jerked up. Hope flashed in her teary brown eyes. He clamped down hard on the need not to hurt her anymore and let her believe for just a little while. "But I don't love you."

She seemed to shrink and retreat before his eyes. He locked his legs and forced himself not to go any closer. "I made up my mind a long time ago that love and marriage weren't for me. I grew up watching the misery and heartache my parents put each other through—and I promised myself, I wasn't going to fall into that trap."

Finally Madelyn lifted her head. "It doesn't have to be that way."

"You're so naive and innocent, I should have seen it before. Love doesn't always survive."

"It can if the people love each other enough."

"Don't confuse lust with love. I wanted you, and love had nothing to do with it." She flinched again, but he was determined to get through this. "I was as cocky as that creep you took down tonight in thinking I could control the situation, that I was actually teaching you a lesson. Instead I took something from you that can never be replaced.

"The only reason I got farther was that you trusted me. I broke that trust. I know you can't stand the sight of me. You probably hate me, and you have every right. What I did was unforgivable. I ask you only one thing: Don't blame yourself. You expect everyone to be as open and as honest as you are. Some of us aren't."

Madelyn didn't know what to say. No matter how he phrased it, he didn't love her. Worse, he wouldn't even try. She was in love with a man who couldn't love her back. Her head fell forward.

"Are you all right?"

She heard the concern in his voice, saw it in his coal-black eyes when she lifted her head: concern, not love. She had given him all she was going to. Somehow she managed to speak with only a minor quiver in her voice, "No, but I will be."

His hands clamped. "I'll call tomorrow."

"I'd rather you didn't."

"I'll call."

The first call came a little after nine Sunday morning. Madelyn lay in bed listening to Daniel's voice and vacillated between anger at herself and at him. She'd known his reputation, and she had let herself get caught up in the moment anyway.

She had never known a kiss could render you mindless, make your body crave for so much more. Once his lips touched hers, thinking became impossible. All her senses took over. Daniel dominated every one.

The touch, the taste, the scent of him wrapped around her—and all she wanted was for the sensation to continue. His voice had dropped to a deep, velvet whisper that sent shivers through her. At the sight of him, his hair hanging down his back, his eyes dangerously alive, she had wanted time to stand still.

The answering machine clicked. She sent the machine a hard glare, then rolled to her side to stare out the sliding glass door leading to her small patio. The large teddy bear Daniel had won for her stared reproachfully back at her from the other side of the glass.

"You're not getting back in here any more than he is," she told the stuffed animal, then tucked her head into the crook of her folded arms. Unlike last time there wasn't a whiff of Daniel's cologne to send her stumbling out of bed. She hadn't stopped until she had laundered the sheets and the pillowcases. She wanted nothing to remind her of her stupidity.

Of all the guys who had tried to talk her into bed in high school or college, she hadn't been tempted, not once. Daniel didn't even have to ask. In the bright light of day, that galled and angered Madelyn more than anything. She had let her feelings for him overshadow every other consideration.

He wouldn't get another chance. She had learned her lesson. But she had paid a high price.

The phone rang. Somehow she knew who the call was from. Her father's cheerful voice came through loud and clear.

"Hi, Kitten. When are you coming home? Seems like a year instead of a month. I guess you're at Sunday school. Today's the pastor's anniversary, and your mother went early to help out." He chuckled. "Probably doing a lot of bragging on how well our baby girl is doing. I better go before I'm late. You know how she hates that. Don't know what time we'll be home, so we'll call back. Bye, Kitten."

The answering machine clicked.

"Oh, Daddy. Your baby girl messed up, and I don't know what to do about it."

"Madelyn, since you won't answer the phone, I'm coming over. I'll be there in twenty minutes."

Madelyn sprang up in bed and stared at the answering machine as if it had turned into a snake. Why couldn't he leave her alone? He had gotten what he wanted.

The thought caused her to wince. She had been ridiculously easy for him. But once she learned something, she never forgot.

Scooting to the edge of the bed, she stuck her foot into her clogs, grabbed her purse off the dresser, and headed for the door. He thought he was so smart. She'd show him.

A smug smile on her face, she turned from locking her door. Her mouth gaped.

"You move faster than I thought," Daniel said.

He was less than ten feet in front of her and closing fast. She glanced toward her car, then back at Daniel. She'd never make it. "I don't want to see you anymore."

"I know and I don't blame you," he answered.

She frowned. "Then why are you here?"

"Because you've been hiding in your apartment and I didn't want that."

"How could . . ." Her voice trailed off as he pulled a cell phone from his pocket. "You've been out here since nine?"

"Actually since eight. I didn't know if you went to early church service."

She couldn't take it in. "I don't understand."

"You're a good, caring woman. What happened last night goes against everything you've been taught. You won't easily forgive yourself, although the fault was mine."

"I was so easy," she whispered in anguish.

Strong hands gripped her shoulders. "Don't say that. Don't you ever say that."

She recoiled. His hands dropped, and he stepped back. "It wasn't your fault. Get that through your head. You depended on me, and I let you down."

There was a question she had to ask. "Did . . . did you plan for . . . for it to happen?"

He gazed at her with steady eyes. "No. I lost control for the first time in my life. I'm not happy about it. Saying I'm sorry won't change things, but I don't want you beating yourself over the head."

She glanced away. "I can't help it."

"Would it help if you beat me over the head instead?" Her gaze jerked back around. "I have a training room in my house."

"No." She had faced disappointments before and survived. She'd survive this time. She had some pride left. He'd never know how much she hurt inside. She held out her hand. "Goodbye, Daniel."

"Take care of yourself." His hand closed around hers.

Nodding, she pulled her hand free and walked to her car. She hadn't missed the electric awareness between them. From the sudden narrowing of his eyes, he hadn't, either. At least she no longer felt used and discarded. She just wished she felt loved.

Daniel watched Madelyn drive away and wondered why he felt worse instead of better. The animosity between them was gone. She had left instead of retreating back into her apartment. He had almost accomplished what he had set out to do. She hadn't smiled or laughed, but she would.

The only problem was, he wouldn't be there to see or hear it.

Madelyn didn't know where she was driving to, and she didn't care. Knowing how hectic the Houston freeways could be, she took the off ramp and simply drove aimlessly until she saw Meyer Park and pulled in.

Too restless to sit, she got out and soon found herself in front of the duck pond, her mind still on Daniel. He was right. She was more angry with herself than she was with him. He had offered nothing, promised nothing. She had wrongly assumed that he felt the same way she did.

He had felt only lust.

Her fault. Despite the idea of being called antiquated by some of her friends, she had always expected to wait until she married to make love. That's why none of the other men in her life ever tempted her to go farther than a few heated kisses.

The moment she had kissed Daniel at the carnival in San Antonio, she had known he was the one she had been waiting for. There was a connection there that even he couldn't deny.

He hadn't tried. She might be inexperienced, but she knew he still wanted her. He just wasn't going to let himself be swayed by his emotions the way she was.

She had three choices: mope and hide from life, chalk up the experience as a bad decision, or go on and pray one day he might stop running from a commitment. Since the possibility of her feelings toward him changing wasn't an option, she really didn't have a choice.

Like her mother, she somehow knew she'd love only once. Considering Daniel's coming over this morning to check on her, and his statement that she was the only woman that had ever made him lose control, things weren't as bleak as they could be.

Returning to her car, Madelyn drove home. Without replaying the messages on the answering machine, she called her parents later that afternoon. At the sound of her mother's voice, her throat stung. The sensation became worse when she talked with her father.

She'd always been Daddy's girl. She'd follow him anywhere. She'd learned to drive by sitting in his lap, caught her first fish with his favorite pole, served him her first mud cake.

Her eyes stinging, she looked straight into the glassy black eyes of the teddy bear. Swallowing, she made up her mind what she was going to do.

After promising she'd be home the following weekend, she put the bear back in the corner of her bedroom. She wasn't a quitter or a coward. Somehow she'd find a way to change Daniel's mind—and maybe, just maybe, win the heart of a falcon.

This has got to stop. Splashing cold water on her face, Madelyn took deep breaths and tried to keep her stomach from emptying anything more. Her lunch was already gone, but that hadn't seemed to matter to her stomach.

The women's rest room door opened, and Cassandra Lincoln came in. "You're feeling better?"

Madelyn sucked in another breath before she answered. "I'm not sure."

The petite blonde frowned. "Today is the second day in a row you've thrown up your lunch. Maybe you're getting an ulcer?"

With one hand on her stomach, Madelyn straightened. "Probably a virus. I've been sick the last couple of mornings also."

Cassandra's blue eyes narrowed, then she smiled. "If I didn't know better, I'd think you might be pregnant."

Madelyn spun toward the other woman, horror written on her face. "What?"

Cassandra held up her hands. "Just kidding. Everyone knows you're the straight-arrow type. I better get back. If you're still sick by tomorrow, you should see a doctor."

Clutching her stomach, Madelyn stared at the closed door. She didn't have to see a doctor for a little virus. She certainly wasn't pregnant. She couldn't be.

Snatching a paper towel from the dispenser, she dried her face and repaired her makeup. She felt better already.

Once at her desk, she went back to working on the specifications for a deep well.

There was a brief knock on her open office door, then Mr. Sampson came in. "Madelyn, I need you and Floyd to fly down to the Gulf. Number fifty-eight is ready to be plugged up and abandoned."

Just the thought of riding in the helicopter sent her stomach into a spasm. Unconsciously she clutched it.

He frowned, coming farther into the room. "You sick?"

She swallowed. "I've picked up a virus."

"That lets you out." He peered at her closely. "Maybe you should stay home tomorrow."

"I'll be fine," she said. "Besides I'm almost finished with new designs for the deep well in zone eight."

"Really?" His eyes brightened. "Then I'd certainly want you to stay and complete that. Cassandra can take your place on the Mexico trip."

"I'll have the report to you by tomorrow afternoon," Madelyn said, her voice wavering only slightly.

By three the next day, Madelyn was trembling and flushed, yet somehow she had managed to finish the report. Despite drinking only a carbonated beverage, she continued to feel queasy.

Mr. Sampson took one look at her when she handed him the report and told her to go home and stay there until she was well. All he needed was the rest of his staff to get sick.

This time she didn't argue. She had never felt worse. Opening the door to her apartment, she stopped only long enough to grab a carbonated beverage from the refrigerator.

Two sips later she was running to the bathroom. After emptying her stomach, she looked into the mirror, refusing to believe what her body was telling her. Eyes shut, she tried to keep the suspicion from forming into thought.

It was useless.

The word formed. Hammered against her skull.

Pregnant.

Unsteady legs refused to hold her. She slid to the cool tile of the bathroom floor. This couldn't be happening to her. She had done it only one time. One time.

No. Her eyes snapped open. Something else was wrong. Maybe she had caught some virus? Her cycles had always been erratic. It was only a coincidence that the Petroleum Ball was a little over six weeks ago. There was no need to panic.

She was overreacting. Daniel had used protection. Just because she had been nauseous for the past few days didn't mean anything. Her breasts being tender was probably due to some hormonal imbalance due to her irregular cycle.

Yes, that was it.

Feeling better, she got up from the floor. The wan, frightened face staring back at her wasn't reassuring.

"I'm not. I'll prove it."

Washing her face and brushing her teeth, she grabbed her purse and rushed out to the car. Not daring to let anyone know her suspicions, she drove to a drugstore on the other side of town.

She sat in the busy parking lot a full five minutes to make sure she didn't see anyone she knew before she went inside. Unwilling to ask a clerk for directions, it took her two frantic minutes of looking over her shoulder before locating the home pregnancy kits.

Grabbing the first one, she went to the counter. When the clerk bagged the kit in a plastic bag and handed it to her, she quickly stuffed it into her purse and left. *You'd think stores would use paper sacks for bagging personal items,* she thought irritably.

Knowing she was being irrational didn't help her to calm down. Always a safe driver, she ran two caution lights and kept the speedometer on seventy on the freeway. Once the test came up negative, she'd be back to her normal self.

Thirty minutes later Madelyn stared at the blue indicator, a growing knot of fear tightening her stomach. No. It was wrong. The kit must have been faulty.

Grabbing her purse again, she went to her car. This time she was too anxious to go very far. She stopped at the first drugstore she saw. Minutes later she was back in the car with three different brands.

The results were the same. Lined up on the marble vanity were four pregnancy tests: each blue, each positive. She was going to have a baby.

"No, I can't—I can't be pregnant. Please, I can't be."

Shoving her hands through her hair, she sat down on the cool floor. One time. She had friends in high school and college who played musical beds and never got caught.

Why her? Why did she have to get pregnant?

She didn't want to be a single mother. Raising a child was a big responsibility. She wasn't ready to be a parent. How could she have been so irresponsible and careless?

Her parents. Her eyes shut tightly. Her parents were so proud of her. How could she tell them that she had messed up? She couldn't. The news would devastate them. She was their sweet little baby girl. Sweet little baby girls didn't have one-night stands and, if they did, they weren't careless enough to get pregnant.

What about her job? She was so proud of her accomplishments and looking forward to being in management by next year. Next year she'd be up to her eyeballs in diapers and formula. It wasn't fair—it just wasn't fair.

Her head dropped into her open palms. Tears freely fell. Lifting her head, she forced herself to get up. She made it to her bed and lay down, curling into a tight ball.

How was she going to get through this?

Madelyn awoke feeling fuzzy and thickheaded. Her mouth was dry. Her eyes hurt. Before she was completely upright, she remembered. Her gaze shot to the bathroom. Anger propelled her across the room.

With an angry swipe of her arm, she swept the test results into the wastebasket, yanked up the plastic lining, and securely tied the end.

She was squeezing the bag when she realized what she was doing. Shame, then guilt, struck her.

"I'm sorry. I'm sorry." Dropping to her knees, she released her hold on the bag.

Her anger was misplaced. The tiny life growing within her wasn't to blame for this. It had nothing to do with its conception.

She had made a decision, consciously or unconsciously, to make love with Daniel. Now she had to take responsibility for the results.

A baby.

Her gaze dropped to her waistline. A life was growing inside her. A life she and Daniel had created. Slowly she reached down and rubbed her abdomen.

"We'll get through this. It's not your fault." Leaning back against the wall she closed her eyes. If she had almost freaked out, what would Daniel's reaction be?

CHAPTER 7

"**I**'m pregnant."

Whatever words Daniel Falcon had expected to hear from Madelyn Taggart's forbidden lips, those definitely were not part of his unwanted fantasy.

With the same control with which he'd held himself since she first walked into his office, Daniel's face reflected none of his anger, his disappointment. Both hands remained negligently atop his neat desk, his face expressionless.

Not that it mattered because once Madelyn had tossed out her bomb, she had tried to take a chunk out of her lower lip, then centered her attention on the bank of windows on the other side of the room. Sunlight poured into his downtown office in Houston like spun gold. He seriously doubted if Madelyn noticed.

"Are you sure?" Daniel asked.

"Yes." Was that a smile or a grimace that quickly swept across the profile of her beautiful face? He couldn't tell. Her dismal expression made it difficult to remember her quick smile, the excited burst of laughter from her mouth, the sparkle in her big brown eyes.

All that was gone now. And it was his fault.

All because that same smile lit up his heart, that same mouth tempted him beyond measure, those same eyes reached inside him and touched his soul. Despite knowing better, he had crossed a line he had no business crossing. "What do you plan to do?"

She looked at him then, her eyes wide. Her teeth clamped down on her lower lip again.

"Stop shredding your lips, for goodness' sake," he told her, the anger he had been trying to control slipping its tenuous hold.

She flinched, and he clenched his teeth to keep the curse words locked behind them. Unable to remain seated, he surged to his feet. Because he wanted as desperately to hold her as much as he wanted to shout at her for being so careless, he shoved his hands in his pockets. "What a mess."

Down went her head again, and he wanted to kick himself. Hell, he should kick himself. This was his fault more than it was hers. Her naivete was alluring to jaded men like him. He had shattered her illusions, and now she was paying the price.

But she had also shattered an illusion he had of her. His fists clenched as a wave of jealousy swept through him. "Have you told the father yet?"

She went as still as a shadow. Daniel could almost feel her pulling into herself. His control slipped. In seconds he was kneeling in front of her, his hands clamped around her upper forearm. "Did that bastard hurt you? Tell me? Who is he?"

Daniel didn't understand the sad smile that transformed Madelyn Taggart's face, but he did understand the words, "You are. You're the father."

Madelyn stared into the stunned face of Daniel Falcon and fought to control the tears that always hovered these days. He had just insulted both of them. "We never really knew each other, did we?"

His face cold, he pushed to his feet. "I can't be the father."

"Biologically or morally?" she managed to choke out.

"Both," he said tightly. "I'm not careless in that area. A man in my position can't afford to be."

Unconsciously Madelyn's hand went to her waist. Daniel saw the gesture and wanted to break something. She had gone straight from his bed to some other man's.

Her memory had never been far from him, and he hadn't meant a damn thing to her. Rage curled inside him, but he had the power to lose it on the woman huddled in front of him or subdue it. He had done enough to her.

"I know this must come as a shock. It was to me," she said quietly, remembering the crazy mix of emotions from fear to sheer terror on watching the tester turn blue. Dark, hopeful eyes lifted to his. "You're the father, Daniel. Nothing is foolproof except abstinence. Failures happen."

Daniel clamped down on the surge of excitement before it could materialize. He wasn't the father. "That's just it, Madelyn. It's never happened in the past."

Madelyn fought against succumbing to the misery and pain and anger assailing her from all sides. Of all the scenarios she had gone over in her mind, denial of paternity was not one of them.

In spite of everything, somehow, in the back of her mind, she had thought he would shout with delight on hearing the news. She had only been fooling herself. Since the morning afterward he hadn't tried to contact her in any way. He had walked out of her life and forgotten she existed.

Her initial instinct was to just get up and leave his office, but she had never been one to walk away from anything, no matter how painful. More than her pride was involved. There was a child to consider.

"Have you told Kane or Matt yet?" Daniel asked abruptly.

Her fingers clutched the handbag in her lap. "No."

"That explains why I'm not in the hospital."

Her sharp gaze locked on his. "My brothers have nothing to do with this."

Daniel snorted. "We both know they'll come looking for me when you tell them."

"I have no intention of telling anyone at the moment," Madelyn said quietly. "As the father I thought you should be the first to know."

"I'm not the father," Daniel repeated adamantly.

Hurt and anger filled her eyes. "I saw the doctor Wednesday, and I'm between seven and eight weeks' pregnant, Daniel. If you'll check your calendar, you'll find that the Petroleum Ball was eight weeks ago tomorrow. You haven't forgotten what happened when you followed me home, have you?"

Pictures of them entwined on her bed flashed into Daniel's mind. His body hardened. He'd go to his grave remembering the softness of her body, the drugging taste of her skin, the soft cries she emitted as he sank into her moist heat.

From the slight parting of her lips, she remembered as well. She had been all the woman he wanted or needed. He hadn't touched another woman since that night. Too bad she hadn't felt the same way.

"What about the next night or the night after?" he asked.

Madelyn flinched. She stared at him in stricken horror. "Are . . . are you saying . . . But you know you were the first."

"It's been my experience that first doesn't always mean only or last," he said tersely.

His words stunned her. She opened her mouth, but nothing came out. Daniel had no such problem.

"How many people do you think are still with their first lover—and if by some miracle they are together, how many of those have remained faithful?" he asked sharply.

"I don't know and I don't care. But I wasn't raised like that. *I'm* not like that—I could never be like that," she told him, her voice rising in anger with each word she spoke.

"And that's the only reason this conversation didn't end the moment you told me why you came. By now you'd be talking to my lawyer."

Outraged, she gasped.

"But good women make bad decisions. I know how naive you are, how hurt you were. You obviously trusted the wrong man."

"Obviously," she said coldly, her meaning all too clear.

A muscle leaped in his jaw. "Do you honestly think you're the first women to walk through my door and make such a claim?" His expression harshened. "I've had two other paternity suits brought against me. The last one less than six months ago. Both claims were proven false."

His implication sent a shaft of red-hot anger through her. "Because their claims were unfounded doesn't mean that you aren't the father of this baby." Hurt beyond measure, Madelyn continued despite the agony she felt. "They probably wanted money. I haven't asked you for anything, nor will I ever."

"They didn't either at first," Daniel said with derision. "Each one went on and on about how they only wanted their child to know its father."

"And you believe I'm just like those women? Trying to get what I can?" The anguish was unmistakable in her thin voice.

"Whatever your reasons, I don't make mistakes like that," he said with biting finality.

"You just made the biggest one of your life. One day you'll realize just how big." Standing, she yanked her purse strap over her shoulder.

Disbelief etched itself on his bronzed face. He took a step toward her. "You're going to have a paternity test and try to bring a suit against me?"

"What kind of woman do you think I am?" she asked infuriated, then continued before he could answer. "To do that I'd have to have testing done now. Amniocentesis can be dangerous, Daniel. I won't risk my baby's life for anything. And despite what you might think, being pregnant and single is not something I want to broadcast to the world."

His black eyes narrowed. "Then what are you going to do?"

She stared at him a long time before she answered. "You gave up your right to ask that question."

His entire body jerked as if he had been struck forcibly. "Don't play games with me, Madelyn."

"I never did and I never will." He was entitled to his doubts, but that didn't mean he could attack her character and suspect her motives. Her chin lifted. "Thank you for seeing me."

His brows bunched in surprise. "You're leaving?"

"I see no reason to stay. There's nothing left to be said. I'd like to re-member our last meeting together at least ending cordially."

His eyes rounded at the full implication of what she was saying. Pleased to leave him looking confused and not so sure of himself, she turned and started from the room.

Dizziness swept over her. She swayed. In her haste to leave, she had forgotten what sudden moves did to her.

"Madelyn!" Daniel's hands circled her forearms.

Eyes closed, she waited for the spinning to stop.

"Madelyn—say something."

The frantic desperation in Daniel's voice more than anything enabled her to open her eyes. "Please take your hands off me and don't shout."

Dismissing the first request, he told her in a commanding tone, "Then stop scaring the hell out of me."

"I wish I could. It's not something I'm overly fond of, either." Her eye-lids fluttered closed again.

"Damnit, Madelyn, don't do this to me again."

"The world doesn't spin so much if I keep my eyes closed," she ex-plained.

Quickly picking her up, he carried her to an overstuffed chair, then carefully set her in it. Her head rested against the high cushioned back. "I'm calling your doctor. What's his name?"

"Dr. Scalar—and Daniel, do you think you could stop talking and ask-ing questions for a few minutes?"

He didn't want to, but he kept his mouth closed. He wanted to help her, and he couldn't do that unless he had more information.

The feeling of helplessness was new to him and completely unaccept-able. He was a man of action, used to seeing a problem and correcting it. But this was completely out of his realm of knowledge. Damn, he didn't know anything about pregnant women!

Except they weren't supposed to get excited. Guilt struck him in the chest like a powerful fist.

He gazed at the beads of perspiration on Madelyn's forehead, her trembling lips, and wanted to strangle the man responsible. His hand flexed and felt her smaller one in his. Tentatively his other hand brushed across her forehead.

Perhaps he should call the doctor. She might not want his help, but obviously she needed someone. Seeing her needing help and being un-able to give it tore at his gut. He'd give her exactly one minute. Sixty sec-onds and if she didn't—

Her eyelids slowly fluttered upward. She moistened dry lips with the tip of her tongue. "Sorry."

"Can I get you something to drink?"

"No, it will only come back up again," she said and slowly sat up. "I can stand now."

He hesitated only a few seconds before assisting her to stand. His attention remained focused on her face to note the slightest change.

"Does this happen often?" he asked when she was completely upright.

She let out a trembling sigh and swept whisps of hair from her cheek. "Depends on what you call often."

"Madelyn," he said in a tight voice that proclaimed he was unwilling to settle for anything other than a straight answer.

"It's more of a nuisance than anything else," she told him, shoving the strap of her handbag over her shoulder.

Black eyes continued to study her. "You're sure you're well enough to leave?"

"I'm fine now."

He frowned, obviously unconvinced. "You don't look fine."

He hit a nerve. Unlike in San Antonio, this time it was *his* fault she wasn't looking her best. "You try being pregnant with your hormones going crazy and throwing up your toenails all the time, and see how great you look."

The sudden tightening of Daniel's features told her she had let her anger undo any ground she might have gained with him in the last minutes. Anger and accusations would solve nothing and perhaps damage what could be salvaged in time.

One of them had to resist the urge to strike out at the other. From the hard glitter in Daniel's eyes, it wasn't going to be him.

He had just shown he wasn't completely indifferent to her. Maybe he just needed time. From the beginning he had told her he didn't want long-term commitments. She couldn't think of anything more long term or more of a heavier responsibility than becoming a parent.

If she didn't believe that he was in heavy denial just as she had been initially, that he'd finally accept the baby as his, she wasn't sure she wouldn't sit down and wail like a child. But that didn't mean she'd hang around waiting until he did.

"Goodbye, Daniel." This time she made sure she didn't make any sudden moves as she left. The door closed softly behind her.

Her body trembling, Madelyn drew in a shaky breath and slowly made her way out of his outer office and down the hallway toward the elevator. She could get through this. She had to.

Daniel stared at the closed door. Emotions swirled through him like a dark cloud. Madelyn had left as quietly as she had come, leaving behind the elusive scent of her perfume and a rage churning inside him.

One tightened his body in remembered pleasure; the other tightened his fists with the almost irresistible urge to smash something.

He silently battled to push both from his mind. He succeeded, but then something more disturbing appeared. Madelyn, faint and pale. That picture would not go away.

Stalking to his door, he jerked it open. "Gwen, cancel my appointment with Ames. Explain to him something came up," he instructed his secretary without breaking his long strides past her desk. Opening the door leading to the hallway, he was just in time to see Madelyn step into the elevator.

Madelyn stepped into the crowded elevator with a sigh of relief. While waiting, the feeling of light-headedness had returned. She had never been sick in her life except for colds, and she was becoming tired and aggravated with her body.

The elevator stopped two floors later, and a well-dressed man in his late fifties wedged himself on despite the sharp looks of the other passengers. Madelyn was just glad the elevator was moving again . . . until she became aware of the cloying scent of his cologne. The muscles of her stomach clenched in protest.

Eyes closed, she started to inhale deeper, caught herself before making the mistake, and exhaled instead. As soon as she breathed in again, the queasiness returned, only worse.

She swallowed, swallowed again. Nothing helped. She needed to get some fresh air. Leaning her head against the cool paneled wall, she opened her eyes and kept her gaze locked on the lit panel clicking off the floors.

Finally the panel blinked 1. Seconds later the doors slid open. Straightening, she started from the elevator. A wave of dizziness hit her halfway across the busy lobby. She paused, blinking her eyes in an attempt to clear her head.

She had to get to her car. She took another step, then another. Faintly she heard someone ask if she was all right. She tried to answer, but found her tongue as uncooperative as her unsteady legs. The last thing she remembered was someone shouting her name.

Time stood still for Daniel when he saw Madelyn falling.

He raced toward her, catching her just as she would have hit the marble floor. Her eyelids were closed, her lips slightly parted.

Daniel thought his heart had stopped. His legs were shaking. Hell, his whole body was shaking. What if he hadn't been worried about her and decided to follow?

Pulling her close, he quickly carried her to a couch on the far side of the spacious lobby and laid her down. Going down beside her, he took her limp hand in his. "Madelyn, please open your eyes."

"Should I call an ambulance, Mr. Falcon?" asked a uniformed security guard who had hurried over.

"No. Just see that we have some privacy." The middle-aged man moved away, but Daniel didn't notice. All his attention was centered on the woman lying so still. "Madelyn—Madelyn, please say something."

Long black lashes fluttered, then opened. "Daniel? W-What happened?"

"You fainted. You can't keep scaring—" Shutting his eyes, he drew in a deep shuddering breath. He jerked them open when he felt the tentative brush of fingertips against his cheek.

"I didn't mean to scare you again. Pregnant women do silly things sometimes."

A soft gasp from behind a crouched Daniel caused Madelyn to glance upward. Directly behind him was a stunning African-American woman elegantly dressed in a pale pink suit.

The gold buttons had the distinctive interlocking CC of Chanel. She wore her short, dark brown hair in a breezy cut that complemented perfectly the contours of her oval face. She appeared to be in her early forties.

Catching Madelyn's gaze on her, the woman smiled and placed a slim, manicured hand on Daniel's shoulder. The square-cut emerald surrounded by diamonds on her ring finger sparkled like green fire. "I see you have been keeping secrets from me again."

Daniel tensed at the sound of the crisp Bostonian accent. He almost groaned. She was supposed to be in New York. But when had Felicia Ann Everett Falcon ever done what was expected of her?

Of all the times for his mother to return unexpectedly, this was the worst. He didn't have to see her face to know she was ecstatic with thoughts of finally getting to bounce a grandchild on her knee. So far he and Dominique both refused to give her any.

She might as well know it wasn't going to happen. He glanced up at her. "It's not what you think."

"I-I'm all right now." Madelyn struggled to rise. "Thank you, but I'll be late meeting my husband."

The smile left his mother's face. She sent Daniel an accusing look.

Daniel didn't know whether to thank Madelyn or shake her. He did know he wasn't letting her out of his sight until he made sure she had stopped all this fainting nonsense. "Can I take the car?" he asked his mother.

"Of course, dear. I'll get a cab back to the house."

He turned his attention back to Madelyn. "Do you think you can walk, or do you want me to carry you?"

"I'd rather not be on the ten P.M. news."

He glanced around the lobby. The security guard might have kept the crowd back, but he and Madelyn remained the center of attention. "Point taken."

Easing her legs over the side of the couch, Madelyn slowly stood with Daniel's help. Thankfully she felt only a brief moment of dizziness.

"Don't you dare go out on me again," he ordered anxiously.

She looked at the frowning woman before answering. "You don't hav—"

"Yes, I do. Ready?"

Madelyn was too conscious of the people watching them, of the unknown woman only a few feet away, to protest any further. She only hoped no one connected with the media was around.

On the sidewalk Madelyn saw the big, silver Mercedes and the chauffeur rushing to open the back door. Her steps faltered. Now she understood what he had meant about "take the car." She had some pride left. "I'm feeling better. I can drive home."

"Humor me. I'll take care of your car after I've taken care of you. Now stop dragging your feet." Exerting more pressure on her arm, he started her toward the waiting sedan.

She didn't protest any further. She was too tired. As soon as she leaned against the luxurious buttery soft leather seat, her eyelids drifted downward. "I hate this."

"Don't blame the baby," Daniel said, a hint of censure in his deep voice.

Thick, black lashes swept upward. She stared at the man she had so easily fallen in love with, the man who didn't love her in return, the man who didn't understand her, the man she was coming to realize she didn't understand, either.

"We never really knew each other, did we?" she said again.

"No," he agreed.

"Well, Daniel Falcon, know this. This child will never hear blame or hatred or mistake or fault or any other words that make a child feel he or she did something wrong. Because I don't want to think of the life growing inside me in those terms. I may have acted irresponsibly, but I plan to take responsibility for my child."

"Raising a child isn't easy," he told her evenly.

"Life isn't easy," Madelyn said and closed her eyes again.

Daniel studied her closely. Was she shutting him out or sick again? He didn't know, but he felt easier since her forehead was dry, her breathing even.

She never acted the way he expected. She hadn't blamed him when she told him of her pregnancy; rather she had informed him. One hell of a difference.

There were so many questions he wanted to ask her—only he wasn't sure if he was ready for the answers. Her betrayal cut deep. Until this afternoon he would have believed it of any woman in his past, anyone except Madelyn.

Although he had known her for only a short while, he had known her brothers for over two years. Kane and Matt Taggart both possessed high standards of integrity and honesty. And while it didn't necessarily mean their sister possessed those same qualities, since they always spoke so highly of her, Daniel hadn't thought differently while he was with her.

But he had been wrong.

Whether out of passion or anger or need, she had gone to another man. In the past Daniel had insisted on loose relationships because he wanted no ties. He wanted to be able to move on whenever he was ready. Although he had wanted Madelyn with a hungry urgency he had never experienced before, he still wasn't ready for anything long term. Ties and commitment didn't fit into his plans.

His parents had shown him how destructive love could be, but it was Jeanette who made sure he never forgot. Poor needy, pitiful Jeanette. She'd wanted so much to be loved and hadn't the foggiest notion of how to love in return.

Madelyn hadn't behaved like Jeanette or any of the other women who had come and gone in his life over the years. Most of them were fascinated with the public's perception of Daniel Falcon, and not the man. He understood their reasons and used them for reasons of his own.

Greedy, selfish women weren't likely to be hurt when a relationship was over. They were in it for the kicks, the prestige, and the benefits of being on the arm and in the bed of a powerful man. The game was to make it seem as if the parting was mutual. Then they'd move on to the next man and the next. "Night crawlers" Luke used to call them.

Daniel glanced at Madelyn. She had been too innocent for him—in mind and body. Yet somehow she had touched him more than the most experienced woman.

Her body had responded to his as if they had always been lovers. There was a knowing, despite the hungry desperation that made each touch, each caress fuel the need for more. Loving her had been the most powerful and the most humbling experience of his life.

No one had ever given him so much of themselves so freely or wanted to please him so much.

That's why he didn't understand. He knew there was a small failure rate using only a prophylactic, but he also knew they hadn't failed him in the past.

Not once.

So why had Madelyn chosen to name him the father and not the real person? He didn't know, but he'd find out who the man was—and if he had done anything to hurt her, Daniel would take care of him in his own unique way. The smile that crossed his face would have chilled a seasoned soldier.

The man should have protected her better. Hell, *he* should have taken better care of her. If he hadn't made love to her, none of this would have happened. No matter who the father was, her life had been irrevocably changed.

Just as no matter how it ate at his insides to think about her with another man, Daniel couldn't leave her alone. That meant he had to stop thinking about the other guy or he'd go crazy.

Yet the craziest thing of all was that he hadn't been able to forget the brief flash of joy he felt when she had told him she was pregnant.

CHAPTER 8

"Madelyn. Madelyn. We're here."

Opening her eyes, Madelyn lifted her head from the seat with difficulty. Although she wanted nothing more than to be able to lie down and stretch out, she couldn't get her body to cooperate.

"Let me help." Once again she was in Daniel's arms. Knowing protest was useless, she leaned her head against his wide chest and closed her eyes. Once inside she'd send him on his way.

"Do you think you can open the door?"

From somewhere she found the strength to open her eyes. Thankfully she found her keys without digging through her perpetually cluttered purse. Key in hand she leaned over. Dizziness struck. Closing her eyes, she slumped against Daniel.

"Easy, Madelyn. Higgins," Daniel called.

"Allow me, miss." Gently the keys were removed from her hands. The lock clicked.

"We're in," Daniel informed her. "Hold on. You'll be in bed in no time."

Madelyn swallowed and remained silent.

With profound tenderness, Daniel placed her on top of the floral comforter. "We'll have you undressed in no time, so you can rest."

Madelyn's eyes blinked open, glad to see at least that the "we" didn't include Higgins. She wasn't quite so sure about the closed bedroom door.

"Just tell me where your nightgown is."

She attempted to sit up, but dizziness and Daniel defeated her.

"Be still. I'll get it for you." He crossed the room and pulled open the top drawer of her triple dresser. "Bingo." The nightgown spilling from his big hand, he came back to the bed.

"Daniel, this is not going to work."

Kneeling on the carpeted floor, he slipped off her dark brown suede heels. "What are you talking about?"

"I'm not about to undress in front of you," she explained, eyeing him wearily.

He stared at her. "You can't do it by yourself. You can hardly raise your head off the pillow."

She couldn't argue with him there. "Maybe after I rest for a little while, I'll feel better," she said, trying not to let herself be lulled into forgetting her decision of sending him home.

"Do you really believe that?"

"I want to believe it," she told him softly.

His hand lifted toward her brow, only to clamp into a fist midway there and settle on the bed. "How about if I help you out of the suit and turn my back while you do the rest?"

Somehow she knew that was as good as she was going to get. Besides, she was too tired to argue. Once she was in her gown, he'd leave. "All . . . all right."

His hands went to the tortoise buttons of her orange suit jacket. "After I finish, I can fix you something to eat."

Her stomach lurched. "Please, I don't want to talk about food."

"Madelyn, I don't think that's an option." Another button slipped free.

"I can't, Daniel."

He stopped and locked at her. "Yes, you can. There isn't much you can't do."

"Once I would have agreed with you," she said slowly.

"Meeting me changed that." Regret flashed across his face. "If I could change things. Go back."

Somehow his words hurt more than they helped. Tears pricked her eyes. She didn't want him to see her weakness.

"Don't cry," he said anxiously. "Everything will be okay."

"Will it, Daniel?"

Not waiting for an answer, she bent her head and slipped the last button free on her jacket, then began unbuttoning her blouse. His fingers were quicker. Despite her intentions of getting this over with quickly, she was glad he didn't try to remove her blouse once it was unbuttoned.

She hesitated only a second before reaching for the side hook on her coffee-brown skirt, then she slid down the zipper. Too vividly she recalled the same rasping sound as Daniel slid the zipper down the back of her gown the night of the Petroleum Ball. As if her mind had a will of its own, she lifted her gaze.

Tight-lipped, he spun away from her. Madelyn didn't have the luxury of trying to figure out if he was angry with her or himself, but angry he was. Shrugging out of her blouse, she pulled her lacy camisole over her head, then unsnapped the front fasteners of her bra, trying to ignore Daniel's presence less than a foot away.

Impossible. Especially when, despite everything, she wanted nothing more than to pull him into bed with her and let him hold her. She wanted, needed to be held. She needed to be told everything was going to be all right. She had never felt so in need of another human's touch in all of her life.

"Everything all right?"

No, she wanted to say. "Yes" slipped out instead.

Grabbing the ecru-colored nightgown on the bed, she slipped it over her head. The heavy satin material pooled in her lap. Now all she had to do was find enough energy to raise up and get out of her skirt and panty hose.

"Decent?"

"Yes, but—" Her words trailed off as he turned. His gaze swept her, instantly seeming to size up her problem.

Standing, he scooped her up in his arms. "Lean against me, and I'll draw the comforter back."

She did, inhaling his scent, glad it didn't make her stomach queasy. Sad because in her weakened state it made her want to keep hanging on.

"I'm going to lay you down again."

He removed her arms from around his neck as soon as her bottom touched the bed, a bottom without her skirt.

Surprised eyes lifted to his. He had the audacity to look pleased with himself. She didn't want to think of how many women he had undressed to perfect such a task.

He pulled the covers over her legs. "Soup, okay? I'm not much good in the kitchen."

"I don't want anything. It'll just come back up."

Hands on his hips, he stared down at her. "What did Dr. Scalar say?"

The fact that he had remembered her doctor's name didn't surprise her. "That it was normal. He gave me some pills, but I can't keep them down, either."

A frown worked its way across his forehead. "How long has this been going on?"

She closed her eyes. She didn't want to see his face when she gave him the answer. "Off and on for several days."

The explosion she expected didn't come. She slowly opened her eyes and cringed. His eyes were saying everything quite eloquently. None of it good.

"Has the dizziness passed? I'd like to talk."

Now she understood why he hadn't said anything. The man never forgot a thing. She scooted down farther in the bed. "I'm really tired, Daniel."

He stared at her a long time. "I'll be here if you need me."

"You don't have to stay." Yet in spite of everything she told herself earlier, she wanted him to. She didn't feel alone when he was with her and being kind.

"Is there anyone who will stay with you if you called?" he asked.

Her lashes lowered. "No. I mean there is, but no one who wouldn't ask questions that I'm not ready to answer."

He nodded. "Then I guess I'm it until you're well enough to throw me out." Bending over, he unnecessarily adjusted the bed covers again. "Close those big brown eyes of yours and go to sleep."

After a moment's hesitation, she turned on her side and did just that.

Now that he was here, Daniel didn't have the foggiest notion of what to do. Hands on hips, he glanced around the small rose and white kitchen. He had mentioned soup because he'd always heard of people trying to give you soup when you were sick. He didn't know if that was what he should be giving Madelyn or not. Obviously she wasn't going to help.

The logical person to ask was another woman who had been pregnant. His mother came to mind. Bad, bad choice.

Leaning against the white countertop, he tried to go through his list of female acquaintances and came to the conclusion that was another bad idea. He could imagine the questions and the gossip to follow.

He was on his own. Looked like soup was on the menu.

Pushing upright, he started opening cabinet door after cabinet door. To his surprise he didn't find any soup or much of anything else. The refrigerator wasn't much better. He thought women stocked food like there was no tomorrow. Obviously he had been misinformed.

He'd have to go to the store. Buying one can of soup didn't seem to make much sense. Madelyn was just going to have to cooperate and give him a list of what she needed.

Opening her bedroom door, he quietly went to the bed. She slept with both hands under her face. She looked peaceful. He pulled the covers back over her shoulder. There was no way he was going to wake her up. He'd just have to find out on his own.

In the living room, he looked for the keys the efficient Higgins would have placed somewhere easy to find. A set of keys was on the cocktail table along with a brass planter filled with a sprawling silk ivy, several women's magazines, and a couple of hardcover books.

He reached for the keys. Inches away his hand paused. Beneath the keys was a book on pregnancy.

The thick book was an unwanted reminder of the guilt and anger he was trying to deal with, but it would also contain the information he needed to take care of Madelyn.

He picked up the book. He was flipping through the glossy pages when he saw the chart on fetal growth and development. Everything inside him stilled for a long moment. Without allowing his gaze to drift down the page, he turned the next page and the next until he reached the index and looked up nutrition.

Fifteen minutes later he left with a list of foods.

"Daniel, I don't want any."

"Come on, Madelyn, just a little," he coaxed. "It can't be good for you not to eat."

She eyed the spoonful of clear yellowish liquid inches from her lips, then Daniel. "I don't remember having any chicken broth."

"I stopped by the store on the way back with your car—now open." He moved the spoon closer.

She opened her mouth to say something, and the broth went in instead. She swallowed. It tasted warm and soothing to her dry throat.

"See, have some more."

She opened her mouth. Maybe the nausea had passed. Several bites later she knew she had deluded herself. She barely made it to the bathroom in time. When her stomach was empty, she wanted nothing more than to curl up into a little ball and roll away in embarrassment.

"I-I'm sorry," she murmured.

"For what? You have no control over being sick." Pulling her gently into his arms, Daniel sat on the side of the bathtub with her in his lap. He ran a moist washcloth over her face. "Better?"

She finally looked at him. He didn't appear disgusted at all. "Yes."

"I'm the one who should be sorry for forcing you to eat." His hand brushed across her moist forehead. "I'll help you brush your teeth, then I'm calling your doctor."

"Daniel, I don't know."

"I don't, either—that's why I'm calling the doctor," he told her, then prepared her toothbrush and handed it to her.

Immediately after she finished she told him, "I feel better already. There is no need to disturb Dr. Scalar on a Friday night. You go on home, too. I'll probably sleep until morning."

He handed her a washcloth to wipe the toothpaste off the side of her mouth. "The book said to call."

"The book?"

Taking the washcloth from her, he placed it on the towel rack, then carried her back to bed. He didn't answer until she was beneath the covers again. "The book on pregnancy," he answered, then he was gone.

Seventeen minutes after Daniel had called Dr. Scalar's answering service, the ob-gyn had yet to return the call. It was six thirty. To Daniel, who was worried he had done more harm than good by forcing Madelyn to eat, it wasn't a good sign. Maybe he should have Madelyn get a new doctor—one who answered calls.

When the phone did ring, he jerked it up. "Yes."

"Dr. Scalar returning your call."

"About time. Madelyn can't keep a thing down, and she fainted twice. I gave her some broth like the book said, and she threw it up. You have to do something now to make her feel better."

"And to whom am I speaking?"

"Daniel Falcon." The name slipped out without a moment's hesitation. He wasn't above using his name to get the man moving.

"And what's your relationship to Madelyn?"

This time the answer came more slowly. "I . . . I'm responsible."

"I should have known that the minute you started rambling. Let me speak to Madelyn."

He never rambled. "She's resting."

"That may be, but until she gives me permission to discuss her case with you, I can't do so," the doctor said evenly.

Daniel wasn't pleased by the man's obstinance. "But I told you I'm responsible."

"I heard you the first time, Mr. Falcon," Dr. Scalar returned calmly. "And I know you've made quite an impression on our city, but your name is not on one piece of information Madelyn filled out—and until it is, I'm going to speak only to her."

"Hold on," he said in rising irritation. Entering the bedroom, he picked up the phone on the nightstand, then touched Madelyn's shoulder. Her eyes opened almost instantly. The weakness in them tore at his heart and dissolved his anger.

"Tell the doctor it's all right to talk with me, then you can try to rest."

Without rising, she took the phone. "Dr. Scalar. It's all right. No, the pill didn't stay down this morning or yesterday. Since Wednesday evening. I don't—" She handed the phone back to Daniel.

"Yes?"

"All right, Mr. Falcon, this is how I see things. Madelyn hasn't been taking care of herself because she's too tired, and the nausea and vomiting are only compounding the matter. Pregnancy is rough when its planned. Unplanned it can be ruthless on the body. You follow me so far?"

Daniel liked the doctor even less. "Yes."

"Good. You did right to give her broth and to call me. If she had been able to keep her pills down, I don't think this would have happened. Give her the pill again with just enough water to get it down. Four hours from now give her a couple of sips of carbonated soda; do the same four hours later."

He paused briefly then continued. "Give her the medicine in the morning as directed. Thirty minutes later give her a couple of saltines and a small amount of carbonated beverage. If she keeps that down, give her some of that chicken broth or something else light. Do this to make up five or six small meals. If it all stays down, good. If not, call me back. Understood?"

"What if she doesn't keep it down?"

"Don't get worried until I get worried. I saw her Wednesday. She's fine and the baby's fine. Anything else?"

Daniel glanced at Madelyn, who was watching him with those big brown eyes of hers. "No, we can take it from here. Good night."

"Good night. By the way, I've known Madelyn since she came to Houston. I'm glad you're there with her. Good night again."

Daniel replaced the receiver.

"What did he say?"

He explained everything the doctor had said, except the possibility that the nausea might continue.

"Didn't you explain you didn't stay here?"

"It wouldn't have mattered. Tell me where the pills are, and I'll get you some fresh water."

"Daniel, I didn't mean for this to happen." She sounded miserable.

"I know."

Thankfully, after a few anxious moments, the pill stayed down. Madelyn was so relieved and so pleased with herself, it didn't take much coaxing on Daniel's part to get her to slide back under the covers.

Switching the lamp on the bedside table to its lowest setting, he walked back into the living room. He hadn't intended this to happen, either, but somehow he was squarely in the middle of Madelyn's life and that of her child.

He didn't want to be there—he just couldn't think of any other place he'd rather be.

Except for one scary moment at Madelyn's second meal, she did fine Saturday and all during the day. She had ceased worrying about Daniel being there and was just thankful he was. She couldn't have taken care of herself.

She had friends in Houston, but as she told Daniel, she wasn't ready to share her pregnancy with anyone else. She went to sleep Saturday night, feeling better than she had in weeks.

She awoke sometime during the night. A muscular arm was flung possessively across her waist, anchoring her to the sculptured male perfection of Daniel's body. His beautiful thick hair tumbled across his powerful bare shoulders. He still wore his pants. Obviously his intent had been to get some rest, not to seduce.

By the light from the lamp on the nightstand, she studied the incredible beauty of his face inches from her own. Since the eyes that had always fascinated her were closed, her gaze centered on his lips. Lips that could steal a woman's will and give her incredible pleasure.

Tentatively her finger traced the shape. His arms tightened, drawing her closer still. She smiled. It seemed natural and right that he would be there for her and their baby. Snuggling closer, she went back to sleep.

Sunday arrived and she continued to improve. Instead of a quick shower, she took a long bath, then ate lunch at the kitchen table. Daniel insisted she rest afterward, and she let him have his way.

Waking later that afternoon, she didn't see him. Curious, she got up and pulled on her robe. Since he had brought her home, he had never been far from her side. She missed him.

She found him in the kitchen. She smiled. "There you are."

He glanced up, then went back to unloading the various sacks spread out on the counter. "Dinner's almost ready."

Going to his side, she opened one of the containers. "Baked chicken. It smells delicious. I'll set the table for us this time."

He shifted uneasily, then looked at her. "Do you think you'll have any trouble from here?"

The smile slid from her face. Trembling fingers set the hard clear plastic container down. "No."

"I'll be going then." He reached into his shirt pocket and pulled out a business card. "My private number is on there. Call me if you need anything."

Her hand clutched the card. Unable to speak, she nodded.

She watched him almost run for the front door. Misery welled up inside her. "Oh, Daniel."

A tense Daniel sat in the backseat of the Mercedes as Higgins pulled out of Madelyn's apartment complex. Daniel hadn't wanted to leave. But he had had to. She possessed the unique ability of slipping past his defenses. Remaining emotionally detached while caring for her was impossible.

He had been doing all right until she became restless Saturday night. He thought he heard a noise coming from her bedroom, so he had gotten up from the sofa where he had been sleeping, pulled on his pants, and went to check on her. She was turning one way, then the other as if she couldn't get comfortable.

Things had started off innocently enough by him feeling her forehead, then her cheek to see if she had a fever. Almost immediately she had pressed her cheek against his hand, deepening the contact, and murmured his name.

The next thing he knew, he was in bed with her, holding her, inhaling her scent, whispering nonsensical words about him being there and she could rest. Unexpectedly being with her calmed him as well.

Waking her every four hours for her meals hadn't been difficult because he had been unable to sleep. Holding Madelyn, he had slept way past his usual hour of rising at six in the morning. He realized then he had to leave.

Sharing the warmth and comfort of another's body could be as addictive as sex. Staying around her would only complicate matters. He had helped her when she needed it, now it was time to get on with his life and she hers.

As soon as the car rolled to a stop in front of his two-story country French mansion on the outskirts of Houston, Daniel got out. He took the four curved brick steps by two, then opened the leaded glass front door and entered the house.

Impatient steps rang loudly on the marble floor as he crossed the seventeen-by-seventeen foyer. He headed for the elegant wood spiral staircase, unmindful of the bright stream of sunlight pouring through floor-to-ceiling windows on the fifty-foot wall of the living room to his immediate right.

He needed a shower, a change of clothes, and to make a phone call. Canceling an appointment ten minutes before time with a man who owned one of the largest rig-manufacturing firms in the country wasn't done. Especially when Daniel needed rigs to bring up oil and gas, and rigs were in short supply and high demand since the energy boom. But not for one second did Daniel regret his decision.

He hit the stairs running, then groaned on seeing his mother coming toward him. Although she enjoyed an active social life and was dressed in something soft and flowing, he didn't hold out much hope she was going out. Because more than anything else, she'd enjoy having a grandchild.

"Good evening, Mother."

"Good evening, Daniel. I'm going to be disappointed in you if that young woman really is married."

It certainly hadn't taken her long to start in on him. "Mother, stay out of it."

She turned and followed him up the stairs. "Don't take that tone of voice with me, Daniel Falcon. I don't care how many boards you sit on."

"I thought you were going to stay in New York until the play you were backing opened," he said, hoping to change the subject.

"Seeing my favorite son is much more important," she said, accompanying him down the wide hallway. "Looks like I returned just in time."

"Mother, unless there's something you haven't told me, I'm your only son, and I'm tired." He opened the door to his room. "Do you mind?"

Apparently she did because she smiled sweetly and stepped past him. Still smiling she sank gracefully onto the maroon silk coverlet on his immense four-poster bed, then crossed her legs at the ankles.

Lilac chiffon fluttered and settled midcalf. "I hope she's feeling better. I never had morning sickness with Dominique, but you were a trial." Her eyes narrowed. "You still are."

A clean shirt in his hand, Daniel paused at the wardrobe, caught between learning more about morning sickness and keeping his mother out of his business. The keenness in her gaze decided him. He'd get the rest of his things later. "I'm going to take a shower."

Leaning back, Felicia braced her hands on the bed. "I suppose I can have Higgins retrace his route and talk to her myself."

He stepped a few feet from the bathroom door. "Mother, please."

"I want to know her. You might as well give in."

Gripping the shirt in his hand, he faced her. "It's not mine."

His mother clearly didn't appear convinced. "You want me to believe that you spent the last two days nursing a pregnant woman—and you're not involved?"

"I'm going to fire Higgins." Daniel had had the chauffeur come back on Saturday to check to see if she needed anything, then Daniel had called him to pick him up this afternoon.

His mother's smile returned. "You can't. I pay him out of my money. Besides, you care for him too much."

"Sometimes I do things I don't want to," Daniel said with suppressed anger.

Rising from the bed, she went to her son and placed a soothing hand on his tense shoulder. "You're an honorable man. Whatever mistakes your father and I might have made in our own lives, we raised you and Dominique right."

He stared out the window draped in maroon silk damask to the towering pin oaks in the distance. "Sometimes I wonder."

"Did this young woman start you to wondering?" she questioned softly.

He glanced down into her expectant face. "You're not going to let this go, are you?"

"No."

He admitted defeat. "Her name is Madelyn Taggart."

"I guess her family is here in Houston," Felicia probed.

"No, she's by herself." The moment the words left his mouth, he knew his mother was going to interfere. "Mother, stay out of this."

"Oh, look. It's almost six." She glanced at the Piaget eighteen-karat gold watch on her slim wrist. "I better let you get your shower or dinner will be late." She hurried from the room.

"Mother."

She kept going. Daniel said one explicit word under his breath.

CHAPTER 9

Monday afternoon Madelyn groaned on hearing her doorbell. She didn't want to talk with anyone, had left work early for that very reason. She had a lot of thinking to do.

Whatever ideas or options she came up with, Daniel wouldn't be a part of them. Foolishly, while he had cared for her over the weekend, she had begun to think he had accepted the baby as his and wanted to be a part of their lives. His quick departure Sunday afternoon proved her wrong.

The doorbell chimed again. Madelyn ignored the sound. He'd left so fast, he probably singed the soles of his expensive loafers.

The memory angered her as much as it confused and saddened her. Who was the real Daniel? The compassionate man who bathed her face and coaxed her into eating or the hard-eyed man who thought she had gone from his bed to that of another man's.

Whatever the answer, his loss.

She didn't want a man who thought her so lacking in morals. He honestly didn't believe her. In his life's experience women moved from man to man with a shameless disregard for propriety—and always, always with an ulterior motive. True, Daniel hadn't known her long, but she felt he *should* have known her character.

She had expected his reaction to be her reaction to their relationship, one of complete faith and trust—and yes, love. She had been so wrong. She should have listened to what he said and not to her own foolish heart.

The bell sounded for the third time. Sighing, Madelyn pushed up from the sofa. Obviously the caller wasn't going away.

Determined to quickly get rid of the person, Madelyn opened the door. Surprise narrowed, then widened her eyes. Her determined visitor was the woman from the lobby of Daniel's office building.

"Hello, Madelyn," the woman greeted with a warm smile. "May I come in?"

Madelyn wasn't in the mood for a confrontation with one of Daniel's lady friends—although so far this one wasn't spitting venom.

"I'm rather busy. What's this about?"

"That's what I was hoping you could tell me," the woman said.

This one might be older and more sophisticated than the other two, but that didn't mean she wouldn't turn into a spiteful shrew. "Could you be more specific?" Madelyn asked, glancing over her shoulder at the sound of a cheer from the TV set.

"Is your husband home?" the woman inquired.

Unprepared for the question, Madelyn answered before she thought. "I'm not married."

The woman beamed. "I knew it. Please, may I come in? I don't think we should talk out here."

"Then you had better tell me your name and what you want," Madelyn told her.

Astonishment flashed across the other woman's attractive brown face. "Daniel didn't tell you?"

The queasiness that had been absent for the past two days returned. "No."

"I'm sorry, I thought you knew." She extended her manicured hand. "I'm Felicia Falcon."

Stunned, Madelyn stared at the other woman in utter horror. Only her grip on the doorknob kept her upright. "You're Daniel's wife?"

"Mother. You better sit down." Stepping inside, Felicia closed the door and led Madelyn to a chair and hovered over her. "Better?"

"Yes," Madelyn answered, unable to keep from staring at the youthful-looking woman. "You're his mother?"

Felicia's smile was one of pleasure and indulgence. "I married when I was eighteen."

Madelyn absorbed the information. Daniel's mother didn't look to be older than her midforties. He was thirty-three. Face-lift or good genes? "Any cosmetic firm, including my brother's, would fight to get you as a spokeswoman."

Felicia laughed, a bright, soothing sound. "Whenever I need a pick-me-up, I shall have to come and see you."

"Why are you here now?" Madelyn asked.

Felicia's gaze touched Madelyn's trim waist before meeting her eyes.

"I've come to ask you something. Something my son says I have no right to ask, but I've never been one to listen to what other people think I should do or say." She paused for only a second. "Are you carrying Daniel's baby?"

Madelyn flushed, then straightened. "I don't want to be rude, but Daniel is right. The answer to that question is none of your business."

To her credit Felicia didn't appear upset by Madelyn's statement. "May I sit down?"

"Of course." Good manners won over nervousness.

Felicia sank gracefully into the jewel-tone floral sofa by Madelyn's chair. Once seated, she placed her black quilted calfskin handbag in her lap, then crossed her long legs at the ankles.

Today she wore another Chanel suit, this one in black minicheck. Deeply etched, small drop sterling silver earrings dangled from her ears. Understated and elegant.

Madelyn sat up even straighter in the antique, Duncan Phyfe armchair given to her by her maternal grandmother and refinished and reupholstered by Kane in seafoam green. She wished she had on something besides a red and white cotton knit striped short set that clashed with her purple slipper socks. At least her hair was combed.

"I have two beautiful children whom I love very much. Dominique is in Paris doing a photo shoot. She says she's having the time of her life." Felicia pressed her lips together. "Sometimes I think she almost believes it herself."

"Mrs. Falcon, perhaps you shouldn't be telling me this," Madelyn said.

Felicia sent her another smile, just not as bright. "I'm not saying anything to you I haven't said to Dominique. Then there is Daniel: aggressive, smart, intelligent, fearless. He took over my father's business interests when he graduated from Harvard, magna cum laude, with an MBA. He has more money than he can spend in ten lifetimes, and he has no one to share it with."

"Mrs. Falcon—"

"It's my fault," she interrupted, her fingers now wrapped around the top of her bag. "Two years ago I would have flayed alive anyone who suggested such a thing to me. Loneliness has a way of making you face the truth."

In his mother's black eyes, Madelyn saw as much misery as in her own. She wondered if Daniel's father loved Felicia as much as she loved Daniel.

"I made mistakes being a mother. I'd like to think I won't do the same with grandchildren," Felicia said softly.

Madelyn moistened her lips. "I didn't say this was Daniel's child."

"You didn't say it wasn't, either," Felicia said, then continued. "Daniel said you have no family here. Is that right?"

"Yes." There was no harm in answering that question.

"I presume you haven't told anyone on your job?" Felicia leaned forward in her seat.

Madelyn's hands clutched in her lap. "No."

"Then you have no one you can talk to about your pregnancy. I'm volunteering." Felicia's eyes sparkled. "I'm not a patient woman by nature, but I promise to try and not badger you too much," Felicia said.

"Daniel won't like us seeing each other." She couldn't believe she was actually considering his mother's proposal.

"Contrary to popular belief by some, Daniel doesn't rule the world," Felicia pointed out with a graceful arch of her brow.

Madelyn laughed, something she hadn't done freely in a week. The take-charge feistiness of Felicia was what Madelyn needed. She wouldn't mope when she was around, and she'd have someone to talk with about the baby.

"I was about to have dinner. Would you care to join me?" Madelyn stood.

Felicia came to her feet, her face wreathed in a wide smile. "I'd love to."

"Where have you been?" Daniel asked as soon as Felicia stepped inside the foyer. "It's almost eight-thirty."

Felicia kissed her hard-looking son on the cheek, said good night, and headed for the stairs.

Daniel was right on her heels. "You've been with her, haven't you?" He tossed the words in accusation.

"By her, do you mean Madelyn?" Felicia started up the stairs.

"You know da—"

His mother whirled, her sharp gaze cutting off the word. Heat climbed up Daniel's neck. Although she knew he didn't curse in front of her, knew he had probably been going to say "darn"—which he was—she also knew one pointed look from her could always make him feel like horse manure. She wasn't above showing him she still had power over him.

"I asked you not to see her."

She smiled, forgiving him. "I'm the parent here."

"You don't understand," Daniel told her.

Folding her arms, she casually leaned against the railing. "Then perhaps you'd like to explain things to me."

Daniel raked his hand through his hair. "Don't you see, being with her only complicates matters?"

"I'm afraid I don't see how it complicates matters any more than when you spent the weekend with her," his mother replied.

A muscle leaped in his jaw. "There was no one else."

His mother's sigh was long and eloquent. "Daniel, if you think that is the only reason you stayed with her, then you're in deeper trouble than I thought."

His hand clamped down on the polished wood of the banister. "Just promise you won't see her again."

Felicia turned and continued up the wide staircase. "I'm afraid I can't do that. We're having dinner tomorrow night."

"Mother, I don't want you seeing her."

At the top of the stairs, she stared down at her son. "There's nothing you can do or say that will keep me away from Madelyn and my grandchild."

"It's not your grandchild," he gritted out.

Sadness touched her face. "As long as there is the slightest possibility it is, I plan to be a part of their lives. You're like your father in so many ways. Please don't make the same mistake." Then she was gone.

He started after her to ask what she was talking about, then decided he'd do better with Madelyn. His mother could be bulldog stubborn. He'd just have to call Madelyn.

Breathless, Madelyn answered on the sixth ring. "Hello?"

"Why didn't you answer the phone sooner?" Daniel barked, her labored breath sending waves of jealously through him.

"I was finishing my exercise. What do you want, Daniel?"

His relief was short-lived. He almost looked at the phone. Madelyn had never sounded impatient with him in the past. "I don't want you seeing my mother."

"Tough."

"Tough?" he repeated incredulously.

"We had a great time talking about fashion, movies, and sometimes just nonsense. I thoroughly enjoyed her company and the baby has a right to know its father's mother."

His grip on the phone tightened. It was all he could do not to tell her again he was not the father.

"Daniel, I have another call coming through. Good night."

The line went dead before he could tell her not to hang up the phone. Angrily he pushed the redial button, only she didn't switch over to talk with him. He barely kept from banging down the phone. He knew what his mother was trying to do. Let them talk and meet all they wanted, but it wasn't going to matter to him.

"Daniel doesn't believe the baby is his," Madelyn said as she sat next to Felicia on the couch, a bowl of unbuttered popcorn between them. Exactly one week had passed since she came into Madelyn's life.

"So history repeats itself." Sighing, Felicia removed her size-six feet from the cocktail table where Madelyn had insisted she place them to get the best effect on watching the black-and-white movie classic on TV.

Madelyn turned wounded eyes to her. "Felicia, I promise I'm not lying. I'm not like those other women who wanted only money from Daniel. This is Daniel's baby."

Felicia's delicate hand covered hers. "Of course not. You misunderstood. I meant Daniel. You see, he was born four months and three weeks after I married his father."

Madelyn's mouth gaped.

"I see I shocked you. It came as a shock to my parents, too. They fully intended me to marry some successful man of my race who was of the same social circle, not fall desperately in love with a full-blooded Muscogee Creek who was as poor as the proverbial church mouse." Felicia sighed. "One look at John Henry, and I knew he was mine.

"As the only child of wealthy parents, 'no' wasn't a word I accepted. I always got what I wanted. My father used to say I demanded my way from the day I was born, and I wouldn't stop until I had it, or those around me would pay."

"You must have changed," Madelyn offered—she hadn't seen Felicia do one selfish thing. She went out of her way to be kind and helpful to Madelyn. She was accepting, nonjudgmental, and respected Madelyn's privacy.

"Thank you, but not until after I lost Daniel's father," she confessed.

"So what happened to make the two of you get together?" Madelyn asked, curious and hopeful at once.

Felicia smiled with the memory. "I sent him a letter, saying my parents were shipping me off to England to marry one of my father's business associates' sons and told him, if he wanted me and his child, he better come and get us."

Madelyn laughed, liking the woman's style. "So he came running."

"In a flash. Two days later I woke up one night with a hand over my mouth. John Henry kidnaped me. We left in his beat-up pickup and were married when we reached Oklahoma. Of course I wasn't that easily gotten back after the way he acted, so he took me to a little cabin and proceeded to try and win me back. I can't ever remember being happier. He ate every bite of burnt food I set before him."

"How romantic," Madelyn said, smiling.

"My parents didn't think so. The only reason they didn't call the police and file kidnaping charges was because they knew I was pregnant and in love with John Henry." She wrinkled her nose. "It probably helped that I called every day for a couple of weeks and sent them a copy of the marriage license."

Madelyn's dark brows drew together. "Obviously they came around."

"Only after Daniel was born. I begged John Henry to call my parents. They fell in love with Daniel and decided they'd rather try and get along with their poor but proud son-in-law than give up their daughter and grandson. I left the hospital thinking all my dreams had come true."

This time it was Madelyn who placed her hand over Felicia's. "You could call him."

"I'm afraid it will take more than a phone call. You see the new improved Felicia. I could be a real rich-bitch when I put my mind to it." Her voice trembled. "I pulled that stunt one time too many. He walked out of my life two years ago, and I haven't heard from him since."

"Does Daniel or Dominique?"

Felicia nodded. "All the time. They split the last Christmas holidays between the two of us. They love their father very much. I wonder why sometimes that they don't hate me for driving him away."

Madelyn remembered Daniel's poor concept of marriage based on his parents' stormy past. She understood him more being around Felicia. Madelyn just wished she loved him less.

"You're too vibrant to hate, and your grandchild is going to love and adore you." Madelyn stood, unwilling to admit there wasn't hope for both of them. "I know what's wrong with us. No butter on the popcorn."

Somehow Madelyn wasn't surprised to see Daniel lounging against a big black truck as she pulled into her parking space in front of her apartment two days later. He looked handsome and dangerous in a black Stetson, white shirt, and sinfully tight jeans.

Truthfully she had expected him or a phone call before now. She and Felicia saw a lot of each other.

Yet, by unspoken agreement, John Henry and Daniel's names were never mentioned in their conversations since Monday night. From his hard expression, Daniel hadn't come to declare his paternity or his affection.

Since she didn't want the entire complex to know her business, she opened her front door and stood back for him to enter. "Daniel."

"Madelyn."

"Have a seat. I have to get out of these heels."

"You should be wearing sensible shoes anyway."

Midway across the room she turned. "What did you say?"

He yanked down the Stetson. "Never mind. I came to talk about my mother."

She was across the room in no time. "Is she all right?"

"Of course she's all right," he admitted, not sounding the least happy about it. "I haven't seen her this happy in a long time. That's why I'm here. You can't keep on giving her false hope."

Madelyn slipped off one of her heels and resisted the urge to throw it at Daniel's head. "I think you better leave."

He didn't budge. "Why are you doing this?"

"Why do you think? I'm not trying to trap you into marriage or ask for a chunk out of your portfolio. I have no reason to lie."

He gave the brim of his Stetson another good yank. "Maybe the father's a jerk."

Slipping off the other shoe, she said, "There's no maybe to it."

His mouth flattened into a straight line. "My mother spends more time with you than she does with me."

"That's because you're out every night."

"Business," he told her and watched her roll her eyes. Gritting his teeth, he gave his hat another yank. He didn't have to hide anything. His life was his own—at least until Madelyn came into his life.

He couldn't stop thinking about her, worrying about her. The women he had taken out hadn't helped. They only made him miss Madelyn more. He could hardly wait to take them home.

Madelyn folded her arms across her chest. "If there is nothing else, it's after seven and I have to get to the gym."

"What! Are you crazy?" he yelled, outraged. "You can't do tae kwon do classes in your condition! What's wrong with you?"

"They're pregnancy exercise classes, Daniel," she said patiently.

"Oh." Damned if he didn't feel his face flush. Flushing, for goodness' sake! She made him act like a raving fool.

"I really must get going."

His gaze locked on her soft lips—lips he was desperately trying not to remember how good they felt on his, how much he wanted to feel them again.

She was too close. The light fragrance she wore beckoned him to lean closer. He had to get out of there before he did something stupid. The book said a woman's breasts changed during this time, becoming more sensitive, larger. The areolae darker.

He wondered. His hand lifted toward her red jacket.

"Daniel, are you all right?"

He snatched his hand down. Disgust rolled through him. He was turning into a pervert. "I'm late for an appointment."

He almost ran from her apartment. He didn't dare look back.

Daniel fully expected his mother to grill him over seeing Madelyn when he arrived home. He had no doubt she knew about his going to see her. He was ready for the interrogation, the prodding. Only his mother wasn't there.

He didn't need to guess where she was. His own mother had gone over to the side of the enemy. She didn't even pretend to be on his side.

He always knew his mother could be stubborn, and he was realizing just *how* stubborn. Her father had told Daniel more than once how stubborn she was. She had grown up thinking everything she wanted, she should have. Usually she wasn't disappointed.

The way the story went, she had seen his father at a Native American rodeo in New Mexico, and that was that. None of them could believe a pampered young woman who had always had servants had lived happily in a little two-room cabin for almost five months, cooking meals over a wooden stove, and sweeping the floor with a straw broom.

John Henry had taken Daniel there once, and he hadn't believed it, either. The log cabin was on a dot of land that scorpions shunned. His father had had to drive fifteen miles one way over rutted roads to work as a ranch hand.

They had certainly loved each other, endured hardships to stay together—yet they hadn't been able to hold their marriage together.

Getting up, Daniel went to stand by the window in his study downstairs. If not for him, they might never have gotten married. Their worlds had collided instead of merging when they left that cabin.

He didn't want that for himself. Or Madelyn.

He had learned at a young age what happened when love wasn't enough. The lesson was reinforced each time his father couldn't take the pressure of his mother trying to turn him into something he wasn't and take off for Oklahoma. Daniel had grown up knowing if not for him, his parents' lives might have taken a different, happier path.

What his parents hadn't taught him about was how easily love could turn into harshly spoken words and accusations, Jeanette had. She had been an expert teacher. Beautiful, vibrant, and poised, Jeanette had been so easy to be with—and then overnight he hadn't been able to stand the sight of her.

She had killed any love he might have had for her, then she had killed herself.

He was never going to let another person depend on him for their emotional well-being and happiness, especially when he knew the high failure rate.

Never. Snapping off the light, he slowly climbed the stairs and went to his room.

Whatever game his mother had going on, he was not going to play.

Daniel was already eating breakfast when Felicia came down the next morning looking elegant as usual in an ice-blue pantsuit. "Good morning, Mother."

"Good morning, Daniel." Kissing his cheek, she took her seat. Almost immediately a servant was at her elbow. "Just juice and toast, please."

Daniel set down his coffee cup. "Eating light?"

"I'm having lunch with Madelyn. I always overindulge. She might be eating for two, but that's no reason for me to gain the pounds." She glanced up and smiled as the servant placed her juice and coffee on the table. "Thank you, Helen."

Here it comes, Daniel thought.

"What are your plans today, dear?" Daintily she lifted her cup and drank.

His smile was pure innocence. "Flexible."

"Good," she commented.

"Is there something you wanted me to do?" he asked, tired of the charade.

"Oh, no. You simply work too hard, and I'm glad you have a light schedule." Getting up from the table, she kissed him on the cheek. "Have a nice day."

Daniel watched his mother leave the room, then grinned. He had walked right into that one. She was enjoying herself at his expense.

Yet there was nothing she wouldn't do to protect her children.

The smile slid from his face. Once that had included almost destroying the man she loved.

CHAPTER 10

Pick up the phone, Madelyn, Daniel silently demanded. His fingers bit into the plastic when the answering machine clicked on. The deep, melodious tone of Kane's voice was starting to irritate him.

Disgusted, Daniel slammed down the phone. There was no sense leaving another message. She hadn't answered the three from yesterday.

Where the hell could she be this early on a Saturday morning? She wasn't at home, that was for sure. He had gone by there before seven this morning and late last night. Both times her Acura was gone.

When he tracked her down, he had something to tell her. This time he wouldn't choke. He'd make sure she understood he wanted her to stop seeing his mother. It was bad enough trying to forget her without his mother being a constant reminder of her.

"What was that noise?"

Daniel whirled to see his mother wearing a navy-blue and white pantsuit, standing in the study doorway. The frown cleared on her face on seeing his hand on the telephone. "Is something wrong?"

His mother would know. She looked too happy with herself for the past two weeks not to be in contact with the woman she thought was carrying her first grandchild. He wasn't going to ask her though.

She'd like nothing better than to see him and Madelyn get together. It wasn't going to happen in this lifetime. Then the picture of Madelyn being hurt and alone somewhere flashed into his mind.

"I can't find Madelyn." Was that his voice that held a mixture of pique and desperation?

Frowning she stepped farther into the room. "Last night she didn't mention she expected to see you."

"You saw her last night?" he questioned, crossing the room. "When? Where?"

"We went to the movies together." His mother shuddered delicately. "I can't believe some of the things that pass for entertainment these days. All that blood and gore."

"You didn't let her see anything that might upset her, did you?" he asked, his tone accusing.

She tilted her head. "I see you weren't worried about me."

He refused to back down. "You're not in her condition." No matter how childish it was, he still couldn't say the word out loud.

His mother had no such problem. "By condition do you mean her pregnancy? Say it, Daniel. It won't turn you into stone."

But it would make him think of the unknown father. As long as he separated Madelyn from the baby, he was fine.

His mother patted his cheek when he remained silent. "Poor Daniel, one day you're going to have to make a decision on this, and I hope it's the right one."

He didn't want to talk about it. "What kind of movie did you see?"

"One that upset us both. A love story that ended tragically. We both cried buckets. Life does imitate art." She looked sad for a moment, then started toward the small dining room off the kitchen.

Daniel didn't know if she was talking about her love life or his, but he was leaving both alone. "If you saw her last night, then you know where she is."

"Of course I do. I must eat breakfast, I'm going sailing this morning," she told him as she entered the dining room.

"Where is she?" he asked, pulling out a peach-covered chair for her.

She took the seat and was immediately served. "Why, she's gone, dear."

The word caught him off guard, plummeting him downward. "Gone?" He plopped into a chair. She couldn't leave him—she couldn't.

"Daniel, are you all right? Maybe Will can take a look at you when he shows up."

"Will?"

"He's a friend of Dr. Scalar and a dermatologist. Dr. Scalar introduced us," she answered, pressing the back of her hand to Daniel's forehead. "You work too hard."

"When did you meet Dr. Scalar?"

"Wednesday, when I went with Madelyn to her appointment," Felicia explained, helping herself to a blueberry muffin.

"Is something wrong?" His heart pounded in his chest.

"No, she's fine." She took a bite of the muffin.

"Then why did she ask you to go?" Daniel asked, still not convinced.

Felicia dabbed her mouth with her napkin before answering. "She didn't ask me to go. I asked her. I wanted to meet the man who's going to deliver my grandchild."

Daniel was caught between reminding his mother he wasn't the father and gaining more information. "If Scalar's going to do the delivery, then why did she leave?"

"She didn't leave. She just flew home for her niece and nephew's birthday party," Felicia told him, sipping her coffee.

The tension snapped back into him. If Kane and Matt found out, there'd be hell to pay. If they upset her, they'd be the ones to pay. "To Hallsville. How long ago did she leave?"

Felicia glanced at the slim gold watch on her wrist. "Her flight left two hours ago, at seven. I offered to take her to the airport since her car wasn't ready as promised. I thought a tune-up was simple. People don't take pride in their work anymore."

Daniel didn't like the way his mother had looked at him when she made her last statement. "How did she get to the airport?"

"She said a friend would take her," answered Felicia. "The sweet thing didn't want me getting up so early since she knew I had a sailing date at nine thirty. Apparently he's an early riser."

"He?"

Now he was sure she was glaring at him. The cup clinked in the saucer. "The man who's taking her to the airport. And don't get that look on your face. You're just like your father. Women do have platonic male friends."

No way was he stepping into that one. "When is she coming back?"

"Her plane gets in tomorrow night around five. She didn't want to be too tired for work. I do hope she has a good time." Felicia looked worried. "She didn't say anything, but I could tell she was a little anxious about seeing her family." The thoughtful expression changed to one of pleasure.

"The only time she perked up in the last few days was when we were trying to stuff those piñatas full of candy to send to the twins." Felicia smiled at the memory. "She put a note on the outside of the box not to open until she arrived. I think she's planning to get a crack at them herself."

"A woman in her condition shouldn't be doing anything like that," he almost shouted.

"Daniel, there is such a thing as too much knowledge." She patted his hand as if he were a small boy trying to get away with something and had been caught. "Perhaps you shouldn't read any more of those books on pregnancy."

Black eyes narrowed. "How do you know what I've been reading?"

"I snooped of course," she answered without the least bit of remorse.

"The surest way to get a mother's curiosity up is to try to hide something from her. Try to remember that in the years to come." With one final pat, she placed her napkin on the table and stood.

"I think you'll like Will. He's going to make a donation to the Children's Wish Ball I'm chairing. He's not as tall as I'd like, but he's quite charming and a good sailor I hear." She sighed. "You can't have everything."

"You can, if you try," Daniel said.

She shook her head. Sadness once again shimmered in her eyes. "No. No, you can't. I tried. Don't make my same mistakes."

Everything was going to be all right. No one suspected anything. Not even a twinge of nausea had hit Madelyn. If she felt guilty about not telling her family, she'd have to live with it. The twins' third birthday party was not the time to broadcast her pregnancy.

Besides, there hadn't been a moment's peace since she had arrived at Kane's ranch house. Matt and Shannon were already there. Her parents drove up just behind her. She had been so happy to see them all. Breakfast was a loud affair, with everyone talking and catching up. Then they had all started trying to get ready for the party at two.

Everyone was given specific duties. They barely finished everything before the first guest arrived. Since then there hadn't been a quiet moment. The party was a roaring success.

Madelyn looked at the forty-odd children racing around the yard, trying to decide what they wanted to do next, and smiled. Unconsciously she placed her hand on her flat abdomen.

"You wonder how they get that much energy, don't you?"

She glanced around into the smiling face of Stewart Yates. Medium height and with nice shoulders and a kind face, Stewart had recently come to work for Kane at the ranch. His five-year-old niece was presently enjoying her third pony ride.

"I certainly do," Madelyn said, returning her attention to her job of watching the three children inside the recently constructed petting area. Only the children weren't doing as much petting as they were hugging the animals. The two goats didn't seem to mind.

"It's good having you back home again," Stewart said.

She smiled at him. "This isn't exactly my home, but it is good being with the family."

Calloused hands settled beside hers on top of the wooden rail. "Any chance of you moving back here?"

"No, I like my job in Houston. Excuse me." Opening the gate, she let the children out and three more in.

"Do you have any plans for tonight?" Stewart asked as soon as she returned.

"Plans?"

He looked uncomfortable. "I thought maybe you'd like to go out to a movie."

"She wouldn't."

Madelyn whirled to see Daniel standing a few feet away. Dressed in jeans and a white shirt and his signature black Stetson, he looked wholly dangerous and too tempting for words. He was also angry. She glanced around to see if any of her family might have heard him.

"I don't seem to remember asking you," Stewart said.

Madelyn swung her head back around. Stewart must have a death wish. Daniel looked ready to explode. "Stewart, do you think you could get me a diet soft drink?"

He didn't budge. "Maybe he'd like to get it?"

A smile crossed Daniel's face. "Good idea." In two strides he was beside Madelyn, taking her arm and leading her away. "Watch the children, would you?"

"Daniel, please," she cried, glancing over her shoulder at Stewart, who was caught between watching the children and coming after them. "That wasn't nice."

"I never said I was nice."

She swallowed. His hand on her bare arm felt too good. If he didn't touch her, she stood a better chance of remaining detached around him. That's the only thing that saved her when he came to her apartment the other day. "I'm assigned to be at the petting area."

"How long have you been on your feet?" He stopped. His gaze swept her. "It's hot out here."

Under his scrutiny, Madelyn's skin prickled in the white, loose-fitting sundress. The man had the most sinful eyes to go along with the rest of him. "I'm fine, but I can't abandon the children."

"That guy was trying to pick you up."

"And . . ."

"And," he shouted. "Have you forgotten you're—"

"Daniel!" she interrupted, looking around wildly. This time several people were watching them, including her two brothers and sisters-in-law. "I hope you're satisfied," she cried, and rushed back toward the petting area.

Hell, he was anything but satisfied. He had never been less satisfied in his life. He hadn't been satisfied since she ran dripping wet into him.

He scowled at her. She was wearing the same innocent-looking dress that had caused him so much trouble in San Antonio.

His gaze lifted to the immense blue Texas sky. Not a rain cloud in sight. His scowl deepened on seeing the other man move closer to Madelyn. He'd put a stop to that.

"Hello, Daniel," Kane greeted, extending his hand. "This is quite a surprise."

"Hello, Kane." Warmly Daniel shook his friend's hand. "I hope I'm not intruding. I was in the neighborhood, so I decided to stop by," Daniel said, almost wincing at his flimsy excuse for being there.

"Glad you did. I'd like you to meet my parents, and Shannon is going to wave her arm off if you don't go say hello." Taking Daniel's arm, Kane led him toward his parents.

Daniel threw one glance over his shoulder, glad to see the cowboy wasn't crowding Madelyn any longer, then turned back to Kane. "Matt might not like that," he said, remembering Matt as the jealous type. It didn't seem fair that Daniel was suffering the misery of the damned all by himself.

"I don't think you have to worry about that."

Daniel simply smiled.

Thirty minutes later Daniel wasn't smiling. He conceded he'd have to suffer by himself. Matt didn't appear the least bit jealous. He was a changed man—not for the better, either.

He didn't seem to be able to keep his hands or his lips off his wife. Kane was just as bad. They were letting themselves in for a lot of heartache, but Daniel wasn't going to tell them that.

Daniel glanced over to where Madelyn stood. The man had moved in again, and this time she'd stayed. Just wait until he got her alone!

"I think we have a problem."

"You noticed too, huh?"

"You'd have to be blind not to."

"I can't believe he thought you'd swallow the story that he happened to be in the area and decided to visit."

"He did tell it looking me straight in the eye. You have to give him points for that."

"He's been in the business world too long."

"Falcon is more than his name. It stands for what he is . . . bird of prey, merciless and ruthless when it comes to going after what he wants."

"That's what I'm afraid of. He won't scare off as easily as the others."

"Don't I know it."

"It might be fun to break his nose after all."

Kane glanced at his brother, Matt, and laughed. "You know he was never romantically interested in Shannon."

"I know, but at the time he gave me some rough moments." Matt pressed his knuckles into his palm. "Maybe Madelyn won't think he's so handsome after I finish."

"Or maybe she'll be as softhearted as Shannon and rush to patch him up."

Matt grunted. "What do you think we should do?"

From their vantage point from the side of the house, they watched Daniel watch Madelyn and Madelyn watch Daniel. "You have to give it to Stewart. He's pretending pretty good he doesn't know what's going on," Kane said. "I think he knows he's out of the running, but is just rubbing it in on Daniel."

"Yeah," Matt said. "At least baby sis and Daniel both look kind of tense. I don't think things have gone too far. Daniel still has that restless, edgy look about him."

"He better keep it until he puts a ring on her finger," Kane growled.

Matt agreed with Kane in principle, and knew Kane had waited until well after the wedding to claim his own bride. Matt hadn't been so gallant or patient. He didn't know if his big brother knew he'd jumped the gun or not, and he sure wasn't telling.

His gaze trained on Daniel again. He wore that same look of denial and desperation Matt knew so well. He had stared at it every morning while shaving. He'd fought his feelings for Shannon for all he was worth. Yet they had been too strong to deny. When they had finally exploded, nothing had been able to hold them back.

"Damn," Matt muttered. "We better have a talk with him."

In unison the men moved toward Daniel. "I'd like to show you something," Kane said.

Without waiting for him to answer, Kane grabbed one arm and Matt the other. Daniel lifted a dark brow, the corner of his mouth tilted. "I wasn't flirting with Shannon or Victoria."

"Wouldn't do you any good if you had," Matt answered.

"Then what is this about?"

"We'll talk in the barn," Kane said.

"Smile at Madelyn, Daniel. She looks upset. Any reason for her to look upset?" Matt asked mildly.

"Why are you asking me?" Daniel said as the three men stepped into the dimness of the barn.

Releasing his arm, Kane faced him. "Because since you've gotten here, you've spent your time between sending killer glances at Stewart and annoyed ones at Madelyn."

Daniel crossed his arms. "Then it seems to me you should be having this conversation with Stewart, since he's been with her since I arrived."

"So far he's the only one doing the looking." Kane thought the look on Daniel's face was much too smug. "But if that should change, he'll be standing where you are in a heartbeat."

Daniel's mouth thinned. Kane and Matt shared a look. It wouldn't hurt to let him know he might not have the inside track.

"I wasn't aware that my actions were being monitored so closely," Daniel finally said.

"Come on, Daniel. You're not talking to two fools. I've seldom seen you look at a woman more than twice. Yet you can't take your eyes off our sister."

He eyed a saddle on the rail. "She's an attractive woman."

Matt threw up his hands. "So are Victoria and Shannon, but you haven't done more than spoken to either of them. And don't say it's because they're married, because two attractive women who aren't have been giving you the eye all afternoon, and you've ignored them, too. What's up between you and Madelyn?"

Unfolding his arms, Daniel faced Matt. "Whether something is up or not, it's between the two of us."

"What if I beat the crap out of you until I get the answer I want?" Matt challenged.

"You can try."

"He can try, but I'll succeed," Kane said, moving his huge body in front of Daniel, towering over him by a good two inches. "I want to know why you didn't mention something was going on between you and Madelyn when we talked. I want answers—and I want them now."

"If there is anything between us, it's none of your business," Daniel said. "But if you upset her, you'll have me to answer to."

"Is that a fact?" Kane snarled.

"Count on it," Daniel answered, not backing down an inch.

Kane suddenly burst out laughing and slapped Daniel on the back. He laughed harder at the bewildered look on the other man's face. "We've been waiting for a man we can't intimidate for our little sister." The laughter stopped and he pinned Daniel with dark, dangerous eyes. "But hear me, Daniel. I don't care about the new moral code. Madelyn is my sister. You step out of bounds, hurt her in any way, and I'm coming after you."

"And when he's finished, I'm next," Matt said.

"I never thought differently," Daniel said.

"Good. Now let's go join the party. It's time to bust the piñatas."

Madelyn was so nervous she had to force herself to keep from wringing her hands. Seeing Daniel and her brothers come out of the barn didn't help. The only two smiling were Matt and Kane. Since Daniel wasn't bruised, she was sure he hadn't told them about her pregnancy. But that left a lot to discuss.

"Time to break the piñatas," Kane yelled, motioning all the children to follow him.

Relief swept through Madelyn as she opened the gate and followed the children. She had to know what they had been talking about.

"I don't have a chance, do I?"

Madelyn turned back to Stewart. Maybe if she had met an uncompli-cated man like Stewart, she wouldn't be going through all of the emo-tional gymnastics Daniel was putting her through.

"That's all right. You don't have to say it," the ranch hand said. "I can see it in your eyes."

"Is it that obvious?" Madelyn asked anxiously.

"Probably just to me, since I wish you would have looked at me that way. But at least I know he's not having an easy time, either, and he's rich."

"Money has nothing to do with anything."

"I know. That's why he's one lucky son of a gun."

She smiled tremulously. "I don't think he would agree with you."

"Some men go down hard—others easy."

"I'll try to remember that."

"I guess I better see if they need any help," he said.

"I hope you find the woman you're looking for soon. I'd say she's the lucky one."

His gaze flickered behind her, then he stepped closer. "I bet your lips taste sweeter than vine-ripe strawberries."

Madelyn's mouth gaped.

"I believe Kane wants you," growled Daniel.

Comprehension snapped Madelyn's mouth shut.

Daniel. Stewart had seen him and given him a little prod—only prod-ding Daniel wasn't recommended for a person's health.

"If there is dancing later on, save me a dance." Tipping the brim of his tanned straw hat, Stewart strutted away.

Daniel turned those lethal black eyes on her. "I hope you've enjoyed yourself this afternoon."

"I might have, if you hadn't shown up. Daniel, what are you doing here? Why did they take you to the barn?" she asked in a frantic rush.

"I came in case you decided to tell your family and needed some moral support," he said tightly. "Obviously you didn't need my help with Stewart hovering all over you."

"Daniel, you can be such a pain in the butt," she snapped and walked off. Unrelenting fingers caught her a few steps away.

"Slow down before you hurt yourself," he admonished. "Mother told me you're thinking about hitting that piñata. Forget it."

She stopped. "What?"

"You'll have to be blindfolded, and I won't have you swinging with a stick and possibly hurting yourself."

"You won't, huh?" Madelyn said, her hands on her hips.

Daniel gave her glare for glare. "No, I won't."

He was magnificent when he was angry, and this time his anger and concern were for her and the baby. *You're getting there, Daniel. Just keep coming.* "Since I want some of that candy, I guess you'd better take my place."

Daniel had taken her place after all the children had had several chances. Much to his surprise, he had enjoyed the encouragement of the children and the teasing from Matt about his pitiful swing. Finally he had landed a solid hit and broken the piñata. Kane had gotten the other one.

Instead of joining in the mad scramble for candy along with the children, Madelyn had stood back smiling until she saw the boys were stuffing candy into their pockets, while the girls had only their hands.

Hitching up the hem of her dress into a makeshift pouch, she waded into the melee, showing the girls how to get more goodies. She was grinning from ear to ear and having the time of her life.

Her parents shook their heads indulgently at her. Her sisters- in-law cheered her on. Her brothers watched Daniel, and Daniel divided his time between sending lethal glances at her and Stewart.

Madelyn happened to glance up and look straight into Daniel's hard black eyes. The fun went out of her. He was more than angry about the candy—he simply didn't trust her.

That hurt. It hurt more to see him abruptly turn to say goodbye to her family, then walk away.

Hungrily her gaze followed.

No matter how much she told herself it shouldn't matter—to forget him—it did matter, and regardless of how hard she tried, forgetting him was impossible.

CHAPTER 11

It was all Madelyn could do to keep a smile on her face as she turned back to the children. She wasn't foolish enough to think that no one had noticed her reaction to Daniel's leaving.

She just hoped they didn't all pounce on her at once. She couldn't take that. Tears pricked her eyes. She was not going to cry. She was not.

Not once, no matter how hurtful the offense had she ever cried in public. Not when Kali Jefferson invited every girl in the sixth grade to her birthday party except Madelyn; not when her date at the senior prom left her to take another, more willing girl home; not when she was repeatedly treated like a nonentity at Sinclair.

Not once. She was stronger than this. A tear formed, hovering on her lower eyelid.

"Madelyn, I need your help setting up things on the back porch," called Victoria.

Madelyn glanced up, blinking rapidly to clear the tears away. Not once because she'd always known her family was one hundred percent behind her. Not once because she had been taught to let no obstacle stand in her way. She sniffed. But Lord, she had never hurt this deeply before.

She sniffed again, her hands digging into the empty pockets of her sundress. Where was a tissue when she needed one?

"Madelyn, come on. I'll meet you on the back porch," Victoria told her, then started for the house. Kane followed.

Her heart sank. Interrogation time.

After walking only a short distance with his wife, Kane kissed her on the cheek and went to stand by his brother. "Baby sis, you better hurry or I might decide to take care of things in my own way."

Madelyn took off. It was a subtle warning. She was being offered a reprieve. The interrogation—and she was sure that was what it was going to be—would come later.

By the time Victoria reached the screened back door, Madelyn had it open for her. "Thank you."

"Don't thank me yet, he still wants to talk with you," Victoria said.

"Matt, too." Shannon Taggart walked up to them. "So do we smuggle you out the front door, or do you want Victoria and me to make the supreme sacrifice and find some other way to take our husbands' minds off their big-brother routine?"

Victoria's hazel eyes narrowed mischievously. "Speak for yourself about sacrifice."

Madelyn laughed as the three of them entered the house. Her brothers' wives were beautiful, loving, and unpretentiously wealthy women in their own right. Victoria owned a chain of six upscale lingerie boutiques called Lavender and Lace. Shannon had inherited her wealth, yet continued to work as a nurse practitioner on a voluntary basis in Jackson Falls where she and Matt lived.

What endeared them to Madelyn was their unfailing love and devotion to their husbands. Husbands who loved them just as much. Her smile died. That was something she might never have.

Shannon's hand gently touched Madelyn's. "Your business is your own, but for what it's worth, some men aren't easy to love or understand."

"Women, either," Victoria added. "Kane didn't give up on me even when another man would have walked away or shook me until my teeth rattled."

Madelyn looked at the two women. "What you're saying is that you have to fight for what you want?"

"If you can answer one question without hesitation," Victoria said.

"What?" Madelyn asked uneasily.

"Can you imagine living your life and being happy without him?"

No matter how much she wished otherwise, there was only one damning answer. "No."

"Then go after him with all you've got," Shannon told her.

"But . . . but what if I already tried, and it didn't work?" Madelyn bit her lip.

"Try again," Victoria said softly. "Kane never gave up on me. He taught me how not to be afraid to trust in loving someone. I never want to think of what might have happened if, at a crucial point in our marriage, we both hadn't put love above pride."

"Matt fought falling in love until the night he proposed," Shannon said with a hint of pride. "I admit I went after him shamelessly."

Laughter erupted. The whole family had been shocked to hear of Matt's engagement. His first marriage had been a disaster, and after swearing not to marry again, he had started going through women like water through a sieve.

"What's taking so long?" Grace Taggart inquired.

"The children are getting restless," Clair Benson added.

"Coming, Mrs. Taggart, Grandmother," Victoria said and rushed toward the kitchen, Shannon right behind her.

Before Madelyn could make her escape, her mother had her by the arm. She swallowed.

She had never been able to hide anything from her mother. She prayed today was the exception. "I'd better help."

"One more minute won't hurt," her mother said. "All I want to know is, was that talk your brothers had with Daniel necessary?"

Swallowing again, Madelyn cut a glance at Victoria's grandmother, Mrs. Benson, who appeared in no hurry to leave. As usual she was in lace and pearls even on a hot summer day. She was a sweet, no-nonsense lady.

"You had only to look at him to know the answer to that question," Clair Benson said. "He needs a haircut."

"He's part Native American," Madelyn said automatically.

Clair regarded her thoughtfully. "My great-grandfather was a Buffalo soldier who fought the Indians."

Madelyn didn't know what to make of that comment. "Yes, ma'am."

"In his diary he said he had never met a fiercer, more determined people. He said he thought they might be like the African tribes." Clair looked at Grace. "I don't know what was said in the barn, but it probably won't do any good." She opened the back door and went back outside.

"Addie," Grace said, her worry obvious in the reprisal of her daughter's old name. "I will be forever thankful for Daniel helping with arrangements for your brother's wedding, but I read the papers. His reputation with women is worse than Matt's used to be."

"And look at Matt now."

"But it took him a long time to find Shannon," her mother said, holding her daughter's gaze.

"Daniel and I are just friends," Madelyn said. The relief on her mother's face was instantaneous. "We better go help in the kitchen."

Grace Taggart palmed her daughter's cheeks. "I love you. If ever you need to talk, call. I'm not so old that I don't remember how it was to be in love and impatient."

"I love you, Mama," Madelyn said, wishing she had enough courage to tell her about her grandchild.

Daniel was in a foul mood. He was also as confused as hell. He had watched Madelyn laughing and giggling with the children, her skirt up over her slim legs, and had been caught off guard by a powerful surge of sexual hunger.

It hadn't mattered that her parents were there or her overprotective brothers or the dozen or so other adults, all he had wanted to do was drag her to him and to the nearest bed. Only he wasn't sure if he would have made it that far.

Lust had snuck up on him when he wasn't looking. It had to be lust. Initially he had been aware of her free, laughing spirit and sense of fair play. It hadn't been a matter of gender. If the girls would have been giving it to the boys, he didn't doubt that she would have waded in for the underdog.

She obviously loved children. She would make a wonderful mother. The sudden thought that he wouldn't be there to be the father hit him like a fist while he was still trying to deal with the lust.

The unexpected longing for her and the baby had sent him back to his rental car and to Meacham International Airport in Fort Worth faster than the lust. He was getting in way over his head.

Looking out the window of his private jet as it made its way to Houston, his mood hadn't changed. He had never run from anything in his life. And he had had plenty of opportunities.

Most of the students in the predominately Anglo-Saxon, prestigious private school in Boston hadn't known what to think of a boy of visible mixed African-American and Native American heritage. Although there were racial mixtures and African-American students, he was the only one of his mixture, an oddity, accepted by some and made to feel an outcast by others.

John Henry Falcon was unapologetically a Native American. He was more comfortable in jeans and a shirt than the suit and tie his wife and in-laws often demanded that he wear. His boots were run-down at the heel and were bought at the local Wal-Mart. No Italian loafers for him.

He believed in the Master of Breath, The People, his family, hard work. From Daniel's earliest memories, he recalled his father telling him stories of The People, of his tribe, the Muscogee Indians, called Creek by the white settlers because their settlement was near creeks. He never let Daniel forget his ancestors had been fearless warriors, brilliant tacticians, and daring leaders.

Daniel had grown up proud of his uniqueness instead of bewildered by the difference. He was sensible enough to realize his outlook might have been different if his maternal grandparents hadn't been wealthy or just as proud of their ancestors who had always been free.

They had migrated from the West Indies to England to America. Intelligence, fortitude, and business savvy had increased the wealth of each generation of Everetts.

His ancestors on both sides had a history of being displaced. His forefathers on his mother's side learned early what rank and wealth and influence could do when Elizabeth I tried to expel blacks from England in 1596. The expulsion movement largely failed, but it served as an indelible reminder that the majority of Britons thought people with dark skin were inferior.

In 1838 on the Trail of Tears, the Muscogee Indians suffered indignities and cruelties and numerous deaths. Then they were made to live on land that was foreign to them.

His ancestors on both sides were thought by some to be inferior, lazy, shiftless. Those small-minded individuals never thought of the intelligence, the perseverance, the determination it took to survive despite constant and overt discrimination and deprivation in a harsh and hostile world.

Both survived, passing down through generations their history through the spoken, chanted, or sung word. One branch of his ancestors had been more financially successful than the other, but both understood the problems inherent to people of color.

His maternal grandparents might have been snobbish in their own way, but they, like his parents, never let him forget money could get you only so far when the hue of your skin didn't come from hours in the sun or a tanning salon. The lesson was brought home one day when he went to the store with his mother, and they couldn't get anyone to wait on them.

Daniel hadn't understood until his mother gave him a smile and asked to speak to the manager. As soon as the man arrived and learned who she was, he had been all apologetic and so were the saleswomen. They left the store without buying anything.

It was only after they arrived home that he noticed his mother hadn't been dressed up the way she usually was. At dinner that night she casually mentioned the incident to his grandfather and suggested they close out the account. They never returned. His lessons had begun. He'd never forgotten.

He was a proud, almost belligerent, kid—big for his age and unwilling to take mess from anyone. If he hadn't had a conscientious teacher in kindergarten, one who ruled the classroom and the playground with rigid standards of fair play—no matter how much money the student's family had—he might have been expelled, or worse labeled "slow" and delegated to a backseat. Instead righteousness, truth, and honor prevailed as the only criteria for justice, in Mr. Kennedy's opinion.

By not being judged, Daniel had learned not to judge. He had no preconceived notions on meeting someone. The person's actions determined how they would be treated from that point on.

Some of his closest friends were still his kindergarten classmates. Since he admired intelligence, his friends were always at the top of the class. Interestingly, as the years progressed, they were the school leaders in academics and extracurricular activities.

Those same friends had grown up to be some of the most influential men in the country: men of integrity and long memory. Each year they got together for a think-tank off the Caribbean, where one of his former classmates owned an island.

None of them would believe that Daniel Falcon had run from a woman he could pick up with one hand. The problem was, after he picked her up, he didn't want to let her go.

Daniel had never in the past had any difficulty in figuring out when someone was trying to put something over on him. His logical mind was telling him he hadn't slipped up. Yet logic was also telling him there was always a tiny risk factor in forming any conclusion dealing with people and emotions.

He had based his decision on his previous experiences with women. But when he looked at Madelyn, as he had that afternoon, he saw an open, caring woman. Not the kind of woman who would name someone else as the father of her child.

That meant he had to reevaluate everything. It wasn't going to be easy—in fact, it was going to be the most difficult, the most gut-wrenching thing he had ever done. Because if he had made a mistake, the possible consequences were just as disturbing.

Something isn't right, and I am going to find out what it is, Bill Taggart thought.

Ever since Daniel Falcon had shown up unexpectedly at the twins' birthday party, people had been acting funny. First it was Madelyn, then his sons, now his wife. Grace bothered him most of all.

After forty-two years of marriage, a man learned to pick up on things if he wanted to stay happy. Grace hadn't asked for her camera back since she came to get everyone for cake and ice cream, nor had she gotten on to him for not snapping photos. She had more pictures of her grandchildren than all of her children put together—doted on the little rascals so much she had to stop going through the children's department to resist buying them something.

Now all her attention was for her daughter. She didn't seem to be able to pass without touching her head, her arm. The trouble was, their daughter was looking sadder and sadder.

His children might be grown, but a man never stopped being a parent until he drew his last breath. Something was wrong with his Kitten, and he was going to find out what it was.

"Kane, Matt—grab some trash bags, and we'll start cleaning up outside."

Bill's determination grew when he saw Madelyn tense and send a worried glance toward her brothers. What made him feel a little better was the slight nod of approval from his wife.

It had bothered him to think Kitten had a problem, and his wife hadn't come to him. He should have known better. They always talked things over. Grace wasn't the secretive type. His sons, on the other hand, could put a rock to shame on giving out information.

Outside he began helping his sons pull the pink and blue crepe paper from the lower branches of the oak tree. "Is Kitten in trouble or heading that way?"

"Daddy, I'm not sure it's either," Kane said. His extra three inches made it easier to remove the paper and not damage the branches. He paused a second, then faced his father. "I think she may be interested in Daniel Falcon, only I'm not sure how far it's gone or if it's going anyplace."

"So that's what the trip to the barn was about?" Bill asked.

"Yes, sir," Matt confirmed, a frown on his handsome face. "Only he isn't as easily intimidated as the others."

"He's not intimidated at all," Kane reminded him.

"Didn't I read he's in Houston now?" Bill asked.

"Yes, sir," Kane said, his sigh long and telling.

Bill stared into the distance for a long time before saying, "All you can do is try your best to raise your kids to know right from wrong, because one day you have to let 'em go on their own." His gaze turned to his eldest. "You were the easiest"—then to Matt—"You were always respectful, but you wanted to push everything to the limits."

Bill lowered his voice and continued. "You worry more about girls, but Kitten has never given your mother and me a moment of worry. I know some of that is because of you two, and I always loved you more because I didn't have to ask you to watch after her.

"Her mother is worried now. So are you two. But all of us jumping on her is not going to help, either." He held up his hand when Matt started to say something. "Sometimes talking makes things worse instead of better. The day Kane stopped talking and hauled you to Wade's ranch was the day you started to heal."

Bill's hand clasped his second child on his wide shoulder. "I hurt for you, but there was nothing I could do but be there for you. I think that's what we have to do now. Just be there for your sister."

"Daniel is my friend, but he can be a coldhearted SOB if he wants to," Kane warned.

Bill looked at his middle child. "So could your brother before Shannon. I want you two to leave Kitten alone."

"And if he hurts her?" Matt asked.

"Then you can have him, after I'm finished," the elder Taggart said.

Gradually Madelyn became aware she wasn't the center of attention anymore. The focus had shifted to Kane Jr. and Chandler. The two show-offs were demonstrating their riding skills.

Victoria, who by her own admission was afraid of horses until she married Kane, was beaming as her children rode their Shetland ponies around the corral. Their father stood nearby, but no one doubted that if he had the slightest doubt of the children's abilities, he wouldn't have given them the ponies for their surprise birthday presents.

"Now we can go riding with you all the time, Daddy," Chandler said.

"Did you get Mama a horse so she can ride by herself?" Kane Jr. asked. "Shadow Walker must be tired of carrying both of you all the time."

Dropping her head, Victoria groaned. Matt whooped. Kane shot him a threatening look. "Shannon, you better get an ice pack ready"

"Now, children," Grace admonished sternly, her lips twitching. "What will Clair and Henry think of us?"

"That Victoria did the right thing when she asked Kane to marry her," Clair answered without a moment's hesitation. Her husband, Henry, not as outspoken as his diminutive wife, smiled in agreement.

This is how it is supposed to be, Madelyn thought. An outpouring of love and affection and warmth. This is what she wanted for her child. Her family might not approve of her single motherhood, but she didn't doubt they'd love her baby.

"That smile looks good on you," her father said, looping his arms over the top rail of the corral.

"Sorry, I've had a lot on my mind." They might love the child, but she wasn't ready to tell them yet.

"Whatever it is, you'll work it out. And if you can't, just remember your family loves you, and we're only a phone call away."

Slowly she turned and gazed up into the eyes of the first man she had loved. In his eyes she saw love just as great. There would be no interrogation.

She'd have time to work through this by herself. Once again her father had come to her rescue, just as he had so many times when she was growing up with scraped knees, broken bikes, back-stabbing friends, callous boys.

She swallowed the growing lump in her throat. "I'm glad you're my father."

"No gladder than I am." His hand left the rail and circled her shoulders. She leaned into him.

From the corral, Kane caught Matt's attention. Silent communication passed between them. For now they'd respect their father's wishes. But if Daniel hurt their baby sister, there wouldn't be much left of him for their father to worry about.

In his black truck, Daniel slowly drove into Madelyn's apartment complex. Catty-cornered to her apartment, he backed in tail first, cut the engine, then tossed his aviator sunglasses on the dash. He wasn't happy about being here, but he hadn't been able to talk himself out of coming.

When he left—all right, ran from Kane's ranch—his primary concern had been with putting as much distance as possible between him and temptation. It was only later, as he had time to think on the flight, that he had thought how his abrupt leave-taking might affect her or make her brothers more suspicious.

She had enough to deal with without their butting in. He didn't delude himself into thinking he had fooled them or gotten them to back off. They were too stubborn and loved their sister too much. He wouldn't, if he we're in their place.

Daniel tossed his Stetson onto the seat beside him. Hell, he had been in their place. Even after all these years, the memory still enraged him. LaSalle had been a smooth-talking snake. Daniel had taken great pleasure in pulling his fangs.

A white Lexus with gold mag wheels and gold trim passed in front of his truck and parked in the space in front of Madelyn's door. Daniel straightened.

The door on the passenger side of the car opened. A jean-clad leg in white sneakers emerged. Moments later the rest of Madelyn appeared, her face wreathed in a smile.

Daniel's attention shifted to the driver. He finally admitted the other reason he was there, to see her "friend." He wasn't pleased.

The other man was of average height and build, and dressed in raw silk black pants and shirt. A diamond glinted in his ear. When he opened the trunk, Daniel noted the heavy gold link bracelet.

Some women liked flashy men. He thought Madelyn had more sense . . . until she laughed and swatted playfully at the arm of the walking jewelry store. Still laughing, they went inside.

The truck's motor came to life. He finally admitted the third reason he had come: to know if seeing her helped him with the turmoil he had been going through since his logic had hit him squarely in the face. It had, only not the way he thought.

He should have trusted his first instinct. There was nothing connecting him to Madelyn except white-hot lust. Madelyn didn't need him, and he wasn't going to make the mistake again of thinking she did.

* * *

"Thanks again, Sid, for picking me up."

"No problem. I'll be here at seven thirty to take you to work," Sid said, setting her overnight case and garment bag on the couch.

"I appreciate it," she told him. "They promised to have my car ready by three tomorrow."

He grunted. "If they don't, let me know."

She grinned. Sid had been her neighbor and friend for two years. He'd passed inspection the first time he met Kane and Matt for the simple reason they could see there was nothing romantic happening. And his collard greens, candied yams, and hot-water corn bread were to die for.

The only boy and youngest child of five children, Sid had grown up with a strong protective instinct where women were concerned. His flight-attendant girlfriend, Gloria, was desperately trying to steer him to the altar. But Sid, an insurance adjuster, was having too much fun living the single life.

"You can depend on it," she finally said.

"See that you do. Hate to run, but the game will be on at six," he said, striding toward the door. "Sure you don't want to come over and watch the Sonics outshoot the Mavericks with me?"

"I'm not sure Gloria trusts me," she told him.

"Her problem. I'm not giving up my friends. Anyway, a relationship won't work without trust."

Madelyn's happy mood deteriorated. "Don't I know it."

He paused with the door open, his gaze openly speculative. "Something tells me you're not talking in generalities."

She studied the toes of her sneakers. "You'll be late for the ball toss."

He crossed back to her. Lean fingers lifted her chin. "Watch yourself, you hear?"

"I hear," she said, then closed the door after him and leaned against it. She heard. The warning had just come too late.

CHAPTER 12

Madelyn frowned on passing empty office after empty office Monday morning. She glanced at her watch: seven fifty-two. Usually everyone was at their desk by now. Putting her briefcase away, she peeped into Floyd Cramer's office. Empty. Dedicated, precise, and punctual to a fault, Floyd arrived at work earlier than anyone and was one of the last to leave.

Her frown deepened. There wasn't a morning meeting, Madelyn was sure of it—at least she hoped there wasn't. Her concentration hadn't been the best the last few weeks.

Hearing faint voices coming from Mr. Sampson's office, she slowly headed in that direction. Finding everyone crowded around a portable TV in her boss's office, she wrinkled her nose. If it was Daniel again, she wasn't staying.

"Good morn—"

Her greeting was shushed. She walked farther into the room. Daniel was hot news, but she couldn't imagine this type of attention.

"What's up?" she softly questioned Mr. Sampson.

His gaze remained fixed on the TV screen. "Mr. Osgood is about to make an announcement."

Madelyn placed her hands on Cassandra's shoulders and leaned closer. Osgood was CEO of Sinclair, and from all the TV stations and microphones jockeying for position, it had to be big news for the regular broadcast to be interrupted.

A distinguished, gray-haired man stepped to the podium and smiled. There was a collective sigh of relief from more than one person.

"Whatever it is, we'll still get a paycheck. Osgood rose up from the ranks. He wouldn't have that 'cat-ate-the-cream-look' if he was about to throw us to the wolves," Floyd announced.

Osgood straightened the mike and began speaking. "Sinclair Petroleum Company, because of its size and savvy, has always been a leader in the energy industry. So it is with great pleasure that I'm unveiling plans to build a two-billion-dollar chemical complex in Singapore, aimed at positioning the company as the low-cost plastics supplier in the booming Asian market."

"Gee whiz," muttered Scotty Jones, who quickly received a collective shush.

Osgood continued. "The four integrated plants in Singapore will eventually employ as many as one thousand people. The huge complex will produce petrochemicals and basic plastics used in a wide range of consumer products. Product prices are at their highest levels in years, and Asian demand is expected to continue to soar."

This time no one said a word.

"The state-of-the-art facility will be supplied primarily from an existing Sinclair refinery in Singapore, Sinclair Petroleum Company in Houston, and other soon to be announced regions." Removing his wire-rimmed glasses, Osgood placed them in his coat pocket. "Questions?"

He was bombarded with them. This time her coworkers weren't listening. They were too excited about the possibility of going to Singapore. Their excitement reached new heights when Mr. Sampson was called upstairs to a meeting.

When he returned two hours later, the first person he asked to see privately was Madelyn. Rising, she barely acknowledged the thumb's-up sign from Cassandra. She was too worried about what she would say if he did offer her a position.

Entering Mr. Sampson's office, she bit her lip and perched on the edge of the chair in front of his desk, "Yes, Mr. Sampson."

He smiled broadly. "I guess you know what this is about. I don't mind telling you, this is a coup for me as well." Leaning forward, he folded his arms on his cluttered desk. "My department has always had a reputation for having the best and the brightest. That's why I wanted you aboard— that's why I asked to see you first."

Madelyn swallowed. The knot remained in her throat and she barely choked out, "Yes, sir."

"Madelyn, you can take that scared look off your face. I didn't call you in here first to tell you you weren't going, but to offer you a position at the Singapore plant." His smile broadened. "Things are still being worked out, but I can tell you now, I'm putting you up for assistant supervisor."

This was worse than she imagined. She'd thought it would take another year before getting into management. Only now she wouldn't be able to accept the position after she had worked so hard.

Leaning back in his chair, he laughed out loud, his blue eyes twinkling. "I see I've shocked you. Well, say something so I can get the next person in here."

Her hand clutching her stomach, she said, "I-I can't go."

He snapped forward in his chair. His was smile gone, in its place was an expression of stunned disbelief. "What did you say?"

"I-I can't go." Saying it the second time wasn't any easier. "I'm pregnant and have no plans of marrying the father." Seeing the shock and disappointment on his face was worse than she'd imagined. "I can't possibly go, but I thank you for considering me."

He didn't say anything but continued to stare at her as if he didn't recognize her anymore. Taking a deep breath, she forged ahead. "I'd appreciate it if you didn't tell anyone else."

"They're going to know sooner or later," he finally pointed out gruffly, his hand clenched on a ballpoint pen.

"Does that mean you're keeping me in your department?"

Tight-lipped, Sampson leaned back in his chair. Leather creaked. "You're bright, intelligent, hardworking. I'm going to need all the help I can get since they asked for three of my top people. Yours was the first name I gave them."

"I'm sorry."

"So am I." He rocked forward. "Please send Kramer in."

Leaving, she did as requested, then went straight to the rest room to be alone. She didn't think she could go through telling anyone else she was pregnant. Certainly not her family. She felt too exposed. Her private sin made public—and it would only get worse.

The next day proved her right. Mr. Sampson, who had always been so warm, seldom acknowledged her unless necessary. Only Cassandra commented.

"He'll get over your turning him down. I'm glad you did, since I was the last one chosen from our department."

Madelyn wasn't so sure. The guilt she thought she had put behind her had risen up again. Even her theater date that night with the irrepressible Felicia couldn't shake her growing melancholy.

All during the two-act play, she thought of Daniel. His picture in the society page of the *Houston Chronicle* with a beautiful young woman tore at her soul. It was plain to see he had moved on with his life, a life that didn't include her and their baby.

She might not be able to imagine a life without Daniel, but he had no difficulty living without her. Somehow she had to do the same.

The next night she made herself go to the monthly church singles Wednesday night potluck dinner. There was always a lot of fun conversation and good food.

It soon became apparent the topic of choice that night was going to be the difficulty of a good woman finding a good man. Of course the men objected to being made the heavies. Where were the good women, they wanted to know.

Unlike usual, Madelyn didn't get into the middle of the heated discussion. Good was relative. Daniel was a good man, she was a good woman, they had created a life, yet they had no future together. Finding didn't count if you couldn't keep him or her.

Tired, she went home early and immediately went to bed. Before falling asleep, her last conscious thought was a wish for her life to be back the way it was.

Pain, sharp and intense in her stomach, jerked Madelyn from a restless sleep. Gasping, she balled into a knot, her arms circling her waist. Nausea sent her staggering to the bathroom. One hand on the toilet, the other clutching her stomach, she went limp when the twin agonies receded.

Breathing erratically, she tried to stand. Just as she pushed to her knees, a twisting pain in her abdomen sent her down again. In the midst of her torment, a mindless fear emerged.

She was losing the baby.

Felicia answered the phone on the second ring. The lateness of the call didn't bother her. She had called Dominique around noon Paris time and she had been out. When her daughter called back, Felicia had been at the club, helping to organize a benefit for literacy. The seven-hour time difference usually worked out well for them since she went to sleep late, and Dominique was an early riser.

"Hello." Popping a tissue from the holder on the bedside stand, Felicia sat up in bed and wiped away the last traces of the chocolate eclair she had indulged herself in. She frowned.

If this was a bad trans-Atlantic connection, there'd be static, not silence. Reaching for the TV remote, she clicked it off. "Dominique? Is that you?"

Hearing labored breathing, she started to hang up until she heard the word "hurt." Swinging her legs over the side of the bed, she stood. Alarm swept through her.

"Dominique! Dominique, say something," she shouted. Covering the mouthpiece, she yelled for her son, praying he had come home and she just hadn't heard him.

"Dominique, honey. It's mother. Talk to me."

"I-It's M-Madelyn," came the thin, wavery voice.

The panic Felicia felt receded only marginally. "Madelyn, what's the matter? I can barely hear you."

"Stomach keeps cramping. I-I don't know if it's the baby or not."

"Are you bleeding?"

"No," came the thankful answer.

"Don't worry—I'm on the way." Disconnecting the call, she dialed her chauffeur and instructed the sleepy-sounding man to bring the car around immediately.

"Where are you going this late?"

Felicia whirled around to see her son in the doorway and almost cried in relief. "Madelyn just called. She's having stomach cramps. She sounded as if she's in a lot of pain."

Terror ripped through Daniel. "Is it the baby?"

With all her heart, Felicia hurt for her son. Fear had done what his stubbornness wouldn't . . . allowed him to accept Madelyn's pregnancy.

Felicia prayed it wasn't too late. "She's doesn't know. She's not bleeding."

"I'm going with you," he said, grabbing his mother's arm and heading down the stairs.

Madelyn and the baby had to be all right. They had to be.

Daniel refused to accept any other possibility. He tried to think of another plausible explanation for her pain, which he might have read about in all the pregnancy manuals he had pored over—yet for the first time in his memory, his calm, concise mind deserted him.

He could form only one thought: *They had to be all right.*

Daniel felt his mother's hand holding his, knew she was offering support and comfort, yet he was unable to respond. It was as if he had been dropped in a black hole.

He exited the Mercedes before it stopped. An eternity seemed to pass before Madelyn's door slowly swung open.

At the first sight of Madelyn, teary and trembling, clutching the doorknob for support, he came hurtling out of the blackness. Panic seized him.

Fear, remorse, guilt plummeted into him from all sides. He couldn't reach her fast enough, hold her tight enough.

"Honey, it's going to be all right."

She buried her face in his chest, her slim body shaking with the force of her sobs. "My baby. My baby."

"Don't cry," he begged. "Our baby is going to be all right. Dr. Scalar's service says he's at the hospital with a delivery, and he'll meet us there."

Scooping her up in his arms, he rushed back to the car. Felicia held the back door open. Once Daniel and Madelyn were inside, she closed the door and quickly got in front.

Higgins put the luxury automobile into a sharp turn and barreled out of the complex. During his youth he had raced stock cars all over the world. He hadn't lost the touch. In no time they were on the freeway, and he made excellent time in the light traffic.

Yet not good enough.

"It's coming again," Madelyn cried, her fingernails biting into the top of Daniel's hand.

Feeling utterly useless, Daniel murmured words of comfort, holding her in his lap, wishing he could take the pain himself.

At the emergency room, still holding her in his arms, he hurried through the automatic doors as quickly as possible without jarring her. "She's pregnant and having severe stomach pain," he told the first medical-looking person he saw.

"Is this Ms. Taggart?" asked the woman garbed in surgical green.

"Yes," Daniel quickly confirmed.

"I'm Nurse McKinnie. Dr. Scalar called." She indicated a wheelchair. "I'll take her back. You can go sign her in."

"I want to go with her," he cried, holding her tighter.

"Are you her husband?"

"No."

"I'm sorry. Regulations."

Reluctantly Daniel lowered her into the chair. She needed help he couldn't give her. The thought was a humbling and scary one. His unsteady fingers pulled her blue terry cloth robe back up over her shoulders. "I'll be here."

Looking small and frightened, Madelyn bit her lip. His last glimpse of her was of tears streaming dawn her pale cheeks just before the nurse wheeled her away through a set of heavy, automatic doors.

Being helpless wasn't something Daniel accepted easily or was used to. "I should be with her."

"Let's go sign her in."

Guilt-filled eyes lifted to his mother's. "How? I don't even know her birthday, her exact address, her . . ." Fist clenched, he swallowed.

"Then we'll do the best we can," Felicia answered reasonably.

He looked at the double doors through which the nurse had disappeared with Madelyn. "I should have been with her."

Daniel paced the waiting room. Luckily Madelyn had preregistered for her delivery, and they had been able to pull her up on the computer. The fact made him feel worse instead of better. His name wasn't anywhere. If she hadn't called his mother, he wouldn't even know she was here. The unsettling thought caused him to break out in a cold sweat.

He should have been with her all through her pregnancy instead of denying his paternity. It had taken this disaster for him to stop fighting what he had always known deep in his heart, his soul.

Duplicity wasn't in Madelyn's makeup. She was open and honest, sometimes too much so. Her sense of fair play was too ingrained for her to place false paternity. He had let his hardheaded logic, then fear of his feelings, then his jealousy at her apartment Sunday afternoon get in the way of that knowledge.

The baby was his. Stopping, he stared up at the ceiling. *Please, God, don't let it be too late for me to make this up to both of them.*

"Felicia."

Daniel whirled abruptly. A black man in his late thirties, in a white lab coat over green surgical garb and a white cloth cap, held out his hands to Felicia. His mother rose immediately.

"She's fine. Food poisoning. Several more of her church members are in the main ER," he said, his voice a smooth baritone.

"Thank God," Felicia said.

"Can I see her?" Daniel asked.

The man turned to him, his hands still holding Felicia's. "Daniel Falcon, I take it?"

"Yes. Dr. Scalar, I presume."

Deep black eyes twinkled. "You presume correctly. I don't suppose you can wait until I grab a cup of coffee? I've been here for ten hours."

"I don't want to, but since you helped Madelyn, I'll wait."

Dr. Scalar's gaze narrowed thoughtfully. "I can't imagine waiting is something you do well."

"No, it isn't."

"In that case, follow me."

"Give her my love," Felicia called.

Daniel followed the broad-shouldered man, resisting the urge to ask him to hurry.

"We've given her something for the pain and the nausea. Since she's in the first trimester of her pregnancy at almost eleven weeks, I'm keeping her in observation overnight," he told Daniel, pushing open a solid green door.

Seeing Madelyn on the bed, Daniel rushed past Dr. Scalar to her side. Unable to resist, he placed his hand on top of hers resting on her sheet-covered abdomen.

He frowned slightly as she removed her hand and put it under the covers. "Mother sends her love."

"I feel like a fool for worrying her. But I'm so relieved I could dance," Madelyn said. "Thank you, Dr. Scalar."

"You just be careful what you eat from now on."

Something was wrong. Her smile was too bright, almost forced. "Do you need anything from your place?" Daniel asked.

"No, we'll be fine now." She patted her abdomen. This time her smile was real.

Daniel wanted to place his hand on hers again, but wasn't sure of his reception.

"I'd better go. I have a patient in labor upstairs." Dr. Scalar gave Daniel a considering look. "The father is a wreck. I hope you hold up better."

"Someone else is going to be my birthing partner," Madelyn quickly said. There wasn't a hint of regret in her steady voice.

Dr. Scalar's face lost its warmth. "Whomever you choose will be fine, I'm sure. I'll stop by before I leave the hospital."

The door swung shut. Daniel didn't know what to say. He suddenly had the feeling he had lost something infinitely precious, and he wasn't sure if he was going to be able to get it back.

"Daniel, I have to ask for your forgiveness," she finally said, her fingers playing with the seam of the sheet.

Surprise knitted his brow. "For what?"

"For being so righteous when I was telling you about the baby." She shook her head, seemingly unconcerned that her hair was spiked over her head like a porcupine. She had never looked more beautiful or precious to him.

"I was going to take care of the baby and not let it grow up feeling guilt or blame because it was unplanned. But the first time the pregnancy interfered with something I wanted to do, I resented it."

Her face clouded. "The last thing I remember before going to sleep tonight was wishing my life was back the way it was."

"That's understandable, Madelyn," he told her, wanting to take her in his arms so badly he ached. "Your life was changing, and you weren't prepared for those changes. My reaction to your pregnancy didn't help. I should have known the baby was mine. I'm sorry. I hope you can forgive me."

"That's the point I'm trying to make." She lowered her head for a moment, then shook her head. "I blamed you for the same thing I was unconsciously doing. Tonight I finally realized I was spouting words. The pregnancy hadn't really sunk in until it interfered with a job assignment to Singapore." She bit her lip.

"I felt sorry for myself. Then I woke up in pain. I was so afraid I was having a miscarriage. In an instant I realized the best job in the world wouldn't make up for that loss. I had no right to expect you to jump up and down when I really hadn't accepted it myself," she said, condemnation heavy in her quiet voice.

"Mad—"

"No," she said, cutting him off. "This has to be said. I was so concerned about what my family would say, how the people at my job would react, how the parishioners at my church would treat me, that I forgot about the most important thing of all. The welfare of my child. Anything else is secondary." She glanced down at her stomach hidden by bedcovers and circled her arms protectively around it.

When she lifted her face, she glowed with happiness. "I won't forget again. I had never told my baby I loved it, only that I would take care of it. Thank God, I now have the chance. My baby is going to know it's loved."

Nowhere in her diatribe did she mention a need or a place for Daniel in her life with the baby. "I never doubted you'd make a great mother. The kids loved you at the twins' birthday party."

"I'm going to do my best," she said with absolute confidence.

Unable to resist, he brushed unsteady fingertips lightly across her cheek. "You better get some sleep."

Dutifully she scooted down in bed. "Would you mind asking the nurse if I could have a phone? Dr. Scalar doesn't want me to go to work tomorrow."

"I'll take care of it," he said, then added silently, and take care of you and the baby if you'll let me.

"Thanks, but I'd rather call," she told him, already shutting him out.

Not knowing what else to say, Daniel slowly left the room. He had tried to convince himself he didn't need Madelyn in his life, only to find out that he did. It was an unexpected twist of fate that she had taken a page from his book and decided the same thing.

The instant his mother saw him, she rushed to him, her face anxious. "Did something happen to Madelyn and the baby?"

"They're fine," he told her.

"Then why aren't you happy? Despite what's happened in the past, I know you care about both of them."

" 'Too little, too late,' as the saying goes."

Taking his arm, his mother led him out of the waiting room into the quiet hallway. "Will you please tell me what went on in there?"

He repeated their conversation. Each word was like a twisting knife in his heart.

"Daniel, I want to ask you something," Felicia continued when he simply stared at her. "Are Madelyn and the baby worth fighting for, worth locking that stubborn pride of yours in a closet and throwing away the key?"

"Yes." There was no longer any doubt. He wanted both of them in his life.

"Then don't make the same mistake I did," she told him fiercely. "Admit your mistakes. Do everything in your power to let her know you love her."

"You still love him, don't you?"

Tears crested in Felicia's eyes. "I must be a better actress than I thought."

"Then you just didn't marry him because of me?"

Shock widened her eyes. "Is that what you thought?" Her eyes closed briefly, then opened. "Naturally I was scared at first, but it didn't take me long to realize I had the means to make John Henry mine. I can see by your face you think I trapped him. At the time, in my selfishness, I didn't see it that way."

Gratefully she accepted the handkerchief Daniel offered her, then dabbed the corners of her eyes before continuing. "I loved your father from almost the first moment he grinned at me from the rodeo arena. Wonder of wonders, he loved me, too. But your grandparents' wealth sometimes made him uncomfortable."

Daniel's eyes narrowed. "Is that why you tried to make him over?"

"Partly. Although I knew he loved us, a part of him would never be satisfied and happy in tailor-made suits and Italian loafers. The idea of losing him scared me."

She bit her lip. "John Henry is the only man I couldn't wrap around my little finger. The knowledge infuriated as much as frightened me." Trembling fingers swept her hair back behind her ear. "I'm not proud of the way I tried to make him into what I thought he should be. I wanted him less proud, more needy. He took it until I did the unforgivable in his eyes."

Daniel had heard a lot of stories about the final breakup between his parents while his mother had been at a two-thousand-dollar-a-week spa in Florida, but both refused to discuss what had happened. Daniel wasn't exactly sure he wanted to hear.

"Don't look back on this months or years from now with regret," his mother said fervently. Her hand closed gently over his jacketed arm. "Don't follow in my footsteps."

Daniel's concern for his mother grew. He had honestly believed the final breakup hadn't affected her one way or the other for long, believed their forced marriage had slowly killed what love they once might have had for one another. It was a startling revelation to find out how wrong he had been.

He loved his parents, but saw no reason for them to be unhappy together when there was some chance for happiness apart. Now he knew that wasn't the case. "Mother, maybe I can talk to Dad."

Shaking her head, her hand dropped to her side. "Your father wouldn't appreciate your interference. I ruined my marriage. I don't want to ruin your relationship with John Henry."

"He's stubborn, but fair."

"No, and that's final." She hitched the strap of her handbag over her shoulder. She was his mother again—in charge, and not to be denied.

He'd forgotten she was as stubborn as his father. "Come on, I'll walk you to the car."

"And then what are you going to do?"

"What else? Go back in there and fight for another chance. I only hope it's not too late."

CHAPTER 13

"Here's the phone you wanted," Daniel said.

Madelyn opened her eyes, a frown forming on her face as she raised up on her elbows in the hospital bed. "What are you still doing here?"

"They're shorthanded and I decided to stay." The lie slipped out easily. Plugging the phone into the wall outlet, he handed the receiver to her. "It's not like I haven't pulled this duty before."

She accepted the phone, her attention still on Daniel. "I could barely lift my head then. Except for a little queasiness, I feel fine."

"Good." He pulled out a straight-back chair and sat down near the bed.

"Daniel, I'm fine."

"I know." He leaned back in the chair and crossed one booted foot over the other. "Just let me get used to the idea. You scared me again."

"I scared myself," she confessed softly.

Standing, he brushed back her hair, his eyes searching hers. "I know."

Brown eyes misted. "I don't know why I'm crying."

"All the tension finally caught up with you." The pad of his thumb caught a tear and wiped it away.

"I suppose." Dialing, she talked briefly with her boss, then hung up.

"You told him?" Daniel asked, gathering as much from the one-sided conversation.

Nodding, Madelyn leaned back in bed. "He wanted me to accept one of the positions in Singapore at the new petrochemical plant Sinclair is going to build. I was the first person he asked once he came back from his meeting."

Daniel placed the phone on the bedside table, then adjusted the bed-covers. "From your expression, I take it he didn't greet the news very well."

"He's really a very nice man. He has a reputation in the company for having the best and the brightest." She picked at the open weave on the blanket. "I let him down. He likes for us to go out and shine."

Casually Daniel picked up her soft hand. "So you'll shine in Houston instead of Singapore."

She sent him a bright smile. "You can count on it. I'm after his job."

"Something tells me you'll get it," he told her with absolute confidence. "Now rest. I'll be here if you need anything."

Uncertain brown eyes watched him. "You really don't have to stay."

"Yes, I do. Now close your eyes and get some rest before they kick me out of here."

"Daniel," she said softly after she had lain down and closed her eyes. "I'm glad the baby's all right, and I'm glad you're here."

His chest ached. A lump formed in his throat. Tonight could have ended much differently. "So am I."

"Daniel, go home. You look ready to drop."

"Felicia's right, Daniel," Madelyn agreed, resting comfortably in her own bed the next morning. "You look more in need of being in bed than I do."

"There's nothing wrong with me," he told them. "You're sure I can't get you something else?"

Madelyn smiled. "No, I think the magazines, candy, and flowers you picked up in the gift shop this morning just about take care of it."

"Daniel, go home and go to bed," Felicia ordered, bodily leading him by the arm out of the bedroom. "I'll be here."

He rubbed the back of his stiff neck. "I guess I could use a shower and change of clothes."

"Don't you dare come back here before this afternoon."

He frowned down at her. "I thought you were on my side."

"I am. That's why I'm sending you home." Felicia regarded him critically. "How much sleep did you get last night?"

"I don't remember."

She pounced on his answer. "Exactly." Opening the front door, she urged him through. "Goodbye, Daniel." She was still laughing when she reentered the bedroom. "I thought he'd never leave."

"He was so sweet and attentive," Madelyn said, a trace of laughter in her voice. "You should have heard him giving the nurse instructions on pushing my wheelchair into the elevator so I wouldn't be jarred. When he went inside the gift shop, the nurse leaned down and told me she hoped she was off the night I delivered." She sobered. "I guess she thought he'd be there."

"He will be, if he knows you want him there," Felicia said softly.

Madelyn shook her dark head. "Daniel has to go the rest of the way on his own."

The doorbell interrupted any comment Felicia might have made. "If that's Daniel . . ." Ruefully shaking her head, she went to open the front door. Instead of her son, a couple in their midsixties stood there. "Yes?"

"Good morning," greeted the gray-haired woman. "We're Mr. and Mrs. Sampson. Is it possible that we see Madelyn for a moment?"

"Is she expecting you?"

"No, but she called last night and told my husband about her illness," the elderly woman explained.

"You must be her boss." Felicia smiled warmly. "Daniel said she called you last night."

"Daniel. Daniel Falcon?" the man questioned, his voice rising in apprehension.

"Who is it, Felicia?" Madelyn called from the bedroom.

"May we see her?" Mrs. Sampson asked. "We'd like to give her these flowers. We promise not to stay long."

"This way." Felicia led them to the bedroom. "You have visitors, Madelyn."

"Mr. and Mrs. Sampson, what are you doing here?" Madelyn questioned, forgetting about the magazine in her lap.

"Howard wanted to tell you something," Mrs. Sampson said.

Madelyn tried to take comfort in the spring bouquet Mrs. Sampson was holding. It wasn't likely she was being fired if they were bringing her flowers, but being asked to transfer to another department would be almost as bad. "Of course. Felicia, could you please excuse us."

Felicia saw the anxious expression on Madelyn's face and gave the Sampsons a pointed look. "The doctor doesn't want her disturbed."

Jane smiled. Howard remained uncomfortable looking.

"I'll add some water." Taking the bouquet, Felicia left.

"Howard?" Jane prompted.

What little confidence Madelyn had that the situation wasn't dire plummeted. Being at a loss for words or unable to speak his mind was not a characteristic of her boss. "Is this about my job?"

"Howard, you're scaring the poor dear," his wife told him.

Mr. Sampson found his voice. "What do you think she did to me? She's the best production engineer I've had in years, and she tossed it all away."

"I won't apologize for my baby," Madelyn told him fiercely. "If you'd like for me to transfer to another department, I'll understand."

"Who said anything about a transfer?" he asked roughly. "You're still the best production engineer I've got."

"I don't understand," she told them.

He finally spit it out. "Babies and our jobs don't mix. We spend too many long hours away from home. You could have been tops in your field. The Singapore tenure would have given you more experience. Now you'll never get to the top."

Madelyn began a slow boil. Throwing back the covers, she got out of bed. The heavy silk blue pajamas more than adequately covered her. "Are you saying when this baby is born, I won't be able to do my job just as well?"

"You'll try." He shook his balding, gray head in dismay. "But the baby will be sick with this or that, and you'll have to take off."

"You better believe it," she said with heat. "That just means I'll have to work twice as hard when I return—something I'm very well used to."

His blue eyes narrowed. "I won't cut you any slack because of the baby."

"I won't ask you to."

Eyeball to eyeball they glared at each other. "Just so we understand each other. Tomorrow is Friday, you might as well take it off, too, because I want you fresh on Monday morning. Number eighty-five in East Texas struck gas and oil. They need the pipes like yesterday to bring up both. I want you to work with me on it."

Although excitement raced though her at the prospect of working beside him, her expression didn't change. "I'll be there at seven forty-five."

Nodding curtly, Mr. Sampson turned to his wife. "Let's go."

Jane smiled and whispered, "He really likes you or he wouldn't be so upset. He'll get over it though. We'll have lunch when you feel better."

Madelyn eyed her boss standing impatiently in her doorway. "Thanks for bringing him."

Astonishment touched Jane's round face. "You have it wrong. Howard isn't the type of man you can make do anything. I'm the Trojan horse, so to speak. He didn't like the strain between the two of you. He's not really as chauvinistic as he sounds."

Mrs. Sampson's eyes twinkled mischievously. "I'm depending on you to do what I and our four daughters and the other women who have worked under him with children have been unable to do—get him to admit motherhood doesn't diminish a woman's brain cells."

"You can count on it." The women shared a smile.

The doorbell rang. "Seems you have another visitor. We'd better go," Jane said.

Grabbing her robe from the foot of the bed, Madelyn followed them into the front room. "Daniel!"

His cutting gaze zeroed in on Madelyn, warmed when he nodded to

Mrs. Sampson, then zipped back to Mr. Sampson. "Good morning, Mr. Sampson. Finding out already you can't get along at the office without Madelyn? I'm afraid you'll have to—the doctor wants her to rest."

Mr. Sampson's blue eyes widened.

"Daniel," Madelyn admonished, "you're meddling into something that is none of your business."

"Shouldn't you be in bed?" he asked her.

Madelyn sent Daniel a glare hot enough to melt steel. "Stay out of this, Daniel, or be prepared for the consequences."

"Mad—" Daniel began, then her eyes narrowed. He snapped his mouth shut.

"I apologize, Mr. Sampson. Mr. Falcon is a family friend, and he sometimes oversteps himself," Madelyn explained.

Daniel's mouth tightened.

A spat of erratic coughing erupted from the kitchen. "Some water would do wonders to clear your throat, Felicia. You met his mother earlier." A smile on her face, Madelyn opened the front door. "I'll see you at seven forty-five sharp, and thanks for the flowers."

Mr. Sampson almost smiled. He cut a quick glance at the silent Daniel Falcon. "You might make it after all."

"Of course she will, Howard. How else is she going to take your job?" his wife asked.

Mr. Sampson appeared exasperated at his petite wife, but Madelyn noticed he held her arm until he had seated her in their blue Cadillac, then gallantly lifted the hem of her floral print dress away from the door frame. He smiled down at her just before shutting the door.

His concern and love for her was obvious. For a moment Madelyn allowed herself to wonder what that must feel like, to know you were loved, wanted, needed.

"I overreacted again, didn't I?" Daniel asked, a note of caution in his voice.

Closing the door, Madelyn faced him. "Next time ask if your help is needed before you go charging in."

"That's a promise," he said, watching her closely as if she were a time bomb and he wasn't sure how to diffuse her. By slow degrees he took her arm, then gently led her toward the bedroom.

Madelyn started to remind him he hadn't asked, then decided to let him get by this one last time. A contrite Daniel was something you didn't see every day. "Why are you back?"

"I thought I recognized him, but it didn't hit me until I was several blocks away."

Pulling off her robe, she climbed into bed. "So you were practicing your rescue skills again?"

"Unnecessarily, it seems. I guess I keep forgetting you can take care of yourself."

"It's always nice to know you have backup if needed."

"What did he mean by exception?"

She made a face. "He thinks women can't cut it in the business world once we become mothers because we lose focus or have to take off too much with sick children." She smiled with satisfaction. "I know it won't be easy, but I can do it. I told him I'd take off if my baby needed me and still get the job done."

"I could help."

She was glad she had leaned forward to pick up a magazine and toss it out of the way. Her heart was almost dancing before she remembered he had taken care of her before until she was able to take care of herself, then he was gone. She didn't want a part-time father for her baby.

Grasping the magazine, she laid it aside. Her face expressionless, she said, "That won't be necessary." Yawning, she scooted down farther into the bed. "I'm really tired. Good-bye, Daniel."

"I'll see you this afternoon."

He informed his mother of the same thing on passing her in the living room. Madelyn was shutting him out again. He could take care of their child as well as anyone.

He'd show her when the time came. In the meantime he was going to swing that door wide open and keep it that way. Even as the thought came to him, Daniel knew it wouldn't be easy.

Madelyn wasn't going to be pushed. Self-reliant and independent, she might occasionally get down, but not for long. She was a survivor. He had never met a woman like her. She was the kind of resilient woman that could take on the world once she made up her mind.

She had made up her mind, only he wasn't sure if she still wanted him standing by her side when she did. He hated to admit it, but he wasn't brave enough to ask her the question in case she gave him an answer he didn't want to hear or accept. Opening the back door of the Mercedes, he climbed inside.

"Where to, Daniel?" the chauffeur asked, looking in the rearview mirror. Higgins had known Daniel since he was born. The elderly driver saw no reason to stand on formalities when they were alone or with just the family. Neither did Daniel.

"I don't know," Daniel said. He waited for a second, then asked, "Why are women so complicated?"

"Don't know. Guess that's why I'm not married. Couldn't find one who would put up with me," he answered.

"You want to run that by me again? Mother and some of her friends would try the patience of a saint. They talk incessantly and sometimes can't decide where they want to go or what they want to do." Daniel leaned forward in the backseat. "I've never seen you get the least perturbed with them. Even dour Mrs. Crenshaw calls you a dream."

Higgins chuckled, laugh lines deepening around his dark eyes. "She doesn't have to go home with me. I like my things to stay where I put them. Most women like a neat place. They say they're gonna leave your things alone—the next thing you know, you can't find a thing." Half turning in the seat, he faced Daniel.

"Nothing starts my day off worse than having to look for something I left out so I wouldn't have to look for it in the first place. A fussy woman can sure ruin a man's day. If I leave my Sunday shoes under the kitchen table, and my running shoes in the hallway, no one bothers them."

Higgins's comments clouded the issue rather than helped. Daniel didn't know how Madelyn felt about shoes left under the kitchen table, or if she usually woke up grumpy or smiling in the morning. The thing that had bothered him was the thought that he might never find out.

Exactly twenty-nine minutes after Daniel left, Madelyn's doorbell rang. She and Felicia exchanged looks.

Madelyn, sitting up in bed, voiced both their thoughts aloud. "Do you think it's Daniel again?"

"I wouldn't doubt it. Thirty minutes seems the limit of his endurance of being away from you," Felicia said, rising from the side of the bed. "But if it is, I'm going to put him over my knee."

"I want to see that," Madelyn said to Felicia's retreating back.

Felicia opened Madelyn's apartment door, still smiling over her shoulder at Madelyn's additional instructions from the bedroom to send Daniel home if it was him. When Felicia faced forward, time stood still.

Two beloved words whispered across her lips: "John Henry."

His impersonal gaze touched her briefly, dismissing her as insignificant, then went beyond her to scan the interior of the room behind her.

Joy turned to pain. Trembling fingers gripped the doorknob as she fought to keep from crying out her anguish.

He was still everything to her, and she was less than nothing to him.

Yet some part of her was unable to dismiss him as easily. Hatless, his thick black hair hung straight down his back, framing a face as masculine as it was ruggedly beautiful.

"I was told I would find Daniel here."

The pain in Felicia's heart deepened. He refused to even greet her or say her name, but the deep timbre of his voice made her ache, made her remember its hoarseness as he'd painted erotic pictures of pleasure in her mind and made each one come true.

His searching gaze finally came back to her. She wished it hadn't. She could have borne his anger, withstood his hatred, but the blankness in his expression sent her deeper into despair. It was as if he had wiped her from his mind.

"Someone at Daniel's house said he was here with a friend." Deep grooves furrowed in his copper-toned forehead. "Is he all right?"

"Dad!" Daniel greeted in excitement from behind his father.

John Henry turned to be enveloped in a hearty hug, which he gave back full measure to his son. Stepping away from each other, they shook hands. Both were smiling.

Daniel couldn't have been happier that instead of leaving, he had walked around the apartment complex trying to figure out how to get Madelyn to let him into hers and the baby's lives again. He wasn't any closer to a solution, but at least his delay hadn't caused him to miss his father.

They hadn't seen each other since the Christmas holidays. Seeing him at Madelyn's door with his mother had been a wonderful surprise.

"You look well," his father said, thumping him soundly on the shoulder.

Daniel grinned. "You expected different?"

The deep frown returned to John Henry's face. Lines formed by time and sun radiated from his midnight-black eyes. "Last night I had a dream you were troubled and in pain. I called, but there was no answer. I got into my truck and started driving."

Daniel's hand tightened in his father's. John Henry had always possessed an uncanny sense of when his family was in pain or troubled. As a child, Daniel had thought it was cool, then as an adult he had rebelled against his father's interference. It had almost taken a tragedy for him to accept his father's gift and be thankful.

"Madelyn was sick," he answered, the memory still painful. "Come on I'd like you to meet her."

Daniel turned and saw the empty doorway. His mother was gone. His puzzlement grew as he led his father inside the apartment and didn't see either woman. "Mother. Madelyn."

"We're in the kitchen," called Madelyn.

"Maybe some other time," his father said, his tone flat, his displeasure evident in his narrowed gaze and stiff shoulders. Guests were greeted, *if* they were welcomed.

Daniel didn't know what was going on, but he knew Madelyn wouldn't judge a man because he wore boots badly in need of a shine and new heels, jeans and blue plaid that were thin and faded from too many washings.

John Henry's muscular arm firmly in his hand, Daniel rounded the five-foot partition separating the kitchen from the living room. Felicia's rigid back was to them. Over her shoulder, he saw one of the magazines he had bought Madelyn.

Daniel frowned. He thought she'd be overjoyed to see his father. "Mother?"

Madelyn in her robe and gown literally jumped up from her seat at the small table and extended her hand. "You must be Daniel's father. My name's Madelyn Taggart."

"So you're Daniel's friend," John Henry said, his gaze probing.

Withdrawing her hand, Madelyn gave Daniel's father a tight smile. "And Felicia's."

John Henry grunted.

Madelyn lifted her chin. "You and Daniel must have a lot to talk about. I won't keep you," Madelyn said and started for the front door.

"She's the reason why you were so worried?" his father asked, his voice dismissive and puzzled.

Daniel watched Madelyn halt abruptly and spin around. His gaze went to his father and knew he was in one of his intractable moods. "Dad, please."

John Henry grunted and shrugged broad shoulders.

Daniel glanced around the room at the three silent people and had no idea how to ease the obvious strain between them. "Let's go to the house and get you settled in."

"I want my own room," John Henry proclaimed.

"Anything you say." Daniel swung back to his silent mother. "I'll ride home with Dad. Should I tell Higgins to wait for you?"

"No, we have some things to discuss," Madelyn answered for Felicia.

Daniel studied the hunched shoulders of his mother, the gritted smile of his father, the narrowed gaze of Madelyn and left. After telling Higgins that Felicia would call, Daniel climbed into the passenger seat of his father's dented, faded blue truck.

The motor purred to life like a well-fed cat, which Daniel thought wasn't far off the mark. The outside of the vehicle might look like it had been rescued from a junkyard, but under the hood was the finest money could buy.

"Your friend is not a good woman."

"You're wrong. She's the best. Better than I deserve," Daniel said, propping his elbow on the open window panel. "Dad, if you were trying to stick it to Madelyn and Mother back there for some slight, you're wrong," Daniel defended. "Neither deserves it."

Shifting the truck into gear, John Henry pulled off. "It wasn't as much fun anyway since I couldn't get a response from either of them."

"Were you trying to?"

"If you didn't care for this woman, I wouldn't have heard your pain." John Henry hit the freeway with a burst of power, the gears slipping smoothly and cleanly. "I wanted to see if she would make your heart bleed as the other tried to do."

"And Mother?"

"To see if she had learned to see with her inner instead of her outer one." Calloused hands tightened on the steering wheel. "She's only gotten worse in the last two years. She was too ashamed to look at me and take me to task as she used to do."

"Dad, you're wrong."

"I'm right—and I've finally come to a decision." He downshifted. "I'm divorcing your mother."

CHAPTER 14

As fast as Felicia wiped, more tears appeared. "I've lost him. I've really lost him."

Her chair pulled up next to Felicia's, Madelyn tried to console the seemingly inconsolable. "You don't know that."

"Yes, I do. I told myself it was over, but deep down I never believed he'd do it."

"You didn't even look at each other or speak. There's still a chance," Madelyn offered, unsure if she was right to offer hope when she wasn't so sure of the outcome.

Felicia looked up sharply, her lashes spiked with moisture. "That's just it. Even when we were ready to push each other over a cliff, we were never able to deny the deep attraction we had for each other. We may not have seen each other in two years, but for me at least, the irresistible allure is still there—stronger because I've missed and dreamed about him so much." Tears crested and flowed down her cheek.

"He made it clear he wants separate bedrooms. In the past we never slept apart under the same roof no matter how long we had been apart. John Henry would always say the bed was big enough for both of us." She sniffed delicately. "Sometimes during the night one of us would reach for the other, and blame didn't matter."

Madelyn knew what she meant. Finding Daniel in bed with her when she was ill had seemed natural, right. Curling up against his hard warmth had been instinctive, as if he completed her. She had felt safe in the haven of his strong arms. That kind of feeling could easily become addictive.

"I secretly hoped that when we saw each other again, the seductive pull we always felt for each other would overshadow the past and enable us to work things out." Felicia bit her lip. "As you saw, it didn't happen. He didn't even want to look at me."

"Maybe your wealth and background intimidate him?"

Abruptly the tears stopped. Felicia's shoulders in an elegant Chanel suit, this one in butterscotch, snapped back. She pinned Madelyn with a look. "John Henry's background to him is just as impressive as mine is to me. He's one of the proudest men I know. His master's thesis on the education of Native American children was published in several journals across the country."

"What!"

"He finished near the top of his class in his undergraduate and graduate studies at Oklahoma State University," Felicia said proudly.

"But the way he was dressed?" Madelyn questioned.

"Clothes have never meant that much to John Henry. At least he didn't try to fake you out the way he did my parents once we arrived back in Boston with Daniel." Felicia shook her head at the memory. "My father was laying it on a little thick about what we had and how grateful John Henry should be until John Henry had enough. I thought my mother would faint when he offered to buy her for his uncle.

"John Henry calmly related that his uncle's wife was toothless and unable to soften the animal hides for clothes and moccasins by chewing them. My mother, on the other hand, had an excellent pair of teeth."

Madelyn burst out laughing.

"My mother, who never drank anything stronger than sherry in her life, had to have a double brandy." Felicia dabbed another tear. "My father almost beat her to the bar when John Henry continued by saying since my father was so prosperous and the front lawn was so big, surely he wouldn't mind his relatives moving their many tepees there."

Madelyn erupted into another fit of laughter. "He doesn't like to be stereotyped. I know how he feels," she said. Perhaps she had misjudged him. On seeing Felicia's tears as she rushed into her bedroom, Madelyn had thought the worst of John Henry. Now it appeared she may have been too hasty in her judgment.

"That—and he knows it makes me crazy. The only thing he can do to make me crazier is to slurp his soup."

Fighting the smile tugging at her lips, Madelyn said, "Eventually your parents must have caught on."

"That only made it worse," Felicia said. "John Henry has a way of causing you to feel inferior with a grunt."

"I noticed," Madelyn said, leaning back in her chair. "No wonder Daniel is the way he is."

"Dominique is the same way," Felicia said with maternal pride, brushing away the last traces of tears from her cheeks.

Madelyn absorbed the information. No one in the Falcon family could be pushed, led, or prodded. Strong willed, a tad shy of arrogant, and as bold as the devil—intelligent and wily enough to give you a head start and then beat you to the finish line. Considering her family possessed some of those same attributes, Madelyn knew she was going to have her hands full raising her child.

Her hand cupped her still flat abdomen. "I'd say I have my work cut out for me."

Felicia finally smiled. "You won't be bored, that's for sure."

"Then I'm going to need all the help I can get." Madelyn's face became shadowed for a moment. "I don't know if my baby's father will be around much, but I'd like to be able to count on his paternal grandmother."

"Daniel cares about you and the baby," Felicia defended.

"He wants me, but a lasting relationship has to be built on more than lust." Madelyn groaned and closed her eyes for a few seconds. "I can't believe I'm talking to you this way."

"I assure you, I've heard the word 'lust' before," Felicia said.

Crossing her arms across her chest, Madelyn studied the other woman's flawless features. "It's because you don't look old enough to be his mother."

"It's in the genes. My mother doesn't look a day over sixty and she's pushing seventy-five. Dominique still gets carded sometimes unless she has on makeup, then watch out," Felicia told her.

Madelyn hung on to the word "parents." "Your parents are still living."

Felicia nodded. "So are John Henry's. So you see the baby will have a lot of people to spoil it."

"But not the father," Madelyn said softly. "And before you start on me about Daniel, I suggest you set your own house in order."

Sadness crossed the older woman's face. "There is nothing I can do."

"Bull," Madelyn said. "You've been handing out advice to me; take some for yourself. If you really are afraid he's going to ask for a divorce, you'll have to act fast and get him back."

Tears crested in Felicia's black eyes again. Madelyn wasn't having it. "Crying won't get him back."

"I don't know what to do," Felicia wailed.

Madelyn stood and took the other woman by the arm. "We'll think of something. In the meantime we're going to stop all this moping and crying and do something just for us."

Felicia resisted every step into the bedroom. "I'm sorry, Madelyn, but going to a day spa would only remind me of John Henry's and my breakup."

"Who said anything about a spa?" Freeing the woman, Madelyn pulled a pair of faded sweatpants from the closet. "We're going to bake bread."

Most of the men Daniel knew relaxed on the golf course or in the gym. Daniel liked riding. There was something about a powerful animal beneath him, the elements around him, and the sky over his head that always calmed him.

Until today. He was worried about his mother. Although John Henry hadn't mentioned anything more about the divorce since he tossed the news out an hour ago, he wasn't given to making idle statements.

Slowing Wind Dancer, his Arabian stallion, to a walk, Daniel glanced over at his father. John Henry was an excellent rider. In fact, he had taught Daniel to ride when he was no older than three.

Whenever his father had taken off, he had always said good-bye to Daniel and Dominique and called every day. They had felt confused more than anything. They couldn't understand why their parents lived apart so much. When they were growing up, divorce hadn't been as prevalent among their friends.

"Dad, are you sure you should ask for a divorce?"

"The dead branch on a tree serves no purpose," his father answered.

This time Daniel knew his father wasn't being obtuse, but conversing in the wisdom of his grandfather. "What if the branch only gives the appearance of being dead? Maybe it just needs a little care."

"It's a wise man who will choose defeat over dishonor and the loss of an ear," John Henry said.

Daniel pulled his horse up abruptly. A Muscogee adulterer in the old days lost an ear. "You want to marry another woman."

John Henry solemnly faced his son. "One has asked."

Daniel hung his head. "You'll break her heart."

"I would never hurt Ann. How can you think that I would hurt any woman?" his father asked indignantly.

Daniel's head shot up. "I'm not talking about your *other* woman. I'm talking about *my* mother."

Sharp black eyes centered on Daniel. "Breaking your mother's heart is impossible. I embarrass her just by entering a room."

"Whose fault is that?" Daniel gestured toward his father. "Dominique and I took you shopping when we visited you for part of the Christmas holidays, and today you show up looking like you don't have two cents to your name."

His face impassive, John Henry remained silent for a long time, then he lifted a dark brow. "Who says I do?"

"All right, Dad, have it your way."

"I fully intend to." He gathered the reins securely in his gloved hands. "Now are we going to ride or talk?" he asked, his horse always a full length ahead.

"I'm sure she's all right," John Henry repeated for the second time in as many minutes as he sat beside Daniel, who was speeding back to Madelyn's apartment later that afternoon.

"Then why does she keep telling me she can't talk every time I call?" Daniel asked.

His father propped his elbow on the door. "Probably because she's busy."

"Doing what?" Daniel asked. "She's supposed to be resting."

John Henry sent his son a sharp glare. "You think there's another man over there?"

"If there is, there's nothing going on," Daniel said without a doubt in his mind. Madelyn was honest and up-front. He might learn slowly, but when he did, he didn't forget.

"So the baby she's carrying is yours," came the calm statement.

Daniel's gaze cut to his father. "How—"

"Watch the road."

Swerving to miss a Honda, Daniel gave his attention back to driving. Luckily they were near his freeway exit. "How did you know?"

"Prenatal vitamins on the kitchen table," John Henry said succinctly.

Daniel shook his head. He should have remembered very little got by his father—including the little dents and door dings he used to get on his father's car. No matter how far away Daniel parked, some nut would always park beside him and always leave his calling card on the side of the car.

"Why didn't you say something sooner?" he questioned, turning into Madelyn's complex.

"I wasn't sure how much you were involved."

"The baby is mine," Daniel admitted, the realization still having the power to make him feel scared and proud at the same time. Parking, Daniel cut the motor and frowned on seeing his father settling back against the leather seat.

"Dad, come inside."

"Neither one of them probably wants to see me," his father answered. "I came only because I knew you were worried."

"Then come all the way," Daniel said softly. "Madelyn means a lot to me, and I'd like for both of you to get to know each other better."

John Henry hesitated only a moment, then opened his door. "When is the wedding?"

Halfway out the door, Daniel paused. "We haven't talked about it."

"Don't wait as long as I did. Felicia's parents never forgave me for her not having a big society wedding," his father said, meeting Daniel at the front of the truck. Silently they walked the rest of the distance together.

Daniel had a great deal more to worry about than Madelyn not having a big wedding. When her family found out she was pregnant, all hell was going to break loose. Once he could stand from the beating her brothers were going to give him, he'd be in front of some minister so fast, his loose teeth would probably rattle.

Frowning he rang the doorbell. Somehow they'd have to understand he cared for her and the baby, but marriage wasn't in his plans. He—

His thoughts stumbled to a halt as his mother answered the door. The always perfectly groomed Felicia had flour on her face, more flour and some pasty-looking substance on the oversized black T-shirt with the Houston Sonics emblazoned on the front, flour-coated sweatpants—and ugly, shocking green knitted booties on her feet.

His mother's eyes widened. Her gaze jerked to John Henry, and Daniel knew if he didn't do something, the door would slam in their faces. "Hi, Mother. Something smells good."

Putting his arm around her shoulders, he led her back inside, giving her a little squeeze to bolster her courage. "I-I'll go get changed."

"Not until you ice these cinnamon rolls," called Madelyn.

His arm still around his mother, Daniel walked to the kitchen. Madelyn, in a T-shirt with the Dallas Stars hockey team logo on front, jeans and another pair of ugly booties, had apparently also been cooking.

But she was considerably cleaner. Dishes were stacked in both sides of the sink, and the counter was lined with various types of tempting-smelling baked bread.

"I missed lunch. Mind if I have a croissant?" Daniel asked, already reaching for one.

"Help yourself," Madelyn said dryly, bagging a loaf of foil-wrapped bread.

"This is good." Midchew, he frowned, then swallowed. "I hope you did-n't overdo it."

Madelyn rolled her eyes as if she had expected the comment. "Felicia did most of the work."

"I'm sure he can tell," his mother mumbled, her head bowed.

"Would you like a croissant, Mr. Falcon?" Madelyn asked, feeling sorry for Felicia. She had hoped he'd stay away until Felicia had her courage up.

"Call me John Henry. If you don't mind, I think I'd rather have one of the cinnamon rolls once Felicia finishes icing them." Pulling out a chair, John Henry took a seat.

Madelyn could tell Felicia wanted to run for it and quickly handed her the bowl of cream cheese icing. "Here you go. I'll fix some coffee."

Daniel was already reaching for the pot. "I'll do it. You sit down."

She sat. "You're as bossy as Kane."

"Thank you," he said. Turning he missed the face Madelyn made at his back.

His father didn't. She tensed until he smiled. "I see you are feeling better."

"Much," she said, hoping Felicia wasn't having too much trouble with the icing. Madelyn could certainly see how she had burnt John Henry's food—she was lost in the kitchen.

A glass of milk plopped in front of her. She shot a glance at Daniel, but he was already pulling mugs from the cabinet. She could only hope his father didn't catch on. John Henry and she were still unsure and circling each other.

"I'll get you a plate for your roll," Madelyn said.

A light touch of John Henry's calloused hand stopped her from rising. "Please, let her do it," he said softly. Louder he asked Daniel to take a seat as well.

John Henry's gaze was locked on Felicia so fiercely that Madelyn didn't see why there wasn't a hole in the back of the other woman's T-shirt. The antagonism and animosity she expected him to display wasn't there. Instead there was a watchfulness that made Madelyn uneasy. She glanced at Daniel, but he was also watching his mother.

More than the icing of cinnamon rolls was at stake here. Madelyn tried to think of one thing that would get Felicia moving to face her husband. To her delight, Felicia took care of the situation herself.

"How many do you want, John Henry?" Felicia asked, her voice slightly shaky, her back still to him.

"Two. I missed lunch, too," he said.

After placing a platter of the iced pastries on the table, she handed him a dessert plate. He took the stoneware, and they stared at each other a long time before he said, "If these aren't burnt on the bottom, you didn't help cook them."

Felicia burst into tears and ran from the kitchen. Madelyn jumped up to go after her.

"Please, let me." John Henry turned to his son. "It seems you may have been right. Excuse me."

Madelyn watched him leave, sadness in her eyes. "I guess you were right, Daniel. Sometimes love isn't enough."

Felicia heard Madelyn's bedroom door open and close, but didn't look up. She was too busy fighting another losing battle with tears. "I'm sorry, Madelyn. I just couldn't stand there and listen to him laugh at me."

"I've never laughed at you."

Everything within her stilled at the sound of John Henry's deep, rich voice. For him to see her so disheveled, and now in tears, completed her humiliation. She would have run into the bathroom and locked the door if getting up wouldn't have offered him another mortifying look at her.

Worn cowboy boots and faded jeans came into her line of downcast vision. "Why are you on the floor?"

The question seemed easier to answer than to think about her embarrassment. "I didn't want to mess up the bed or the chair."

"Felicia, always worrying about what is proper, about being clean and neat."

Instinctively she reacted to the slight censor in his deep voice. "All of us can't thumb our nose at convention the way you do."

"There's a difference between thumbing your nose and living by your standards and not someone else's."

She opened her mouth for a comeback, but out of the corner of her eye she saw him easing down on the floor beside her. Her thoughts scattered.

Pressing his broad back against the foot of the bed, John Henry stretched his long, muscular legs in front of him. Although they weren't touching, he was close enough for her to catch a faint hint of his Aramis cologne. The scent on him always made her want to lick her lips, then lick him . . . all over.

She chastised herself, but it did little good. John Henry had always fascinated her.

His muscular strength and size was never more in evidence. She'd always liked the way their bodies complemented each other: her slimness to his brawn. It was only later in their marriage that it intimidated her. Madelyn had it backwards—John Henry intimidated *her*. He was a man who didn't bend to her will.

Self-consciously, she wiped her cheek and felt the stickiness of the icing. Her desperation to flee increased. She moistened dry lips. "If you'll leave, I'd liked to get dressed."

John Henry crossed his booted feet at the ankles and braced his large hand on the carpet a tiny inch away from her hip. "You and Madelyn still have the dishes to do, unless you plan to let her do them by herself."

"Of course not," Felicia snapped, hurt that he thought she was that inconsiderate.

"Then why change?" He nodded toward the Chanel suit hanging on the back of the closet door. "I don't think that was made to wash dishes in."

Felicia didn't know how to respond. She couldn't very well explain to him that she felt more in control in her own clothes. She never wanted him to see her at less than her best.

"Do you remember what a hard time I had getting you to wade in the creek at the back of the house?" Out of the corner of her eye she saw his sensual mouth curve upward. "You never liked being dirty or mussed. The only time you didn't care what you looked like was when we were making love."

Heat splintered through Felicia like a stoked furnace. Her hand clenched in her lap. Vivid images of them entwined in bed flashed into her mind. The sudden need, the hunger was almost unbearable. Unconsciously she pressed her legs closer together.

"I'm hungry. You want to go get a hamburger or something?"

She jerked her head around. "You're asking me to go to dinner with you?"

"I don't see anyone else, and I don't mean dinner where I have to dress up," he told her.

Felicia couldn't take it all in. He was looking at her, talking to her, asking her to dinner. "Yes, I'd love to." She was up in a flash, rushing across the room toward her suit.

"If we go, you wear what you have on."

She whirled just before her grasping fingers touched the linen. "What? You can't mean for me to go out looking like this?"

"I've seen how long it takes you to dress, and I'm hungry now." Gracefully he came to his feet, his black hair swinging around his wide shoulders. "Are you coming or not?"

Felicia heard more than the words spoken. She heard, "I won't ask again."

"I'll get my purse."

"You won't need it."

She looked at him, and his gaze was steady and hard. She couldn't tell if he wanted to see her humiliated further, or was simply being impatient. She knew only that she had to take this last chance, no matter the consequences.

Walking toward him in her flour-and-dough-stained T-shirt and faded sweatpants, her face almost as bad, took every bit of Felicia's courage. Moistening her lips, she tasted icing at the corner. The Joy perfume she had splashed on that morning was probably no match for the aroma of freshly baked bread. Swallowing, she kept going.

She didn't need a mirror to know what five hours in the kitchen had done to her makeup, her hair. In fact, she preferred not to see one.

"Can I borrow the truck, Daniel?" John Henry asked the instant they entered the kitchen. "Your mother and I are going to get something to eat."

The twist of irony of his father asking for the car keys while his date, Daniel's mother, stood by and stared at her booted feet, lifted Daniel's spirits considerably. He wished he could enjoy it.

Madelyn had sipped her milk and played with the crust of a croissant ever since she had tossed out her opinion on love not being enough. For once, Daniel didn't want her agreeing with him.

Daniel studied the uneasiness of his mother, the self-assurance of his father. He couldn't begin to guess how his father had managed to get his mother to go out in public the way she looked. No matter what his mother did, she did it with style.

And now she was going out looking as if she had been attacked by a bread machine and wearing the ugliest booties he had ever seen. His father didn't miss much, and it was a sure bet he knew what his mother had on her feet.

He flipped the keys. "No dents, no dings, no tickets. Be back at a reasonable hour."

His father merely lifted a heavy brow. "I'll listen to you as much as you listened to me."

Daniel looked uneasy. "Wasn't my fault other people can't drive."

"So you always said. Help Madelyn with the dishes." He turned to Felicia. "Let's go."

Felicia didn't say a word, just started for the door as if she had been given her last rites and she was walking the last mile.

CHAPTER 15

"**A**re you just going to sit there and eat another cinnamon roll?" Madelyn asked as soon as the door closed.

Daniel frowned, not liking the glint in her eyes. "What is it you want me to do?" he asked cautiously.

Chocolate-brown eyes widened in disbelief. Planting both hands on the table, she stood. "Go after them of course. Felicia was terrified."

Daniel blinked. "What?"

Rounding the table, she tried to drag him up by the arm. "I try to stay out of family business, but Felicia is my friend. Being a man, maybe you didn't notice, but she didn't look too happy to be going with your father."

Daniel allowed himself to be pulled to his feet because he didn't want her to hurt herself. "You really think Mother didn't want to go?" he asked, trying hard to keep the smile off his face.

"Of course she didn't," Madelyn told him. "Now go get her before they leave."

Settling both hands on her shoulders, he turned her to him. The smile he had been trying to hold worked itself loose. "Thank you for caring about my mother, but in the short time you've known her, has she ever done anything she didn't want to do?"

"No, but she wanted another chance."

"Exactly," Daniel said. "If we try to stop her from leaving with Dad, she's not going to be happy with either of us."

Madelyn glanced toward the door. "She looked so unhappy, Daniel."

Her continued concern for his mother touched him. "Probably because she's not looking her best. Have you ever seen her less than perfect?"

Madelyn's shoulders relaxed. "Come to think of it, no. I had to push her hands into the bread dough. But whenever I'd turn away, she'd wipe them on paper towels. She probably went through half a roll."

"Don't worry, Mother is fine."

Madelyn shifted restlessly under his hands. It felt good to have his hands on her again. "Do you think they can settle their differences?"

"I hope so," Daniel said, the pad of his thumb absently stroking her shoulder. "He said some other woman asked him to marry her."

"Oh, no." Madelyn cried. "Poor Felicia."

"Don't count Mother out. Some woman may have asked to marry him, but Dad didn't say he had said yes."

Madelyn's eyes brightened. "Then there's a chance?"

"There's always a chance," he said looking down into her eyes.

Swallowing, she stepped back. "I guess so."

He wasn't buoyed by her mild agreement, but it was better than a resounding no. "You want to go out to get something to eat or cook in?"

Folding her arms, Madelyn lifted a delicate brow. "I wasn't aware of inviting you to dinner."

She looked so adorable and cute with a smattering of flour across her forehead, he wanted to take her into his arms and cuddle her. Too soon. "Dad has my truck."

"Felicia said you have a five-car garage, and all the bays are full. You had to move one out to make room for her Mercedes."

"True, but they're there, and I'm here and hungry." He smiled. Dimples winked. "If you'll recall, Mother gave Higgins the rest of the day off."

She eyed him for a long time. Was it possible that last night at the hospital heralded a new beginning for them? "If you stay, you're helping do the dishes and we eat out."

"You've got yourself a deal."

Felicia couldn't relax. She tried taking deep breaths, creating a soothing picture in her mind, closing her eyes. Nothing worked. She finally had John Henry to herself, and she looked like an apprentice baker on her first day.

"You're going to stretch Madelyn's T-shirt out of shape if you keep pulling on it," John Henry said mildly.

Felicia released the ball of black material and glanced out the window of the truck. This so-called date was turning into a disaster.

"What do you want to eat?" he asked, pulling up behind another vehicle in the drive-thru window of a fast-food restaurant.

"Nothing for me," she said, knowing the food would stick in her throat.

"Did you eat while you were baking?" he asked, shifting the gears and pulling up.

She shook her head. "I wasn't hungry then, either."

"Why? You're worried about Madelyn and the baby?"

"You know?" she questioned. "Daniel told you?"

"May I have your order, please?" asked the disembodied voice.

"A hamburger with mustard, no onions, a grilled chicken sandwich, two fries, and two chocolate shakes."

"Thank you. Please drive to the first window."

"John Henry," Felicia prodded. "How did you find out?"

Answering her question, he shifted to pull his wallet from his pocket and pay the cashier. Felicia's heart sank.

The only reason she had noticed the vitamins was because she had watched Madelyn take one that morning. There probably wasn't a speck of flour or batter or a myriad of other things on her that he hadn't seen.

"Hold these."

Taking the shakes, she sat quietly while John Henry pulled into a space at the far end of the parking lot.

"I hope she didn't forget the ketchup."

"You don't like ketchup on your fries," she said absently.

"You do. Here it is," he said, pulling the package from the sack. "Pop some straws into our shakes."

Felicia was peeling the paper from the straw before it hit her. "You don't like chocolate shakes, you like strawberry."

Coal-black eyes stared into hers. "A man can change his mind."

Felicia's breath fluttered out over her lips.

"Eat your chicken sandwich," John Henry said, unwrapping his hamburger. "Then maybe we can go someplace and talk."

Her eyes brightened with hope that displaced her growing fear and helplessness. She unwrapped her sandwich. "I'd like that, John Henry. I'd like that a lot."

John Henry decided Daniel's house was the best place to have their conversation. He wanted a place where both of them could seek some privacy if things went wrong. A lot could go wrong. Maybe he was setting himself up for another disappointment. Maybe Daniel was wrong.

Yet seeing Felicia this afternoon, all mussed and in disarray, had been so reminiscent of the day he had come home from work to their small house to see her grinning and so proud of a batch of misshapen biscuits she had baked for him. In that moment he knew she no longer regretted their hasty marriage, regretted being separated from her parents, regretted not having the luxuries he couldn't afford.

Knowing her family would use any means necessary to get her back, he had quit his job with the Bureau of Indian Affairs in Flagstaff and brought his bride to the tiny community in Oklahoma where he had grown up. The only job available was as a ranch hand. He had gladly taken it to keep Felicia with him.

The first weeks were nothing short of pure hell. Nothing he did pleased her except when they made love. He had left her asleep that morning after a particularly satisfying night of lovemaking and had expected to come home again to a silent, sullen wife.

Instead she had met him at the door with a kiss, a smile, and the worst-looking biscuits he had ever seen.

The biscuits were as hard as rocks and as tasteless because she had left out the baking powder and the salt. To him, it hadn't mattered.

He couldn't have been more pleased and proud. He had drowned them in syrup and eaten every one, out of love, out of not wanting her to eat one herself and get sick because she was four and a half months pregnant with Daniel.

Remembering that day, John Henry felt the familiar tug of happiness in his heart, the unwanted ache of loving a woman he had never been sure of.

They walked side by side without touching until they reached the edge of the immense backyard. Felicia headed for the white wrought-iron bench under a hundred-foot oak.

"Let's sit over there."

Warily Felicia eyed the base of the towering oak tree with several of its foot-thick roots protruding aboveground. Without glancing his way, she walked over and sank down on the sparse grass, drawing her slim legs under her. "All right, John Henry, you've pushed and ordered and subtly threatened—so what now?"

He hadn't expected her to be agreeable for long. Even at the spa two years ago, when rage had consumed him, she had stood up to him.

"Were you having an affair with Randolph Sims?" he asked. It wasn't what he had intended, but he needed to know nonetheless.

"No," she answered softly. "But I wanted you to think I was on the brink."

"Why?"

Hands pressed together in her lap, she looked out across the well-tended lawn. "I-I thought you didn't care. I wanted to make you jealous."

John Henry remembered going to the spa to surprise her, and he was the one who had been surprised. "Try again. You didn't know I was coming."

"Yes, I did," she answered quietly. "Dominique had called me that morning."

"So you invited Sims to your suite," he said tightly.

Her head swung around. "I thought he was you when I answered the door."

"And I suppose you gave him no provocation to think his visit might be welcomed," he bit out.

She flinched from the anger in his harsh face, but she didn't look away. "I'm not proud of the way I behaved, but I gave him no indication to expect anything else."

Hands on hips, his long black hair swirling wildly around him in the wind, John Henry glared down at her. "No indication! Damnit, Felicia, you're not that naive. Randolph had wanted you as long as I can remember."

"I admit I was wrong. I'm sorry."

He gave a short bark of hollow laughter. "You flirt with a known womanizer, a man who likes to brag about his conquests, and you think saying 'I'm sorry' is supposed to rectify the situation?"

"I don't know what else to say." Her gaze searched his face. "At least it never got out."

"Because I waited until Sims came out of your room and promised him if he said one word about you he'd regret it," John Henry said, his face hard and unrelenting.

"Then you know he didn't stay," she said joyfully.

"Not that night, but what about the other nights before I arrived? You asked me to leave while he stayed. Do you know how that made me feel, to see slime like Sims smirking?" he questioned harshly.

She came to her feet, her face and eyes imploring. "Nothing happened that night or ever. You've got to believe me. You might forgive me a lot of things, but adultery isn't one of them."

"I could have killed you both," he said, his fists clenched.

"You could never physically hurt me, but I realized if you harmed Randolph, you'd be the one to pay. That's why I told you I didn't love you. You were too proud to want a woman who didn't want you." Tears sparkled in her eyes and rolled down her cheeks. "I've paid for my foolishness every day and night since then."

"I've paid, too," he said.

John Henry had lived with her rejection day and night for two years. It was a hurt, a pain that wouldn't go away, a pain that knew no source of comfort. How could there be when his beautiful wife sent him away while she prepared to take another man to her bed? "I hated you. I hated you as much as I once loved you."

"C-Can't we start over?" she asked.

"And what will you do the next time I don't heel when you snap your fingers?"

Anger blazed in her eyes to match his. "How dare you say something like that to me? You're the one who kept popping in and out of mine and the children's lives. Heel, my foot.

"You don't know the meaning of the words 'submission' or 'compromise.' You're as arrogant and as proud as ever. Did you ever stop to think how I felt knowing that sooner or later you'd get restless and go back to Oklahoma to that farm you bought a couple of years after we were married? Or how I felt hearing my friends whisper behind my back about my glaring lack of ability to keep my husband satisfied and at home?" she raged.

"You and the children could have come, but you were too busy being Miss Society and living the pampered lifestyle your parents' money allowed you," he told her.

"I was not going to raise my children in a two-room cabin with the nearest school twelve miles away with only one teacher for each grade," she flared. "I wanted better for them."

John Henry's face contorted, rage mixed with despair. "So the truth is finally out. I was good enough to screw, but not good enough to take care of my kids."

Horror washed across Felicia's face. "No. I didn't mean it that way. I wanted them to have every advantage to succeed in life, and that meant the right schools, the right social standings."

"Things I couldn't give them," John Henry said. He stepped back and lifted his arms from his sides. "This is who I am, Felicia. A simple man, a Muscogee Indian. Not much to people like you, but I'm proud of who I am. I'll never be happy being anything else. I'll be damned if I'll try anymore." His hands lowered. "As quick as possible, I want a divorce. Get one or I will."

"John Henry," Felicia cried, tears streaming down her cheek, her hands reaching for him.

He stepped back. "I don't ever want to feel your touch again, to know that I let you trample my pride underfoot. Get that divorce—and when it's final, I'm marrying a woman who wants me the way I am."

With a soundless cry, Felicia crumpled. Sobs racked her body.

John Henry looked down on the woman he'd loved since the first moment his eyes touched her, the woman who had given him more joy than he ever expected, more sorrow than he thought at times he could bear. Through it all he had stayed because of that love, stayed because of the children, then after they were grown, he kept hoping he would be enough for her. He needed a woman who needed him. Felicia never would.

"You have two months." Turning, he walked back to the house.

Madelyn was impressed with Daniel's dinner arrangements that night, but she didn't intend for him to know. Opening her front door, she didn't act the least surprised to see a tuxedoed waiter with several silver domes on a serving cart and a second waiter behind him with a collapsible table. Her expression never changed.

In less than five minutes, the table was set with white linen, sparkling water was chilling in an ice bucket, and Daniel was holding her chair for her. By her plate was a pink orchid.

She remained cool through her crab claws sauteed in lemon sauce—thawed a little when served her garden salad loaded with artichokes, mushrooms, scallions, and cucumbers. He made points, however, when he asked what she was digging in her salad for, and she said, "more cucumbers," and he gave her his.

She kept up the pretense until the first bite of the most mouth-watering lobster she had ever closed her lips over. She moaned. Ignoring Daniel's knowing smile, she kept eating. Dessert was something rich and decadent and chocolate. Stuffed, she managed only a couple of spoonfuls. Daniel had no such trouble. He finished off his and hers.

The best part of the dinner was she didn't have to clean up afterward or groan all the way to the car to drive home. Sitting on the couch, one hand holding the orchid, she watched Daniel let the waiters out. She didn't think she'd move until morning.

"Can I get you anything?" he asked.

Madelyn looked the long way up to his bronzed, smiling face. He'd been smiling all evening. The smile looked good on him. "Not unless you want me to pop."

He squatted down in front of her and took her free hand. "You're tired."

"A little," she confessed, then yawned.

He grinned. Dimples winked. He stood and pulled her to her feet. "Come on, and lock the door so you can get some rest."

"How are you going to get home?"

"I'll call Higgins. Dad certainly seems to have forgotten me," he said, his tone light.

Madelyn came to a decision. "Take my car. There's no reason to disturb Higgins."

"You're sure?"

"I'm sure." Going into the bedroom, she returned shortly with her keys. "No dents. No dings."

"I'll be extra careful." Leaning over, he kissed her on the cheek. "Good night."

Following him to the door, she didn't know why she suddenly felt sad. "Drive carefully."

"I will." He reached for the door, then turned back, drawing her into his arms. She went willingly. There was no need to urge her lips apart, to coax her.

Finally he lifted his head, his breathing labored. "I'd better go."

He was out the door before she remembered to say, "Please call and let me know if Felicia is all right."

"I will. Now go back inside and lock up."

"Good night," she whispered, then stepped back, closing and locking the door. If only it was as easy to close her heart against hoping for something that might never be. She prayed that Felicia's heart was safe.

Madelyn's had been lost the first time Daniel kissed her.

Felicia cried until there were no tears left. The whimpering sobs took longer to subside. She'd never known a despair so deep, so yawning with no hope. Always in life she had hope and the courage to take what she wanted.

Hope and courage were gone. She no longer cared.

"Felicia."

Something in her sparked before she realized the voice was Higgins' and not John Henry's. She curled tighter.

A frail hand patted her on the shoulder. "Now, now."

"Oh, Higgins. I was such a fool."

"Your parents indulged you too much. Told them to let you throw a tantrum or two. They acted like I had asked them to lock you in a closet."

Sniffing, she sat up and leaned against him. "Maybe they should have."

"I've been thinking we'd take the car and drive down the coast to Galveston, maybe stay at this little bed and breakfast I read about for a few days," he suggested. "Just until you feel better."

"I don't think I'll ever feel better."

"Yes you will." Awkwardly he helped her to her feet. His frail arms around her shoulders, they started for the house.

Stoic, John Henry watched them approach the back of the house. He had stood and watched Felicia until he couldn't stand it anymore. He had called Higgins and asked him to go to her.

The chauffeur knew all the family secrets, and he could be trusted. He also loved Felicia like the daughter he'd never had. She needed someone who loved her. John Henry's love had never been enough.

Opening the glass door, John Henry took the path leading to the stables. He needed a long, hard ride. Maybe if he rode hard enough, fast enough, he'd stop hearing Felicia's sobs, stop tearing his heart out over a woman he couldn't stop loving.

Daniel sensed something was wrong the instant he entered the house. It wasn't just the quietness. It was something else he couldn't put a name to.

Taking the stairs two at a time, he went to his mother's room. The door was open. Seeing her packing, he knew. He crossed to her and took her in his arms.

"Mother."

He caught a brief glimpse of her defeated expression before she grabbed fistfuls of his shirt and pressed her face against his chest. "Your father asked for a divorce."

His arms tightened. He had hoped they could work things out. "I'm sorry. Maybe—"

"No. It's over. Please don't say anything else, or I'll start crying again."

Feeling utterly helpless, he continued holding her. "Is it all right to say I love you?"

He felt her nod against his shirt. "Higgins is taking me to a bed and breakfast in Galveston. I-I'd like to be gone before your father gets back."

Strong hands gently pushed her away. A frown knitted Daniel's brow. "Where is he? His truck is out front and so is mine."

"I don't know. Higgins said he saw John Henry tear out of the stables on one of your horses, but that was at sundown." Fear crossed her delicate face. "Daniel, you don't think he's hurt, do you?"

"Dad's the best rider I know. Don't worry," Daniel advised, but he was already turning away. His father knew better than to ride at night. Yet what if something had happened before nightfall? If the unthinkable had occurred, none of the horses had been stabled long enough to come home on their own.

Fighting a rising fear, Daniel ran into the stable and hit the light switch, already moving swiftly down the aisle, counting horses. Seeing one missing, his heart stopped—Jabel, the fiery Arabian stallion he had purchased last week.

"Daniel?"

He swung around to see his mother, her arms wrapped around her, her eyes begging him to say the word to put her mind at ease. He couldn't. "One of the horses is missing."

"No, no."

"Mother—Dad!"

Felicia whirled. With a shout of pure joy, she launched herself at John Henry, who was walking and leading Jabal by the reins to the stable; her frantic arms circled her husband's neck. Jabal shied from all the noise. Felicia didn't seem to notice John Henry had to release the horse in order to keep them upright, keep them from falling beneath the stallion's deadly hooves.

Daniel grabbed the animals dragging reins.

Felicia kept right on planting kisses on John Henry's dirt-smeared face and crying. It took her a minute to notice he wasn't kissing her back. Her body tensed.

Slowly her arms slid down from around his neck. She took one, then another step backward. Seeing his expressionless face, she ran out of the stable.

Fists clenched, John Henry remained unmoved.

"We thought you'd been thrown," Daniel said matter-of-factly. The look on his father's face said they should have known better. "You're dirty enough."

"I stayed out longer than I expected. Since it was dark, I walked the horse, tripped and fell."

Now Daniel was the one wearing a look of disbelief. "You see like a cat in the dark."

"I had other things on my mind," John Henry explained tightly.

Daniel had a good idea what those things were. "The main thing is that you're unhurt. We jumped to conclusions since Higgins had seen you ride out earlier. Mother stopped packing and followed me out here."

Surprise widened his father's eyes. "Packing?"

"What did you expect after asking for a divorce?" Daniel said, not bothering to keep the anger out of his voice. "Now you can marry what's-her-name."

"If only I could." Turning, John Henry left the stable.

CHAPTER 16

Felicia lay prone across the antique linen hand-embroidered bed-spread. She hadn't thought she had any more tears. She had been wrong.

A hand lightly touched her head. She flinched. "Please, go away."

"If only I could."

Recognizing John Henry's voice caused the tears to flow faster. "Please."

The pressure of his calloused hand increased as he continued stroking her hair. "Do you know you're dirtying up Daniel's fancy bedspread?"

"That's what they have dry cleaners for," she sobbed, hating the almost aching need to press her head into his strong hand.

"Your suit will have to go to the cleaners, too. I guess you didn't think about that when you were hugging me."

"I thought you had been hurt. Who cares about a stupid suit."

"You were really scared, weren't you?"

Felicia stopped long enough to stare up at him in disbelief. "How can you ask such a question?"

"Because you always acted like I was an embarrassment to you."

She came up like a spring, her face horrified. "I never!" she began, only to stop, her eyes shutting as she recalled the conversation with Daniel at the hospital. Slowly her eyes opened. John Henry watched her intently.

The time for the whole truth had finally arrived. John Henry couldn't hate her any more than he already did. At least she might stop hating herself for what she had tried to do to him.

"I was never ashamed of you. But you were the only man I was never sure of." She swallowed. "At first I tried to make you over because I wanted you to forget about going back to Oklahoma. I was terrified you'd get tired of me and leave, then I did it to protect you against snide, ignorant remarks."

A muscle leaped in his jaw. "Come on, Felicia. You know I never gave a rat's behind about what your family or friends thought about me."

"I know that's what you said. Sometimes you went out of your way to play the uneducated Indian, but I'd see you sometimes looking at a group of men in a conversation you were excluded from, and I'd ache for you."

He shook his head. "You had it all wrong. Most of the time I was thinking how bored I was or what a waste of time it was to be there." His expression grew hard. "Your friends might have been wealthy, but a lot of them were bankrupt in the real things that matter in life."

"Including me," she said softly.

"I tried to make myself think so, but I did a lot of thinking this afternoon and realized something." He glanced around the lavishly decorated room. "Daniel might have obtained this without the private schools and the privileged life, but he couldn't have grown up to be the man I'm proud to call my son without you. I'm just as proud of Dominique."

His gaze returned to Felicia. "Whenever I showed up, there were never any recriminations from either of them. They were always happy and eager to be with me, no matter how I was dressed or what I drove. They still are. They had to learn that from someone. We might not have gotten along at times, but you never tried to teach my children to hate me."

Felicia sniffed. "I hated the farm in Oklahoma. You seemed to need it more than me and the children."

John Henry's hand tenderly stroked her cheek. "I never acclimated to Boston. The weather, the crowds, the food. I felt utterly useless working a token job for your father, living in his house. A Muscogee is taught to take care of his wife, his children. I felt less than a man."

"Forgive me. I never knew."

"Looks like we both have a lot to forgive," he said, picking her up. Her eyes widened, but her arms closed around his neck. "I take it that door leads to the bathroom."

"Y-Yes."

"Good. Hope your bathtub is as big as mine."

"John Henry, what are you doing?"

"Hell if I know. I only know I have to make love to you or go stark raving mad." He stopped and looked down at her. "Any objections?"

She bit her lip. "I don't want to lose you again."

"Our track record hasn't been the best."

Felicia's hold tightened. "I'm willing to try if you are. I'll do whatever it takes."

Shoving the door open to the bathroom, John Henry set her on her feet and began unbuttoning the buttons on her suit. "Whatever covers a lot of territory."

Felicia's fingers went to his shirt. Her hands trembling, her voice unsteady, "I hope it does, because it's been two long years."

His hands stilled at the implication of what she had just said sinking into him like tender claws. "I—"

"Sheee." Her lips gently grazed his. "You are the heart of my heart. I'll keep on saying the words until you hear it in your heart as well."

"Felicia, I can't lose again."

"You don't have to." Stepping back, she undressed for him, her eyes glowing with a desire that was matched in his.

He pulled her to him, his mouth and hands devouring her. "I've waited so long."

"So have I." Her hands began unbuttoning his shirt, anxious to feel the heat and muscled warmth of his body. "Don't make either of us wait any longer."

He didn't. Quickly he finished undressing and drew her down on their scattered clothes on the floor, joining them in one powerful thrust. Her body accepted him as it always had, with hungry eagerness.

Mingled sighs of pleasure escaped from their lips. Sensations, powerful and exquisite, ran through them. They stared into each other's eyes, not moving, prolonging the exquisite moment each had waited for, hoped for, prayed for.

Then his hips began to move, slowly at first, then with quick, powerful movements. Heat built like a raging inferno, sweeping them both down its path. Completion came too soon, shaking them both with its violence. But there was also a rightness.

Trembling fingers swept John Henry's heavy mane of black hair away from his perspiration-dampened face. "Welcome home."

"In my heart. I never left."

Tears formed in Felicia's eyes. Tenderly John Henry kissed every one away, then moved to other, softer parts of her body. It was a long satisfying time before they got into the tub, longer still until they went to sleep locked in each other's arms.

In the other wing of the house, Daniel called Madelyn from his bedroom to tell her his parents were trying to work things out. He was glad she didn't ask for any details. His mother and father had been behind closed doors together in the past, but until tonight he had never actually considered what they might be doing. He didn't want to tonight, either.

Reluctantly he ended the conversation less than a minute later. Madelyn sounded sleepy. Lying down, his hands behind his head, he could almost see her curled up in her bed, her hands pillowing her cheek.

With a fierce yearning he wished he was there with her, to hold her, to love her. Soon, he promised himself. Very soon.

"Not yet, Mrs. Falcon, wait until the batter bubbles and the ends turn up just slightly," instructed Mrs. Hargrove, Daniel's cook.

With all the concentration of a mother watching her child take its first steps, Felicia's eyes never left the four circles of pancake batter.

"Bacon needs turning. You want me to do it?" asked Mrs. Hargrove.

"No, please, I want to do this by myself." Giving one last look at the pancakes, Felicia turned the bacon, her attention zeroing back in on the grill. Taking a deep breath, she flipped first one, then the others over. They weren't the perfect round shapes she would have liked, but they held together.

"I did it—I did it."

"You certainly did, Mrs. Falcon. We'll have you cooking in no time."

"Thank you, I couldn't have done it without your help." Smelling the bacon, Felicia took it out of the skillet and placed the strips on paper towels to drain, then removed the pancakes, adding them to her stack. Picking up a bowl, she whisked the contents, eyed the butter heating in the skillet.

"It's ready," instructed the cook.

The egg batter began to sizzle the instant it hit. Using the spatula handed to her by the other woman, Felicia soft-scrambled the eggs.

"Mother?"

"Good morning, Daniel," Felicia called, her attention on her cooking.

"It's barely eight," he said. Since she went to sleep late, she usually slept until around ten unless she had an appointment.

"I know." Felicia put the food in the divided chafing dish, covered it with the sterling silver dome lid, then placed the dish on the tray beside a plate and a carafe of coffee. "I wanted to surprise your father with breakfast."

Daniel stared at his mother. She was glowing. She was also in a flowing aqua robe. In his memory she had never come downstairs until she was dressed. "You two are going to work things out?"

"I'm going to do whatever it takes to make him happy," she said, then blushed. "I better take this upstairs before your father wakes up."

"He's still asleep?" Daniel questioned. His father never slept past five.

Felicia blushed again, her hands tightening on the sides of the wooden tray. Her gaze dropped to the middle of his chest.

"Must be the long drive," Daniel said helpfully, trying not to think of the implication of the robe or the blush. "You better get going."

Nodding, Felicia turned away, walking slowly. Still slightly bemused, Daniel followed into the dining room as she headed for the sweeping staircase. His mouth opened to ask her if she wanted him to help, but the words were never spoken.

His mother stopped, her gaze lifting. At the top of the stairs stood his father in jeans and an open shirt. For an interminable amount of time, they simply stared at each other, then his father quickly moved down the stairs. Without a word being spoken between them that Daniel could hear, his father swept up his mother in his arms, tray and all, and started back up the stairs.

Seeing them disappear, Daniel's thoughts returned to Madelyn. He wanted to be with her in the morning, to hold her, to eat breakfast in bed with her.

"Here's your coffee, Mr. Falcon. Breakfast will be ready in a few minutes," said the housekeeper, handing him a cup. She looked toward the empty staircase. "I've never seen a woman more happy to be cooking breakfast for her husband."

"Did Mother make this coffee?" he asked mildly, taking a sip. "It's not half bad."

"I bet your father thinks it's the best coffee he's ever tasted," Mrs. Hargrove noted before going back into the kitchen.

Daniel followed, his brow furrowed. He didn't particularly care for sweets, but he had downed a half dozen cinnamon rolls yesterday because Madelyn had helped make them.

He placed the cup on the counter. "Nothing for me, Mrs. Hargrove. I have an early appointment."

"You're sure?" she questioned. "The whole-grain muffins should be ready to take out of the oven shortly."

"No, thank you," he said, opening the back door leading around the side of the house to the garage. "My appetite is craving something sweeter this morning."

"Good morning."

No man had a right to look so gorgeous in the morning, Madelyn thought. His chiseled features were perfect. His glorious hair was secured at the base of his neck.

Daniel's smile faltered when she didn't say anything. "I didn't catch you at a bad time, did I?"

"No," she answered, wondering if she'd ever come close to stopping loving him.

He shifted uneasily. "I brought your car back, in case you needed it to do some errands, since it's Friday and you have the day off."

"Thank you," she answered, still not moving aside to let him in. Loving Daniel was one thing, opening herself up to more heartache was quite another. She held out her open palm.

"I thought we might have breakfast," he said.

"I don't feel like getting dressed."

"I could go get something."

"Too much trouble. Besides, breakfast food gets cold easily." She wiggled her fingers impatiently.

Another frown worked its way across Daniel's brow. "I bet Dad didn't have this much trouble getting Mother to cook his breakfast."

Madelyn's eyes widened. She pulled Daniel across the threshold and closed the door. "Felicia cooked breakfast?"

"Pancakes, bacon, sausage patties, the works," Daniel smiled. Dimples winked, and it was all Madelyn could do not to sigh and ask him to do it again. "Her coffee wasn't half bad, either."

Madelyn folded her arms and eyed him suspiciously. "And you thought you might come over for some of the same?"

A flush rose up in his face. Madelyn could just imagine what he was thinking. Trying to settle her own erratic heart rate, she said, "This may come as a surprise to you, but all women can't cook."

They looked at each other and burst out laughing. "With Felicia as a mother, I guess not. Come on, I'll see what we can find," she said.

After taking off his jacket, Daniel followed her into the kitchen. "If the selection isn't any better than when you were sick, we better risk it being cold."

Throwing him a frown, Madelyn opened the cabinet and took out a box of instant Cream of Wheat and grabbed a pot. "It'll have to be hot cereal, croissants, cinnamon rolls, and juice—if there's any juice left."

Daniel opened the refrigerator. Sounded like a plan to him. "No juice. You need milk with that?"

"Yes." Pouring a small amount of milk in the pot, she turned on the gas burner. "Grab the croissants and cinnamon rolls in the plastic container. I'll slice the bread for the toast."

In a matter of minutes, they were seated and eating. "How is it you can cook bread that tastes this good and not much of anything else?" Daniel asked, on his third piece of toast. The only thing left of his two cinnamon rolls were a few crumbs.

She grinned. "I love fresh-baked bread. I took time enough long ago to learn the old-fashioned way, before quick-rising yeast. The whole process soothes me."

"What were you and Matt doing while Kane was learning to cook?" asked Daniel.

An impish smile crossed her brown face. "Anything that kept us out of housework. I was Daddy's girl. Loved tagging behind him and taking apart things to see how they worked. Matt loved doing anything on horseback, and the girls loved him. His mission was to make as many happy as possible"

Daniel chuckled. "Your poor parents."

Madelyn laughed and took the last bit of her toast. "They loved us and our differences. They're so proud—" Her face became shadowed.

Daniel saw the pain in her face, her hand clenched atop the table, and wanted nothing more than to never see her sad again. "I have a couple of hours before my first appointment this morning. You want me to take you grocery shopping?"

She smiled, but it wasn't as bright. "Bite your tongue. Shannon and Victoria are still trying to get my brothers into the grocery store and longer than ten minutes in a dress shop. They're too impatient. I imagine you're the same way."

"You need food," he answered simply.

"I'll do it later on this morning." She rose, gathering the dishes. "Anyway, it's about time for another care package from my mother."

Daniel took his plate to the sink. "Care package?"

This time the smile was real. "A tradition that started when Kane went to college of sending a box every month filled with goodies. It continued with Matt, and now it's my time."

"But you're out of college."

"Yes, but I work long hours, and my cooking skills aren't what they should be. Mama knows it." Turning on the faucet, Madelyn squirted dish-washing liquid into the rushing water. "She did the same for Matt until he got married to that woman." Derision coated the last two words.

Daniel knew "that woman" was Matt's first wife. Her treachery had almost ruined Matt's career in the rodeo and had ruined his life until he met Shannon.

Opening a drawer, Daniel took out a dish towel and began drying the dishes. "The wrong woman can make a man's life hell."

Madelyn looked at him closely. "You sound as if you're speaking from experience."

He shouldn't have been surprised that she could read him so easily. "Jeanette Pearson. I met her when I was a sophomore at Harvard. Her family had recently moved to Boston. It wasn't until later that I learned they left San Francisco because of Jeanette's problem.

"She was beautiful, vivacious, manipulative, and possessive—only I didn't know it until I tried to break off the relationship after I got tired of her jealous rages. The next day she slashed the tires of my car." He balled the dishcloth in his fist.

"A week later she got into my apartment and trashed the place. She kept calling, begging for me to take her back or I'd be sorry. I thought she meant me personally." His eyes became shadowed. "She overdosed. She left a note blaming me."

"Daniel, no!" Madelyn cried, her hand gently on his arm, her heart aching for him.

"Her parents blamed me despite knowing Jeanette was mentally ill. She'd tried the same thing with a man in California. The maid found her." His hands unclamped and clamped. "Instead of getting her the help she needed, they tried to hush it up. She died for their stupidity and mine."

"How can you say something like that?" Madelyn questioned. "You had no idea she had mental problems."

"One part of me knows that—another part looks at the senseless waste of a life." He tossed the cloth on the counter. "Love can be as treacherous as it can be beautiful. Sometimes you don't know it until it's too late."

Madelyn fought hard to keep the despair from her face. He didn't believe in love—had been hurt by it, had seen his parents' misery because of it. Love to him was something to be avoided.

Daniel kept on talking, unaware that he was shredding her heart while he went on about how fortunate she was to have grown up with a happy, loving family. Didn't he understand that for her it would never take the place of being loved and cherished by him?

"I shouldn't have told you," he said. "Don't look so sad. It was a long time ago."

And you'll remember it always, she thought.

"Madelyn?" he questioned, his hand touching her cheek.

"I'm all right," she managed. "You'd better get going or you'll be late for work, and I need to get to the grocery store."

"You're sure you don't want me to go with you?" He frowned. "You don't want to overdo things."

"I promise to take things easy." Turning away, she went to the front door and opened it. "How are you getting back to your office?" she asked, striving for normalcy.

"Higgins is waiting for me." He seemed reluctant to leave. "I didn't mean to upset you."

"I know. Have a good day."

"I'll call you later. Rest after you come back," he told her.

"Good-bye, Daniel." He cared about her and the baby, wanted what was best for them, he just didn't love them.

Leaning over, he brushed his lips against her forehead, then walked to the waiting Mercedes. Stepping back, she closed the door, feeling empty and alone.

CHAPTER 17

Daniel didn't expect to see the "walking jewelry store" open Madelyn's door that afternoon. A Houston Sonics T-shirt stretched across an impressive chest. Daniel remembered his mother wearing one similar.

"Is Madelyn here?"

The man didn't move an inch. "Who wants to know?"

"I might ask you the same question," Daniel said, irritated by the man's attitude.

"Yeah, but I'm not moving until I get an answer," the other man said.

Daniel studied the broad-shouldered man. He wasn't a threat to him with Madelyn, and if he was that protective of her, Daniel could stand his rudeness. "Daniel Falcon. I believe she's expecting me."

A smile broke across his dark face. He extended his hand. "Hey, man. I have you to thank for helping Madelyn while I was out of town."

"She told you about being sick?" Daniel asked cautiously.

"Sure," the man said, breaking the handshake and standing aside for Daniel to enter. "My name is Sid Wright. I live two doors down. Madelyn told me you're a friend of the family."

"She did, huh?"

"Food poisoning is nothing to play with," Sid said, continuing to the kitchen. "I just got back into town this morning. Saw her car out front on a Friday and came over to check on her. After she told me, I figured she needed a good meal."

Daniel eyed the various simmering pots on the stove. "You cooked."

"Yes," Sid said laughing. "Mrs. Taggert's care package didn't come today. I thought I better chip in. You like fresh black-eyed peas, collard greens, and candied yams?"

The tantalizing aromas drew Daniel closer. "Her family must really appreciate you."

Sid's booming laughter filled the small kitchen. "Between you and me, I think it's the only reason her brothers didn't send me packing the first time we met. They knew I wouldn't let her starve."

Another person who cared. It wasn't difficult to feel protective of a woman as warm and gracious as Madelyn. "Thank you for caring for her."

At Daniel's fervent words, horror replaced the smile on Sid's face. "Geez, no."

"Is something wrong?" Daniel asked, already aware of the answer.

"You hurt her, and I'll be on you like white on rice."

"That was never my intention," Daniel said earnestly, wondering if others could read his feelings for Madelyn so easily.

"Keep it that way," Sid turned off all the burners and removed a covered roasting pan from the oven. "Madelyn is in her office, working on some project with pipelines. I told her I'd call her for dinner. She works with headphones on sometimes."

"You're leaving?" Daniel asked.

"Three's a crowd. Madelyn knows how to reach me." He opened the door. "I meant what I said about not hurting her."

"So did I."

"I don't suppose you can cook?" Sid inquired.

Daniel had to smile, liking the man. "About the same as Matt."

"Heaven help us all." Shaking his head, Sid closed the door.

A smile on his lips, Daniel loosened his tie, removed his jacket, and went to find Madelyn. Since there was only one other room he hadn't been in, locating her office wasn't difficult.

Headphones on, she was transcribing scribbled notes into the computer. Absently unbuttoning his shirt collar and rolling up his sleeves, he watched her work. She appeared totally engrossed in what she was doing. Every once in a while, she'd stop, prop both elbows on the desk, and stare at the screen, then back she'd go.

He hated being disturbed when he was working on something, but she needed to eat. Pushing away from the door, he walked over and gently tapped her on the shoulder.

Her slim hand did a flicking motion, which he was sure meant to leave her alone. Smiling, he tapped her on the shoulder again.

"Go away, Sid."

Gently he removed the headphones. "It's not Sid."

She jumped, swinging around. "Daniel!"

"Dinner is ready."

Moistening her lips, she rubbed her hands on her sweatpants. "Where's Sid?"

"Gone. He thought three was a crowd."

Her expressive eyes widened. "You told him."

"He guessed." Daniel laid the headset aside. "I'll go set the table."

Saving her file, Madelyn shut off the computer and followed. He looked better each time she saw him. "Felicia called before she and your father left for Galveston."

"They went in Dad's truck." Daniel opened the refrigerator, glad to see it stocked better than it had been that morning. "Higgins said Mother had on her first pair of blue jeans and was grinning like a kid on Christmas morning."

"I'm glad for them," Madelyn said.

"Me too. I called Dominique, and as soon as she wraps things up in Paris, she's heading home."

"That's wonderful," Madelyn said, pausing with the plate she had picked up in her hand.

Setting a glass of milk on the table, Daniel came to her. "Then why do you look as if you've lost your best friend?"

She studied the buttons on his blue pinstriped shirt. "Long day I guess."

His forefinger lifted her chin. "Then we both deserve something special."

His head slowly descended, his lips closing over hers. Somehow the plate was out of her hands, and they were free to go around his neck—her body was free to nestle against his.

Slowly his head lifted. "Very special. Now sit down before I forget my good intentions. Do you want some of everything?"

"Whatever you want," she said.

"A dangerous thing to say to a man who wants a woman as bad as I want you."

She tucked her head. *Want*—not love.

"When is your next appointment to see Dr. Scalar?"

"Why?" Her head came up.

"If you don't mind, I thought I'd go with you. I imagine I should know your exercise schedule as well."

She frowned. "Why should you want to know that?"

"I plan to go with you of course."

"You can't," she told him, her voice rising. "People would figure out in no time."

The plate of food plunked none too gently in front of her. "You don't want me with you?"

She heard the hurt in his voice, but she was hurting, too. "That isn't it. You're too well known."

He sighed. "All right. I'll start searching for a birthing coach who can give us private lessons."

"I-I've thought about that, and I've decided to ask Sid."

"No." The word was flat, inflexible.

"Dan—"

"No." Coming down on his haunches, his hand pressed possessively against her abdomen. "I know I messed up. I was a fool to doubt you. This is my child, and I care about the both of you. I know you have a right, but please, please don't shut me out."

"Daniel."

He kissed her on the eye, the lips, the arch of her neck. "Please don't shut me out." His mouth fastened on hers.

Thought slipped and faltered under the onslaught of his kiss, the disturbing heat of his touch. His body urged her closer. Her sensitive breasts pushed against his chest, causing them to ache sweetly. Needing to get closer, her arms slid around his neck, bringing him nearer, anchoring him.

The shrill ring of the phone was like a blast of cold air. Hastily withdrawing her arms, Madelyn looked into brilliant black eyes deep and intense with passion. The shrill, impatient ring came again.

Pushing to his feet, Daniel stepped back. Grateful to him and the caller, she went to answer the phone in the living room. "Hello."

"Addie, are you all right? Why didn't you call?"

"Mother."

"Why didn't you call and let us know you had food poisoning and had to go to the hospital?" Mrs. Taggart asked, concern and hurt mingled in her voice.

Madelyn moistened her lips. Sid must have called her mother. It was a good thing she hadn't mentioned being admitted. "I didn't want to worry you."

"Mothers are conditioned to worry," said her father. "On the other hand, I've got enough gray hairs."

Madelyn plopped down on the sofa, silently thanking her father for trying to defuse the situation. "I won't do it again."

"We're on our way. We just thought we'd call first," he said.

"No, please," Madelyn almost screeched, then sought to calm herself. So much for thanking him. "I've never felt better. My boss gave me today off, and we're starting on a new project Monday, and I need all the time I have to be ready."

"We won't be in the way," her mother said, the hurt returning to her voice.

"Mama, I didn't mean it that way. You know you're always welcome."

"We just want to make sure you're all right," her mother told her. "You never minded us visiting before."

Elbow on her knee, Madelyn propped her forehead in her open palm. "Mama, I don't mind your visiting. I'm just a little busy at the moment."

Daniel motioned for the phone. She shook her head. "Hello, Mr. and Mrs. Taggart," he called loudly.

"Who was that?" her parents chorused.

Glaring at Daniel, Madelyn gritted out, "Daniel Falcon."

Silence stretched for long moments before her mother asked, "Why is it all right for him to be there and we can't come?"

"He just dropped by. I was about to send him on his way when you called," she said.

The grin on Daniel's face was part leer, part recrimination—and all seductive. He held out his hand for the phone. She took great pleasure in slapping the receiver into his palm.

To her disappointment, he didn't even wince. "Mr. and Mrs. Taggart, this is Daniel Falcon. I believe I have the perfect solution. If I remember correctly, Tyler has an airfield. I can have her there and back in a matter of hours, saving you the drive, and she can work on a laptop during the flight."

"I see," Mrs. Taggart said. "Thank you, Mr. Falcon. May I speak with my daughter, please."

He handed her the phone, making a cutting motion across his throat. She caught back a giggle. "Yes, Mama?"

"He said he'd bring you, but I don't want you in one of those crop dusters," Mrs. Taggart said firmly. "Do you know anything about his plane or his skills as a pilot?"

"No, but I'm sure he's a good pilot." Madelyn wrinkled her nose as Daniel mouthed "the best."

"I don't want you flying at night in a small plane. Can he bring you tomorrow morning?" her mother continued.

She didn't need to ask. "Yes."

"Call with the time, and we'll meet you at the airport."

"Yes, ma'am. Good-bye, Mama, Daddy."

"I don't think your mother likes me," Daniel said when she hung up the phone.

"She doesn't trust you," Madelyn told him.

"She might have been right at one time, but I'll make things right, I promise."

Madelyn shook her head. "No promises."

His face grew harsh. "I wouldn't lie to you."

"I never thought you would." Sighing, she glanced at the phone.

"What's the matter?" He hunkered down in front of her.

"The reprimands and inquisitions aren't over."

"Kane and Matt."

"Exactly," she stated, and reached for the ringing phone. She closed her eyes on discovering both brothers on the line. It wasn't too long before they asked to speak to Daniel. He didn't look too happy when he hung up.

"Well?" she questioned when he didn't say anything.

"If you ever get sick again and I don't call them, there won't be enough left of me to . . . you get the general, gory idea."

"I'm sorry."

"The one who's going to be sorry is Sid. He's going to learn to keep his big mouth shut where you are concerned." Daniel headed for the door.

Madelyn was right behind him. "You don't know where he lives."

"He said two doors down. How difficult can it be?"

Following an irate Daniel out the door, she hoped one of them would listen to reason, but didn't hold out much hope. Sid, despite his easy-going manner, could be just as volatile as Daniel.

Luckily Sid wasn't at home. Unluckily she received three more phone calls from her family during the next hour. Daniel left by seven, saying he'd pick her up at ten the next morning.

When she received the next phone call from Matt shortly after Daniel had left, she informed her brother to spread the word that if they kept calling, she wouldn't be able to come at all because they were keeping her from working. If they were worried about Daniel, he had gone home. The phone calls stopped.

A little after ten that night, Madelyn climbed into bed. Thankfully she had advanced further on working out the specifications for the pipes than she had imagined. By Monday she'd be able to give some important data to Mr. Sampson.

The ringing phone set her teeth on edge. She jerked up the receiver. "This does it. I'm not coming home."

"Give 'em hell," chuckled Daniel.

Grinning, she scooted down in bed, her knees tenting the bedcovers. "They mean well."

"They love you," he told her.

"I love them, too."

"The both of you okay?"

A blossoming warmth unfurled beneath her heart. Smiling at the teddy bear across the room, she laid her hand across her stomach and mouthed, he's getting closer. Out loud she said, "Great."

"Then don't fret about tomorrow. Things will work out."

Worry she had tried to ignore crept into her voice. "They've always been so proud of me."

"With every right."

"That might change when I tell them."

"Nonsense. From what I saw at the birthday party and heard tonight, their love is the kind that gets stronger, not weaker, when there's a problem," he told her. "Parents aren't as harsh on us as we are on ourselves. They tend to want to heal rather than hurt. Mine included. Despite their differences when Dominique and I were growing up and making mistakes, I think they loved us the most."

"I guess I'll find out. Good night, Daniel."

"I'll be there with you. Good night."

Hanging up the phone, she shut off the light and lay down again, dreading the coming morning and knowing there was nothing she could do about it.

Madelyn's parents were waiting for them Saturday morning at Pounds airport in Tyler. The small Cessna Daniel piloted didn't appear to impress either of them. Grace Taggart pulled her daughter into her arms seconds after she reached her. Bill Taggart stared at mother and daughter, waiting patiently for his turn.

Daniel watched the three closely. There was no doubt that the trio loved and respected each other. It didn't sit well with him that he might have jeopardized their relationship. He didn't doubt that eventually they'd come to forgive, but the forgetting part worried him. Madelyn loved her family, and their love in return was paramount to her happiness.

"Good morning, Mr. Taggart."

"Hello, Mr. Falcon," Mr. Taggart said.

"Please call me Daniel," he said, extending his hand. The grip was firm, the eye contact direct. Here was a man Daniel could respect.

At the twins' birthday party, he had been too concerned with Madelyn to pay much attention to anyone else. He should have realized sooner, three extraordinary adults would have extraordinary parents.

"Mrs. Taggart, nice to meet you again," Daniel acknowledged, turning to the older woman.

"Thank you for bringing our baby home," she said, looking pleasingly plump and pretty in a soft blue cotton skirt and blouse.

Madelyn blushed. Her father chuckled. "Now, Mama, you know she doesn't like to be reminded she's the baby."

"Well, she shouldn't act like one," her mother admonished, her arms still around her daughter's still slim waist.

"I won't again, Mama," Madelyn promised, glancing around for her brothers.

"They're not here," her father said as if reading her mind.

Madelyn sighed her relief. "Thanks, Dad."

Her father stared at Daniel. "They said there wasn't a need."

Daniel accepted the hard gaze of Mr. Taggart. "They were very explicit and thorough in our conversation."

"Good, then I won't have to be," Mr. Taggart said, ignoring Madelyn's shocked expression. "Come on, the car is over here. By the way, what is it you do exactly, Daniel?"

Madelyn groaned. It seemed she was going to be spared the inquisition. Daniel wasn't.

Daniel—who hadn't been grilled by concerned parents since high school—answered the myriad of questions with ease. It wasn't until halfway through their lunch that he understood why. He honestly liked the Taggarts and wanted them to like him.

The reason was sitting across from him, happy and teasing, as he had seen her few times. She rolled her eyes as her father told him about having to hide his tools when she was growing up to keep her from taking the electrical appliances apart.

She was beautiful and alluring. She was also wearing another one of those gauzy, off-the-shoulder dresses she'd worn when he'd first seen her. His mind had no difficulty seeing her again, wet and tempting, her breasts high, her nipples proud and erect, her body lush. Glad he was sitting down, he gulped his tea.

Later sitting in the comfortable living room, half watching a golf tournament, Daniel saw the many photographs of the Taggart children progressing from infancy into adulthood on the piano, the mantel, the side tables. Scattered among the photographs were pictures of their twin grandchildren and wedding photos of their two sons.

Graduation pictures of Kane, Matt, and Madelyn and their subsequent diplomas were proudly displayed on one wall. Daniel had given his diplomas to his parents as well. During the important events in his and his sister's lives, they had always been together. The family unit was important to children, and he planned to be there for his child.

A blip ran across the bottom of the TV screen, predicting severe storms moving into the area.

Instantly Daniel was alert and on his feet. "May I use your phone?"

"I'll show you," Madelyn said.

In less than five minutes, Daniel had the information he needed. "There's a storm cell moving in from the south—it shouldn't get here for another hour. By that time we could be in Houston."

"Then you think we should leave?"

"At any other time I wouldn't think anything about taking off, but storms can be unpredictable and with you and—" Her startled gaze alerted him they weren't alone.

He turned to see her parents standing in the doorway and explained the situation. "It's up to Madelyn if she wants to leave now or wait it out and go back in the morning."

"Of course you'll wait," Mrs. Taggart said.

"We're leaving," Madelyn said. "Daniel says we'll be back in Houston by then."

"No," her mother protested.

"You're sure?" Daniel's attention centered on Madelyn.

"I'm sure," Madelyn answered without hesitation.

"Is it safe?" Mr. Taggart asked, his eyes direct and probing.

Daniel faced her father. "I wouldn't take off if it wasn't."

The older man nodded. "Come on then, let's get you two to the airport. Every minute probably counts."

"I'll take care of her."

"You better," chorused her parents.

Madelyn watched her parents on the runway until they disappeared from sight. Her mother had looked terrified.

"We can still turn back," Daniel told her.

"I'm not afraid for us." She straightened in her seat. "I'm just sorry she has to worry."

"You have that much confidence in me?" he asked, clearly surprised.

She cut her gaze toward him. "A braggart and a fool you're not."

Daniel laughed. "That leaves room for a lot of other faults."

"I know, but I'm keeping quiet until you land this baby."

The flight and landing were as smooth returning as it had been going. Madelyn called her parents from Daniel's car. They didn't talk long because the predicted storms had reached Tyler, and there was lightning. She didn't want to tell her mother, but an unexpected storm was moving fast into their part of Houston as well. They barely made it inside her apartment before the hard rains hit.

"That's what I call cutting it close," she said, looking out the window at the torrent of wind and rain lashing the cars in the parking lot. "Out-running two storms in a day has to be some kind of record."

"I kind of hoped we wouldn't make the last one," Daniel said.

Jerking her gaze from the parking lot, she saw Daniel coming toward her, a dangerous glint in his coal-black eyes. She swallowed. "W-What are you talking about?"

His hands settled gently on her waist. "I like this dress. It reveals and conceals and tantalizes. You were wearing one similar when we first met."

"It was plastered to me," she said, then flushed with embarrassment in remembrance.

"I remember. You were beautiful. I wanted to take you away and do wicked things to your delicious body. I still do."

Madelyn trembled.

"Do you know, most of the day I've been fantasizing about your being wet and helpless in my arms."

Madelyn gulped.

He reached out one long finger and traced her nipple. The point immediately hardened. His head bent, his teeth gently closed around the turgid point to lave and tug.

Madelyn sagged in his arms, her breathing erratic.

He lifted his head slightly and stared at the results. "On second thought, I may like getting you wet better myself."

CHAPTER 18

The seductive inference of Daniel's words caused Madelyn's body to shake. She stared into his hot eyes and felt her resistance crumbling, then his mouth closed over her nipple again. She was lost.

All she could do was feel the exquisite sensations sweeping through her, but somehow it wasn't enough. She wanted his hot, knowing mouth on her bare breast. Even as the shock of her thought went through her, he was pulling the wet cloth away and granting her unspoken desire. His mouth closed on her taut nipple.

Her knees buckled. Her back arched. A ragged moan slipped past her lips.

His head lifted. If his eyes were hot before, they were a blazing inferno now. Swiftly he carried her into the bedroom, pausing only long enough to pull back the covers before laying her crossways on the bed, her legs hanging over the side.

Dry mouthed she stared up as he removed the band securing his hair and unbuttoned his shirt. Naked from the waist up, his thick hair hanging down his back, he looked like a magnificent warrior, strong enough to bend anyone's will to his. His gaze moved over her in blatant hunger.

Instead of fear Madelyn felt a rush of greedy anticipation.

Pleasure, not domination, was his intent. The irrefutable proof of his ability pushed insolently against his pants. The thought should have sent her rolling from the bed—instead heat and moisture pooled in her lower body. Her heart drummed.

Slowly Daniel came down over her, bracing his hands on either side of her face, holding his body away from hers. "I've never wanted another woman as much as I want you. I've never wanted to give as much as I want to give to you."

As soft as a whisper, his lips touched Madelyn's. Instinctively she opened her mouth to his. He didn't take her up on her offer, but was seemingly content to nibble and taste her lips. Restless she moved under him, wanting and afraid to ask until his lips moved away from her mouth.

"No." Her arms left her sides and wrapped around his neck, holding him to her.

"Tell me what you want, Madelyn."

She moistened her lips. "You know."

"I know I want to make a feast of every sweet inch of you. I know I want your mouth greedy and hot on mine. I know I want to bury myself deep inside your silken heat, then do it all over again in a variety of ways, but I don't know what you want."

Madelyn shivered from need, from his erotic words. This time when they made love, she wouldn't be able to tell herself she was swept off her feet. She wanted him, and she was tired of denying herself.

Tomorrow could take care of itself. She just wasn't ready to say the words. "How . . . how about all of the above?"

"That'll do for a start."

She opened her mouth to ask what he meant, but then his mouth closed on hers again, his tongue plunging inside. Figuring she'd find out later, she joined in the blatantly arousing kiss.

Lifting himself away, he grabbed her dress and pulled it over her head, leaving her in only a strapless, ice-blue lacy bra and panties that were just as quickly disposed of. Before she could get nervous, he was kissing her again, drugging her with the ecstasy of his touch.

He began to slide downward, past her breasts, her stomach. The first touch of him *there* set her bucking. His hands beneath her buttocks kept her in place. Shock and pleasure rippled through her—she tried to scoot away, then his tongue flicked. She cried out—not in shame, but in rapture.

Helpless, her hips moved toward him, her hands clutched the sheet. All she could do was moan his name, and soon she could not even do that. When it was over, she lay sprawled on the bed.

"Open your eyes." Daniel's voice sounded strained, gritty. "Open your eyes."

From somewhere she found the strength to comply. His eyes looked like glowing coals. She shivered, then shivered for another reason as he began to slide into her. Unblinking eyes captured hers as he joined them completely.

His moan of intense pleasure heightened hers. Her legs locked around his waist, bringing him deeper, closer. His hips began to move, slowly at first, then with a relentless rhythm she matched effortlessly. This time they reached satisfaction together.

In the aftermath, her body sated and languid, reality came crashing back. Daniel's touch sent her heart racing, her thoughts tumbling, but he had yet to speak of more than erotic, hot sex, and a child between them. He loved her body, but did he love her?

Madelyn was already afraid she knew the painful answer.

She snuggled closer, fighting the agonizing knowledge. He was afraid to love. Loving meant being vulnerable. He'd risk anything except his heart, which he defended with an unshakable iron will.

She could wail against fate for letting her fall in love with a man who considered love a liability, or she could take this time together to build memories. Angling her head up, her lips sought his.

Daniel and Madelyn lay curled up together in her bed. They had made love most of the afternoon and into the night. Earlier they had taken a shower, then fixed a quick meal before tumbling back into bed.

Madelyn was so responsive and giving, he hadn't been able to keep his hands off her. She had been the same with him. The more he made love to her, the more his body wanted.

He loved the way her breasts responded to his mouth, his touch. Interestingly he also just liked looking at them—at her. The restless feeling he had with other women after sex didn't come—he was content to lie there with her in his arms.

"Marry me," he said, not realizing what he was going to say until it slipped out. He tensed, but hearing the words aloud didn't bring the fear and uneasiness he always imagined.

His lips brushed the top of her head. Moving her things to his place would be simple. The teddy bear could go into the baby's room. They'd have a good life—

"No."

Daniel's warm thoughts crashed to a halt with the softly spoken word. Jerking upward, he stared down at her in disbelief. "What did you say?"

"No." She had the nerve to say the word again, this time lifting her small chin for emphasis.

He couldn't believe what he was hearing. "You don't want to marry me?" he asked tightly, knowing anger was no way to get her to change her mind, but unable to help himself.

"I didn't say that," Madelyn replied.

"It sounded like it to me," he yelled, watching her through narrowed eyes as she pulled the sheet over her breasts. He felt an urge to snatch the bedding away. On top of rejecting him, she was hiding her body from him.

"Daniel, there's no reason to yell."

He stared at her. How could she be so calm when she had just blind-sided him? She added insult to injury by patting his cheek.

"Come on and get dressed," she told him, climbing out of bed and showing him a tempting picture of the elegant curve of her back and lush buttocks before slipping on her nightshirt he had hurriedly re-moved an hour ago.

He gritted his teeth. One day he was going to have her naked and keep her that way.

"Daniel, move." She handed him his shirt. "I have to get rested for church early in the morning."

"You're throwing me out?"

She smiled as if she were talking to the simpleminded. "Don't be dra-matic. I need my sleep."

He didn't move. "You can't sleep with me?"

"You might snore."

"I don't," he snapped, affronted.

"How would you know?" Not waiting for an answer, she acted as if he were the simpleminded person again and put his arms into the shirt.

Finished, she handed him his black briefs with one hand and with the other patted back a yawn as if his naked body did nothing for her, while the sight of the narrow line of brown silken flesh between her unbut-toned nightshirt had him hard and throbbing. "I don't snore."

She picked up his pants and shoes and gave them to him. Once again he was the recipient of that smile. "Thank you for being so understand-ing."

Standing, he pulled on his briefs, pants, then shoved his feet into his shoes. If she didn't want him, he wasn't begging to stay.

"Good night, Daniel."

Brushing past her, he stalked to his car. She had thrown him out. No woman had ever thrown him out. Women had been trying to get him to the altar since he was eighteen, and the first woman he asked threw him out.

His jabbed the key in the ignition hard enough for it to snap, then he snatched it out and stalked back to her apartment. His fist pounded on the door. He was too angry for a doorbell.

Immediately the door opened. Her hands clutching her pink silk nightshirt, she stared up at him with wide eyes. "Why don't you want to marry me?" he asked.

"Because you don't love me." The door closed.

His fist hit the door again. He was through the door before it opened completely. "How can you say that? I'd do anything for you."

"I don't doubt you'd fight the devil to keep me safe, but there's one thing you won't do"—a weary determination came over her face—"give me your heart, totally, completely with nothing held back. I won't trap you into marriage."

"You're not trapping me—I'm asking," he told her, aware he hadn't reassured her about loving her.

"You didn't want to ask me, Daniel. You were feeling warm and magnanimous after some good sex. You stiffened like a board after asking me." The memory still hurt. She had wanted to kick him out of bed—she had wanted to bawl her eyes out. Instead she had tried to act as if she weren't dying inside.

"The sex was fantastic, and I admit to being thrown a little at first, but I meant it when I asked you to marry me," he railed.

She had learned early when people were the loudest, they were often the most wrong or the most scared. "If I had said yes, you'd be backpeddling as fast as you could by now. As it is, you're upset because I'm refusing you."

"You're wrong."

"Daniel, I don't want to argue." She was tired to the bone and finally resigned to what she had to do. "I think it's best that we don't see each other."

"You can't be serious."

"I am. I'll let you know when the baby is born. You and your parents can visit as often as you want."

Anger flashed in his dark eyes. "You expect me to just walk out and leave you and my baby?"

"You didn't want me or the baby when I first told you," she reminded him.

"I was a cynical fool. I'll always regret not believing you, but the fact remains you're carrying my child. I have a right to be a part of his life before he's born. If I had the skill, I'd deliver our baby with my own hands when the time comes. Since I don't, I'm going to do the next best thing—be there when it happens."

She shivered. "No."

"Yes," he countered, looking dark and menacing, a warrior refusing to be denied.

Madelyn refused to cower. Her chin lifted again. "You don't own me, Daniel."

He stepped closer, bringing with him the heat and hardness of his body. "I don't own you, but you belong to me, just as I belong to you. That irrefutable fact has been between us since we first met, since our first kiss, since I first made love to you."

"I belong to myself," Madelyn said, her arms circling her stomach, glancing away.

"What's the matter?" he asked frantically, his gaze swiftly running over. "Are you sick?"

"I'm just tired."

"What a fool I am," he said, picking her up despite her startled protests and depositing her gently on the couch. "I forgot what a long day you've had. I didn't mean to make it worse."

Slowly, carefully, she clenched her hands in her lap and looked away from his anxious face. "Daniel, I really think we shouldn't see each other for a while."

"Tell me what it is you want me to do or say," he implored, frustration in every word.

"You'll have to figure it out for yourself."

"And if I can't?" he asked.

Biting her lip, she finally looked at him. "Good night, Daniel."

He didn't move. He couldn't. How did he prove to a woman he loved her when he wasn't sure he knew what love was between a man and a woman? He wanted her, needed her—he didn't know about loving her.

Love was infinitely scarier. Loving a person was dangerous. Jeanette, his parents, Dominique, too many friends to count had proved that.

"You've never said you loved me, either," he said, aware he was grabbing at straws.

She gazed at him a long time before saying, "Yes, I have. With every touch, every smile, every gesture, every tear." Her sigh was long and telling. "I loved you when you hurt me more than I thought I could bear, I'll love you until the day I die—but I can't love you enough for the both of us."

His head fell, his hair falling over his shoulders. Despair, like a brutal fist, closed around him. "Why can't you take what I can offer?" he asked in a hushed whisper.

"I deserve more." The answer was as simple as it was complicated.

Madelyn was like no other woman he had met. She was loving and generous and fiercely loyal. She was also independent and a fighter. She could have taken a secure job with her brother, instead she had struck out on her own, using her intelligence and her skills to make her own way in the cutthroat business world.

Her strong work ethic enabled her to accomplish a great deal in a relatively short time. She eagerly sought to achieve more. Motherhood wasn't going to stop her from reaching the top of her field.

Neither would a man called Daniel Falcon.

Pushing to his feet, he stared down at her downcast head. "I don't know how, but I'm going to win you back." Without another word, he opened the door and left.

* * *

Desolate, Madelyn curled up against the teddy bear, her cheek pressed against the prickly fur, her arms around the wide middle. She loved Daniel, wanted to marry him. But she wanted more than a "have-to" marriage.

Daniel was still holding back, protecting himself. Until he could trust her not to betray him, take the risk of being hurt, they'd never have a happy life together. As she'd told him, she couldn't love enough for both of them. She'd grown up seeing how wonderful a marriage could be. Settling for anything less was unthinkable.

Madelyn wanted all or nothing. Untangling herself from the stuffed animal, she went to stand by the open doorway of her bedroom. The silent front door mocked her.

Looked like it was going to be nothing.

Daniel didn't sleep at all Saturday night and he was sure Madelyn hadn't fared any better. She had looked totally dejected when he left. The thought of her crying and upset kept him awake. It had taken every bit of his willpower to wait until morning to return and try to get her to listen to reason. The least she could do was not shut him out while they worked out their problems. There was no sense in them being this miserable.

Daniel pulled into Madelyn's apartment complex with the firm belief she was in bed, bereft and heartbroken. Parking several doors down, he got out and started toward her apartment.

Madelyn's laughter, light and teasing, reached him first, then he saw her as she emerged from her apartment. Dressed in a hot pink linen suit she looked beautiful and joyously happy. Shocked he stopped in his tracks. A well-dressed Sid in a light gray tailored suit came out behind her. In a matter of seconds, they were leaving in Sid's car.

Daniel watched until the Lexus disappeared. Only then did he slowly make his way back to his truck. Madelyn wasn't crying and waiting for him, she was going on with her life. He was human enough to admit he wished it hadn't been so easy for her, but man enough to admit he was glad she had the resilience and courage to take control of her life, glad she had friends who cared. But he'd be damned if any other man was going to be her birthing partner when she delivered their child.

Madelyn might have gone on with her life, but Daniel was going to make sure there was a place in it for him. He paused and looked to where he had last seen Sid's car, then concluded silently that making his wish a reality might be the most difficult thing he had ever done.

Daniel was in trouble, and he knew it. Pacing the length of his bedroom long after midnight, he discarded one idea after the other. Three days had passed since he had seen Madelyn and Sid drive away from her apartment.

Of course he'd called. She was coolly polite and continued refusing to see him. Since he didn't want to upset her, he complied. But he wasn't sure how much longer he could take not seeing her. He missed her, worried about her.

His parents had called, and he had given them the good news/bad news. His proposal; her refusal. He hadn't gone into any other details. They were due back Saturday morning. If he was still clueless, he might have to ask his mother for advice.

Even as the idea came to him, he rejected it. Somehow he knew he had to come up with the answer himself. Obtaining help from an outside source would diminish whatever plan he put into action. The usual things that enticed a woman—flowers, candy, expensive gifts or trips— wouldn't work on Madelyn. But what would?

She kept on saying it had to come from his heart. So he was reasonably sure it had to be something just for her, but again what?

He tried to think of what his married friends did and drew a blank. He had made a point of staying away from weddings since he didn't believe ninety percent of them would last ten years. He sent his gift on the happy occasion and his condolences on learning of the divorce.

Staring down at the landscaped, lighted backyard, Daniel tried to think of something. His business was ideas. But at a time when one was the most important, he drew a blank.

The thought went through him like an electrical shock. His body tensed. It couldn't be. Yet he knew it was. He had been running from the idea since their first kiss.

It was important because he loved her.

He loved her: totally, irrevocably.

Daniel went to sleep thinking of Madelyn. He woke up thinking about her. She occupied most of his thoughts during the day. He worried, he wondered, he ached with a loneliness for her which nothing else could appease.

Usually, at this time of year, he was getting ready to begin his documentary on African-American and Native American history and contributions. This time he had assigned someone else to the project. The thought of leaving town and not being near Madelyn if she needed him made him physically ill.

She had become the most important thing in his life.

His parents were acting like lovesick teenagers, his wandering sister was due home soon, his business was flourishing, he had friends, he was in good health—yet he didn't remember ever being so . . . so melancholy and lonely.

Damn! It had to be true. He laughed with the sweet knowledge. "Look out, Madelyn, I'm coming after you. And I know the perfect day."

CHAPTER 19

"Happy birthday, Madelyn," yelled her family. All of them—her parents, Kane and Victoria and the twins, Matt and Shannon—were crowded in front of her door.

Surprised, pleased, and lonelier than she thought possible, Madelyn couldn't keep the sparkle of tears from her eyes. Her palms covered her mouth and nose. She had felt so sorry for herself lately, she hadn't remembered her birthday.

"I think she thought we forgot," said Kane, holding a huge boxed sheet cake in his hands.

"We've never forgotten one in the past," said her mother, her hands holding a beautiful gold-foil-wrapped package. "Are you going to ask us in, or are we going to have this party in the doorway?"

Stepping aside, Madelyn brushed back tears. Now she wouldn't have to spend a miserable Friday night by herself, thinking and aching for Daniel. It seemed an eternity instead of only six days since she had last seen him.

The twins came barreling through the door dressed in matching jumpers appliqued with apples and ABC's. "Happy birthday, Auntie," Chandler said, a beautiful replica of her mother. "I helped picked out the cake."

Not to be outdone, Kane Jr. said, "Me, too."

"Thank you both." Leaning down, she hugged them both. She thought of holding her own child one day. Her throat tightened.

"I picked out your gift by myself," Victoria said, handing her sister-in-law a box wrapped in lavender-colored paper with a silk orchid on top.

Another box was handed to Madelyn, then another and another until her arms were full. Although she knew tradition forbade her from opening the gifts until after they had dinner at some exclusive restaurant and cut the cake, the outpouring of her family's love caused her throat to constrict just a little more.

"Hurry up and go change," Shannon said, eyeing Madelyn's T-shirt and sweatpants. "I'm starving."

Matt threw his arms around his wife and hugged her to his side. "You always are these days."

Something clicked in Madelyn's brain. "You're pregnant?"

Her sister-in-law beamed. "Isn't it wonderful? We decided to wait and tell you in person."

"You're going to be an aunt again," Matt told her proudly.

Her parents looked at them lovingly. Kane pulled Victoria into his arms. That was how it should be. Her eyes closed in adjunct misery.

"Kitten, what's the matter?" her father asked, coming to her.

Tears flowed down her cheek. "I messed up, Daddy. I let all of you down."

"Kane Jr., Chandler. Why don't you go outside on Aunt Madelyn's patio and ride her stone elephant," asked Kane quietly.

"Me first."

"No, me."

Madelyn swallowed the knot in her throat. She didn't want to see the disappointment in the faces of those she loved. "I'm pregnant."

She expected the broken cry from her mother, the sizzling epithet from her brothers. The tears in the eyes of her father broke the last of her restraint. "I'm sorry. Please, please don't hate me or the baby."

"Oh, my baby," her mother cried, drawing her daughter into her arms. "We could never hate you or the baby."

"I'm going to kill him," Matt growled.

"Not if I get to him first," Kane said.

Madelyn heard the threats and lifted her head from her mother's shoulder. "Please, just stay out of this."

"I warned Daniel, and he didn't listen," Kane said.

"It . . . it was too late then," she confessed, her voice strained and embarrassed.

Her brothers' faces hardened. They turned as one toward the front door. Clearly they weren't going to listen. Dread swept through Madelyn. "Let it go. It's over between us."

"Are you defending him?" asked her father, his voice and gaze cutting.

"Beating up Daniel isn't going to solve anything," she said, dashing away tears. "He's their friend."

"Was," Kane said, opening the door. Matt followed. Their wives threw one sympathetic look at Madelyn and rushed after their husbands.

Madelyn covered her face with her hands. What a mess.

Daniel was in a good mood. Everything was set for his surprise. Whistling, he bounced down the stairs, heading for the garage. The pounding on his front door changed his direction.

The housekeeper reached the door first. In strode a visibly irate Matt and Kane, their wives ineffectually trying to hold on to their arms.

In an instant Daniel knew. "I take full responsibility."

"You should have listened to me," Kane said, anger in every word he spit out.

"Kane, she cares about him," Victoria told her husband.

"She picked the wrong man to cry over," Matt stated, trying to shake off Shannon's hold without jarring her.

"Crying. What did you do to her?" Daniel asked, closing the distance separating them. "If you upset her, I'll tear you apart."

"Me? You're the one who got her pregnant and dumped her," Kane said, having just as much difficulty untangling Victoria's arms from around his neck as his brother was having with Shannon.

"I didn't dump Madelyn, she dumped me," Daniel said.

"I don't believe you, Daniel," Shannon said, hanging on to Matt's neck. "Madelyn loves you."

"That's why she dumped me," he explained. "She didn't believe I loved her in return."

"Was she right?" Victoria demanded.

"No!" Daniel said. "It just took me a little time to realize it. I was on my way over there now to ask her to marry me again."

Matt stopped struggling with his wife and almost smiled. "Daddy will be glad to see you."

Madelyn's eyes widened on seeing Daniel and her brothers and sisters-in-law enter her apartment. He didn't appear bruised or intimidated. Immediately his dark gaze locked on her. There was something softer, warmer in the way he looked at her.

"You've got some nerve coming here," greeted her father, advancing purposely toward Daniel.

Her father's angry expression caused Madelyn to spring up from the sofa, where she had been sitting with her mother, and place herself in his path. She dreaded doing so because she would have to look into his face again and see the disappointment and pain in his eyes and know she had put it there.

She didn't think it was a coincidence that he was the one to go and check on the twins after her brothers left. He hadn't returned until now. "Daddy, please—this will only make things worse."

With gentle but determined hands, Daniel moved Madelyn out of the way. "Stay out of this before you get hurt."

"Get away from him," her father ordered when Madelyn moved back in front of Daniel.

"Daddy, maybe you should know Daniel asked Madelyn to marry him, and she refused," Kane said.

"What?" Mrs. Taggart said, moving around the sofa to her daughter. "Is this true?"

Madelyn couldn't stand much more of this. She glanced from one to the other. "I know you mean well, but this is my life—and I'm going to live it the way I want."

"They're angry at me, not you." Daniel's fingers entwined with hers. "You can do your worst to me if you want, but leave Madelyn alone. She's been through enough."

"You caused it," her father shouted, his voice as sharp and biting as a whip.

"Yes, I did. I take full responsibility. I'm not proud of the way I behaved, but I'm proud of your daughter and our child she's carrying," Daniel said, tightening his hold on Madelyn's hand when she attempted to pull away. "I made a mistake. I won't make another one. If I can convince Madelyn to marry me, I'll cherish her always."

Her head fell. She bit her lip. "I won't marry you, Daniel."

"You said you would if I could prove to you I loved you," he reminded her, wanting to hold her so badly his arms ached.

Madelyn's head came up, heat flushed her face. No one seemed inclined to leave. "This isn't the time."

"I disagree." He glanced at his watch. "It should be arriving about now."

The doorbell rang. Kane opened the door. A man in a dark brown uniform stood there. "Delivery for Miss Madelyn June Taggart."

"There she is," supplied Shannon, nodding toward an unmoving Madelyn.

"Could you sign this while I start unloading?" he asked.

Kane took the clipboard, since his sister didn't appear inclined to move. "It'll be signed by the time you return."

His hand in hers, Daniel tugged her to the doorway. "I promise you'll like it."

She signed her name, then cautiously took a step forward. The man jumped out of the back of the truck, then reached in to pull out a large white box with a huge red bow on top. She looked at Daniel.

He smiled. "I'll hold it."

Trembling fingers untied the bow and removed the lid. She glanced from Daniel back to the dozens of colorful slips of paper inside. She picked up one, read it, then held it to her erratically beating heart, her gaze on Daniel.

Victoria and Shannon both rushed over, wanting to know what was written on the paper.

Madelyn swallowed before she could whisper an answer. "It's a promise from Daniel to fulfill whatever wish or fantasy I have that's just for me. Anytime, anyplace."

Victoria and Shannon glanced at their husbands. They simply folded their arms and smiled. The women grinned.

The deliveryman returned and handed Madelyn a slightly smaller box with a red bow. Opening the top, she pulled back the white tissue paper to reveal a beautiful cherry chest.

Her heart rate going crazy, she lifted the lid. On a bed of red velvet lay a ring of keys. Lifting the heavy gold ring, she stared at Daniel.

"They're to all my properties, my safe-deposit boxes—everything I have. If you'll look, I had your initial engraved on all of them." He held up a small key to show her. "Of course your signature will be needed on file in some cases, but a representative can fly out so you won't have to take off work."

Her hand fisted over the keys. Sadness touched her eyes. "It wasn't about money."

"I know that. It's about love and trust." He nodded toward the keys in her hand. "You asked me to give you the heart of the falcon. You have it. Everything that I have—all that I've accumulated over the years—is in your hands. In the bottom of the case is the location and the access codes. All my life I've worked to be the best there was, but I realized nothing meant anything if I couldn't have you."

Pulling a flawless, five-carat pink, heart-shaped diamond from his pocket, he picked up her left hand and slid the ring on her third finger. "I give you my heart, my love, my life. Please marry me."

A tear slipped past her lashes. For countless moments she gazed at him, then her head lowered. The fingers of her other hand closed over the ring and began slipping it from her hand. Panic assailed him.

"No—wait—please." He rushed out the door. Everyone in the room except Madelyn went to watch Daniel climb inside the delivery truck. Seeing him emerge moments later, they were even more puzzled.

Daniel was slightly winded from his dash. He knew time was running out, and this might be his last chance. More frightened than he had been in his entire life, he prayed every step of the way to Madelyn. He knew she loved him. He just had to find a way for her to know he loved her.

"You don't know how much trouble I had tracking this fellow down. I was so nervous, it took me three tries to win him in Brownsville."

He took a step closer, bringing with him the scruffy teddy bear from the carnival in San Antonio. "Everyone does need love. I was wrong. Don't shut me out. Nothing I have means anything without you."

He racked his brain to come up with something else when she remained unmoved, staring at the stuffed animal. "Madelyn, you have to believe me." Jamming his hand into his pocket, he pulled out the tattered remains of the targets. "I swear it's the same teddy bear—the mate to the one I won for you."

Her head remained bowed.

He looked around desperately as if seeking help from her family members. The sad expressions in Shannon and Victoria's eyes escalated his fear.

"Madelyn, please. I even tracked down Jerome and gave him a job because I knew you wanted to give him another chance." In rising frustration, he shoved his hand through his hair, dislodging the band. "I've resigned from half the boards I'm on so I can stay home with the baby since I know you want to work. Madelyn, I love you. I'll even learn how to cook if you want."

She finally lifted her head. In her teary eyes he saw love and hope and a lifetime shining back at him. With a cry of happiness, she launched herself into his arms . . . where she belonged. "Oh, Daniel, you really do love me. Give me a little time, and I'm going to cook you the best meals you've ever tasted."

"She must love him," Kane quipped.

"He must love her if he's going to eat her cooking," Matt said, not even grunting when his wife elbowed him in his side.

"Kitten?"

Madelyn briefly glanced at her father. "I love him, Daddy."

"I'll be watching," Mr. Taggart promised.

"I wouldn't have it any other way." Daniel smiled down into Madelyn's glowing face. "We can be in Nevada and married in three hours."

"There is not going to be another elopement," Mrs. Taggart said firmly.

"Mrs. Taggart, Madelyn deserves to have the wedding of her dreams, but I think it's more expedient if we are married as soon as possible, then leak the information to the press in a couple of weeks with an earlier date," he explained. "My mother can take care of the arrangements for the second wedding."

Mrs. Taggart humphed. "I have a few suggestions."

Everyone in the room groaned. Daniel didn't know or care why. The most important thing was Madelyn and the baby were going to belong to him and he to them. "Whatever you want—although I've never been to a wedding, I read a couple of books Rhona helped me pick out at Nia's, and I think I have everything planned for this one."

His future mother-in-law sent him a stern look. "I hope you don't think this absolves you."

"No, ma'am. I'm just glad you and Mr. Taggart will come to the wedding and give me another chance." His arm tightened around Madelyn's waist. "The wedding plans I made for tomorrow wouldn't mean very much to her if her family wouldn't be there and happy for her."

Grace Taggart unbent only slightly. "On that we agree. Just to make sure everything is in order, I'd like to go over those plans with you."

Again there was a chorus of groans. "Anything you say," Daniel agreed quickly.

Madelyn smiled up into her future husband's puzzled face. "Remember, you asked for it."

"And thank God I'm going to get it," he said, kissing her with tender restraint and love.

EPILOGUE

Daniel's plans for their Saturday afternoon began spectacularly. With surprise and delight, Madelyn used one of the keys on her gold ring to open the massive front door of a magnificent ten-thousand-square-foot, six-bedroom, seven-bath home outside Las Vegas. The turn-of-the-century Mexican colonial hacienda with its beautiful grounds on two private acres with lush greenery, koi ponds, tennis courts, swimming pools, and majestic mountain view was the perfect setting for a romantic wedding.

Daniel insisted the wedding be informal and that Madelyn wear the white gauzy sundress she had worn when they first met. Beneath the arched foyer, he had welcomed everyone to their home, but his gaze never left Madelyn's.

The passionate look in his eyes caused her to blush, and her parents to glare at their future son-in-law. But the tender way he placed the plastic-enclosed sundress in her arms, then kissed her lightly on the cheek, had her parents nodding in approval.

Moments later the housekeeper escorted Madelyn upstairs to a spacious suite, overlooking an enclosed garden, where she could dress and relax. Daniel watched until she disappeared, knowing that it was the last time he'd ever unwillingly be separated from her.

While the women fussed over Madelyn and helped her to get ready, Daniel listened to the advice of the men and kept his eyes on the magnificent black wrought-iron staircase for his bride. He couldn't stop smiling.

Somehow he had gotten his parents and their parents, Victoria Taggart's grandparents, Sid, and even Octavia Ralston and Cleve Redmon from Matt's ranch in Jackson Falls to his house for the wedding. Daniel was determined that Madelyn know she was loved and cherished, and enjoy their nuptials. He had checked and rechecked every detail. Interestingly enough, Mrs. Tagg—

His thoughts came to an abrupt halt when he saw Victoria and her daughter, hand in hand, coming down the stairs. They made a beautiful sight. He didn't have to look around to know Kane wore a proud expression on his face. Mother and child. Daniel's chest hurt. He couldn't wait for Madelyn to belong completely to him and to hold his own child.

"Daniel, you have to wait for Madelyn in the gazebo," Victoria instructed with a smile, then turned to Mr. Taggart. "If you'll come with me, Madelyn is waiting for you to escort her."

Mr. Taggart swallowed, placed the glass he was holding on the table, and started from the room. Daniel's voice stopped him. "Thank you."

The older man turned. Daniel's gaze was as steady as his extended hand.

Slowly Mr. Taggart lifted his hand. The handshake was sure and strong. "She'll always be my little girl."

"I know," Daniel said. "That's why I'm thanking you for trusting me to take care of her."

"Come on," Kane said, taking Daniel by the arm as his father started for the stairs again with Victoria and Chandler. "You don't want to keep baby sis waiting, do you?"

Daniel was the first one out the terrace door. He completely missed Kane and Matt's pleased smiles.

The initial sight of Madelyn literally stole Daniel's breath. She had always been beautiful to him, but today she glowed. He didn't know if it was her pregnancy, her happiness, or that in his eyes she could never be less than perfect. He didn't care.

Daniel noticed her glancing around as she slowly came toward him and silently went over his list again. She was carrying the water lilies bridal bouquet; all the women held a single water lily.

From his vantage point he could see the buffet table, the three-tiered wedding cake with small, gold-foil boxes nearby for their guests to take cake home as mementoes. A more lasting memento in the form of a Baccarat crystal heart paperweight was probably being placed in each guests's room at this very moment. He'd even slipped a blue garter to Madelyn while they were on the plane.

Finally she reached his side beneath the flower-draped gazebo. "What's the matter?" he asked anxiously.

"Where's Dominique?"

"Between here and the airport in Vegas, I hope," he said. "I have a helicopter standing by to bring her here as soon as her plane lands from New York."

"Could we please wait for her, Daniel?" Madelyn asked. "I'd like all of our immediate family to be here."

Pleased and unsurprised by her thoughtfulness, Daniel ignored everyone and everything and pulled Madelyn into his arms. "I'd like for her to be here, too. As long as I don't have to let you out of my sight again, I don't see why not. Today is your day."

"And yours," Madelyn said, smiling up at him, their faces inches apart.

"Oh, no, I'm too late," proclaimed an out of breath female voice from behind them.

Everyone turned toward the sound. More than one might have thought it, but only Sid mumbled, "Goodness gracious."

The woman standing at the back of the small wedding party was absolutely stunning. A glorious mane of jet-black hair framed a sensually exotic face. The hot-pink Versace dress flowed flawlessly over a curvacious body and stopped midthigh to reveal long, sleek legs.

"You didn't miss the wedding, Dominique. Madelyn wanted to wait for you," Daniel told his sister. "Now be a good girl and be quiet while I marry the woman I love."

Instead of doing as he requested, Dominique's gaze flicked from Daniel to Madelyn. "I was thinking of kidnaping you until you came to your senses, but I can see that would take a lifetime."

There were shocked gasps from the Taggart side of the family and groans from the Falcon side.

"Be happy for me," Daniel said.

"I will because I see the same love shining in her eyes. I pray that the Master of Breath will bless your love for all of your lifetimes," Dominique proclaimed, then glanced around. "Hello, Mother, Daddy, and all the grands. Where's my flower?"

The double-ring ceremony proceeded without further interruptions. Madelyn took great pride and pleasure in sliding a heavily carved gold band engraved with their initials onto Daniel's finger. No one was surprised when Grace Taggart and Felicia Falcon began to weep softly during the exchange of vows.

After many toasts were made for their happiness, after dinner and dancing, it was time to toss the bouquet and the garter. The only single adults were Octavia, Dominique, Cleve, and Sid. When Madelyn tossed the bouquet, Dominique just happened to lean down to speak to the twins. The flowers landed at her feet. Chandler picked them up. Sid was watching Dominique, and the garter popped off his forehead. Kane Jr. nabbed that one.

Bidding their guests good night, the newlyweds retired to the guest house, leaving the main house to their still partying guests. As soon as

Daniel carried Madelyn across the threshold, he kissed her. They were both breathing hard when he lifted his head.

"Thank you for believing in me," Daniel said fervently, "I won't let you down."

"I know. I love you, Daniel."

"I love you, too." He set her on her feet. "Why don't you get changed. I left something for you to put on in the bathroom."

Madelyn blushed, then laughed. "Did Victoria help you?"

He kissed her on the nose. "Nope, I did this all by myself."

Still smiling, Madelyn went into the bathroom. The smile slowly faded. Tears pricked her eyes as her hand touched the white bathrobe. Somehow she knew it was the same one from his hotel room in San Antonio. The entire day had been reminiscent of their first meeting. He couldn't have expressed his love more eloquently.

Dashing away tears, she quickly undressed and put on the robe. As before, Daniel was waiting for her.

"Daniel." It was the only word she could get past the constriction in her throat.

His large hands tenderly cupped her face. "I envisioned sliding this off you, envisioned making you mine. Even knowing it wasn't possible, I wasn't able to leave the robe behind."

"I'm glad you didn't."

"I love and need you so much."

Her hands palmed his cheeks. "I'm yours, now and forever. Make me yours again."

He needed no further urging. "Now and forever," he murmured just before his lips closed over hers.

A falcon had lost his heart and found his soul mate. He might soar in the clouds, but his mate would always be by his side. Love didn't bind, it freed.

The heart of Daniel Falcon was at peace.

His sister Dominique's was another story.

Break Every
Rule

DEDICATION

Velma Lee Radford and Mc Radford Sr., rule breakers who loved unconditionally. I miss you still.

SPECIAL THANKS

William H. Ray and Ron Reagan for their photographic expertise and invaluable insight.

Ronaldo Cordova, President of Royal Choice Carriers, for his never-ending patience and knowledge of the trucking industry.

Leo Wesley, a full blood American Indian and a citizen of the Muscogee Creek Indian Nation, and educator for the Dallas Public School for American Indian Studies.

Karen Thomas, for remembering a long ago promise.

Angela Washington-Blair and Carolyn Michelle Ray for always being there for me.

Bless and thank you all from the bottom of my heart. This book couldn't have been written without you.

PROLOGUE

It was a night the elite of Houston society would never forget.
Felicia Falcon and Grace Taggart wouldn't have had it any other way.
After all, over two hundred guests were invited to a black tie affair with
the promise that something spectacular was going to happen. They had
better deliver if they wanted to hold their heads up again.

The heavy vellum invitation stated quite clearly that the doors of the
grand ballroom at the posh hotel where the affair was being held would
close precisely at eight P.M., with no further admittance allowed. That the
invitees were given only two weeks notice was nothing short of unheard
of.

Not one single person declined. And those who didn't receive invitations tried to attach themselves to those who did. Here again, they were
stymied—Invited Guests Only.

No exceptions.

The seating was carefully arranged so that guests of Felicia and Grace
were kept apart. Speculations at the linen-draped tables flew fast and furious. Those who knew the stylish and elegant Felicia Falcon, a trans-
planted Bostonian, also knew that she and her husband had reconciled
after a two-year separation.

Could they be repeating their vows, since they had eloped—much to
the chagrin of her wealthy and influential parents?

On the other side of the lavishly appointed room, those who knew the
down-to-earth native Texan Grace Taggart as a devoted wife and loving
mother guessed the affair was to announce the engagement of her

youngest child and only daughter, Madelyn. Grace's two older sons, Kane and Matt, were already happily married.

All of them were wrong.

The two black-jacketed waiters assigned to every five tables kept the guests plied with tasty tidbits and vintage wine as the clocked ticked closer to eight. At precisely eight P.M., exactly three minutes after the last hurried guests were seated, the swish of a pure white satin curtain on the far left of the immense room revealed thirty-seven elegantly attired people standing side-by-side.

Instantly, members of the Falcon and Taggart families were recognized. The faint whispers became more pronounced. With a lift of his large hand which held a fluted champagne glass, Bill Taggart, in a tailored black tuxedo, stepped forward.

The murmurs hushed as if a switch had been flipped.

"Ladies and gentlemen, it is with a great deal of pride and an equal amount of pleasure that I welcome and greet you tonight. Those standing beside me join me in thanking you for coming. Would you please stand with us as I make this toast?"

Chairs scraped the polished hardwood floor as people stood, their glasses already topped off by an efficient stream of additional waiters. When everyone was standing, glasses raised, Bill Taggart visibly swallowed, but his voice rang loud and sure and proud as he said, "Please join me in wishing health and happiness to Mr. and Mrs. Daniel Falcon."

A gasp was completely obliterated by the swish of another white satin curtain in the center of the room. Standing on the balcony at the end of a spiral staircase were Daniel and Madelyn.

Daniel, his long, salt-and-pepper hair tied at the back of his neck, wore his tuxedo with the casual elegance of a man who is confident about who he is and his place in the world. Madelyn wore a showstopping, jeweled, hand-embroidered jacket over a full-length, gold satin gown with equal confidence and elegance.

The audience erupted into thunderous applause. The couple smiled joyously. As soon as the applause had died down and the forgotten toast was drunk, an unseen man stepped out and handed Daniel a cordless mike.

"Good evening, everyone. Thanks for sharing in this happy occasion with us. To those of you who know me, I'm sure this comes as quite a surprise. It did to me, as well." Daniel looked at Madelyn, who smiled bashfully at the knowing laughter of the audience. "Maybe that's why it's taken me so long to face the truth—that there is only one woman I'm ever going to love, and you're looking at her."

The applause lasted for a full minute.

Madelyn leaned naturally, trustingly, against her husband. "Those of you who know me also know how stubborn I can be. Those of you who know Madelyn and her family know she doesn't take crap from any man, Daniel Falcon included."

More laughter and applause.

Daniel glanced at Grace and she nodded. "Madelyn is strong and independent, just as her parents and her brothers taught her to be. So it came as no surprise that shortly after we were secretly married almost five months ago that she showed the good sense to—I believe the phrase is, kick me to the curb."

"I don't mind telling you that I had to work hard to get her back. You'll never know my dismal feeling of utter despair when I thought I couldn't have her back in my life. Finding out she was carrying our first child made the pain all the more intense."

Although he paused, not a whisper could be heard in the room.

"I'm baring my soul tonight to publicly apologize to Madelyn, but also to let you know that she and our child mean everything to me. I'll do anything to make sure both are safe and happy." His piercing black eyes roamed over the room. Each person got the message: to harm the wife and child was to bring down the wrath of the father. No one doubted the retribution would be quick and merciless.

At Daniel's nod a waiter returned with a champagne flute. Daniel lifted the glass high and said, "Please join me in saluting my wife, Madelyn June Taggart-Falcon, a woman of extraordinary patience and a boundless capacity for love. I'll go to my grave thanking God for both."

Daniel took a sip of wine, then handed the glass to the waiter. His arm securely around Madelyn's burgeoning waist at four-and-a-half months pregnant, he led her down the stairs to the sniffles and applause and whistles of the guests.

The moment their feet touched the gleaming ballroom floor, a waltz began to play. Folding doors moved aside to reveal a full string orchestra.

The guests continued to applaud as the couple twirled around the floor. The beautiful woman and handsome man—their eyes locked in eternal love.

Grace Taggart, in a periwinkle-blue gown, clutched the hand of her husband and watched her daughter in the arms of the man she loved. She knew the mother and daughter relationship had changed and taken another direction, but that was as it should be. The main thing was that her daughter loved and was loved in return. Madelyn didn't need the formal wedding Grace had always wanted for her daughter.

She had Daniel.

Next to Grace, Felicia Falcon, elegant in a sky-blue Valentino gown, let the tears freely fall from her eyes. Her son was happy at last. She felt the callused hand of her husband on her bare arm and stared up into his jet-black eyes. Thick black hair hung bone straight down his back and brushed across strong shoulders encased in the first tuxedo he had ever willingly worn.

How she loved this man—a man she'd almost lost because of foolish pride. Needing to be close to him, she leaned into John Henry's strong embrace, his arm pulling her close.

Daniel and Madelyn stopped and invited their guests to join them on the dance floor. Felicia watched as several young men in the extended Taggart family rushed toward their youngest child and only daughter, Dominique.

Dominique, exquisite in a sophisticated and flattering long-sleeved Mizrahi gown, put one red, manicured nail to her chin as if considering her choice of man. From beneath impossibly thick lashes she looked from one to the other, causing her long, lustrous black hair to skim over her shoulders and down her back.

Several other men joined the group. Her exotically beautiful face drew men like the proverbial moth to a flame. Only Dominique didn't let the men stay around long enough to feel the heat, let alone become singed or burned, Felicia thought.

Her daughter had inherited the best features from her Muscogee Indian father and African-American mother. Unfortunately, she had also inherited their stubbornness.

Dominique's laughter, low and husky, teased as much as her banter—about being unable to choose from so many handsome men, so she might just sit out the dance. Protests from the men rang loud and clear.

"After all these years she still hasn't healed," John Henry said softly to his wife.

"I'm afraid not. Worse, I'm not sure if she ever will, or how I can help her," Felicia admitted, her gaze on her daughter as she dazzled her admirers with ease.

"Do you think she will stay this time?" John Henry asked.

Felicia's hand tightened on her husband's. "If we're lucky. She seems serious about her photography, and wants to open her own studio. She's passionate about something for the first time in years."

"But not about a man?"

Felicia said nothing. The answer was obviously clear as Dominique chose the youngest person in the group, a boy of about sixteen, to be her dance partner. Felicia glanced at the disappointed faces of the men not chosen, nor would they be.

Daniel had found love. Dominique was still running.

CHAPTER 1

"I do hope this is what you wanted," said Janice Yates, a thread of anxiety evident in her crisp Bostonian accent as she took the Second Avenue exit off Hawn Freeway in Dallas, Texas.

Sitting beside Janice in the vintage Mercedes, Dominique Falcon nodded, her pulse kicking up a notch. Her future might be riding on what she saw in the next few minutes. It could be the beginning of what she hoped was a career, not another disappointment. After facing five such disappointments in the past month, she wasn't looking forward to a sixth.

"We'll be there in two minutes," Janice told her, taking a left into Deep Ellum, an avant guarde art district near downtown. "The neighborhood is in transition from residential to commercial, so you have an eclectic mix."

"It's the studio that counts," Dominique said, hearing the doubt in her godmother's voice. In her search she had seen a wide range of photography studios from lavish to run-down, but it was the atmosphere for the work created within that counted, not the outer trappings.

"It's the building at the corner with the glass front and side."

Dominique, in a chocolate, double-breasted jacket, matching cuffed trousers, and long-sleeved silk bodysuit, eagerly scooted forward on the smooth, leather seat of the Mercedes. Automatically, her hand closed around the Nikon that was never far from her reach these days. She came out of the car as soon as Janice brought the vehicle to a parallel stop in front of the building.

Janice, stylish and slim in a fringed, glen plaid jacket and skirt, was almost as fast. She took exceptional care of her fifty-three-year-old body and liked to think she could still keep up with anyone half her age. She usually did.

Unlocking the clear glass door, she stepped back. "Stop staring from the outside and come on in."

With a smile, Dominique's long legs quickly closed the distance between them. But once she was at the entrance, her steps slowed. She wanted this to be the place.

Her right hand trailed along the S-shaped Plexiglas that separated the tiled entryway from the polished concrete flooring of the main part of the studio. Glancing back at her godmother, who looked as anxious as Dominique felt, she faced forward and stepped around the glass . . . and into her dream.

It was as if the room had been waiting for her, and she for it. She felt right. It felt right.

Sometimes it takes a little longer for some of us to find what we're looking for. The thought raced through Dominique's head. Her search had taken twenty-nine years.

Dominique slowly let her gaze roam over the enormous studio. White walls glistened. Immense, plate glass windows reaching thirty-feet high in front of her provided an unobstructed view of a small, well-tended park across the street that had a piece of modern art, three black, wrought iron benches, and several small oak trees. Working in the studio would be almost like being outside.

One of the other properties she was shown had had a glass front, but had looked out onto a dreary office building. Perhaps because she was part Muscogee Indian, she liked space and the ability to see the faces Mother Nature painted on the landscape. Here, she could have both.

Overhead track lights were spaced every seven feet. In the far corner of the wall were bare rods waiting for canvasses and backgrounds. Next to them was a sliding steel door for deliveries. The setup was a photographer's dream.

"You're sure this place is for lease?" Dominique asked.

"I sure am," Janice said with a smile. "The man who was the previous tenant went to California with his wife after she was transferred there."

Dominique turned to the older woman, suspicion creeping in. "And you just happened to hear about it, when I've had realtors across Texas and the bordering states looking for a place exactly like this?"

"Don't you still believe in the power of a fairy godmother?" Janice asked, raising a finely arched brow.

Dominique laughed, a rich, throaty sound. "I believe you and my family would do anything to keep me close. Houston and Oklahoma are both less than an hour's flight from here."

"Is that so bad?"

"No. I've missed all of you." She folded her arms. "But I need to know if Daniel or one of his associates owns the building. And if they do, please don't tell me the tenant lost his lease because of me."

"What a suspicious mind you have. As far as I know, Daniel and the owner of this building have never met. I knew you were looking for a place, and I put out the word that if anyone heard of anything to let me know. I may have lost some clout in the Boston community, but I have contacts here." The hurt was unmistakable in Janice's voice.

Instantly contrite, Dominique hugged Janice affectionately. Dominique hadn't meant to bring up bad memories. Janice had been on a social and financial par with Dominique's mother until Janice's womanizing husband decided he wanted a younger wife four years ago. Greedy as well as immoral, Wayne Yates started a smear campaign about Janice's character that nearly devastated her.

When the messy and public divorce was over, her reputation was tarnished, the lavish home she had lovingly decorated and cared for had been taken away from her, leaving her bank balance pitifully low. She had left Boston, moving first to New York and then finally to Dallas three years ago to open an antique store.

"I know that," Dominique finally said. "But I also know my family is skeptical about this newest goal of mine, and with my track record they have every right to be. But I also know they realize how much I want to succeed and will do whatever they can to help me achieve what I set out to do. I've let them help in the past, but this time I want to do it on my own."

"So, do it," Janice said, the words a challenge.

Dominique searched the steady, brown gaze of her godmother for only a moment. Duplicity wasn't in Janice's nature. She was too sensitive and too caring to be dishonest.

Joy and, yes, a tiny shred of fear, raced through Dominique. This was it. All she had to do was to be bold enough to step out and take the challenge. If she were going to make a name for herself in photography, she had the place to do it.

It meant moving, as she had so many times in the past, but this time she had a definite goal, a purpose in mind. That hadn't always been the case, she ruefully admitted as she gazed around the room.

Her wandering had initially begun as a means of getting away from the pain in her family's eyes every time they looked at her. By the time she had finally taken a good look at her life, eight years had passed. Eight wasted years.

Her delicate hands lifted and closed around the Nikon N90 hanging from her neck. Such a small object, but its power was irrefutable. With it, she felt powerful. Through the camera lens she saw what was, saw endless possibilities of what could be.

"I hope that smile means you're going to rent this studio and stay in Dallas with me."

Dominique turned toward the stylishly dressed woman a few feet behind her. "It's perfect. I couldn't have dreamed of better." She smiled down at her petite godmother. "All I need now are some clients."

"You'll have them once I start telling my friends here and in the surrounding Metroplex about you," Janice said with confidence.

A frown worked its way across Dominique's brow. "Remember, I'm Dominique *Everette.*"

Janice let out an exasperated sigh. "I don't know why you don't use your name. People would fall all over themselves to have Dominique Falcon do their portrait."

"That's exactly what I'm afraid of. You, of all people, know what I'm talking about," Dominique reminded her. "Mother was so worried about you when you left Boston. She would have done anything to help you. You accepted nothing but friendship." Dominique tilted her head to one side. "You didn't try to influence anyone with the Falcon name, either."

"I had something to prove," she said with a trace of bitterness in her voice.

"And you did. Janice's Antique Attic has done well." Dominique sighed. "Try to understand that I want to make it on my own merit, just as you did."

"In your case it's different. People would have probably cluttered up my shop not buying a thing, but they'll stand in line for the sister of Daniel Falcon and the daughter of Felicia Falcon to take their picture, and you know I'm right."

Dominique was unfazed. "Believe me, I've thought this through very carefully. I've been out of the country and my picture hasn't been in a fashion magazine for some time, so no one should recognize me. I've planned and budgeted. I have two years to turn a profit before the money I've allotted myself runs out."

"And that's another thing. I can't believe you want to pay me rent," Janice said testily.

"If I lived anywhere else I'd have to pay." Dominique refused to back down. "Don't fight me on this. I was looking forward to spending some time with you."

"All right, but I don't like it. The way you explained things last night, paying me rent leaves you with very little working capital to keep your business going."

Dominique's fingers tunneled though her thick black hair. "That's the way it has to be. Dominique Falcon may have access to unlimited capital, but Dominique Everette is an entrepreneur with a tight budget."

"I wish there was some way for you to show those fabulous wedding photographs of Daniel and Madelyn," Janice pointed out ruefully. "The way his hand was touching her face was almost erotic."

Dominique had felt the same way on seeing her brother and his bride in the forest glen she had created just for that shoot. It had been imperative that people believe the wedding had taken place much earlier than it had. She had achieved her goal and more.

Watching them, she had almost felt like a voyeur. After the session was finished, Daniel had stated he and his bride were going to stay a while and not to come looking for them.

Dominique could still remember Madelyn's shocked protest, and Daniel's answering laughter. Two hours later they had finally come home, looking disheveled and utterly happy until they spotted her. Madelyn blushed, but Daniel grinned like a rogue, picked up his wife and started up the stairs to their bedroom, whistling. She didn't see them until the next day.

It had been a fantastic picture because the subjects were amazingly photogenic, madly in love, and beautiful. All Dominique had to do was press the button. The camera, Daniel, and Madelyn did the rest. She knew that wouldn't always be the case. Yet, she eagerly wanted the chance to try.

"No, I'll do it on my own or not at all," Dominique said. "There is already enough speculation on the identity of the photographer. You're the only one outside the immediate family who knows I took those pictures, and it has to stay that way."

Janice made a face. "I suppose."

"I may not be able to show that picture, but I've an idea of another one that's going to be just as memorable."

"What?"

Dominique grinned. "Not what. Who? And the answer is you."

"Oh my," Janice said, her face glowing with obvious pleasure.

"Oh my is right. Let's go create some magic." Taking her godmother by the arm, Dominique started across the room.

After signing the contracts for a two-year lease which took a hefty chunk out of Dominique's budget, they dropped the film off at the photographic lab, then headed home. Dominique's spirits were higher than they had been in weeks.

Things were coming together. When she'd received Janice's call a week ago she had no idea she'd have a studio by the next Monday. Photographing her godmother had made her dream seem real and obtainable.

Janice parked in the detached garage of the one-level, ranch style home. Arm in arm the women walked beneath the ivy-covered breezeway leading to the back door of the kitchen.

Janice opened the door and they were greeted by the light scent of bayberry in the welcoming brightness of the spotless yellow and slate kitchen. Those colors were joined by mauve and hunter green as they passed through the spacious, antique-filled living room and continued down the hall on the way to the guest bedroom.

"If you don't like anything, we can change it," Janice said on opening the door.

"You have exquisite taste, Janice," Dominique said, already knowing she'd love the room. She wasn't disappointed.

The genteel elegance of the bedroom reminded her of an English garden. The walls were done in a dusty pink to complement the soft floral print of the woven damask drapes tied back on either side of an upholstered Victorian window seat.

But the focal point was the elegant, eighteenth century mahogany bed with a shaped headboard and high posts with urn finials. The bed was lavish, with a matching comforter and mounds of decorative pillows that invited a person to lie down in luxury and comfort.

And everything looked new and fresh.

Dominique turned to her godmother. "What if I hadn't liked the studio?"

"I refused to let myself think you wouldn't," Janice said simply. "I'm behind you all the way in this."

"Thank you," Dominique said, giving the woman another hug. It felt good to have another person believe in her dream, to believe her vision could become a reality.

Although her parents and brothers loved her and were making the right overtures, they weren't completely sold on the idea that she wouldn't become bored and change her mind in a year or less, just as she had done in the past. Dominique's Place, a little bistro in New York, was just beginning to show a profit when she became restless and sold out in nine months. The Afrikan Art Gallery in Seattle only lasted seven and a half months.

She had been assisting some of the best photographers in Europe for the past two years, but this was the first time she was going to be on her own.

"I have faith in you. We all do," Janice said. "I'll go start dinner. Call your parents and Daniel, and meet me in the kitchen. We have some celebrating to do."

Setting her Louis Vuitton overnight bag on the bed, Dominique picked up the phone and called her parents in Oklahoma and her brother in Houston. Each one caught the excitement in her voice and wanted studio portraits done. Laughing, she had asked them to give her a little time.

Hanging up ten minutes later, she changed into white shorts and an off-the-shoulder knit top that skimmed a couple of inches above her navel. Humming, she headed for the kitchen.

The celebration dinner was a two-inch thick porterhouse grilled to perfection over charcoal, stuffed baked potato with the works, spinach salad, and butter pound cake topped with freshly made whipped cream and lush, ripe strawberries. Dominique teased Janice about making her fat, but she ate every bite.

Dominique had thought she'd miss the fresh vegetables and fruits she got daily from the Paris market. Janice was quick to point out that Dallas had its own Farmer's Market, and she shopped there at least twice a week.

Deciding they were too stuffed to tackle the kitchen, they had taken their glasses of chardonnay and gone outside to relax by the pool. The backyard was awash with flowering begonias and petunias.

Despite it being September, the temperature in Dallas still soared into the high double digits. Placing their drinks on the umbrella table that separated them, both women settled into chaise lounges several feet from the edge of the sparkling blue water.

"Evening, ladies."

At the unexpected deep male voice, Dominique sprang upright and almost fell out of the lounge chair. Regaining her balance if not her dignity, she whipped off her sunglasses and jerked her head toward the sound.

Her gaze traveled up taut, muscular thighs encased in tight denim jeans, past a narrow waist, over an impressive chest to a sinfully handsome face sculpted in bronzed mahogany that an angel would have wept over. Her hand lifted and closed around thin air. She almost groaned over the loss. The photograph would have been sensational.

Unexpectedly, as she gazed into rich, chocolate brown eyes, she experienced the sense of being knocked off balance. Her hand clutched the edge of the chaise lounge. The irrefutable awareness annoyed her almost as much as her idiotic impulse to slip her shades back on to shield herself from his hot gaze, which prowled over her as if it had every right to do so.

The belated greeting that she had been about to utter died in her throat. She detested men who openly ogled her.

Her hard glare elicited a deepening smile that made her think of how a cat must look just before licking his chops and pouncing on his prey. As that thought raced through her mind an unfamiliar something stirred deep inside her. His impact on her senses was totally unexpected and totally unacceptable. She felt . . . restless.

In the past she'd had no trouble dismissing such ill-mannered men. Yet, this particular man with his deep, molasses voice flowing like a lazy, sun-kissed river and too handsome face made it difficult for her to do so.

"Hello, Trent," Janice greeted warmly. "You're off early today. It's only a little past seven."

He chuckled, a deep baritone sound that did strange things to Dominique's stomach. Maybe it was the second helping of pound cake overflowing with whipped cream and strawberries.

"Don't remind me," he answered, but his gaze never left Dominique.

Janice saw his attention on Dominique, frowned, and swung her legs over the side of the lounge chair. "Forgive me. Dominique Everette, Trent Masters—my friend and next door neighbor."

"Hello." His grin widening, he extended his hand.

Uncharacteristically, Dominique ignored the gesture. She didn't let herself think her refusal to take his hand was anything more than a firm rebuttal against his earlier rudeness. "Do you usually come over unannounced?"

The welcoming smile on Trent's handsome face froze. His outstretched hand dug in the front pocket of his tight jeans. Dominique considered the accomplishment a minor miracle. "It hasn't been a problem in the past."

"Trent has been a lifesaver to me since I've moved here, Dominique," Janice said, her gaze whipping back and forth between the two tense people.

Dominique caught the placating note in her godmother's voice and heeded it. If the man had helped her godmother, he must not be as rude and crude as he appeared. That didn't mean she wanted to be best buddies with him.

"If you'll excuse me, I have some things inside I need to take care of." She stood. "Good-bye, Mr. Masters." Her voice was cool and final.

Trent had never been in a blizzard, but he now had a pretty good idea how it must feel to step from the warm confines of the indoors into a blast of frigid air. Nonplussed, he watched the stunning woman brush by him as if he were the lowest kind of life form. Noting her head held high and her regal bearing, he had the irrational urge to either bow or laugh.

Looking at her sleek, golden brown body moving away from him, the wind whipping her wild mane of midnight-black hair as it skimmed the top of her swaying hips in the white shorts, another thought struck—how much he enjoyed eating chocolate swirl ice cream in a cone. Licking from the top to the bottom, then taking a good bite.

"Trent? Trent?"

Guiltily, Trent brought his rampaging mind back, then turned toward Janice and took the seat Dominique had vacated. The canvas was still warm. It didn't take much imagination on his part to recall her utterly feminine and alluring body stretched out on the lounge and the turmoil it created within his own body or to imagine his fitted over hers.

"Not you too?" Janice almost groaned.

"What?" he asked.

Janice rolled her eyes. "Most men see Dominique and start acting as if they have a screw loose. I thought you had more sense."

Trent reached for the drink nearest him, sniffed, then put the glass back on the table. He needed something stronger than wine to fortify him. "So did I."

The older woman laughed. "At least you're honest about it."

"The drool on my chin would have probably given me away."

She smiled indulgently. "It's about time you started thinking about something else other than those trucks of yours."

"Just because I'm thinking doesn't mean I'm going to do anything about it." Trent shook his dark head and gave a long, telling sigh. "Women take too much time. Dominique more than most, I imagine."

Janice straightened her shoulders and sent him a stern look. "And why would you think that?"

"It obvious," Trent said, leaning back in the chair and crossing his long legs. "She has to know she's gorgeous, with a body to match. She probably could have any man she wanted. A man is going to have to put in a lot of overtime to keep her happy."

"I never thought I'd see the day you'd judge someone on appearance," Janice said ruefully.

Trent frowned, his gaze going back to the closed patio door Dominique had disappeared through. "Are you trying to tell me there aren't at least ten guys lined up to take her out?"

"As far as I know there's not one."

His frown deepened instead of clearing. "It's worse than I thought."

"What are you talking about?"

"Barracuda. Eat a man up and spits him out."

Janice surged to her feet. "If you say one more unkind word about my goddaughter, you'll find yourself unwelcome in my house or on my property."

He came to his feet as well. "Goddaughter. You've never mentioned a goddaughter."

"That didn't mean I didn't have one," Janice said. "She's opening a business in Deep Ellum, and will be living with me for an indefinite period of time, so I expect you to be courteous." Janice picked up the two glasses. "If not, you'll have to find someone else's pool to swim in and another place to eat." With that she swept into the house.

Dominique was in the kitchen washing up the dinner dishes. Setting the glasses on the blue tile countertop, Janice picked up a drying towel. "Despite that display of male stupidity, he's a nice, intelligent man."

Dominique clinked a china plate none too gently in the dishrack. "I hate being stared at as if I'm on display."

"I know. You may not believe this, but Trent seldom pays attention to women. It's kind of odd to see the turnabout. He's usually the object of female attention."

"Some women have no taste," Dominique said, trying hard to forget her own reaction to Trent. With her heart still thudding, it was impossible.

Putting the plate away, Janice reached for another. "On the contrary, Trent is considered a very good catch. He's in his mid-thirties, has a successful transport trucking business, he's handsome, and has a body that has been known to create a stir when he wears swim trunks."

Dominique didn't want to think of Trent in swim trunks. She was having enough trouble trying to forget his broad shoulders and the muscled hardness of his thighs in those disgraceful jeans. "He probably knows it and uses it to his advantage."

"Quite the opposite," Janice said, pausing between drying two forks. "He seldom dates. Says he's too busy running his business to socialize."

"With his attitude, who would have him?" Dominique asked, determined to dislike the man.

"Half the single women I know, that's who." Janice chuckled, then sobered. "If I know Trent, his conscience is already giving him a good talking to and he'll probably apologize the next time you see him."

"I hope that's in the year two thousand," Dominique said, snatching a wineglass from the counter.

Wearily Janice eyed Dominique's agitated motions. "If you cut your hand, you won't be able to use your camera."

Instantly, Dominique's hands stilled. "He made me so angry."

"Men were acting much worse at Daniel and Madelyn's reception, and they didn't faze you," Janice reminded her.

Head down, Dominique slowly began washing the glass. "I knew I didn't have to see them again. Masters is different," she explained.

"That he is, in many ways. I just hope you won't hold this afternoon against him, and will allow yourself to find out." Janice placed a hand on Dominique's rigid shoulder. When Dominique looked at her, she continued speaking. "You both mean a lot to me, and I'd like you to be friends."

"Friends might be asking too much," Dominique said with a wry twist of her mouth. "How about we don't draw blood?"

"It's a start."

Not moving as Janice stalked away, Trent had winced on hearing the angry thud of the patio door closing. If she got the blasted thing off the track again he wasn't going to fix it.

Even as that thought came to him, he knew he'd do anything Janice asked him because of two things: he liked and respected her, and she had been right to ream him out about Dominique.

He wasn't surprised by how easily Dominique's name rolled off his lips. In his business you had to remember names. What did surprise him was his initial reaction. Hard and hot and stupid.

He shook his head ruefully. He was too old and he hoped too intelligent to act that way. He owed both women an apology, but watching the loosely woven patio curtains swoosh closed, he didn't think now was the time.

Looked as if he was on his own for dinner. He sniffed the air and recalled the smell of charcoal-cooked meat that had brought him over in the first place. Janice had probably cooked steaks on the grill he had spent all day setting up last summer while she stood under the protective covering he had built so she didn't have to cook in the sun.

With a last, longing look at the curtained door, he started home. Served him right.

But he couldn't help wondering how he was going to face his meat loaf again. There wasn't enough sauce in the world to disguise the bland tasting concoction he'd stirred together two days before. Grimacing, he tried to remember if he had eaten the last of the warmed up chili Friday night.

CHAPTER 2

Trent was on his porch sipping coffee early the next morning when Dominique sprinted by, her long, sleek legs quickly taking her away from him. Today she wore a red and white nylon short set. A loosely woven braid as thick as his fist and as shiny and black as a raven's wing hung down her slim back.

Without breaking her measured stride she started up the sharp incline of the street. Her movements were graceful, effortless, and in perfect harmony.

He grunted. That was more than he could say for himself. He had had a restless night and this morning didn't seem to be any better.

He hadn't nicked himself shaving or stubbed his toe on the corner of his dresser in years. This morning he had been so preoccupied with thoughts about Dominique he had done both.

What was it about the woman that annoyed and excited him at the same time? Whatever it was, he had better find the answer and quick. Friends, good friends like Janice, were too hard to come by.

Stepping off the porch, he dashed the bitter, three day old coffee into the grass. It was time to eat some humble pie.

He rapped once on Janice's kitchen back door.

"Come on in, Trent," Janice called.

Opening the half-glass door, he walked inside. Janice, her back to him, was at the stove stirring something. Eggs, he guessed. The rich smell of coffee and bacon had him salivating. "I'm sorry about yesterday."

Sliding the contents of the skillet into a plate, she picked up the slate blue stoneware and placed it on the table. "I knew you would be. Sit down and eat, since you missed your steak last night."

Trent thought longingly of the steak he could have eaten instead of the burnt chili he'd tried to reheat, then pulled out a caneback chair and reached for a fork. Eggs and crisp bacon filled the plate. He almost licked his lips.

His blessing was quick. The second he opened his eyes, he reached for a fluffy biscuit.

"Tsk, Tsk. If I didn't know any better, I'd think my cooking brought you over here this morning with your hat in your hand instead of decency."

He had the grace to flush. "I'd like to think it's more of the latter than the former, but you are the best cook in Texas."

"Humph," Janice said. Picking up his cup, she filled it with freshly brewed coffee. "You might be able to get by me with flattery, but Dominique is another matter. She'll try for my sake, but if you blow it the next time this might be the last of my cooking you're going to get for a while."

"If any man knows the value of a second chance, I do," Trent said with feeling. His life had always been that way—a series of events that at first looked bleak, then eventually worked in his favor.

Initially all he had understood growing up in the foster home was that his mother hadn't wanted him. It had taken years of counseling for him to see that perhaps leaving him warm, clean, and dry in a hospital bathroom was the best she could do for him.

The note—Keep him safe. I can't. Tell him I loved him, I did, but he won't remember.—and a new, blue baby blanket were the only legacies his mother had left him. She had never been found. The authorities suspected she was in an abusive situation, and might have feared for his life.

The social worker and others had helped him realize that he could be bitter and angry, or he could take every opportunity that came his way and make a place for himself in a sometimes harsh, cruel world. It wasn't easy, but he had succeeded.

Janice pulled out a chair and sat down. "Believe it or not, Dominique is looking for her chance, too."

Trent stopped eating. It had struck him odd last evening and then now, that a caring, nurturing person like Janice had never mentioned a goddaughter she was obviously very fond of. "Is she in some kind of trouble?"

"No, and that's all I'm going to say."

He studied the stubborn set of Janice's chin and knew he wasn't going to get anything else out of her. His gut instinct warned him to leave it alone. He had his hands full running his business. He couldn't save the world. He'd tried.

He went back to eating his breakfast, but not with as much enjoyment. The thought of Dominique being in trouble was oddly disquieting.

Trent was waiting for Dominique when she returned thirty minutes later. Although he had tried, he hadn't been able to keep himself from trying to figure out what her story was, and why Janice had never mentioned her.

He was too up front and honest for secrets. But he respected people's privacy. And he readily admitted to himself that if Dominique didn't bother him in a purely masculine way he wouldn't have given the matter a second thought.

So basically the problem was his, not theirs. There was never a problem in life that he hadn't been able to work through, and he didn't see Dominique Everette as any different. He'd just wait until she finished her cooling down regimen. Then he'd go over, apologize, and get back to his peaceful life.

The first part of his plan was going smoothly until she started bending over, touching her toes. The red nylon shorts lifted and clung to her nicely rounded hips, and all his good intentions of ignoring his utterly sensual new neighbor slipped away.

Instead, he remembered one of the treats he liked best at the foster home was peppermint sticks at Christmas. Most of the other kids got tired of sucking on theirs and started biting.

Not Trent. He knew how to savor his all day long with long, slow licks. Up and down, up and down. Down one side, and then down the other. He had the best tongue twirl at the foster home.

A dog barked, drawing Trent out of his musing. Damn. He had done it again.

He was a better man than this. Women didn't faze him. He certainly didn't fantasize about them. He had normal sexual drives, but he controlled them, not the other way around. A man who couldn't control his sexual urges wasn't much of a man.

They certainly didn't get very far in the competitive business world. Especially if he had to build his business, the way Trent had.

Masters Trucking got him up in the morning and made him feel alive. He didn't have time for a woman. He needed to put a stop to whatever this was. His number one rule was his business had to be his number one priority.

Determined not to waste another moment, he strode down the steps and crossed Janice's yard. "Dominique."

She whirled around on the small porch. "Do you always sneak up on people?"

"Sorry. I wasn't aware that I walked that softly." His gaze didn't drop below her sweat-dampened face. He was actually proud of himself.

"If you'll excuse me." She turned toward the door and somehow he managed to step in front of her. Abruptly, she staggered back. "What are you doing?"

"Trying to apologize, and doing a poor job of it," he admitted ruefully. "Look," he said, running his hand over his close cropped hair. "I usually get along with everyone, but we seem to rub each other the wrong way."

Black eyes widened. Up went her cute little chin.

Trent thought, *Bad choice of words.* If they were ever rubbing each other, he was sure it would be the right way, and they wouldn't be having a problem. He cleared his throat and his mind of everything but getting his apology out before he messed up even more.

"I was out of line yesterday. It's not my practice to stare at women, even ones as beautiful as you."

"Now it's my fault for your bad manners," she said frostily.

"Will you stop twisting everything I say?"

She crossed her arms over her heaving breasts. "They're your words, not mine."

"Have it your way. I'm the lowest form of life for daring to look at you in anything but a respectful manner. You're a guest of Janice's, and her goddaughter. I value her friendship, and I wouldn't want to lose it."

"She's quite fond of you," Dominique admitted reluctantly.

"Something you apparently don't understand."

"I don't have to."

"That's where you're wrong," Trent said. "In case you've forgotten, Janice has few family members, and those friends who are close to her, she values highly. She won't like us being at odds."

Dominique glanced away. He might be rude, but he was also perceptive.

One of Janice's regrets about her failed marriage was that she didn't have any children. Felicia always maintained that Janice had left Boston because her ex-husband's new wife had a baby four months after their divorce was final, and three months after they married.

Janice had made her friends her family. She was generous and compassionate, and could always be counted on to help anyone in need, just as she had helped Dominique.

Trent continued, "All I'm asking for is a truce, for Janice's sake. We don't have to be best buddies or anything."

Dominique's head came around. His words were almost her own. She was in Janice's house, and as such she had to respect her hostesses' guest and friend, no matter how much he irritated her. Most of all, she knew he was right.

For reasons that completely escaped Dominique, Janice thought highly of the brash, insolent Trent Masters. Dominique didn't see why, but snubbing the man wasn't worth upsetting her godmother.

Her hand lifted.

Almost immediately his rough hand closed around hers. Heat like a sunburst splintered through her. It took all her control not to jerk her hand free of the firm but surprisingly gentle grip. "Truce. Now, if you will excuse me, Mr. Masters."

She started to brush by him. He moved again. This time she wasn't able to stop her forward momentum. The front of her body collided firmly with his. Breasts to thighs. Air hissed through her clenched teeth. She jumped back.

The look she sent him would have melted steel. "Mr. Masters, you're beginning to annoy me again."

"That's just the point. Janice is not going to believe everything is all right if you keep calling me Mr. Masters like you have a bad taste in your mouth," Trent pointed out, trying to forget the softness of her rounded breasts pressed against him or the silkiness of her skin.

Dominique conceded the point with a curt nod of her head.

"Is it me, or are you always this reticent?" he asked.

"I don't particularly like you."

"I gathered that, and I don't blame you. I admire honesty," he told her frankly. "I expect the same of myself. I was totally over the line yesterday, and if there's anything I can do to make up for it, I'm willing—except move to another planet."

She stared at his handsome face and silently wondered if the earnestness she saw reflected in his steady, brown eyes was real or part of a calculated act. Then she decided to give him enough rope to hang himself.

"All right. Trent. Now if you'll excuse me."

Trent watched Dominique close the door on him again. His hand rubbed across his chest where he still felt the lush softness of her breasts. His heart rate was erratic, his breathing more so. He wondered if she felt the intense sexual pull, then dismissed the idea.

Despite what Janice had said, he was beginning to believe Dominique was a barracuda. Her only problem was probably a love affair that had ended badly. Trent suspected the man had gotten the worst of it. Dominique had kicked the unfortunate brother in the teeth and left him in shreds.

Shaking his head, Trent started back to his house. Of all the women to send his body into hyperdrive, he had to pick Miss Ice Princess of 1998.

No matter how hard Dominique scrubbed her body in the shower, the sensation of Trent's touch would not go away. No matter how much of her scented bath gel and soap she used, she still smelled his spicy cologne, and another scent that was uniquely his.

Throwing back her head, Dominique let the blast of warm water beat down on her upturned face. Of all the times for her body to remember its gender now was the worst, and with the worst kind of man.

Her only concern had to be with establishing herself as a portrait photographer, not with discouraging the unwanted advances of some Neanderthal.

She knew how to handle men like Trent—remain calm and cool, and above all never let them know they got to you. Dismissive without being cutting. The male ego was too big and too fragile to stand being rejected outright. If they stepped over the boundary as Trent had, then you cut them off at the knees. She should have looked down her nose at Trent, slipped her glasses back on, and acted as if he didn't exist.

Instead, her body had reacted to his before she had time to breathe. Eight years ago she had made a vow that her body would never rule her mind. The consequences were too painful. She had never broken that rule until now.

Straightening, she shut the water off and reached for a fluffy, rose-colored, bath towel. She could handle Trent, just as she had all the other men who wanted to take with no thought of giving.

She didn't dare let herself think of the consequences if she could not.

"I can't believe this," Janice said, twisting the ignition key again and getting even less results. This time the motor turned over only once. Another switch of the ignition key elicited nothing. "I can't believe this. You're going to miss your plane."

"I'll call a cab," Dominique said. At any other time she would have taken a later flight, but she was anxious to leave. She refused to think Trent might be the reason. She had never run from a man in her life, and she didn't intend to start.

Janice shook her cap of dark curls. "This isn't a usual cab route. It'll take forever." Pulling her cell phone out of her oversized Gucci bag, she punched in a number. "Trent, my car won't start and . . . thank you."

"He'll be right over," Janice said, deactivating the phone. "It's a good thing you had an early flight and we caught him before he left for work."

Dominique was going to reserve judgment. In a matter of seconds a metallic green truck with tinted windows pulled up behind them. By the time the driver's door opened, Janice was halfway to him. Dominique stared straight ahead and remained unmoved.

"It won't start," Janice told him again. "It was fine yesterday."

"Let me try." Long, muscled legs clad in sharply creased denim jeans preceded Trent into the sports car. Dominique's hands tightened around her purse. For some reason the air in the car seemed harder to draw in, the interior smaller.

Trent flicked the key. Nothing.

"It has to start. Dominique will miss her plane," Janice wailed, standing beside the open driver's door.

"You're leaving?"

The question sounded like an accusation. Dominique didn't want to face him, yet she found herself doing so. "Yes."

Hard, brown eyes impaled her. "I'm usually at the office more than I'm here."

It took a few moments for the implication of his words to sink in. He thought she was leaving because of him. On one hand, it irritated her that he thought he had that much power over her, on the other his statement showed he really cared for her godmother.

She responded to the latter. "I'm going home to pick up my things and then I'm returning."

For a long moment, their gazes clung. She couldn't look away nor did she want to.

Trent nodded once, emphatically. "You won't be sorry." Before she could answer he was out of the car and lifting the hood.

Dominique sagged against the leather seat and wondered if the ozone level was higher in Dallas than Houston. Something had to be wrong to make her act like a teenager with her first crush.

While she was trying to figure things out, her door opened. Trent stared down at her. "The battery is as dry as a sucked chicken bone. I'm not sure if I put a charge on it it'll hold. I'll have to take you to the airport."

"That won't—"

"Oh, thank you, Trent," Janice said, cutting Dominique off. "I'll call the auto club to come see about the car."

"I'll have Smitty come over, too," he said, then stared down at Dominique. "What time is your flight?"

"Nine-thirty," answered Janice. "Her case is in the trunk."

Trent glanced at the gold-and-silver-toned bracelet watch on his wrist. "Eight-fifteen. You still don't believe in giving yourself enough time, do you, Janice?"

The older woman looked chagrined. "It would have been fine if the car hadn't died."

Trent didn't comment, just looked back at Dominique. "If you want to make your flight we need to get going. It's a fifty minute drive without the morning rush hour."

She didn't move. "What about Janice?"

"I'll have someone come over."

Again he looked meaningfully at his watch. "I hate to rush you, but I have an early morning appointment myself."

She was a woman, not a child. "Then, as you said, we'd better get going."

Getting out of the car, she hugged Janice good-bye and went to Trent's truck and got in. She was a Falcon, she thought as she buckled her seat belt. Her female ancestors on both sides of her family were as brave and as resourceful as their male counterparts.

They'd needed to be. Ignorant and sadistic individuals saw the color of their skin and deemed African-American and American Indian women fair game to be used and abused. Despite tremendous odds, they had survived degradations and injustices no human should have to endure.

Her ancestors were princesses and medicine women, rulers and healers, fearless and daring. Not one would have given Trent a second thought.

Opening the door, Trent climbed inside and buckled his seatbelt. The roomy cab seemed to shrink. Tinted windows created a disturbing atmosphere of intimacy. She drew in a nervous breath and inhaled the faint, spicy scent of his cologne. For some insane reason she had the sudden urge to lick her lips. She groaned instead.

"You say something?" Trent asked as he backed out of the driveway.

"No," she said quickly, glad when seconds ticked by and he didn't say anything else. Something was definitely wrong with her. The only thing in her favor was that Trent didn't have a clue. Lord help her if he ever did.

Neither spoke until Trent passed through the ticket booth at Dallas-Ft. Worth International Airport. "Don't you think you had better tell me the airline, terminal, and gate?"

Dominique realized on hearing the question that she had forgotten to check the night before to make sure the gate hadn't changed. She gave him the airline, then checked her ticket to give him the other information he requested.

Trent moved over a lane and took the next exit. She was still gripping the envelope when Trent pulled into the parking lot on the upper level for departing flights. "You don't have to park," she told him hurriedly.

"Your flight leaves in ten minutes. I suggest we run instead of arguing." Grabbing her case out of the back-seat, he took her arm and steered her across the street into the terminal.

The heat of his hand easily penetrated her light blue, linen jacket. She cut a glance sideways at him and saw the rigid profile of his face. He was just being courteous, nothing more. A few more minutes and she'd be on the plane.

The security buzzer sounded. She glanced back as a male security guard moved toward Trent. "Please try again, Sir."

"Go ahead, Dominique. I'll catch up with you," Trent said. He stepped through and the security buzzer sounded again. "Must be the keys."

"Beep again, Brother, and you're mine," said a statuesque female security guard a few feet from Dominique. Her dark eyes gleamed with interest as they traveled slowly over Trent's muscular body.

"I'll buy you lunch if you let me do him," stated another female security guard, her gold-tipped nails tapping restlessly against the metal detector in her hand.

The women looked at each other and burst out laughing.

"Dominique, go on," Trent told her again as he jammed his hand into his pocket and removed his keys, then tossed them into the waiting container the guard held.

Holding his hands up in the air, he walked through the security checkpoint again. Silence.

"Dog," said the first security guard who had spoken. "Did that brother have a body on him. I was looking forward to—"

"Come on," Trent said, retrieving his keys with one hand and reaching for Dominique with the other. His steps were hurried as he led her away from the disappointed security women. "Why didn't you go on?"

Telling him about the two woman ogling him would inflate his probably already huge ego. "It would have been rude," she answered instead.

He grunted. "If you miss your plane, Janice is not going to be happy." He expertly steered her through the early morning crowd of business and vacation travelers.

Hearing the announcement for boarding for her flight, their pace increased. When they arrived at the check-in counter, only one customer service representative remained, and a long line of passengers waited to board.

"Seems I just made it," Dominique said, the huskiness of her voice more pronounced from rushing.

Before the words were halfway out of her mouth the agent abruptly lifted his head. Thin shoulders snapped to erectness. His professional smile warmed considerably as he greeted her, then went about checking her in.

Handing her a boarding pass he said, "I'm sorry, the other first class passengers have already boarded. It will be just a moment."

"That's all right. I'm just glad I didn't miss my plane."

"So am I," he said, his voice just shy of crossing the line between professionalism and flirtation.

Dominique felt a hand clamp on her arm and looked up at Trent. Her brows bunched. He was glaring at the too thin man. Not for one second did she think Trent was jealous. Rudeness just came naturally to him.

Freeing her arm, she walked to the window to wait to board. "Are you always like this?"

"What did I do now?"

"You looked at that poor man as if you wanted to take his head off."

"He deserved it."

"For what? Being nice to me?"

"For peeping down your blouse," he answered tightly.

"What?" Dominique exclaimed, glancing down. The lacy cup of her blue bra peeked from between the opening of her unfastened buttons. She quickly redid them, then remembered the man's gaze dropping.

She flushed. "Thanks."

Trent's brown eyes rounded. "What did you say?"

"You heard me, and I'm not repeating it."

He smiled. "I guess I can live with that."

Her heart rate kicked up. He really did have a nice smile.

"Last call for passengers boarding Flight six seven six for Houston. Last call."

Dragging her gaze away she glanced toward the thinning passengers, then reached for her overnight bag. "I'd better get going."

Slowly, almost reluctantly, he handed her the luggage. Their fingertips brushed, and this time neither could deny the transfer of heat.

She moistened her dry lips. "Thanks for the ride."

"When are you coming back?" he asked, telling himself he was asking for Janice.

She bit her lip before answering. "I don't know, but I'll be busy when I do."

To Trent, she couldn't have said it any plainer. They might have a truce, but she still wanted to steer clear of him. He had never pushed himself on a woman, and he wasn't about to start.

"You don't believe in second chances, do you?" he said, then continued before she could answer. "As I said, I'm gone a great deal. Have a good flight." Tipping the brim of his Texas Rangers' baseball cap, he walked away.

Dominique watched him leave and felt oddly bereft.

"Miss Falcon, you'll have to board now."

Dominique jerked her head around to see the ticket agent. "Thank you," she said coolly. The smile on his narrow face turned to puzzlement as she brushed past him and headed for the gate.

She didn't look back.

If she had she would have seen Trent stop and turn around. He stayed there until the gate closed and the airplane taxied down the runway.

Dominique wasn't as cold as he had thought, but the realization didn't make him any happier. Apparently neither one of them was looking for an affair, yet the attraction between them was getting stronger each time they were together.

So there was only one thing to do. Keep the hell away from her and pray she did the same with him.

CHAPTER 3

As soon as the flight attendant gave the clearance to make in-flight calls, Dominique dialed Janice's home number. She was mildly surprised when her godmother answered the phone. Trent's assessment was correct, she informed Dominique. His mechanic, Smitty, had brought a battery and installed it for her.

Trent always took care of her. He was such a fine, conscientious man, she said. You didn't find too many young people who were concerned with older people, especially if they weren't related to them.

Dominique didn't want to hear about the sterling qualities of a man who confused, irritated, and excited her in equal measure, but Janice was on a roll. Dominique mumbled the appropriate words politely when it was time for an answer, but as soon as Janice started winding down Dominique told her godmother she'd call that night.

Replacing the receiver, she sat back in her seat and tried to think of anything but intense brown eyes that could melt stone and make her body tremble.

"Excuse me, Miss. I know this must sound like a line, but don't I know you?"

He didn't, but that didn't keep the suave and polished business executive sitting next to her from trying to pick her up. She resorted to her old standby of pleading a headache, putting on her shades, and turning her shoulder to him during the rest of the flight.

The second the FASTEN SEAT BELT sign blinked off after landing forty-eight long minutes later in Houston, Dominique pushed her glasses atop her head, stood, and reached for her bag. Her seatmate, the two men across the aisle, and the male flight attendant hurried to help her. Restraining herself from telling them that if they moved out of the way she could do it better and faster, she kept a smile plastered on her face.

Overnighter in hand, she left the airplane at a brisk pace. The business executive sprinted to catch up with her. Unfortunately, Dominique was beginning to develop a real headache.

Her gaze was glacial. "I don't know any more ways to indicate I'm not interested, and I don't intend to try. Good-bye."

Gripping her luggage, she started out of the portable boarding tunnel. The other two men who had tried to help her with her bag hurried by.

She spotted Higgins—now her mother's chauffeur, and her grandparents' before that—as soon as she came out of the tunnel. Despite his seventy-two years his shoulders were straight beneath his tailored, two-button pinstripe navy suit. The gray abstract tie was silk, the shoes Bally.

She smiled warmly. More than one man watched enviously as she hugged the elderly man.

"Hello, Higgins. I was afraid you might forget me since you have so much time on your hands now," she teased.

"Shame on you, Dominique, for saying such a thing," he greeted, reaching for her case. He might be formal with the rest of the family when their guests or associates were around, but Dominique had always been Dominique. "When I talk to your mother again I'll have to tell her she still has work to do."

She hugged his frail arm, her steps slowed to match his. "You miss her a lot, don't you?"

He nodded. "But her place is with your father and I couldn't be happier. Besides, what would I do on a ranch?"

"I seem to remember Daddy had about five hundred head of cattle and a few fields that needed plowing," she chided affectionately.

Allowing her to go through the outside revolving door first, he followed. "I'm a city boy."

Dominique smiled, secretly wondering if he knew her mother had said Higgins might have stood anything except the fact that the nearest store that stocked his favorite brand of Scotch was sixty miles away.

He would have stayed if her mother needed him, though. She hadn't. Felicia was no longer afraid to lean on her husband or share her innermost thoughts with him. She had finally progressed from an indulged young woman to a happy, contented adult, secure in the love of the only man she had ever loved.

After storing the luggage in the trunk of the shiny gray Mercedes, Higgins opened the passenger door for Dominique. Once she was settled he went around and got inside. "Have a nice stay with Ms. Yates?"

"Most of it," she said, then grimaced. She was not going to let Trent interfere with her happiness.

Higgins backed out of the parking space and merged with the airport traffic. "I thought Daniel said you found a studio."

"I did. There were some other matters that I didn't expect," she told him evasively.

"Anything I can do to help?" he asked.

She sent him a warm smile. "No, but thanks. I have to do this by myself."

"I hope that doesn't mean you're going to go off again," he told her, stopping at a signal light. "It's been nice having you these weeks. I've hated to see you always leaving, and so did your family."

She took the slight reprimand with the affection behind it. "I hated it just as much, but something always pushed me to go."

"And now?"

She searched her heart, her mind. There wasn't quite the peace she wanted, but neither was the restlessness that usually haunted her. "This time I'm going to stay put. In Dallas."

He sent her a pleased look. "It's about time."

"Don't I know it," she agreed.

"You might even find a nice young man."

She stiffened. Not Higgins, too. Since Daniel had gotten married her mother had really been dropping hints for Dominique to find 'some nice young man.'

Dominique glanced at Higgins suspiciously. He and her mother were as thick as thieves. "I'm too busy for that."

"Nobody was busier than your brother, and look what happened to him," Higgins reminded her and took the on ramp to the freeway.

"That won't happen to me," she said emphatically.

The chauffeur shot her an indulgent look. "Seems I remember your brother thinking the same thing. I'd sure hate for you to go through what he went through."

"Could we talk about something else?" she asked.

"None is so blind as he who will not see."

"Higgins." She turned in her seat toward him. "What has gotten into you?"

"Nothing. Just remembering your brother, and remembering how much alike you two are." He sent her a sideways glance. "I'd like to see you just as happy."

She straightened. "I am happy."

"There's happy, and there's happy," he said cryptically. "If you want to know the difference ask your parents and Daniel."

Dominique leaned back against her seat. She didn't have to ask.

Her parents had spent two years estranged and hating every second of it, and neither she nor her brother had suspected they still loved each other and were miserable apart. Her hard-nosed brother seemed to have everything a man could want, yet she hadn't the slightest doubt his wife had given him a happiness that was clearly his greatest joy.

"Everyone wasn't meant to find that someone special," she told him. "Just look at you."

"I do every morning when I shave, and every night when I pass the mirror on the dresser and climb into an empty bed. There's no one there staring back at me except me. Once it didn't matter," he told her. "Seeing the excitement in Daniel and Madelyn as they get ready for that baby kind of makes me wish I hadn't been so finicky in my younger years. At my age a man sees his immortality and it's scary as hell. I don't want that for you."

"Higgins." She turned in her seat toward him. She couldn't think of anything else to say or do. She had always thought he was happy, his singleness something he had chosen. To think he now regretted the decision and was lonely was unsettling.

A frail hand reached over and patted hers affectionately a couple of times before returning to the steering wheel. "Don't fret. I've a good life, and the good Lord willing I've got some years left. Just promise me you won't look back on your life with a 'should have,' or an 'if only,' like I'm doing now. Live your life, go after your dreams, but remember dreams can't love you back. Promise me."

"Higgi—"

"Promise me."

"You know you're like family to us," she said, meaning every word. He was included in vacations and special events as one of the family, not as an employee.

He nodded his graying head. "I know. Sometimes I've thought of your mother as mine. She and I have been through a lot over the years." He sighed. "But there's a special bond between husband and wife, parent and child, that I can't transcend, that I'll never know. You can't tell me you haven't watched your brother and Madelyn and felt like an intruder."

She couldn't, but that didn't mean everyone would be as lucky. She ought to know. She had tried and failed miserably.

"Promise me," he urged.

"I promise to try."

He almost smiled. "You're as cagey as that brother of yours."

"Thanks for the compliment," she said, feeling more in control. She didn't need a man in her life, not now, not ever. So why did a picture of Trent Masters flash before her?

* * *

Trent couldn't concentrate. He'd tried. But a black-eyed temptress with long, black hair and a voluptuous body kept getting in the way.

Tossing the pen down on the bid he'd been trying to work on for the past two hours, Trent finally gave up. He'd bet dollars to donuts she wasn't thinking about him. She probably had every guy on the plane salivating.

Just as she had that ticket agent drooling. Trent got angry all over again. At himself and the agent.

He had noticed the man's gaze dropping and thought he was eyeing her breasts. It wasn't until after he turned her around to lead her away that he had seen the delicate blue lace as fragile as a spider web flirting with concealing her breasts.

Flirting, because the lace left the top swell deliciously bare. His blood had heated: his anger had risen.

He surged to his feet. He had promised Dominique they would be friends. Friends did not lust after each other.

The wooden chair creaked as he spun it around and plopped back down again. He was going to finish this report. No woman was going to interfere with his business.

The roar of a powerful diesel engine clearly came through the double office window. Trent lifted his head. The huge, black, seventy-foot eighteen wheeler with a two-foot-wide slash of red and yellow down the sides with Masters Trucking imprinted upon it slowly pulled into the complex.

Seeing one of his rigs never ceased to fill him with a sense of pride and accomplishment. There were forty-nine in all, scattered across the United States, Mexico, and Canada.

Pretty good for a man who had started out with a blanket and a note. But he never forgot things might have ended differently if people along the way hadn't helped him. Sure, people had tried to stick it to him—the woman he thought he loved for one—but somehow things had always worked out in his favor.

He had left West Memphis with the clothes on his back, a shattered dream, and a broken heart. On the way his new sports car had burst a water hose.

Randle Hodge, in a fifteen-year-old rig, admittedly stopped to harass the pretty boy in the sports car, but had taken pity on him instead. After jerry-rigging his hose, Randle had followed Trent to the nearest service station. Pulling a card that had seen better years out of his back pocket, he had handed it to Trent and told him to call him if he ever needed help.

Trent had tried to pay him. Randle had looked affronted and told him to just pass on the kindness if the opportunity ever presented itself.

In Dallas, Trent had found the job market slim. Needing money more than he did a fancy car, he had contacted Randle to see if he knew some-place reliable to sell the automobile. Randle had told him to come see him.

Randle hadn't been at home when Trent arrived, but his wife, Helen, had. After feeding him his first home-cooked meal in years, she had asked if he knew anything about bookkeeping. He should, he said—he had majored in finance in college.

Before he knew it Trent was living in the former bedroom of their old-est son and working as a sales rep, accountant, manager, and whatever else was needed for H&H Trucking Company. By the end of six months their profit margin had quadrupled.

On their first Christmas together they handed him a large box. He had hardly been able to contain his emotions when he saw the toy truck with Masters Trucking on the side.

They said Masters sounded better than H&H. Besides, Randle had a greedy brother who would try to hit him up if he knew the company was turning a profit. Their children were all grown and had no interest in the trucking business. So, how about it? With the lump in his throat all Trent had been able to do was nod.

Trent had worked harder than ever. They had gone from one eigh-teen wheeler to two, and eventually to fifteen by the time the Hodges dis-solved their partnership three years later.

Randle and Helen said they wanted to enjoy their money, and let Trent buy them out. He had hated to see them go, but wished them well. He had enjoyed talking over decisions with Randle, but as Randle had pointed out with a gap-toothed smile, all he ever did was listen, anyway.

That was ten years ago. Randle and Helen lived near Big Sur in a huge house that easily accommodated their six children and twenty-three grandchildren when they came to visit. They were a noisy, rowdy group when they got together. Trent was looking forward to spending Christ-mas with them, as he had every year since they first met.

As usual, Helen would ask if he had met a nice woman. Usually he had an answer—not this time. Picking up the pen, he went back to working on the report. It remained to be seen if Dominique was nice or not. The only thing he was sure of was that she played hell with his concentration.

Dominique was waiting at the bottom of the spiral staircase for Daniel and Madelyn when they stepped into the spacious foyer of their home. As usual she was struck by what a magnificent couple they made. Daniel, handsome as sin, in a charcoal gray, tailored suit that fit his muscular build flawlessly; Madelyn, her skin glowing and classically beautiful in a stylish, lavender maternity dress with a white collar.

Hand in hand, they smiled at each other with an expression that could only be characterized as pure bliss. Dominique's fingers closed on nothing. Her camera was in her bedroom. She sighed over the loss.

One thing was certain. Higgins had been right about that, at least. They did make her feel as if she were intruding on something uniquely private and profoundly special.

Daniel saw her first, his smile broadening. "Hi, Sis."

"Hello, Dominique," Madelyn said, moving closer to Daniel as he released her hand only to curve his arm around her thickening waist.

"Hello." Dominique came to her feet. "Daniel, if you have a moment there's something important I need to talk to you about."

"What's the matter?" he queried, a frown marring his handsome face.

Madelyn saw the serious expression on Dominique's face and eased away from her husband's loose embrace. "I'll go upstairs and change."

"That's not necessary, Madelyn," Dominique said. "I'd like you to stay."

Daniel sent his sister a pleased smile and pulled Madelyn back into his arms. She came easily, her head resting against his wide chest as if it instinctively knew it belonged there.

"Perhaps we should go into the study," Dominique suggested. "Madelyn, you've been at work all day."

Daniel's frowned deepened. "Maybe you should go upstairs and lie down."

"I'm fine." Madelyn patted her protruding abdomen. "Better if your son hadn't played kick all day."

He kissed her on the cheek. "I'll have a talk with him tonight."

Madelyn tucked her head and Dominique knew her brother was being playful and naughty—two things she had never known him to be with any of his women friends in the past. Turning, she went into Daniel's study, then closed the sliding doors behind them.

As soon as Daniel and Madelyn were seated on a small sofa, Dominique repeated her conversation with Higgins on the way from the airport and ended by saying, "I think he's feeling lonely and a bit left out."

"I distinctly remember him telling me he was too set in his ways for a woman," Daniel told her.

"That may be, but seeing your happiness and Mother and Daddy's has given him second thoughts. Especially when he goes home alone," Dominique explained.

Madelyn bit her lower lip. "I think Cleve sometimes felt the same way before Matt made him foreman of the ranch after Matt married Shannon. Just taking care of things around the ranchhouse and stables wasn't enough for his still agile mind, and somehow I think it made him think he was taking charity."

Distracted, Dominique ran a hand through her long, black hair. "I think Higgins feels the same way. A part of the family and yet separate."

"Well, it looks like we have to straighten him out." Daniel stood and dialed Higgins number. "Can you please come to the study? Yes, now."

"Daniel, what are you going to do?" Dominique asked.

"You'll find out," he said.

In a few minutes, Higgins knocked on the door. Receiving permission, he entered. His gaze leaped from one person to the next. "You wanted to see me, Daniel?"

"Yes. I need your help."

Higgins expression cleared. "You know I'll do anything I can."

"I knew I could count on you. When the contractors start renovating the room next to ours for the nursery, and I'd like you to take charge to make sure things are done right," Daniel explained.

"I thought you wanted to take care of that personally," Higgins said.

Dominique's gaze went to her brother. So did everyone else. Daniel had interviewed representatives from five top architectural firms before making a final decision about which one to hire. No one doubted the newest little Falcon would be lavished with love and have the swankiest nursery possible.

Daniel looked straight into Higgins's eyes. "I could use some help."

"Please, Higgins. Maybe you can help Daniel remember moderation is good in all things," Madelyn suggested.

"I took out the sky dome, didn't I?" Daniel said matter-of-factly.

"Yes, and I love you for it." Madelyn turned to the elderly man. "You see. I need some help on this. That is, if you don't think it will be too much trouble?"

"No. Not at all," Higgins hastened to reassure her.

"You might as well move into the house. I want you nearby. That way we can discuss how things are going when I get home." Daniel hugged Madelyn. "Then, too, if Madelyn needs something and I'm not here, you'll be closer."

"All right." Higgins appeared dazed.

"You think you can move in tonight?" Daniel continued. "They start in the morning, and Dominique will be too busy packing for her return to Dallas to keep an eye on things. I know this is sudden notice, but I really need you."

"That doesn't matter, Daniel."

Daniel grinned. "Good. I can go help, and then we can eat dinner."

Higgins took a few steps toward the door, then stopped and looked Daniel straight in the eye. "I know what you're trying to do."

"And I could kick myself that I haven't done it before. I'm ashamed to say I took you for granted, but that didn't mean I valued you less," Daniel told the older man.

"I don't want busy work," he said, his carriage proud.

Daniel pinned him with a look. "You know how much I love my wife and our child she's carrying. Does entrusting their welfare to anyone else sound like busy work?"

"No."

"Glad that's settled. I'll help you move."

Higgins gave Dominique a long level look, then threw his shoulders back. "I can move myself."

He was at the door when Daniel called, "You can have Dad's old room. Dinner in twenty minutes."

The door closed softly behind him, but his shoulders were erect.

Dominique had never been prouder of Daniel. "I'm glad to call you brother."

He shook his head. Thick, lustrous hair moved. "I only hate I didn't see it myself."

"Don't blame yourself." Dominique folded her arms. "I'd say you had a few other things on your mind. Were you really going to build a sky dome in the baby's room?"

"No, but it's a thou—"

"Don't you dare even think of changing anything," Madelyn chided, cutting Daniel off. "Poor Mr. Lawrence is about to pull out the few strands of hair he has left now."

Daniel's hands circled her rounded stomach from behind. His teeth nipped her playfully on the ear. "If Dominique doesn't mind telling Mrs. Hargrove there will be one more for dinner, I might let you persuade me."

"Daniel," Madelyn admonished, but she was smiling.

Dominique laughed and started from the room. "You might as well give up, Madelyn. He's a rogue and he enjoys making you blush."

"I know," Came Madelyn's reply. "One day I'm going to turn the tables."

That would be impossible, thought Dominique as she opened the door. Then she glanced over her shoulder to see her brother, a man known to make grown men quake, press his cheek tenderly against his wife's.

Then again, maybe not. Dominique hadn't thought Daniel would ever marry, let alone fall so deeply and irrevocably in love. Love changed people. Her face harshened. Sometimes it also made fools of them.

No matter what, she was not going to let herself ever be that vulnerable. Closing the door softly, she headed for the kitchen. She never made it.

"Surprise!"

She whirled around to see her parents and her grandparents on both sides grinning at her. Before she could do more than gape, they had all converged on her. By the time she had gotten the last hug, Daniel and Madelyn were also there.

"You could have said soemthing," she told them.

Daniel held up his hands. "Mother swore me to secrecy."

"We just wanted you to know we're behind you and wish you well," her mother said, looking elegant as usual in a cranberry colored, silk Dior pants outfit. "Here."

Dominique took the box and opened it. Inside was a heavy gold card holder for her desk and a monogrammed gold case which held a single vellum business card with Photographs by Dominique slanted at an angle in elegant script.

"As soon as you get your phone and the e-mail address Daniel says you have to have, you'll have a neverending supply," her father proudly told her.

"We thought it best if we had ours delivered," Daniel told her. "It's a complete computer set-up with your web site."

By the time her maternal grandparents had given her a beautiful leather portfolio with her single initial, and her paternal grandparents a Mont Blanc pen set and gold-leafed appointment book, her eyes were misty. "Thank you."

"You haven't received mine yet." Higgins handed her a gold bag from an exclusive gift shop.

Inside was a heavy lucite piece inscribed: "Follow your dream, but never forget your heart."

"Higgins, I didn't know you were such a romantic," said her maternal grandmother.

"A man must have some secrets," he said.

"One of them is how to get out of the sand trap," her maternal grandfather said. "How about coming back with us to Palm Springs for a little vacation? We could pair up and trounce Murphy and Thomas."

"I was hoping he'd come back with *me.*" Felicia took Higgins by the arm.

"Then you come over and we could finish our game of horseshoes," suggested John Henry's father.

"And stay for some of my famous pan bread," added John Henry's mother.

"Sorry, you'll all have to wait," Higgins told them. "I've got to make sure the nursery is built right. Felicia, you have John Henry. And before you leave tomorrow, Edgar, I'll show you a sand trap secret or two. Mary and Leon, I'll be happy to visit when I've taken care of things here. Now, we should probably go in to dinner. Madelyn has been on her feet a long time." Reaching for the smiling young woman, Higgins led her slowly to the dining room.

Daniel shook his head, but he had a smile on his face. "I think I've created a monster."

"But you've made him happy," Felicia said warmly.

Dominique looked between her mother and brother. "You knew!"

"Suspected," Daniel confided. "You were the only one he shared his feelings with."

"Because he was worried about me," Dominique confessed. "But not everyone needs a significant other to be happy."

"Maybe not everyone, but I think Higgins is right. You weren't meant to live alone. One day some man is going to break through that wall you've built."

"I don't need a man."

"I didn't need a woman, but I can't imagine living my life without Madelyn," Daniel said with feeling. "Come on, let's go have dinner. I don't want to spoil tonight for you."

"You haven't. I know what I want out of life, and a man is not it."

CHAPTER 4

Camera in hand, Dominique bounded up the stairs to get another roll of film from her room. It was almost ten that evening, yet no one seemed inclined to call it a night. Daniel had tried. He had asked Madelyn if she was tired so many times that when he had done so again shortly before Dominique went upstairs, everyone in the room had answered in unison for her—"No."

With his usual self-assurance, Daniel had smiled and leaned back on the couch beside Madelyn. His arm around her shoulder, his fingers playing in her hair, he'd said, "Just checking."

Shaking her head at the memory, Dominique decided to call Janice as promised. There was no telling what time she'd finally come back upstairs. Sitting on the side of the bed she picked up the gold and white phone.

After the sixth ring, Dominique was concerned. After the tenth, she really began to worry. Janice hadn't mentioned going out. Absently, Dominique tapped the roll of film on her crossed knee. Where could Janice be?

She was about to hang up after the twelfth ring and redial when an out of breath male answered. "Hello."

Her grip on the receiver tightened. She'd recognize that deep molasses voice anywhere. And if her mind didn't, her body would.

"Hello," Trent repeated impatiently. "Look, whoever this is I'm standing here dripping wet from the shower, and I'm not in the mood to play games."

"What?" Dominique shouted, uncrossing her legs and jerking erect.

"Dominique?" Trent asked. "Dominique, is that you?"

"I wish to speak to Janice," she answered crisply.

"I hope you're not thinking what it sounds like you're thinking," he said, his voice taking on a stinging tone.

"Don't flatter yourself. Janice has better taste," she shot back, and meant every word. She didn't know the reason for his taking a shower in Janice's home, but she knew it was innocent. Janice didn't sneak around, nor was she two-faced.

Laughter flowed through the line. "You sure know how to keep a guy humble."

She hadn't expected the laughter or the strange flurry it created in her stomach. Restlessly she shifted on the handwoven bedspread. "I thought you said you weren't there very much."

"I'm not," came the reply. "I haven't been home ten minutes."

She frowned her confusion. "Home? I dialed Janice's number. I couldn't have misdialed. I don't even know your number."

"Janice had her calls forwarded over here. She had to meet an out of town client at her store," he explained.

Dominique cast the ornate clock on the bedside table a worried glance. "It's ten o'clock."

"The Nelson's could only make it tonight. They're good customers from Denton and she's met them at night before. Both teach at Texas Woman's University and can't make it until late."

"I still don't like it," Dominique said. She knew how defenseless a woman could be.

"Don't worry. The street her antique shop is on is filled with shops and restaurants, and well lit. Besides, the Nelsons always arrive first and always follow Janice to the freeway," Trent told her. "She has her cell phone, and if I hadn't thought it would be safe I would have gone with her."

Another thought struck Dominique. "If she had her cell phone, why didn't she just have her calls forwarded to it?"

"Because she gets so involved in phone conversations she doesn't watch where she's going." Dominique could hear the exasperation in his tone. "After two fender benders, the insurance company and I convinced her the phone should be used for emergency purposes only."

Dominique pulled her legs under her Indian style. "You do watch over her."

"I try."

"Thank you."

He chuckled, a deep sound that made her entire body tingle. She moistened her dry lips and wished he'd stop doing that. "Twice in one day. Something tells me I might be looking at some kind of record," he said, a note of amusement rolling through his voice.

She couldn't help the smile that formed on her face. "You might, at that."

"When are you coming back?" he asked, then added, "Janice told me to ask you."

"Thursday."

"Flying?"

"Driving."

"Start out early," he advised. "They're doing a lot of construction and the traffic getting in and out of Houston can be maddening. My truckers complain about it all the time."

"My brother, my father, and Higgins and I have already had this talk."

"Who's Higgins?"

"An old friend of the family," she answered, telling herself she wasn't pleased that he sounded jealous.

"How old is old?"

Dominique laughed. It just slipped out. He sounded so annoyed. "Seventy-two."

"You have a nice laugh."

Smiling, she slipped off her heels, scooted up against the headboard padded in silk brocade, then crossed her long legs. "So do you."

"Does most of your family live in Houston?" he asked.

"Just my brother. My father and his parents live in Oklahoma, my mother's parents in Boston," she explained, thinking of how they had all dropped everything to be with her tonight.

"You're lucky."

"Extremely. What about your family?"

"It's just me. I never knew my parents. I grew up in foster homes."

"Oh. I'm sorry." She felt an odd clutch in the region of her heart that he had had to grow up without the love and support of a family. She couldn't imagine where she would be without hers.

"Don't be. I've met a lot of good people through the years, and made some lifetime friends."

"Janice is one of them. She mentioned how successful you are. What you've accomplished is remarkable," Dominique returned, true admiration in her voice. She hoped she could do half as well.

"A lot of good people helped me along the way," he told her. "I don't want you to think I did it all on my own."

"Still, it must have been difficult."

"Sometimes, but I learned early that life wasn't going to give me anything. I've worked long and hard for what I have, and never regretted a moment of it," he said with feeling. "You can succeed just like I did."

"I'm going to give it my best shot," she said, her confidence soaring.

"Good. Hey, can you believe we've been talking for five minutes and neither one of us has gotten angry?"

"Maybe it's because we can't see each other," she said, and immediately a picture of him staring at her lips at the airport filled her mind. She got that restless feeling again.

"Maybe," he said, his voice oddly husky as if he were thinking of the same thing, "I'd better go. I'm getting goose bumps on my goose bumps."

She flushed and sat up in bed to swing her legs to the carpeted floor. "I'm sorry. I should have ended the call earlier."

"Don't be. If I hadn't wanted to talk to you, I would have ended the call myself."

"You're very frank."

"I've been told that, but then lies and secrets can destroy a person's life. I can't see a reason to lie."

While Dominique agreed with him in principal, she was harboring secrets of her own. "Sometimes extenuating circumstances demand bending the truth a little."

"Lying is lying no matter how you dress it up," came the emphatic answer. Trent obviously didn't even believe in little white lies.

"I suppose."

"Glad you agree. I wouldn't want our friendship to suffer because we couldn't trust each other."

"You think we can be friends face-to-face?"

"The best. Goodnight, Dominique. I'll tell Janice you called."

"Goodnight." Dominique slowly hung up, fine tremors rippling through her, and it wasn't the prospect of opening her studio that caused the reaction.

"Trent Masters, you could be a real problem," she said. Silence was her only, unsettling answer.

In Dallas, Trent began whistling as he finished drying on the way to the bathroom. He wasn't aware that a broad smile accompanied the whistle until he passed the tri-fold mirror in his bedroom. He stopped, his gaze fastened on his reflection as if he was seeing it for the first time.

He didn't like what he saw.

"Oh, no you don't. Don't you even try to go there. Dominique and I are going to be friends. Nothing else." The second the last words left his mouth, he knew he was fooling himself.

Naked shoulders slumped. He had never lied to himself in the past, and he wasn't about to start. Dominique got to him on every level, and not just the obvious ones of her face and body. Her haughtiness challenged, her throaty voice intrigued.

What really got to him was that she needed a second chance—the one thing he believed every person deserved. How was a guy supposed to resist?

She was like no woman he had ever known. And she was making him do things he had never done before. Not once in his life had he ever been jealous about a woman . . . until Dominique.

He had known her barely a day and he was ready to defend her honor and keep her safe. He could discount the airline clerk, but he couldn't discount that he had been jealous when Dominique mentioned the guy named Higgins.

He could still hear her sweet laughter, part teasing and part surprise. His body had hardened instantly. If she had been there, he would have pulled her into his arms and tasted the laughter on her lips, then the passion and need.

Trent spun away from the mirror. Jerking open a dresser drawer, he yanked out a pair of white cotton briefs and pulled them on. He then reached for a fresh pair of jeans. They were at a strategic point and going no further without discomfort when he glanced down.

His head lolled back and he stared up at the ceiling. *Why me, Lord?*

Dominique Everette could turn out to be a real problem and a test of everything he believed in.

Trent gave Janice five minutes to deactivate her alarm, grab a diet drink, and make it to her bedroom before he punched in her number. She answered on the second ring.

"Hello."

"Hi, Janice. Dominique called around ten. She's driving back Thursday."

"Thanks for taking the call," Janice said. "I thought you were coming for some strawberry shortcake."

Trent refused to glance down. "I'm not hungry."

"Could you repeat that?"

He knew Dominique could be trouble. Never in the past had he had to think before he spoke. "I had something before I left work."

"Since when has that changed anything?" she asked.

He rubbed his throbbing temple. "Sometimes things happen when you least expect them."

"Trent, you know I'm very fond of you, but you're not making very much sense. You sound distracted. You and Dominique didn't have words, did you?"

"No. We're going to be friends."

"You don't sound too happy about it."

"I just have something on my mind tonight. Did the Nelsons buy anything?" he asked, grasping for a way to change the conversation.

"The Queen Anne secretary for Mrs. Nelson's office."

"Good. I'd better get some sleep," he said.

"It's only ten-thirty. Are you feeling all right?"

"I'm fine."

"Well, goodnight, and thanks again. I'll call her in the morning."

"Goodnight." Trent hung up and headed for the shower. Exercise sure hadn't helped.

Dominique's brow arched on seeing Daniel waiting for her in the dining room the next morning. A perfect, deep red rosebud lay on the pristine, white linen tablecloth by his coffee cup. She only needed one guess to know who the fresly picked flower was for. "Good morning."

"Good morning." Standing, he pulled out a chair for her, then retook his seat next to hers. "You seem surprised to see me."

She picked up her napkin and spread it on her lap. "As I said yesterday you have a lot on your mind, and I'm two years older since we had our last big brother little sister conversation before I left for Paris."

His large hand brushed back a strand of heavy, black hair from her face. "No amount of years will ever make me stop worrying about you."

"You and life taught me to take care of myself, remember?" she said, spearing a cube of honeydew in her fruit cup.

"I remember a lot of things," he said softly. "The trouble is, so do you."

She couldn't deny his words. Her hand stilled, but thank goodness it didn't tremble when she turned to him. "I won't be made a fool of again," she told him, her eyes and voice as cold as ice.

"You're so much like I used to be it scares me." He held up his hand when she opened her mouth to speak. "I was so busy judging Madelyn on the basis of all the other lying, scheming women I had met, I didn't see her for the honest woman she is until it was almost too late. Be careful you don't do the same thing and let the past ruin your chance for happiness."

Despite her best effort an image of Trent crystalized in her mind. In rising irritation she firmly pushed the image away. "I'm happy for you and Madelyn, but a man in my life is the last thing I need."

He shook his head, his salt-and-pepper hair sliding over his broad shoulders. "As I said, you're just like me."

"Excuse me, Mr. Falcon, Mrs. Falcon's tray is ready," said a slim, young maid in a black and white uniform.

"Thank you." Standing, Daniel placed the rose on the tray, then took it from the servant.

"You'd better get that up to Madelyn," Dominique said, smiling that her guess had been right.

"Trying to get rid of me?" he asked, but he was smiling.

"No, but it's a thought. I like Madelyn," she said, leaning back in her chair. "She was all set to send her brother, Kane, and his family into the studio until I told her I wanted to keep a low profile."

"She's really big on family."

"Sounds just like the man she married. I've never seen you this happy."

"I didn't know I could be." His black eyes probed hers. "Don't let what happened eight years ago steal *your* chance for happiness."

Before she could speak he whirled and walked out of the room. *Just like Daniel to want the last word,* she thought. She watched him head toward the stairs, then she dug back into her fruit. Why was everyone so eager for her to have a man?

The answer came almost instantly. They loved her and wanted her to be happy. To them that meant a man in her life.

Before her disastrous marriage she had agreed with them. Now she knew better. The only thing that was going to make her happy was a successful photographic studio. Her mind firmly made up, she speared another cube of melon.

Finished with breakfast twenty minutes later, Dominique was rushing out the door when the maid informed her she had a telephone call from Janice Yates. Sprinting back, she picked up the phone in the living room. "Hi, Janice."

Janice didn't waste any time. She wanted to know every single detail about the surprise party. Dominique delighted in telling her. Teasingly, Janice told Dominique she had a present for her, but she had to wait until she came back to Dallas. Since Dominique loved surprises but hated to wait, she tried every way she knew to get the information out of her godmother. No luck.

"Stop fishing. My lips are sealed," Janice said, laughing, then sobered. "Trent phoned me last night to tell me you had called. He had sounded distracted, and he wasn't hungry."

Dominique barely kept from rolling her eyes. "Janice, Trent is a big boy and can take care of himself."

"I know, but he just didn't seem himself. Did you two have an argument or something?" Janice inquired.

"No we didn't. We were quite civil and mature." She glanced at her watch. "Gotta run. I have an appointment. See you tomorrow around eleven. Love you. Bye." Hanging up, Dominique shoved the thick strap of her oversized bag over her shoulder and headed for the front door.

Outside, she started down the curved stone steps just as the architect, Robert Lawrence, drove up. The short, compact man emerged from his metallic green Jeep carrying several cylindrical tubes beneath his jacketed arm, his movements slow and methodical.

When he saw her, his round face resigned, he tried to smile as he greeted her, but the results looked more like a grimace. He started up the steps.

Dominique said hello and got into her Jaguar convertible. She thought of telling the harassed looking man that Daniel had turned the project over to someone else, then decided to let him find out the good news for himself. Because no matter what Daniel said, he wanted nothing less than perfection for his first child.

Driving past the recessed double doors, she saw the architect being greeted by Daniel, Madelyn, and Higgins. Daniel had stayed to introduce Higgins. Madelyn had stayed to make sure Daniel didn't institute any last minute changes. Her grandparents remained in their rooms. Good thinking on their parts. The next five weeks were going to be very interesting in the Falcon household.

Her life in Dallas would be just as interesting. Downshifting, she pressed on the gas and zipped through the high, black, iron security gates of the estate. The red sports car gave her all the power and maneuverability she wanted. Although the vehicle was eleven-years-old, it had been meticulously cared for.

She hit the freeway with a burst of speed and merged with the traffic. Moments later an eighteen wheeler pulled beside her and tooted its horn. Her heart lurched. She glanced around sharply.

A bearded man wearing a once beige, straw cowboy hat grinned down at her. She waved and willed her heart to calm down. She was not disappointed, she told herself, but that day she spent an unprecedented amount of time glancing at the drivers of eighteen wheelers.

She also spent the day doing something else she had never had to do before—comparative price shopping. The owner of the third photographic equipment shop introduced her to price matching, turned his office over to her, and gave her a phone book, a pad and pencil, and a soft drink.

By early afternoon the trunk and backseat of her car were almost filled to capacity. She had purchased cameras, lenses, power packs, umbrella, soft boxes, stands, backgrounds, and the cases to store them. She couldn't remember ever having as much fun.

Pulling up in the circular driveway at Daniel's house, she got out of the car and went inside. Since she was leaving early the next morning there was no need to unpack the car. Heading for the stairs, her smile broadened. Her equipment took up so much room, she was going to have to take a small suitcase and ship the rest of her things.

"Miss Falcon, I'm glad you're here," said Mr. Lawrence, looking even more unhappy than he had that moring.

Her brow furrowed. "Is Daniel still here?"

"I wish he were. It's Higgins."

Her eyes widened in surprise. "Higgins?"

"Yes, Ma'am. Mr. Falcon said to follow his instructions, but I can't believe he wants to do something like this."

"Not the sky dome?" she asked, trying to keep a smile off her face.

The man's eyes widened for a fraction of a second, then shut.

"It was only a thought my brother had. Are my grandparents here?"

His eyes opened. Dominique couldn't figure out if he looked desperate or resigned. "No, they left shortly after I arrived and haven't returned."

Dominique's lips twitched. She'd always known the grands were intelligent people. "I'll go explain to Higgins."

The harassed man's appreciative gaze found hers. "Thank you. He's in the bedroom we're remodeling, watching every move my guys make."

"Higgins takes his responsibilities very seriously. My family has always relied heavily on him." She started up the stairs and the architect fell into step beside her.

"I heard you were leaving tomorrow with your grandparents. I don't suppose your trip can be postponed?" he asked hopefully.

"Sorry, I waited a lifetime for this. You're on your own."

His shoulders slumped. "I knew I should have been a dentist, the way my mother wanted me to be."

Dominique laughed, thinking she couldn't wait to call Daniel. He had never spoken truer words than when he said he had created a monster. Mr. Lawrence might not be happy, but Higgins would know he was loved and needed, and he wouldn't be lonely any more.

Out of nowhere came the questioning thought *When will I know the same thing?*

Dominique arrived at Janice's house shortly after noon, Thursday. Climbing from the low slung car, she stretched her hands over her head, then went around to the passenger side and got the one suitcase she'd managed to bring.

Janice, in a black gabardine coatdress with white collar and cuffs, met her at the kitchen door with a warm greeting and a hug. "You're an hour late."

"Traffic," she said succinctly, and set the small Louis Vuitton pullman down. "I have to be at the studio at twelve-thirty to let the telephone man in and receive some equipment I had to have shipped."

"What about lunch?" Janice asked.

"I'll grab a bite later," she said, and started back out the door.

"Here. Your present." Janice handed her a gold ring with three keys and the initial D. "The small one is for the glass storm door. The other two are for the double locks on the front and back doors."

Dominique clutched the keys in her hands. One more symbol that her dream was becoming a reality. "Thanks for this, and everything."

"You know you're more than welcome. As I told you, I'm going to enjoy having you here."

"I'm looking forward to living here, too." Dominique reached for the door. "I'm not sure when I'll be home."

"It had better be before dark," Janice said with a tinge of worry. "As I said, the area is in transition. It has a lot of traffic in the daytime, but things close up at night."

"Yes, Godmother."

Janice smiled. "Get on out of here. I have to get to the shop myself."

Smiling, Dominique hurried back outside and drove away. If she stared at Trent's house as she passed it was no one's concern but her own.

Everyone was late, and calling on her cell phone elicited little information. Worse, the electricity had not been turned on as promised, so there was no air-conditioning. She had long since plaited her hair, tied the pink silk top in a knot beneath her breasts and rolled up another two cuffs in her khaki walking shorts.

By five that afternoon she was hot, thirsty, and tired, and her temper was on a very fragile leash. Hearing the buzzer for admittance, she hit the control in her hand. Trent strolled in, looking cool and sinfully handsome in oatmeal linen slacks and a tan shirt, the long sleeves were rolled back to reveal the fine sprinkling of black hair on his arms.

Puzzlement drew her brows together. "What are you doing here?"

"Hello to you, too."

Irritated, she shoved a hand over her hair. "Sorry. This day has not been one of my best."

"Janice called and said you were still waiting on some service people and asked me to check on you," he explained. "My trucking company is a couple of miles from here."

"Thanks. I can't believe it's taken this long," she said, trying to keep her eyes from the white sack in his hand and not salivate at the smell of food coming from it.

"There's a tie-up on Hawn Freeway going in both directions, and one on Central Expressway as well," he explained, the sack still firmly in his hand.

"I hate to be gauche, but are you planning to share whatever's in that sack that smells so delicious?"

"Here," he said, handing her the bag and wondering if there might ever be a time when seeing her didn't hit him like a hard punch.

"Thanks," she said, hurriedly opening the bag. The aroma of fresh baked bread and spices wafted up to her.

Using one of her camera cases as a makeshift table, she placed the sack on top to use as a tablecloth and unwrapped her hot roast beef sandwich. Her mouth open, she glanced up to see Trent watching her intently. Her stomach did a predictable flip-flop.

She swallowed, then asked, "Do you want a bite?"

Yes, he thought *but not of the sandwich.* Gracefully, he came down on the other side of the case. "I've eaten."

She bit into the sandwich. The bread was soft; the beef juicy and delicious. She was aware of Trent watching her eat, but she was too hungry to bother worrying about it. Finished, she sat back and sipped on her drink.

"Missed breakfast, huh?" Trent said, his gaze running lightly over her mouth. The way she sometimes flicked her tongue out was driving him absolutely crazy.

"And lunch." She took another sip of her drink. The sweetened iced tea didn't help her dry throat. She wished he'd stop staring at her mouth. "I really appreciate your taking off work."

"I was closer than Janice," he explained easily.

For some reason his answer irritated her. "Thanks, anyway," she said, getting to her feet.

"You're welcome." He rose with her and walked farther into the interior of the studio. "Your studio has a lot of glass."

"That's what makes the place so great. It's like working outside."

He glanced over his shoulders. "I would have thought you were more the indoor type."

Her hand clutched the sack. "Somehow I think you mean the useless type."

"And what do you like to do outside?" he asked, ignoring her dig.

"Take long walks. Jog. Ride."

His gaze swept back over her before lifting to her face. "You certainly have the legs for it."

A spear of heat lanced through her. The door buzzer saved her from answering. She whirled away and went to pick up the automatic opener on her desk.

"Don't you think you should check before letting them in?" he asked.

She wanted to tell him to mind his own business, but anger was no reason to act irrational. She went to the door. "Yes."

"Telephone company."

She buzzed a tall, black man inside. After giving him instructions she turned to Trent. "Thank you for coming, and for the food."

"Trying to get rid of me?" he asked.

"Yes."

"Not a chance, Buttercup." Folding his arms over his wide chest, he leaned against the white beam separating the glass in front of the studio.

She was so startled by the nickname that she didn't say anything for a moment. "I beg your pardon?"

"Janice would skin me alive if I left you by yourself."

Janice again. "I'm a big girl."

His gaze intensified. "That's the problem."

Once again she felt the heat, this time more intensely.

"What kind of pictures do you plan to take?"

"Portraits mostly," she answered, her voice not quite steady.

"How long have you been in the business?"

"Not very long," she answered, unable to keep the worry out of her voice. Perhaps she should have given herself three years.

"Dallas has a healthy economy. You should do well." He unfolded his arms. "I might even break down and have you do a photograph of me, although I don't know who might want it."

"The usual recipients are friends, family, lovers," she said, knowing she was delicately probing.

He inclined his head toward the front. "An office supply truck just pulled up."

"Oh." Dominique went to answer the door, wishing the two men had waited a few minutes longer, then began chastising herself. She didn't want to know anything about Trent's personal life.

After that everyone seemed to come at once. She didn't have time to talk to Trent, but he was always there, a silent, disturbing, almost brooding presence. The workers obviously felt it, too, because they kept glancing in his direction.

It was after eight when she locked the front door. Darkness had descended. Janice was right. The area had a creepy, deserted quality at night.

A silent Trent walked her to her car parked parallel to the studio. He regarded the shiny, red Jaguar with a frown, then swung his gaze to her. "I thought you were just starting out."

She glanced from her car to the hard glint in Trent's eyes. "It's eleven years old, and the only car I've ever owned."

He didn't say it but the question was there in his expressive face, the narrow line of his mouth. How had she earned that kind of money?

"I paid for it myself with money I earned as a model in Europe, just out of high school," she told him, each word tightly controlled with simmering anger. She started to turn away, but his hand on her bare arm stopped her.

Intense heat radiated from his fingertips. He released her instantly, his hand balling into a fist. "You don't owe me an explanation."

"I wasn't giving you one. I was just stating a fact." This time she opened her door and got in. Tires spun as she sped away from the curb.

The hard blast of a horn from directly behind her had her gripping the steering wheel, but she slowed down, annoyed with herself that his opinion of her mattered, irritated that she had reacted so foolishly.

Trent meant nothing to her, she thought, totally ignoring the little voice that asked, *Then why am I so hurt?*

CHAPTER 5

Tires squealed. Trent was out of his truck and striding toward Dominique before her car engine died. His face hard, he jerked open her car door and glared down at her. "What the hell is the matter with you, driving like that?"

Calmly, Dominique picked up her purse from the seat and got out of the car. She angled her head back to meet his irate gaze. "I slowed down."

"Since when is seventy slowing down?" he snapped, wanting to shake her for being so reckless and scaring him half to death, disgusted with himself for making her angry in the first place. He had stepped way over the line. Somehow, though, instead of his apologizing as he knew he should, he let his temper get the best of him.

Midnight-black eyes gave him glare for glare. "I was going sixty-five."

"Yeah, and zipping in and out of traffic like a jumping jack."

"You're exaggerating. I drive fast, but I'm competent." She pinned him with a look. "Since you arrived when I did, you must have been driving the same way."

He refused to back down. "How else was I going to keep up with you?"

Up went her delicate chin. "No one asked you to keep up with me. I told you, I'm a big gi—" She stopped abruptly.

His searing gaze lowered to her heaving breasts in the bright pink blouse. His hands clenched. He wanted to test their weight and resilience in his hand. Among other things.

A car passed. His gaze snapped up. Wide-eyed, she stared back at him.

He didn't blame her. His anger was displaced. He was totally out of line.

For the second time that night he had taken his anger out on her. "I know you won't believe me, but I'm usually a nice guy."

A satiny brow arched on her beautiful face. The wind tossed wisps of her black hair playfully. It was all he could do not to reach out, take it down, and run his hand through its thick, glossy length. "You've said that before," she reminded him.

"I know, and believe me I've never had to repeat myself in the past." He hesitated, trying to find a way out of his dilemma without compromising his principle about never lying, without admitting to his unreasonable jealously of the men watching her that had sparked his poor behavior. "You want to go get some ice cream?"

"No, thank you."

He hadn't thought it would be that easy. "Janice likes lemon custard. I'm sure if we went, she'd want some."

For a long time, Dominique studied his earnest expression. No one in her family was shy about speaking their mind, so his outburst hadn't bothered her. Considering what she had gone through eight years ago, her reaction surprised her. She hadn't cowered; she had faced him unflinchingly. It was as if on some basic level she instinctively trusted him not to harm her physically.

Another surprise. Rule Number Two: Give no man your trust until he's earned it several times over. Rule Number Three was also on shaky ground: Trust your first instinct.

"If that was an apology it's the sorriest one I've ever heard."

He tugged on the brim of his Negro League baseball cap. "Probably because I'm out of practice."

Up went that brow again.

"*Now* who's jumping to conclusions?" he asked. "The reason I'm out of practice is that I try hard not to put myself in the position of offering them."

The porch light clicked on. Janice stepped outside, her hand still holding the glass storm door. "Hello, you two. Dominique, I'm glad you're home. Everything get finished?"

Dominique turned. "Hello, Janice. Yes, thank you."

"Hi, Janice," Trent called. "I was trying to talk Dominique into going and getting some ice cream. You want your favorite?"

Janice's hand went to her slim hip in teal blue, wide-leg pants. "I probably shouldn't, but I can't resist. Go on, Dominique. You've had a trying day."

"I don't want it to become more trying," she muttered to herself.

"It won't."

She spun toward him. His hearing must be as acute as hers and her father's.

Trent met her inquiring gaze with that intense way he had of looking at her that left her restless and wanting something she didn't dare let herself think about. He was not a restful man to be around. "I don—"

"Please."

In her experience, a lot of men asked for a second chance, they even said *please,* but none made her stomach do flip-flops while doing so. At any other time, it would have been a clear signal to stay as far away from the man as possible.

With Trent living next door that wasn't going to be an option. Since she hadn't had these feeling in nine years, and never this strong, the best thing she could come up with was to stand her ground and hope familiarity bred disinterest.

"All right."

"Great." He grinned like a kid who had been granted a favorite treat. Taking her by the arm he led her back to his truck. "We'll be back in a little bit, Janice."

"Take your time. I have some paperwork to do," she said, then went inside.

Dominique climbed into the cab of the truck, wondering what she had gotten herself into. The door closed, and with it came the feeling of intimacy she'd experienced the first time she was with him in his truck.

The engine came on and she buckled her seat belt, wishing she could harness her erratic emotions as easily.

"Thank you for coming," he said, pulling off.

"Janice wanted some ice cream."

"I would have brought it back to her."

She turned toward him. "I know. Despite what's going on between us, you and Janice are genuinely fond of each other."

He stopped at a signal light. His gaze, searing and hot, found hers again. "What is going on between us?"

Her uneasiness on the topic clearly showed in her voice, "Perhaps you should answer that. You're the one who became angry this afternoon and tonight for no reason."

The light flashed to green. He pulled away. If he told her he was jealous of the men this afternoon, he'd be in more trouble than he was now.

"Well," she prompted.

"Those men annoyed me the way they were looking at you," he admitted, hoping he didn't have to be more specific.

"*Me?* They could hardly work for watching you," she told him. "You were like a dark, avenging angel waiting to dispense judgment and punishment on any person who displeased you."

Flicking on his signal light, he pulled into the parking lot of the ice cream shop, searching for a space. He had never been very good at hiding his thoughts. "It couldn't have been that bad."

"The phone company said the rewiring would take no longer than an hour. It took three. The cleaning crew promised to be out in two hours. They brought extra help because they were late, and it still took that long. Th—"

"You win," he said, holding up his hand as he parked. "You made your point."

"Good." Opening the door, she got out.

He met her at the front of the truck. His hand lightly touched her shoulder. "Wait." His hand fell to his side when she did as requested.

"You'll never know how sorry I am about what happened, especially the incident outside by your car. I have no excuse for such bad behavior." He stuck out his hand. "But if you can see your way clear to forgiving me and starting over again, I promise never to jump to conclusions again, and you'll never be sorry."

Dominique looked from Trent's steady hand to the steadfast gaze. His unspoken accusations had touched a hidden memory that had hurled her back into the past. She didn't like the journey, nor how vulnerable it had made her feel.

"Be very sure, Trent. You were right. I'm not much on giving second chances."

Neither his hand nor his gaze wavered. "I'm sure. We'll seal the promise with a double dip of chocolate pecan."

"Make it French vanilla and you have a deal." She lifted her hand.

"Deal." His callused hand closed securely around hers.

The line moved with quick efficiency. Before long, they were leaving the store with a hand-packed pint of Lemon Custard for Janice while eating their own double dip cones.

"Between you and Janice, I'm going to be fat," Dominique said, climbing into the truck.

"You have a long way to go." Trent slammed the door and got in.

"You want me to hold that?" Dominique asked, watching closely as Trent slid his tongue around the side of the cone. She felt funny again.

"Naw. After years of practice, I have this down pat." He proved as good as his word as he managed to fasten his seat belt, start the truck, and back out of the crowded parking lot with ease. "You're dripping."

"What?" She flushed.

"Your ice cream."

"Oh," she said, licking up the sides, feeling strange sensations growing, gathering inside her like forces of energy.

"You have to have good tongue actions. You need more practice," he told her.

The force zipped like chain lightning through her, pooling in her lower body. She shifted on the smooth leather seat. *Girl, get a hold of yourself. He's talking about ice cream.*

"Here. Watch me," he said, and proceeded to slide his tongue expertly around the ice cream. "You have to go slow, so you won't miss a spot and drip."

She didn't want to think about dripping. Her teeth bit into the cone, relishing the coldness.

"Hey. You cheated."

She swallowed. "You didn't say anything about rules."

He glanced at her briefly, then centered his attention on the street. "I thought I did."

Dominique was grateful for the ice cream. It gave her a reason not to talk and something to cool her down. The moment the truck stopped in Janice's driveway, she was out the door. As before, Trent easily caught up with her.

"Do you always run wherever you go?"

"Sorry," she said, but she kept walking fast. At the front door, he held the hand-packed ice cream for Dominique while she unlocked the door, then gave it back to her.

"Goodnight," he said.

"You aren't coming in?"

"You've had a long day, and I promised not to make it any longer."

"You didn't." She smiled, meaning it. "Thanks for the ice cream."

"I still have to teach you how to eat it properly," he told her.

The urge to lick her lips was too strong for her to ignore. She didn't. She tasted vanilla, but it left her wanting. She had a sudden craving to know how Chocolate Pecan tasted . . . on Trent's lips.

"You missed a spot." The pad of his finger grazed across the corner of her mouth and stayed there.

The strange feeling she had started having in the truck crystallized into desire. It would be ridiculously easy and so unthinkably foolish to turn her head and close her lips over his finger.

"Thanks again." She averted her head and quickly went inside. Leaning against the door, she closed her eyes and tried to control the wild, pulsing need raging through her.

She hadn't had to deal with those emotions since her divorce, since her life had turned into a nightmare. She didn't want to deal with them now, but she didn't have a choice. Trent wasn't going away, and she wasn't running from another thing in her life.

She straightened. She had overcome problems in the past. Trent should be no different. Even as she went in search of Janice, she couldn't quite convince herself.

Head bowed, Trent placed both hands on the closed door. Every muscle in his body tensed. His heart raced. Desire pulsed through him.

He hadn't thought just touching her lip could make every cell in his body quiver with need, hadn't thought he'd see a matching need reflected in her midnight-black eyes.

What a mess!

Pushing away from the door, he walked slowly to his truck, drove the short distance next door to his house, and went inside. He didn't stop until he was stripped naked and standing under the powerful blast of shower water.

If he didn't learn to control himself around Dominique, he'd have the highest water bill in Dallas.

Trent felt like a Peeping Tom, but that didn't stop him from watching Dominique through the sheer curtains in his living room as she passed by on her morning jog. It wasn't difficult to imagine her as a model. She was graceful and moved with a fluid elegance. He enjoyed watching her.

"That's not all you enjoy watching," he said aloud and dropped the curtain, aware he had done so because she had disappeared from sight.

He just didn't understand himself. Two weeks had passed since Dominique returned and he was still as hot and as bothered as ever. Each time he saw her he wanted her. Each time, the wanting was becoming harder to deny.

It wasn't as if he hadn't been around beautiful women before. Although Margo didn't have the unconscious sensuality of Dominique, she was gorgeous. And as dishonest as they came.

She'd had him so wrapped around her little finger that he hadn't known up from down. He had sent resumés all over the country in his senior year in college. His grades were good enough so that a few Fortune 500 companies were interested in him, but he had wanted to work in a midsized company where the advancement opportunity was greater.

Margo's father knew his daughter's charm, and had brought her along when he came to his university. Five minutes after Trent took her fragile hand in his, he would have done anything legal to please her.

He had taken the position of manager before even seeing the machinery company, and at less pay then he had been offered by other companies. He'd been caught by the entreaty in Margo's big, brown eyes and outrageously pleased that she thought he could bring her father's company out of its slump.

Once he was on board Margo had become more obvious with touches, low-cut dresses, the elusive scent of expensive perfume. She'd dangled her lush body in front of him as the prize while Trent put her father's company in the black again.

Fool that he was, he'd believed in her—his nose was "wide open." He worked like a dog—sixteen hour days, sometimes longer, seven days a week—until the manufacturing firm slowly turned a profit for one quarter, then another.

On one of those long nights he found out just what Margo and her dear father thought of him. Trent had been working late and had cut the lights off just to bask in what he had accomplished in ten short months. He was congratulating himself on how far he had come in twenty-one years. Soon he'd have a wife and family. He'd belong.

He had heard her laughter first. When he first heard it at the university he had thought the sound a bit shrill, but after falling in love with her, he thought it had a childlike quality.

The mention of his name had Trent sitting up and smiling, sure that they were going to say what a good job he had done and that Margo's father was finally going to give them permission to start planning their wedding, since the company was on solid ground.

He was wrong.

"Can you believe a nobody like Trent actually thinks I'm going to marry him?" Margo said, her voice scornful. "He could have insanity in his family."

"You've handled him very well, Margo," said her father. "A few more months and we can get rid of him." He laughed. "He was so easy to manage. Thanks to you."

"I hope you remember what a sacrifice I'm making when the dividends come in at the end of the next quarter. There's a fabulous diamond bracelet and matching earrings I've been wanting."

"You'll have that, and more. Just keep playing him along."

The voices had faded after that. Trent had stayed in his dark office, angrier than he'd ever thought possible, until the night cleaning man had come in. Getting up, he had shoved all the papers on the desk in his briefcase and walked out.

He hadn't looked back.

Outside, he had stared at the ridiculously expensive sports car that he was struggling to pay for on his salary, one Margo insisted he drive—her future fiancé had an image to uphold.

Once back in his furnished apartment, he had looked around and knew there was nothing to keep him there. Packing his clothes, he had awakened his disgruntled manager to give her the key. His one stop was at the ATM machine, to draw out his $356.64.

He had taken the first interstate highway, then the next exit, and the next, stopping only for gas, until he ended up outside of Texarkana, Texas, with a busted water hose. Randle Hodge had come along, and once again, adversity had turned into opportunity.

Sighing, Trent released the past. He thought Margo had taught him to be wary of beautiful women who were financially unstable. He now steered clear of needy women like the plague.

He didn't mind lending a hand to anyone getting started, but that was all. He wasn't going to be used again by a greedy, unscrupulous woman, no matter how beautiful she was.

All that had been fine in theory until he had seen Dominique reclining on the lounger, heard her husky voice, watched the swing of her hips as she walked away from him. Lust, certainly, foolishness, most definitely, tested his rule each time he saw her.

Sipping the forgotten coffee, he headed to the kitchen and his breakfast. There was nothing worse than cold eggs, unless it was cold poached eggs. At least the coffee didn't taste so bad. Either that, or he had killed his taste buds.

He grimaced. He hoped not. His mind, like a treacherous boomerang, homed in on Dominique. He had gone to bed more than one night speculating about the taste of her lips.

Something deliciously sweet and maddeningly elusive, he imagined— like cotton candy, each taste always enticing him back for another taste, then another, yet never quite fulfilling the promise, always leaving him with the hope that the next time his lips closed over the sugary confection his hunger would be appeased.

He wouldn't mind coming back again and again, he was sure. The pleasure would be in the quest he would never want to end.

The ringing phone jerked him out of his musing. "Hello."

"Trent. We got a call from the electric company. They have a hot load of transformers that need to go to Ohio. A storm just blew through this morning. Who do you want to send?" asked the dispatcher, who then proceeded to tell him who was available.

"I'll take it," Trent said, dumping the egg in the garbage disposal.

Surprise registered in the woman's voice over the sound of the running disposal. "You haven't made a run in over nine months."

"So, I'm long overdue." A few days away from Dominique might give him some perspective. "Be there in twenty. Have everything ready for me to pull out."

Hanging up, he rinsed the dishes, stacked them in the dishwasher, grabbed his keys with one hand and his baseball cap with the other.

In minutes he was speeding away.

Janice was speaking on the kitchen wall phone when Dominique returned from her jog. Opening the refrigerator, she poured herself a large glass of orange juice. After taking a sip she rolled the cool glass over her hot forehead.

"I'll take care of the mail and newspaper. Don't worry about anything. You just be careful. Good-bye," Janice said.

"Someone had to go out of town unexpectedly?" Dominique asked, sipping her juice again.

Janice bit her lip. "Trent."

"What's the matter?" Dominique asked, her heart lurching.

"He said he had to make a run with a hot load of transformers to Ohio," Janice explained, pulling her silk jacket over her leopard print blouse.

"He deals in stolen merchandise?" Dominique squeaked.

A smile took the lines of worry from Janice's face. "Hot in trucker language just means they should have been there days ago. Trent is honest, and has the highest integrity. I just wish I knew why he's taking off this way."

Dominique sat the glass on the counter. "You said he had to make a run."

"But he hasn't been on the road in months. I hope everything is all right."

"I'm sure it is." Dominique picked up Janice's purse and handed it to her. "Scoot. You have an eight o'clock appointment."

"Your breakfast is in the oven," Janice called, opening the back kitchen door.

"I told you I could fix my own."

"I enjoy cooking. You know that. I'll have to fix Trent something nice for his homecoming. Truck stop food ranges from excellent to awful."

"Janice. Will you stop worrying?"

"I'll try. It's just that he's been acting strange for the past few days." Coming back inside, she kissed Dominique on the cheek. "Have a wonderful day."

"I will," Dominique said, waving good-bye. Heading for the shower, she tried to run over the list of things she planned to do that day, but she couldn't put her godmother's concern about Trent's behavior out of her mind.

Most of all, she couldn't help wondering if she had anything to do with his leaving.

Dominique's studio was perfect. The curved rosewood desk Daniel had included with the computer system was elegant and graceful. On its polished surface were the black Mont Blanc desk set, her appointment book, her engraved cards, and the lucite piece Higgins had given her. She had found just the right small couch and a table and chair within her budget for the previewing room, where she planned to show her proofs and slides to her clients.

If she ever got any.

Trying not to sigh, Dominique glanced around the studio. The only sounds were the gurgle of the water cooler and the soulful voice of Anita Baker on the CD player. Even the usually busy traffic seemed to have disappeared. Along with the potential customers.

She knew three weeks in business wasn't a long time, but she had thought she'd get some response from her radio ads on a popular R&B station or her web site. Well, she'd had some calls, but after she told people her prices they either tried to haggle with her or simply hung up.

Silver bracelets jingled on her arm as she picked up the slick brochure listing her prices, then leaned back in her leather chair. If she cut her prices, she wouldn't be able to meet expenses. If she didn't get some customers, she'd be out of business, anyway. This was where it got tough.

Either she could start second-guessing herself or figure out a way to get people into the studio. Her budget wouldn't allow for any more large expenditures after the radio ads.

She thought of her dynamic, stubborn family. Not one of them would hesitate to go down fighting for what they believed in. This time she was going to do the same. She set the brochure aside. Not one price was changing. That left her only one alternative—to develop a marketing plan that was inexpensive and effective.

Her front door buzzer rang. She spun around in her chair away from the computer and pressed the buzzer for the person to enter. In came a rather austere looking woman, elegantly dressed in a lilac designer suit, carrying a small white poodle covered with tiny, lilac-colored bows.

"Good evening. Welcome to Dominique's. Can I help you?"

"Yes, I'm Mrs. Hightower. Mrs. Harold Hightower. Janice mentioned you had just returned from Paris doing photography, and I want you to do Scarlet."

"Scarlet?"

"Scarlet," Mrs. Hightower repeated, lifting the dog.

Dominique didn't hesitate. Business was business. "Please have a seat and tell me if you have anything specific in mind."

Thirty minutes later Mrs. Hightower left, saying she'd call. Dominique doubted it. Her eyes had widened like saucers when she saw the price list. As the saying went, another one bit the dust.

The buzzer rang and she automatically glanced up. Her body tightened. Her heart rate increased. The sound came again, and she finally moved to deactivate the lock.

"Hi," Trent said, strolling in as if he hadn't been gone almost a week without a word. "I haven't been gone so long that you didn't recognize me, have I?"

"No, of course not." Did she appear as flustered as she sounded? Had the past five days passed so slowly because she had missed Trent, or because business was so slow? She didn't know and she wasn't looking too closely to find the answer.

Her hand swept over her hair and encountered the heavy silver and turquoise barrette at the base of her neck. The action was a sure sign of a woman primping for a man. Maybe she already knew the answer to why the past days had been so trying. "Hello, Trent."

He glanced around, noting the canvas and props. He wore a chambray shirt and the usual tight jeans that defined his long, muscular legs perfectly. "Looks good."

So do you, she almost said, and clamped her teeth together.

He turned back to her. "How's it going?"

"As well as can be expected," she said evasively. "How was your trip? Janice said you don't usually go on runs."

"I don't like getting rusty." He tugged the brim of his black baseball cap with Masters Trucking in red block lettering on the front of the crown. "I'd better be going. Thought I'd stop by and say 'Hi,' since it's on the way home."

"I understand. I have to get back to work myself."

"Bye."

"Bye," Dominique said, and turned to the computer. After the door closed, her hands remained immobile and slightly unsteady. She had been so sure that she was over whatever it was that had affected her when Trent was around. She had been wrong.

One glimpse, one smile, and she was back where she started—sinking fast, and not a life preserver in sight.

Trent got into his truck and knew five days away had accomplished one thing—made his body hungrier. Flicking on the ignition, he drove home.

All he wanted was to sleep for the next twenty-four hours. After the run to Ohio he had headed to Rochester, New York, then to Laredo, Texas, then back to Dallas. Every mile of the way Dominique had ridden with him. At night she was there when he went to sleep, and she was waiting for him when he woke up. The past five days were the loneliest he had ever spent.

Now he was back, and wishing he hadn't gone. He didn't like the shadows in her eyes. He planned a little talk with Janice to see how Dominique's business was going.

Something told him it *wasn't.* If there was anything he could do to help, it was as good as done. Helping her out wouldn't hurt anything. They weren't dating or anything.

Once home, he showered and plopped down nude across his king-size bed. He had just settled his body comfortably when the phone rang.

He ignored the sound, knowing the answering machine would pick it up, and wished he had unplugged the thing. He was too tired to talk to anyone, and if it was business his staff could run things as well as he.

"Trent, this is Frank Lloyd. Just wanted to remind you that my wife and I are looking forward to seeing you and your guest Thursday night at the dinner party. Please call."

Trent groaned into the pillow as the answering machine clicked off. Lloyd was a business associate and a friend. He owned the company that had supplied Trent with diesel fuel at a very reasonable rate for the past five years. Since diesel was Trent's highest outlay, he liked to keep Frank Lloyd happy.

Showing up without a woman on his arm tomorrow night was definitely not going to win points. Scowling, he rolled onto his back. He hadn't dated in months. Had no desire to do so.

But he needed a woman.

One popped into his mind. Instead of his scowl deepening, he smiled, tired of fighting the inevitable. There was only one woman he wanted to take out, and somehow he was going to make it happen.

Dominique Everette broke just about every rule he had about women: She was struggling in her business. Worse, she interfered in his business. But something told him she was well worth the risks involved.

With a smile on his face, he rolled onto his side and went to sleep.

CHAPTER 6

"Good morning, Janice," Trent said Thursday morning as he strolled into her office at the antique store, trying to be casual. He was anything but.

"Good morning, Trent." She greeted him with a smile, resting her silk-clad arms on the papers strewn over the wide surface of the Chippendale desk, which was polished to a high sheen. "Dominique told me you were home."

"I need your help." He didn't believe in wasting time.

Since awakening that morning he thought of little else except how to get Dominique to go with him tonight. He was convinced that a straightforward approach, his usual way, wouldn't work this time. Breaking another rule seemed par for the course.

Janice frowned. "I knew something was bothering you. I called last night, but got your machine."

"I was beat from the trip. Sorry."

"That's all right. I simply wanted to invite you over for dinner," Janice assured him. "As for my help, you know you only have to ask."

Trent lifted his cap, then ran his large hand across his head. Now came the hard part. "I hate to put you in this position, but I can't figure out another way," he admitted, then proceeded to pace on the Aubusson rug in front of her desk.

Janice's worry and concern deepened. Trent was always calm no matter the circumstances. "It can't be that bad."

Stopping, Trent looked at her with true desperation in his dark brown eyes. "I need your to help get me a date for tonight."

She relaxed. "Trent, you should be ashamed of yourself for scaring me. Any young woman you know would be happy to go out with you."

"Yeah, but they'd expect me to call again. I need a date with no strings." Placing both hands on the desk, he stared across the surface at her. "That's why I need you to help me."

Her shoulders pressed against the high back of the woven, upholstered chair. "Me?"

"I know you've sometimes matched up a few neighbors and friends. I thought you might help me out."

Janice lowered her gaze and began straightening the papers on her desk. "I don't know where you could have heard such a thing."

"Come on, Janice. I wouldn't ask if I didn't need your help," Trent admitted. "Mr. Scoggins stopped by the house last fall while he was out for a walk and decided to stay and watch a football game with me. He had one too many beers cheering the Cowboys on to a victory against the Redskins, and told me everything."

That got her attention. She lifted her head. "And just what is everything?"

Trent straightened. "That you have an unofficial dating service for people over fifty called No Strings. You've met a lot of your clients through your business. It's very exclusive and private."

"Apparently not private enough."

"Please don't be upset with Mr. Scoggins," Trent said. "As I said, he had one too many beers. I gathered he's very pleased with a Mrs. Taylor who lives in East Dallas. I just hope you can do the same for me. On a one-time basis, of course."

Janice settled back in her chair. "Trent, you said it yourself. I deal with people over fifty."

Trent shoved his hand into his front pocket. "As desperate as I am, I'll take anyone at the moment." He sent her a speculative look. "You have any plans for tonight?"

Her perfectly arched brows lifted regally. "A woman, no matter her age or the length of acquaintance, does not like to hear a man state he's desperate and then ask if she's available in practically the same breath."

Trent winced. Maybe he should have gone for the straightforward approach, after all. "Sorry. You know I didn't mean it like that. I forgot about the dinner party tonight until the host called me yesterday afternoon. The last time I showed up without a date at a dinner party, the hostess glared at me and the empty chair beside me all evening."

"Surely you can explain to him that your date had to cancel," Janice offered.

"I could, except it wouldn't be the truth. In any case some of the people coming tonight were at a dinner party last month, and I didn't have a date then either. I always intend to invite someone, then I get busy and forget."

"Freud said there are no accidents, Trent."

Broad shoulders shrugged. "Maybe. I told you I don't have time to keep a woman happy. I'm too busy with my business. Anyway, Mr. Lloyd, tonight's host, made it a point when I returned his call today to mention that his wife hoped the same thing didn't happen tonight."

"Then cancel entirely," Janice suggested.

"I tried. No go." Trent shook his dark head, glad he didn't have to fabricate this part. "Mr. Lloyd said his wife had gone to a lot of trouble and wanted everything to run smoothly. Two empty seats would be upsetting."

Entwining her fingers, Janice braced her arms on her desk. "How important is this man to your business?"

"Very," Trent answered. "Fuel is the major outlay in my business. Frank Lloyd in my only supplier, and sells me what I need at a price where I can still make a profit. If I lost the account and had to go to another supplier, I wouldn't get as good a deal."

She peered at him closely. "But is he the vindictive type?"

"I don't think so, but I don't think his call yesterday was a coincidence, either," he said slowly.

"A warning?" Janice guessed.

"That's my guess." Trent moved a delicate Sevres porcelain figurine aside and propped a hip on the corner of the desk. "My guess is he wants to make sure things go well."

Janice eyed the entwined porcelain lovers to make sure they hadn't survived two-and-a-half centuries only to meet disaster a continent away from the factory in England, then switched her attention back to Trent. "I don't blame him. I have to say I admire him for wanting to make his wife happy. Do you know how much behind the scene planning and effort it takes to make a dinner party seem effortless?"

"No, I don't, but if she's going to get this worked up about it she shouldn't have one," he said with obvious impatience.

"Being a successful hostess can be just as important to a woman as being a successful businessman is to you. She is often a reflection of her husband, and it is important that she shine brilliantly," Janice said from experience.

"If you say so." Trent stood. "Can you help me?"

"Sorry, I don't know anyone."

"You know someone."

Her eyes widened. "You can't possibly mean Dominique?"

"She's under fifty."

"She has also made it clear that she doesn't want any entanglements."

"Neither do I. That's what makes this so perfect. I don't have time to court a woman, and I don't want one to get the wrong impression when I take her out. This way, with Dominique, it's perfect," he said, knowing he was skimming the thin line of truthfulness.

Janice shook her head. "I don't know, Trent. Dominique doesn't do blind dates."

"This isn't a blind date. She knows me."

Both brows arched. "May I remind you that you two didn't exactly hit it off?"

"I know, but lately we've gotten along better. I'd ask her myself, but I thought she might take it better coming from you."

"So, Dominique was your choice from the first?"

"Yes," he answered.

"Mind if I ask why you had to back your way into this?" Janice asked, watching him closely.

"I wanted you to see how desperate I am before you said no automatically. Dominique would get something out of it, too," he rushed on to say. "The dinner party would be a great chance for her to meet some of the movers and shakers in the city. I don't think her business is going too well."

Janice bit her lower lip. "It has been slow, despite the referrals I've made. I don't understand. Her photographs are beautiful."

"So is she, and that could be a problem. Some women aren't going to want the competition. She needs to find clients who are secure in themselves and their relationships, who don't have to worry about paying their bill," he said.

"I suppose you're right."

"I know I am. All the couples tonight are successful and have been married for years. We'll be the youngest people there, and the only singles." His tone increased in excitement. "This could be mutually beneficial to both of us. All I ask is that you ask her, give her the facts, and let her decide for herself."

"I guess I could do that."

"Thanks, Janice. I knew I could count on you once you had all the facts." With a smile, he was out the door. It was only when he reached his truck that his elation began to wane.

He didn't know much about Dominique, but one thing he knew instinctively was that she wouldn't liked being pushed into anything. She made her own decisions. Trent had to admit that he wasn't sure how he'd react if the tables were turned.

Turning, he went back inside the shop. What seemed like a good plan this morning suddenly had flaws. Lack of sleep must have dulled his mind. Just as he opened the shop's door, Janice came out of her office and greeted two elderly ladies.

She glanced toward him and he shook his head and retraced his steps to his truck. He'd just have to take care of things himself, but how? One thing he knew—he needed a date for tonight, and Dominique was it.

Dominique was at a low point. She had yet to come up with a marketing plan, and the order for the sitting she had done that morning wouldn't pay a day's rent.

She had to find a way to break into the overcrowded Dallas photography market. But how? Leaning back in her chair, she stared at the computer's blank screen as if it could tell her the answer.

The phone and the front door buzzer sounded at the same time. She glanced up to see Trent at the door. He was in a black tux. Even from thirty feet away she cold see that the perfect cut of the suit accented his muscular build.

Automatically she buzzed him in. Seeing his silhouette in the doorway for a moment gave her pause. The formal attire somehow made him appear more intimidating, more dangerous, more sensual. Perhaps letting him in wasn't the wisest thing to do. Trent made her body react in a totally unacceptable way.

"Hi. You want to get that?"

Flushing, she reached for the ringing phone. "Photographs by Dominique. Hi, Janice."

"May I speak with her?" Trent requested, holding out his hand.

"Janice, Trent wishes to speak with you." Her gaze flickered to Trent perched on the the corner of her desk. "Yes, he's right here." She held out the phone. "She wants to speak with you, too."

Accepting the phone, Trent said, "Hi, Janice. I decided to take care of things myself. Thanks. Good-bye." Replacing the receiver, he glanced around. "Things have really shaped up."

"I'm sure you didn't come here to talk about the studio. You were here yesterday."

He turned back to her, his gaze intent and more disturbing than any man's had a right to be. "Why not?"

He had her there. "You're too busy to take the time."

"A man is never too busy to take the time for the things that interest him."

Dominique felt her insides shiver. She didn't need this complication in her life. Her only concern had to be her business. "If you don't mind, I'd like to get back to work."

"Doing what, might I ask?"

For some reason she didn't want him to know she was floundering. Worse, she had no idea of how to fix things. "Working on a marketing plan."

"I'm pretty good at that. Maybe I can help," he said.

"No, that—"

He was off the desk and standing behind her before she could stop him. Her hands clenched as she waited for his derisive remark once he saw the blank screen.

"Just starting, huh?" His hand rested on the back of her chair, the back of his fingers brushing her arm.

"Yes." Unobtrusively, she leaned forward. Trent followed the movements, bringing with him the disturbing scent of his cologne and his own unique scent. Both had her wanting to lick her lips again.

"You have to show the public something different. Something unique."

Dominique propped one arm on the desk beside the keyboard. "But what?"

"Whatever sets your work apart from all the other photographers," he answered simply. "In my business it was consistent, dependable, honest service. My customers had to learn to trust me, and know that I was going to deliver their merchandise intact and on time. You have to show them that each picture is as important and precious to you as it is to them. You've got to sell your uniqueness."

Without thought she tilted her head and turned around. His lips were in her direct line of vision and mere inches away. She drew in a shaky breath and inhaled something minty. Jerking her gaze back around, she asked, "How do you know I'm unique?"

"I saw the pictures you took of Janice," he answered. "They weren't stiff, formal poses. They were fun shots. They captured Janice's love of people and life."

She felt enormously pleased. That was exactly what she had tried to do. Slowly she faced him, this time making sure her gaze didn't drop below his eyes. "Thank you."

He straightened. "You're the one who took the shots."

"And very few since," she finally admitted ruefully.

"That's because your work hasn't circulated enough." Facing her, he folded his arms, leaned back against her desk, and stared down at her. "You need people to know what you can do."

"I'm going to do an ad in the newspapers. I've already tried radio."

"I have a better idea."

She frowned. "What?"

"Take your product to the people. People see your product, but they don't see you."

She folded her arms across her chest. "I'm selling photography."

"Don't get testy on me. People respond to things beautiful and alluring. You're both."

She didn't know how to take the compliment. She did know that for the first time in years she was thankful for the way she looked. "I want my work to speak for itself."

"It will, but you have to get them to look first. I have the perfect solution," he told her, coming around to the front of the desk and staring down at her.

Warily, he eyed the tux. "Does the way you're dressed have anything to do with it?"

"Always knew you were smart."

"And busy. So if you'll just tell me what this is all about, I can get back to work."

"And impatient," he rushed on when she frowned, "I have an important dinner party to attend tonight and I need a da—"

"I don't have time to date," she said, cutting him off.

"Neither do I. That's why I'm asking you."

Surprise was clearly written on her face.

His smile made her want to hit him. "The dinner party tonight is strictly business. I had asked Janice to speak to you for me, then I decided to ask myself."

She folded her arms. "Why?"

"I didn't want you to feel as if you were under an obligation to go, or think I was pushing you," he answered truthfully. "We're still testing the waters of our friendship, and I didn't want them muddied."

That hadn't been what she wanted to know. "Why didn't you get your own date?"

He grinned like a little boy who knows he can charm any female who has a heartbeat. "Promise not to get angry."

Dominique definitely had a heartbeat, and it was galloping at the moment. "I promise to try."

"Fair enough. I work long hours and seldom have time for anything that isn't connected to business. The dinner party tonight is a case in point. Most women want a lot of attention, or are demanding. You take them out once, and if you don't call again their feelings are hurt," he explained.

"You aren't interested in me, so there would be no chance for either of us to get the wrong idea or of having our feelings hurt. Plus, I might be able to help your business."

He flashed his heart-pounding smile. "Believe it or not, I really am a nice guy. Janice said you needed a second chance without explaining why." He grew serious. "I own Masters Trucking because Randle Hodge gave me a second chance. I promised him if I ever saw anyone else who needed a hand, I'd pass on the favor."

"Sounds very touching."

"It's the truth. I don't lie," he told her tightly.

Instantly contrite, she said, "I'm sorry if it sounded that way."

"Apology accepted. Will you go?"

She leaned back in her chair and stared at him. Temptingly sinful. Her hands itched to grab the Hasselblad on the desk. She clenched them instead, glancing at his tux. "You must have been pretty sure of yourself."

"This is part of plan A."

"Plan A?"

"I was going to pose for some shots for Randle as sort of a joke. He's a great guy, and the reason I got into the trucking business. I owe him more than I can ever repay," Trent explained, then grinned. "He can't stand anything but his overalls. I used to handle sales for that very reason. But this afternoon I got to thinking, and decided you needed someone who could really draw attention to your work."

Just then the buzzer rang. Dominique looked around Trent to see a mountain of a black man in the doorway. She glanced up at Trent in confusion.

He grinned. "This is Cowboy country, and you're about to meet one. Buzz him in."

The huge man didn't look like a cowboy to her. She shuddered just to think of the poor horse that had to carry him all day. Besides, he was dressed in what looked like a white silk, bandless shirt and black linen slacks. Definitely not the attire of any cowboy she had ever seen.

"Dominique, don't keep the man waiting."

She buzzed him in. He wasn't alone. Two adorable little girls who appeared to be about five and three years old were with him. Their outfits matched from the headbands in their short Afros to their shorts sets, to the abstract cuffs of their white socks. Each child had her small hand curled trustingly around one of the man's fingers.

"Hey, Man," greeted the cowboy. "My wife had to go on an errand, and I had to babysit. Hope that's not a problem?"

Trent reached up the long distance and slapped the man on the back. "Just so you're here. Isn't that right, Dominique?"

Not sure of what was going on, but ingrained with good manners, Dominique came around her desk and extended her hand. "That's right. I'm Dominique."

His jaw unhinged slightly. Distractedly he lifted his hand. "Pleased to meet you." The little girls took off for an old leather trunk filled with ladies' antique clothes. "You got anything in there they can mess up?"

"No," she answered.

"Good. Ready to shoot."

Her gaze swept over him again. He looked rather stiff and intimidating. Maybe if he were in his regular clothes—"You want to take your picture dressed like that?"

"What the matter with the way I'm dressed?" he said, not sounding at all pleased.

"Nothing," she hastened to reassure the towering man.

"He looks fine, Dominique," Trent said, almost glaring at her.

"Of course he does," she said to Trent, then faced the man glaring down at her and swallowed. "Trent said you were a cowboy, and I just thought you'd want to have your picture taken in your boots, or at least your Stetson."

Both men stared at Dominique for what seemed countless moments, then met each other's gazes and burst out laughing. Dominique suddenly felt as if she were the brunt of a joke. "Did I say something funny?"

"Not at all," Trent said, struggling to stop laughing. "It's my fault for not making the introductions sooner." Trent quickly corrected the matter. Dominique's expression didn't change.

He and the man exchanged looks again. "You still have no idea who he is, do you?"

"I'm sorry if you're someone I should recognize," she said, knowing how some people's egos were easily bruised when the world didn't know them. "I've been out of touch lately."

"You'd have to have been out of the country not to know about the world champion Dallas Cowboys, and one of their star team members," Trent offered.

She had been in Europe, but didn't think this was the time to tell Trent.

"That's all ri—girls, get out of there."

Dominique turned to watch the man move with surprising speed and agility toward the two giggling girls who were in a tangle of clothes and beads. Scooping up one in each arm, he faced her.

The oldest child had a three-foot strand of pearls dangling around her neck; her hand was clamped on the wide brim of a ladies' straw hat encircled in large poppies. The youngest had a ladies' shoe dangling from her foot, a pink boa around her neck.

"Sorry, Dominique. I'll pay for any damage to the clothes and other things."

Dominique wasn't thinking about damages. The brawny man holding the two small, giggling girls so tenderly was such a contrast that she knew she had to capture the moment. Reaching for her Hasselblad 503CW, she raised the viewfinder to her eye. The adjustments were smooth, automatic. The motordrive whirled as she took several rapid shots.

The camera lowered. "Please, sit down with the girls in front of the trunk."

He did so easily, attesting to his strength and also to ease of practice. Here was a loving father who took time with his children. That was what she wanted to capture.

She knew she was right about the relationship as she watched the youngest cup her father's face with her small hands and kiss him while the oldest leaned contentedly against his wide chest. The camera shutter whirred and whirred.

Ten minutes and seventy-two shots later, she sat back on her booted heels, a satisfied smile on her face. "You have two precious daughters."

He beamed and hugged the giggling girls to him. "Thanks. They are something, but I thought you wanted to take a picture of me."

"Your children are an extension of you. Obviously you're a loving father, and that shows. That's what I want people to see."

"What about the Dallas Cowboys?" he asked.

"I know Texas is supposed to be bigger and better, and you've obviously shown it by being on the team of the world champions cowboy event, but is a Dallas cowboy really any different from thousands of other cowboys all over the country?" she asked seriously.

Trent's groan could be heard loud and clear.

Dominique heard the sound and forged ahead, anyway. "I simply think being a loving father speaks more highly of you than your occupation or anything else."

"So do I." On bended knees, he untangled the girls from the props and picked them up in his arms. "How soon can you have the proofs ready?"

She came to her feet, the camera clutched securely in her hands. The cost would double to have the slides printed in under seventy-two hours, but she had a feeling the results would be worth it.

"Anytime after noon tomorrow. You can come in at this same time if it's convenient," she said, feeling as if her feet were dancing a happy jig although they were still on the floor.

"Good. I'll bring my wife."

"I look forward to seeing you then."

The man looked toward Trent. "If these pictures come out as well as I think, I'll still be in your debt."

Trent stuck out his hand. "Why don't we call it even and start fresh?"

The handshake was sure and strong. "Thought you might say that. Dominique, I'll see you tomorrow."

As soon as the door closed Trent picked Dominique up and twirled her around. "You were really awesome. You know that!"

"Put me down," she told him, but she was smiling.

He sat her down, but kept his hands on her small waist. "You don't have any idea of what you've done, do you?"

His happy mood matched hers. "No, but I've taken some very good shots. One of them just has to be a twenty by twenty-four or at least a sixteen by twenty." She groaned as a thought hit. Her happiness took a nosedive. "Oh, no. I forgot to give him a price list. Janice's friend's eyes almost popped out this morning when I showed it to *her.* Do you think he and his wife will be the same way?"

Trent shook his head. "I can't believe you."

"What?"

"To you he was just a man and his children."

Her shoulders slumped. "I'm sorry I didn't recognize him, but he seemed to take it well."

Trent laughed, sending her stomach into another flurry. "The main thing is that everyone we meet tonight will know who he is. You're going to be the talk of the party. You'd better take lots of business cards."

Her eyes glowed. "You really think so?"

"I know so. Come on, I'll help you pack things up so we can get to the party." Releasing her, he went to the trunk and began putting the clothes away. "I can't wait to tell Frank Lloyd why we're late. He has season tickets to see his favorite team play."

"Play what?" she asked, pressing the button to remove the film.

He didn't answer until he stood before her again, a mischievous smile on his face. "Football."

Predictably her stomach fluttered, but there was something else to be considered. One thing she had learned since her return from Paris was how seriously men in America took football—her father and Daniel included. "I'm ruined."

"Just the opposite," Trent said. "Dallas loves the Cowboys, and anybody *they* love. I'd say business is about to increase."

"Thanks to you."

"We're friends, remember?"

"Friends."

CHAPTER 7

Eyeing herself critically in the full-length mirror, Dominique admitted she wanted to look spectacular and didn't question the reason why. There was no guarantee that the afternoon's shoot would develop into a sale, but she felt like celebrating, anyway. The red silk gown she chose was sophisticated, elegant, and sensual.

Grabbing her tiny, red satin handbag shaped like a tulip, she strolled out of the bedroom. Trent was in the living room with Janice. He must have heard her because he glanced toward the door while bringing a glass of iced tea toward his mouth. His mouth gaped.

Dominique finally admitted the real reason she wanted to look good. If the stunned look on Trent's face was any indication, she had outdone herself.

"You look lovely," Janice said.

Lovely meant nice and peaceful, Trent thought. There was nothing nice or peaceful about the beguiling woman in red smiling at him. She knew her power, and wasn't afraid to use it. She was absolutely stunning. Evocative was another word that came to mind. A living fantasy come to life.

He had never seen a woman more alluring, more confident in herself. Her hair was loose and flowing around her shoulders like coiled silk. Hunger hit him hard and fast. He reluctantly admitted Dominique had a way of taking him further, faster, than any woman had. It wasn't a comforting thought.

The glass clinked as he set it on the coffee table and stood. "I'll apologize early for staring."

She smiled. "It's the dress."

Immediately his gaze swept back over the gown that covered her from neck to knees but also displayed the flawless perfection of the wearer. His mind got him into trouble again—there wasn't a line anywhere to indicate undergarments. He swallowed. Hard.

"Shall we go? I don't want us to be too late."

"Have fun," Janice told them.

"Goodnight," Dominique called.

Trent mumbled something, he wasn't sure what. Dominique could definitely be a problem.

Her skin is like warm velvet, he thought as he led her to his parked car. She smelled exotic and forbidden. He caught himself wanting to lean closer to inhale her fragrance, to touch her in other places to see if she was that soft all over.

"I thought we were going in your truck," she said, sliding in on the passenger seat of the roomy, champagne-colored Lincoln Towncar.

The dress skimmed up above her knees. He'd like nothing better than to place his hands on her sleek legs and slide the gown up further.

He cleared his throat. "Might have been a tight fit." She glanced up at him sharply. "Getting in the truck, I mean."

Closing the door, he went around and got in, hoping he'd have pulled it together better by the time they reached the Lloyd's.

He did, with Dominique's help. She was in a playful mood, and thirty minutes later when he parked in front of the Tudor style mansion in far North Dallas, he was back in control.

At the handcarved front door they were greeted by a servant and immediately shown into the living room. All the guests turned to see the new arrivals, who were twenty minutes late.

From the relieved expression on Frank and Ann Lloyd's faces, Trent knew his and Dominique's tardiness had worried them. He extended his hand. "Sorry we're late. Mr. and Mrs. Lloyd, I'd like you to meet Dominique Everette."

Even at sixty-five, Mr. Lloyd was a typical male. His eyes rounded. He recovered nicely. "Glad you could both make it."

"Welcome to our home," Mrs. Lloyd said graciously. "Let me introduce you to the rest of our guests."

The other four couples' reaction was predictably dictated by gender on seeing Dominique for the first time—the men with open admiration, the women with distrust.

Trent found himself annoyed at all of them, until he remembered his own reaction and noticed that Dominique didn't appear to mind. She was gracious and charming. When they were shown into dinner, she was complimentary of the table and the room without being effusive.

During dinner the women gradually thawed. By the time the main entree was being served everyone was chatting amicably. It didn't escape Trent that the reason was probably because Dominique wasn't paying any more attention to the men than they were paying to her.

They were male enough to enjoy looking at a beautiful woman, but that didn't mean they loved and cared for their wives any less. Finally Trent was able to relax enough to enjoy his succulent prime rib and baby potatoes.

They were finishing dessert when Mr. Lloyd gave Trent the opening he had been waiting for all evening. "My box is open to any of you who want to come and watch the Cowboys beat up on the Philadelphia Eagles Monday night. Should be a massacre," he said gleefully.

Ann shot him a pained look. Her husband grinned. Ruefully shaking her head, she asked, "What did you men do before football?"

Frank shook his head of graying hair. "I don't even want to think about it."

Everyone laughed.

Trent placed his fork on the empty dessert plate where there had been a large wedge of pecan pie and took the plunge. "Dominique, for one, is glad. Her latest client plays for the Cowboys."

All eyes turned to her. "Trent, why don't *you* tell them?" she suggested easily.

He was only too happy to give them the details. "I had seen the fantastic pictures Dominique took of her godmother and I suggested he come by. But Dominique took one look at his daughters playing dress up and decided to do a family shot."

All eyes focused on her again. "They were about three and five years-old, and just precious," she said. "I can't wait until I see the prints."

"Neither could he. He's coming back with his wife tomorrow afternoon," Trent said.

"Are portraits your specialty?" one of the other dinner guests asked.

"Yes, but I don't like formal poses. I'd much rather create something unique that says something about the individual," Dominique explained. "The photos this afternoon just happened. It wasn't planned, but that's what is going to make them great."

"How do you know?" asked the man to her left, who was vice-president of a bank.

"I just know. The way a tennis player knows a particular shot is going to win the game. The way you know when the stock is going to plunge or rise. You just know," she said simply.

He nodded. "I have a six-year-old grandson who loves to fish more than eat. What do you think would fit him?"

"A tattered straw hat, old-fashioned overalls rolled up midway on his legs, a cane fishing pole in one hand, and a tin minnow bucket in the other."

"Oh," said the perfectly coiffured woman in a black gown beside him.

Dominique flushed. "Sorry. I didn't mean to offend you by mentioning the bait."

"You didn't," the woman hastened to say. "I could just see Michael as you pictured."

"My son likes fishing, too," said the man across from her. She remembered him as an investment broker.

"Now, Charles," said the banker. "Our Michael already has the overalls, and I don't want his picture looking like anyone else's."

"Since neither of you have made an appointment with Dominique, I don't see how you can have pictures alike, and I'm sure you wouldn't get an idea and let another photographer take the pictures," Trent said smoothly.

"Of course not," they chorused.

Dominique caught Trent's wink and hoped no one else had. The odds were in his favor. She was the center of attention again.

She spoke to the second man. "Perhaps your son likes fishing, but he may have other interests. Reading under a shady tree, drawing, or perhaps he considers it his duty to find every puddle of water on a rainy day and making sure he splashes all the way through them."

The heavyset man laughed. "Are you sure you haven't met Ben?"

She smiled, as did everyone. "Although it's just my brother and I, I grew up with a lot of friends and family around."

"So how do you work?" asked the first man.

"I like to meet with potential clients first, to get a feel for what they like. The consultation visit is free, of course. If I don't come up with an idea then, I give the person a call later, when I do."

"From what I've heard tonight, I don't think there is a chance of having to wait." He glanced at his wife who nodded. "How soon can you schedule Michael?"

She saw no reason for being coy. "I'm open."

"You have a card?"

Her expression saddened. "No."

"Here you go," Trent said, handing the man her heavily embossed card. "I picked up some while I was in Dominique's studio this afternoon. I have some friends who are football fanatics who are going to insist she take their picture, as well."

"May I have one?"

"Yes, me too."

"Certainly, ladies. Take extra if you need them," Trent suggested with a smile.

"Maybe you should have her do your picture, Ann," Frank suggested to his wife. "You know the children and I both have asked you."

"You know why I haven't, Frank." Ann turned toward Dominique. "No offense, Miss Everette, but my pictures don't turn out too well."

"Please call me Dominique, and that's the photographer's fault, not yours. It's imperative that the photographer not only have a solid understanding of their equipment, but of lighting and composition, as well. For your clear complexion I'd use soft lighting and put you in a setting that you enjoyed so you'd be at ease. My bet is it would be your flower garden."

Her eyes widened. "How did you know?"

"From what I've seen of your lovely home the rooms are marked by soft colors, fresh flowers, and light," Dominique said. "The botanical prints are as proudly displayed as the other pieces of framed art on your walls."

Dominique leaned forward to stress her point. "The living room is an easy mix of antiques, plush, upholstered pieces with pink pillows, and fresh flowers in china pots. Despite the elegance, there is a hominess that invites everyone to sit and enjoy. Like this room, it has richness and charm."

Obviously pleased, Mrs. Lloyd smiled. "Thank you. You're very observant."

Dominique sat back in her chair. "A photographer has to be a decorator, as well. The picture has to appear effortless, yet capture the essence of the people in the shot." She glanced around the dining room. "Just as the refinement here appears effortless, although I'd be willing to bet you put a lot of time and effort into creating the effect."

"It has taken me years of collecting to finally have the house the way I want it," Mrs. Lloyd admitted.

"You've succeeded admirably." Dominique nodded toward the French doors. "Decorative lighting outside allows dining room guests to enjoy the flowering gardens and terrace at night. From the size of those brass urns filled with pink geraniums by the doors, I don't think they were brought in just for tonight."

"No, they weren't." The hostess turned to Trent. "May I please have one of those cards?"

He passed one to her with a smile. "Something tells me Dominique is going to be busy, so tell your friends early so they can beat the rush. I'm thinking about letting her do me."

"How would you pose Trent?" asked Mr. Lloyd.

All eyes turned to her. For the first time that night Dominique didn't like the attention on her. "Doing something he obviously loves." His dark eyebrows lifted in silent query. "Stepping from one of his trucks."

It was obvious from everyone's expressions that they were disappointed with her answer. That was fine with Dominique. It was better than shocking them with her first thought—Trent stepping dripping wet from the shower, and not a towel in sight.

He was displeased with her.

She knew it from the stiff way he held his body as he walked her to Janice's front door, knew it from the implacable line of his mouth where a curve had lingered until an hour ago. His disapproval bothered her more than she wanted to admit.

She had every reason to celebrate and she thought he did, too. When they left the party a short while ago, Mr. and Mrs. Lloyd couldn't have been more amicable.

That's why she didn't understand. That's why she was walking slowly toward the front door. "You're very quiet."

"Long day."

She stopped in the arch of light through the half-glass of the door. "Why did it get longer an hour ago?"

For a moment she thought he wasn't going to answer. Then he blurted, "Why couldn't you think of something more exciting for me?"

She blinked. "I beg your pardon?"

"I mean, you only met Mrs. Lloyd tonight, haven't even seen the children, and you came up with great ideas. You made me seem boring," he told her, digging one hand into the front pocket of his trousers.

"Boring?" Not unless they had changed the meaning of the word in the dictionary. He was mind-blowing sexy, with a hard, powerful body and eyes that could melt stone.

"Did you see the way they looked at me?" he asked, his voice irate. Then he rushed on before she had a chance to answer. "They probably think the reason I haven't had a date before is because no woman would have me."

She started to laugh, then caught his hard expression in the faint light. "You're serious?"

"Darn right."

"I thought the idea was good."

"It would have been if you hadn't suggested it."

"You're losing me."

He jerked his hand out of his pocket and thrust it toward her, his gaze running from the wild mane of black hair to her red satin heels. "You stand there looking absolutely sinful, and you want to take my picture getting out of a truck, and I'm your date."

The woman in her was wildly pleased that he thought she looked sinful. On the other hand, she wasn't about to let him know it. "Would you rather I'd said naked on a bear skin rug?"

"It would have been better," he retorted.

Her chin lifted. "I don't have one in stock, but I'm sure I can rent one. Will Thursday at five be convenient?"

"What?"

"Thursday at five," she repeated, enjoying the shocked expression on his handsome face. "I hope you're not shy, because as you remember I have glass on the front and side. I'm sure you'll attract lots of attention in the buff. Of course, I'll try to finish quickly—the air-conditioning is a bear."

Hands on narrow hips, he glared at her. "You're serious, aren't you?"

"As a heart attack."

The stared at each other for a long time. Trent cracked first. "I guess I sounded kind of childish, huh?"

"A bit, but then friends can be a bit childish with each other."

He reached out and brushed an errant curl away from her face. "Friends, huh?"

She shivered. When she spoke her voice wasn't quite steady. "Y-Yes. I don't know how to thank you for tonight, and everything."

He chuckled, his good humor returning. "I thought they were going to come to blows over you."

Her laughter joined his. "I was surprised and pleased. They were really possessive and territorial."

He stepped closer, bringing with him the disturbing warmth of his body, the irresistible and forbidden allure that was uniquely his. "Being possessive and territorial where you're concerned would be exceptionally easy." The back of his knuckles skimmed across her cheek.

A painful memory flickered in her subconscious, but it was no match for the sudden flare of heat in her belly. Her vision narrowed down to him, more specifically his well-sculptured lips. Air became difficult to draw in. His breathing appeared just as labored.

His head titled, bringing his mouth closer. Danger signals went off in her head.

Hastily she stepped back from beckoning temptation, but Lord, it was difficult. "I'd better go in."

Hot brown eyes regarded her intently. He wanted to touch her, caress her, kiss her. He wanted to feel the softness of her skin against his, to heat the surface with his kisses, to make her forget to be wary of him.

The last thought was the only reason he didn't close the distance between them and take her into his arms. He stepped back, giving them both space. "Goodnight. I'll see you in the morning."

"Oh," she said, her thoughts going back to that morning. She had jogged as usual, and had been keenly aware that he watched her as she departed and returned. She'd felt his gaze as if it were a tangible thing.

"Janice invited me over for breakfast."

"I see." She couldn't possibly be disappointed. "Goodnight."

"Goodnight," he said, trying not to howl his frustration.

Turning her back on temptation, she unlocked the front door and went in, glad somehow that Janice was in her bedroom. Entering her own bedroom, she tossed her purse on the bed and reached for the zipper in the back of her dress.

She should be elated about the latest developments in her business, but all she could think of was how sensuous and soft Trent's lips looked, and how she had wanted to feel them on hers.

A dangerous thought.

LaSalle should have cured her of letting emotions rule over common sense. LaSalle—elegant, handsome, suave, rich. At thirty-one, everything a naive young woman could want in a husband, unless he went into one of his rages—then he became a demon unleashed.

Merciless and cruel.

He had taken a malicious, sadistic pleasure in shredding her self-esteem, alienating her from her friends and family, and making her shamelessly dependent on him. She had been pitiful in seeking his approval.

All in the name of love.

He said he loved her, lavished her with expensive gifts, haute couture clothes, a luxurious home to prove it. The fault had to lie in her.

All her friends were envious when at twenty she had captured one of the most eligible bachelors in the country. She despised leaving her family to move to Atlanta, but she had hated the thought of being without LaSalle more.

Their June wedding had been a spectacular social event. She came home from their honeymoon on St. Thomas happy and wanting to please him in every way. She soon learned that meant dressing more alluringly and entertaining his business friends and associates on a moment's notice.

She was a trophy wife before she knew what the term meant—a thing to be put on display to ensure the envy of other men and thus the admiration of the man who possessed her. Her growing discontent soon affected her responsiveness in bed. One night, eight months after they were married, he went into a jealous rage because she didn't want to have sex. Positive she was having an affair, he threatened to kill her and her lover.

Then he forced himself on her, hurting her in mind and body. Afterward, he had apologized and begged her forgiveness.

The next day he sent her a double strand of perfectly matched pearls and flowers, and that night took her to an exclusive restaurant.

She forgave him, but she knew he had killed something in her for him that nothing could ever revive. He seemed to sense it, and became more demanding of her time, his jealous outbursts more frequent.

She tried, she really did, but she had not been brought up to equate cruelty with love. She knew that even with love marriages sometimes had problems. Her parents sure had their share. Yet not once could she remember them arguing in front of her and Daniel, or saying one derogatory word against the other.

A month later when LaSalle arrived home from work, she was packed and ready to leave. When begging had proved ineffectual, he had hit her. She had fought back, but it had done little good.

She had blacked out. When she had come to, she was tied to the bed. He'd free her if she promised not to leave him or tell her family what had happened.

She'd promised only to hate him until her dying breath.

Dominique came back to the present. Her hands were trembling.

She remembered that LaSalle had been courteous, a gentleman. Her friends and family had thought highly of him. Then he had turned and made her life a hellish nightmare.

Worse, the shame of her stupidity and weakness made it difficult to face her family, sending her on an endless journey of finding peace, finding herself. Finally, both were within her grasp.

Only another man was slipping insidiously into her life, though, making her feel things she had promised herself never to feel again. She couldn't let that happen.

She could handle friendship; she couldn't handle anything more. She never wanted to be that vulnerable again.

Sweat should not be erotic. But Trent's unruly body was living proof that it was.

That morning he had intentionally waited until Dominique went inside after her jog and had enough time to go to her room before he went over to Janice's kitchen door. His plan was to grab a quick cup of coffee and split. After a restless night, he wasn't ready to face the reason so soon.

After his brief knock and Janice's "Come in" he opened the kitchen door and felt as if he had run into a wall. He had calculated wrong.

Dominique was dressed in black leggings with a sweat-dampened, pink top that clung to her honey-bronzed skin and skimmed just above the impossibly sexy indentation of her navel. She must have had a good run, because more sweat ran from her high cheekbones to her soft chin before dropping onto the lush curve of her breasts, dampening the spandex material.

He had the irrational urge to walk over and lick every drop of moisture away. Very, very, slowly.

"Dominique, do you want a bagel or bran muffin?" Janice asked.

"Dominique jerked around, her eyes wide, her breathing uneven. "Nothing. I have a lot to do today."

Janice turned from the refrigerator. "Domini—"

"I'd better get going," she interrupted. "Good morning, Trent."

"Good morning." He watched her practically run from the room. He had probably embarrassed her by drooling again.

"Sit down. You're not going to go anywhere," Janice told him. "May-be you can tell me about last night. I fell asleep reading, and Dominique had gone for her jog by the time I got up this morning."

Trent had never known his hearing was so acute, but somehow he heard water rushing through pipes. Dominique was in the shower, naked and wet. His eyes shut.

"Are you all right?" Janice asked with a frown.

"No," Trent answered truthfully.

Pulling out a chair, Janice practically pushed him down into it. "Are you sick?"

"I wish I were," he answered, his gaze going toward the back bedroom.

Her gaze narrowed with understanding and unease. "Oh, Trent. No you didn't?"

"I'm not sure what it is I've done," he said.

"Then there is hope for both of you," Janice said, taking a seat beside him, her gaze direct. "Dominique isn't ready for a relationship. I'm not sure if she'll ever be. You push her and she'll run."

The question of "why" popped into his head, but he knew he wouldn't get the answer from Janice. He didn't mind, because he wanted Dominique to tell him herself. "I don't want her to leave."

"I believe you, and I know you'll do what's right for her. You're a good man." Janice stood, straightening her apron over her black skirt and zebra print blouse. "Now, tell me about last night while I fix your break-fast."

He did, glad of the diversion. This time when he remembered her idea for his photograph, he realized something he had missed last night.

Dominique might be attracted to him, but she wasn't ready to let her-self become involved. She would accept friendship, but nothing else.

But no matter what they were telling each other, their body language was saying something entirely different. The heat, the need, the hunger, was there waiting. Simmering just beneath the surface.

Sooner or later it was going to come to a boil and they were going to become lovers. When the time came, he wanted no hesitation, no regrets.

Trent wanted her as wild and as hot and as needy as he was going to be. But just as much, he wanted her to be sure of herself, of him.

He wanted them to remain friends afterward. With everything in him he was determined not to jeopardize one for the other.

The best way to ensure that was to make sure she trusted him, trusted herself with him.

He sensed her return as if they were physically connected. He glanced up. She stood several feet away. She looked beautiful and a bit wary in a fuchsia pantsuit.

Her face said it all: he could have her as a friend or alienate her by trying to take it farther before she was ready. Somehow he knew she allowed very few people to see her inner emotions. The knowledge humbled him and gave him hope.

"I think you should eat before you leave. You're going to have a long day," he said.

Her grip on the wide strap of her purse eased. "Maybe you're right."

"Sure I am. That's what friends are for," he reminded her.

She took her seat and reached for the muffin Janice handed her. As the older woman passed, he felt her hand on his shoulder. She trusted him. Before he was through, Dominique would, too.

CHAPTER 8

The phone was ringing when Dominique entered her studio. Hurriedly closing the door she sprinted across the room, tossed her bag on the desk, took a calming breath, and answered, "Photographs by Dominique, Dominique speaking. How may I help you?"

After a warm greeting, Samuel Jacobs, the banker she had met the night before, quickly got down to business. He wanted to schedule an appointment for his grandson and granddaughter. He and his wife didn't want to show favoritism.

Five-year-old Gia was in ballet, and could wear her recital costume. They needed to know if she had the overalls, cane fishing pole, and minnow bucket for six-year-old Michael?

"I'd prefer you get the overalls. The rest I can take care of," she said, wondering where she was going to come up with the items.

"No problem. Is Monday at eleven still open?" he asked.

"Yes," she answered, opening the crisp, new leather-bound appointment book.

"Good. Please put the children down. Their mother will probably come with us. If that isn't too many?"

"Oh, no. That's fine." Taking another deep breath, she asked the dreaded question. "Would you like me to fax you a copy of the price list, or go over it when you come in?"

"You can show it to us then, but I don't really see that as a factor here," he stated simply.

Dominique gave a silent yell. She liked Mr. Jacobs's style. "I look forward to seeing you all Monday at eleven."

"Thank you, Dominique. Good-bye."

"Thank *you*, Mr. Jacobs." Hanging up the phone, she grinned and brought both elbows down sharply with clenched fists. "Yes!"

The phone rang again. She was almost afraid to hope it might be another customer. This time she was much slower in picking up the phone. "Photographs by Dominique, Dominique speaking. How may I help you?"

Mrs. Lloyd wanted to schedule an appointment. While they were talking, the line beeped for another call coming in, but Dominique didn't click over. She wanted each client to feel that when she was talking to them they had her undivided attention.

Ten minutes later when the call was finished, Mrs. Lloyd had scheduled a ten o'clock Wednesday appointment at her home for her garden photograph. Dominique was thrilled. Two appointments weren't going to keep the wolf from the door, but she had a chance to show what she knew. That's all she had ever wanted, a chance.

Opening the drawer, she reached for the yellow pages to look up fishing equipment. Before she could find the listing she had another call, then another, both from the other women guests at the dinner party. Coincidentally, their daughters were Idlewild debutantes, and they wanted something unique for their formal photographs in their white gowns.

Ideas formed in Dominique's mind while she was talking to each woman. She had no doubt that once she saw the gowns on the young ladies she could give them a photograph they'd cherish for a lifetime. Tuesday morning and afternoon were booked.

Hanging up the phone, she was ecstatic. Picking up the other yellow pages she turned to T. Finding the number, she dialed. "May I speak with Mr. Masters?"

"Whom shall I say is calling?" asked a woman in a slow Southern drawl.

"Dominique Everette," she answered, wondering how many women worked at the trucking company.

"Hi, Dominique. Everything all right?" Trent asked as soon as he came on the line.

"Hi. Couldn't be better, thanks to you." Leaning back in the chair, she smiled and told him about the calls. "My appointment book finally has something in it."

He chuckled. "I told you going to the dinner party with me would be good for business."

"Yes, you did," she said, enjoying the sound of his laughter and his voice. "I don't know how to thank you."

"Friends help each other."

"I'm beginning to find that out," she said softly.

"Stick with me, Buttercup. You ain't seen nothing yet."

"That's the second time you've called me that. Why?"

"You sure you want to know?" he asked, his voice wary.

"Yes."

"A buttercup is a wild yellow flower that is as beautiful as it is delicate, and can adapt and flourish in the harshest conditions," he explained.

"Oh." She felt flattered and immensely pleased. "I guess I'd better go. I have to find a place that sells minnow buckets and cane fishing poles."

"Travis Bait House on Lake Ray Hubbard should have everything," he said. "How soon do you need them?"

"Monday morning."

"We can take a drive out there Sunday and pick up everything you need," he suggested.

"You don't have to do that. Just tell me how to get there and I can find it by myself," she said.

"I'm sure you could, but the problem would be fitting the pole into your car."

She bit her lower lip. She hadn't thought of that. "I'm sure the salesperson will have some idea."

"Yeah. Stick it in the car and hope it makes it to wherever you're going. In the meantime, you're watching the fishing pole instead of where you're going," he said curtly. "I'm taking you."

She laughed, surprising herself again at her easy acceptance of his taking charge. "You're as bossy as my brother."

"I'd like to meet him sometime. Is he in the business sector?" Trent asked.

"He works for an oil company," Dominique said, uneasy about telling half-truths to a man who valued honesty so much.

"You have another call coming in. See you tonight." He clicked off.

Dominique clicked over to another call. It was the investment broker from the Lloyd's party. Minutes later his son was scheduled for Friday afternoon. Hanging up the phone, she smiled. Trent had certainly gotten her business rolling. Just wait until she told him tonight.

Her smile faded as she realized what she was thinking. What she had done. The first person she had wanted to share news of her business turning around with had been Trent. Not her family, not Janice.

She could tell herself that the reason was that he was mainly responsible for the increase in her business, but she knew it went deeper than that. Somehow he had managed to do what no other man had done in eight years, make her forget caution and act instinctively.

Perhaps he had been able to do so because she didn't have to worry if he liked her for herself or her family's wealth and connections. To him she was Dominique Everette, a struggling photographer who needed a second chance. And he was determined to help her get it.

A man who thought of and cared for others without expecting something in return was difficult to dismiss. Add to that Trent's handsomeness and his knee-weakening smile, and any woman was in trouble. Dominique wasn't any different. She had been around wealthier, more sophisticated men, but never one who called to her in so many ways.

But there were other, more dangerous, reasons. She wasn't going to fool herself. He was attracted to her just as she was attracted to him. Yet, unlike other men in the past, who'd wanted to use her for their own selfish lust, Trent seemed willing to wait. A man who placed a woman's needs before his own was a rarity in her life's experiences.

But for how long?

Putting away the phone book and her purse, she leaned back in her chair. The question she should be asking herself was how long she could hold out against him and the yearning of her own body.

The answer wasn't comforting, and neither was the thought of what she had to do.

Trent leaned back in his chair, a wide grin on his face. Dominique had sounded happy and proud. He was pretty proud of himself the way he had maneuvered his way into taking her to get her props. Maybe after they finished he could take her ri—

"That grin is even goofier than the one you had this morning, when you came in whistling."

Trent rocked forward in his chair and stared at his secretary, Anita Tabor, in the doorway. Of all the people to catch him off guard, Anita was the worst.

Besides being on his case about finding a woman and getting married, she was an incurable romantic. Her eyes still misted when she found one of the notes her husband invariably left in her purse.

Anita maintained she intended to keep the romance in her marriage by refusing to grow old. She wore light brown contact lenses and kept her gray hair dyed a startling shade of red that matched her inch-long nails.

Trent didn't remember ever seeing her in anything that wasn't fitted to her mature figure. Today she wore a white rayon blouse with ruffles in the front and a straight burgundy skirt.

She was the best secretary he had ever had. She got things right the first time and could work independently. He didn't think anyone could beat her on the word processor. She had a knack for remembering facts and dates, spoke three languages, and her computer skills were almost as good as his.

He had always been grateful he had let his chief mechanic Herb talk him into interviewing his wife when she had lost her job due to downsizing. Today, Trent wasn't so sure. Anita had a tenacity for badgering until she got the answer she wanted.

"Did you need something?"

Her brightly polished nails clicked against the faux pearls around her neck as she advanced farther into the room. "To see how far you had gotten on that bid. But that can wait." She placed surprisingly smooth hands on the cluttered desk. "So who is she?"

"A friend," he said, leaning over the inch-thick bid proposal for a lucrative contract with the Dallas-Ft. Worth International Airport that was only a third finished.

"Does this friend have a face and figure to match that siren's voice of hers?"

"Anita, don't you have work to do?" he asked, turning a page without seeing what was written. Instead he saw Dominique as she had been that morning—sensuously alluring, her skin damp with perspiration—he had wanted to press his lips to every tempting inch of her. His chair squeaked as he twisted in his seat.

"Since you didn't deny it, she must have. So I guess this means I won't have to worry about you as much, or try and set you up with some of the women who have been bugging me for an introduction."

His head came up. "What?"

"Thought that might get your attention." She shook her head of shoulder-length, twisted curls. "Don't worry. None of them seemed right for you. On the other hand, this Dominique Everette sounded mighty interesting."

Trent went back to studying the report. Anita also never forgot a name. "She's just a friend."

"From that grin on your face earlier I'd say you don't plan on staying 'just friends,' " Anita said, giving him a broad, knowing smile.

His head came back up, something hard glittered in his eyes. "Dominique is a lady. I don't—"

"Don't go caveman on me," she interrupted smoothly. "You know I'll respect any friend of yours. It's about time you thought about something other than these trucks."

Trent relaxed. "Herb wouldn't agree with you."

A sultry smile played across Anita's red lips. "You wanna bet?"

Trent couldn't keep the smile from his face. Anita was as saucy as they came. "Get to work."

"So I don't guess you'll be taking any more long hauls in the near future?" she asked.

"You could say that's a safe assumption."

A frown worked its away across Anita's faintly lined face. "Watch yourself, Trent. You've been out of circulation for a long time. You're more likely to fall harder and faster, and be a lot more gullible."

He gave his secretary a long, disbelieving stare. "You can't be serious."

"It happens all the time. People aren't as honest and up front as they used to be, and it's getting worse," she told him, then nodded her head for emphasis. "So take it slow and easy. You're the best there is."

"You just remember what I said," Anita said indignantly and walked to the door. "There are no rules these days. I don't want to see you hurt."

Watching Anita leave, Trent dismissed her misgivings. No one was going to get hurt. They were two consenting adults. When it was over it was over—even as the thought came to him, he realized it wouldn't be that easy or that cut-and-dried.

But for the life of him, he couldn't imagine turning away from Dominique, or trying to stop whatever forces were hurtling them toward a foregone conclusion.

Several hours later he learned Dominique had other ideas. Standing in Janice's kitchen with a bouquet of flowers in his clutched fist, the happiness he had carried with him all day went from disbelief to anger.

"Dominique's in her room with a headache and asked not to be disturbed." Janice's usually direct gaze wavered.

"I see," he said, his voice stiff.

"She said to tell you she'd pick up the fishing equipment herself tomorrow," Janice continued, obviously uncomfortable with the situation.

"You tried to warn me," he said, his mouth a narrow line.

"Trent, I'm sorry." Janice laid her hand on his tense forearm.

"Anita did, too. Shows how much I know." Thrusting the flowers and bottle of vintage champagne into her hands, he swung toward the back kitchen door.

Janice wheeled around and stalked to Dominique's bedroom. After a brief knock she entered. Dominique sat on the Victorian windowseat, her arms wrapped around her updrawn knees, staring out the window. "These are for you. Obviously, he thought you two had something to celebrate."

Slowly, Dominique turned, her gaze touching the bouquet of pink roses nestled in baby's breath, the hand-painted, pale pink and white blossoms on the bottle of Perrier-Jouet. The knot that had formed in her throat—when she told Janice earlier she didn't wish to see Trent again—thickened.

There was nothing Dominique wanted more than to bury her face in the heady floral fragrance, toast the success of the day with Trent, hear him laugh, laugh with him.

Too foolish. Too dangerous. Her eyes shut and she turned away.

Little by little he was scaling her defenses, making her feel things she had thought she'd never experience again. She might have been able to fight the sexual urges, but the urge to share with him her thoughts, her dreams, was what gave her the will to shut him out of her life. He was becoming too important.

The realization scared her. Need made a person vulnerable. She'd sworn to herself that she'd never be at the mercy of another man.

"One day you're going to have to stop running, Dominique," Janice told her and shut the door softly behind her.

"I thought I had," came the soft reply. "I thought I had."

Seventeen short minutes later Trent strode through his outer office, his face hard, his booted heels crackling like rifle shots against the vinyl flooring. Ninety minutes earlier he had left with a happy wave and a grin on his face. Wisely, no one commented. More than one person looked at Anita, but the angry expression on her face didn't invite questions.

Trent slammed his office door, jerked out his desk chair, and flung himself into the seat. His mind was in a tumult.

What the hell had happened between that morning and this afternoon? She couldn't have been stringing him along. The thought that she might have sent a shaft of red hot anger through him before he dismissed the idea.

Something else was going on with Dominique, and he was going to find out what it was. He wasn't a quitter. He'd learned long ago to fight for what he wanted. He wanted Dominique. He was coming out of the chair when his office door burst open.

Anita stood poised in the opening. "Haskall jackknifed outside of Richland near Richland Creek."

Trent came the rest of the way in one controlled rush, his mind clicking. The day was clear and sunny, the roads good. If Haskall had been hitting the bottle after he swore he had cleaned up—"Status?"

"Unknown. Haskall was carrying high-end office furniture. The trucker behind him called," Anita informed Trent, following him out to the driveway.

"Have Simons follow me with a truck. Don't call Haskall's wife until you have some facts to give her." Jerking open the door of his truck, he climbed in and started the motor.

"The driver who called said there might be a fuel leak. Richland Creek feeds into Richland-Chambers Lake." Anita had saved the worst for last.

Trent said one explicit word before pulling out. Rubber burned. He had thought the day couldn't possibly get worse. He was wrong.

Dominique couldn't sleep. After an hour or more of tossing in bed she had given up around one A.M. and gone outside. She should be sound asleep after such a wonderful day.

She was booked for most of next week, and the football player and his wife had been thrilled with the pictures and ordered extra for both sets of grandparents. She found no joy in either. She had no illusions as to the reason why, she had gone outside.

Over the six-foot cedar fence and blooming pink crepe myrtles, she could see Trent's dark house. Her slim arms wrapped around her. Her concern for him had mounted with each passing hour.

She had hurt him, and now he had more problems to deal with. The accident had been on the Ten O'clock News. Briefly Trent had been interviewed, his face grim. The cause of the accident remained unclear, but the threat of hundreds of gallons of diesel fuel leaking into the nearby Richland Creek and then contaminating the lake it fed into had local officials worried.

The cleanup of Richland-Chambers lake, if necessary, would be very costly, and would be the sole responsibility of the trucking company. Already contacted in Dallas and watching the situation closely were representatives from the Environmental Protection Agency. Frantically, she had switched the channel, seeking more information, but learned little more.

She didn't need to feel Janice's condemning gaze to know she couldn't have picked a worse time to push Trent out of her life. Protecting herself didn't seem all that important at the moment.

"Trent, why aren't you home by now?"

"I am."

Dominique spun around. In the half shadows of the light cast by the lamp in the backyard he stood silhouetted. She took two running steps before she realized she had been about to run into his arms.

Uncertain and uneasy now that he was here, she pulled the long silk kimono up over her bare shoulders. Trent's dark gaze followed the motion, then lifted to her face. She felt his searing look from fifteen feet away.

"W-What are you doing here?" she asked, her voice unsteady.

"Coming to see you."

Surprise widened her eyes. "Me?"

He nodded toward the light in the last window at the back of the house. "I didn't want to wake Janice."

"There are three bedrooms besides Janice's. How did you know which one?" she asked.

For a moment, his face harshened, then cleared. "The wallpaper came in the evening before your first arrival. The hanger couldn't come on such short notice. I volunteered to help. After meeting you the next day, I realized why Janice was so anxious about getting everything ready for the room."

"I see." His statement only made her feel worse. He was one of the most thoughtful men she had ever met.

"I wish I did. What did I do to upset you?" he asked, taking a step closer. "I'd apologize, but for the life of me I can't think of a reason, and believe me, I've tried."

Shame and guilt slumped her shoulders. "Nothing."

He took another step. "Then why didn't you want to see me?"

She could run, or face the truth. "You make me feel things I don't want to feel."

In the dim light she could feel him studying her closely. "He hurt you badly, didn't he?"

He was too perceptive. "I don't want to talk about it."

"If that's the way you want it," he said, taking another step closer. "Why are you out here?"

"I—I couldn't sleep until I knew everything was all right," she told him, wishing she had the courage to add, "that *you* were all right."

"It is now," he said, and slowly closed the distance between them. His hands lifted, settling gently on her shoulders. He stared down into her wide, uncertain eyes a long time before he slowly, gently, pulled her into his arms.

Her palms flattened against the hard wall of his wide chest, felt the unsteady beat of his heart, knew hers was equally unsteady. He seemed to surround her with his masculinity.

Instead of fear, she felt an inexorable need to press closer. "W—We were worried about you."

He rubbed his cheek against her tousled hair, the palm of his hands pressed against her back. "Sorry."

She let the pads of her fingertips stroke him absently through his shirt. She tilted her head back to look at at him. "Was it serious?"

"Could have been worse," he said, his thumb stroking her shoulder.

"How much worse?" she asked, barely able to string a sentence together with him touching her.

He stared down at her beautiful face, saw the worry she didn't try to hide. He didn't remember a time he'd wanted to share his thoughts—he did now.

"The driver wasn't drunk, as the policeman first thought. He was in acidosis from undiagnosed diabetes. The fuel spill was contained and cleaned up before it reached the creek. And, thanks to all of my trucks being equipped with air ride, the load didn't sustain any damage."

"You've been at the scene all this time?" she asked, knowing she should step away but enjoying the heat, the solidity of his body, too much.

His hand swept away an errant curl from her face before answering,

"Most of the time. Then I went to the hospital to see Haskall. They care-flighted him to Baylor here in Dallas. I wanted to check on him and assure his wife about insurance taking care of his bill, and tell her that the accident was not his fault."

"Did you think it was?"

His face hardened for a fraction of a second. "Yes. Haskall had a drinking problem, but he swore to me he had been sober for six months. I gave him the short run to Waco to test him."

Dominique felt the chill again. "And if he hadn't told the truth, and been drinking?"

Trent's face hardened. "I would have helped prosecute him to the fullest extent of the law. Drinking and driving don't mix."

"I agree, but something tells me more is involved."

"My customers depend on me getting their merchandise there on time and safely, and I depend on my people to be honest and conscientious. Any time one of those factors is in question, the company suffers," he told her. "I won't allow that."

"That was Haskall's second chance?" she asked, fearing she already knew the answer.

"Actually, it was his first. His brother, Carl, is one of my best drivers. When I hired Haskall, I told him one slip and he was history. I can abide almost anything—except a liar."

Dominique finally had the strength to move away. What would Trent say when he found out the half-truths she had been telling him? "I'd better go in."

"You think I'm too severe?" he asked.

"No." The answer came softly. In any other circumstances, he'd have her admiration. How many other employees would have given the driver a chance? "Actually, I think you're a very nice man."

He scowled. "That's a terrible thing to say."

Because she now understood where he was coming from, she smiled. "Not when you consider I haven't met someone like you in a very long time."

Everything in Trent stilled except his galloping heart. There were so many questions he wanted to ask about her past, about the men in her life, but right now he just wanted to feel her softness, inhale the light fragrance she wore.

"I was thinking the same thing about you."

"Is that good or bad?" she asked, a slight quiver in her voice.

His hands settled possessively on the curve of her waist. "Definitely good."

She licked her dry lips, her body trembling. "Trent, I—"

"It's all right. We'll go as slow as you need to," he said, his head bending, his lips brushing softly against her cheek. Then he released her and stepped back. "Thanks for worrying about me and staying up. No one has ever done that before."

Her eyes widened in surprise and sorrow.

He must have seen the sorrow because he said, "No one has ever tucked me into bed, either. You want to come over and make that a first, too?"

The words were said half teasingly, but the image of Trent in bed and reaching for her flashed through her mind. Heat splintered through her. "I think you can manage on your own. Goodnight."

Turning, she fled back into the house, closing the sliding glass door behind her. *One day you're going to run all the way to me,* thought Trent.

He stood waiting for the light to go off in her room, to know Dominique was in bed. Instead, the light came on in the den. A frown worked its way across his forehead. He had taken a step toward the house to see if things were all right when Dominique came rushing out, carrying something in her hand.

Breathless, her hair tousled around her face, she stopped in front of him. "I was afraid you'd be gone. I thought you might be hungry."

Trent felt an odd twist of his heart. He accepted the tray covered with a linen napkin with shaky hands. "I am. Thanks."

Moistening her lips, she stepped back. "Goodnight, and thanks for the flowers and champagne."

"You're welcome. Goodnight, Dominique. Sleep well."

"You, too."

"I will now," he confessed.

"So will I," she whispered softly, then ran back into the house soundlessly.

CHAPTER 9

Dominique knew she was dragging Saturday morning and acknowl-edged the reason: she wanted to see Trent before she went to work. She had slowly jogged by his house, but this time she hadn't seen the slight flicker of the curtain or felt his gaze. Somehow the run hadn't been the same.

Returning home, she had showered, dressed, and gone to the kitchen. As usual, Janice was there preparing breakfast. While helping her Dominique had told her that she and Trent had talked and everything was fine between them.

Janice had turned from slicing grapefruit and given Dominique a hug and a kiss on the cheek. The pride in her godmother's brown eyes touched her. They both had expected Trent to show up for breakfast. He hadn't.

Janice had left at nine for her antique store. Finally, at nine-thirty, Dominique couldn't wait any longer. She reasoned that he was probably still asleep after all he had been through. She'd see him that afternoon, surely, but somehow that seemed a long time away.

Outside, she got into her car, tossed her purse onto the passenger seat, and backed out. The Jaguar had barely straightened when she heard her name.

She hit the brakes sharply, sending her purse sliding to the floor. Her gaze locked on Trent sprinting across his yard toward her in a pair of faded denim jeans, the tail of his open blue shirt flapping. His long feet were bare. He looked sleep-rumpled and huggable.

"Hey, I almost missed you," he said, grinning down at her, one hand on the hood of the car.

Dominique felt her heart rate increase, and smiled up at him. "Good morning. I'm glad you didn't."

His face softened at her admission. "Once I check on Haskall and the cleanup site, I'm going to watch the football team I sponsor today. Care to come with me?"

"What time?" She didn't even have to think. She had decided last night, when she handed him the tray and he had looked so stunned and pleased, that she wasn't running anymore. Such a small thing, but it had apparently meant so much to him. A man who could appreciate such a simple gesture could be trusted with her newly awakening feelings.

"Around three," he answered.

"I have a few errands to run, but I should be home by two-thirty."

"Good. I'll pick you up then. I have to get the drinks. What should I get for you?" he asked.

"Bottled water."

"Any particular kind?" he asked.

"Anything you choose will be fine," she said.

"A man likes an agreeable woman."

"With the right man that isn't difficult," she bantered easily.

His gaze centered on her lips, then he stepped back. "See you at two-thirty."

Dominique drove away with a silly smile on her face, and she wasn't going to worry about it. She was going to enjoy her time with Trent and take one day at a time. If that broke every rule in her book, so be it.

Trent, in jeans, black polo shirt, and baseball cap was waiting for Dominique on Janice's front porch when she drove into the driveway at 2:45. Slamming out of the car, she hurried toward him. "Sorry, I'm late. Traffic was a snarled mess."

Standing, he smiled easily at her. "As long as you're here."

Opening the door, she waved him to a seat in the living room. "I won't be but a minute."

He laughed. "Somehow I doubt that." He laughed harder when she frowned at him over her retreating shoulder. "These games never start on time, so don't worry."

"It's just that I hate people to wait for me," she said, rounding the hall corner.

"Some things are worth the wait."

She paused, threw a smile over her shoulder, then quickly entered her room. She had already decided what she would wear, so it was a matter of throwing off her oyster pleated slacks and blouse and pulling on a raspberry-colored camp shirt and khaki walking shorts. Next came switching her handbag, jewelry, and shoes. Her room was a mess, but in less than three minutes she was back in the living room.

"Ready."

Trent glanced up from the magazine he was flipping through. His gaze tracked her from the raspberry sun visor to the colorful scarf tied on the strap of her purse to the white tennis shoes, then back up again. She had knockout legs that made a man's hands itch.

"Isn't this all right?"

"More than all right. You're beautiful."

Dominique blushed—something she couldn't remember doing since she was a teenager. "Thank you. It's in the genes. My mother's family is very striking. When she married my father, a full-blooded Muscogee Indian, it made an interesting mix."

Trent studied her intently. As if unable to help himself, he stroked the knuckle of his hand down her cheek and let it remain there. "Fascinating and exquisite would be more like it."

The reverence in his tone as much as his touch made her shiver. He smelled good. She wanted to move closer and wrap herself in his scent, in him. All she had to do was lean forward and—

"If you do we'll never make it to the game," Trent growled, his eyes dark and intense.

She took all her courage in her hands. "Would that be so bad?"

"I promised." His hand fell.

Dominique watched the need mixed with regret in his dark chocolate eyes. Here was a man any woman or child or friend could count on. "Then let's go. On the way, I can tell you about the fantastic sale I made with Bruiser and his wife, and you can tell me why you didn't mention his nickname."

Throwing his arm around her shoulders, Trent started to lead her out of the room. "If I had told you I wanted you to photograph a Cowboy named Bruiser you would have tossed me out of your studio."

"Point taken."

"On the other hand, the teenagers on the football team you're going to meet think Bruiser and his teammates are the coolest guys anywhere." Trent opened the front door and locked the glass door after them. "And when they learn you took his picture, you're going to be besieged by every player there."

Dominique's eyes widened.

Trent kissed her quickly on the lips. "Don't worry, I'll protect you."

Twenty-five minutes later when they arrived at Kiest Park, Dominique's insides were still quivering like gelatin in an earthquake. Trent hadn't acted as if the kiss bothered him at all. If she hadn't noticed the slight trembling of his hand when he put the key in the ignition, she might have thought it hadn't.

As it was, she was already anticipating the next kiss. This time, he wasn't going to get away with a little peck. Since she had decided to stop running last night after they met in Janice's backyard, she was rather anxious to see what she had gotten herself into.

She smiled secretly. Shameless and eager.

Trent cut the motor and glanced over at her. "That kind of smile has been known to get a woman in trouble."

"Only the woman?"

Trent's eyes blazed. The easy smile slid off his face. He twisted in his seat toward her.

"Trent, I'm glad you're here!" cried a happy male voice.

Dominique could almost read Trent's mind. It wasn't pretty. But when he turned to the man approaching the truck, his voice was warm and friendly.

"Hi, Charles. All the team here?" he asked, climbing out of the truck.

"Every one," Charles said, his gaze following Dominique as she rounded the truck and came to stand beside Trent.

"Dominique Everette, Charles Powell, the coach of The Tigers, the next divisional champions."

"Hello, Dominique," he greeted, taking off a cap with a "T" on its front and nodding.

"Hello, Charles." She held up her Nikon. "Mind if I take some pictures?"

"No. Help yourself." The older man turned to Trent. "Heard about one of your trucks, and know you had your hands full. I appreciate you coming."

"I promised to bring the drinks. Besides, I wanted to see them play," he said simply.

"You won't be disappointed." Charles slapped Trent on the back.

"Come on. We'd better get these drinks over there before they come looking for us." Easily lifting the large cooler from the back of the truck, the men started toward a group of loud teenagers.

"You know anything about football?" Charles glanced over his shoulder.

"Very little," she admitted. She had graduated from an all girls private school and college. Although Daniel had excelled in sports, his boy's prep school had only offered tennis and golf. In college he had concentrated on getting his MBA in three years. He succeeded with a perfect grade point average.

"Don't worry, Charles," Trent said. "I intend to teach her all she needs to know."

She glanced up sharply. Trent had a smile on his face that made her knees weak. He winked and continued toward the bench.

Dominique slowly followed and wished she knew more about football. Like how long the game lasted.

Ninety-three minutes and counting in the last minutes of the fourth quarter, she later learned. Cheering from the sidelines next to Trent, Dominique didn't mind. She was having a wonderful time. The thirteen and fourteen year-old boys had been predictable in their initial reaction to her; they had all given Trent the thumb's up sign.

He'd grinned and slung his arm around her shoulder. It was a good thing he had, because he chose that moment to tell the boys about her taking Bruiser's photograph. Suddenly she was surrounded, the entire team wanting to be near her, wanting her to take their picture.

Seeing their eager faces, she volunteered to be the team's official photographer and take all of their pictures. A wild whoop went up. The only reason she wasn't lifted up too was Trent's admonishment for them not to.

The Tigers had taken to the field and dominated it. Charles was right. He had a good team. Even with Dominique's limited knowledge of the game, she knew The Tigers played with skill and intelligence. She found herself cheering the teenagers along with Trent, and giving the referee just as hard a time.

When the clock ran out, The Tigers were ahead by nine points. Their side went wild. The coach was hoisted into the air. Trent picked Dominique up and spun her around. By the time he put her down, several team members were there, wanting to lift her up again.

Trent placed his arm protectively around her, a wide grin on his face. "Told you I'd protect you."

"My hero," she said.

"You'd better believe it," he bantered, then turned to a beaming Charles. "You think this calls for pizza?"

Charles's "Yes," was drowned by the team's roar of approval. "I can follow you with the team in the van."

He glanced down at Dominique. "You don't mind, do you?"

"No. They played hard."

"That's my girl," he said, giving her a brief squeeze before releasing her and picking up the cooler. "Charles, we'll meet you at the regular place."

Dominique couldn't resist. As soon as Trent turned, she raised the camera, lowered the lens, and clicked.

Stopping, he glanced over his shoulder. "What's the matter?"

"Nothing. Something caught my interest," she said, catching up with him. "I think it might be my best shot of the day."

* * *

As expected the pizza celebration was a wild, happy affair, with the teenage boys trying to talk with their mouths full and replaying the moments when they had shone and ignoring the times they fumbled or missed a tackle. Trent listened attentively to each player, his interest and concern for them obvious.

At the moment he was feeding the jukebox. Dominique had never heard some of the selections, but from the way Trent bobbed his head to the beat of the music, he had.

"He's good with the boys, isn't he?" Charles commented.

"Very," Dominique said, raising her camera to take a picture of Trent standing in the midst of the youths.

"It was a fortunate day for us when he came by the Y years ago to become a sponsor." Charles nodded toward the laughing group. "Most of them are from single parent families and live in situations that would make most adults shudder. Playing team sports they learn the value of hard work and discipline."

Her camera lowered. "They also learn someone else cares about them. You. And Trent."

The tall, lean man nodded. "But Trent is their hero. He made it through the system. He has promised each of them a scholarship if they keep their grades up and stay clean. Only one kid had to be dropped from the program."

"What happened?"

His eyes saddened. "Joyriding in a stolen car. He said he didn't know the car was stolen, but the rules for players are clear. Any infraction with the law and you're off the team and out of the program."

"Did you believe him?"

"Yes. I think his cousin Isaac orchestrated the entire thing to get him thrown off the team, so his control over him would be total. Isaac is a rebellious, angry teenager. We couldn't help him at the Y." Charles slumped back in the booth. "We might have been able to help his young cousin, Jessie. He's a good kid. Trent liked the boy. It tore him up to put Jessie off the team. But rules are rules. You start bending them for one, and discipline is shot to hell."

"Where is he now?" she asked.

"Following Isaac straight to the pen or an early grave. They live in the area, as do the other kids." Leaning forward, he twisted the paper his straw came in. "Isaac is an accident waiting to happen. Unfortunately, when it does Jessie is going to be right along beside him."

"Hey, why the long faces?" Trent asked, sliding in the booth beside her.

"I was telling her about Isaac and Jessie," Charles explained.

The smile faded from Trent's face. "Isaac is going to drag Jessie right along with him until they're of age, and then some judge is going to throw the book at them both. If they live that long."

"Can't you do anything?" she asked.

Hard eyes stabbed her. "What? Until Jessie is more afraid of the consequences than he is of Isaac, there's nothing I can do. I've gone by there a couple of times, talked to his mother, but she isn't much help."

She touched his arm. "You tried."

"It wasn't good enough," he bit out.

"It was for them," she said, nodding toward the youths who were either clustered around the juke box, talking to a group of girls who had come in, or playing arcade games. "You made a difference for them. It hurts, but sometimes you can't save them all."

"I know, but I don't have to like it."

She gently placed her hand on his. "You wouldn't be the man you are if you did."

"Domini—"

"Hey, look at the babe."

Dominique glanced up to see four youths wearing oversized shirts, baggy pants, and sideways baseball caps. Gold chains glittered around their necks. The oldest appeared to be about seventeen or eighteen, with a scraggly goatee. Beside her, Trent tensed.

"You want a real man, Honey, to rock your world."

Trent came out of the booth in a rush. Grinning, the young man who had spoken held up his hands. "Be cool, Dude. Be cool."

"One day, if we're both lucky, you're going to reach adulthood and I'll be waiting," Trent said.

The teenager chuckled and glanced around the restaurant. "Did you hear this old man threaten me? I oughta call the cops."

"You mean you know your numbers, Isaac?" Trent asked mildly.

Laughter erupted in the restaurant, then ebbed just as quickly when Isaac turned toward the sound. His brown eyes narrowed, he faced Trent again. "Watch it, Old Man. I might forget my mama taught me to respect my elders." He snickered and glanced around. "I forgot you wouldn't know anything about *that,* since your mama threw you away like trash."

Dominique gasped and tried to come out of the booth. Trent blocked her way and it was like trying to move the bolted down booth.

Charles had no such problem. "Say another word, Isaac, and I'll gladly spend the night in jail," he warned.

Dominique glared over Trent's rigid shoulder. "Leave him alone!"

"You let everybody do your fighting for you, Old Man." Isaac sneered. "See, Jessie, he ain't nothing, just like I said."

An overweight black teenager with a cherubic face glanced at them, then away. Head bowed, he dug both hands into his pockets.

Isaac didn't notice. He was too busy looking Trent up and down in distaste. He sneered again. "Ain't nothing. I could screw the bitc—"

Trent struck without warning. Isaac found himself a foot off the floor, Trent's hand clutching the collar of his jersey. His eyes bugged, then watered. Only a strangled gasp managed to slip past his gasping lips.

"Trent. Trent, please," Dominique pleaded, trying to peel Trent's hand away from Isaac's neck without success. No one else moved. "Trent, please."

"I hate to do this, but she's right, Mr. Masters."

Dominique turned to see two policemen coming toward them. Relief surged through her until she thought of the consequences. "He was provoked."

"Never doubted it, Miss," said the older of the two—Officer Bolder was on his gold nameplate. "Mr. Masters, he's going to pass out in a second and we're going to have to take him to the hospital, and there's going to be a lot of paperwork. I hate doing paperwork. Keeps me off my beat."

"Trent, *please!*" Dominique pleaded.

His hand opened. Isaac crumpled to the floor. Gasping for breath, he held both hands to his throat.

"I can either assume Mr. Masters was teaching you a new judo technique, or there was some type of altercation," said Officer Bolden. Isaac was already nodding his head.

"If there was an altercation your parole officer would have to be notified. I'd have to take statements from all the witnesses involved, and if I learned you caused this in any way, I'm positive your parole officer would consider it a clear violation of your parole, and back in juvenile you'd go."

The policeman looked thoughtful. "Then again, your overworked parole officer might decide he's tired of fooling with you and let you be classified as an adult, and off to Lew Sterrett jail you'd go. Seems I remember from all our associations that you turned seventeen last week, and to the courts you're now considered an adult."

Trent moved. The second policeman stepped in front of him.

"Your call, Isaac," Officer Bolden said.

The young man grabbed his baseball cap from the floor, then pulled himself to his feet. His cold eyes were savage and promised retribution. His gaze moved past Trent, who towered a good five inches over the policeman, to Dominique by his side.

"You made a mistake, Old Man." Holding his throat, he shoved his way through the crowd that parted to allow him to pass. Silently the three youths with him followed. The youngest and heaviest of the three stopped and stared back at Trent briefly, then followed the others.

"The action is over, folks. Take your seats," the policeman ordered, then said, "Charles, why don't you get the boys together and take them home?"

"I'll call you later, Trent." With a slight squeeze of the younger man's arm, Charles passed and motioned for the players. They were almost out the door before Trent moved.

The policemen and Dominique followed closely. Trent stopped in front of the group of wide-eyed teenagers.

"I broke a rule. What I did was wrong. I let my temper get the best of me. That's not how you settle differences. Violence creates problems, not solve them," he said. "If Sergeant Bolden weren't a good man, I'd be in trouble and off the team. I wouldn't have liked that."

"We understand, Mr. Masters," said Kent, the captain and quarterback of The Tigers. "You couldn't let Isaac call Miss Everette out of her name. A man's got to protect his woman. We'll see you at practice next week if you can make it." He held up his hand, palm out.

Trent slapped the palm, then in turn each of the subsequent players'.

"I told you you made a difference," Dominique said, taking his arm as the last player left the restaurant. He flinched. She frowned up at him. "Trent?"

His face grim, he turned to the policeman. "Sorry, Officer Bolden."

"Like the lady said, you were provoked. Why don't you take her home so the place can get back to normal?" he suggested.

"Did you just happen by, or did someone call you?" Trent asked, not moving.

"The manager. Now, good-bye."

Nodding, he closed his fingers loosely around Dominique's arm, then led her from the restaurant. Outside he opened the door of his truck and helped her in. Without a word he came around, started the engine, and drove off.

Silently, Dominique sat in the truck, hoping to give him time to work through his feelings. He was angry, but she thought there was hurt and embarrassment as well.

A short while later he pulled into Janice's driveway behind her Mercedes. Leaving the motor running, he walked Dominique to the front door. "Good-bye." Spinning on his heels, he went back to his truck and drove off.

Dominique didn't move until the truck disappeared. Sighing, she slowly went inside. Trent was doing his best to shut her out. She didn't like the reversal of roles.

"Dominique, is that you?"

"Yes." Janice always asked the same thing, Dominique thought. She took another step across the marble entryway and could go no further. There was no way she could leave Trent alone and in pain.

Placing her handbag on the couch, she fished until she found her keys, took off her sun visor and the silver barrette holding her hair in a ponytail, then swung toward the door. "I'm going over to Trent's. Don't wait dinner."

"I may be gone when you get back," Janice said, coming into the living room as she fastened the sleeve of a figure-flattering, gold gown.

Her hand on the knob, Dominique glanced around and whistled. "You look fantastic."

Janice blushed prettily. "Paul Osgood—he owns the restaurant across the street from my shop—invited me to the Meyerson Symphony Center to see Porgy and Bess." She bit her lower lip. "I'm kind of nervous. It's the first time I've been out on a date in over a year."

"Wish I could give you some pointers, but it's been longer for me," Dominique said, then grinned. "But if it's any consolation, you're going to knock his eyes out."

Janice laughed. "That's the idea."

"Have fun."

"Thanks, Dear."

Opening the door, Dominique headed for Trent's house. Obviously he didn't want to talk with her. Too bad. They were friends. He was in misery, and she'd be damned if she'd let him stay that way or allow him to shut her out.

CHAPTER 10

It took nine rings of the doorbell to get Trent to answer. His face wasn't reassuring when he did. From his imposing height of six-feet, brown eyes that had been warm and teasing before Isaac's arrival were as icy as his clipped voice. "Yes?"

On hearing the harsh sound she wanted to weep. She swallowed. Trent didn't need tears. "I'd like to speak to you for a minute. You can time me if you want."

For an uncertain moment she thought he would deny her entrance and close the door in her face. When he simply stepped back, she didn't hesitate to step inside. Her gaze never left his stiff, unyielding face, nor his hers.

There was anger there, but there was also something deeper, shutting her and everything and everyone else out. She thought of him growing up without the support of a family, and had to fight harder to keep her tears from falling.

How much worse would her nightmarish marriage have been if she hadn't had her family, if all her life she hadn't known that they would always be there for her? Whether Isaac spoke the truth or not, his spiteful words had wounded Trent deeply.

"Trent." She said his name softly, her voice trying to convey that she was there for him.

"I don't want your pity, or anyone else's," he clipped out. "Your minute is almost up."

So he didn't want to listen. Then maybe . . . Even as the idea of what she was going to do came to her, she realized she was about to break another rule—that of never being the aggressor in a relationship. She smiled.

Her slim arms lifted. She felt the tenseness in Trent's shoulders as her hands slid around his neck. His deep brown eyes widened, but he didn't step back. She took that as a good sign and closed her hands around his neck, bringing his head downward while lifting herself on tiptoe to meet his descending lips.

They weren't cold as she expected, but warm and incredibly gentle. The kiss needed to be just as soft and gentle and giving. Trent needed comfort from someone who cared, someone who thought he mattered, and she intended him to have it.

His past didn't make the man. He did. He—the man he had become despite now knowing his origin, despite tremendous odds, despite obstacles that would have crushed a lesser man—was the only thing that mattered.

That was her intention until Trent's body shuddered and his lips parted. Her tongue slipped naturally inside his mouth, tasting him, savoring the different flavors and textures and the pleasure. The unexpected shock was staggering, the need to dive deeper and explore unbearably tempting.

Somehow she managed to resist and lean her head back. Stepping away was impossible. His strong, muscular arms were locked tightly around her, keeping her flush against his lean, hard body. She felt him from the tingling of her nipples to the throbbing of her midsection, to the quivering of her thighs.

Swallowing, she stared up into eyes dark with passion and felt a tiny thrill of pleasure that she had put it there. More importantly, the shadows were gone. "Is my minute up?" Her voice was husky, deep.

"I forgot to keep track." This time he was the aggressor, eagerly taking her lips, her thoughts, until she was all want and need caught in a riptide of passion. She gloried in every sensation rippling through her body.

"Dominique," he whispered, his lips nibbling hers, then tracing a path to the pulse hammering in her throat. "You smell and taste like my dreams."

His lips came back to hers, rough and demanding, and she matched him effortlessly, endlessly. Warm, callused hands slid beneath her blouse and closed over her aching breasts. She shuddered, pressing closer, somehow knowing he could make the sweet ache go away.

Suddenly she was lifted. She had a fleeting moment of seeing an arched foyer and high ceiling, then Trent's mouth was on hers again, and with it came the mindless need and passion.

She sank back into his arms and their passion. She was as greedy for him as he was for her.

Then his mouth was gone and he was clinging to her, his grip almost bruising. "I don't want our first time to be this way."

Dominique slowly came out of her desire-induced daze to find herself in Trent's lap in a big, oversized upholstered chair. Her head was pressed against his wide chest, her legs drawn up beside her.

His large hand released its tight hold on her and stroked her from her neck to her hips, then back again. That wasn't what she wanted stroked. She made an inarticulate murmur of protest.

"Please, Dominique. Don't move. If you do, I'm not going to be able to stop this time," Trent told her, his voice gritty.

Dominique stilled, thinking of the incongruency of the situation. She had been the one running from a relationship and now it was Trent. Somehow in her inexperience she must have read him wrong.

Shame swept through her. "I—if you'll let me up. I'll leave and won't bother you anymore."

"You're not going anyplace, and you bother me even when I can't see you."

"I do?" she asked, angling her head up and brushing her breast against his chest.

"Dominique," he groaned. "Honey, please don't do that."

She eased back down, her fingers playing with the button on his polo shirt. "Then why did you stop?"

"A lot of reasons. Believe me, I still don't know how I did it."

"Are you going to tell me?" she asked, a bit of pique in her voice when he didn't continue.

"You have as much fire and temper in you as you have passion and tenderness. You're a unique woman."

Dominique melted against him again.

"I've tried to resist you, and when it didn't work I bowed to the inevitable. And before you get angry, no, I didn't think you were easy." His hand tunneled through her luxurious, unbound hair. "The attraction we had for each other was too strong for us to resist for long. It might have been different if we didn't live next door to each other."

"Janice would have been heartbroken if I moved," she said.

"I know. I wouldn't have liked it much, either." He sighed. "Janice knows I'm attracted to you, but she was worried you'd run. And she was right."

Dominique felt she had to defend herself and sat up in his lap. "Not for long."

His smile was sad. "I know, but that was only yesterday. Can you really say with all honesty you came over here ready to accept us being lovers?"

Dominique started to twist, felt an unmistakable bulge beneath her and stilled. "No."

"I thought not. You were coming to comfort a friend who is becoming more than a friend. But once we step over that line there's no going back." His gaze was searing, his voice gentle. "I want you like I've never wanted a woman, but I don't want to risk losing you as a friend, or to have either of us dreading coming home for fear of seeing the other, or one of us moving."

Tenderly, his large hands cupped her face. "We have to go into this with our eyes open and be very sure what we feel isn't going to wear off in a couple of weeks."

Dominique folded her hands in her lap. "I'm not much on relationships since my marriage ended badly."

"You're divorced? You want to talk about it?"

She hadn't talked about LaSalle to anyone since the weekend Daniel rescued her. She had felt too ashamed. "I was such a fool. I let him control me and humiliate me, and did nothing. All in the name of love."

Trent's eyes blazed. "Sounds like the fault was his, not yours. Love makes a person blind to other people's flaws. I thought I loved a caring, beautiful woman named Margo, thought we were going to be married one day. Turned out she was selfish and manipulative. The only reason she wanted me around was to help her father head off bankruptcy."

Anger flared in Dominique's eyes. "Don't worry. People like that usually get what's coming to them."

"I'm not. She's no longer of any consequence to me, although it took a long time for me to come to terms with the situation. Overhearing her and her father talking about using me was actually the best thing for me. It caused me to leave West Memphis." His thumb stroked Dominique's cheek. "Being married must have made it more difficult and much harder for you to leave."

His understanding enabled her to tell him the rest. "I kept hoping he'd stop being jealous, stop demanding perfection. I had finally had enough. Only LaSalle didn't want to let me go. He kept me tied to the bed for two days before Daniel showed up." Somehow she couldn't tell him of the rape.

"Where is he now?" Trent asked, his voice dangerously quiet, his face savage.

"He died in an automobile crash three years later." She didn't add *a broken, ruined man*. Daniel had seen to that.

Once again she was gathered tenderly against Trent's chest. "We don't have the best track records for choosing the right people, do we?"

"No."

"We certainly know what we don't want, so choosing what we want shouldn't be too difficult. I'm holding what I want."

Pleasure and uncertainty went through her. "So, the problem is me?"

"Yes."

An audible sigh slipped past her lips. "After all the doubts and reflections and worry I've gone through to get this far, you tell me I still have a ways to go."

Warm lips pressed against her forehead. "You'll get there."

"How do you know?"

"Because I believe in you, and I refuse to let myself think otherwise." He leaned her away from him to study her anxious face. "You're going to come to me one day with no regrets, no hesitations, and I'll be waiting." His mouth claimed hers, the claiming tender and passionate.

Afterward, she nestled against his chest. "You kiss very well."

"As the saying goes, 'You ain't seen nothing yet.' "

She laughed, as he'd intended. "You know you're setting a lot of high expectations in my mind."

"Good. It will keep you thinking about me."

"You certainly don't lack confidence," she said, sitting up to look at him.

"I learned early to believe in myself," he told her simply.

The shadows weren't back in his eyes, but she heard them in his voice. "Do you want to talk about her?"

There was no need to clarify. "She left me clean and in a new diaper and blanket in a hospital bathroom, with a note that said, "Keep him safe. I can't. Tell him I loved him. I did, but he won't remember." They think she was in an abusive situation. I work with a lot of kids. It's no secret that I grew up in foster care. Isaac guessed right that my mother didn't want me."

Indignation flashed in her eyes. "I don't believe that, and neither do you. Isaac was trying to hurt you in the only area where he sees you as vulnerable, the only area he has something you don't—a mother he knows. Don't let him succeed." Tears crested in her eyes. "Do you know how hard it must have been for her to give you up and not know if the people who found you would be kind, or indifferent, or cruel?"

"Shush. I didn't mean to make you cry. I don't think about her very much anymore."

Dominique heard the words "very much" and she fought to keep tears from falling. "Did you ever try to find her when you were an adult?"

"Yeah, but no luck."

"My cousin, Luke, might be abl—"

"No," Trent stated flatly. "It's over." As if to punctuate his words, he stood and sat her on her feet. "How about going to a movie, then out to dinner?"

She lifted a brow. "Is that how you end a discussion when you don't want to talk? By changing the subject?"

"Seems it might not work with you."

He wasn't ready, and she wasn't about to push the issue. She knew how difficult the past could be to look back on. "It might if I can have buttered popcorn, a hot dog, and a large drink."

"You don't come cheap."

"Nope, and don't you dare forget it." Lifting on tiptoe, she kissed him on the lips and started for the door.

This time she noted the polished hardwood floors, the Turkish area rug in front of the white traditional sofa, the rich bronze, floor-to-ceiling, custom swag drapes over sheers, the pair of graceful wing chairs framing the windows. Across the hall in the formal dining room, a sparkling crystal chandelier hung over a floral centerpiece on the double pedestal dining table.

"I like your place."

"Thanks, and thank Janice." He chuckled. "Once we got to know each other, she politely suggested my house needed a few things and volunteered to help."

"That's our Janice. I'll be ready in fifteen minutes."

"Dominique?"

She turned.

"Thanks."

"That's what friends are for." The door closed softly behind her.

The movie was a popular sci-fi one that had been in the top ten for months. The monsters were grotesque, quick, and deadly. The first time one popped out unexpectedly, Dominique screamed and wrapped herself around Trent's neck. Since her scream wasn't the only one she heard in the crowded theater, she hadn't felt bad. By the third time, she decided she liked where she was and stayed there.

"You want to see another movie?" Trent asked, his lips brushing against the top of her head.

"I'm enjoying this one," she said.

He angled his head down to look at her in puzzlement. Another chorus of female screams and a few male gasps went up. Although Dominique wasn't watching the screen, she dutifully buried her face in the side of his neck.

Chuckling, he kissed her on the forehead. "You're right. This may be the most enjoyable movie I've seen in years."

"Definitely," she agreed, chancing a one-eyed glance at the screen. Not a monster in sight. Smiling, she snuggled against Trent. They never stayed gone for long.

Almost two hours later the hero and heroine finally dispatched the last pesky monster, save one for a sequel. Trent and Dominique filed out of the theatre along with the rest of the audience into the cool night air.

"I still owe you, since all you had before the movie was a hot dog and a cola. What would you like to eat?" he asked, opening the door to his Lincoln.

"Chinese."

"I'm lousy with chopsticks," he confessed.

"I'm an expert," she said, getting into the car. "Since you protected me, the least I can do is feed you."

"You're on."

Good at her word, Dominique handled the chopsticks as if she had been born with them in her hand. Trent didn't like the look of some of the food she put in his mouth, but since Dominique was feeding him he ate it, anyway.

Too soon they were back at Janice's house. Silence fell between them as Trent cut the motor and switched off the headlights. Dominique pulled her lower lip between her teeth, her hands curled around the small, red, calfskin bag in her lap. Her legs shifted and the sound of her red gabardine pants rubbing against the seat seemed unnaturally loud.

"Don't get nervous on me," Trent said, his strong fingers circling the back of her neck beneath the collar of her white, appliquéd linen blouse and turning her toward him.

"I just don't know what to expect. What to do," she admitted.

"What would you like to do?" Her gaze went to his lips. "Come here."

She went. No sooner had his lips settled on hers than a bright beam of light engulfed the car. They both jerked apart. The lights shut off. Doors slammed.

"Stay here," Trent ordered and got out of the car. He might as well have been talking to the wind.

She almost beat him out of the car. She watched his tense body relax as Janice and a distinguished looking black man got out of a 850 BMW.

"Trent, who did you think it was?" she asked.

"Doesn't hurt to be cautious," he told her and curved his arm easily around her slim shoulder and pulled her to his side.

"Dominique, Trent. We're sorry," said Janice, hurrying to them, looking beautiful and flustered.

"Please accept my apology," said the gray-haired man with her.

"I'm the one who should apologize to you and to Dominique, for acting like a teenager." Trent held out his hand. "Trent Masters, and this is Dominique Everette."

"Paul Osgood." He smiled warmly at Dominique and shook hands with Trent. "It's a pleasure."

"Paul was coming inside for some coffee. You two want to join us?" Janice asked.

"No thanks," Trent said. "I'd better be going."

"I'll move my car." Keys jingled in Paul's hand.

"Don't bother. I live next door. I'll just walk over in the morning and pick it up, if it's all right, Janice?" Trent asked.

"You know it is." Janice's gaze switched between him and Dominique. "Are you sure you don't want to come in for a little while?"

"Yes, thanks." With a brief kiss on Dominique's cheek, he walked away. Dominique stared after him, and was glad she had when she saw him point to the backyard. With a secret smile on her face she headed inside. Paul, his hand on Janice's elbow, followed.

As soon as they were in the foyer, Dominique yawned. "Goodness. I'd better not drink any coffee. Nice meeting you, Paul. Goodnight to both of you."

"Run along, Dominique," Janice said, her look knowing. "I wouldn't want you to miss any sleep, or anything else important."

Trying not to laugh, Dominique quickly went to her room, threw her purse on the bed, then raced to the window and lifted it. Trent was there. Trying not to giggle, she leaned over and he lifted her out.

"Do you think we fooled them?' he asked.

"No."

"Then we might as well make this worth it." His lips took hers and the world around her receded. He was the focus of her universe.

His tongue expertly probed and searched the sweet, dark interior of her mouth. His hands were no less busy, seeking and giving pleasure as they skimmed and teased and pleased.

When both were near their limit, he tore his mouth from hers, their breathing ragged and harsh in the cool night air. They clung to each other until their breathing slowed, the throbbing of their bodies dulled.

"Maybe we should have said good-bye for real." His lips nibbled her neck, her ear, as if he could not force himself to stop tasting her, stop touching her, stop kissing her. "Neither one of us is going to sleep worth a damn."

"I—I could come over after she's asleep."

Finally he lifted his head. "No. This is the limit of our sneaking. We're definitely not sneaking into each other's beds. Besides, if I correctly read the gleam in Paul's eyes, Janice might be spending her nights someplace else soon, too."

"You think?" Dominique asked excitedly. Janice deserved a man to love and cherish her. Funny, the words didn't seem so impossible anymore.

"I think." Trent kissed her on the lips, picked her up and sat her back inside her room. "Tomorrow after church we can go pick up your props."

"Thanks for a wonderful evening, Trent."

"Goodnight, Honey. Sleep tight." He shut the window and waited until she closed the latch and pulled the curtains.

* * *

Trent thought he might get used to seeing men get that stunned look when they saw Dominique, and hoped it would be soon. He wasn't used to being possessive or jealous. He was both with Dominique, pitifully so. This morning at church had tested his endurance, when men he barely knew had clustered around him after the service to greet Dominique.

Considering how fantastic she had looked, in a rose pink suit with a fitted short skirt, he had tried to remember where he was and not to glare at the men waiting to be introduced. It had helped that Janice was there, and that Dominique had treated them all with polite courtesy and nothing more.

But he had stayed by her side.

He hadn't thought that would be necessary at the small bait store on Lake Ray Hubbard he had taken her to after they had lunch at Paul's seafood restaurant with him and Janice. Now, Trent wasn't so sure.

Casually, he leaned against the scarred, plywood counter of Travis Bait Store, a twenty by fifteen wooden structure with a tin roof, and listened as the elderly owner told Dominique more than she'd ever need to know about picking out a cane fishing pole. She didn't appear to mind.

Considering Travis had a belly from years of drinking too much beer and doing too little exercise, a total of five, scrawny, white hairs sticking up on the top of his otherwise bald head, and only came up to Dominique's shoulder, Trent wasn't worried.

The other two men in the store were a different matter.

Both were in their early thirties, had all their hair, and concave stomachs annoyingly displayed in their shorts and unzipped windbreakers, and—from what Trent could determine—were almost as tall as he was.

They had told Travis they had come in for lures. The only lures they were interested in were ones with which to catch Dominique's attention.

Not in this lifetime, thought Trent.

But they were trying. If he heard one more inference about how much money one or the other had made, or how fast their world-class boats could go, or about the customized work added to their new luxury sports cars, Trent was going to stuff cotton in his ears. Since there was no cotton in sight, he decided leaving might be a better idea.

"Travis, I really appreciate you taking time to help, but she just needs one for a picture. She's not writing a book on the subject," Trent said.

Both Dominique and Travis turned to Trent with a frown. "Information is never wasted," Dominique said, then smiled brilliantly at Travis. "You were saying?"

The elderly man's Adam's apple bobbed. He'd once told Trent while they were trading fishing yarns and sipping beer that looking at a beautiful woman made a man feel ten years younger. Gauging from the rapt way Travis was staring at Dominique, he had regressed to puberty.

"Excuse me. I didn't mean to eavesdrop, but did I hear that you do portraits?" asked the taller and more boisterous of the two men.

Trent came away from the counter. He couldn't believe the audacity of the man, but he planned to set him straight about trying to pick up Dominique.

"Yes," Dominique said.

Trent stopped midway across the room and glared at Dominique and the man. Didn't she know when a man was trying to hand her a line? He thought of lures, and his jaw tightened.

"What kind?" the stranger asked.

"Photography."

"She's buying a cane pole and a minnow bucket for a portrait tomorrow," Travis supplied, his voice rich with pride.

"Really," the man said, walking closer. "This is fortunate. My mother has been after me to send her a portrait. She's in Europe on an extended vacation. Do you have a card?"

Dominique opened her oversized bag and rummaged inside. "Sorry, I appear to be out. I can write out the number." Walking over to the counter near Trent, she took out a pen, scribbled on a small notepad, then ripped out the sheet. "Here."

"Thanks. You'll be hearing from me." He strode to the door and turned. "I almost forgot. What's your name?"

"It's on the paper. It's French."

The man glanced back at the paper, frowned, then smiled. "Oh, yes. I didn't see it." The door closed behind them.

"I'll wait in the truck," Trent said, his expression sour.

"I shouldn't be much longer," she told him.

"Take your time."

"Trent," she called as he reached the door. "Is something wrong?"

His gaze flickered to Travis. "We'll talk about it later."

Travis hadn't lived to the ripe old age of seventy-five without knowing when to make himself scarce. "I'll go restock the cooler."

Neither seemed to notice the store owner leaving. "That man was trying to pick you up and you gave him your number. He could be a maniac, for all you know."

Dominique folded her arms across her chest, tightening the yellow T-shirt across her breasts. "And you think I'm too naive or too stupid to figure that out for myself? Or maybe both?"

Trent had always thought of himself as a smart man—at least, until Dominique. How had he been put on the defensive with such a no win question? "I didn't say that."

"You implied it," she said, her black eyes narrowed.

"You're in that studio by yourself. I simply meant you should be less trusting." He tugged on his baseball cap. "I was worried about you. He had shifty eyes."

Dominique's lips twitched. "Shifty eyes?"

"He did, and when you schedule him make sure someone is there with you," he said.

She placed both hands on his chest. "I gave him a wrong number, and the words in French were 'no sale.' "

Trent brightened, his hands settling on her narrow waist. "That's my girl." The doorbell chimed and a customer came in. "Pick out your pole so we can go. I have a surprise for you."

"What?"

"If I told you it wouldn't be a surprise." Laughing at her mutinous look, he pushed her toward the cane poles.

CHAPTER 11

Dominique couldn't quite believe it when Trent drove beneath a sign that read Lowell Riding Stable. She stared at him, then back to the stables directly in front of them. "Does this mean what I think it does?" she asked.

"Why do you think I insisted you wear jeans and boots?" he asked.

She bit her lip, but laughter bubbled forth, anyway. "I thought the bait shop might be in a swampy area and you were worried about snakes."

"The two-legged variety sure put in an appearance at the bait shop," Trent said, and pulled to a stop.

"Hello, folks," greeted a bowlegged young man of about twenty, a wide grin on his face and an even wider straw hat shading his freckled face. "What can I do for you?"

"Hello. I'm Trent Masters. I reserved a few horses for this afternoon."

"A few?" Dominique repeated incredulously.

Trent shrugged. "I didn't know what kind of horse you were used to riding, so I reserved the entire stable."

She gasped. "You didn't."

He looked embarrassed. "Afraid so."

She threw her arms around his neck and kissed him before she could think of a reason not to. "Thank you. I don't think anyone has ever given me anything nicer."

"I was just thinking the same thing," he said, his arms going around her waist.

"If you'll come this way, I'll show you the horses," said the young man.

Trent reluctantly released Dominique and pulled her from the cab. "I hope he's not as longwinded as Travis."

Dominique curved her arm unconsciously around Trent's waist. "No need. This time I'm the expert."

Minutes later Trent knew Dominique had spoken the truth. She and the young man—who identified himself as the owner's son, Johnny— threw out words like *deep chest, strong foreleg,* and *long neck,* which all obviously meant something to them, but nothing to him.

The closest he had gotten to a horse when he was a child was seeing one in the pasture as he passed on the highway. His adult association was about the same.

"I'll take this one," Dominique said, stroking the white face of a huge, black gelding.

"You have a good eye, Ms. Everette. He's the best of the bunch," commented Johnny, opening the stall and leading the horse out. Head high, his velvet nostrils drinking in air, the animal pranced behind Johnny.

A frown of uncertainty on his face, Trent stepped back as they passed. "You're sure? He's kind of big."

"Don't worry. I was riding before I was walking. Did you decide which one you want?" she asked, glancing around the stables again.

"I, er think I'll just watch," he said evasively.

Her attention came back to him. "You aren't going with me?" Disappointment coated her words.

Somehow he managed to hold her stare. "No. I'll just wait here."

Her midnight-black eyes studied him for a long time, noting his hands stuffed in his front pockets. She remembered his quietness once they entered the stables. "You don't ride, do you?"

"I've never been on a horse in my life," he admitted.

His calm words shocked her. "Then why bring me here?"

"Because you said you liked riding, and I wanted to give you something you enjoyed," he explained easily.

Warmth at his words curved her lips upward. She could think of few instances where a man had offered her pleasure that wasn't to be shared or didn't ultimately benefit him in some way—fewer men still who openly admitted that a woman possessed a skill they lacked.

Standing on tiptoe, she brushed her lips across his cheek. "Thank you."

"You're welcome." Lacing her hand with his, he led her to the saddled gelding. "I can't say I missed the experience until now."

Dominique swung gracefully into the saddle. Gathering the reins handed to her by Johnny, she stared down at Trent.

"What are you waiting for?"

"I wish you could go."

His hand rested on her thigh. "So do I." He stepped back. "I'll be here."

Nodding, she spoke to Johnny standing several feet away. "Can Rio take the fence?"

"Like a cat," came the proud answer.

"Now, Dom—" Trent began, but Dominique had wheeled the animal and was racing toward a white, wooden fence twenty yards away. He wanted to call her back, but prayed instead. Her unbound black hair streamed behind her back as she leaned low over the animal's neck and aimed straight for the five-foot fence.

He knew a moment of fear and helplessness as the horse started over the obstacle. For a nerve-shattering moment animal and rider seemed suspended in midair. Then they were over, and racing hell-bent for the next fence.

Fear turned to amazement and pride as Dominique and the gelding took the next fence as easily as they had taken the first. He heard her shout in triumph and watched them disappear over a hill.

"Damn, that lady can ride."

"You can say that again."

Fifteen minutes later Trent wasn't so sure about Dominique's riding ability. He hadn't moved very far from the spot where he had watched her disappear. Seventeen minutes after she had ridden away, he went inside the stable in search of Johnny. He found him cleaning out the hoof of a cinnamon-colored horse.

"Shouldn't she be back by now?"

"Hard to say. The ranch has thirty acres." Johnny never glanced up from his task.

Trent went back outside, only to come back three minutes later. "Saddle me a horse."

Johnny's shaggy eyebrows bunched. Releasing the horse's hoof, he came out of the stall. "Didn't I hear you say you don't ride?"

"I don't see where it would be all that difficult once you got on," Trent said, hoping he was right.

"You're sure?" To his credit, the young man didn't laugh. "We aren't liable for injuries."

"I take full responsibility for my actions."

Johnny turned and walked toward the back of the stable. "I'll get Bitsy."

Trent hoped Bitsy was as small and biddable as her name sounded. When Johnny led the small roan mare outside the stable, Trent breathed a little easier.

"If you're worried about Ms. Everette, I'll go look for her," Johnny offered. "But like I said, she rides well."

"I know, but even the best riders can fall," he said, the thought making his stomach knot.

"Not this time." Johnny nodded toward the hill. "Here she comes."

She came slower this time, almost at a lope, her hair bouncing around her erect shoulders. The sun was behind her, silhouetting her. She and the blaze-faced horse were a magnificent pair. Even as a nonrider, Trent could tell she rode well. The closer she came, the more he had the insane notion he'd like to be on the horse with her.

She rode straight to him. This time Trent took the bridle instead of stepping away. "You were gone a long time."

"I've been known to stay out for a couple of hours or more."

"What brought you back sooner?"

Throwing her long legs over the saddle, she slid down. "I kept thinking about a man who gives without asking for anything in return. I decided it didn't make much sense to think about him when I could be with him."

His hand gently touched her cheek. "I missed you, too."

She glanced at the saddled horse Johnny was leading back into the stables. "You were sending Johnny after me?"

"I was coming myself," he confessed. "I needed to know you were safe."

Her hands palmed his cheeks. "Except for the men in my family or close to us, I've met few men like you."

One hand closed over hers, his thumb caressing the back of her hand. "Is that good or bad?"

"Both," she admitted softly.

"I don't think so."

"Why do you say that?" she asked, genuinely puzzled.

He smiled slowly and tenderly. "Because this time you ran *to* me instead of away."

Realization widened her eyes. Reflexively she tried to draw back, but found herself firmly anchored against him, one of his arms securely around her waist. He had moved extremely fast and knew her too well.

"Don't get scared on me."

"The thought crossed my mind," she answered honestly.

"I know." Trent studied her face intently. "Just give us a chance."

She thought of her friends' failed marriages, her parent's rocky relationship until recently, and then she thought of Daniel and her promise to Higgins. Mostly she thought of the man holding her with equal amounts of strength and tenderness, and relaxed in his embrace. "I believe that's what I'm doing."

"You won't ever be sorry." One arm around her waist, he led the horse inside and handed the reins to Johnny. After thanking the young man and bidding him good-bye, they walked slowly to the truck.

* * *

Trent knew his jaw was slack, but he couldn't help it. He was human and Dominique was the quintessential woman, sensuous, alluring and provocative, and she was walking toward him in a bikini designed to bring a man to his knees.

The little white nothing had three scraps of material covering strategic areas and none of them wider than his hand. Worse, the bottom was high on the sides and scooped in front to show that incredible, sexy navel of hers.

He was trying not to remember thinking the first time he saw her how much he liked chocolate swirl, how much he liked licking it from top to bottom, but goodness, he was only a man. And Dominique was very much a woman.

"I take it you approve of my swimsuit selection," she said, her arms going around his neck.

His trembling hands braced themselves on her trim waist to keep her from coming any closer. "Like I once said, I'll apologize early."

She smiled, a siren's smile. "Good. Then I'm glad I bought it yesterday."

"Yesterday," he echoed.

"The frame shop in Arlington was next door to a swim shop."

"So you decided to punish me for my rudeness the first time we met by getting a suit to give me a coronary, huh?" he teased.

Her regard grew serious. "I did buy it with you in mind, but not as punishment."

The significance of her statement sunk into Trent. "You wanted to please me."

"Yes."

The answer was so simple yet carried such a wealth of meaning behind it that Trent felt humbled and proud and scared all at once. Gently he enfolded her in his arms. "You're one special lady. I'll never abuse your trust."

"I think I realized that even before I bought the suit." Her cheek nuzzled his wide, bare chest that was sprinkled with black hair. "Janice was right. You are something in swim trunks."

"Stop that." He set her away, then grabbed her by the hand and started toward the pool. "We're going swimming."

Her laugh was sultry and bold. "Why, Trent, I do believe you're afraid of me sometimes."

He stopped so fast she almost bumped into him. "No I'm not," he said and dove into the pool. Emerging several feet away he said, "It's all the time."

A wide grin on her face, she dove in the pool after him.

They spent the afternoon playing in the pool and lounging, and when hunger and the encroaching shadows of darkness drove them inside they went to Janice's well-stocked kitchen. While Trent slowly chopped and diced his way through making a mixed green salad, Dominique prepared boneless chicken breasts to grill.

"You want me to do anything else?" Trent asked, dumping everything to a clear glass bowl.

Dominique glanced at the haphazard way he had thrown things together and smiled. It would taste the same. "No. I'll do the rest."

Trent walked over to the stove watching her every movement. "Your mother teach you how to cook?"

Dominique laughed before she could help herself. "Until recently, my mother couldn't cook an egg."

Frowning, Trent folded his arms across his shirted chest. "Then who did the cooking?"

Hearing the wonderment in his voice, she glanced up, ready to tell him about the cook. Then she remembered that Dominique Falcon had a cook, but Dominique Everette did not. Her gaze went back to the broccoli. "We managed."

Trent's arms went around her waist. "Every woman can't cook. From what I've heard, sounds like you and your parents are close. That's what counts."

He was comforting her. His thoughtfulness never ceased to touch her. She wanted so much to not have any secrets between them, but she didn't want to take a chance of disturbing the delicate balance of their relationship. Then, too, she liked being liked for herself and not the Falcon name.

"Yes. That what counts." She turned in his arms. "I'm going to take a shower."

He made a face. "I don't suppose it would do me any more good to ask to wash your back than it did when I asked you when we got back earlier."

Dominique regarded his disgruntled expression with a smile. "No."

"Thought not." He kissed her on the cheek. "One of these days you're going to say yes."

She quivered inside. "There is that distinct possibility."

"I love it when you talk dirty to me." Grinning, he went to the kitchen door. "If you change your mind I'm only a phone call away."

"Be back to eat in ten minutes. I don't want to reheat the food."

"I'll be back in six, and maybe we can use the other four minutes to heat each other up." The door closed behind him.

Dominique didn't waste time. Quickly sliding the meat under the grill she checked the broccoli and rice, then headed for the shower. She wanted Trent so much she was trembling inside and she was tired of fighting it. Somehow she'd make him understand later the reason for not disclosing her identity.

Tossing off her cover-up, she hooked her thumbs in her spandex bikini bottoms. Maybe if they were lucky they'd have five minutes.

Trent made it back in five minutes, but Janice and Paul had returned in four from their date. The only reason Trent managed to greet them cordially was the look of disappointment on Dominique's face when she met him at the back door wearing an off the shoulder, hot pink, knit top and skintight black jeans. Somehow he knew she had purchased the top at the same time she purchased the swimsuit.

He let his gaze speak his approval. She flushed, but didn't look away.

"Dominique may rival you as the best cook in Texas, Janice," he said easily.

"According to Dominique you haven't eaten," Janice said from her seat at the round oak table.

Trent stared down at Dominique's. "A man doesn't always have to taste something to know it's going to be good."

"Trent," Dominique admonished, but she was smiling. "For that you have to serve yourself."

"Don't mind at all," he said, his eyes conveying a wealth of meaning.

Blushing, she turned away and asked Janice about the mutual friends she and Paul had gone to visit that afternoon. All the time Dominique was aware of Trent, and wished they could be alone.

It was not to be.

Janice and Paul sat with them while they ate, then remained as Trent and Dominique cleaned up the kitchen. Long before then, Dominique and Trent had begun giving each other covert looks.

Janice, usually talkative and smiling, sat grim-faced and silent. Paul, who had been charming and a bit of a tease at his restaurant, had retreated behind a troubled expression. He sat arrow straight in his chair, sneaking glances at Janice which she steadfastly refused to acknowledge.

Finally, Dominique had had enough. "Janice, there's a button off the suit I plan to wear tomorrow. Do you have a needle and thread?"

If Dominique had any doubt about there being a problem it vanished when Janice almost jumped up from the chair. "I'll get it for you."

Once in Janice's bedroom, Dominique asked, "What's the matter? Did he make a move on you?"

Janice's lower lip began to tremble.

Dominique saw red, and whirled toward the bedroom door.

Janice's hand on her arm stopped her. "Please wait."

"No man is going to treat you badly again," Dominique said fiercely.

Janice shook her head. "You don't understand. It isn't that he kissed me. It's that . . . that he called me Lilly. Lilly is the wife he lost fifteen years ago."

"Oh, Janice," Dominique said, pulling the other woman into her arms. She came easily.

"I just can't seem to get it right. First Wayne dumped me for someone younger, then Paul uses me for a stand-in for his dead wife." She sniffed. "I guess that says a lot about me."

Dominique set Janice away from her. "It says you're a goodhearted, loving woman. It's not your fault Wayne was trying to hang on to his youth, and Paul his past. If they didn't value you for the woman you are, it's their loss."

Janice stared at Dominique, her tears abating. "You've finally let go of the past."

"You can't look to the future without letting go," Dominique answered firmly. "I'm just beginning to see that."

"Trent helped, didn't he?"

"Yes."

"I'm glad." She touched Dominique's cheek. "Do you mind saying goodnight to Paul and Trent for me?"

"No. Can I bring you anything?" she said, her own eyes starting to tear. She'd never seen Janice look so desolate, so lost.

"Nothing. I'll say goodnight to you, too."

Squeezing her hands, Dominique closed the bedroom door and went back to the kitchen. She was ready to flay Paul alive until she saw the anxiety in his face as he came to his feet, his gaze going beyond her to an empty room.

"Where's Janice?"

She didn't remember his voice being that shaky. "She asked me to say goodnight to you."

For a moment he stared at Dominique as if he didn't understand what she had said, then he plopped back down in his seat. "I messed up."

The utter desolation in his words so closely echoed those in Janice's that Dominique felt tears sting her eyes again, but this time there was also anger. "You should have thought about that before you called her your dead wife's name."

"What?" His graying head came up sharply.

"You don't kiss a woman and call her by your dead wife's name," she repeated.

"I didn't," he defended, surging to his feet.

"You called her Lilly," Dominique said, her anger mounting when he shut his eyes.

"I think you'd better go," Trent said, his voice cold as he came to stand by Dominique.

Slowly Paul's eyes came open. "Lilly was my wife's first name, but I called her by her middle name—Ann."

"That's worse," Dominique riled. "At least she could understand why you called her by your wife's name. Please leave."

Paul didn't move. His shaky hand ran over his head. "Please, can I speak with her? She misunderstood me."

Dominique crossed her arms and glared at the man. "A likely story."

"When I called her Lily, I didn't mean the name, I meant the flower. Janice has an innocent, pure quality like the flower. The Song of Solomon is my favorite book of the Bible. She is like a lily to me, with all its fragility and its uncompromising strength," he said passionately. "I called her my lily. My deceased wife was a wonderful woman, the mother of my children. I mourned her. But there is no way I'd confuse her with Janice."

Dominique's arms slowly uncrossed. She didn't know what to say.

"First door on the right," Trent told him.

"Thank you," Paul said.

Dominique placed her hand on Paul's jacketed arm as he started past her. "I hope for her sake you're telling the truth. You'd better hope for yours that you are."

His gaze didn't waver. "I am." Dominique's fingers slid from the fine gray wool. He continued out of the room.

She was still watching Paul when Trent's arms curved around her waist from behind, bringing her body against his. He placed his chin on top of her head. "I believe him, Dominique."

Her arms circled his. She leaned back against him. She couldn't see Janice's bedroom door, but she heard Paul's knock. "Why does caring for someone have to hurt?"

"It doesn't always."

"Tell that to Janice," Dominique said. "Or to me."

He turned her in his arms and stared down into her troubled eyes. "One of my foster parents' grandmother lived on a farm. We went there one summer to pick blueberries. Grandma Hawkins always said the sweetest berries were always deeper into the briar, and it stung like the dickens getting them, but one taste of the blueberry cobbler and you'd forget all the hurt you had to go through."

"Dominique. Trent."

They pivoted at the sound of Janice's soft voice. She was standing by Paul, his arm around her waist.

Janice's lipstick was smeared. Paul wore a smile. "I—" she began.

"I was just going over to Trent's," Dominique interrupted. "He was telling me about blueberry cobbler, and I want some."

Trent grabbed Dominique by the arm and headed for the back door. "Makes me hungry just thinking about it. I'll make sure she gets back safely. Goodnight Janice, Paul."

"Wait." Dominique opened the refrigerator door and pulled out the bottle of champagne Trent had given her. "Champagne and blueberries sounds like a natural combination to me."

"A natural," Trent agreed.

Giggling, Dominique followed. She was still laughing when Trent opened the door to his house and pulled her into his arms and silenced her with his lips.

CHAPTER 12

"What do you want to do first?" Trent asked on lifting his head. Dominique's eyes widened in surprise. She had expected him to take her straight to bed.

"Since you don't seem to have a preference, maybe we should drink that champagne. Hunting for berries, as I remember, can make a person thirsty." Picking her up in his arms, he started toward the kitchen.

One arm hooked around his neck, her other hand holding the bottle of champagne, she stared up into his face with growing confusion. "Trent?"

"Don't worry. I won't be selfish and take all the berries for myself." He stared at her with dark, hungry eyes as he sat her on the white tile counter. "You trust me not to do that, don't you?"

She finally understood. Trent wasn't going to jump on her and take, thinking only of himself. He valued her. Was there ever a man who understood her more? "Yes," the word trembled over her lips as she drew the cold bottle of champagne against her.

"I'll get the glasses."

"As much as we've jostled it you'd better get the mop while you're at it," she called, trying to match his mood.

"Ye of little faith," he said, opening a drawer for a corkscrew, then reaching into the glass-fronted blue cabinets and removing two wineglasses. "Besides, I've been curious about something."

"What?" she asked, releasing the bottle to him.

"How champagne would taste on your skin."

Dominique was extremely glad she was sitting. Her body seemed to go all soft inside. "Trent." She wanted to kiss him again, taste him.

"Champagne first."

Dominique barely managed to nod. They both knew what would come before the night was over.

The cork came out with a pop. Wine fizzled and foamed over the sides. Trent regarded the small amount of wine on the counter with a frown. "Maybe I should have shaken it again?"

Dominique accepted the long-stemmed glass, pleased her fingers trembled only slightly. "There's always next time."

His dark brown eyes seemed to narrow. "I'll hold you to that."

She swallowed, then moistened her dry lips. "What should we drink to?"

"To second chances and new beginnings." His glass clinked against hers.

"Second chances and new beginnings." She drank the wine, her gaze unable to leave his.

Slowly he took the glass from her hand and stepped between her legs and framed her face with hands that trembled. "I look at you and ache all over."

Her hands covered his, her gaze steady and sure. "I feel the same way and I'm tired of fighting it." Her lips gently touched his. "I want to be here with you. Only you."

A fierce pleasure ripped through Trent. His forehead touched hers. "Despite what I said, I sometimes doubted."

She exerted enough pressure to lift his head until their eyes met. "Now that you've shamelessly worn down my resistance, I hope you'll live up to the promises you made each time you looked at me the way you're now looking at me."

"How am I looking at you?" he asked, his voice rough and strained.

"As if you could eat me with a spoon and lick your lips afterward," she said, her voice shaky.

"That about covers it." His lips met hers, warm and gentle, then with increased hunger. Dominique matched his hunger and tested the limits of his control.

He had intended to go slowly, make the night one they'd both remember and cherish. As soon as his tongue slipped into the dark interior of Dominique's mouth and her tongue swirled around his, he knew he had overestimated himself and underestimated her.

He didn't waste time thinking about his miscalculations. He just tightened his hold and enjoyed his downfall.

Need trampled through her. She strained to be closer. Trent helped by sliding her hips forward. His blunt arousal brushed teasingly against the notch of her thighs.

So close and yet too far.

His hands swept up her sides, closing over her breasts. His thumb flicked once, twice, across her nipple. She arched, pressing closer to the sweet pain. It was all the encouragement he needed. Lifting his head for an instant, he grabbed her top and jerked it up over her head.

He caught a glimpse of a wisp of pink, lacy perfection masquerading as a bra just before his teeth closed over her dusky brown nipple and tugged. A cry of pleasure broke over her lips.

She heard him murmur something about berries, but couldn't understand. She had only a heartbeat to wonder why, since her hearing was so acute. His mouth closed over the other nipple, his tongue sliding across the turgid point, and her thoughts scattered.

Unconsciously, her hands wrapped around his head, anchoring him in place. The sensation was exquisite.

She wanted to kiss him the same way. She wanted him to feel the same sharp urgency, so intense it was almost painful but filled with so much pleasure she was light-headed.

Releasing him, she jerked his shirt out of his jeans. Unsteady fingers fumbled the buttons free. Unerringly, her lips found his nipple buried in the soft texture of his chest hair.

Trent groaned.

Dominique smiled like a well-fed cat. She suddenly realized what he meant about berries.

"No more." Trent pulled her head up and saw the pleasure in her face from giving him pleasure, and his knees almost buckled.

"Unless things have changed in eight years, there's a lot more."

Shock went through him at her words, and then another deeper, more complex emotion he couldn't define. He felt weak and strong, the seducer and the protector. "You're everything I've ever wanted in a woman, and so much more." Sweeping her up in his arms, he grabbed the bottle of champagne and headed for the master bedroom at the back of the house.

The spacious room lay in semi-darkness, but he had no difficulty finding the king-size bed. Setting the champagne on the nightstand, he pulled back the multicolored, Kente-inspired bedspread, then tenderly placed her on the cool, black cotton sheets. "Stay here."

Dominique would have laughed if she'd had enough breath. Her knees wouldn't support her even if she had any inclination to leave. She didn't.

The snap of his jeans coming undone sounded overly loud in the charged atmosphere, as did the rustle of the denim material sliding down his legs. Her calming heart hitched.

Somewhere in the shadowed room she heard the faint hiss of a match. By the time Trent finished lighting the candles on the six arm, double candelabras on the mahogany mantel, her heart was racing. Faint whiffs of cinnamon drifted out to her. Golden embers from the gas logs glowed in the open, polished, brick fireplace.

She was being seduced. The fact that he didn't have to go to such measures endeared him to her more.

Crossing the room, Trent turned down the thermostat and shut the door. Gaslight and candlelight, the only illuminations, played over his conditioned muscles and created shadows on his handsome face and lean body.

Silently he came to her, naked and majestic. She trembled at the sight of him, but not from fear.

A knee dug into the mattress beside her, and his hands cupped her face again. "I knew you'd look even more beautiful with candlelight dancing on your skin."

A long, lean finger brushed across her lip, the curve of her jaw, then curved until reaching her nipple. She trembled. "I've imagined how you'd taste, but all my fantasies and speculations were pitifully inadequate. It's not just the taste, it's how you make me feel when my mouth is on you and I hear your cries of pleasure, and know they're just for me." His head bent, taking the pebbly point into his mouth.

A shudder went through Dominique. Her body went liquid. Before she knew it she was minus her jeans and panties and Trent's powerful body was crouched over hers. In a moment of panic a distant memory pricked up, but before she could respond to the fear his hand swept up her bare leg to the center of her body. A finger dipped inside.

A ragged moan of pleasure, not fear, slipped over her lips.

"I knew the fire was there. Waiting to be stoked, waiting to be found."

He unhooked the front fasteners of her bra, his hands covering the silky firmness of her breasts, kneading the resilient flesh. His mouth came back to hers, his tongue dipping, twirling, in her mouth as his lower body touched hers maddeningly.

The ravenous and deeply erotic kiss stole what little control Dominique had left. Trent was right about the fire, only it was raging in one spot. She whimpered, twisting on the bed, her arms straining to bring him closer.

His mouth left hers again. She moaned her protest, then gasped in shocked pleasure as he kissed her in the most intimate of places. She was helpless to fight the tightening of her body being pushed over the edge. When it came she cried out Trent's name in helpless surrender.

He was there.

Gathering her still trembling body in his arms, he slid into her moist warmth, only to retreat and return again. His body set up a relentless rhythm that she matched and followed effortlessly. This time, when completion came they were together.

Rolling to his side, Trent took Dominique with him, his breathing labored. He had never known making love could be so explosive or satisfying. Never had he experienced anything like it. Somehow he sensed he never would with another woman. Dominique had challenged and broken rules he had established to live by. Tonight she had done it again.

Perhaps because he had had to share a bed until he was in his teens he liked sleeping alone, and he liked doing it in spacious comfort. His gaze returned to the woman in his arms, her black hair spilling over his pillow, her bare shoulders. His arms tightened. He couldn't imagine leaving her.

Warm lips pressed a kiss to her lips. "You're all right?"

Her eyelids fluttered open to reveal languid black eyes. "Wonderful."

"Good." He reached for the bottle of champagne and splashed a dab over her navel. "Time for dessert."

Dominique stretched luxuriously in Trent's large bed early the next morning, then hastily drew her bare arms back beneath the covers. The bedroom was still chilly. Trent had forgotten to turn the thermostat back up until a couple of hours ago.

Her pleased smile broadened. It wasn't that he had forgotten. He had been busy with other things. All of them fantastic.

She thought she knew her body, knew about sexual pleasure, but with a mixture of tenderness and aggression Trent had shown her much more. She had absolutely no desire to be anyplace except where she was.

Content for the first time in years, she smiled and snuggled against Trent's muscled warmth. His arm came around her waist dragging her closer.

He spoke without lifting his head, "If you want to go jogging, I'll go with you."

"I'd rather go riding."

His head came up, a frown on his face until she threw one long leg over his waist. His eyes darkened to tiny points of desire. Catching her by the waist he shifted, allowing her to straddle him.

She captured the pulsating warmth of his manhood and guided him. Eyes closed, she savored the exquisite pleasure of them being joined inch by incredible inch.

"Look at me."

Her eyelids fluttered opened. What she saw in the depth of his gaze filled her in an entirely different way. She wanted to tell him, but no words came. She knew a way.

Her body moved against his, with his. Her knees locked at his sides, felt the power and the passion of his body beneath her, felt her own power as a shudder ripped through him. Her hands braced against his chest, she took them to the point of no return.

She collapsed on his chest. His hand stroked the damp, smooth curve of her back to the roundness of her hips.

"Lady, what you do to me," he said, when he had enough breath to do so.

Satisfaction curled through Dominique. "I'm glad, because you've given so much to me." She felt him smile. "I didn't mean *that.*"

Chuckling, he put his arms around her and she found herself hoisted in his arms. He started to the shower. "I told you I love it when you talk dirty to me."

Dominique was nervous. Janice would surely be up by seven-thirty, and once she saw Dominique wearing the same clothes she'd know. Then, there was another problem. Her hand lifted to her damp, tangled hair.

"It really looks fine," Trent said, brushing his hand across her head.

Dominique knew her hair was a tangled mess. She didn't regret helping to get it that way, but she did regret having to face her godmother.

"Come on," Trent said, tugging her hand.

"Maybe I should go in alone," she suggested, biting her lip.

"No deal. We're in this together. Janice is not going to crucify you." Stopping, he stared down into her troubled face, then took her into his arms. "It will be all right."

"I hope so."

"Have I let you down yet?"

Raising her head, she quirked an eyebrow. "That, I believe, is the reason I'm in the predicament I'm in."

"I told you I aim to please." Kissing her on the nose, he continued the short distance to the door and knocked.

"Come in," called Janice.

Squeezing Dominique's hand, Trent opened the door and curved his arm around her waist so they walked through the door together. "Good morning, Janice."

"Morning, Janice," Dominique greeted slowly.

Janice glanced up from behind the refrigerator door. "Good morning. Breakfast is almost ready."

"Is there anything I can do?" Dominique offered, breathing easier since her godmother didn't look at her any differently.

"If you can handle the French toast, Trent can set the table," Janice said, closing the refrigerator door and placing a package of breakfast ham on the counter.

Both jumped to do as she asked. Soon they were all sitting at the table. After Janice had given the blessing, she looked at Trent and said, "I guess we'll be seeing more of you."

Dominique almost choked on her toast. Her gaze went to Trent, and knew they were both thinking of the term literally.

Clearing his throat he answered, "Yes. I hope that'll be all right with you?"

Janice turned to Dominique. "You're sure?"

"I'm sure," she said, feeling Trent's approving gaze on her.

Janice picked up her coffee cup. "Looks like I'd better double up on the groceries."

"Hey, I don't eat that much," Trent protested.

"No, but you and Paul will together," she told him.

"You're sure?" Dominique asked.

Janice set her cup down before answering. "The only thing I'm sure of is that I'm not sure of anything."

"Sounds like me after I met Dominique," Trent said thoughtfully.

"And look how that turned out," Janice commented.

Dominique blushed.

Trent grinned.

She wanted to throw her toast at him. Instead, she stood. "I need to get to the studio. I have a lot to do before Samuel Jacobs and his family arrive."

"Give Samuel and his wife my best," Trent told her.

"I will." Dominique went to her room with a smile on her face. Life was definitely on an upswing.

Samuel Jacobs's grandson, Michael, was a rascal. But a cute rascal. It was obvious five minutes after he came into Dominique's studio already dressed in his new gray, striped overalls that his grandparents doted on him. It was just as obvious that his mother made sure her son knew she was in charge.

His sister, Gia, was a chubby five-year-old with a sunny disposition and a giggly laugh that was infectious. Dominique looked at the beautiful little girl in the snug fitting purple tutu, tiara and rouged cheeks, and knew the outfit was all wrong.

"Mrs. Marshall, may I see you a moment, please?"

"Of course." Frowning, the mother followed.

Dominique dug her hands into the front pockets of her navy trousers. This wasn't going to be easy.

Dominique's mother, Felicia, had taught her all about the fierceness of a mother's love. Dominique didn't think Mrs. Marshall was any different. One wrong word and she would be out the door.

Dissatisfied customers, especially those as influential as the Lloyds, could ruin her business. But she had to take the chance.

"I don't think the costume is right for Gia. She has too much energy."

Mrs. Marshall's lips tightened. "What do you suggest?"

Dominique took a deep breath and plunged in. "The classic setting for such a photograph would suggest serenity. That's not Gia. She bubbles over with life. I want to show that. I'd like her to come back in a long, white summer dress and small white straw hat, and shoot her in front of a background of wildflowers with the sun setting in the distance, with a kite in her hand."

The mother emitted a startled outcry—"Oh!"

"What is it, Carolyn?" asked Mrs. Jacobs.

Dominique thought, *Here it comes,* but held her ground. If she were going to be a photographer she had to do it without compromising her principles.

"Ms. Everette just suggested another pose for Gia instead of the ballet costume, and I agree with her," Mrs. Marshall said. She turned to her daughter. "You get to fly a kite, Sweetie."

Gia smiled broadly, then glanced at the ceiling. "Will it fly in here?"

Mrs. Marshall faced Dominique. "I'm sure Ms. Everette will think of something. Isn't that right?"

"You just leave everything to me."

How do you get yourself into these things? Dominique thought as she tried to figure out a way to suspend the kite with the illusion of the wind tugging at it in the studio. A fan might work if it were far enough awa—

The buzzer sounded. She glanced up. Her face broke into a wide smile. Pressing the buzzer for admittance, she hurried to meet Trent halfway. Seconds later she was in his arms, his lips on hers.

He smiled down into her upturned face. "Now, that's what I call a welcome."

"I suppose you just happened to be passing by?" she teased, her fingers twined around the back of his neck.

"No, I missed you and I didn't want to wait until tonight to see you," he told her frankly. "If not for all this glass, I'd show you exactly how much."

Her heart sped up. "I'd let you, too."

"You're making it awfully difficult for me to behave."

She grinned. "I could say the same thing about you."

"You'd better." He kissed her on the nose. "I have a surprise for you tonight."

"What?"

"If I told you—"

"It wouldn't be a surprise," she finished with a pout.

He laughed and hugged her to him. "I love teasing you."

I love you. The words popped into Dominique's head and almost tumbled over her lips.

"Honey, what's wrong?" he asked, staring down into her troubled face. "You're trembling."

"I—" She couldn't tell him. That would mean the ultimate in being vulnerable. With an effort she brought a smile to her lips. "I guess I'm a little tired."

"My fault. You'll get a good night's sleep tonight," he promised.

She pulled her arms down. She tried to tell herself that she should be pleased that he was being thoughtful again, but somehow she felt abandoned. "I should get back to work."

His hands on her waist held her in place. His gaze intent, he said, "If this is going to work we have to be honest with each other."

Some secrets she wasn't ready to divulge, but he was right. "I guess I didn't think you'd get tired of me so soon." She wasn't prepared for the anger that flashed across his face or to find herself off the floor and staring into his blazing eyes.

"Tired of you? What gave you such a crazy idea?"

She would have been indignant if his anger hadn't stunned her. "You—you said I'd get a good night's sleep."

"That's right. So we'd better get to bed early. Any objections?"

She shook her head. "None."

"Good." He set her on her feet. "Then I trust there won't be a reason to have this conversation again."

"I'm sorry," she said. "I just . . ." Her voice trailed off. She glanced away.

A lean, hard finger brought her head back around. "Don't start doubting me or yourself. And remember, whatever it is we talk about it, no jumping to conclusions. All we have to do is be honest with each other, and things will be fine."

She shifted restlessly. "Things aren't as simple for some of us," she told him while thinking of her real identity, her love.

"They can be if you let them."

"Perhaps," she said evasively.

"Sounds as if you need convincing." He kissed her hard on the lips, then went to the door. "It's a good thing I enjoy a challenge."

Dominique watched his truck pull away from the curb, her thoughts troubled. He might enjoy a challenge, but he detested dishonesty. Somehow she had to find a way to tell him about her identity. The longer she waited, the harder it was going to be for both of them.

Trent deserved total honesty. She could give him nothing less. Somehow she'd make him understand she hadn't intentionally deceived him, that she had simply been trying to make it on her own.

Tonight. She'd tell him tonight. Her mind made up, she turned toward her desk.

The buzzer sounded. She glanced around. Her hand, already reaching for the control, froze.

Standing outside the glass door were Isaac and three other male teenagers, including Jessie. Isaac twisted the doorknob, pounded on the glass. When the door didn't open, the teenagers began making lewd, suggestive motions with their bodies and hands while mouthing the foul words.

Disgusted, she jerked up the phone. They should be in school instead of bothering her. She was calling the police.

Her gaze switching from the youths to the phone, she punched in 9, then 1, then 1. Frantically pointing to her, three of the boys ran out of sight, leaving Isaac to make one last hand gesture before following.

Moments later a fast moving, battered, red Camaro sped past the front of the studio with Isaac and another teenagers hanging out of the windows, yelling what she was sure were obscenities. Her hand trembling, she dropped the receiver back into place.

What could she tell the police? That some teenagers had made suggestive gestures and then run? Hardly enough to warrant the call.

Yet, if Trent found out about the incident there was no telling what he might do. It wasn't worth the possibility of his getting into trouble with the police. She was safe inside the studio, and she always left before dark. She wasn't worried about them coming back. They had fled too quickly when she had picked up the phone. Cowards, all of them.

Rounding her desk, she sat down and wondered how they had found her, then decided it didn't matter. Determined to forget them, she went back to working on the photo shoot for Gia.

Trent was smiling broadly when he entered his outer office. With a wave to Anita, who was on the phone, he went to his private office and sat behind his desk. Scooting his chair closer, he picked up the ballpoint pen he had left on top of the bid proposal earlier.

Seconds ticked away. The pen remained immobile. His mind was three point, seven miles away in Deep Ellum, more specifically on Dominique Everette.

By nature, he wasn't an impulsive person. Yet, he had wanted to see her and had simply given into the urge to do so. He leaned back in his chair and freely admitted he hadn't been a lot of things before he met Dominique. He didn't mind the new Trent one bit. He couldn't remember being happier.

In his mind he replayed the happy expression on Dominique's beautiful face when she saw him, the utterly beguiling taste of her lips, the way her body melted against him. He didn't see how it could get any better than this.

Every moment with her was fantastic. And when he wasn't with her, he wanted to be. He loved everything about her.

He loved her.

The realization didn't shock him. Since he had first seen her, he had been falling. He'd gone to the mat and stayed there when she came over to comfort him after his confrontation with Isaac. However, he didn't think she was ready to hear the words.

Her jumping to conclusions when he mentioned letting her get a good night's sleep was evidence that she remained unsure about their relationship. She wouldn't for long. He was going to show her in every possible way that they had a future together. He was used to working hard for what he wanted, and Dominique Everette was definitely at the top of his want list.

This time things were going to turn out differently. This time he didn't have to worry about deceit and dishonesty from the woman he loved. This time his second chance at happiness was just the beginning.

CHAPTER 13

Dominique had planned to tell Trent the moment she saw him. Her plans were altered when he came over after six that evening and insisted she come with him at once. Janice, planning to go out later with Paul to a movie, waved them off with a smile.

Dominique had gone willingly, prepared to explain everything to him, until he showed her her first surprise in his bedroom. Two dozen pink and white roses sat in a delicately etched, crystal vase on the dresser. Beside the flowers were a sterling silver comb and brush. Her unsteady hand picked up the comb, then the brush.

"There's another present over there."

A long, pink, silk robe lay on the bed. Beside it was a pair of matching slippers.

"There's one more." Tugging her hand, he took her into the large bathroom that held an oversized sunken tub and a glass enclosed shower, then pointed to the top of the black marbled vanity.

A *dryer.* A lump formed in her throat. She turned to him, the brush still clutched to her chest.

"I knew you were upset this morning about your hair. I hope you don't mind."

"Mind?" Her arms went around his neck. She gazed up at him. "Thank you. Your thoughtfulness always makes me feel special."

"You *are* special." His arms circled her waist. "But I benefit, too. We can make love in the shower or the tub and neither of us has to worry about your hair."

"T—Trent." His name trembled on her lips. A familiar heat began to build inside her.

His hands lifted and began unbuttoning her white blouse. "What do you say we test the dryer? You never know when you might get a dud."

Placing the brush on the vanity, she smiled up at him, her hand closing around his masculinity. "A problem you don't have."

He nipped her on the ear. "And aren't you pleased?"

"Very."

His fingers made short work of her cotton blouse and lacy bra. "Then I know you'll be happy about something else."

She was almost as quick with his shirt. "What?"

He reached for the button on her slacks. "Ice cream."

Her hands paused on the snap of his jeans. "Ice cream?"

He grinned wickedly. "Trust me."

For a long, satisfying time Dominique could barely lift her eyelashes. She did, though, just enough to see Trent's slumbering face inches from hers on the pillow they shared. She felt the sheet on her and knew he had pulled it over them. She hadn't had the strength.

She should have known when he said "Trust me" with a gleam in his eyes that he was going to do things to her body that still made her blush. Her lashes closed as she remembered doing similar things—and enjoying every sensual, erotic-filled moment.

She'd never think of ice cream in the same way again.

"I'm going to help with your hair as soon as I can sit up."

Dominique opened her eyes to find herself staring into Trent's dark gaze. She loved him more with each passing moment. Somehow she found the strength to move enough to touch his face with her fingertips. "We need to talk."

"Later." His mouth found hers again and once again she was taken to a place only Trent could take her. By the time he joined her, she had ceased to think.

The next morning Dominique didn't think about telling Trent until she was halfway to work. She'd just have to tell him that evening. When she arrived home Janice put her to work helping prepare for the neighborhood block party in their backyard. During the laughter-filled gathering, she was too busy meeting the mostly elderly neighbors and helping Janice and the other ladies make sure they didn't run out of food or drink to think of much else.

It was almost eleven when the last couple left. Trent had taken her back to his house and straight to bed. The following night they double-dated with Janice and Paul and went to a dinner show at the Venetian Room in the Fairmont Hotel. This time she took Trent straight to bed.

She really planned to talk with him when she arrived home Thursday, but they went to watch The Tigers practice and show them their pictures. They stayed at home Friday night, but by then her courage had decreased dramatically. She didn't want to chance ruining their relationship.

Her days were filled with doing a job she loved: her nights in the arms of a man she loved. She had waited so long for the former and hadn't known how much she wanted the latter until Trent had walked into her life.

As days turned into weeks, she knew she had no choice. Her family was becoming suspicious, since she was gone so much at night. Dominique expected them to pay her a visit any day. Before that happened, she had to tell Trent.

"A penny for your thoughts?" Trent said beside her one night in bed, their heads on the same pillow.

Her fingertips grazed his lips, traced his dark brow. "I guess it's time I told you."

Frowning, his hand caught hers. He kissed her palm. "What is it, Honey?"

"I know you think of everything in black and white with no shades of gray, but that isn't always the case with some of us," she said carefully.

"Is this about your marriage?"

"No. You banished LaSalle completely," she told him truthfully. "I didn't think that was possible before I met you."

"Then this isn't about another man?"

"This is about us. If . . . if afterwards you still want there to be an us."

His arms closed tightly around her, dragging her to him. "Don't ever scare me like that again. You had me thinking you were going to leave me."

"You may want me to after I've finished."

He sat her away from him, his gaze searching. "This sounds serious."

"It is."

"I'm listening."

She bit her lower lip. "I think we should get dressed first."

His hands tightened for a split second, then opened. "You can get dressed, but you're not leaving me."

She had to touch him one last time. She laid her hand on his chest. "That will be up to you." She turned away from him, gathered up her clothes, and dressed in silence.

Finished, she went down the hallway and perched on the edge of the chair framing the window in the living room. It wasn't lost on either of them that the seat was only a few feet from the door.

Trent stared at her choice of seats, then pulled the matching chair around her, effectively blocking her escape, and sat down. He didn't know what was going on, but she was not running away from him. There was another surprise he intended to give her tonight, and nothing she said was going to change that.

"Whenever you're ready."

Dominique clasped her hands together. Nothing had been this hard, not even telling Daniel about the horrors LaSalle had put her through.

"If you want to, we can forget this, do your hair, then have the dinner I picked up on my way home," he suggested. "It's Chinese."

She didn't even think of taking his offer. It was now or never. She moistened her dry lips. "Janice was right about a second chance. I needed one desperately. I needed to find something that brought peace and permanence. I had been looking and wandering for eight years."

"Since your divorce?" he asked.

"Yes. It . . . it wasn't pleasant."

He came out of his seat to kneel in front of her. His hands gripped hers. "You don't have to tell me anything more about that. It isn't hard to imagine what happened when you were tied up."

Shame went through her. She tried to tug her hands free. It was impossible.

"Listen, Dominique. You have nothing to be ashamed of. Don't you think I felt you tense sometimes when I touched you? If that bastard hadn't been dead, he would be now," Trent said fiercely. "But you're past that now. In the past weeks we've been as intimate as a man and woman can get, and you were with me all the way. He's behind you. You're independent and strong. You're free."

"Now." she said, continuing slowly, "but when I came to Dallas all I had were dreams. I was running from who I am, and trying to prove to the world I was as talented as anyone in my family." Her hands clutched his. "To the people who loved me it didn't matter, and I shouldn't have let others influence me into thinking it did."

"He made you think it did," Trent told her.

"Yes. During the nine months of our marriage my best was never good enough, and afterward I was never quite as sure of myself."

"It's over. You're stronger now. You can accomplish anything you want."

She pulled her hands free. "I know that now, but it took caring about you, being around you, to make me realize that. I don't regret how I handled things. I regret thinking it was the only way."

"What are you talking about?"

"I wanted to make it on my own as a portrait photographer. I didn't want another failure in my life," she told him tightly. "I wanted no one to be able to say I had used my family connections, as they did in Paris."

"Paris?" He straightened. "I thought you modeled after high school."

"I did, then off and on since then," she told him watching him stand and move back a step. So it had begun already.

"So when did you start taking pictures?" he asked.

"Two years ago we were on location for a fashion shoot for a European magazine at a small fishing village, and the photographer's assistant became ill. I was finished for the day so I volunteered to help. Looking through the lens instead of being on the other side opened a whole new world. Most photographers start very young, but I was determined."

"Apparently you learned well."

A chill went through her. His controlled words hadn't sounded like a compliment. "I like to think so. It was past time for me to find something I enjoyed, and was good at. I tried a couple of other business ventures, became bored, then sold out. In the meantime I wandered around the world."

"It takes money to do both."

She started to drag her hand through her hair, encountered the tangles, and put her hand in her lap. "Yes, it does. But I have money."

"How did you get it?" he asked, taking a step toward her.

"The old-fashioned way. I inherited it."

His brown eyes narrowed. "If you have money, why were you so worried about your business?"

"Because I want to succeed on my own," she reminded him. "For once in my life I want to stand and accomplish something on my own merits and know it's not because of my last name."

His hand brushed across his head. "Come on, Dominique. I keep up on African-Americans who are the movers and shakers in the business world, and I don't remember seeing Everette on the list."

"That's because my grandfather retired years ago. I'm sure the name Falcon was on the list."

He went still. "What did you say?"

She pushed to her feet. "Everette is my mother's maiden name. My given name is Dominique Nicole Falcon."

"What is Daniel Falcon to you, your cousin or something?"

"My brother."

Trent said one explicit word before turning away, then whipping back around so fast that she jumped. "You really had me going," he said, his face and voice hard. "You must have had a great time laughing at me trying to help you with your business. You can probably buy the entire building—no, make that the block—and not put a dent in your checkbook."

There was only one accusation she wanted to talk about. "I never laughed at you. I had given myself two years to succ—"

Dry laughter cut her off. "Two years! If you hadn't succeeded, what would you have done?" His hands lifted when she opened her mouth.

"Don't tell me. I think I can guess the answer. Go back to wandering and being a part-time model and living a life most people can only dream about."

"When I first came here you might have been right," she told him frankly, and rushed on when his expression hardened. "That's not true anymore. I'm tired of moving from one place to the other. I want more out of life."

His temper flared higher. "So what was I? Your entertainment to keep you from being bored?"

"You know that isn't true!" she cried. "I care about you. You're the first man I've made love to since I left my husband."

"So I'm supposed to be grateful for the privilege, is that it?" Cold eyes swept from her tousled head to her booted feet. "The sister of Daniel Falcon allowed herself to condescend to make love with a man whose income is pocket change to him."

"Don't you see? You just said it yourself. Before I told you who I was, I was Dominique. Once I did, I'm relegated to being Daniel Falcon's sister," she said fighting her own anger, fighting tears. "I love my brother, but I hate being in his shadow. I wanted to make it on my own, but I failed. If you hadn't stepped in to help, I'd still be looking for my first big customer."

"Yeah, good ol' Trent, being suckered in by another beautiful woman to help her business." He laughed bitterly. "I was so sure you were different, but you're worse than Margo. At least she had a real need. But you just used me."

Her own temper finally slipped free. "That's nonsense. I never asked for your help."

"You didn't have to ask. Most men would do anything to help you, and you know it."

Black eyes narrowed. "Yes, and you know what they expect in return."

His head snapped back. "That's not the reason I helped you, and you damn well know that," he yelled.

"Then you should damn well know the only reason I went to bed with you is that I care about you!" she shouted just as loudly.

"Not enough to be honest with me."

The fight went out of her. She reached for him. "I was afraid you wouldn't understand."

He pulled his arm away. "Oh, I understand perfectly. I don't want to hear any more."

"Why won't you listen?" she asked.

"I *did* listen. You should have listened to me." His voice had a final ring.

Fear made her tremble. "I thought you were so big on second chances. Don't you think I deserve one?"

Trent gazed into the depths of her eyes and knew if she didn't leave soon she wouldn't until he had compromised another principle and taken her on any terms. "Good-bye, Dominique. Tell Janice to stop buying extra groceries. I won't be coming over anymore."

Dominique shook her head, accepting defeat. "No, don't do that to her. I'll leave. There's a loft apartment next door to the studio."

"That area isn't safe at night," he flared.

She wanted to take comfort because he still worried about her, then she remembered he was a caring man. He cared about her, but he didn't love her, and he wasn't going to forgive her. "Good-bye, Trent." She stepped around him, opened the door, then closed it softly behind her.

Hearing the door close was like hearing the sound of his heart being ripped out. Dominique Falcon. Another rich, spoiled socialite had stuck it to him. How could he have been so stupid? At least he had found out before he had given her his surprise.

He stalked back to his bedroom and went straight to the fresh vase of roses. Pushing aside one tight bud, then another, he finally located the pink rose he sought.

Laying in the center of the perfect, open flower was a two-carat, flawless diamond ring in a heavy platinum band encrusted with gemstones. The ring was as unusual and as beautiful as the woman he had intended to give it to—a friendship ring that he had hoped in time would represent a deeper, more lasting commitment.

He scowled. Grabbing the ring, he opened the drawer and tossed it inside. The brush set followed. He whirled and picked up the robe, intending to trash it, but found himself clutching it instead. Sitting on the bed, he let his forehead fall into the palm of his hand.

He had never hurt this much in his life. His chest felt strangely tight; his throat ached. Why couldn't Dominique be who she'd pretended to be—a struggling photographer needing a second chance—instead of an incredibly wealthy woman who didn't need him?

And that was what tore at him. She didn't need him. There wasn't one single thing in the world he could give her that she couldn't get for herself.

Her wealthy and powerful family dated back centuries; he didn't even know who his mother was. Dominique could toss him aside just as easily and carelessly as his mother had.

The pressure on his chest increased.

He couldn't stay here. Standing, he tossed the robe onto the bench at the foot of the bed, grabbed his keys, and left the room. There was always paperwork at the offi—

A woman's scream pierced the night.

Less than a heartbeat later Trent knew it was Dominique. Terror ripped through him. Heart pounding, more frightened than he had ever been in his life, he raced to the front door and jerked it open.

What he saw sent raw fear coursing through him. He was off the porch and running all out toward Isaac, who was trying to drag the struggling Dominique into the open back door of a battered Camaro.

"Stay back, Old Man, or I'll cut the bitch," Isaac warned, his eyes wild, his unsteady hand holding the handle of a six-inch knife to Dominique's throat.

Trent's blood went cold. His gaze briefly flickered to Dominique, trying to reassure her. Her gaze locked on his. She stopped struggling. "Let her go. It's me you want."

"Yeah, but you want her," Isaac sneered. "I've been watching you since the first night you spent together, waiting for this chance. I knew an old man like you couldn't keep going."

"Come on, Man, let's get out of here," yelled the driver. "The porch light across the street came on."

"Maybe you should let her go?" suggested an unsteady voice.

"Shut up, Jessie. I'm running this." Isaac took another step backward. Trent followed. "I told you to stay back, unless you want me to slash her pretty throat. You can have her back after I'm through with her."

"You'll have to kill me first."

"That could be arranged." Isaac thrust the knife out toward him.

Trent couldn't believe what happened next. Dominique thrust her left elbow sharply into Isaac's stomach, dropped, whirled, and grabbed his arm, spinning him around so that he was between her and the three teenagers in the car, then pushed his arm high up behind his back.

"Ow! Let go of my arm!"

"Drop the knife." Dominique didn't have to say it but once. Metal clattered to the sidewalk.

"Get this bit—ohhh!"

"I wouldn't say that word again if you want to use your arm again," Dominique warned, her voice steady.

A police siren sounded in the distance.

"I'm getting outta here," said the driver, reaching for the gearshift.

Trent moved, grabbing the young man through the open window and dragging him out of the car. With his other hand, Trent cut the motor and pocketed the keys. "I don't think so."

The passenger door abruptly swung open. Out jumped another teenager. He ran down the street without looking back. Less than fifty feet away he stumbled and fell when his baggy pants slid down around his knees.

By the time he managed to get up he was pinned by the high beam light of a police car. Another police vehicle came from the other direction. The wail of a third car grew louder.

"Dominique, are you all right? Did he hurt you?" Trent asked, keeping the teenager he'd subdued on the grass.

No answer.

"Dammit, be pissed at me tomorrow, but please turn around and tell me you're all right." he said, his voice ragged with fear.

A policeman and a policewoman jumped out of the second car and ran over, "What's going on here?"

"He tried to force her into that car with his friends," Trent explained, dragging his prisoner to his feet and handing the officer the car keys.

"He's lying," Isaac yelled.

"Turn them loose," ordered the slender black policewoman, her hair in microbraids.

"What?" Trent yelled.

"You heard me," said the officer.

Dominique released Isaac. The instant he was free, he swung at her with his fist. She blocked the blow and sent a quick jab to his nose with the heel of her hand.

He went down, rolling and cursing.

With a savage curse, Trent started for Isaac. The two officers grabbed him, then were aided by another policeman who had arrived in the third patrol car.

"You see, they're both crazy. I just brought my cousin over here and they went medieval on us," Isaac cried, his words muffled from holding his hands over his bleeding nose.

"That's a lie!" Trent yelled. "I heard Dominique scream and came out, and you were trying to pull her into that car."

"You saw what she did to me," Isaac said, moaning. "I couldn't have dragged her unless she wanted to come. Maybe she wanted a real man between the sheets."

Trent lunged for Isaac. The officers tightened their holds.

"See, what did I tell you? I need a doctor," Isaac wailed. "My cousin will tell you. Tell him Jessie. We were just coming over for him to visit and try and get back on the football team."

Jessie, in a black sweatshirt, oversized jeans, and a sideways baseball cap, eyes wide, was trembling as he got out of the car. "I—I don't want to go to jail."

"Jessie, don't lie for him," Trent said. "You don't have to go the same way as Isaac. I'll help you."

"Now he's trying to bribe my cousin," Isaac flared. "He has money." The youth glanced around at the growing crowd gathering on Trent's lawn and across the street. "His neighbors will probably lie for him. We're just poor, honest kids."

"Cut the crap, Isaac," said the policeman, who came up with the other teenager who had tried to run. "I don't know about the rest of these kids, but Isaac has a long rap sheet. I arrested him myself for car theft when I worked the Southwest Division."

"I've been going straight," Isaac whined.

Dominique stepped forward. "If you'll look on the curb by the car you'll find a knife with Isaac's fingerprints. And if that isn't enough to prove Trent told you the truth, I don't think I would have gotten this if I were willing."

She tilted her head to the side. Blood welled from a two-inch cut on the side of her neck.

CHAPTER 14

Trent exploded in a cry of rage. Another policeman rushed to help with subduing him.

"Trent," Dominique said calmly. "If you're in jail, who's going to take me to the doctor?"

"Oh, Lord." He started toward her, then found himself unable to do so. He gazed at the police officers. "Please, let me go to her. I won't touch him."

The officers looked at the lone female officer, who had two stripes on her sleeve. She nodded.

As soon as Trent was free he rushed to Dominique, picked her up in his arms, and ran back to the house.

Several neighbors Dominique recognized from the block party followed—which proved to be for the best, Dominique realized, because Trent had completely lost it. An elderly woman whom Dominique remembered as Mrs. Garland, a retired nurse, finally got him to put her down on the sofa. When Dominique protested she might get blood on the white material, Trent picked her up again and hugged her so tight she had difficulty breathing.

Once again Mrs. Garland took control. She sent her husband for her first aid kid, then said, "Trent, I can't see how to take care of her if you don't put her down."

Reluctantly, Trent did so, but he knelt beside her, his hand clutching hers. He didn't move when Mr. Garland returned and handed the kit to his wife. He did when Dominique turned her head to one side for the retired nurse to clean the wound.

With a gutteral curse, he started for the door. Neighbors hastened to get out of the way.

"Trent, please hold my hand," Dominique requested softly.

He was back in seconds, kneeling, gathering her hand in his. His were shaking. "It's going to be all right. You're going to be all right." He looked at Mrs. Garland. "Do you think we need to take her in for shock or something?"

"Just keep her warm and quiet," Mrs. Garland advised. "I don't think you'll have any trouble doing that. Mr. Scoggins is going to wait on the porch for Janice to come home."

"Here," said a middle-aged, pudgy neighbor wearing a fuzzy robe that resembled a horse blanket. She recalled his name was Mr. Carol, and that he was a history professor at the local university. "Some of my best Scotch."

Trent went to lift Dominique. An arthritic hand on his shoulder stopped him. "That's for you."

"I don't want any." Troubled, he gazed down at Dominique, and with his free hand pulled up the blanket someone had brought to cover her with to her chin. "You're warm enough? Can I get you anything?"

Now that it was over, the aftershock was getting to her. "If you're not going to drink that, I will."

Sitting her up, he let her take a sip, then another. The amber-colored drink disappeared.

A whistle of approval went up from Mr. Carol. "Now, that's a woman."

At his comment, people began talking about her subduing Isaac. His hand in hers, Trent felt her tremble. "Thank you all for helping, but I think Dominique needs to rest. Mrs. Garland, will you please see everyone out for me?"

"Of course." She lightly touched his shoulder. "You know how to contact me if you need to."

"Thank you, again," Trent said.

"You've helped us enough times," she said, then left.

No sooner had the door closed than the doorbell rang. "It's Officer Blair. I need to speak with you," called a female voice.

Trent scowled at the closed door. "If she hadn't ordered us to let those punks go, Isaac couldn't have taken a swing at you."

Dominique's fingertips touched his tense shoulder. She wanted to touch his face and crawl into his lap, but she wasn't sure of her reception. Helping her didn't mean he had forgiven her. "Isaac got the worst of it. Besides, she more than made up for it when she let you go."

His dark eyes centered on her for a long moment. The doorbell rang again.

"I don't think she's leaving," Dominique said.

Releasing her hand, Trent opened the door, then went back to sit beside Dominique and hold her hand. "The nurse said she should rest."

Officer Blair's expression didn't change at the brusque statement. She took a seat across from them and flipped open a small spiral tablet. "Of course. I just need some information for my report. Why don't we start with you, Sir?"

Trent gave the officer the information she requested, then it was Dominique's turn. She wasn't sure about the use of her assumed name, so she gave Everette as her professional name and Falcon as her legal name.

Trent tensed on hearing *Falcon,* but he didn't release her hand. Officer Blair's pen stilled, her head came up. Dominique could see realization dawning in her narrow, dark brown face.

Falcon wasn't a common name, and when Daniel Falcon hit Houston several months before, the city and state took notice. They still did.

"Any relation to Daniel Falcon?"

"My brother."

Officer Blair's eyes widened, her fingers clenched on the pen. "Sorry about the punch the kid threw at you."

"As I told Trent, you more than made up for it when you let him go." Dominique smiled. "Thank you."

The young woman's shoulders relaxed. "If you can tell me what happened, I can let you rest."

"There's not very much to tell. I was leaving here, going back home, and Isaac came from behind the shrubbery by the side of the house and grabbed me. I screamed."

Trent's hand clenched in hers.

Officer Blair frowned. "You handled yourself well. How did he get a jump on you?"

Dominique glanced at Trent. "I was thinking of something else."

"I see. That's when Mr. Masters came out?"

"Yes." This time it was Dominique who trembled.

The policewoman flipped the small notebook closed and stood. "I have all I need. An investigative officer will be assigned to the case and contact you."

"I'll be out of the studio tomorrow morning with a photo shoot," she said.

"Dominique, you're not going to work tomorrow," Trent ordered.

Calm eyes turned to him. "I beg to differ."

"I'll show myself out. Don't worry about Isaac. He finally made it to the big time with attempted kidnapping, and assault with a deadly weapon," Officer Blair told them.

"What about Jessie?" Dominique asked, remembering the frightened boy.

"He's underage, but he *was* an accessory. The court will decide." The policewoman opened the door. "By the way, you've got some nice moves."

"Thank you. My brother is an excellent teacher."

"Goodnight." The door closed after her.

Trent tucked her hand under the light blanket and pulled it to her chin. "You're sure you're warm enough?"

"Fine." *I'd be warmer if you held me, looked at me.*

"Can I get you anything?"

You. "No thanks."

He nodded, then fiddled with her covers again before his gaze locked on the small, white bandage on her neck. "I should have made sure you reached home safely."

Automatically she lifted her hand to touch his tense features, but the blanket prevented her. "You had no way of knowing Isaac would try something like that."

A muscle leaped in his jaw. "That's no excuse." His eyes finally met hers. They were filled with regret and misery. "I should have protected you better."

This time the blanket was no match for a determined woman. Trent needed her. Her hands touched his face. "You can't possibly blame yourself for Isaac's behavior. I certainly don't."

His long forefinger trembled as it lightly grazed the bandage. "He could have—" His eyes shut, his hand clenched into a tight fist.

"It's over," Dominique said, taking Trent's cold hand in hers. "I'm safe, thanks to you. If you hadn't come out, he might have succeeded in getting me into that car."

His eyes opened and they were no less haunted. "He only came after you because of me."

"Trent, stop blaming yourself." She sat up. "If it's anyone's fault, it's mine. I should have called the police the afternoon they showed up at my studio."

"What? Why didn't you tell me?" he shouted. "What afternoon?"

"The day after we slept together for the first time he and his pals came by the studio and made some crude gestures when I refused to admit them. They ran when I picked up the phone to call the police," she explained, not liking the way Trent was glaring at her.

"What stopped you from completing the call?" he asked.

She bit her lower lip. No way was she fooled by the quietness of his voice. His eyes were blazing. She had a feeling that if she weren't hurt her feet would be dangling off the floor again.

"Dominique?"

"You're not going to like it."

"I don't imagine I will, but I want to hear it, anyway."

She lay back down and drew the blanket up to her chin. "I didn't want you to get into trouble. I was safe in the studio, and I always leave before dark."

His brow furrowed. "You were trying to protect me?"

"Yes."

"I can—" he began, only to stop abruptly and stare at her, his gaze studying her more closely. "What I'm thinking can't possibly be true. You wouldn't do anything so idiotic." He pushed to his feet, took a few steps away, then quickly came back and crouched down. "You jumped Isaac when he pointed the knife at me. Why?"

She moistened her lips. This was going to be tricky. "It was the opening I had been waiting for. I wasn't going to get into that car."

"You're lying!" he shouted, pushing to his feet and glaring down at her. "You were trying to protect me again. Don't you ever take it into your head to do something like that. I can take care of myself. Do you hear me?"

She didn't think it wise to point out that the entire neighborhood could probably hear him. "Yes. Someone is at the door."

"I mean it, Dominique."

"It's probably Janice." Dominique sat up and swung her legs over the side of the sofa.

"What are you doing?" Trent asked, coming back to her.

"If Janice sees me lying down she'll think the worse. I don't want to upset her more than this is going to already," Dominique explained, reaching for the bandage.

Trent's hand stopped her. "Leave that alone."

"She'll se—"

"The bandage stays."

"Trent, be reasonable."

"Believe me, I'm giving it my best shot. Now leave that alone." Pushing to his feet, he went to answer the door. "But don't think we've finished our conversation. I still have a few things to say to you."

Dominique didn't mind the omnious threat. As long as Trent was talking to her there was a chance he might forgive her.

As soon as Trent opened the door Janice rushed inside. Paul was directly behind her. Her godmother took one look at Dominique, began fussing over her, and insisted she be taken home and put to bed. Dominique started to tell her that wasn't necessary, but Janice looked so distressed that she consented.

She had barely stood when Trent picked her up in his arms. The stubborn look in his eyes warned her to not protest.

Since she didn't know if that would be the last time she'd be held by him, be able to hold him, protesting was the furthest thing from her mind. Circling her arms around his neck, she leaned her head against his chest. Paul followed them out and closed Trent's door, while Janice rushed ahead to open her front door.

As soon as they entered Janice's house they heard the phone ringing. Dominique had expected the call. "That will be for me. Please place me on the couch by the phone."

Frowning, Trent did as she requested. "How do you know it's for you?"

"Unfortunately, from experience," she told him. Taking a deep breath, she picked up the receiver. "I'm all right Dad, Mother."

"Dominique!" Felicia cried. "We've been frantic for the past forty minutes. No one would answer the phone."

"What happened?" her practical father asked.

Dominique bit her lip and tried to think of a way to tell her parents without upsetting them, then realized that they already were. Her father's unique ability to tell when his children were deeply troubled or frightened had saved her from LaSalle, had helped Daniel out of a bad situation.

"Baby, say something?" Felicia said, her voice shaky.

"A teenager tried to make me go someplace I didn't want to," she told them. "It was over before it began."

"We're on our way," John Henry said.

"There's no need for you to come."

"There is *every* need. The helicopter Daniel sent just landed. Be safe, and know you are loved," her father said.

"Be safe, and know I love both of you, too." Her eyes misted for the first time. She hung up the phone. From her earliest memories, her father had always said good-bye to her the same way.

"You're all right?" Trent asked.

"My family is coming, and the craziness is about to begin." Her hand swept over her mussed hair. It was too late to worry about what the neighbors or the police thought. "I'd better get ready. We'll need coffee."

"And food for the hoard," Janice said.

"I'll take care of everything, Janice." Paul took her hand in his. "You just take care of Dominique."

"Thank you, Paul." She kissed his cheek.

Dominique glanced at Trent, then stood and walked toward her bedroom. There was no sense waiting. She wasn't likely to get a kiss.

Trent had never seen anything like it in his life.

Apparently, neither had Paul, because Trent had caught the amazed look on the older man's face once or twice as the evening progressed. No wonder Dominique and Janice had suggested food and drinks. He had thought they meant for her family.

Since mud had more flavor than his coffee and about the same texture, he had gladly let Paul make it. Then Paul had called his restaurant
and had them deliver food. Trent never thought of leaving. He had a few
things he wanted to say to Dominique.

Almost to the moment she came out of the bedroom—looking re-
markably calm and breathtakingly beautiful in a white turtleneck pull-
over and matching pants—the doorbell had rung. Taking a seat on the
Duncan Phyfe couch, she had grimaced and said, "Open the door and
let the show begin."

Janice nodded. In walked the police field supervisor, who had come by
to express his regret of the "unfortunate incident" and wish her well.
From then on, the doorbell and the phone rang constantly.

Some of the calls were from anxious relatives, others from city or police officials who wanted to "express their regrets and drop by." She had
thanked each one for calling and told them she'd be delighted to see
them.

More than one official brought his wife with him. They had sipped
coffee, nibbled on quiche and cherry tarts, and invited Dominique to become a member of most of the prestigious organizations in the city.
Trent couldn't help but remember that Dominique Everette had not
been asked.

Dominique handled them all with easy assurance, and thanked them
for coming. Elegant and poised, she made a point of stating that she
hoped the media did not learn what happened.

Repeatedly, she was reassured. Neither the police nor the city officials
were anxious for word to circulate that a wealthy socialite had been attacked fifty feet from her home.

Janice was waving good-bye to the final guests when *they* arrived. Trent
thought he had prepared himself for her brother and parents, but one
look at the powerfully built men with thick hair rippling down their
backs and the exquisite woman between them, and he knew he had been
wrong.

They were an exotic trio. They'd stand out in any crowd, not only for
their handsomeness but for their proud carriage. Here were three people who could probably spit in the devil's eye, then laugh.

He didn't know who the beautiful young pregnant woman was, or for
that matter who the well-dressed elderly man was, but they definitely
weren't related by blood to the Falcons or Everettes. They didn't have
the coloring or the itensity.

"Mother, Dad!" Dominique cried, jumping up from the sofa and running to meet her parents. She was enveloped in a hug and rocked.

"You're sure you're all right?" Felicia asked, stepping back to look at
her daughter and touching her face.

"I'm fin—" She stopped abruptly as her mother's hand slid downward and encountered the bandage.

Eyes wide, her hands shaking, Felicia slowly peeled away the collar of the turtleneck. "How bad is it? And are there any more? I want the truth."

"Just this scratch, Mother."

"Where is he?" John Henry asked, his eyes as cold as black ice.

"In jail, Dad." She smiled to soothe him. "You didn't have to fly here."

"Stop talking nonsense," Daniel said. His hand trembled as it touched her neck. His jaw clenched. "I thought I taught you better."

"If you hadn't, she would have been in a lot more trouble."

Everyone in the room turned. Trent stood in the kitchen doorway, his stance combative.

"Who are you?" Daniel asked.

"This is Trent Masters, my neighbor," Janice supplied. "Next to him is Paul Osgood. Dominique was coming from Trent's house when it happened."

Paul received no more than a cursory nod. Trent remained the center of attention. "Why didn't you see that she got home safely?" Daniel asked, his voice hard.

"At the time I thought I had good reasons." Trent's gaze was fixed on Dominique. "Now—" His hands flexed helplessly. "I'd do anything to change things."

"Trent, it wasn't your fault," Dominique cried, stepping around her parents and going to him. "Please stop blaming yourself."

"He should," John Henry said. "He should have protected you better."

Trent turned to face her family. They were all glaring at him, even the pregnant woman. Once again it struck him how little Dominique needed him. She had a family that obviously loved her very much. She certainly hadn't needed him to protect her against Isaac. If not for him, she would never have been in danger in the first place. She needed him like a fish needed a bicycle.

But he realized something. He needed her. His attention came back to her. "I'd like to talk to you alone. Will you come back to the house with me?"

"Yes," she answered without hesitation.

The vise around his heart eased. But there was still another hurdle. He turned toward Dominique's parents. She caught him by the arm. "Where are you going?"

"To ask permission. We wouldn't get two feet." This time he didn't stop until he stood in front of her unsmiling father. "Sir, you're right. I should have protected her better. My punishment is that I'll go to my grave knowing I didn't. But I'd like you to give me a second chance. I'd like your permission to speak to her privately."

"Give me one good reason why I should." John Henry asked.

"There are lots of reasons, but I'd like Dominique to hear them first," Trent told him.

"Go on, Dad, I recognize the look," Daniel said with a smile, his arm going around the pregnant woman's waist.

Trent's brow arched. He hadn't expected an ally in Daniel, nor to see his face soften as his cheek rested against the woman's head. But he was finding love had a way of changing a person and breaking all the rules. "Please, Mr. Falcon."

"If you go, Dominique, remember your promise," said the elderly man.

Trent figured the man who had spoken must be Higgins, the family friend. He was certainly outnumbered, but he wasn't giving up.

"Are you the reason she's been out every night?" Felicia asked.

"Yes, Ma'am."

"If my daughter returns upset in any way, you'll answer to me," Felicia promised.

"I want her home and safe in an hour," John Henry said flatly.

"Da—"

"Yes, Sir," Trent said, cutting Dominique off. Taking her hand, he guided her through the back kitchen door.

Trent seated Dominique on the couch in his living room. He was too nervous to sit. "Your father didn't give us much time, so I'd better get started. I'm sorry I blew up at you, and for comparing you to Margo. She had everything handed to her, and she always had her hand out, wanting more. She never worked a day in her life, never did anything during the time I knew her for someone else."

He ran his hand over his head, stopped, and stared down at Dominique. "There's no way she wouldn't have used what little influence her father had to advance herself socially. She certainly wouldn't have risked her life for me, or anyone else. You're nothing like her. Forgive me for even thinking so for a moment. You chose to make it on your own. That took courage."

"I was scared," Dominique admitted.

He sat down and took her hands. "But you didn't let that stop you. You didn't give up."

"I'm not sure what would have happened if you handn't helped me get started."

"I might have given you the opportunity, but it was your unique ability to visualize concepts and create images that made people want you to do their portraits." He smiled proudly. "You didn't let them down. Your pictures reflect the essence of the subjects. I might have helped you get started, but you did the rest. Please say you'll forgive me."

She drew in an unsteady breath. "I do. So where do we go from here?"

"That depends on you."

"Me?"

"I'll be right back," he stated, then went down the hall into his bedroom and came back. Kneeling in front of her, he held the diamond ring between his thumb and forefinger. "I want you to have this."

Her eyes widened. She gazed from the white fire dancing in the center stone to him.

"I was going to ask you to wear it as a friendship ring."

She could barely get the words past her dry throat. *"Was?* You don't want me to have it now, since you know who I am?"

"No."

Her eyes closed in misery.

"I want you to have it because I love you, and want you to be my wife."

Her eyelids flew up. Grinning, she launched herself into his arms, almost toppling him over on the floor. Crying and kissing him, she said, "Yes. Yes. And if you ever scare me like that again I'll make you drink your own coffee for the rest of our lives together."

His arms tightened. "Dominique, I love you so much."

"You'd better, because I love you so much I ache sometimes." She held out her left hand and he slid the ring on her third finger. "It fits perfectly, just like us."

"Just like us." His eyes grew haunted. "I was so scared you wouldn't learn to love me. Then when you told me who you are, my fears escalated. You family has such a history, and so much wealth."

Her hands stroked his face. "And it doesn't mean squat if you aren't happy and don't have love. I know. Remember?"

"I only know I can't live without you. I only know that I'll love you and protect you through eternity."

"Good, because I feel the same way." Her fingers began unbuttoning his shirt.

His hands grabbed hers. "I promised to have you back in an hour."

She lifted an eyebrow. "Unless you've developed a problem I'm not aware of, that should be just enough time."

Chuckling, he picked her up in his arms and started for the bedroom. "Oh, Buttercup, I just love the way you talk."

EPILOGUE

The wedding announcement of Dominique Nicole Falcon and Trent Jacob Masters made headlines across the country. The media might have been caught napping and let Daniel Falcon's wedding slip past them, but they were determined to more than make up for that loss by covering every facet of his sister's engagement and nuptials.

They had a lot to cover. From the elegant announcement party at the lavish Mansion Hotel to the bridal showers held from one end of the country to the other to the hand-beaded crystal and seed pearl wedding gown to the spectacular five-foot wedding cake with blooming cascades of sugar flowers, the wedding was clearly going to be an event.

The couple was clearly in love and wanted everyone to share in their happiness. Dominique was heard saying more than once that it would be difficult for a woman *not* to fall in love with a sensitive, caring man like Trent. The incredible thing was that somehow he had fallen in love with her as well. The Master of Breath had blessed her beyond belief.

Trent was not used to the spotlight, but he was comfortable with, and had confidence in, his future bride. On being asked about Dominique's statement, Trent always replied *he* was the blessed one. She was as courageous as she was beautiful and talented. He thought it incredible such a unique woman had fallen in love with him.

The wedding day was perfect. Sun poured from the cloudless sky like spun gold. Barely a breeze ruffled the yards of netting in Dominique's beaded headpiece or her upswept hair as she rode in the open carriage with her father. A hush fell over the church when the doors were opened and she stood silhouetted in the light.

Always beautiful, in the ivory satin and organza gown she appeared even more so with the glow of happiness and love on her face. As her father led her down the aisle strewn with rose petals in the crowded church filled with flowers and the soft glow of candles, her twenty-five yard, cathedral train trailed softly behind her.

Finally they reached the altar and it was time for her father to hand her to Trent and leave. John Henry didn't hesitate. "Be safe, and know that you are loved," he whispered, kissed her on the cheek, and stepped back.

Tears misting in her eyes, she looked at her father, her teary-eyed and happy mother, Daniel, his arm around Madelyn, who was holding their sleeping, three week-old son, Daniel Jr., Higgins with a lady friend, and Janice and Paul. Love *was* possible, and infinitely preferable to being alone.

Love didn't make you vulnerable. It made you strong.

Turning, she caught sight of the stony face of her cousin, Luke, at the end of the pew. *Your time is coming,* she thought.

Smiling, she blinked back tears and reached her gloved hand out to Trent, who stood tall and proud. His hand closed securely around hers.

I love you, he mouthed.

I love you, she returned.

Slouched in his seat, Luke barely kept a grimace off his face.

He had yet to learn about love, but he would.

In time.